~~Daughter~~

of Blood

"Prince Aranraith," he husked, as though his mouth was as dry as Faro's. "You honor this house."

He bowed forward until his forehead touched the floor, and after a moment's hesitation the old man, clearly bewildered, did the same. Faro lay absolutely still, aware that this hall, too, had grown cold. He was trying to breathe shallowly, but he could see the air misting just past his lips.

All three strangers lifted back their hoods, and Faro stifled a cry because now he could see why the tallest man's hood had moved. He closed his eyes, hoping that he had fallen asleep in the temple porch and when he looked again the nightmare would be gone. But the stranger was still there, a powerfully built man in gold-washed black mail, with long coils of hair falling down his back. Except that the coils were not hair at all, but a sinuous twist of blue-black snakes, their forked tongues a perpetual flicker about the stranger's head and shoulders.

Nauseated, Faro screwed his eyelids shut again, but his heart still hammered painfully and he had to fight to control his trembling. Outside, the rain began to drum.

"Where is Nirn?" The voice that spoke was darkness and shadow, with a rustling sibilance through it, and Faro knew without opening his eyes that it belonged to the man with the serpent hair.

HELEN LOWE

Daughter of Blood

The Wall of Night: Book Three

www.orbitbooks.net

ORBIT

First published in Great Britain in 2016 by Orbit

1 3 5 7 9 10 8 6 4 2

A CIP catalogue record for this book
is available from the British Library.

ISBN 978-0-356-50005-8

Typeset in Times by M Rules
Printed and bound by CPI Group (UK) Ltd, Croydon, CR0 4YY

Papers used by Orbit are from well-managed forests
and other responsible sources.

MIX
Paper from
responsible sources
FSC® C104740

Orbit
An imprint of
Little, Brown Book Group
Carmelite House
50 Victoria Embankment
London EC4Y 0DZ

An Hachette UK Company
www.hachette.co.uk

www.orbitbooks.net

*This one has always been for my sister,
Jennifer, who shares my love
of fantastic stories.*

Contents

PART VII: *The Sundered Web*

PART VIII: *The Shield of Heaven*

Prologue

Tongues of lightning flashed out of a bruised sky, the wildfire flickering along a broken colonnade before splitting apart around a man's tall figure. Dead leaves drifted to either side as the rift in the air closed, but no ripple disturbed the length of the newcomer's surcote, white over blue-black mail, or the fall of his long hair as he passed beneath a crumbing arch and into an open court, bounded by twelve paired pillars. A wide pool lay on its far side, with shallow steps leading out onto a stone platform where a woman gazed into the motionless depths. Her gossamer sleeves stirred in a slight breeze, but otherwise she was as still as the surrounding water and did not turn when the man joined her.

"Nindorith told me you were here." His voice was layered with muted power. "There is no secret for you to find, heart of my heart. It has been as we see it now since Amaliannarath departed."

The woman's gaze remained on the water. "Died, is what the others say. Even Salar holds that Amaliannarath extinguished herself, trying to carry the whole of Fire through the void."

"Those of Sun will always say what suits their current purpose, especially Salar. Ask me, or Nindorith, if you have questions about Amaliannarath."

One of her hands clenched. "I have spoken with Nindorith, as it happens." Each word was a weight, dropped into the air between them. "He said that she and Fire vanished, passing beyond even his ability, or Salar's, to trace, which makes it probable they all perished." She paused. "Only the great Prince Ilkerineth, it seems, does not agree."

Oh, my heart, Ilkerineth thought: striking at me over Amaliannarath's long-ago fate will not bring our son back.

Our son. Even the words were a fist of pain, closing around his heart. For an instant he was half form, half wildfire, as his banked-down power strained to break free—not just clear of this sad place, caught in its pocket outside time, but tearing through the barrier Wall and into Haarth. With Nindorith at his side and Lightning at his back he might even be able to do it, since the Derai had neglected the foundations of their Wall for so long ... But a split second later Ilkerineth had caught himself, the wildfire dying as he forced grief and rage back down.

I have lived too long, he thought. They lay my son's dead body at my feet and still I will not obliterate another world, even if I could.

And Nherenor had loved Haarth. That must be weighed in the scales, too, when avenging his death. The Derai, though— Briefly, the wildfire flared again, because the ancient enemy were another matter entirely. Despite that, Ilkerineth kept his voice even and the timbre of power quiet, as it always was when he spoke to the woman before him: Nherenor's mother, whose eyes shifted with the colors of the sea. "The facts we know only make death the most likely answer, not the certain one."

Sun, Lightning, Fire: one of the Sworn's three nations gone, just like that. Why did you do it, Amaliannarath? he demanded silently. Why didn't you appeal to me or to Nindorith, if you thought Aranraith and Salar were behind the assault on Fire? "I know what Salar has come whispering, under the pretext of sorrow for our grief," he said aloud, "but no matter what the basilisk may suggest, this place is a ghost—no more than an echo of what it was when Amaliannarath lived. And even she, in her full power, could not have brought Nherenor back from the dead."

The woman beside him moved restlessly. "Would Salar lie outright? He swears that Amaliannarath may have known how to move through time. And this was her place, so if she did . . ." Her chin lifted. "If I delve into its memories deep enough, if I plumb the pool—" When she broke off, he knew her eyes would be storm dark. "What if I could open a way into that power? What if we could go back and slay Nherenor's killer before he was slain?"

"'What if,'" Ilkerineth repeated, but checked his headshake. "Salar might not lie outright, but every word will have an alternate interpretation. Few know better, too, just how immensely strong Amaliannarath was. So if even she could be obliterated by the void, how do you think a lesser power would fare, attempting the same feat?"

Both her hands shut this time, into fists so tight the knuckles gleamed. "Do you think I care for that? Our son has been slain in a Haarth backwater by a Derai spy. Yet all you speak of is what cannot be done. Perhaps you have lived so long and seen so much death that even your son's killing ceases to matter. But if Salar is right and a way exists that may undo his death, then I *shall* find it."

The blade of loss turned in Ilkerineth's heart, sharper than any words that she could hone against him out of her pain. But he continued to hold the rein on his power tight, because it was true that he had seen death—aeons of it. He had also observed Salar's sly hand at work many times and knew that if he answered her rage and despair out of his own, a good part of the basilisk's work would be done.

I should not have let Salar come anywhere near us, he reflected grimly, even under the pretext of observing our ancient mourning ceremonies. Nindorith had warned him, but he had been determined to honor Nherenor with the full rites, thus proving what he had long suspected: that of the two of them, Nindorith was by far the wiser.

"At least when it comes to Salar."

"So you are here," Ilkerineth replied.

"Even you should be wary, my Prince, given it was Salar who

pointed the Lady toward this place. Whatever it may have been when Amaliannarath came here, it is largely unprotected now."

"Do you suspect treachery, despite Sun's current litany of co-operation?" Ilkerineth let dryness tinge his mindspeech. They both knew that Aranraith's envoy, Arcolin, had actively undone their work toward alliance with Emer—and contingent hope of cutting off the Derai's trade with Haarth—as soon as Nindorith withdrew following Nherenor's death. They also suspected Aranraith's agents in northern Emer of killing their own operative there, the shapechanger known as Malisande. Her death had appeared to be the work of native assassins, but could well have been engineered by Sun adepts seeking to repli-cate her infiltration of the Emerian Oakward.

A flicker of Nindorith's power, also banked down, acknowledged the dryness. *"Still, Aranraith could be right in the short term. Setting this world alight with local wars may serve our ends just as well as alliances."*

"It's too often the short term, with Aranraith." Ilkerineth frowned. *"But he would only move against me if he felt sure you and Lightning would then come over to him."*

"I would rather follow Amaliannarath's path than join Aranraith." Nindorith's reply was a pulse of muted thunder, but Ilkerineth felt his regard shift to the black-clad figure at the edge of the pool. *"Far better for all of us, if you stay alive."*

"I'll do my best." The breeze eddied as Nindorith withdrew, although Ilkerineth guessed that he would not have gone far.

"Nuithe." He spoke the woman's name softly, and this time she turned as he stepped close, her eyes falling to his extended hand. Slowly, her fists uncurled and she placed a hand in his, although she hesitated before coming into the circle of his arms. Ilkerineth kept his clasp light, because of the mail, and felt his usual amaze-ment that the top of her head barely reached his shoulder. Briefly, he closed his eyes, breathing in the scent of her hair. "One reason I have lived this long," he said finally, "is because I never forget what Salar is. Any hope the basilisk held out to you will have been proffered to feed Aranraith's hatred, or bait a trap." Involuntarily, his arms tightened. "You are strong and valiant, but this dead place could still leach all the power out of you until you follow our son to the grave."

Nuithe was silent so long that he wondered if she had heard him. When she did finally speak, her voice was a whisper. "My heart cries out for him: my Nherenor, my son." Her hands, clenched back into fists, pressed against his chest. "But if I cannot have him back, I will have vengeance for his death."

Ilkerineth let his arms tighten again, just a little. "Nherenor shall be avenged. I am still of the Sworn and would have to live a great deal longer than I have for the fires of vengeance to grow cold." For the first time, he let himself feel the wind's chill, answering his mood. "But this place is dangerous. The maelstrom is waking again; we all feel it. Once it rouses fully, it will suck all lesser powers into itself, making no distinction between friend and foe."

"The maelstrom ..." Nuithe's voice trailed off. "So that's why Aranraith is bent on larger plans, testing the Wall's ability to constrain the Sworn again."

"Given what's brewing, he may be wise." Ilkerineth frowned, because although the way Nuithe herself had opened through the Wall, nearly two decades ago, had greatly increased the Sworn's ability to access Haarth, Aranraith's raid on the Keep of Winds had still failed, six years before. Yet the raiders had also exposed Derai weakness, striking into the heart of what should have been their enemy's greatest stronghold.

Nuithe's frown mirrored his. "I heard what he said to you during the mourning rites: that we must cease skulking in the shadows and waiting on uncertain prophecy to favor our cause. I assume he meant Nindorith's foreseeing, a child of my blood driven like a death-stake into the heart of the Derai Alliance." Her voice flattened. "But now Nherenor is dead."

And as early as his funeral, Ilkerineth thought, Salar came whispering ... Seeing the trouble in her expression, he could guess what the basilisk might have been whispering about, besides Amaliannarath.

As if their thoughts marched together, Nuithe stepped clear of his embrace. "Aranraith hates me. With the foreseeing come to nothing, he will try and use me as a wedge. Initially between Sun and Lightning, but he'll drive it between you and Lightning, too, if he can." She crossed her arms, her gaze steady. "Many years ago you granted me sanctuary among the Sworn, and then the protection of your name. And however wildly I may have spoken, just now, I know you will never forget the blood debt owed for Nherenor's death." The wind keened, catching at her hair and trailing sleeves. "But I will understand, with my value to the Sworn cause diminished, if you wish to cut me loose, to achieve what I can on my own."

Ilkerineth's lightning sparked in answer, and Nuithe's eyes flickered, although she did not flinch away. She had never shrunk from him, not even when Nindorith first brought her half dead into Lightning's hall—and he had transformed out of wildfire before her eyes in order to deal with Aranraith's outrage, baying at their heels. Now, Ilkerineth let his anger die, since it was directed at Salar's meddling and he knew all too well just how persuasive the basilisk could be. Even if Nuithe had refused to listen at the time, the words would still have kept working away in her: because Salar, like Nindorith, was an Ascendant, one of the great powers of the Sworn.

"Diminished value," Ilkerineth observed. "Yes, indeed—except as an opener of ways, a power we have not numbered among our ranks for millennia. And it was you who brought down the barriers into the Old Keep of Winds, so the Sworn could attack Night in their greatest stronghold." He let his smile gleam as he regarded her. "You also swore to Lightning, as our Lady of Ways, before you agreed to marry me. Rest assured, I shall not release you from that oath. Especially," he added, humor fading, "when letting you go would be as good as delivering you back into Aranraith's hand."

Nuithe was looking down now, so he could no longer read her expression, but he let his voice grow soft. "I am the Prince of

Lightning, so might well offer a woman sanctuary to advantage my cause and spite my enemies. But I would not need to marry her to achieve either end. I am not a liar either, the reason I call you my beloved is because it's true." A single step closed the gap between them again. When she did not move away, Ilkerineth brushed his fingertips across her hair, much as the wind had done. "I asked you to marry me because I love you." Pain roughened the softness in his voice. "I will release you from that bond if you wish it—*because* you wish it—but not without a plea. We have lost our son; must we lose each other as well?"

Nuithe shook her head, which might be as close as she would come to saying what she wanted. Heart of my heart, Ilkerineth thought, but waited for her to come to him.

He, too, was a great power of the Sworn and could make her do so with a word if he chose, binding her will to his. That was the course Aranraith would choose—and had raged against Ilkerineth for neglecting ever since he learned of Nuithe's ability with ways and Nindorith's foreseeing. Because my brother Prince of the Sun, Ilkerineth thought fiercely, has never been interested in trust, only power and obedience to his will, just as he has forgotten why we came to be fighting this war in the first place.

Nuithe's arms slid around his neck and her lips met his with an answering fierceness. Ilkerineth savored its edge against the softness of her mouth, their kiss lengthening, before he drew away to murmur against her ear: "Besides, think how much greater a vengeance you can encompass as my wife, with all of Lightning at your back."

Her arms tightened. "I am thinking of it. Every minute of every hour, the hope of retribution sustains me, both for my old vengeance and now the new."

Just as it was hate, he reflected, that had sustained her when she first joined Lightning, driving her will to survive with all the potency of a once great love turned on itself. He guessed she might have been able to speak words of affection, too, in that former life—but Nuithe, the name she had chosen for herself, meant "dark heart" in the oldest language of the Sworn. She had seemed well named, too, until Nherenor had given her a reason to love again.

Yet now Nherenor was dead and both love and hope turned to ashes. Ilkerineth felt his expression cloud, the storm within him brewing, as her hands wound themselves into his hair. "Nindorith or our agents *will* hunt out Nherenor's slayer," she whispered. "He cannot elude us forever. Yet Night has found some means to prevent any more ways being opened into the abandoned Old Keep. And their Earl still lives and has not yet lost all that he holds dear." She pulled his mouth down to hers again, and this time the kiss was all ferocity until her grip on his hair eased. "You and Nindorith have sworn to observe the ancient mourning period for Nherenor in full, but let me honor our son equally, Prince of the Lightning, by resuming the hunt. I may not find the assassin, but I shall rend Night's friends and paint their names onto Lightning's banners in their own lifeblood."

She hates well, I'll give her that. Aranraith's observation, because hatred spoke to the Prince of the Sun. Ilkerineth let wildfire crackle around them both, but kept his voice soft. "How fierce you are, my Lady of Ways. But we have other hunters, a nation of them."

"'*If Night falls, all fall.*' The old prophecy hangs by a single thread now." Their kissing had drawn blood, the trickle dark against her lip. "Let me be the one to drive home the blade." Nuithe's hands tightened again in his hair, her body urgent against his. "Give me an army if you must, but let me hunt."

He bent his head and licked away the blood. "So be it," he whispered—and caught a flicker in the corner of his eyes, a slow powerful turn of shadow within the glass-smooth water. His head came up as he drew her within one mailed arm, while the other went to his sword. Lightning still flickered in the bruised sky, but the light had faded and fog was boiling up around the perimeter of the pool. Beneath its surface, the long shadow turned again.

"Back," Ilkerineth said, and they retreated across the platform and up the steps to the space between the twelve paired pillars. He held a shimmer of protective wildfire about them both, but although the shadow passed close to the steps, nothing broke the surface of the water. Yet, he thought grimly, and did not stop until they reached the crumbling arch. The surrounding quiet was so intense that it reverberated, like the afternote from a great bell. Already the fog was rolling across the pool, although so far only tendrils had crept past the pillars. A quick glance around showed streamers of mist creeping into the colonnade as well.

"Is it a Sun trap?" Nuithe's whisper was loud as a shout against the silence.

Ilkerineth jerked his head in a quick negative and gathered his power. Lightning crackled as the void whispered in answer, low and eerie from every corner of the dim space. Nuithe wiped away the blood that had welled again on her lip. Of course, Ilkerineth thought: blood. He ground his teeth at his own carelessness, even as he channeled a mindcall to Nindorith. *To me, my brother!*

Wind shrilled across the open court and shadows oozed from the fog, snaking past the pillars. Ilkerineth drew his power in closer still as a dark shape began to heave out of the pool and the fog raced forward—to engulf Nuithe, he guessed, drawn by the blood. Towering taller than the pillars, he summoned a blue-white blaze of lightning and hurled it toward the onrushing shadows. The wind shrieked and the waters churned as Ilkerineth extended both arms and more lightning crackled, immolating both fog and shadow before he asserted his will and compelled the small world of Amaliannarath's pool back into calm.

"Impressive," Nindorith murmured, his power an invisible rampart along the colonnade and around the arch. *"You did not need me after all."*

"Apparently not." Wildfire was still blazing along Ilkerineth's arms, and he let it burn, an aftermath to the surge of magic through his body. Nuithe was bone white, the delicate angles of her face pressing sharply through skin, and her nose was bleeding. She tilted her head back and wadded a trailing sleeve against the flow, but her

eyes were fixed on him. "What was that?" Fabric and blood muffled her voice.

Ilkerineth let the wildfire die so he could wrap both arms around her and hold her close, *close*, until the pounding of his heart stilled. But it was Nindorith who answered, a roll of quiet thunder out of the air.

"The maelstrom stirs, Lady." He paused, and Ilkerineth knew they were both listening, waiting for another chill whisper out of the void. "It begins again."

PART I

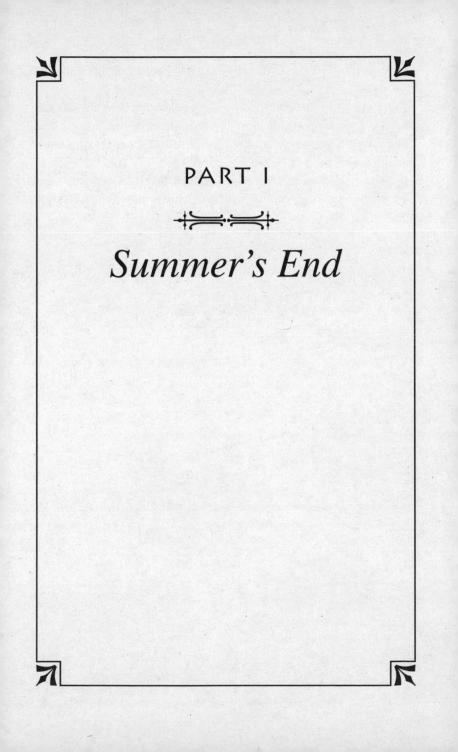

Summer's End

1

Lady Mouse

Outside, the latest Wall storm had blown itself into a brief respite of calm weather, but inside the Red Keep the storm that had been raging between the ruling kin for weeks continued to generate acrimony and raised voices. Although, Myr thought, wrapping her arms around her drawn-up knees, "raised voices" was only her former governess Ise's way of being polite. Anyone else would say shouting, usually over the top of whoever else was yelling at the same time.

She stared out over league on league of cloud wrack and bitter peaks toward the dark smudge that concealed the farthest limit of the Wall of Night. Sometimes, when the sky was more overcast, she caught the flicker of lightning through the smudge and would shiver, thinking about all those who kept watch over that dark boundary. Today, though, the sky was as close to clear as it ever got on the Wall of Night.

Peaceful, Myr told herself, thinking of the dispute that still rumbled in the keep below her. It was not a comparison she had ever thought to make in favor of the Wall, even if all eight of her strong-willed siblings were resident in the keep at one time. Yet argument seemed too mild a term for the tempest that had broken the moment their father, Sardon, the Earl of Blood, announced that one of his daughters would marry the Earl of Night before the year was out. Myr knew the marriage was only happening because the Earl of Night's outsider leman was dead. Assassinated, Ise had told her, by members of the Earl's own Honor Guard—and Myr couldn't blame her older sisters for not wanting to marry into a House so lost to the Derai Code.

After very brief consideration, she amended the latter reflection to exclude her two eldest sisters. Hatha, the Earl's eldest, warrior daughter, had guffawed when she heard the news and observed that she doubted the Earl of Night envisaged a battle-scarred veteran like herself arriving in his wedding caravan. The Heir of Blood, Kharalthor the Battlemaster, had roared with answering laughter and punched his twin on her mailed shoulder with a gauntleted fist. From what Myr could tell, watching from as close to the door of the council chamber and flight as possible, that confirmed the Earl of Night's bride wasn't going to be Hatha. And she did find it impossible to imagine Hatha ever wearing anything but armor, or living anywhere but in a barracks. In fact, mostly Hatha didn't live in the keep at all, but served with Kharalthor on Blood's borders.

The bride was not going to be Liankhara either, because the Earl's second daughter had served as a Blood spymaster since she was younger than Myr was now. Neither the Earl nor his council would countenance her loss from Blood's ranks, or the potential subversion of her loyalties, no matter how strategic the marriage offered. So that left Sardonya and Sarein, as well as Myr herself.

Myr grimaced, because she knew no one would contemplate her for the role. Not that she wanted to be considered, but she was weary of hearing "weak" whispered behind her back. One of her former household guards, Kolthis, had not even bothered to whisper when he called her the Half-Blood. To be fair, he had been dicing with his cronies at the time and probably not known that she was close enough to overhear. Myr was not sure he would have cared, though, even if he had. And although the House of the Rose was just as much part of the Derai Alliance as the House of Blood, Myr would never dare utter that small defiance aloud. Not even when alone and on the pinnacle of the Red Keep's tallest watchtower as she was now. Besides, it would not change anything. No one would consider her suitable for the role of Countess of Night, with its unprecedented opportunity to further Blood's sway within the Derai Alliance.

I've only just come of age anyway, Myr told herself. Blood might use strategic marriage to seal its alliances, but the ruling kin always served within their own House for at least five years after reaching their majority. With her eighteenth birthday only a month behind her, Myr had not even endured the public celebration yet, let alone chosen the role in which she would serve her House. She had assumed that her half-sister Sarein would be the Bride, since she was not only five years past her majority but already an adept player in Blood's councils. Since the Earl's remaining daughter, Sardonya, had made the last strategic marriage into the House of Swords, that also made it Sarein's turn . . .

Except Sarein was refusing the honor—or rather, dishonor, as both she and Sardonya had been saying at length and volume for weeks now. Offers of gold, jewels, and ongoing revenue from Blood's mines had failed to appease either sister, although eventually, Myr supposed, one of them would have to give in. Once an agreement between Houses had been signed, especially a marriage contract, breaking it would not just mean a loss of honor and prestige for the defaulting party, but heavy reparations, and possibly blood feud or even war.

The Derai Alliance can't afford that sort of schism between Blood and Night, Myr reflected somberly. "I wonder what they're holding out for, before deciding the matter between them?" She murmured the words to the vast expanse of the Wall, her voice falling away into emptiness. Given what had already been offered, it must be staggeringly large, and Myr wondered why her father had not just issued a command weeks ago and ended all the disputation right then. As for the Earl of Night, Myr's secret opinion was that if he only knew what the next seven years held for him with either Sardonya or Sarein, he'd be praying to all Nine Gods for Blood's arguments to remain unresolved.

A boot scraped at the foot of the lookout stair, followed by ascending footsteps. "Lady Mouse." Myr recognized the voice before she saw Taly, one of the guards assigned to her household. Taly's watch partner, Dabnor, had coined the nickname "Lady Mouse"—but Taly, new to the keep and with an equally new ensign's knot on her shoulder, had taken over a year to begin using it. Now she squatted on her heels beside Myr, studying the bleak terrain. "Dab said he'd seen you heading this way." Myr suspected Dab would have said "scampering," but even at her most relaxed it was not a term Taly would use, or repeat, in relation to one of the Earl's children. "It *is* quiet up here today," she added.

By comparison with the inner keep? Myr wanted to say, but knew Taly would just clam up, her expression stolid as the stone in the keep's walls.

"Your sister has sent for you," the ensign continued, when Myr did not speak. "Captain-Lady Hatha wants to see how your weapons practice is progressing."

Myr groaned. "Do I have to?"

Taly's expression did not change. "She said I was to flush you out, wherever you were hiding. And that my failure would not be acceptable to her."

I hate the way Hatha does that, Myr thought: makes it clear that Taly, Dab, or whoever else she corners will get punishment detail if *I* don't do what she wants. "I loathe weapons practice," she said, and caught Taly's slight headshake before the guard checked the gesture.

"You're a Daughter of the House of Blood, Lady Myrathis. You need to know your weapons."

Myr pulled a face, because she much preferred learning how to treat others' aches and bruises, rather than sustaining them herself. The arts of Meraun, she thought, rather than those of Kharalth, the Battle Goddess. But Blood followed the latter, not only first among the Nine but largely ignoring the rest, so forswearing the arts of war was not an option for a Daughter of Blood.

"Your eye–hand coordination is good; you just need to apply yourself more." Taly stood up. "Dab thinks so, too, and Captain-Lady Hatha is a good teacher."

For you maybe, Myr thought, although she stood up as well, shaking out her skirts. "She loves sparring with you," she said aloud. "I wish I could dress you up in my clothes and add a glamour, so she thinks you *are* me. Then everyone would be happy."

Taly put out a mailed arm, blocking the entrance to the stair. "Never say such a thing again, Lady Mouse, not even in jest. I've heard of folk exiled for less, including those of high blood." A shadow touched the ensign's hazel eyes. "And darker stories, too, from some of the hardline holds: whispers of those with even a hint of the old taint, including children, being murdered rather than exiled."

Myr swallowed. "My father would never allow anyone to harm me—" she began, but stopped at Taly's expression.

"And your siblings?" The guard spoke softly. "The Lords Anvin and Parannis? Lady Sardonya or Lady Sarein?"

Myr shivered. "All right," she said, but Taly did not lower her arm.

"What if I refused to let you leave? What if I said I was in the pay of your enemies, the House of Adamant or the House of Stars? Or I could be a Swarm minion, ridden in on the back of a storm and secreted here? What would you do then?"

"I'd be dead anyway," Myr told her. "No matter how much I practice, I'll never be anywhere near as good as you."

Taly clicked her tongue. "You'll be dead because you think that way. The more you practice, the more likely you are to find a way to survive." She lifted her arm clear. "After you, Lady Mouse."

At least, Myr reflected, Taly did not try and trip her as she went by, the way Kolthis had liked to do, before the happy day when he and his cohort had been rotated into her brother Huern's guard. Now she held up her skirt to avoid stumbling on the steep stairs, only speaking once she reached the first landing. "Besides, the demons that ride the storms are just fireside tales, everyone says that." In fact, she was not sure Mistress Ise supported the popular view on storm demons, but she wanted to delay getting to the training hall, in the hope Hatha would grow tired of waiting. "I'll have to return to my rooms and change if I'm going to train," she added, when Taly remained silent.

This time the ensign did reply. "I sent Dab to fetch your attendants and your training clothes." Myr did not need to look back to know she would be grinning. Sighing inwardly, she resigned herself to an afternoon of misery.

Hatha was nowhere to be seen when they reached the training hall, and it was Mistress Ise, rather than one of Myr's attendants, who waited beside Dab. The guard towered over the diminutive Rose woman, who had been governess and was now senior companion to Myr, exactly as she had been to her mother, Lady Mayaraní of the Rose. Myr could not see any training clothes, but she did catch the hand signal Dab flashed Taly. She had worked out enough of their hand codes to know it was a warning, although not the finer shadings that would have conveyed what the warning meant. But Ise's presence had already told her there was trouble, even if the old Rose woman's tone and expression were as noncommittal as Dab's lean countenance.

"Where's Hatha?" Myr asked, and was pleased with the calm way her voice came out.

"She has been summoned to attend your father." Ise spoke in the formal, well-modulated tone she had tried to instill in Myr. "As have you, Lady Myrathis."

"Just with Hatha?" Myr asked, clinging to a thread of hope. "Or—"

"I believe all your family will be there."

"Nine!" Myr ignored the old woman's reproving look. According to Ise, only the poorly brought up invoked the collective numeral for the Derai's Nine Gods. "Are they all still shouting?" She could feel her head start to ache, just thinking about being in the same room.

"Your sister was already shouting when she left here," Dab said, straight-faced. Ise's reproving look shifted to him, although she said nothing as Taly placed one hand on Myr's shoulder, turning her toward the door.

"Best not keep your father waiting, Lady Myrathis."

No, Myr thought, although she desperately wanted to drag her feet. She straightened her back and tried to imagine that she was as physically strong as Hatha, or subtle like Liankhara. Or even, she added tartly, as self-serving as Sardonya and Sarein. Her resolution lasted until the first sounds of shouting reached them, at the far end of a long somber corridor that led to her father's war room. The granite walls dwarfed them all, and the lamps were set so high on the evenly spaced columns that little light reached the floor of dark polished stone. Myr stopped, gazing along an avenue of ancient war banners, their colors quenched in shadow, toward the stony expressions of the honor guards outside her father's door.

Kharalthor, she thought, listening to the Heir's familiar roar. The subsequent bellow was Anvin, shouting back. Taly's gloved fist rapped her shoulder gently. "Heart up, Lady Mouse." Myr sighed, but started forward, very conscious of her guards' stolid presence and Ise's cane, tapping its rhythm against the stone. Blood's hydra emblem was carved above the war room door and Myr felt as though every one of its nine heads was staring directly at her. She was so busy trying to avoid the stone stare that she almost walked into the Honor Lieutenant on duty. He stepped swiftly away, saluting, and she recollected herself sufficiently to incline her head in acknowledgment.

The shouting hit her like a wall as soon as the door opened. Her father was sitting back in his great chair with his eyes closed, but he opened them as she entered. Huern and Liankhara both looked around, and Hatha nodded from where she sat, using a small dagger to clean beneath her nails. Kharalthor and Anvin were still shouting, and Sardonya and Parannis had joined in while Sarein watched them all with her chin on her hands. Myr envied her companions, who got to wait outside, and wondered if she dared slip into a chair close by the door. She hesitated—and her father waved her to a place between Sarein and Sardonya. Myr bowed to him, the deep salute that even a Daughter of Blood must make to the head of her House, but fixed her eyes on the tabletop as soon as she was seated.

"It's only a seven-year contract." Kharalthor pounded his fist against the carved arm of his chair. "That means in seven years' time one of you can return here a very wealthy woman."

"We'll have to live *there* for seven years first," Sardonya yelled back, "in a keep where *honor* guards have murdered a member of their Earl's household."

"Put down his outsider bitch, you mean," Parannis said, below the roar. Sarein mimed applause.

Anvin rested both fists on the table, glaring at Kharalthor. "What better sign that the rot's really set in, when an Earl forgets himself to the extent of rutting with outsiders and his guards realize they've no honor to defend anymore? Yet you ask one of our sisters to enter such a den?"

"I'm not asking!" Kharalthor's fist pounded again, and Myr wondered how long the chair would survive such treatment. "The contract's been signed. Blood's honor is at stake!"

"And what about Sarein's and my honor?" Sardonya flung back. "Perhaps our father should have thought about that before putting his name and seal to the agreement." Her glare was wasted, though, because the Earl had closed his eyes again, his expression unyielding as a slab of stone.

Why does he let them rage at each other like this? Myr wondered. *Is it a test, to see who is strongest, or most determined, or simply the most virulent?* Almost involuntarily, her gaze slid to Parannis and Sarein, although she kept her lashes lowered like a protective veil. The younger pair of twins had their heads close together, whispering behind their hands. Myr looked away, feeling a headache begin to press. She knew the drug Ise would prescribe for it, and where to find it in the Rose woman's store, but that did her no good now. Instead she focused her breathing into the rhythm Ise had taught her, trying to stave off the worst of the pain until she could escape.

Sardonya had continued to scowl at the Earl's unresponsive face, but now she tapped her foot. "Besides, I've already made one marriage of convenience outside of Blood. It's someone else's turn." The gaze she turned on Liankhara was steel. "Yours, perhaps, Sister Spider?"

"The Earl of Night's clearly not particular." Parannis began cracking his knuckles. "Perhaps he'd take you, Kharalthor, since you're so keen on the match?"

Hatha chuckled, but the look her twin leveled at Parannis was hard. "Huern, Anvin, and I have all made strategic marriages, cementing our line's bonds with Blood's satellite holds—something you have yet to do. So step carefully, little brother."

Parannis shrugged, but did not respond. Even Hatha, Myr knew, had made a marriage of policy when she was younger, and had a son growing up in his father's Hold. Liankhara looked around the table. "The agreement specifies a child from the union, an Heir for the House of Night. I think Earl Tasarion may prove quite particular about that."

This time Parannis sniggered, while Sarein pursed her lips—but until the meeting got down to serious business, Myr knew she would leave the talking to her twin.

"He should have shown his particularity a little sooner, then." Sardonya spoke more quietly than before, although every word was acid-etched. "I don't see how you can expect either Sarein or me to bed, let alone bear children to an Earl who has sullied himself with an outsider. We'd spend another seven years after we got home cleansing ourselves of the pollution."

"More like fourteen!" Anvin scowled from Kharalthor to Liankhara.

"No amount of wealth," Parannis added, "could be expected to compensate either of my sisters for that."

His comment had come just a little too quickly, Myr decided. That suggested Sardonya and Sarein must be working together, either to carve out more concessions, or simply to win a decisive round against Kharalthor and their older siblings. In which case they were playing a dangerous game, with the agreement between the two Houses already signed. She concentrated on keeping her breathing calm and the headache's pain dull as Kharalthor spread his great hands wide.

"For the Nine's sake! The child would be heir to the Derai Alliance itself, not just the House of Night."

Huern spoke for the first time since Myr arrived, his tone reflective. "And if anything should happen to the father, the mother becomes regent."

"And would then have to dwell in the Keep of Winds until her child was of age." Sardonya curled her lip at him. "Marrying the Sword Earl's brother and living in their keep for three years was more than bad enough." She paused, her expression growing thoughtful. "Mind you, if the contract had been with the son rather than the father . . ."

"Only it wasn't. And no one in the Keep of Swords showed any desire to prolong your stay once the three years were up." Liankhara regarded her sister dispassionately. "Try not to show yourself up for a fool, Sardonya. A Daughter of Blood standing as regent to the Heir of both Night and the Derai Alliance—we've been awaiting an opportunity like this for centuries."

Parannis and Sarein smirked in unison as Sardonya's expression darkened, but it was Anvin who replied. "Do you intend to make sure it bears fruit, Sister Spy?"

Liankhara raised one shoulder in a half shrug. "For now, the alliance itself is sufficient for our purpose. The Heir of Night will be our blood relative, and if we bind his or her marriage back into our own kinship web as well . . . " She shrugged again, her smile thin. "A circumstance the Heir's mother will undoubtedly be able to influence. If we play the hand this marriage deals us well, we shall see the leadership of the Derai pass to *our* bloodline within a generation."

"Where it should be," Kharalthor agreed. His heavy gaze swung between Sardonya and Sarein. "A true Daughter of Blood would put the good of her House before self-interest."

Sardonya snorted, but Anvin was frowning. "What of the taint? How can we keep our line free of that?"

He sees the greater advantage, Myr thought. Possibly because they were the children of the Earl's second wife, Paranna of Oath Hold, and half-siblings to the rest, Sarein and Parannis were only ever for themselves. But Anvin might be won over—and despite Liankhara's accusation, Sardonya was no fool. She would detect Anvin's potential defection and the advantage shifting to Sarein, who could rely on her twin's unswerving allegiance. Myr's headache pulsed in anticipation of Sardonya's fury, darkness hovering at the periphery of her vision. Doggedly, she concentrated on a scratch in the tabletop and pushed both pain and darkness back.

"The taint came into their line from Earl Tasarion's first, Sea House wife." Kharalthor was dismissive, but Parannis laughed.

"How glib you are, brother. Earl Tasarion also has a Night kins-woman with the taint, one who resides in the Keep of Winds' Temple quarter. So the only sure way to keep our line and House pure is to make no marriage and allow no child that will expose us to risk." His smile widened as Sarein extended a hand, crooking long fingernails into his forearm. "Although we could argue that the integrity of our bloodline has already been compromised."

Myr's head throbbed as Kharalthor surged to his feet, knocking his chair to the floor. "How *dare* you insult our father!" Two more chairs grated back as Anvin and Parannis leapt up, too, the latter laughing—until Earl Sardon spoke above the uproar, flat as iron.

"Sit down, all of you." He waited until they were seated before leaning forward, his stare boring into Parannis. "Be warned: I will not have your barbs—or those your sister has sharpened for you—on this matter. As for the rest, I am out of patience with your intermi-nable arguments."

Liankhara bowed from her chair. "The matter must be settled, my Father, otherwise word of our reluctance may trickle back to Night."

"Does that matter, Sister Spider?" Now Parannis was cool, and Myr's stomach muscles clenched. "Perhaps they need to know how little we care for what they think."

Earl Sardon held up his hand, commanding silence. "Not before this marriage is secured and the advantage it will bring us consolidated." He frowned around the table. "I said that I would have a decision today and I mean it. Sardonya, Sarein: ask for whatever gilding will sweeten this bargain for you and I will consider it favorably. But be very sure, if you do not reach a decision between yourselves, then I will choose for you."

Sardonya, spear-straight in her chair, tossed back her long auburn hair. "Perhaps, Father, you should have consulted with us before pledging your honor and that of our House to this path. You may compel all you like, but neither of us will go willingly."

Myr did not dare look at her father, but despite the pain behind her eyes she did turn at Sarein's delicate cough. "We have heard that this Night Earl, amongst his many peculiarities, is a stickler for our Derai law." Her half-sister's tone was demur. "Laws that forbid any Derai being forced into marriage, even to aid the cause of Earl and House."

The silence that followed was infinitely worse than the shouting had been, and even Sarein, Myr noticed, was not quite brave enough to meet their father's stare. "So you both refuse?" The Earl's voice was a blade, and the pain in Myr's head cut deeper. Across the table, Huern and Liankhara made an elaborate show of looking at each other.

Of course, Myr thought, the deal makers—and felt sure that any scheme these two proposed would have been dreamed up long before. The only question was who else they had enlisted to back their play, since they would not show their hand until certain it would win the game. Despite the headache, she made herself focus as Liankhara spoke. "One of our line must make the sacrifice for Earl and House."

Here it comes, Myr thought, keeping her eyes on the tabletop.

"So if Sardonya and Sarein continue to refuse their duty . . ." Liankhara's pause stretched—until Myr's head lifted to find not only her sister's gaze, but Huern's and the Earl's, also fixed on her. Mesmerized, she stared back.

"Then," Huern finished smoothly, "the Bride must be Myrathis, now that she's old enough."

I'm not ... Myr struggled to stay upright, to continue breathing evenly despite all their eyes fixed on her. *I can't ... I haven't ... No—* Darkness wavered at the edge of her vision again, but odd details intruded: Hatha's little knife, hanging motionless above her sister's nails, and Sardonya's scornful look.

"Her?" Sarein said finally. "The Half-Blood?"

"Who can barely use a sword," Parannis added, "and dabbles with healing under the ill-advised tutelage of the Rose crone? You cannot be serious."

The silence endured an instant longer before all her siblings' voices clamored, shouting over the top of each other. Unable to move or speak, let alone think coherently, Myr gave in to the hovering darkness and fainted.

2

The Serpent Prince

The three hooded figures came up Grayharbor's Sailcloth Street just as the rain swept in off the sea for the second time that day. The deluge brought a swirl of leaves and rubbish down the deep gutters on either side of the cobbled thoroughfare, and all three leapt for the portico of Seruth's temple where Faro had taken shelter. He heard one of the strangers curse as his boot came down in the flood. The fine black leather was soaked in an instant, and the man cursed again as he followed his companions into the porch. Faro moved further back, into the corner closest to the temple door, wary of the long black cloaks and deep hoods that did not fall back even when the newcomers sprang for shelter. They were carrying swords, too. He recognized the shape of hilt and scabbard beneath their cloaks and knew that likely meant other weapons as well.

The man who had stepped in the gutter said something, half under his breath, but his companions did not reply. Faro shivered, feeling chilled, although Summer's End rain was seldom icy. He registered the man's unfamiliar accent, too, when he had thought he knew all the nationalities that brought their ships into harbor and hawked their wares among the trading houses. He had even seen an Ishnapuri mariner once, with wide silk trousers, curved knives thrust into her waistband, and curled toes to her shoes. She had winked when she caught him staring and tossed him a small silver coin with the lion and stars of Ishnapur on one side, and a ship on the other. He had drilled a hole through it and wore it still, on a leather thong around his neck.

Faro stared at the downpour and contemplated edging inside the temple itself, but feared the movement might draw the strangers' attention. He studied them covertly, noticing both their height and the way the tallest man's hood was constantly moving. That fascinated him—until he realized that the leather of the soaked boot was already dry. He would have bolted then, except the boot's owner turned and stared straight at him from within the concealing hood. The chill around Faro intensified and he tried hard to look past the hood, rather than directly into the face beneath it.

"Guttersnipe." The man spoke in the River tongue, which was also the language of Grayharbor, but still with the unknown accent. Faro recognized the lordly tone, though, from listening to the mercantile nobility of Ij. "Do you know where the Ship House may be found?"

Faro regarded him warily. "D'you mean Ship's Prow House, sir?"

"Ship, Ship's Prow," the man returned. "Surely it's all the same?"

"Nossir." Faro kept both face and tone neutral. "The Ship House is an inn down harborside. Ship's Prow House is a merchant's place that gets rented out to River folk with business here. It's not far," he added, when the man remained silent. "You go up Awl Lane, off the top of this street." He shivered, rubbing at his arms, and wished the rain would stop so his uncomfortable companions would leave.

"You will take us there," the stranger said.

Not for nothing, I won't, Faro thought. The nearer of the other two, the one without the moving hood, turned as though overhearing his thought and held up a copper coin between black-gloved fingers. Faro hesitated, aware of the sharpness within his stomach and that an Ijiri penny would buy him both a meat pie and an unblemished apple at the market.

"Well?" the first man demanded, and Faro nodded reluctantly, snatching the coin out of the air when the second stranger flipped it to him. After that it was a matter of waiting for the rain to slacken sufficiently to venture out, while trying not to look at his companions at all. Once they did set out up Sailcloth Street, the cobbles still dark with rain, the two strangers walked to either side of him, with their companion in the moving hood immediately behind. Silently, Faro cursed himself for having given in to the coin's temptation.

Awl Lane was steeper and narrower than Sailcloth Street, hemmed in by tall stone walls with narrow gray houses rising behind, which forced them to walk single file. The first stranger trod close on Faro's heels, a heavy hand resting on his shoulder. Once he closed his fingers, steel biting into flesh and muscle, and Faro bit the inside of his mouth so as not to cry out. I won't give him the satisfaction, he resolved, but was conscious of the accelerated thumping of his heart, and the chill sweat filming his skin.

The lane ended in a small square, with more of the tall, narrow houses set around it and short flights of steps up to wooden doors. The fountain in the middle of the square was dry, except for the water left by the rain. A bronze archer rose from its central plinth, suggesting that this must have been a prosperous quarter once. Now all the houses, like the fountain, had a slightly shabby air, the paint on their shutters and doors faded.

The ship's figurehead that gave their destination its name was set over the door of the largest house on the square. It always made Faro shiver, because rather than being the usual depiction of a heroine or hero out of a story, it was a fierce-eyed mer-horse, with a long horn spiraling from its forehead and ears pressed flat to its skull so it looked half serpent. The colors of the savage head and horn, and the scaled body, must have been brilliant once—gilt and scarlet and deeps-of-the-sea green—but had grown as faded as the house's flaking woodwork. The door was framed and banded with iron, and despite the heavy hand on his shoulder, Faro still noted that both looked new. The hinges and lock, too, as well as the hasps on the shutters, he thought, squinting up—and saw that some wag, a 'prentice most likely, had left a chisel blade stuck into the figure-head's spiraled horn.

I'll come back for that later, Faro promised himself, so I'll have something to stick into the likes of these three, next time someone tries to nab me. "The Ship's Prow House," he said, and tried to pull clear, but the stranger was quicker. His grip clamped down, forcing Faro to his knees.

"Not so fast," his captor said.

Faro felt the chill from the temple porch bite deep into his flesh, and had to ball his hands into fists to prevent them shaking. The three hooded figures stood in a semicircle around him, studying the figurehead and the door. No one knocked, but eventually Faro heard the sound of a bolt being drawn back. A moment later the door opened slightly and a boy his own age peered through the crack. "The master's not at home to visitors."

The man with his hand on Faro's shoulder laughed, short and hard. "He'll see us." He shoved Faro ahead of him. "Up you go."

Faro twisted and struggled, despite the pain of the man's grip, aware that the other boy was trying to close the door. The man holding him laughed again and uttered a single, unrecognizable word—and immediately, Faro froze in place. His throat was locked, too, as his captor shouldered the door wide and thrust him bodily inside. The door banged into the other boy's face, knocking him backward.

His nose is broken, Faro thought, seeing its crookedness and the gush of blood. But he's frozen, the same as me; he can't do anything to help himself.

As the door closed behind them, his captor spoke another, inde-cipherable word and Faro's rigid body went limp. The man shoved him away at the same time, and he collapsed in a sprawl of arms and legs, gasping for breath. Running footsteps sounded, then came to an abrupt halt. Still sucking in breath, Faro peered up at the new arrivals: an elderly servant, and a much younger man with dark shoulder-length hair and an ascetic expression.

"This is an outrage," the servant began, but his voice was shaking.

Don't be a fool, old man, Faro thought. The three who had entered the house with him said nothing, but the dark-haired man sank to his knees, dragging the old man down with him.

"Prince Aranraith," he husked, as though his mouth was as dry as Faro's. "You honor this house." He bowed forward until his forehead touched the floor, and after a moment's hesitation the old man, clearly bewildered, did the same. Faro lay absolutely still, aware that this hall, too, had grown cold. He was trying to breathe shallowly, but he could see the air misting just past his lips.

All three strangers lifted back their hoods—and Faro stifled a cry, because now he could see why the tallest man's hood had moved. He closed his eyes, hoping that he had fallen asleep in the temple porch and when he looked again the nightmare would be gone. But the stranger was still there, a powerfully built man in gold-washed black mail, with long coils of hair falling down his back. Except that the coils were not hair at all, but a sinuous twist of blue-black snakes, their forked tongues a perpetual flicker about the stranger's head and shoulders.

Nauseated, Faro screwed his eyelids shut again, but his heart still hammered painfully and he had to fight to control his trembling. Outside, the rain began to drum.

"Where is Nirn?" The voice that spoke was darkness and shadow, with a rustling sibilance through it, and Faro knew without opening his eyes that it belonged to the man with the serpent hair. This time he understood the strangely accented words, although he had to concentrate to make them out.

"Forgive me, Prince Aranraith," the dark-haired man replied in the same language. "But he has ordered us not to disturb him. Under any circumstances, he said."

"Fool." Faro heard the first stranger's fingers snap as he switched back to the River dialect. His tone was that of a man commanding a dog. "You, boy! Fetch your master."

For a moment Faro thought the stranger meant him, but when his eyes flew wide the other boy was lurching to his feet, his nose still bleeding. "Now, dolt!" the stranger snapped. The boy ran, scrambling up the dark wooden stairs at the far end of the large chamber. Before he reached the upper level, another tall figure with startling, bone-white hair had appeared at the balustrade. A flare of lightning reflected through the windows in a way that made it seem to emanate from the white-haired man, but no rumble of thunder followed. The only sounds were the rain, and a hissing from the snakes as Prince Aranraith and the newcomer stared at each other.

The prince's two companions had fanned out to his left and right, and now Faro saw the last of the strangers clearly for the first time. His black armor was honed to spur points at elbow and shoulder, while the sword at his hip was long and curved toward the tip. The eyes that rested on Faro were set slantwise in a face that was all austere planes and sculpted angles, their expression dark and impenetrable as the void. Faro froze again, unable to look away.

He did not see the boot coming, only screamed as agony exploded across his body. The force of the kick propelled him several yards across the floor, into a carved wooden chest. He was aware, through the pain and the sobs that he could not check, that the first stranger was staring down at him. The man's eyes were as darkly blue as sapphires in a gem merchant's window, and their color bored through the pain until it was all Faro could see. "You do not look at us without leave, gutter vermin. It will go worse still if I hear you speak."

Beyond the blue of the stranger's eyes, someone was laughing. At first Faro thought it was the serpent prince, because even above the rain he could hear the laughter's hissing note, but then realized that the sound was coming from the balcony. "How you do despise the natives, Arcolin, beneath your envoy's veneer." Despite the hissing laugh, the white-haired man's voice was ice: "And here in company with my kinsman, Aranraith, and the great Thanir—a delegation indeed."

"As you say." Arcolin turned toward the balcony, releasing Faro. "You've made us work to find you, Nirn, but the time for games is over. We're here to discuss treachery: your hound Emuun's treachery."

Lightning snapped blue-white from the gallery and fractured the flagstones between Arcolin and the stairs. Faro nearly bit through his lip, because this time there could be no question, the lightning had definitely been inside. When his vision recovered from the flash, the dark-haired man, who had been kneeling a moment before, was standing at the foot of the stairs. The old servant still lay with his hands over his head, moaning.

Darkness rose about the three intruders and flowed between them and the staircase. Faro, enthralled and terrified together, found he could not look away from the shadows that writhed through it, or block out their sibilant whispers. The susurration echoed the prince's serpent locks, which had risen as one, their fangs extended, when the lightning seared. They hissed again as the prince held up a hand weighted with jeweled rings, the gemstones glittering in the afterdazzle.

"Your adept's behavior suggests he fears us, Nirn." The prince's eyes glinted, garnet red beneath heavy lids, and the dark-haired man paled. "Or believes we mean you harm—as if we were Derai, tearing ourselves apart with petty feuding."

"Petty?" Nirn's voice was still ice. "When you accuse one who is my blood kinsman, his service to our cause well proven, of treachery?"

"They also entered your house without leave, Master," the dark-haired man said, although his voice shook as the serpents twisted his way.

The warrior spoke for the first time, pitching his words to carry above the rain. "Rhike is dead, Nirn—we believe by Emuun's hand."

Faro was still finding it painful to breathe as Nirn descended the stairs. Despite Arcolin's threat, he could not stop his gaze returning to the sorcerer's emaciated countenance and the fine scar that cut from temple to chin. "Rhike?" Nirn said finally. "That *is* a loss. And she, too, was kin." The scar, livid against his pallor, twitched as his pale gaze settled on Arcolin. "I heard you were wounded, Poisoner. Did one of those brands you were busy thrusting into southern fires leap back out and burn you?"

"Retract your fangs, Nirn." Aranraith's command resonated through the hall as he crossed to the table at its center and pulled out a chair. His serpent hair subsided as he sat. "Sit, all of you."

Only the warrior hesitated, frowning as he studied the dark-haired man on the stairs, although he addressed Nirn. "You had two adepts when last we met: Jharin, here, and another one—Amarn. Where's he right now?"

"Sheltering from the rain, no doubt." Nirn made a business of taking the chair opposite Aranraith's, his smile thin. "He went down to the port with orders for the ship's captain that brought us here. Ostensibly a coastal trader, but a smuggler on the side and useful, so we let him live."

Arcolin had seated himself on Aranraith's left, so Faro could only see his back and long black braid. "What if he or his crew talks?"

Nirn placed a jade rod on the table as Jharin, the dark-haired adept, came to stand behind his chair. Finally, he nodded toward the other boy, huddled halfway up the stair. "We have the captain's only son as hostage, in case my compulsion on him and his crew wears thin."

"And the old man who welcomed us?" Arcolin's drawl was pronounced.

"Comes with the house." Nirn shrugged, indifferent. "He and the boy are also under compulsion, but they can't understand us in any case."

"Can they not?" the black-armored warrior asked. Briefly, he glanced at Faro, who shrank back against the chest, as if he could disappear into the carved wood.

"Leave them for now. We have business to discuss." Something in the heavy velvet of Aranraith's tone, and the lazy way the snakes curled and uncurled, turned Faro's throat into a lump around which he struggled to breathe. In that moment he knew that none of them—not the boy on the stair, or the old man still prone on the flagstones, or himself, pressed against the chest—would be allowed to live.

Outside, the rain had become a tumult. Lightning illuminated the room again, and this time the crash of thunder followed within seconds. Nirn waved a hand, and flame leapt in every glass-enclosed lamp around the room. The brightness pushed the shadows back, except around Aranraith, while the white-haired sorcerer's fingers tapped on the jade rod. "So, Thanir. Unfold me this business of Rhike's death and your accusation against Emuun."

The warrior seated himself on Aranraith's right. "Rhike was slain at midsummer, by a warrior who was immune to magic."

"And blood," Aranraith added, "demands blood."

"Always," the others intoned as one. The snakes bared their fangs, but any sound they made was lost beneath the storm. The gutters would all be overflowing, Faro knew, every steep street and wynd a torrent of water and filth. If only he could get clear of the house, he would disappear into the darkness and back alleys where he had a dozen hideaways, places these strangers would never find him. He gritted his teeth to prevent them chattering and struggled to concentrate the way his mam had taught him, observing both people and his surroundings closely.

Briefly, he fought back tears, as grief for his mam joined with fear and pain. Focusing on the old discipline helped, even if the strangers' conversation was a confusion of strange accents and incomprehensible discussion—of enemies and magic, and a warrior immune to it who had sabotaged something called a coterie in some distant place. Occasionally, names would swirl to the surface, like debris in a flood, including Emuun and Rhike again, but also Orriyn, who seemed to be Selia as well . . . And someone called Nherenor, who had been killed and whose death mattered, for reasons that Faro could not make out. He felt the tension that weighted their silence, though, when eventually the talking stopped.

Lightning had continued to flare throughout their exchange, but now Faro noticed how closely the thunderclap followed the latest flash. "Emuun accompanied me here from Ij," Nirn said, once the rumble died away. "By the time I dispatched him south again, hunting those accursed couriers . . . It would have been early summer, at least, before he returned to the River."

Aranraith's serpent hair hissed. "This is Emuun we're talking about. If his quarry went south then he would have arrived shortly afterward."

"In fact," Arcolin took him up, "we know he did. Rhike reported that he had the couriers you're so obsessed by within his hand several times in Emer, yet on each occasion his fist refused to close—difficult behavior to explain away."

Nirn's fingers tapped against the jade. "Sometimes the simplest explanation is the correct one. Whoever Rhike encountered cannot have been Emuun."

"Sometimes," Arcolin mimicked, "the simplest explanation *is* the correct one. Emuun is the only immune warrior we have left with sufficient experience to overcome an adept of Rhike's caliber, especially when she knew who she was dealing with. And she *saw* him, openly working with the native agents who undid our work. Admit it, Nirn: you've lost control of him."

Thanir leaned forward. "Nindorith did allege a Derai taint to Nherenor's death, although even he could not track its source. But it was definitely one of the native agents seen working with Emuun that wounded Arcolin."

Arcolin's response was lost as thunder crashed again, but Nirn was frowning. "Ilkerineth's son is dead, yet afterward Nindorith could not hunt the killer down? There's no Derai with that sort of power, not anymore."

"What's the alternative? It's even less likely that a native could accomplish such a thing." Arcolin shrugged. "The agent who wounded me got lucky, that's all. Still, regrettable though the boy's death was, it diverted Nindorith and Ilkerineth's attention into the mourning rituals. That left us free to deal with the Southern Realms in our own way."

"Yet here you are." Nirn's malice was obvious, even to Faro, tensed against the chest. "And wounded, however unluckily, by one of the natives. Or is that somehow Emuun's doing as well?"

Every serpent on Aranraith's head uncoiled, spitting. Momentarily, even the storm stilled, although Faro only realized he was holding his breath when his ears began to roar. Thanir's chair scraped back, his head turning toward the door. "Someone's coming," the warrior said.

3

Against the Wall

"Amarn!" Jharin started forward, but Aranraith waved him back. "Thanir will deal with it," he said, as the warrior crossed to the entrance and lifted the bar. As soon as he turned the handle, the force of the storm banged the door wide and a sodden figure fell through. Thanir kicked the door closed again, but did not rebar it as he draped the newcomer's arm across his shoulders and part carried, part dragged him to a settle by the fire. All the strangers were on their feet now, their attention on the newcomer—but Faro's eyes remained on the door.

Not barred, he told himself. His eyes returned to the group about the settle, all with their backs to him. Very slowly, he began inching toward the door, only to freeze as Jharin turned and hauled the old servant to his feet.

"Fetch hot water," the adept ordered, reverting to the Grayharbor dialect. "And wine. You!" he snapped at the boy on the stairs. "Get down here and tend the fire."

If I were that old man, Faro thought, edging closer to the entrance as the servant made his unsteady way out of the room, I would just keep on walking. The other boy, the smuggling sea captain's son, scuttled down to the wood stacked beside the hearth. Flame licked upward as the first log went in the grate, highlighting the injured man's slack expression and blue-tinged mouth.

"If you don't do something," Thanir told Nirn, "you'll find yourself short an acolyte. Someone's snapped this one's strings."

Nirn had been standing very still, his posture suggestive of someone listening to a distant conversation, but now he shrugged and rested his fingertips against his adept's forehead. Faro could have sworn that pale flame wreathed the sorcerer's hand at the same time as Amarn spasmed, all his limbs jumping as though a lightning bolt had gone into him. His eyes remained closed, but as soon as the spasm ceased he began to breathe more evenly and a healthier color crept into his face.

Flames began to roar up the chimney, and Arcolin rounded on the sea captain's son—still doggedly placing logs on the fire—and hurled him away. "Half-wit!" Terrified of being noticed, Faro froze in place. He was almost glad of the respite because his injured ribs were in agony, but equally relieved when the intruders' focus remained on Nirn.

"You use your adepts hard," Thanir said. "Our supply is not so plentiful, these days, that we can afford to throw them away."

The scar on Nirn's face writhed—as though it were alive, Faro thought, repelled—but otherwise his expression was indifferent. "He'll live. You can see that for yourself."

"What matters," Arcolin agreed, his vivid gaze narrow, "is who did this."

Jharin cleared his throat. The serpents around Aranraith's head stirred in answer, and the acolyte looked toward Nirn, waiting for his nod before speaking. "Derai ships come and go as they please here, seldom keeping to any schedule . . . " Again, Jharin cleared his throat. "The day before yesterday, we saw one of their weatherworkers near the *Sea Mew*. He did not see us, but Amarn and I decided to take turns keeping watch, just to be sure."

"If a weatherworker's been showing interest, then you've been sloppy." Arcolin was contemptuous. "You need to supervise your acolytes more closely, Nirn."

Faro tensed, expecting Nirn to hurl lightning again, but the sorcerer's gaze remained hooded. Aranraith stepped close to him, and although Nirn was tall, the serpent-haired prince loomed taller. "Arcolin's right. Most of the thrice-cursed weatherworkers seem to be at least half mad, but they're powerful still, as well as unpredictable. If this ship drew their attention, they may have already tracked down your lair. Did you think of that before letting your acolytes run loose?" His sibilance had grown more pronounced, the garnet gaze glittering. "I have indulged your eccentricities until now, but I won't tolerate another debacle like the one you oversaw in Ij."

Faro lay petrified, watching a vein in Nirn's temple throb. Arcolin and Thanir could have been statues, looking on. Only the wind-tossed shadows of the storm moved—that and the serpents, coiling and uncoiling around Aranraith's head. The sorcerer's hand was clenched white around the jade wand, but slowly relaxed. "You know what happened in Ij," he said finally. "There were imponderables, threads that never showed up along the lines of foreseeing."

"So you say." The serpents all hissed as one, and the temperature dropped again as Aranraith brought his face close to the bone-white sorcerer's. "But the threads should have been there, shouldn't they, if you were seeing true? When did imponderables ever escape you in the past, even if you could not fully weigh their influence? You *promised* me success, kinsman—then conveyed some farrago of the Derai-backed minstrel and a native militia turning that success to failure. Meanwhile, the River lands sail on, largely undisturbed. And now you—*you*, my kinsman—have drawn the Sea House's attention through your adepts' carelessness, a debacle we must now clean up." Aranraith's lip curled. "The Nirn I lured from Ilkerineth and Lightning to stand at my side would have disdained such incompetence—and remembered we have a war to win."

This time Nirn hissed back. "I forget nothing! But sometimes the wise course is to retreat and gather more intelligence, especially when you cannot discern the nature of what opposes you."

Aranraith's sneer deepened, but it was Thanir who spoke. "To be fair, my Prince, too much about recent events remains opaque, not only to Nirn." The serpents whipped around on him, but the warrior met the garnet glare steadily. "Salar and Nindorith agree that the thread that is this Patrol, the River soldiery, has risen to the surface of the pattern. But otherwise the Patrol is a blank, even to them. It's the same," he said to Arcolin, "with the native agent who opposed you in Emer. Despite having his knife, the one that wounded you, he remains invisible to our scrying."

Nirn's pale stare shifted to Arcolin, both assessing and malicious. "Not just mischance, then? The native agent actually stood firm against your power?"

Arcolin looked dark, but Thanir nodded. "That, together with the way he's vanished so completely, are equally intriguing."

"A puzzle." Nirn's voice acquired a singsong note as his expression turned inward looking. "Everyone has a face, a name, however deep it's buried. But who could block me and Nindorith, both? Not you, Arcolin. Not even you, Aranraith, not without Salar."

Aranraith's serpent hair was quiet, coiled close about his head, while Arcolin and Thanir watched the sorcerer with similar, intent expressions. "Something new, then?" Thanir prompted.

"Or something old . . ." Nirn's face was skull-like in the next jagged lightning flash, and the light reflected off his eyes as though he had grown blind. "Something moves in the current, quick as a fish turning between light and shadow, but more than that I cannot yet discern."

He sees with the inner eye, Faro thought, riveted despite his fear. Hanging about Seruth's temple, one heard whispers of such power, but only as a mystery confined to the sworn priesthood or belonging in the same tales as ghosts and heroes. Now Faro shuddered as he watched Nirn sway—and even if the others' attention had not been locked on the sorcerer, he did not think he could have stopped himself crawling away. Cautiously, he eased into movement again.

The old man chose that moment to re-enter the room, struggling to hold a tray with a steaming jug, a stoppered wine jar, and five earthenware goblets. His progress was unsteady and his hands began to shake, the contents of the tray rattling together as all three visitors turned their eyes toward him. When he stooped to set the tray down, the weight tipped too far forward and the whole array spilled onto the tabletop. The hot water flooded across the wooden surface, while the goblets bounced and rolled until one finally fell to the flagstones, shattering into fragments. Nirn's head jerked and his eyes widened, the blindness gone.

Faro understood, then, that he had not fully appreciated just how large Aranraith was—not until the prince's right hand shot out and seized the servant around the neck, hoisting him off his feet. Faro could see the old man choking, his eyes bulging out as Aranraith's hand closed on his throat, while the serpents sunk their fangs into cheeks and forehead and lips. Each bite left angry puncture marks behind, with red inflammation spreading rapidly away from the wounds. Yet Faro knew the old man was already dead, his windpipe crushed, even before Aranraith threw his body away like a broken toy.

You should have run, old man, Faro thought, tears sliding down his face. You should have run.

"*Almost*, we had what we need," Aranraith said, and his voice was shadow and power, equal to that of the storm. "But that's why I need you back with us, Nirn, and all of us working together again with Salar, as we did when we wrought our will with Aikanor."

Nirn's smile was thin as the whiplash scar. "I've always thought Aikanor was among our finest work."

Aranraith laughed, the sound slicing through the room. "It was. We can achieve such results again, too, if we combine our efforts." His tone grew silken, but the note of power deepened. "I am weary of skulking in shadows, especially with the maelstrom rising again at last."

Maelstrom . . . The word resonated, and Faro felt every hair rise across his skin. Aranraith's garnet gaze swept the old man's body, then the sea captain's boy curled into a fetal ball with his eyes screwed shut, before stopping at Faro, rigid against the wall.

I should run, Faro told himself: right now. But even if he could have moved—could have overcome the agony of his ribs and his shallow, pain-filled breathing—the door was still too far away. Even uninjured, he would never reach it and flee through before they caught him.

Aranraith laughed again. "Behold the gutter rat, slinking along the wall while we look the other way." Directly overhead now, the thunder pounded out its counterpoint to Faro's terrified heart as the serpent prince turned to Arcolin. "You've had your fill of native vermin lately. You dispose of the ratlings. As for you, Nirn—" Again the serpents hissed, echoing the sibilance in the dark voice. "I want you back with us, as I said. It's a small enough price to pay for your recent failures."

The bone-white sorcerer looked back at him, his eyes unreadable in the skull-like face. "I could give you Emuun. That should be recompense enough."

Aranraith's smile was half a snarl as lightning turned the room blue-white. The brilliance flickered on Arcolin's knife as he moved toward the sea captain's son, who remained curled into his ball. *Because he doesn't understand their speech,* Faro thought, *so he doesn't know* . . . He wanted to scream out, to warn the other boy, but remained frozen as Aranraith spoke again, his voice sinewy with power. "You are not going to *give* me Emuun, Nirn. I am going to *take* him. Thanir will do that job, not these benighted acolytes that your immune henchman would eat alive."

Lightning forked again and thunder crashed almost simultaneously, so that Faro could see, but not hear, as Arcolin wrapped one hand in the other boy's hair, dragging the head up and back to cut his throat. *So much blood,* Faro thought numbly, as Arcolin let the twitching body fall: *so much blood* . . .

"The only recompense I consider acceptable," Aranraith said, as the thunder ended, "is for you to make yourself useful to me again. And to Salar, who also insists on your return."

Nirn's head jerked back. "Salar? You would bring the basilisk against me, *kinsman*?"

Shadows moved in Aranraith's face. "No one commands Salar, not even me. But neither of us will brook your refusal. Too much is at stake and we are running out of time. So be wise: come with us freely." Without waiting for a reply, the serpent head turned back to Arcolin. "We'll go now, before any Sea scum arrive. Finish up here, then follow."

"A pleasure," Arcolin murmured, his blue gaze fixed on Faro. Smiling, he drew a white cloth from his pocket and wiped the knife clean.

Faro's brain was screaming at him to get away, but the best he could manage was the same leaden crawl toward the door. Pain and tears blurred his gaze and he was aware that snot was trailing from his nose—like a crying baby—but he could see no point in wiping it away. Over his shoulder, he watched his killer's catlike approach.

An icy blast whipped through the house and a line of garnet flame split the air before the fireplace, dazzling him. When Faro's vision cleared, the figures gathered there had disappeared. Black magic, he thought, gritting his teeth to silence their chattering. They told tales about that, too, in Seruth's temple. He had shivered along with all the other listeners, delighted by the thrill of darkness and danger, never dreaming he might find himself at the center of such a story.

Arcolin was standing over him now. Faro did not need the lightning's glow to see the black leather boots or the gleam of mail beneath the long black cloak. He did not need to hear above the thunder either, because Arcolin's voice spoke inside his head. *"Does one blunt a good blade on a rat? I think not. One just kicks it to death, against the wall."*

Instinctively, Faro curled tight, even though he knew it would do no good. He was aware, in a small, detached recess of his mind, that he hated Arcolin—hated his handsome face and vividly blue gaze—as much as he feared him. But he was far beyond the pride of trying not to scream as the first kick landed hard against his drawn-up knees. Outside, lightning seared simultaneously with the thunder's crack, drowning his scream as the boot connected again, and then again, each blow precise and almost leisurely. *"Let's see,"* the voice inside his head said, *"if we can't kick you apart like a chest full of wormwood."*

Another kick landed, this time against Faro's arms, wrapped close about his head. His body jerked and the next kick drove into the small of his back, booting him away from the protection of the wall. Arcolin laughed as Faro shrieked, the sound torn out of his throat and lost against the boom of the storm—then laughed again, delivering another, harder blow. Pain and darkness exploded across Faro's mind as well as his body. He could almost see the thin line that was his cry, spiraling out beyond the hall and the door with the ship's prow above it, into the wild dark of the storm until it reached the next fork of lightning, flickering between heaven and earth.

And the lightning answered, tearing the sky apart in a blue-white blaze of power that leapt down the path of his scream and into the chisel blade left in the mer-horse's horn. The ship's prow exploded as the lightning tore through the head and neck of the mer-horse—and the door disintegrated, every nail in it hurtling outward. Faro shrieked again, his mind and body on fire as the smell of melting metal and burning flesh assaulted him.

I'm dead, he thought. I'm dead. When the dazzle of the lightning faded, he let his mind follow, down into darkness.

But the darkness, it seemed, did not want a scrawny street brat and spat him back out again. Faro tried to move, groaning as every bruise and muscle protested. His eyelids were glued shut and his tongue felt swollen; when he licked at his lips, he could taste blood. He could smell blood, too, and smoke, and melted iron. Slowly and painfully, he raised his hands and worked the gummed lids apart.

Faro blinked, orientating himself, then gritted his teeth against the pain and pushed himself up. Fires burned close by, mainly above pools of metal where the door had been. The rain was still falling, although the thunder and lightning seemed to have stopped, but Faro shivered anyway, remembering the spear of lightning splitting the heavens. His eyes slid to where Arcolin had been, but found him sprawled about ten paces away, where he must have been hurled by the force of the explosion. More fire burned between Faro and the body, making it impossible to determine whether his attacker was dead or unconscious.

Either way, Faro knew he needed to be gone, but did not trust his ability to stand upright. He crawled toward the doorway instead, and a gust blew rain through the opening and into his face. The chill shocked him wide enough awake to use first the floor and then the wall to propel himself upright. He could feel every place where Arcolin's boot had connected, and clung to the wall, shivering— then jumped violently as a shadow fell across him. Shaking, Faro turned his head and met Thanir's dark regard. The warrior stood by the fireplace, with one hand resting on the hilt of his curved-tip sword, and a helmet, crowned with horn and talons, tucked beneath his arm. He studied Faro, his expression incalculable. "Well, well. Here's an unexpected turn of events. You, little rat, are supposed to be dead."

"It was the lightning," Faro whispered, as Thanir strolled closer.

"Was it?" Thanir was meditative. "But what am I to do now, having found you alive? Undoubtedly, you should be dead. But then again, my instructions were precise: to find out what had delayed our poison master." His brows drew together and he angled his head as though listening to another speaker. Faro, in equal parts mesmerized and terrified, noticed for the first time that the warrior had jeweled clips in his hair, an odd contrast against the barbed armor. "Agreed," Thanir murmured. "If spared he will owe me a debt for his life. But of what value is that?"

Faro licked at his lips and slid sideways again, but Thanir took one long stride and occupied the empty doorway. He spared a brief glance for the remains of the door, scattered at his feet, then extended a hand to hold Faro in place. Seen this close, the decorations in his hair were not clips at all but the heads of long pins, each one the preserved body of a beetle with a jewel-bright carapace. Faro stared at them doggedly—but Thanir's other hand tilted his chin, so he could no longer avoid the warrior's dark searching gaze.

"The lightning, you say? Intriguing." Thanir was still meditative. "And a street rat in my debt for his life; that will be a new thing." Faro tried to open his mouth—to say that he would honor the debt, that the great warrior would not regret it—but Thanir laid two fingers across his lips. "Never speak of it, little rat. Let it be our secret, yours and mine." He lifted his hand and stepped clear of the doorway, the shadows thickening around him. "Well," he said softly, when Faro did not move. "What are you waiting for? Run, if you value your life."

Faro did not run, he could not, but he bowed his head and staggered through the door, to lose himself in the rain.

4

Lost

At first Nhairin fled blindly, filled with the mysterious song that had woken her out of darkness and opened her prison door, leading her past oblivious guards and through gates that opened at a touch. Gradually, as both the song and then the memory of it faded, fear replaced both: the terror that now she was awake, Nerion would find her again, because Nerion had *always* been able to find her.

Whenever those memories crowded in, Nhairin would run before them, even if instinct insisted some things could never be outdistanced. Turning away from the Wall of Night, she zigzagged across the Gray Lands in an effort to confuse pursuit. Sometimes she would double back for the same reason, or lie hidden beneath straggling scrub when her lame leg gave out. She was badly out of condition, but whenever she stopped fear would swirl to the surface again, driving her on as soon as scant breath and her leg permitted.

She might be unfit and only just released from the darkness—the Madness, Nhairin thought, shuddering because release brought knowledge together with memory—but at least she had snatched up some weapons and supplies as the song led her out of Westwind Hold. As well as a water bottle and a pouch of food, she had a dagger, a bow, and a quiver full of arrows, and was soon thankful for all three.

Gray Lands' game might be scant and wary, but Nhairin saw plenty of 'spawn sign, far more than she remembered when fleeing this way with Malian and the small company from Night.

Her face, already disfigured by the old scar that cut across it from temple to chin, twisted further as she recalled the end of that journey, when Nerion's mind-whisper had urged her to kill Malian's friend, Kalan, with his inconvenient ability to turn away seeking minds. She had tried to do it, too . . . Nhairin swallowed against the dust that clogged her throat and sipped tepid water from the flask, reflecting that she would much prefer not to remember. And, in fact, the Madness had flooded in very soon after that.

Perhaps, she thought now—stoppering the bottle without a second sip, to ensure it lasted—because it was easier to give in to the roiling chaos of Jaransor, which had begun pressing at her mind as soon as she crossed the Telimbras, than to live with the shame of her actions. She recalled, too, how other whisperers had reinforced Nerion's compulsion after the attempt to knife the boy had failed. Their combined pressure had sliced through Nhairin's mind like blades, insisting that she "pursue" and "slay" after Kalan and Malian had fled from her into low-lying cloud.

From what Nhairin could remember of her guards' conversation, the background to her long sojourn in the Madness, Malian and Kalan had died later anyway, just as Kyr and Lira had fallen while attempting to delay the Swarm pursuit. So it was all for nothing, Nhairin thought. If Malian had lived, she might have contemplated returning to the Wall for her sake, but not now. In fact, she would not go anyplace those from her past might think to look, especially Nerion.

Terror welled again as Nhairin recalled her childhood friend's unerring ability to locate her, however carefully she hid. But I can't dwell on that, she told herself: I mustn't think about Nerion at all. I have to keep moving or find somewhere safe, someplace she would never associate with me.

The extent of darkspawn sign ruled out travel by night, since darkness would aid most 'spawn's stalking abilities more than it concealed her. Instead, Nhairin found night-time hideouts where an enemy could only come at her from one direction. She hunted for water, too, but preferred seeps found in shallow scrapes of rock, rather than waterholes or streams where both darkspawn and Derai patrols might come—including patrols specifically hunting her.

If possible, Nhairin would not have stopped at all, because as soon as she halted for any length of time the fear would return. The pain in her leg became a constant, like the wind and dust, but she still pushed on until the muscles spasmed, because when her leg was on fire and exhaustion closed in, the memories were also held at bay. Her other constants were the certainty that the Wall offered no succor, and the reluctant conviction that she would be safer if she kept close to Jaransor. Nhairin would never willingly go into those hills again, but although even their silhouette, seen through the Gray Lands' haze, made her shudder, she knew both 'spawn and other Derai would feel the same aversion. Besides, proximity to the Telimbras and the hills beyond, however dangerous, meant more game to hunt.

On my way to where, though? Nhairin thought, peering at her dirty face and bedraggled hair in another shallow pool. As soon as she stopped, she noticed the chill in the wind, blowing down out of the Winter Country. For the first time, she realized that autumn was upon her, and she needed to think beyond her crisscross traverse and the imperative to keep moving. To where? she asked herself again. If she turned north, into the face of the wind and oncoming winter, she might eventually find the nomads of the Winter steppe. But death seemed a more likely prospect, even if the Winter People were prepared to take her in.

Nhairin frowned at her reflection, because despite erratic progress she had gradually been working her way southwest. Eventually, she would reach the Border Mark—although not, given her lameness and recollection of distance, before winter overtook her. Yet even if she survived that far, only the unknown lay beyond the Border Mark: first the Barren Hills and then all the alien realms of Haarth.

The reflected face wavered, as if disturbed by Nhairin's doubt rather than the wind—because until the evening when Malian's company crossed into the Gray Lands, she had never left Night's territory, let alone the Wall. She had not traveled with Tasarion and Asantir to the River lands, all those years ago, in the time before Tasarion and Nerion even talked of being married. She had wanted to go, but Nerion had intended visiting her Sea Keep kin and wanted Nhairin to come with her—

"And I always did what Nerion wanted." Nhairin whispered the words aloud, and the wind caught them up. *Always, always, always,* it sighed back at her.

Ay, always, Nhairin thought—just as I could never hide from her when we were children, playing truant in the Old Keep. She shivered, remembering how she had never liked to go far into the echoing, lightless halls. At the time, she had thought that was why Nerion always discovered her hiding places so easily, although she could never find her friend.

Nerion always wanted to explore further into the darkness, too, Nhairin reflected, and she never got lost, while I always did. She shivered again and huddled her arms close, remembering how the Westwind song had not only cleared her mind of the Madness, but illuminated secrets she had previously kept hidden from herself.

No. Nhairin shook her head sharply. Not secrets—truths that I would not *allow* myself to know. This time she shuddered, reliving how Nerion's voice had whispered into her dreams on the night the Keep of Winds was attacked and so many had been slain, Malian's household among them. The whisper had told Nhairin what she must do, how the keep's alarms could be silenced. Later, the same whisper had held her immobile, staring into the fire, while a siren worm crept close to kill Malian as she slept. In both cases Nhairin had barely recalled either the whisper or the compulsion afterward, beyond fragments she assumed were dark dreams.

Because I always did what Nerion wanted, Nhairin repeated silently, and she bade me forget. The song had illuminated that truth, too, when it dispersed the darkness that shrouded her mind. Nhairin rocked back and forward on her heels, because she now knew the whispers had not ended with the worm, but increased—while the part of her that loved Malian, and was Derai to the core, struggled to break free of what seemed a waking nightmare.

Instead, Nhairin thought, I led Nerion straight to Malian when we fled, as unerringly as if she held a compass and I was north. My oldest friend, she added, rocking again, made me into a traitor to Earl and Heir and House, as well as to myself—Nerion, in whose cause both my face and my leg were cut open, holding the door against the Old Earl when he was bent on her murder.

The sense of betrayal was gall. Nhairin could taste its bitterness in her mouth.

The Madness of Jaransor had finally shut out Nerion's whisper, but the words the Westwind guards called Nhairin—traitor, betrayer, scum—could always work their way into the core of the darkness and find her there, no matter how she had crouched and rocked, trying to hold them out. *Traitor, betrayer, scum*, Nhairin repeated silently: not because I helped Malian flee Night, but because of what I did at Nerion's behest. Stilling, she pressed scratched hands to her face, because now that she had stopped long enough to think, she knew it did not matter whether she stayed ahead of winter or not. The Derai Alliance had no tolerance for traitors, and the outsider world, from what little she understood of it, had little truck for the Derai. "So I may have woken," Nhairin whispered to the grit-laden wind, "but I'm still lost."

Lost, the wind whispered back: *friendless, homeless, lost* ... Slowly, Nhairin lowered her hands as another thought took hold: she could take her own life. The Honor Code allowed it where a Derai sought to atone for compromised honor or broken oaths. No one would know if she committed suicide out here, and few would care if she was never found, but it was the one way to be certain Nerion could never whisper into her mind again.

And compel me to do her will, betraying honor and every oath I ever swore, Nhairin thought, drawing her dagger. Besides, the act of restitution was what counted, not whether anyone knew of it.

"Lost." The murmur gusted out of the wind as it veered around, blowing off Jaransor instead of down from the north. Nhairin's heart thudded sharply, but the voice was a sigh against her ear rather than a compulsion in her mind. Yet although she remembered the Gray Lands' wind well from crossing the plain with Malian, she did not think this voice had been in it then. *"A filament for the lost . . . to find their way home by. May it find you out, Nhairin, wherever you are."*

May it find *me*? Nhairin thought, the knife forgotten. Wonder was a ball, lodged in her throat, the stinging in her eyes more than blown grit as dust spiraled about her. Hiding me, Nhairin realized—and although she could not see the filament the wind-voice spoke of, she could sense its presence, unraveling through the swirl of debris. And if she could keep moving, keep following where the thread led . . . Slowly, Nhairin sheathed the blade and rose, grimacing at the flare of pain from her leg, before turning into the wind.

It occurred to her, as she started out, her sense of a voice within the wind, hiding and guiding her, could simply be the Madness reasserting itself. Some people, she thought—the sort of reflection Nhairin-that-was would have entertained—might say that hope itself was a form of madness, and clinging to it further proof she was deranged. Regardless, she plodded on, and gradually another realization intruded. It was not just that the Madness, once she let it in, had been stronger than Nerion's hold on her mind. Nhairin could not shake the sense that fact mattered, in some way she could not discern. As though it's a story I need to tell, she thought, other than to the wind.

Yet even if she dared return to the Wall, Nhairin doubted anyone there would believe her tale. All she could do, she decided finally, was hope and plod on, following the thread spun for her out of dust and wind—even if that was a sure sign the Madness still held her in its grip.

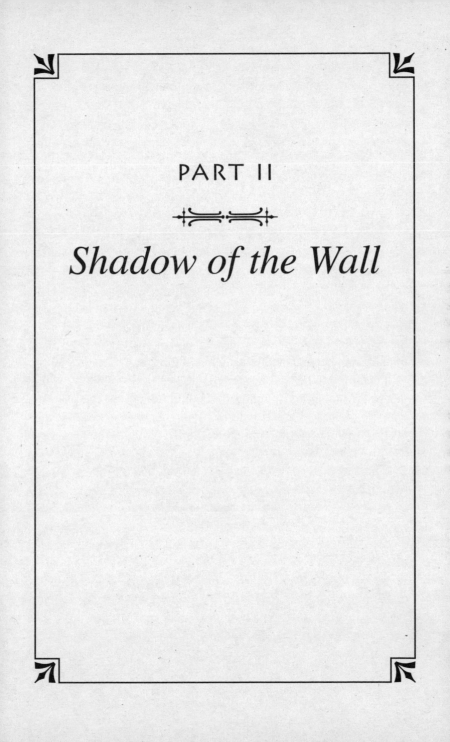

PART II

Shadow of the Wall

5

Blood Warrior

Kalan's dream was of a brisk blue-and-white morning in the great seaport of Ij, with the city's domes and spires gleaming against a bright sky. In his dream, the Aralorni ship *Halcyon*'s gangway thumped onto a wharf and the heralds' great gray horses clattered down the tarred planks. Kalan would be leaving with the *Halcyon* again on the afternoon tide, but he followed the horses onto the dock to bid the heralds farewell. Inside his dream, he knew this was all as it had been: the smell of tar and salt, the cries of seabirds, and the voices of sailors, dock workers, and clerks from the Ijiri trading houses all raised about their own business, while Jehane Mor and Tarathan of Ar waited at their horses' heads.

In the waking world, they had spoken of everyday matters, mainly the heralds' advice, as experienced travelers, for Kalan's continuing journey. He, in his turn, had queried how safe it was for them to be back in Ij after events there in the spring, even if all they intended was traversing the long canal from the harbor to the river port. But now, in Kalan's dream, he gazed into the impassive mask of the heralds' faces, which could have been wrought out of sculptor's bronze, and asked: "Before we left Emer, why did you send the dream to Jarna? The one that said my fate led me away from Emer and from her?"

Even immersed in the dream, Kalan knew that he had never asked that question—not on that blue-and-white morning in Ij, and not at any time during the journey from Caer Argent. He had wanted to, but the time never seemed right. Now, though, the light in the heralds' eyes pierced him as they spoke as one, their voices weaving in and out of each other in the manner of their Guild. "Because you did not love her, not in the way that she loved you." The sculpted masks softened, although their eyes still looked deep into his. "But you asked us to save her life and she needed to be able to heal."

Perhaps, the dreaming Kalan reflected, the reason I could never bring myself to ask the question was because I already knew the answer. Briefly, the dream showed him Jarna again, lying below Imuln's sanctuary in Caer Argent with her lifeblood soaking through leather and mail. He had thought she would die in that gray dawn, and the heralds had expended a great deal of power to hold her body and spirit to life.

Soft as a whisper, the dream shifted into his last memory of Jarna, with her face turned to the infirmary wall so she did not have to watch him leave. Reliving that moment, Kalan knew that the heralds had spoken truth: he cared for Jarna deeply and always had, enough to beg for her life in Caer Argent, but he had never loved her as she loved him. Oh Jarn, he thought, knowing this was as much a goodbye as their last farewell in Caer Argent—but the tide of the dream had turned, and the blue-and-white day in Ij was drifting away from him.

The heralds' faces dissolved into a blaze of light, and Kalan came awake to the bump of the *Halcyon*'s hull against timber, followed by the thud of a hawser and a sailor's call, answered by a jest in an unfamiliar accent. Grayharbor, Kalan told himself, but remained in his hammock while more sailors called news to those on shore. The gangway would go down soon, just as it had in Ij, although it would be some time before the captain and port authorities worked through the *Halcyon*'s bill of lading and he could disembark the horses. But when he did walk onto the Grayharbor dock, he would be wearing Derai armor for the first time.

Coming home, Kalan thought—ironically, because although he had been born into the warrior House of Blood, he also possessed the old Derai powers. For the past five hundred years, the Derai Alliance's Blood Oath had forbidden his kind from becoming warriors. Among the warrior Houses, those with power were also barred from mainstream Derai life and confined to the Temple quarters in Keep and Hold. It was the Blood Oath, as much as Darksworn assassins, that had driven Kalan into exile with Malian of Night six years before. Now, his bond to Malian and the debt of honor they owed the Winter Woman, Rowan Birchmoon—who had been murdered by Night honor guards—brought him back to the Derai Wall. But Kalan remained a renegade under the Oath, so although he would disembark wearing Derai armor, he could not use his true name.

An imposter as well as a renegade, Kalan reflected dryly. He had been uncertain how he would manage the transition from Emerian knight to Derai warrior, until the heralds had taken him to the great harborside market in Port Farewell. The market was famous for its trade in armor and weapons sourced from every corner of Haarth, which Tarathan had assured him would include Derai equipment. Kalan had found the herald was right, although most of what he examined had been the generic armament the Derai Alliance traded with the River and Southern Realms of Haarth. But because more Derai had been traveling south in recent years, mainly to the River, but a handful into Emer and Lathayra as well, he was able to find a scabbard with the House of Blood's hydra stamp and a cuirass in the distinctive deep-red steel particular to the warrior House.

The cuirass had given Kalan pause, because he could not imagine a Derai voluntarily parting with House armor, especially when careful examination showed that the owner's personal device had been removed. The job had been well done, though: he had to look closely to find the evidence. Besides, the pieces were too good to pass up. With the red steel and the hydra device on his scabbard, few would question that he was anything but a Blood warrior returning home.

Another trader had been keen to acquire Kalan's Emerian armor, so he had broken even overall. The only weapon he would not trade was the dagger that Lord Falk had given him, on the first anniversary of his arrival at Normarch. It was a fine weapon, with a blade of damascened Ishnapuri steel, a ball of Winter Country amber for a pommel, and Lord Falk's own red fox device stamped into the scabbard. Currently, the dagger lay at the bottom of his travel roll, together with the oak-tree buckle Audin had given Kalan for his last birthday, and the yellow tourney favor bearing Ghiselaine of Ormond's lily insignia. All three were wrapped in waterproof cloth and stitched closed—underlining that the Emerian life, like Kalan's armor, belonged in the past.

Like Jarna, too, he supposed, although it was not a happy thought. Similarly, when he had farewelled Tarathan and Jehane Mor on the Ij quayside, their embrace had been that of friends who do not know if they will meet again. But they had not spoken of that, or where the heralds' next commission might take them.

Into danger, Kalan reflected, as likely as not—just as he intended walking into the heart of the warrior House that was bitterest in its suppression of those with the old Derai powers. Still, given the opportunity for advancement the contest of arms represented, warriors would be flooding into the Red Keep from all Blood's holds and outlying forts. And on the road from Caer Argent to Port Farewell, the heralds had helped him layer a series of wards in place, designed to lock his powers deep beneath the outward seeming of one more warrior among many. The protective layers were an Oakward art, but Jehane Mor's aptitude for concealment, woven together with Kalan's own, had achieved a result that was close to invisible. Detection would require either a powerful spellworker or a level of scrutiny he was unlikely to encounter in the Red Keep.

"Unlikely," Kalan murmured now, "but not impossible." Listening to the activity above deck, he considered the other question he could not bring himself to ask: not on the ride from Caer Argent to Port Farewell, or on the voyage to Ij. He had glanced Tarathan's way several times toward the sea journey's end, but each time his will to ask had dissipated like the *Halcyon*'s wake, creaming away southward beneath an escort of seabirds. Something *had* happened between the heralds and Malian in Caer Argent, though, he was sure of it—and almost certain that it had more to do with Tarathan than Jehane Mor, despite the fair herald gifting the Heir of Night a medallion.

"Keep it," she had told Malian, "for my sake."

"For both our sakes," was all Tarathan had added—but then he had kissed Malian on the mouth. Kalan had a fair idea what the Normarch damosels, and also Jarna, would have said about that. Nonetheless, his question had remained unasked.

Outside, the *Halcyon*'s gangway thudded down onto the Grayharbor dock and someone came up it, whistling. Time to move, Kalan thought—but he still took care over his armor, paying attention to every buckle and binding. In Emer, a knight learned how to arm himself, but it felt odd to be doing so without any of the comrades he had lived and fought alongside for the past five years. Kalan slid the longsword and scabbard with the hydra device onto his belt and buckled it on, realizing that it was almost the first time since he had fled the Keep of Winds with Malian that he could recall being alone. Yet the most disconcerting step was donning the crimson cuirass of Blood, the House that had expelled him as soon as his old powers manifested at seven years of age.

"What are you, boy? Who? . . . None of our family ever had such powers!" Kalan heard his father's voice again, from that long ago day when he had been banished from family, Hold, and House. *"You are no more son of mine."*

No, he thought. Falk of Normarch was far more of a father to me, even if I was just one of a castle full of aspiring squires. Yet when he gazed down at the crimson breastplate and Derai-made armor, it still felt right, as though this was indeed his birthright, no matter how much House and family might wish to deny him. Kalan pulled his shoulder-length hair clear of his face with a leather tie—and hoped those in Grayharbor who had dealings with the Alliance really would see a Derai warrior and not an Emerian imposter.

"So you are awake." The *Halcyon*'s bosun greeted Kalan with a wink as he emerged onto the deck with his saddlebags and travel roll on one shoulder, and his helmet hooked over the other arm by its strap. "And ready for business, I see." The man's expression was friendly enough, but Kalan could see he was re-evaluating former impressions. "Their honors said you were a northerner, but I had my doubts until now."

"I've spent some time in the south." The ship must have crossed the bar at dawn, because despite a gray sky the day was already fully light. Kalan wanted to scan the port for any sign of Sea House vessels and take in details of the town, but instead nodded toward the hold, where wool bales were being hoisted clear and swung onto the dock. "And my horses are Emerian. How long before I can take them off?"

The bosun glanced over the gunwale. "If you can wait until the tide's high enough to use the lower ramp, that'll make disembarking 'em easier. Otherwise we'll have to use the hoist and your roan devil won't like that."

"I'll wait," Kalan said, but checked on the horses anyway. They had objected to coming on board, Madder in particular evincing a strong desire to kick his stall to matchwood and hole the ship's hull. Eventually both horses had adjusted to the enclosed space and the movement of the ship, but Kalan had still needed to spend a great deal of time with them, especially when a squall blew up a day out of Port Farewell. "Because Jarna," he murmured to the roan destrier now, "would curse me in this life and into the next if I let any harm come to you. As for you," he added to Tercel, offering the bay a slice of the apple he had kept back from his previous night's supper, "we've known each other a few years now, so we have to stick together. And keep this fire-eater in his place," he added, as Madder thrust his head over the divide to demand more of both the attention and the treats.

Since anything further must wait on the tide, Kalan decided to visit the shipping offices and if necessary find an inn. The bosun assured him they would keep watch over both the horses and his belongings, so he left his gear in Madder's stall and walked down onto the dock. The first few moments were disorientating, as the apparently solid quay continued to move with the same rhythm as the harbor swell. He had experienced something similar in Ij, but the heralds had promised him the sensation would pass, so Kalan placed a steadying hand against a wool bale while he gained his bearings.

Ports, he decided after a few minutes, must be much the same everywhere. Of the three harbors he had now seen, Grayharbor was distinguished only by being much the smallest. His initial impression of the town was one of narrow houses crowded close together, interspersed by only the occasional dome or spire. The buildings he could see clearly were built chiefly of grayed timber, with shingle roofs sloping sharply up toward the overcast sky. Even the harbor was a dull gray-green, almost as though the Wall were casting its long shadow this far south.

Don't be fanciful, Kalan told himself: it's just the weather today.

The nearest shipping office was little different from the one in Port Farewell, a small room just inside the wide double doors of a ship chandler's warehouse. The names of ships were chalked onto a blackboard beside the office door, but the clerk pursed his lips, assessing Kalan much as the *Halcyon*'s bosun had done. He looked like he might have been a sailor himself once, with a silver ring in one ear and callused hands that reached for a leather-bound ledger. "You'll be wanting a Derai ship, then? I take it you're going north?"

Kalan nodded, watching the man flip through the ledger while his keen hearing sifted the rustle of the pages from the drone of another clerk's voice deeper in the warehouse, checking off stores. He caught a back door's creak as well, and the scuffle of mice around grain bins. The clerk placed a metal rule on the pages, to hold them flat, then pushed the ledger across the counter. "Here you are." He watched closely as Kalan swiveled the ledger around.

Does he think I'm unlettered? Kalan wondered. Even in the House of Blood, with its fixation on warrior training, every child learned to read. Or perhaps the clerk was checking that he could read Derai. If the man had dealings with the Alliance, he might well be wary of those he did not know. Kalan examined the page. "Nothing for a week. Is that certain?"

"The ledger records the sailings we know about, as I told the warriors who arrived the other day. But a Derai ship can arrive at any time." The clerk's eyes, a faded blue between deep crow's-feet, were still assessing. "We can't sell you a passage either, just give you a token for the ship's captain. Your Sea House mariners decide who they do and don't take."

If they would not let him embark, then Kalan would have no choice but to travel overland, which would take weeks, maybe even months if the weather turned against him. In which case, he reflected ruefully, the Bride of Blood might reach the Keep of Winds before he even sighted the Red Keep. He took the metal tag the man was holding out, nodding as he saw the ship engraved into one side and the Sea Houses's mer-dragon device on the other. "Thank you. Other Derai warriors, did you say?" he added.

The clerk nodded. "Seeking passage north, like you. They said they'd been following the tourney circuit in the Southern Realms. We get a few like that these days."

It wasn't just mice in the warehouse, Kalan thought, catching the whisper of a footfall. Wood scraped faintly against wood—a bin lid being shifted, he suspected—as the clerk's lips pursed. "They're staying at the Marlinspike, if you want to find them. I don't recommend it, though," he added, taking the ledger back.

The stealthy footsteps were retreating toward the rear of the warehouse. "The Marlinspike?" Kalan inquired. "Or finding these warriors?"

"Oh, very good." The clerk's faded eyes studied him a moment longer. "I'd try the Anchor if you want somewhere clean and honest. They've hosted Derai guests before."

Kalan heard the rear door creak open and then as softly close. "Thank you," he said again. "I take it the Anchor has a stable?"

The lips pursed again. "Horses, is it? Yes, they do. But you may find transporting horses will cost you a great deal more, depending on which Sea House ship you strike." He tapped the ledger with his forefinger. The nail was deformed, Kalan noticed, as though it had been torn off and grown back warped. "The *Elv'Ar-i-Anor*'s due soon and has a reputation for fair dealing."

I'm still feeling the motion of the sea, Kalan told himself—but it did not quite cover his disconnect at hearing the Sea House name spoken in a Grayharbor accent. "I'll go to the Anchor." He pulled out what he hoped would be an appropriate sized coin. "If a ship arrives before the *Elv'Ar-i-Anor*, could you send me word there?"

The clerk shook his head, the silver earring glinting. "No need for the coin, not in Grayharbor. I'll send word, though I doubt you'll need it, staying that close to the port." He paused, before adding slowly, "You'll have been in the south awhile, then?" This time he did smile, a very dry expression, when Kalan nodded. "I thought that must be the case. Most Derai who come here, even the mariners, don't say thank you. Not to us."

6

The Pastry Thief

Of course they wouldn't, Kalan thought, emerging into the wharf's bustle. He wondered what else he was going to give away without realizing, simply because he had been too-long away from Derai society. The breastplate he wore might be crimson, but he had been seven years old when he last dwelt in the House of Blood. Still, Malian's foreseeing had not only placed him on the Wall of Night, but as part of a wedding caravan. He could not be sure it was the Daughter of Blood's wedding caravan, of course—especially since Tarathan, who was also a seer, had told him that the paths of seeing were always fluid and no outcome ever set in stone.

There'll always be risk, Kalan told himself, but at least Malian's vision offers hope I'll succeed. I just need to be more careful, that's all.

A lot more careful, he added silently. He had been tempted to repay the clerk's advice about inns and—inadvertently—Derai behavior, by informing him that someone was using the warehouse's back door to pilfer. Doing so, though, would have raised too many questions around how he knew. Still, Kalan was sufficiently curious to investigate the alley behind the building before going to the Anchor. The narrow strip of dirt was a dead end, confined between the rear walls of warehouses on three sides. He could see nowhere for a thief to come and go, except via the alley entrance or slipping from one warehouse into another. The latter was the most likely explanation, he reflected, turning away. The pilferer had been drawn to the same bins as the mice, probably also looking for food, and Kalan began to feel glad he had kept silent.

By the time he reached the inn, he had dismissed the matter from his mind. The Anchor was comfortable, rather than well-appointed, but the inn-wife looked him over with care before confirming that she had both a room and stabling for the horses. The tariff fitted the unpretentious style of the accommodation, but Kalan was grateful to have both his share of the Caer Argent tourney prize and the journey money Lord Falk had given him. He had known the Castellan was being generous, paying him a knight's fee for his service between Summer's Eve and the Midsummer festival, on top of the Aldermere revenue that was his by right. Nonetheless, he would need to be careful if he had to wait long for a Sea House vessel, then buy passage to the Wall for himself and two horses.

"We're plain here, both the rooms and the food, which comes at set hours if you want it." The inn-wife's look sharpened as she handed him a room key. "And we're no Marlinspike. We'll not have abuse or brawling in common room or yard."

Kalan thought she looked brawny enough to deal with disorderly guests at need, although he was also forming an unflattering picture of the Derai warriors who had arrived in port before him. He kept a lookout for both them and the Marlinspike on his way back to the *Halcyon*, but did not see either. Mostly, he wanted to eat now rather than waiting for the Anchor's next set meal, in the hope that food might banish the world's slight, persistent sway—but the *Halcyon*'s bosun waved him over as soon as he appeared on the dock. "Tide's right," the man said. "Let's get this done."

Madder came down the ramp with a squeal, trying to rear against Kalan's hand on his bridle, before sidling sideways to bare long yellow teeth at a nearby stevedore. "They're warhorses," Kalan warned, keeping his other hand close to Tercel's bit and maintaining a safe distance between the destriers and interested bystanders. These were mostly sailors and traders, although a band of urchins loitered close to the warehouses, and midday drinkers lounged in a tavern that was little more than an awning stretched above coopers' barrels.

"Earl Sardon must have taken to breeding horses now, as well as offspring." Despite Madder's nervous excitement, Kalan heard the comment in Derai at once. He kept the horses walking and picked out the warriors as he turned, counting four of them beneath the awning. One was sitting in the deep gloom cast by an adjoining warehouse wall, but the three to the front were all unshaven, their leather and mail well-worn. Yet it wasn't until the horses' circle took him away again that their faces and appearance clicked into place. These were House of Sword warriors from the contingent that had been in Caer Argent for the Midsummer tournament.

Kalan's thoughts raced, realizing they had to be a remnant of the group who had broken their tourney oath and fought the Darksworn Lightning knights in the ruins of the old Sondcendre mansion. Many had died there, and he had thought, when the bodies were found, that the Lightning knights seemed to have the upper hand. Clearly, though, these warriors had gotten away.

They must, Kalan decided, have been just ahead of the heralds and himself on the road to Port Farewell, and taken ship before they arrived. "Easy, my braveheart," he murmured to Madder. "Steady, brother," he told Tercel, keenly aware that they had not found the giant Orth's body among the dead: Orth, who had tried to kill Audin in the sword ring and later sought to force a fight on Tarathan of Ar, despite the inviolability of heralds in every realm from Ij to Ishnapur.

An oath breaker and a murderer, Kalan thought, as the horses' circle brought the dockside tavern back into view. More importantly right now, all the Sword warriors had seen him in Caer Argent, so the question—regardless of whether Orth was among them or not—was if they would see past the Derai armor and House of Blood trappings to the young Emerian knight. And Orth *was* with them. He was the one in deep shadow beside the wall, his height disguised by the fact that he was sitting down. While the horses circled, he had turned to face the dock, and now Kalan recognized him despite the gloom.

The Sword warrior's expression was bleary, his eyes bloodshot, and although he was watching Kalan and the horses, his demeanor remained incurious. One of his companions leaned forward. "I'm Kelyr," he called in Derai, "of the House of Swords. Honor on you and on your House."

His voice, Kalan noted, was not the one that had made the observation about Earl Sardon. "Khar," he replied, using a common House of Blood name, one of the many diminutives of Kharalth, the Battle Goddess. It could easily be a shortening of Kalan as well. "Light and safety on your road," he added, observing the formalities.

Kelyr rose and moved out onto the wharf. "Those are fine horses you have there." His tone was friendly, although the warmth did not touch his eyes. "Are they great horses, out of Emer?"

"They were both bred there," Kalan replied, matching the friendly tone. "Have you been in the south?"

"Following the tourney circuit, ay, as well as about our Earl's business." Kelyr's tone hardened. "Some of our number stayed, but we four are to report the loss of our captain, Tirorn, who was also our Earl's nephew."

First Kin, Kalan thought, suppressing a whistle. When confronting Tarathan, Orth had blamed the heralds for the disappearance of his captain, who was also a blood relative, in Ij. If the captain had been First Kin to the Earl of Swords as well, that would explain the giant's determination to be revenged—although it didn't justify Orth and his comrades' indifference to identifying the right culprit.

"A difficult homecoming for you, bearing such news." Kalan halted the horses so as not to seem disrespectful. Madder shook out his mane, but otherwise both chargers had quieted and stood with their heads up and ears pricked toward Kelyr.

"Ay." The Sword warrior looked away, toward the waterfront with its forest of masts and rigging, and the gray firth beyond. "But our Earl needs to know, so we'll take a ship if we can, rather than traveling overland."

"If we do all end taking the long road, you can ride with us," another of the warriors said. "Tawrin," he added, indicating himself. Like Kelyr, his tone was friendly but his eyes less so. Kalan nodded in response, letting the Sword warriors interpret the gesture how they chose. The road might be dangerous for solitary travelers, but no more so, he suspected, than traveling with a group of oath-breaking warriors that included Orth. The prospect of making his way through wild country while they were on the same road was equally unappealing, and additional reason for hoping there *would* be a ship.

At least none of the four seemed to connect the Blood warrior before them with one of the many knights of Emer they had encountered briefly in Caer Argent. People saw what they expected to, though, so all things considered, it would probably have been more surprising if they *had* recognized him.

Orth and the warrior opposite him, introduced as Malar, returned to their drinking, but Kelyr and Tawrin seemed disposed to talk. Most of the watchers were drifting away, although Kalan was aware that the urchins had crept closer once the horses stopped moving. They were a scruffy bunch, and like any dock loiterers could well be pickpockets. "Keep clear," he warned them again, switching back to the language of Emer, which was similar enough to all the other dialects spoken in the Southern Realms to make him understood from Grayharbor to Aralorn. "These horses are trained to fight and could attack if startled."

A server moved out from beneath the awning and snapped a dish-cloth at the urchins. "Be off! We've no pickings for your kind here."

One of the youngsters skirled a challenge, shrill as the gulls overhead—and then the whole bunch charged as one, shrieking and snatching up food and coins left on the barrel tops. Orth surged to his feet, roaring, as a small thief seized the half-eaten pastry from his plate, while the server and other patrons cursed and grabbed at darting bodies. Those who sat further back, or had already eaten, laughed and called encouragement to either side, only swiping out if any urchin came too near. The vagabonds twisted and dodged clear, racing away with their booty.

Safety, Kalan saw, was a tangle of godowns at the town end of the dock, and the raiders took full advantage of wharf traffic to make their escape. All, that is, except the ragged lad who had snatched Orth's pastry. His swerve to avoid one of the alejack drinkers brought him too close to Tawrin, who stuck out a foot and brought him down flat. The boy sprang up again immediately, the pastry still clutched in his hand—but it was too late. Orth's giant hand had closed on the tattered tunic and now hoisted the thief high, his other fist poised to smash into the dirty, terrified face.

"Stand!" Kalan ordered the horses in Emerian—one of Jarna's painstakingly inculcated commands—and sprang forward, intercepting Orth's blow. The giant snarled and tried to hammer the fist into Kalan's face instead. Checking the strike's momentum felt like trying to prevent a mountain toppling, and Kalan called on the combined strength of five years working in the Normarch forge, and training in full Emerian armor with sword and lance, battle-axe and mace. His arm and shoulders were rock, his mind cool as his eyes met Orth's. "He's just a child," he said, keeping his voice level.

The Sword giant's expression was almost comical as he glared from Kalan's hand, locked on his wrist, into his face. "He's a sniveling Haarth thief!"

"He's hungry," Kalan answered, countering Orth's shift in weight and alert for a head butt, or knee to the groin. "Look at him."

Orth glared, his head lowered. "A thief!" he roared, and shook his captive so violently that the boy's head snapped back, his teeth jarring together. But the threadbare tunic, unequal to such treatment, tore apart—and the boy's body dropped clear, leaving Orth with a handful of fabric. The warrior gaped, a second bellow cut off as the boy scrabbled to get away. Kalan stepped back, but not so far that he could not intervene again if necessary. Kelyr and Tawrin threw him a hard look as they moved in to flank their comrade, who remained standing with his head lowered.

His breath sobbing, the boy regained his feet and darted toward a clear space between the curious onlookers and Kalan's horses, swerving away from the snake of Madder's head just as a watcher turned to boot him on his way. The kick caught the boy's rear a glancing blow, enough to send him sprawling along the wharf, stopping short of a pair of black-booted feet.

Kalan, turning with the rest of the bystanders, saw the boy's gaze lift from the boots to the hem of a long black tunic. A sword in a silver-worked scabbard was belted around slim hips; a hand in an embroidered gauntlet rested on its hilt. The newcomer's face was framed by cables of twisted, shoulder-length black hair and her expression was stern as she studied the urchin at her feet. She wore a mail corselet and steel breastplate over the black tunic, with the twelve-pointed star of a Sea House navigator worked into the bright metal. Slowly, the stern gaze traveled from Kalan, to Orth and his companions, then around the gathered watchers, before returning to the boy.

"Begone," she told him, a single word in the Grayharbor dialect, and he was up and running as though released from a spell. No one turned to watch him go. Like Kalan, they were all looking at the navigator and her companions. The clerk from the shipping office stood close by her right hand, while two men and another woman were ranged at her back. The device on their breastplates was a pair of crossed swords rather than a star, and all three wore steel caps on their heads and carried crossbows. Sea House marines, Kalan supposed—but it was the figure to the first woman's left who held his attention. The man was tall, with the same twisted hair as his companion, although his was mostly gray, framing a deeply weathered face. The breeze rippled the folds of his sea-green robe, the deep border a wave design in indigo and black. Power stirred, too, telling Kalan that he was in the presence of a Sea House weatherworker.

Orth's attention had swung to the robed figure and now he

growled, low in his throat, before spitting onto the dock. "Priest-kind! By the Oath that binds the Derai, you've no right to walk here."

"The ship decides who quits its decks, no one else." The navigator's voice rang cold, and her eyes, dark as a storm at sea, held Orth's glare. The wharf stilled, its quiet filled by the cry of seabirds and creak of the moored ships. Kelyr's fingers closed on his comrade's sword wrist, and Kalan wondered which imperative would win out: the giant warrior's hatred of priest-kind, or the realization that the fastest way to travel north was on a Sea House ship.

The matter hung in the balance a moment longer before Orth growled again, but in defeat this time. Throwing off Kelyr's hand, he turned on his heel and stalked away. Malar's head swiveled, tracking Orth's departure, before he tossed back the last of his ale and followed. The Sea woman's gaze lingered on Kelyr and Tawrin, before considering Kalan. "Swords," she said meditatively. "And Blood." She inclined her head gravely. "Honor on you and both your Houses. I am Che'Ryl-g-Raham of the Sea House, navigator to the ship of the same name."

Kalan saluted. "Khar, of the House of Blood. Light and safety on your path, Navigator."

"Honor on you and on your Houses, light and safety on all your roads," Kelyr said, as though trying to smooth over the tension by giving the salutation in full. "I am Kelyr and this is my shield comrade, Tawrin. Our companions are Malar"—he paused—"and Orth, who is Second Kin to our Earl."

Che'Ryl-g-Raham's expression was thoughtful. "Orth of House Swords: that name has reached us in the Sea Keep." The navigator's tone was neutral, but the Sword warriors stiffened. Her gaze returned to Kalan, then circled the bystanders again. "What business was it that we interrupted here?"

She spoke as though she had a right to know, using the Grayharbor dialect as she had throughout, and the watching locals shuffled their feet. As though they recognize her right, Kalan thought, intrigued. He glanced at the Sword warriors, curious to see how they would respond. Kelyr's lips were compressed, but his tone gave nothing away. "The brat stole from our table, Navigator." The look he shot Kalan was hard. "But our brother of Blood took exception when Orth sought to punish the fault."

"The boy snatched half a pastry," Kalan said. "If Orth's blow had connected, it would have killed him."

"Theft is theft," Kelyr replied. "If one overlooks small infractions, larger ones will quickly follow."

"Punishment should also be appropriate to the crime." Che'Ryl-g-Raham extracted a copper coin from the wallet at her belt. "Perhaps I bade the thief depart too soon, but will this make good the House of Swords' loss?"

"The coin will pay for the food," Kelyr agreed, taking it, then switched to Derai. "But the Haarth vermin stole from Derai, when our Wall and our watch are what keep these scum and their world safe. A copper coin doesn't set that right."

Kalan glanced at the clerk, but if the man understood spoken Derai, as well as reading it, he was giving nothing away. Che'Ryl-g-Raham frowned. "You would have me invoke our treaty with Grayharbor and get the boy taken up for theft?" She shook her head. "I am of Khar of Blood's mind: your reaction is out of proportion to the provocation."

"Unusual." The weatherworker's voice was deep and filled with nuance—like the ocean, Kalan thought, aware of Che'Ryl-g-Raham's inquiring expression and the two Sword warriors' distaste. The weatherworker's eyes looked past Kalan rather than at him, the wind plucking at the sea-green robe. "I would not have expected a Blood warrior to intervene for one not of his own House, let alone a pastry thief who is not even our kind."

So much, Kalan thought, for not drawing attention to myself. The weatherworker might appear indifferent, his eyes continuing to gaze into the distance, but Kalan could feel his psychic scrutiny. The sensation was similar to a spider crawling across his skin and he had to fight to keep his expression unchanged, letting his thoughts take their texture from the timbers of the wharf and the soft slap of the water below it, their color gray as the sky.

The crawl of power vanished, although outwardly the weather-worker remained exactly as he had before, his eyes focused on the middle distance. The onlookers, as if feeling that the Derai drama had run its course, began to disperse. Madder took a step forward, butting his head into Kalan's shoulder.

"Ah, Rayn told me there were horses as well as Derai requiring passage." Che'Ryl-g-Raham glanced at the clerk, then back to Kalan and the horses. "That need not preclude our reaching an agreement, so long as the rest of our Grayharbor cargo can be accommodated." Her gaze returned to the Sword warriors. "I will need to consult with Rayn and his clients over that. If you come to the ship tomorrow morning, I will let you know then whether we have berths, and set the fare."

Her tone was neutral, but Kalan sensed that the cost was likely to be high, especially if the ship was pushed for hold space. Tawrin shifted his weight, while Kelyr cleared his throat. "Our journey," he said, still speaking in Derai, "is a Matter of Kin and Blood."

And that, Kalan thought, as Che'Ryl-g-Raham bowed, acknowledging the claim, will override all other considerations—including whatever the navigator has heard about Orth. A Matter of Kin and Blood was one of the first and oldest rights acknowledged by the Derai, and warriors returning to their House under such circumstances would always be given priority. Reluctantly, he inclined his head, accepting the Sword warriors' claim as the navigator had done. "Until tomorrow," he said, but rather than the gray sea road, he suspected his future held the long slow route north through the Barren Hills.

7

Fire and Water

The mariners retired with Rayn to the shipping office, while the two Sword warriors departed in the same direction their comrades had taken. Curious to see a Sea House vessel, Kalan led the horses back past the *Halcyon* until he sighted the lean lines of the Derai ship, berthed at the far end of the wharf. The tall black prow rose above the dock like a swan's neck, although unlike the ships of Haarth it was not carved into any shape of beast, bird, or mythic creature. Once Kalan came right up to it, he saw that the ship's name, *Che'Ryl-g-Raham*, was indeed the same as that of its navigator. Was it the same for all ships and navigators? he wondered. At the same time, he noted the eyes painted on either side of the black prow. The lines were drawn in sea-green, indigo, and silver to resemble the dawn eyes of Terennin, the far-seeing god, but when Kalan looked away from them to study the rest of the vessel, he found that he was being observed in return.

The watcher, a woman in a sleeveless, sea-green tunic and leggings, was standing on the fo'c'sle deck with one hand resting against the ship's prow. She had lines about her eyes but otherwise her face was smooth, and her head was shaven, which made it difficult to place her age. A fine silver chain, hung with charms, shone against one ankle, and silver bracelets twisted up her arms. More silver gleamed in her ears, but like the weatherworker she kept her gaze fixed on a point somewhere past Kalan's shoulder. He felt the spider's crawl across his skin again, but inclined his head as courtesy demanded. "Honor on you and on your House."

She did not reply, just continued to stare. Madder shifted, trying to turn as footsteps sounded behind them. Turning himself, Kalan saw one of Che'Ryl-g-Raham's marines, who stopped clear of the horses. "Temorn." The newcomer indicated himself, before his gaze lifted to the woman by the prow. "She won't speak to you," he said. "Best if you stand clear, Khar of Blood, until you've been accepted as a passenger."

If I'm accepted, Kalan thought. The marine's look was neutral as he took up position by the gang ramp, but his manner, while not unfriendly, made it clear that he was serious about Kalan leaving. Neither he nor the woman on the fo'c'sle deck spoke or moved again, but Kalan felt their eyes at his back for the length of the quay. The female marine watched him from the ship chandler's door, nodding as he passed, but she did not speak either, and although the ale drinkers glanced around, none showed any further interest.

The tangle of godowns at the town end of the quay was quiet, and Kalan guessed that the urchins must have gone to ground. Once clear of the quay, he swung into Madder's saddle, checking the roan's sly attempt to nip a passerby who brushed too close. Now that the adrenaline from the wharf confrontation was subsiding, he realized that the swaying sensation had dissipated as well and decided he could wait to eat, after all. When he paused at an intersection close by the Anchor to let a bustle of apprentices and warehouse clerks pass, his attention was caught by a temple down the side lane. The frontage was constricted, comprising little more than a narrow portico with a weathered door, and the stone facing was so worn that even his keen sight could not make out what god it was dedicated to. The statue niches to either side of the door were empty, too, although the obscure location suggested a shrine to the Haarth deity, Karn.

Except the people here will say Kan, Kalan reminded himself, as they do on the River. Thinking of the dark god, however he was named, put him in mind of Malian, who had followed Kan when she served as an adept in the Shadow Band of Ar. *"What are you doing now?"* he thought, while knowing there was little chance the mindspeech would reach her at such a distance. *"Did you find the sword, I wonder? And will it lead you to Yorindesarinen's shield more readily than Nhenir led you to her blade?"*

He had been angry with her when he left Caer Argent, believing she had held out the illusion of choice about his return to the Wall, when her seer's vision showed him back there all along. Yet if what Tarathan had said about foreseeing being uncertain was correct, then Kalan could see that, by her lights, Malian truly had been trying to leave him free to choose. *"When,"* as Jehane Mor had pointed out, by one of their quiet campfires on the road to Port Farewell, *"she has very little choice herself. Who asked her if she wanted to be Heir of Night, let alone the Chosen of Mhaelanar, the One of your ancient prophecy?"*

"She accepts her duty," Kalan had replied, all three of them using mindspeech so the only sound was the whisper of the flames, and the small rustlings of the Emerian night. *"As do I. But—"*

"If you may affect your fate, despite her foreseeing, so too may she. That is our hope also." The heralds' mindspeech had whispered together as one, but when Tarathan leaned forward to place another branch on the blaze his expression had been so— Guarded, Kalan thought now, memory paring away any concealment afforded by that distant fireside's light and shadow. As though there might be some part of the foreseer's truth that Tarathan had been withholding.

Kalan twitched his shoulders, much as the horses would if a fly settled on them, and put both the small temple and the past out of his mind. Right now he needed to concentrate on the present: stabling the horses and then eating, checking his weapons, and trying to ensure he was on the *Che'Ryl-g-Raham* when her prow turned north again. Even, he told himself, as Madder moved forward, if it means sharing a cabin with Orth.

The inn-wife's lips compressed when Kalan asked about the midday meal, her pointed glance traveling to the position of the sun, however muted by cloud cover. Yet by the time she looked back at him, her expression had relented. "I suppose the cook could make you a sandwich, but the common room's closed until dinner so you'll have to eat in the kitchen."

"Our candlemaker's lad was on the wharf when the ruckus happened," the cook said, explaining the inn-wife's willingness to make an exception as he sliced a generous amount of bread and cold beef onto a plate. "Those wharf larrikins are nothing but trouble and need to be set to proper work." He laid the knife aside, adding pickle and salad greens. "But young Myron said that northern brute might have killed the lad he caught if you hadn't stopped him." The cook paused in the act of putting the plate before Kalan, his face uncertain. "No offense intended."

Since I'm a northerner myself, Kalan thought. "None taken," he said.

The cook set the plate down. "I didn't think so, given you intervened. But you nor—" He stopped, looking conscious again.

We northerners can be a touchy lot, Kalan interpreted, concentrating on the serious business of eating as the cook became busy, rewrapping the beef. "This is good," Kalan said, checking a *thank you*.

The cook's expression eased. "There's more bread and cheese here if you want it, and I've a slice of pear pie left over from yesterday."

Kalan wanted both, very much, and when he had finished, the tapster pulled him a beer, which he drank on a bench outside the common room door. The gray morning had given way to an afternoon of intermittent sunshine, but the tapster's opinion was for rain tomorrow. "Still, the wind should stay fair now we're coming into the more settled time of year."

After his years in northern Emer—where even before the Ash Days that marked the turning point between Autumn's Eve and Karn's great festival of Autumn's Night, chill rain would have turned the few roads into bogs—Kalan found it hard to adjust to fall bringing more settled weather. But the Wall of Night had its own distinct weather system, with spring and summer turbulence driving the great storms—so perhaps the shadow of the Wall really was stretching south, if Grayharbor was influenced by the same pattern. He found that possibility disturbing, even if it could work in his favor now.

"And," the tapster added, "the good weather means we get more Sea Keep ships in port."

Kalan resisted the offer of a second beer, leaving his armor and most of his weapons in his room before returning to the stable to groom the horses. Despite the cool day he warmed up quickly and was soon working in his sleeveless undershirt as he had during the Normarch days. The tune he whistled beneath his breath was from one of the Emerian songs of springtime love. For a few moments he could have been back in the small gray castle with Audin and Jarna working close at hand, while Girvase and Raher sparred in the yard and the damosels called out encouragement. The suppressed giggles, too, usually meant damosels at hand—and then both his whistling and the brush paused as Kalan realized the giggling was real and not memory.

When he glanced up, two stable lasses grinned back at him from the loft. The taller of the two held a pitchfork, although he did not recall hearing the sounds of hay being shifted. Taking a mid-afternoon break, he guessed. The oldest would be no more than fourteen, while her companion appeared several years younger, her thin face eager beneath a dusting of freckles. "Hello," he said, and they giggled again.

"Hello," the younger girl replied, bolder than her companion, whose face had suffused with a mix of color and shyness. "Myron said you must be strong, to stop that giant hitting Faro. We didn't believe it could really be you, though, when we saw you bring the horses in."

Kalan kept his face serious. "But now you do?"

She nodded, her expression equally solemn, although the grin returned as soon as she glanced at her companion. "Without your armor you look as strong as Andron—doesn't he, Leti?" Leti nodded. "Andron," the speaker informed him, "is the watch's smith and the strongest man in Grayharbor."

"I'm honored you think I could be as strong," Kalan said as he resumed grooming Tercel. "You said Myron knew the boy this morning. Faro, was it?"

Both girls nodded as one, but this time it was Leti who spoke. "We all know Faro. He used to help us here sometimes, when his mam was still alive." Her frown made her look older. "We were all in the Dame School together."

"He always said his mam taught him more," the younger girl said. "She mostly repaired armor, but Andron said there was nothing she couldn't make or mend. He wanted to marry her, too." Again she addressed Leti. "I heard Andron's sister telling our mam so—but that she wouldn't have him. 'Too good for the likes of us,'" she added, in what Kalan suspected was mimicry of Andron's sister.

"Stefa!" Leti said, but the younger girl shrugged.

"That's what she said." She picked up a hank of straw and began to plait it.

"What about Faro?" Kalan asked, as Leti looked away. When she looked back, her eyes were troubled.

"He was turned out of their rooms after his mam died of the fever, but was sleeping in the old Seruth temple and earning coin from odd jobs and running messages, enough to eat. So he seemed all right."

"We told him to come here," Stefa put in, without looking up from her plaiting. "But he said that would be charity, because our mam didn't have a real job for him."

"Our mam," Kalan realized, must be the inn-wife. "Stiff-necked," he observed, with a parting pat for Tercel. He moved into Madder's stall and the roan rolled an eye at him, but otherwise stood quietly, his ears swiveling between Kalan and the girls' voices. "So what was he doing with today's miscreants?"

The question was as much for himself as the girls, but Leti looked away again, as though she might find an answer caught between the pitchfork's tines. "We don't know. He disappeared a few weeks back. At first we thought he'd gone completely, but then Myron saw him down by the docks. But Faro ran away as soon as he called out."

"Hiding," Stefa added.

Hungry and terrified as well, Kalan reflected, although the latter could simply have been because of his proximity to Orth's fist. He was not quite sure why he was giving the vagabond further thought, except that he knew what it was to be both outcast and exile, thrown on the kindness of strangers. In both cases he had been fortunate, first in the Temple of Night under Sister Korriya's tutelage—although he had not appreciated his fortune at the time—and later as Falk of Normarch's foster son. But he had seen enough of the world to know that it could be far from kind, especially to those without money, or kin and clan to call on in need.

The girls returned to their work, while Kalan checked the horses' hooves and shoes. The rest of the afternoon he spent in his room, going over his weapons and armor. His hands were as busy as Stefa's had been, about her plaiting, but random images kept reasserting themselves: the woman on the *Che'Ryl-g-Raham*'s fo'c'sle, with her unfathomable expression; Faro's scrawny body, his face contorted into a scream but no sound emerging; and stealthy movement about a grain bin, unobtrusive as the warehouse mice. A hungry intruder . . . But here Kalan shook his head, because every urchin on the dock was probably equally hungry, so that on its own did not make the pilferer likely to be Faro. He frowned, too, remembering Lord Falk's maxim that starvation was as great an enemy on the Northern March of Emer as anything a knight might slay with arrow or sword.

The reflection made him take his time over the plain meal put before him in the Anchor's common room that evening, savoring every mouthful. The room was half full, with a scattering of farmers come in from the surrounding countryside, townsfolk either going on or just off shift, and a handful of sailors and traders from other ports. Without his armor to draw attention, no one took any notice of

Kalan. The talk was desultory, although he did hear a few remarks about the incident on the wharf, with opinion evenly divided between amusement at the urchin gang's impudence and headshaking over the entire business.

Afterward, Kalan went to bed early. He slept deeply, the dreams taking a long time to intrude. When they did, the first images were jumbled: a house with a mer-horse's head above the door, a slender horn projecting from its forehead. A storm blew up and lightning crackled, exploding down through the horn. The front door disintegrated into ash and flaming splinters, and he smelled burning metal and burned flesh—before the dream shifted and a young woman turned against a halo of fire, her expression as shy as Leti's in a face tinted by the flames.

"Who are you?" she asked, as the fire roared and a hound belled in the distance. Another young woman turned, this time against a sky filled with storm wrack, and Kalan could not escape the impression that he had seen her somewhere before, although he did not know where. Her hair was twisted up into a fine mesh of amethysts and silver, and pearls the color of smoke hung in her ears, but the face beneath the jeweled net was blotched with tears.

"I'm sorry," she whispered. *"I'm sorry, I'm sorry."* The single hound became a baying pack and Kalan's dream filled with smoke and burning again. Because, he realized, shaking himself clear of the Gate of Dreams, it wasn't just a dream. Somewhere in Grayharbor, a fire raged.

Kalan sprang from the bed to a furor of bells, shouting, and barking dogs. He still smelled smoke, but a quick glance out the window confirmed that it was not the Anchor on fire. The sky above the port was a red glare, and the bells clamored from that direction, too, borne on the wind like the smoke. Which means, Kalan thought, pulling on his boots, that the fire will be blowing toward the town as well.

A bell began to ring nearby—summoning fire-watches from farther afield, he guessed—while voices shouted along the street and in the yard below. Kalan pounded down the stairs to where the inn-wife had gathered her daughters and the rest of the staff. "Get to the port," she said, when Kalan asked what he could do. "We'll look to the inn and your horses, but they'll need every pair of hands there if the blaze is not to reach us—" She broke off as the cook ran into the yard, and Kalan left, not needing to be told that the port was full of timber and tar, with goods from every part of Haarth stored around the quay, at least some of which would be highly flammable.

By the time he arrived, the ship closest to the town end of the wharf was an inferno and the blaze had spread to the godown warren. Like the ship, several buildings were already well beyond saving, the flames licking skyward. A barge was standing off from the burning vessel, with the crew working a pump and arcing water from long leather hoses over the blaze—but all along the wharf ships were slipping their moorings and heading downharbor.

On the wharf, what had to be most of the town's fire-watches were working frantically around a series of water-wagons, some pumping on the flatbeds while others dragged more of the leather hoses to direct water onto the conflagration. Teams with leather helmets and protective hauberks were working to create a firebreak, pulling down the nearest buildings while others dragged the wreckage clear. Every sound building past the firebreak had a bucket brigade on its roof, ready to douse windborne sparks, and citizens were forming bucket lines from the harbor as a second barge nosed into the space closest to the water wagons.

When Kalan looked toward the far end of the wharf, he saw that the *Che'Ryl-g-Raham* was still in place but with a cordon of marines deployed along the dock. A horn blew frantically and he leapt clear as two more water wagons careered onto the quay and the fire-watch clinging to the sides leapt down. "Here!" a man yelled, gesturing for help with the heavy hoses, but Kalan pushed past, jogging toward the *Che'Ryl-g-Raham*'s picket. He recognized both Temorn and the marine from the ship chandler's door, but his eyes were on the navigator where she stood just behind their line. The reflected glow tinted her face with the same lurid colors as the woman in his dream, except her expression was hard, every bone a chiseled edge.

"That's close enough," Temorn said, but Kalan had already stopped.

"Your weatherworker," he said, pitching his voice to reach Che'Ryl-g-Raham without shouting. "He could put the fire out. You have goods here," he continued, when she said nothing, just regarded him without any change of expression. "This is the Alliance's main trading port. Getting the fire under control is in your interests as well."

For Serrut's sake, he thought, when the navigator remained unmoving—but then she stepped through the line of marines, her unsmiling gaze boring into his. "Do you presume to tell us our business, Blood warrior? Or perhaps you think we are all poured from the same mold as *your* kind?" She bared her teeth: a challenge, not a smile. "Why do you think we're still here? But weatherworking is not the snap-of-a-warrior's-fingers business. So go and hazard yourself keeping the fire contained if you're so eager to help. We'll protect our *interests* as we see fit."

The look Temorn shot him was decidedly sympathetic, but Kalan still gritted his teeth as he started back. Clearly, he had made a fool of himself. But she's right, he thought, still smarting as he helped drag the final hose down from the last-come wagons: *nothing* is probably exactly what the House of Blood would do under similar circumstances.

A woman with a pickaxe shoved a dripping cloth at him, in lieu of a leather helmet, and he wrapped it around his head and face. The next half hour was spent helping bring the hose as close to the conflagration as they dared without being beaten back by smoke and heat. Despite the cloth, Kalan's eyes and lungs ached, and the water being poured into the burning buildings seemed to have little effect.

"You look like you can swing an axe." A watch captain grasped his arm, pointing toward one of the wider lanes through the godowns. "We need to get those lean-tos down. They're too close to the buildings on this side and we risk losing the lot."

So Kalan gave up his place on the hose to the next smoke-grimed face and seized the axe, plunging deeper into the nightmare of heat and smoke and sweat, aching muscles and aching lungs. In the end, he barely registered the first fat drop of rain splashing onto his hand, or a second that snuffed out a wind-borne spark in midair. By the time he did, the rain was on them in earnest, striking with such force it felt close to being hail. The man beside Kalan thrust both arms and his axe heavenward. "Thank Imulun!" he shouted, hoarse from the smoke.

No, Kalan thought: thank the weatherworker. Now he could feel the torrent of power being released through the deluge, and sense the strength that had pulled the rainstorm in off the deep ocean to break over Grayharbor. In time to be useful, he reflected, his face raised to the downpour while his chest heaved. The wind had also died away completely, so quite possibly the weatherworking had saved the town.

Once the lean-to demolition was complete, the axe team retreated to the open wharf. Kalan's first look around, once he had stacked his axe beside the others and stripped the smoke-blackened cloth from his face, was to locate the weatherworker. The flow of power was so strong he had assumed the man must be close by, but he had to look the full length of the wharf, to the *Che'Ryl-g-Raham*'s poop deck, before picking out the cables of gray hair—drenched to rattails by the deluge—and a rain-sodden length of robe. He did not know if the weatherworker could see him through the downpour, but raised a hand in salute anyway.

Others along the docks were looking the same way, but the marine cordon remained in place. Besides, there was too much to be done to delay for courtesies yet. The water wagons had to be refilled and a firebreak encircling the godown area completed, in case the blaze reignited once the rain stopped. But the downpour continued throughout the night and rain was still falling when dawn broke. By that time the captains were of the opinion that it was safe to begin standing the firewatch teams down. Food and ale were set out in a nearby warehouse, but like most of his sweat- and grime-streaked companions, Kalan ate mechanically and was too exhausted for conversation.

Afterward, the firefighters sluiced the worst of the muck from their bodies, before trudging their separate ways. Despite Kalan's efforts at the pump, the inn-wife insisted he take a proper bath in the Anchor's washhouse before coming indoors. She also sent the tapster to make sure he kept his head above the soapy water. By the time Kalan finally reached his room, rather than removing the clean clothes Stefa had brought him, he simply collapsed onto the bed, falling into a sleep so deep that no dreams intruded.

8

Puzzles

Kalan woke to the rain's soft swish and a filtering of gray through the shutters. Although impossible to be sure in the overcast weather, he guessed the day was growing late. His muscles ached as much as they had after the Caer Argent tourney, and this time his lungs and eyes were smarting, too. He eased his feet onto the floor, trying to recall whether he had taken his boots off or left them in the washhouse—and realized that he had forgotten the Sea House navigator's instruction to present himself at the ship that morning, in order to negotiate his passage north. Given her sharp words the previous night, he could only imagine that he was not going to be a passenger when the *Che'Ryl-g-Raham* did sail. Always assuming the black-prowed ship had not already left.

He stretched, groaning again, then forced himself upright and straightened his rumpled clothes. His boots, he recalled, *had* been left by the bathtub, but when he opened his door he found them sitting neatly beside it, cleaned of debris and freshly oiled. He pulled them on and buckled his sword and daggers about his waist, but left off the armor. Leti was watching from the stable door as he went past, so he waved, calling out that he would be back for dinner. She nodded, but he thought she looked as though she had been crying.

It might just be from the smoke, Kalan told himself, conscious of his own red eyes, but on impulse he turned back. "Is something wrong?"

Definitely crying, he decided, as she bit her lip and looked away. "A lot of people died. They got trapped on the ship and in the buildings." Her voice was a thread, and faltered before she resumed again. "And Myron's missing. After what happened yesterday, he told us he was going to hunt through the godown area until he found Faro. But he wasn't free until last night." She hugged her arms about herself. "We're afraid he got caught in there, the fire took hold so fast."

Recalling the heat and fury, Kalan thought it probable no one in the affected buildings had escaped. "I'm sorry," he said, aware of the futility of the words. They woke another recollection: the young woman with her hair twisted into a silver net, who had appeared in his dream. *"I'm sorry,"* had been her words, too. *"I'm sorry. I'm sorry."*

Did she feel as inadequate as I do right now, when she uttered them? he wondered. And what was she sorry for anyway?

"The fire captains," Leti added, "think it might not have been an accident. That's what people are saying." She ducked back inside the stable door, her hands pressed to her mouth as though the information had escaped against her will, but the words stayed with Kalan. He had seen death before, both in the Keep of Winds and on Emer's Northern March, where he had lost a great many friends fighting Swarm agents earlier in the year. But the death of children always hit hard.

On reaching the harbor, Kalan took shelter beneath a warehouse eave and studied the rainswept dock. The smell of burning was still strong, but the ships that had stood off during the night were either remoored or had departed altogether. The *Halcyon* was back and the *Che'Ryl-g-Raham* still in place, this time with only one marine on watch. At the opposite end of the dock the remains of the burned ship had been towed clear of the pier, while the port's fire-watch was still working in the area where the conflagration had taken hold. Kalan could see covered-over drays in the warehouse where he had eaten as dawn broke, and guessed they must contain the remains of the dead. He felt no need to examine them for himself, crossing to the chandler's warehouse instead.

Rayn was peering at a ledger through round, wire-rimmed spectacles when Kalan walked in, but this time the clerk offered him a tall stool to sit on before pouring a clear, aromatic liquor into narrow glasses. "The *Che'Ryl-g-Raham*," he said, raising his, and pursed his lips when Kalan hesitated. "Not all of your people's ships and crew would risk themselves for port and town, young man, despite their trade here."

So it appears some of the Sea House *are* like Blood, Kalan reflected, as he raised his glass and drank. The liquor's tang filled his mouth, before tracing a line of fire from throat to gut. He sipped again, listening to the rain and all the soft warehouse noises, but heard no sly creak from the back door, or any other sound out of place. The liquor seared his throat again as Rayn lowered his own glass. "I heard you worked all night among the fire teams. Andron said you did a hero's work with an axe."

Andron must have been the captain who handed him the axe, Kalan supposed. It would not be unusual for a smith to captain a fire-watch, especially since Leti and Stefa had said he was in the town guard. "I'm no hero." Kalan sampled the drink again, the sip no less fiery than its predecessors. "I heard that the blaze might have been arson. Did Andron say anything about that?"

Rayn shook his head, his expression lengthening. "It seems hard to believe, but when Andron and his team finally got on board what was left of the *Sea Mew*, it looked as though the hatches had been wedged shut. And the human remains in what was left of the hold would account for captain and crew." He shook his head again. "*Sea Mew* was a coastal trader and the captain's son disappeared a few weeks back. The crew had been searching everywhere for him, even along the landward route to Ij."

"And now this," Kalan said softly.

"Now this," Rayn echoed. "There's talk the *Sea Mew* was not above smuggling on the side, and the Captain of the City Watch has taken over the investigation." The clerk set his empty glass down with a small clink. "But the business doesn't look good, whichever way you examine it."

"Whoever did this," Che'Ryl-g-Raham said, coming in out of the rain, "either has no regard for the Grayharbor authorities or is sending a message. Or both." Her expression was reflective as well as stern, so much so that Kalan wondered if she knew more than she was saying.

"No regard, eh?" Rayn frowned. "Do you think this might be the School of Assassins' work?"

"I think it could be interesting to look in their famous book," the navigator replied, "although Dancers of Kan are by no means the only option. Some might say the method was too crude for them. Or too arrogant."

They were all silent, and Kalan contemplated what was left of his drink before speaking. "I thought you might have sailed by now."

"Not without a functioning weatherworker. And after bringing the rain early, ours needs complete rest." Her gaze measured him, almost as expressionless as she had been in the fireglow of last night's wharf. "Given the loss of stored goods, we should have space for you and your horses, as well as your fellow warriors with their Matter of Kin and Blood."

Despite inward relief, Kalan kept his face composed and bit back his thanks. "They're not my fellows," he said instead, and sensed the glance that the Derai navigator and Grayharbor clerk did not exchange.

"No," Rayn said finally. "When the smoke got too much in the Marlinspike area last night, they shifted their gaming and drinking to the Drover, near the landward gate."

Kalan stopped himself from shaking his head, but his features must have been less composed than he thought, because Che'Ryl-g-Raham's smile held a glimmer of malice.

"Don't worry, everyone saw you fighting the blaze, so the honor of the warrior kind is not completely in the mud. And if the mood does turn that way, no one will look in your direction for a scapegoat to string up."

Rayn studied her over his spectacles. "The honorable navigator has an excellent sense of humor," he observed, very dryly, before his gaze shifted to Kalan. "There is no question of that, either in your case or that of the Sword warriors. Arson is a serious charge, and lives, buildings, and goods have all been lost, but I hope we still have enough justice in Grayharbor to make sure it's those responsible we punish."

A little to Kalan's surprise, Che'Ryl-g-Raham's edge of malice faded. "Still, better for all of us that Derai were not implicated in starting the blaze and that some of us were seen to help fight it. I know it's not Grayharbor's way, friend Rayn, but it would not be the first time the mob has answered a disaster of this kind."

Better for all of us indeed, Kalan thought, seeing the look that passed between them. He understood what they did not say: that if Derai were hanged in Grayharbor, it would mean blood feud with the Derai Alliance and most likely armed retribution as well. "Blood price," he murmured, and the navigator nodded.

"Best it doesn't happen," she agreed, before turning back to Rayn. "I'll let you sort out Khar of Blood's fare once we have the rest of the manifest in order. Don't go too easy on him," she added, a grin crooking. "He does have two warhorses." Her gaze returned to Kalan. "As for when we sail, it'll be when our weatherworker's recovered. Rayn will send word to your lodging when the time comes."

She glanced over her shoulder at the rain, and Rayn reached for a third glass. "A drink?" he suggested, and she nodded, pulling up another stool and settling onto it so her scabbard swung clear. Rayn turned to Kalan. "You'll have another?"

"Why not?" Outside, the late afternoon was fading to dusk, but he had at least an hour before dinner would be served in the Anchor's common room. He watched the clerk fill all three glasses, before raising his in unison with theirs.

"Health," Rayn murmured, and both Kalan and the Sea woman echoed the word. In Emer they would have drunk to friendship and glory; on the Wall to Earl, House, and honor. In Grayharbor, with an outsider and two Derai whose Houses were at best neutral to each other, health had the advantage of being a safe pledge. Although friendship, Kalan thought, listening while the navigator and clerk talked of goods and manifests, shipping movements and weather conditions beneath the drum of the rain, would probably be as true a toast.

He swallowed the last of his liquor and stretched, feeling a pleasant warmth in his belly. Further down the wharf, men conversed idly as a warehouse's doors screeched closed; the sound almost disguised the tiny opening creak of the chandlery's rear entrance. Kalan lowered his arms, listening intently until the creak sounded again. A brief silence followed before he heard the creep of carefully placed feet. Casually, he stood up and asked for directions to the privy.

Rayn pointed, and Kalan started that way, pacing quietly between rows of shelves but angling toward the furtive sounds. He listened for a careless footfall or yesterday's betraying scuff of a bin lid, but whoever had crept in was also adept at stealth. When he paused to look down another long aisle, he saw the rear door standing ajar and considered closing it, except that might panic his quarry. A few paces more brought him in sight of the grain bins, which stood several rows deep along the warehouse wall. A chain hung down from the gantry above them, part of a mezzanine loft that in turn joined a narrow walkway running along two sides of the warehouse.

Plenty of pathways for a pilferer, Kalan thought, his gaze traveling casually across the dimly lit space. And plenty of places to hide among the stored goods. He could see the privy door built into one corner and separated from the grain barrels by stacks of sail canvas. Continuing in that direction, he picked out a variation in the dust between the last two rows of barrels—the suggestion that a mark might have been brushed away. A glance along the barrels revealed that one lid was very slightly raised, as though it had been partially lifted clear then hastily replaced.

So where are you? Kalan thought. Are you crouched between

the barrels, or do you have a better bolthole? He pretended to be distracted by a pallet of axe-handles, picking one up while in reality studying the surrounding area. A half turn, as he tested the handle for heft, showed him a pile of abandoned creels and crates behind the sail canvas. The loose stack offered crawlways for anyone small enough, as well as potential hiding spaces. Replacing the axe handle, he crossed to the pile and examined a creel instead. If someone was hiding there, however, even Kalan's acute sight could not make them out.

Thoughtfully, he set the creel down again, aware that Rayn and Che'Ryl-g-Raham had fallen quiet. Even so, the exhalation as he turned away was so soft that few others would have caught it. Kalan was sure it came from within the pile of crates, yet still could not see anything out of place. Frowning, he considered the possibility that he was dealing with an aptitude similar to his own: someone who was adept at taking on the appearance of his or her surroundings, while turning a hunter's eyes and mind away. The ability was one most Derai would only expect to find among their own ranks, but Kalan's time beyond the Wall had taught him otherwise. All the same, a gift that matched his shielding power, or Jehane Mor's, would still be rare.

But if he *was* dealing with another shielder, then the power use itself would also be concealed. Hiding in plain sight, Kalan thought: it does fit—yet how to flush the quarry out?

Turning back to the crates, he sank onto his heels, which brought him eye level with the gaps between them. He was no seeker, like Malian and Tarathan, but suspected that separating illusion from reality would be like standing between the waking world and the Gate of Dreams, able to see one and both at the same time. So rather than using power, he concentrated on looking both at, and through, the tangle of wickerwork and planks.

At first the loose pile appeared the same, but eventually Kalan began to see how the shadows clung more densely to one cluster of creels. Narrowing his focus, he gradually pulled what initially looked like disparate elements into a coherent physical form: first the outline of hands wrapped around knees, then a head hunched down onto shoulders. Finally, a face emerged from the pattern of substance and shadow, darkness and light, and two wide, frightened eyes stared back into his.

"Ah," said Kalan. "Found you."

He thought his quarry might flee at once, but the boy remained frozen in place. "We met yesterday, on the wharf," Kalan said, keeping his manner easy. "You're Faro, aren't you?"

The boy continued to stare, but gave no sign of having heard him. "I've met some friends of yours," Kalan went on, still casual. "Leti and Stefa at the Anchor Inn: they're worried about you." Best, he decided, not to mention Myron. "If you were to make your way there, I could buy you a meal and ask the inn-wife to find you a real job." He paused, but the boy's set face remained blank. "Or I could leave some money for you, since I'll be leaving Grayharbor soon."

He tried to think of a good place to leave it, where the boy would not have to deal with those who meant him well—the inn-wife, or Andron, or even Rayn—unless he chose to. Somewhere out of the way, Kalan thought. "There's a temple before you reach the Anchor," he said. "It's the small old one, down a side lane off the crossroads. The god niches on either side of the door are empty, so I'll put the money in one of them. Say at noon tomorrow, if you haven't come to the inn."

The small body stirred. " 'Tisn't a temple." His voice was small, too, and hoarse, although that could be the aftermath of smoke. "It's a tomb. A god's tomb, some of Seruth's priests say, from the time before time."

"Is it now?" But Kalan was recalling a moonless mountainside in Emer and the ancient darkness that had crept out to waylay Malian in her guise as Carick the scholar. "The niches are outside, though, and I'll be leaving the money when the sun is high." He made a move to stand.

"I like horses." A tremble shook the hoarse voice as Kalan

resettled onto his heels. "And I'm fast to run messages. I could work for you."

Kalan shook his head, but the hoarse voice spoke quickly before he could reply.

"You wouldn't have to pay me or anything." The boy was shaking now, enough to stir the creels. "I'll work for just my keep, if you'll take me away with you."

Pity twisted in Kalan's gut, but he kept his tone reasonable. "Faro, the place I'm going is the Derai Wall and that's no place for you." Or anyone who's not Derai, he added silently, remembering Rowan Birchmoon. "Come to the Anchor or take the money I'll leave for you. You have friends here and can make a life for yourself again."

The head amid the enclosing crates jerked—*no*—before Faro turned his face aside. Kalan sighed inwardly. "I'm going to stand up now and move away," he said, addressing the resolutely averted head. "You go when you're ready. But I've accepted Rayn's hospitality, which means I'll have to tell him about your pilfering, so best you don't come back."

If Rayn is wise, he thought, he'll keep that rear door bolted from now on. And if you're wise, he added silently to Faro, you'll let your friends at the Anchor help you. But the feeling in his gut, where the twist of pity had dispelled the warmth of Rayn's liquor, told him that Faro was unlikely to be wise. He shook his head again, about to withdraw as promised—and only heard Che'Ryl-g-Raham's soft tread a moment before she unshuttered the lantern off Rayn's desk.

She crept up on me, Kalan thought, astonished, as the navigator set the lantern down on a grain bin and turned toward him. Her silhouette, a shadow warrior with cabled hair twisted around her head like serpents, and a long, curve-tipped sword at her hip, loomed across roof and wall—and Faro screamed, erupting from his hideaway. Kalan caught one glimpse of his terrified face before the boy darted over the top of the sail stack and swung the gantry's hanging chain at Che'Ryl-g-Raham. She and Kalan both jumped back, and Faro fled through the door, slamming it shut behind him.

"I thought I heard voices." Che'Ryl-g-Raham's surprise was reflected in the lantern's glass panes. "Was that your pastry thief from yesterday?"

Kalan nodded. He was wondering why the navigator had terrified the boy so much now when she had not done so the previous day, even before she let him go free. Che'Ryl-g-Raham glanced from him to the door. "You're not going after him?"

"No, he's frightened enough as it is. Poor little rat," Kalan added.

Curiosity replaced the navigator's surprise. "You know, I think our weatherworker may be right about you." Her tone was reflective. "You're not like any other Blood warrior I've met."

"You've met a lot, I take it?' Kalan replied coolly, although his heart had begun to hammer.

Che'Ryl-g-Raham's smile glinted. "Enough to decide that you're a puzzle." The smile deepened as he kept his expression impassive, and she spoke softly, leaning forward so that her lips almost—but not quite—brushed his ear. "Don't let it trouble you, Blood warrior. I like puzzles."

9

Sepulchre

Attendance at the Anchor's dinner was sparse and Kalan had a table to himself, one that commanded a view of both the common room door and a window onto the yard outside. Afterward he lingered over his beer, but although he waited until the inn gates were closed for the night, Faro did not come. The tapster had shot more than one speculative look his way as the evening lengthened, his manner shifting to heavy sympathy as he closed up. "Girl let you down, did she? It's probably nothing personal. Even if *she* liked you, most families are wary of northerners."

Kalan stared. "It wasn't that," he said stiffly, but could tell the man was unconvinced, especially when his color heightened, remembering Che'Ryl-g-Raham's murmur against his ear. Her eyes had been alight with amusement and something more as she stepped back, but she left immediately afterward, striding out into the rain as though she did not notice it—which she probably didn't, being used to walking a deck in all weathers.

Ignoring the tapster's knowing look, Kalan returned to his room, where sleep eluded him. Admittedly he had slept most of the day, but part of his wakefulness was chagrin, because between intervening on Faro's behalf, fighting fires, and catching a Sea House navigator's attention, he was not doing well at staying in the background. And why, he asked himself, am I so concerned about this Faro anyway? What's makes one Grayharbor foundling different from a world full of starving and abandoned children? I can't look out for them all.

He thumped his pillow, trying to get more comfortable, and supposed that unlike all the other foundlings, this one had crossed his path. But if he wouldn't take a trained knight like Jarna with him to the Wall, he certainly couldn't take a Grayharbor street brat. Still, if Faro did come to the inn tomorrow, he would speak to Andron on the boy's behalf. The smith might be willing to get Faro some sort of apprenticeship in the watch's compound, especially if he really had been fond of the boy's mother.

Despite forming this resolution, it was near dawn before Kalan fell into a light uneasy sleep—and swift as a dam breaking, the white mists of the Gate of Dreams flooded into his mind. The hounds he had been hearing more frequently since leaving Emer were silent, but a woman spoke in Derai, her intonation exasperated. "I'll be glad when we're done with this nursemaiding detail."

A man replied, sounding weary despite his good-humored tone. "We all will, Innor. But riding escort allows us to scout out this country like the Captain wants, especially up around Dread Pass, so . . . " Kalan never heard what the so was, because a gap opened in the mist and he found himself standing on a plain that reminded him of the Gray Lands, although sheer mountain walls rose on either side and he was gazing toward a massif that had to be part of the Wall of Night. He thought he could make out what looked like a narrow pass between the heights, with dark clouds boiling above it.

"Dread Pass," he whispered. Foreboding prickled across his skin, but the brume rolled in and the plain gave way to a forest of vast, silhouetted trunks. A voice sang through the blank world, a low vibration of blood and danger, and he knew without needing to look that the black-pearl ring on his hand would be glowing. He waited, half reluctant, half with a rising sense of anticipation, for the Gate of Dreams to reveal the Great Spear that he had first encountered six years before ... *"Soon,"* the voice sang, exultant and fierce: *"soon."* But the spear did not materialize and gradually both the song and the glow from the ring faded. Although there was no breath of wind, the fog began to blow apart, the forest dissipating into the gentle slap of water, a creak of rigging, and the smell of salt and tar. A shadow loomed through the whiteness as a gull mewed nearby, perhaps disturbed by the coming dawn.

The shadow darkened, acquiring form through the dream, much as Kalan had distinguished Faro from his surroundings the previous evening. The wooden planks beneath his feet became the Grayharbor dock, while the black swan's neck rising above his head was the prow of the *Che'Ryl-g-Raham*. Beyond the mist, the gull called again, greeting the day. Kalan could see the bird's wings in his mind, turning against the first light, even as a wave lifted the ship's crest high—and the eye painted on the side of the black prow opened, gazing down at him.

The dream fled, or Kalan did, back to the dawn's pale light filling his room at the Anchor. Che'Ryl-g-Raham's voice followed him, an echo out of the ship chandler's the night before, the same note of laughter infusing her tone: *"Don't let it trouble you, Blood warrior. I like puzzles."*

I'm not sure I do, Kalan thought, waking up. He found he could not shake the memory of the eye on the ship's prow opening to look at him, or of the navigator's words, however long he lingered over breakfast. The spear song with its promise of *"Soon"* also unsettled him, and eventually the common room discussions of soil conditions and crops drove him to the stable. He groomed the horses, keeping a watchful eye on the yard through the open double doors, before polishing their tack to a high gloss. When he was done with his own gear, he began on the inn's harness, sitting on an upturned tub just inside the stable door while Leti and Stefa came and went, exchanging glances as they worked around him.

I must have a face like an overcast day, Kalan realized, finally rousing himself sufficiently to decipher Stefa's whisper, wondering what could have made him so out of sorts. Che'Ryl-g-Raham, he thought wryly. He had also been hoping that Faro would show up, despite the odds against it. But now it was time to weigh the money he thought Faro needed against how much he could spare, before leaving it at the old temple—or tomb—as promised.

Kalan counted out the coins in his room, taking account of Faro's food and shelter as well as the cost of purchasing an apprentice-ship—although he doubted what he could spare would stretch that far without the inn-wife or Andron's goodwill. As much as possible, he chose smaller coins that were unlikely to generate accusations of theft, and was replacing the balance when his hand brushed against the package containing Lord Falk's dagger. It, too, would fit into the empty god niches, and both the dagger and Audin's silver buckle would fetch a good price if the right person negotiated with an armorer . . .

Kalan hesitated, because the parcel's contents were gifts that meant a great deal to him, as well as being the last ties to a life he had loved. That life was over, though, and none of them—Lord Falk, or Audin, or Ghiselaine—would think their gifts ill-used if they bought Faro a better life. Or even just a life, Kalan reflected, knowing the likely fate of a child living on the street. After further consideration, he decided not to leave the package in the niche with the coins. Instead he would ask Rayn to have the smith, Andron, sell the buckle and dagger on Faro's behalf and secure him that appren-ticeship—once, Kalan thought, exasperated, the little fool realizes he can't go on living the way he is.

And then, he told himself, closing the saddlebag, I really will have done all I can for the boy.

The sun had come out by the time he reached the side lane, although the portico that formed its far end remained in shadow. Coolness reached out, engulfing his approach, and although Kalan was certain Faro would be watching, he also guessed that the boy's vantage point would be sufficiently far away to prevent him being easily trapped.

Seen up close, the plaster on the pillars was cracked, with lichen growing over both their surface and the stone slab that served as a door. It was the door that made Kalan decide it really must be a tomb, because he could see no hinge or handle, and it would be unusual to build a temple that did not open. When he looked for an inscription he found nothing, not even the suggestion of a device or dedication eroded by time. Curious, he laid his palm against the stone—and almost jumped back as power flickered across the wards suppressing his magic.

The power had come from the door or whatever lay beyond it. Kalan kept his hand in place, but although his pearl ring gleamed against the lichen with the iridescence of a crow's wing, no glow of power answered the tremor from the door. He waited, letting out his breath as a second frisson of power rippled against his wards and the slab beneath his hand began to grate open. The sound echoed in the narrow lane, and Kalan felt sure people would come running to investigate. But although stone continued to grind against stone, no one came.

The light from behind him lanced into the dark interior, dust motes speckling its path, and Kalan took the precaution of prying a few looser cobbles from the edge of the lane and piling them against the jamb, to prevent the door closing while he was inside. Then he waited for several minutes, every sense alert for danger, before stepping into the gloom.

The contrast with the shaft of light made the darkness to either side more impenetrable, but after his vision adjusted, Kalan realized that the interior was little more than a nave, with another empty god niche at its far end. The space was stark, the roof, walls, and pillars constructed from undecorated stone, while the floor was broken only by a steel panel the height of an infantryman's shield, set into the flagstones. Kalan's breath misted on the chill air as he walked forward, his boots leaving prints in the surface dust.

He studied the austere interior again once he reached the panel, but could detect no sign of the power that had ignited when he touched the door. It was possible, he supposed, that a ward had been bound into the slab alone, serving as a magical lock. The metal of the panel was also filmed with dust, but when Kalan crouched to look more closely, he could detect no inscription. If the place really was a sepulchre, then a crypt or coffin, or even a skeleton wrapped in a rotting shroud, could lie beneath the steel. But he felt no inclination to disturb the dead, and was no grave robber either, greedy for treasures interred to give the deceased comfort in whatever afterlife those who made the tomb believed in. In any case, the join between panel and stone was seamless and he could see no easy way to lift it clear.

All the same, it did seem strange that whoever lay here merited a mausoleum but not an inscription, not to mention a warding spell on the door but none elsewhere in the tomb. Kalan's attention returned to the god niche, speculating on why it might have been provided and then left empty. When he looked away, his eyes traveled back along the shaft of daylight to a shadow hovering just outside the entrance. "Hop inside, little sparrow, if you dare. I've brought the money I promised you."

Faro, it seemed, did not dare. His shadow advanced, but only until his scrawny person stood in the doorway, poised for flight. "I don't want your money." His voice was a whisper, as though he feared to startle the shadows, his grimy face a mix of curiosity and fear as his eyes darted around the dark interior. Wonder crept in when he fixed his gaze on Kalan. "No one's ever been able to open the door before. Not ever, though lots have tried: priests and sages, princes and merchants, and even one of those weatherworkers. So they say." He ran the tip of his tongue across cracked lips. "But it's never budged. Not once."

Kalan shrugged, surveying the narrow space again. "It opened as soon as I touched it, so maybe those others were trying too hard." Yet if the ripple of power *had* acted like a lock set to keep all but the right person out, then why would he—whether Kalan, an outcast from the House of Blood, or Hamar of Aldermere, Falk of Normarch's foster son—be that person? Automatically, his mind went to the black-pearl ring—except it had not been affected by the door.

Faro's stare was almost painful in its intensity. "But it *opened*," he whispered. "For *you*. And then you went in. I thought—I didn't know ..." He wiped his hands down his ragged shirt, the whisper fading away.

"Did you come to make sure I was safe?" Kalan smiled at the small, hovering figure. "I think we'll both be all right. Whatever mystery governs the door, the inside's just an empty space."

The boy nodded, with another quick glance around before his gaze returned to Kalan. The darting movement might be reminiscent of the sparrow Kalan had called him, but his gaze was an owl's, large-eyed and solemn. When he spoke, his whisper was urgent. "You can't go with them, the Sea people. You won't be safe."

"On the Sea House ship, you mean?" Kalan waited for Faro's nod. "I have to, I'm afraid. Their vessels are the only ones that sail to the Wall of Night. Besides, I'm Derai, like they are. Our people take passage on their ships all the time." Those few who journey to the outside lands, at any rate, he added silently.

Faro shook his head. "But *you* can't. Not if the door opened for you, because that means you're special, no matter how ordinary you seem on the outside."

Kalan recalled the ship's eye from his dream, opening to look at him, and the way Che'Ryl-g-Raham's words from the previous night had pursued him: *I like puzzles.* A coolness feathered along his spine, but all he said was: "Why's that, Faro? Is it because of the weather-workers?" He could well imagine that many Haarth people, not just warrior Derai, might be afraid of their powers. "Was that why you were so frightened of the navigator last night?"

The grimy face contorted, as though the boy was trying to shape words but could not quite manage it. "I thought she was ... someone else," he forced out finally. "Her hair ... and the sword ..." His voice trailed away, then strengthened again. "But the Sea people are stealers. That's what my mam said. If you're not ordinary you have to stay clear of them, else they'll steal you away."

Kalan considered it unlikely that Sea House mariners would

steal Grayharbor children, or concern themselves with any Haarth business beyond their trade. Although— Here he paused, because Faro's ability to conceal himself was far from usual. If there were others like him, then Grayharbor might wish to conceal the fact that weatherworkers did not have a monopoly on arcane power. But stealers ... Kalan shook his head, until it occurred to him that if fugitive Derai priests, those called the Lost, had been discovered in the port town, Sea House mariners could well have returned them forcibly to the Wall.

He frowned, contemplating another possibility, but kept it to himself. "I'm grateful for the warning," he told Faro, "but my business is pressing, so I shall have to chance the Sea House ship." He looked around the stark space one more time, his manner casual. "There's really nothing here as far as I can see. What do you think, time to leave?"

The boy vanished at once, and Kalan grinned as he rose to his feet. By the time he reached the door, Faro was crouched on a nearby roof, close by a drainpipe that had clearly been his means of ascent. Kalan removed the cobbles from the jamb, and as soon as he stepped clear the stone slab grated back into place. He frowned at it briefly, before smiling up at Faro. "Another puzzle," he said lightly, extracting the money from his coat. "Grayharbor is full of them."

He thought the boy might smile in answer, but when Faro saw the bag of coins, sullenness closed over his grimy face. "Here." Kalan tossed the bag up to him and wondered, momentarily, if Faro was going to let it fall back—but at the last moment he snatched it from the air.

"Take me with you," he said fiercely, not even looking at the coins. "I can watch your back."

Kalan shook his head. "It's not possible, Faro. I told you that last night." He paused. "The money will keep you going for a while, but I'll leave something more with Rayn, the clerk at the shipping office. That should bring enough for a decent apprenticeship, which is a better future than you'll find with me." The set expression above him was not encouraging, but Kalan persisted. "Once the *Che'Ryl-g-Raham*'s gone you can walk in the front door whenever you're ready and talk to Rayn about it."

The knuckles around the coin bag clenched white as Faro's face twisted. "I don't want your better future," he cried. "I want to come with you!" When Kalan said nothing, just continued to gaze steadily up at him, he raised his arm as though intending to fling the coins back into the lane, but checked the gesture. Instead he sprang up and hurled himself along the eave, disappearing between the adjoining roofs without looking back.

At least he kept the money, Kalan told himself, but his frame of mind was bleak as he quit the lane. Like the weather, the mood did not lift, even when his fare on the *Che'Ryl-g-Raham* turned out to be more reasonable than he had feared. Rayn listened without interruption to his explanation about Faro and agreed to dispose of the contents of Kalan's package for the boy's benefit. Yet striding back to the Anchor afterward, Kalan still felt as dour as the day. I couldn't possibly take Faro with me, he thought, and I've done all I can: I have to put him out of my mind and concentrate on my own business. But this, he found, was more easily resolved upon than done. Faro's despairing *I want to come with you!* stayed with him as tenaciously as Che'Ryl-g-Raham's murmur about liking puzzles.

Curse the brat! Kalan thought, rather savagely, when an afternoon's walk around the landward perimeter of the town brought him back to the Anchor, and his dinner, in as morose a temper as when he left it. A Grayharbor urchin would not survive long on the Derai Wall, that was all there was to it. And if, as he had begun to suspect, Faro was the result of a liaison between one of the Derai Lost and a local woman, that was even more reason to keep him away from the Wall of Night.

I'm doing you a favor, boy, even if you don't see it, Kalan thought, mopping up his gravy. He could only hope that Faro would understand, one day—assuming that Malian found both sword and shield and they could stop the darkness from swarming over Haarth. For if they did not, there would be no better future for anyone, from a street urchin in Grayharbor to the Shah on Ishnapur's Lion Throne.

Kalan slept without dreaming and woke to the previous day's grim mood, which only lifted when he found Rayn waiting in the Anchor's yard. "The *Che'Ryl-g-Raham* sails on tomorrow's dawn tide," the shipping clerk said, and Kalan nodded, relieved that the waiting was over. No dreams disturbed his sleep that night either, and he woke in darkness to collect up his gear and prepare the horses for the voyage. A tousled, sleepy Leti let him out the inn gate, and she was still in the entrance when he looked back from the street corner. A fine, misting rain haloed the night lantern above her head as they both lifted a hand in farewell.

When Kalan reached the dock, the charred remains of the *Sea Mew* were no more than a shadow seen through intermittent drizzle. Lanterns glowed saffron on the wharf adjoining the *Che'Ryl-g-Raham*, as well as along the ship's bulwark and in her rigging, illuminating the mariners' work. Orth and his Sword comrades were waiting in the lee of the nearest warehouse, but as much as possible in the confined area, they ignored Kalan's arrival. He shrugged inwardly, conscious of Che'Ryl-g-Raham's presence on the poop deck as the crew came and went. Even with his own powers suppressed, he could almost see the shimmer of magic when the weatherworker joined her. Orth glowered in the same direction, his arms folded, but Kalan imagined that the Sword warriors' desire to reach the Wall— together with the ship's marines—would deter a confrontation. He was also aware that the Sword band's restraint would not extend to a Blood warrior without comrades or kin to back him.

Dawn was imminent when word came to embark. Kalan got the horses on board with far less fuss than in Port Farewell, although both regarded their accommodation in the hold with suspicion. He spent time getting them settled, listening to the voices of the mariners working cargo and the footsteps crisscrossing the deck overhead until whistles piped, indicating they were about to sail. When metal clinked softly behind him he spun around, expecting a Sword warrior, but instead saw the woman with the shaven head, her stare unblinking as she watched him from beside the hold ladder. "Honor on you," Kalan said automatically, although he was also remembering that the marine, Temorn, had told him she would not reply. Could she be mute? he wondered. In the gloom, her gaze was as opaque as a blind woman's, but she raised her hands, pressing the palms together and bowing in an ancient gesture of greeting and salute.

Madder snorted, his ears pricking forward as Che'Ryl-g-Raham swung down the ladder, her frown shifting from Kalan to the shaven-headed woman. Kalan thought she was going to speak sharply to one or both of them, but despite the frown her words were calm. "You should not be here," she told the woman. "Your place is on deck, with Laer."

The woman turned away immediately and ascended the ladder, the charms on her ankle bracelet tinkling. Che'Ryl-g-Raham watched until she disappeared through the hatch, before directing her frown at Kalan. "Is she not allowed down here?" he asked.

Che'Ryl-g-Raham hesitated. "She is the Ship's Luck," she said finally, "whose place is with the weatherworker once a ship puts to sea. Ship's business," she added brusquely, forestalling questions. "But if she bothers you again, do as I did just now and send her back to Laer."

Kalan was about to say that the Luck had not been bothering him, but honesty made him admit that he found her disconcerting. Che'Ryl-g-Raham nodded, as if reading the admission in his face.

"When your horses are settled," she said, "find Temorn. We don't usually carry this many passengers, so we've had to give you a bunk in the marines' quarters. He'll show you where to stow your gear. We'll refund part of your fare, of course," she added.

It was only afterward, when Kalan was back on deck and the *Che'Ryl-g-Raham* was slipping seaward in the gray dawn, that he wondered whether he had been assigned comrades to watch his back, after all.

10

Ship's Business

The voice of the sea filled Kalan's dreams, a whisper and bubble along wooden planking, although the timber on which he walked was hidden by fog. His footsteps were muted, but despite the whiteness he felt sure it was a dock he paced, rather than a deck. It was like the Grayharbor dream again, he thought: the vision of mist with a gull's cry beyond it, and the *Che'Ryl-g-Raham*'s eye opening to gaze down at him. This time, though, it was not just one curved black prow rising through the fog, but a fleet of them, all with the same dawn eyes painted on their prows.

When Kalan turned to gaze back the way he had come, he saw that the fog had thinned. Now he could make out masts and rigging, harpoons and ballistas, as well as the ominous nozzles used to spray what the Derai called Sea House fire. When he looked more closely, he saw that many of the ships appeared to have recently been in battle, with gouged and holed hulls and snapped masts. A storm could also inflict such damage, but these were fighting ships and Kalan guessed he was seeing the Sea House navy, the warships that sailed into the heart of the Great Ocean's storm zone to hold the Swarm-born monsters that dwelt there in check. Ship's business, he thought, repeating Che'Ryl-g-Raham's phrase—except if the Gate of

Dreams was showing him this, then something about the fleet must be his business, too.

"Or you are our business." If he had been awake, Kalan knew every hair on his body would have stood on end, because the whisper had not only spoken into his dream, but from within the wards he and the heralds had woven with such care. Wary, he placed a dream hand against the nearest black prow.

"What business would that be?" he asked.

"We know who you are, Kalan of House Blood, Ser Hamar of Aldermere. We know the Token you bear upon your hand. But we are good at keeping secrets."

So Yorindesarinen was wrong, Kalan reflected, when she said that no one would remember the black-pearl ring anymore. Clearly someone, or something, did—which just went to show that gifts from dead heroes should never be taken at face value.

"Secrets . . . " The voice was a shiver across his mind, and beyond it Kalan could hear a song that rose and dipped with the waves. It was in his dream and so he could not tell himself it was just a song, but he pulled his mind back to the more pressing matter: how either a single ship, or a dream of the Sea House fleet, could discern who he was beneath the guise of Khar of Blood. Or, he added grimly, recognize the ring that Yorindesarinen gave me.

"All those who come within the ambit of our power we comprehend fully," the dream voice replied, *"just as we comprehend you now, waking or dreaming. The star-bright hero we remember from the days before, as we recall the one who last wore your ring upon his hand."* Momentarily, the voice paused. *"We remember everything."*

Kalan sensed the parts to a puzzle shifting around him as the fog began to fray apart. The distant song acquired a wilder note, while all along the dream quay the ships rose high and then fell again on an unseen tide—and the eyes on every curved prow opened as one, piercing him with their vision. *"Need presses, Kalan-hamar. You must wake."*

His mind framed a demand for explanations, but the fog streamed

away until the only contact with the dream was his hand, still resting on the warship's black prow. A shudder ran through both and
an instant later he was fully awake, staring into the darkness of
the marines' quarters with his palm resting against the *Che'Ryl-g-
Raham*'s hull. Kalan told himself the shudder was only in the dream,
but held still for several seconds anyway, expanding his awareness
to encompass the ship. He could feel the rhythm as it ran before the
wind and identify distinct sounds: the swish of the sea along the hull,
the creak of sail and rigging, and the murmur of the crew keeping
the quiet watch. It was their second night out from Grayharbor,
and those marines not on duty were sleeping all around him, some
distinguished only by the in-and-out of their breath, while others
punctuated the darkness with snores. All seemed as it should be, yet
uneasiness persisted, keeping Kalan's focus on the ship despite the
dream still niggling for his attention.

"Vermin: I can always smell 'em." Kalan almost jumped when the
voice muttered, as close as if the speaker were right beside him. He
placed the Swords' accent at once, although he was unsure whether it
was Orth or his equally surly comrade, Malar, who had spoken—but
recognized Kelyr, speaking in reply.

"All Sea House ships carry weatherworkers. We knew that before
we embarked."

"Don't forget their so-called Luck, Kel." That was Tawrin. "You
don't need a wyr hound baying to know there's something off about
her."

"Makes me want to puke when either one comes near." That's
Malar, Kalan decided, which means the first speaker must have
been Orth.

"Stay away from them, then." Kelyr sounded exasperated. "We
want to survive this voyage, not end being hung from the ship's
yardarm."

Malar muttered something indecipherable, which Kalan suspected
was profane. Even taking into account his acute hearing and the way
sound traveled, he was certain they must be close by and not in the

guest cabin beneath the poop deck. The most likely explanation was that they were on the deck immediately above the marines' quarters, and a trick of the ship's structure was funneling their voices—which might be why none of the marines stirred, being used to the phenomenon. Kalan frowned, concentrating, as Malar spoke again.

"... can't even have a go at that cursed Blood snot. Every time I look around there's a marine watching."

"They gave him a berth in their quarters, too." Kelyr sounded amused. "Someone on this tub has our measure."

Che'Ryl-g-Raham, at least, Kalan thought, although Temorn had observed that the Sword warriors reeked of ill will. Malar's further expletives did not surprise him, but Orth telling his comrade to "stow it" did.

"Khar will keep." Will I now? Kalan thought, as Malar fell silent. "The weatherworker and his pet are vermin we know, but whatever I spotted in the dusk was lurking near the hold and moved too quickly for me to get a good look." Orth paused. "I saw the mariners looking, too, when they thought I wasn't paying attention. By the time I got close enough, there was nothing to find." He paused again. "But you know that feeling you get, the twitch when there's any kind of 'spawn about."

Reluctantly, Kalan had to concede that he did, although he had not detected anything amiss on the ship.

"You should tell young Khar," Tawrin drawled. "Oh, that's right, I keep forgetting. Blood don't believe in darkspawn anymore."

"They call them Wallspawn these days." Kelyr ignored a snort from one of his comrades. "And they rely too much on wyr hounds, rather than their warrior instincts."

"That's because they think hunting 'spawn's like tracking their renegade priest-kind." Malar cleared his throat, then spat.

Interesting, Kalan thought—but Tawrin was speaking again. "Perhaps we should show these Sea Keepers what hunting 'spawn is really all about."

Kalan recalled the battered warships in his dream and doubted the mariners needed help with that. "I thought we were going to lie low. But if a dark minion has got on board ..." Kalan could hear the shrug in Kelyr's voice. "Besides, I'm always up for a good hunt."

"Show these ship scum why they still need warrior kind," Malar muttered. As if, Kalan thought, the marines are anything else—but he was already swinging out of his bunk as their footsteps moved away. Even if Che'Ryl-g-Raham had someone monitoring the Sword warriors, the dream had mentioned need, and they were heading toward the hold and his horses. Cursing inwardly, he reached for his boots, leather hauberk, and sword belt, but in the interests of speed and stealth left the rest of his armor behind. He would have to rely on his hearing and night vision to avoid being ambushed; besides, it would only take a shout to bring those on watch running.

As he came on deck, Kalan saw a shifting glimmer near the hold, but both the light and the Sword warriors had disappeared before he reached the hatch. They had left the cover open, so he flattened himself to one side and peered into the swaying shadows below, that were suggestive of a lantern being shone from one side of the hold to the other. A moment later Malar cursed as someone stepped on a chain, although the expletive was immediately bitten off. The swing of the lantern stilled.

The Sword warriors were listening, Kalan guessed, as he was. Mostly, he could hear Madder and Tercel's restlessness, disturbed by both the jumping lanternlight, with its associated threat of fire, and the warriors' stealth. He only hoped the Sword warriors had seen enough of warhorses in the south to stay clear of the stalls.

"I can't see anything here at all." Tawrin's voice was pitched just above a whisper.

"There's a pack of cards back in our cabin," Kelyr murmured. "And a few good bottles ... "

Malar cursed him, but beneath his breath. "When is Orth ever wrong?"

"I can think of a few times," Kelyr muttered back, as the lantern swung again.

"All this tells us is that the 'spawn's good at hiding." When Orth stepped into Kalan's view, his sword was drawn. "There's vermin here all right. I don't need to see it to be sure."

"If we skewer every shadow, we'll flush it out. If we don't, then we go through every coop and crate until we find it." Malar's tone made it clear what would happen then, but Kalan was imagining Che'Ryl-g-Raham's reaction to all the hold's goods being opened or run through with swords. Orth was already stabbing methodically as he moved along the bulkhead, and the play of shadows suggested another warrior was doing the same on the hold's opposite side.

"What's that?" Tawrin exclaimed. "There, by the horses!" Shadows leapt and Madder screamed, not in terror, but a warhorse's cry of defiance and rage. That war cry would rouse the dead, let alone the ship, Kalan thought, catapulting down the ladder as Tawrin backed away from Madder's stall. The destrier half reared, his hooves striking at the wooden barrier between them before he lunged forward, his ears well back and his teeth snapping at the Sword warrior. Beside him, Tercel tossed up his head and stamped, snorting his own readiness to defend their territory.

"Who needs a warhorse on the Wall anyway?" Orth's sword arm drew back as Madder trumpeted out both warning and challenge.

"Keep away, all of you!" Kalan shouted. "Madder, stand down!" he commanded in Emerian, as whistles shrilled and feet pounded overhead. He countered Malar's attempted intercept with a stiff-armed shove, thrusting him into Kelyr. Tawrin jumped clear of Kalan's elbow to his throat, opening a path to Orth. Kalan closed the intervening gap in a single stride, drawing his sword and beating Orth's blade aside as the Sword warrior turned on him.

Marines thundered down both the fore and aft ladders into the hold. Peripherally, Kalan was aware of steel caps and crossbows, but kept his focus on Orth. Footsteps scuffed, followed almost instantly by a thud and a groan as Che'Ryl-g-Raham strode forward. "What in the Nine's name is going on?" she demanded.

"I need to calm my horses." Kalan spoke to her, but did not look away from Orth—or Madder as the roan's head snaked forward again, more in warning than threat this time. Orth's expression was ugly, a red gleam very like the warhorse's in his eyes, but he stayed where he was.

"Orth says there's 'spawn in there." Kelyr was terse. "Khar's horse is protecting it."

"The horse is still contained by the stall." Che'Ryl-g-Raham sounded remarkably calm given the situation. "And we have cross-bows here, so you two can put your swords away."

She had not drawn her own weapon, Kalan realized. Then again, she must realize they didn't need any more blades in the mix. Slowly, he sheathed his sword.

"Orth," Kelyr said, and the giant warrior finally did the same, moving a reluctant half step away as Madder rolled an ill-intentioned eye in his direction.

"Whatever's in there," Kalan said, matching the navigator's com-posure, "can't be darkspawn. Madder would have killed it if it was."

"We already know it's not darkspawn." Now Kalan detected the anger beneath Che'Ryl-g-Raham's surface calm. "We've been aware for some time that we have a stowaway, but that's ship's business to deal with, not an excuse for a bunch of warrior kind to run amok."

Kalan flushed, but Orth glowered at her. "It's 'spawn," he insisted. "I know the vermin taint."

"Orth," Kelyr warned again, while Tawrin shifted uneasily.

"Let me settle Madder down," Kalan said, striving for reasonable-ness. "Then we can see what, if anything, he's protecting."

Che'Ryl-g-Raham regarded him a moment longer before she nodded. The marines with her lowered their crossbows as the Sword warriors shifted back—all except Malar, who Kalan now saw was sprawled facedown with Temorn's boot on his back. That must have been the scuff and thud, he realized. He wondered who Malar had swung at, but spoke soothingly in Emerian, employing the language both horses were most familiar with. "Well done, my bold hearts. Bravely done, my beauties, but the danger's past now. All's well, my valiants."

Finally, he placed his hand on Madder's halter and studied the rumpled hay at the rear of the stall. Nothing moved, but he could see no escape route, except for a creature small enough to squeeze through the narrow gap between stall divide and bulkhead, and into Tercel's space. Carefully, he scrutinized the bay's stall.

"Can he see it?" a marine behind him muttered.

Orth scowled. "Why all this waiting? Let me run my sword through the straw."

The hay beneath Tercel's manger stirred, then immediately stilled. Both horses turned toward the movement, their ears pricked at an identical angle of interest. Definitely not darkspawn, Kalan thought, surveying the narrow gap, but something—or someone—small. Suspicion hardened closer to certainty as he recalled Orth's observation about the 'spawn being good at hiding. Keeping his voice even, Kalan switched to Derai. "There's nowhere left for you to go, so give yourself up or we'll beat the straw. Be wise, Faro: show yourself."

The hay beneath the manger whispered, then rustled, and finally heaved aside. Faro stood, his expression a mix of fear, defiance, and a sullenness that matched Orth's. "Vermin!" the Sword warrior snarled. "I told you!"

"Even if it's a Grayharbor louse rather than darkspawn," Tawrin added smoothly. "Hiding with Khar's horses, though ... That suggests he smuggled the boy on board."

"For his own good reasons, no doubt." Kelyr's tone implied that Kalan's motivation could only be dark.

Under the circumstances, Kalan reflected grimly, their insinuations must seem plausible. Yet Che'Ryl-g-Raham was shaking her head with a certainty that surprised him.

"I'm confident Khar knew nothing of this until now." Her gaze traveled from Kalan to the Sword warriors as she signaled Temorn to let Malar rise. "Stowaways are ship's business, but regardless, passengers do not take any shipboard matter into their own hands. You're all confined to quarters until I say otherwise. You, Faro, must come with me."

The Sword warriors all began protesting, both against her assessment of Kalan's involvement and being confined to quarters. Faro shot forward and flung his arms around Kalan's knees, clinging to him like a spar in a storm. "Don't let them steal me," he begged. "If you tell them I'm yours, they can't take me away."

"He is right, Kalan-hamar." The voice from Kalan's dream whispered in his mind. *"Stowaways are ship's business, but if you claim him as yours then he becomes Blood business, even on a Sea House ship."*

How would a Grayharbor brat know that? Kalan wondered. However extensive the dealings between the Sea House and the port town, he doubted that level of lore was common knowledge, if known at all. He was also reasonably sure that no harm would come to the boy at Che'Ryl-g-Raham's hands. Most likely, Faro would just be shipped back to Grayharbor. On the other hand, Kalan could not be certain of that. He also felt responsible, because he should have made sure Faro's future was settled before leaving Grayharbor, not left the business to others. Remembering the boy's warning against the Sea Keepers, Kalan could only imagine the desperation that had led him to stow away—and now surrendered to what had begun to feel like the inevitable. "I didn't smuggle him on board," he told Che'Ryl-g-Raham, "but now he's here, I feel a duty toward him. By your leave, Navigator, I claim Faro as mine: the House of Blood's responsibility from now on, not yours or the ship's."

"By my leave," she said, as though examining the words. When she smiled, her expression held as much steel as humor. "I think you already know that you don't need my leave." She held his gaze, her own impossible to read, then nodded. "So be it. Faro is yours, Khar of House Blood, to do with as you will, subject to the laws of the Derai."

Said like that, the formal words were a judgment—but both Orth and Kelyr protested at once. The giant's shout was pure outrage: "A Haarth louse can't be taken into the Derai!"

Kelyr was cooler. "With respect, Navigator, I question your wisdom regarding Khar, as well as his right to sponsor anyone.

Let alone"—his lip curled—"introducing Grayharbor dregs into an honorable House."

Che'Ryl-g-Raham's brows rose. "You question my judgment, do you, Kelyr of House Swords? On the ship whose name I bear?"

Kelyr swallowed, but he must, Kalan thought, be a brave man in his way. "With all proper respect for you and your ship, Navigator, but this Khar— He bears a Blood name and wears their harness, yet he has not only come from the Southern Realms, along with horses of the kind we don't use on the Wall, but speaks to them in some southern tongue. You all heard him, just now. Also," the Sword warrior's tone suggested this was the most compelling reason for misgiving, "he shows a most un-Bloodlike kindness for vermin like this boy."

Kalan's heart thudded, wondering if he was about to fail in his mission without even setting foot on the Wall of Night. Che'Ryl-g-Raham's expression, however, was dry rather than doubting. "I've observed the kindness. But neither Khar, nor you and your comrades, are the first Derai to have sought return passage from the Southern Realms in recent years. Nor is there any law that precludes outsiders dwelling among the Derai. The Earl of Night himself has an outsider minstrel, and had an outsider consort, too, before she was murdered."

Malar looked as though he would like to spit again, but Kelyr shook his head, his expression dark. "Yet who *is* he, Navigator? Khar of House Blood, yes: but what is his lineage? Who are his clan and kin?" Now he spoke directly to Kalan. "What device should be blazoned on that Blood harness of yours?"

It was a fair question, one any Derai should be able to answer. Faro's upturned face was worried now, as if realizing that a failure to respond satisfactorily would place him back in Sea House hands. Kalan hesitated, because giving his family name and lineage might avoid immediate disaster, but would only result in a worse fate if he tried to enter Blood territory under his true colors. Yet a lie would not only stain his honor in both Derai and Emerian eyes, but could easily be investigated and proven false.

"See," Kelyr said, and Kalan saw triumph in all the Sword faces, a counter to the flicker of doubt in Che'Ryl-g-Raham's expression, and the trouble in Temorn's, standing behind her.

"We know who he is. We recognize the lineage he brings back into the ranks of the Derai." For a moment Kalan thought it was the dream voice, clear and inflectionless, that had spoken aloud—but Che'Ryl-g-Raham and the marines were looking toward Laer and the Luck, standing by the aft ladder. Laer's face was almost as impassive as the Luck's emotionless countenance, but the marines' dumbfounded expressions confirmed that it was she who had spoken, not the weatherworker. The Sword warriors just stared, puzzled and hostile at the same time.

The Luck pressed her palms together in the ancient salute she had made to Kalan two dawns before. "Honor to you and to your House, scion of Blood, son of the line of Tavaral, the Faithkeeper, of the fellowship of the Storm Spears. Light and safety on your road to the Red Keep."

11

✦━━✦

Storm Spear

S*torm Spear, Storm Spear, Storm Spear* ... Hours later, when
Kalan lay awake in the cabin that was rightly Temorn's, as the
ship's captain of marines—but given over to him now that Faro
must be accommodated as well—the whisper still seemed to echo
through the ship. The reference to the fellowship had obviously meant
something positive to the ship's crew, since they treated the Luck's
greeting as both settling Kelyr's challenge and sufficient explanation
for Kalan's reluctance to identify himself. But *I'll undo everything
she achieved,* he thought now, *if I ask questions—the largest of which
has to be why she intervened at all.*

He was aware, too, that the Luck had never used his name, only
spoken in epithets: scion, son, warrior ... In fact, she had not actually
said he was a Storm Spear. Her words could equally well have meant
that Tavaral had been of the fellowship of the Storm Spears. Everyone
present had just assumed she meant Kalan. *And I keep saying* she, he
reflected, *when what the Luck said was* we. *Probably, she had been
referring to herself and the weatherworker* ... Regardless, Kalan *was*
a scion of the House of Blood, and his clan name, before his exile, had
been Tavar. So it was possible his family line went back to a Tavaral,
somewhere in the mists of Derai history. But he had never heard of

the Storm Spears before, let alone being one himself—which brought him back to the mystery of what the Luck had been about.

Frowning, Kalan watched the darkness beyond the cabin's porthole until the sky began to gray and Faro stirred in the hammock Temorn had slung for him. Earlier, the boy had tossed and turned, crying out warnings in his sleep. As well he might, Kalan thought, given his second encounter with the Sword warriors. For now, though, Faro's expression was peaceful, and although his limbs twitched again, he did not wake.

Kalan shook his head, but let his thoughts drift into the rhythm of the sea until the ship's bell rang the change of watch. Boots tramped overhead, followed by a clatter down the nearest companionway, and Kalan swung to his feet as brisk footsteps started toward his cabin. He was already opening the door as the marine outside raised her hand to knock.

Rin, he reminded himself. Like Temorn, she had been with Che'Ryl-g-Raham that first day on the Grayharbor dock. Briefly, she glanced past him into the cabin, before stepping back. "The navigator requests that you take breakfast with her in the great cabin, at your earliest convenience." Rin kept her voice low. "I'm to stand watch here while you're away."

"Whatever the Sword warriors may say about Matters of Kin and Blood, they were effectively banished into the Southern Realms." Che'Ryl-g-Raham spoke starkly, one hand resting on the charts that littered the main table in her great cabin. "They betrayed the honor of Earl and House, letting darkspawn slay the Keep of Bells' priests they were supposed to be escorting." Her lips pursed. "The report we heard named Orth as the ringleader in that endeavor."

An account that fits, Kalan thought, with their oath breaking in Emer. But Che'Ryl-g-Raham had resumed speaking. "Although you would say Wallspawn these days, in the House of Blood." Her manner was noncommittal. "The official Red Keep line is that the Swarm is a myth designed to keep us from the pleasanter realms of

Haarth." The Sword warriors had alluded to the same thing, Kalan recalled, although clearly it was not a view they shared. But then Blood was the rearguard of the warrior Houses, while Swords was the farthest forward of all the Derai Houses except Night and Stars. "Not," Che'Ryl-g-Raham said, "that one would expect a Storm Spear to share that view."

Wouldn't you? Kalan thought. Inwardly, he cursed his ignorance, particularly since the navigator's intent gaze belied her neutral manner—although she let the pause when he might have answered pass. "We shouldn't let the food get cold," she said instead, and joined him at the cabin's smaller table. They both sat, and she lifted the cover off the tureen between them. "Please, eat."

The dish, Kalan thought, savoring the first hot mouthful, was remarkably good, with eggs and some kind of grain mixed in with smoked fish. As he ate, he studied his surroundings: not just the size of the cabin or the line of square windows along the ship's stern, but the mellow woodwork and a star chart engraved in silver along one wall. His eyes kept returning to the chart, impressed by the detail but puzzled because all the constellations were unfamiliar. Eventually, Che'Ryl-g-Raham's gaze followed his. "Do you recognize them?"

Kalan hesitated before shaking his head, thinking it might be a test. But the navigator just nodded and gestured for him to take more food. "Star maps are our business, I suppose, not that of the warrior kind."

"Was there a reason you thought I might know them?" Kalan asked, refilling his plate.

Che'Ryl-g-Raham was studying the chart. "There's a memorial with twelve sides in the Sea Keep, located at the entrance to the Temple quarter." Her dark gaze flicked back to his. "Each side depicts a distinctive pattern of stars, none of which belong to this world. They chart every star system we've traversed in our war with the Swarm until we came through the Great Gate, and may even extend back to the beginnings of the Derai. I commissioned the engraving when

I was made navigator. To remind me," she finished gravely, "of that possibility."

From the stars we came. As navigator, Che'Ryl-g-Raham would be more attuned than most to that tradition. Kalan studied her openly and wondered what she saw in return: a travelworn Blood warrior, or someone more mysterious, the Luck's Storm Spear ... Every question he asked her was a risk, but then again, the heralds would say risk was the logical extension of being alive. And he needed information. "I'm still puzzled," he said, "why you thought I might recognize these stars."

Che'Ryl-g-Raham set her empty plate aside. "The monument commemorates the Sea House navigators that charted the route through the Great Gate, together with those who aided them, including the rearguard that held the Swarm at bay until all our ancestors had passed through. Names from every House in the Alliance are engraved upon its stone." She paused, her expression unrevealing. "But all the Blood names are from one fellowship, that of the Storm Spears."

The Great Gate, Kalan thought, which saved the Derai but almost destroyed Haarth. He was still Derai enough to feel awe—accompanied by unease as he wondered whether the Storm Spears had fought solely as elite warriors or been a military order that employed the old powers. A great many warrior orders had, of course, before the Betrayal and the Oath. But if the Storm Spears were one of them, then the Luck had just increased his danger, since even a historical association with the old powers would alienate many in the House of Blood.

"I was not aware of the memorial," he said, hoping it explained his frown. "I would like to see it, though."

"Would you?" Che'Ryl-g-Raham continued to study him. "I like puzzles, Khar, but I am also a navigator of the Sea House, which means I value truth more."

Sometimes, Kalan decided, the only path forward *was* truth, or at least as much of it as safety and his adherence to Malian's cause allowed. "I've been away from the Wall for some time and I have never visited the Sea Keep before, which is why I don't know your memorial." He paused, thinking what else he dared reveal. "While your Luck's greeting honors me, I do not know if there are any others she would salute as Storm Spear, either on the Derai Wall or among the realms of Haarth." Kalan wanted to spread his hands, a gesture that sought exculpation for all he had not said, and could not, but held himself still. "The reason I'm traveling to the Red Keep now is to compete in the Bride of Blood's Honor Contest."

"All truth, I don't doubt." Che'Ryl-g-Raham was dry. "While remaining as full of gaps as facts, I feel sure of that, too." She rose and opened a drawer, removing a package stitched into waterproof cloth. Recognizing it, Kalan's brows drew together.

"I gave that to Rayn."

"Rayn's business, and the loyalties that stem from that, lie with the Sea House." Returning to the table, she placed the package down. "I gave him money to fulfill his agreement with you regarding its contents. But a rank-and-file—by his appearance—Blood warrior carrying items that once belonged to the highest nobility of Emer is more than a private puzzle. Rayn judged that it might not only affect my ship, but also my House and possibly our wider Alliance."

Kalan maintained his outward calm. The Luck had acknowledged him, and whatever reservations she might harbor, Che'Ryl-g-Raham was raising the package privately. "What do you judge?" he asked.

Her smile was edged. "By *my* leave, you said last night, and now ask what *I* judge, as if that were the beginning and end of the matter. So perhaps you are just another thickheaded Blood warrior, after all." She folded her arms, regarding him with a mix of mockery and steel. "But if you can answer *my* puzzle, Khar of Blood, I'll let you keep your secrets."

You may like puzzles, Kalan thought, but if you agree with Rayn, why give me the chance to keep my own counsel—unless that's part of your riddle, too? He frowned, considering both his visions and recent events. The Luck *had* to be the key, he decided. She had not only spoken to him—when Temorn had been adamant, that day in

Grayharbor, that she would not—but her voice was uncannily similar to the one in his second dream of the Sea Keep fleet. He was also remembering the way both navigator and ship had the same name, and what Che'Ryl-g-Raham had said to Orth, that first day in Grayharbor: "The ship decides who quits its decks, no one else."

Not the navigator, he thought now, or any member of the crew: the *ship*. "We," the Luck had said as well. "*We* know who he is." The voice in his dream, though, had said something more: *"We remember everything."*

It was obvious once you looked at the puzzle pieces the right way—but Kalan still felt shaken, his emotions a turmoil of excitement and wonder. *"And now I,"* he said silently, knowing that no amount of wards, however deeply layered, would prevent the one he addressed from hearing his mindspeech, *"know who* you *are."*

"Well?" Che'Ryl-g-Raham demanded softly. "Do you understand, Storm Spear?"

Her dark gaze was intent, and Kalan guessed that she had already read the emotions he could not keep from his face. "The Ship's Luck spoke, but it was the ship that vouched for me." He waited for her nod. "That's also how you knew that Faro was no darkspawn and I had nothing to do with his being on board."

She nodded again. "It's not possible to stow away on a Sea House ship. *Che'Ryl-g-Raham* allowed the boy to board and concealed his presence until now, even from me. Ship's business," she added, although the twist to her lips suggested she was not happy about the course this particular affair had taken. "Which is now Blood—or at least Storm Spear—business."

The implication of that, at least, was clear. The ship—or ships, Kalan was not yet sure on that point—wanted Faro with him. He grimaced, and her mockery glimmered again.

"Look on the bright side. When the Luck spoke, she didn't just answer Kelyr's challenge. Effectively, the ship has sponsored you." Che'Ryl-g-Raham laughed, only a little grimly, at his expression. "Believe me, I was taken by surprise, too."

"So what does sponsorship mean?" This time Kalan did open his hands. "Consider me just another thickheaded Blood warrior who is well and truly out of his depth."

"Somehow I doubt that," she said. "But think of the sponsorship as a form of guest friendship, at the very highest level of our House." She must have seen him swallow, because her mockery returned. "Oh yes, Sea Count and High Priest level. So when we send our embassy to this Red Keep contest, you and Faro will be able to travel in their company."

Which means a far safer journey, Kalan reflected, including not having to watch my back trail for the Sword warriors. Yet he was surprised as well. "Will Sea really send an envoy to honor the new Bride, when the Earl of Night's first wife, the one he set aside, was blood kin to your Count?"

Che'Ryl-g-Raham's last glint of mockery vanished. "We have not forgotten Lady Nerion or her wrongs, but this union between Blood and Night is too large for any allied House to overlook. Whatever the circumstances, Sea will pay its respects." She hesitated. "Laer said to warn you that the Red Keep may not welcome the return of a Storm Spear. Our envoy should be able to advise you further, since it's the sort of thing ambassadors know about."

Kalan frowned, his misgivings about the Storm Spear designation returning. "I can't just ask Laer what he meant?"

"You can try." She shrugged. "But weatherworkers have their own ways, and holding sensible conversations isn't always one of them. Personally, I'd save my breath for bending our envoy's ear."

She seemed convinced the envoy would be forthcoming, which Kalan found encouraging. And although he might have to wait for the embassy to depart, the delay would allow him to see the Great Gate memorial and more of the Sea House fleet, a reflection that returned his focus to the dream ships. *We remember everything*, they had told him, but what Kalan recalled now was the damage to almost every vessel. Fear touched him, chill as winter. "What happens if a ship is lost? Can it be replaced?"

"I see you really do understand." Che'Ryl-g-Raham's gaze was on the gray heave of ocean beyond the cabin's square windows. "If both ship and crew are entirely lost, and there is no one to carry even a spark of the ship's essence back to the Sea Keep, to be rekindled within a new vessel, then yes, the whole of what our fleet is diminishes." Her somber gaze swung back to him. "But the fleet cannot stay in port. For House and Keep and the Derai Alliance itself, the ships must sail."

For Haarth, too, Kalan thought, although he knew that was rarely foremost in Derai thinking. "I'm sorry," he said.

"I believe you are." She pushed the waterproof package toward him. "Take back your belongings, Khar of House Blood. I will retrieve the money I gave Rayn when I'm next in Grayharbor."

The package's contents had betrayed him once, and Kalan did not want to risk it happening again, particularly in the Red Keep. He moved the package back. "Will you keep them for me, until I return again?"

"And if you don't?"

He considered that. "Then return them to Falk of Normarch, the lord who gave me the dagger, together with whatever word you may learn of my fate."

Che'Ryl-g-Raham was silent, before finally nodding. "I will keep them for you. Until you return again or news of your passing reaches us."

"Thank you." Kalan rose and bowed. "When I do return"—he would not say *if*—"the coin I shall offer to redeem them will be the whole of my truth."

Her smile was warm this time, with no edge to it, whether of steel or mockery. "You name a fair price, Storm Spear. I shall look forward to that day."

"*As shall I.*" The mindvoice was light rippling on water. "*In the meantime, Kalan-hamar, I bid you carry our name with you, as we shall remember yours.*" The voice sighed, or it could have been the sea, curving along either side of the ship.

I know who you are, Kalan had said only a few minutes before, but now doubt seized him and he waited for the voice to name itself.

"Now we are many, but once, in the time before, we were Yelusin, the Golden Fire that infused the Sea Keep." Stillness and light enclosed Kalan, the voices of wind and wave ebbing away. *"It is not only our name that we ask you to bear, but a spark of our power concealed within yours so that we may join again with our brother, Hylcarian. We were severed from him and all our conjoined Fires on the Night of Death, in the instant before Yelusin-that-was disintegrated. Afterward, we thought we alone had survived—until we saw our brother in your memories, alive still in the Old Keep of Winds."*

The Night of Death, Kalan repeated silently, feeling the full weight of that bitter, five-hundred-year-old history. Every Derai child learned it young: how the peace feast meant to end the civil war had ended in bloody slaughter, and the priestess, Xeria, had broken the Alliance's oldest law, calling down the Golden Fire against the Derai. Kalan had been with Malian, six years before, when Hylcarian, the now-remnant Golden Fire of the Keep of Winds, had described Xeria's act as a soul wound that nearly destroyed him. *"And dispersed* you *among the Sea House fleet at the same time,"* Kalan said now.

"Without the ships, nothing of Yelusin-that-was would have survived. Even then, it was a long time before our fractured consciousness re-emerged."

A time, Kalan knew, in which the starvation and plague that followed the loss of the Golden Fire had continued the civil war's decimation of the Alliance. He frowned, recalling how he could not touch Hylcarian's twelve-sided table in the heart of the Old Keep—because although born to the House of Blood, he was not of *the* Blood, the kindred of power bound to the Golden Fire since the beginning. *"So I may not be able to carry your power."*

"You are of the line of Tavaral, the Faithkeeper. That is as much honor as most Derai who call themselves the Blood can lay claim to, in these days. And the power you will carry is no more than the fragment of a fragment." The murmur of memory and regret

strengthened. *"We have also seen who* you *are, Kalan-hamar, and that your road leads to the Keep of Winds and our brother. It is enough."*

"*By way of the Red Keep,*" Kalan cautioned, as the sounds of the day returned. He registered Che'Ryl-g-Raham's focused look and wondered how much she had absorbed of his exchange with her ship.

"Am I her *ship? It would be as true to say that she is* my *navigator."* The voice of light was amused. *"As for the Red Keep, you'll need me, as well as your layered wards, if the wyr hounds there are not to bay whenever you pass by."*

Wyr hounds: Kalan felt the trail of winter's fingers down his spine. *"And this business of being a Storm Spear?"*

"For that reason, too," Yelusin replied, as Che'Ryl-g-Raham spoke.

"The ship holds that if a Storm Spear is to enter the Sea Keep again and visit our memorial, then he should do so under his true colors." She smiled faintly. "In this matter, we are of one mind. With your permission, I'll have our ship's armorer engrave the Storm Spear device onto your mail and weapons before we make landfall."

Kalan was about to say he could do it himself, then realized he did not know what the device was. Che'Ryl-g-Raham's smile was so bland that he guessed she suspected his dilemma, while beneath wind and wave and the fall of light, he caught the ghost of Yelusin's laughter—echoed by the firefly spark settling deep within his mind.

PART III

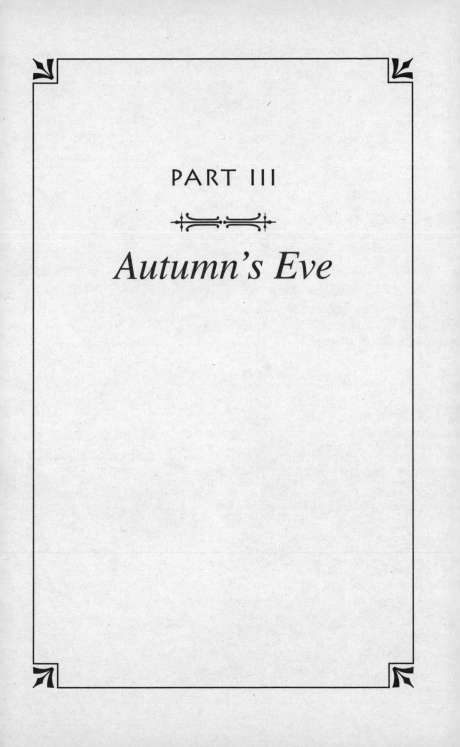

Autumn's Eve

12

The Lonely Grave

Nhairin's leg, overworked from constant travel and too many detours to avoid long-range patrols, finally gave out when she was crossing a bare stretch of plain. To stop where she was meant death, so Nhairin crawled on for what felt like hours, until she reached a pile of tumbledown rocks. Once she had worked her way between the outlying stones, she found a narrow path among the larger boulders that eventually led into a small cave where the ground was more sand than pebbles.

Once inside, Nhairin collapsed into the sleep of exhaustion, despite the agony of her leg. When she woke—whether hours or days later, she could not be sure—her entire body was so stiff that moving was anguish and the lame leg still would not bear her. But it was only when thirst, and the need to relieve herself, made her crawl outside, that she realized the sense of an invisible thread guiding her was gone.

Initially she was too exhausted, and then too hungry, to feel the same level of fear that had driven her away from Westwind Hold. The first few days among the rocks she mostly slept, only dragging herself as far as the small seep of brackish water on the Jaransor side of the rock pile before crawling back into her hideaway. Once, she roused to the sound of voices. Derai voices, Nhairin thought, but the wind blew the voices away and she decided they must have been a hallucination. She thought the hound was a hallucination, too, when she woke to a rare, clear dawn and saw it standing in the entrance to her cave.

I know you, Nhairin thought. By the time she was fully awake the hound was gone. Later, though, she found pawprints in the entrance, so knew the dog had not been either the aftermath of a dream or a figment born of exhaustion and gnawing hunger. Curiosity drove her outside, and this time she climbed higher up the rockpile in an attempt to work out where she was.

Closer to the Wall than I would like, Nhairin decided, frowning. She had not realized the thread was leading her back that way. A cairn lay in the opposite direction, marking the far side of a hollow that lay just beyond the seep. She did not have to get closer to recognize the cairn as a Derai burial marker, the sort raised for captains or ruling kin who fell a long way from House and keep. The hound was lying in front of the cairn as though keeping watch, its nose on outstretched paws. And although it did not look her way, Nhairin felt certain it knew she was there.

I really do know you, she thought, studying the hound's long, graceful body and white, feathery coat. I might, she added, even be able to name you, in which case . . . She stopped, reluctant to pursue what the identity of the hound and its presence here suggested, but eventually moistened her cracked lips. "Falath," she whispered. Nhairin thought she had barely spoken aloud, but the hound's elegant head lifted, turning as though the dark eyes could look through rock, straight to where she lay.

"You're Falath," Nhairin whispered again. Her hunger, weariness, and fear were all temporarily forgotten, for if this was Falath, then the cairn the hound guarded must mark Rowan Birchmoon's grave. Yet the Winter Woman, Earl Tasarion's consort, had been alive and well when Nhairin left the Keep of Winds . . . Which made her wonder again, as she had several times on her stumbling progress across the plain, exactly how long the Madness had held her in its thrall. Still, at least she knew now that it could not be longer than a hound's lifetime.

We were friends once, the Winter Woman and I, Nhairin thought—in our way. Or perhaps, honesty compelled her to admit, in my way. She had liked Rowan Birchmoon well enough, while simultaneously resenting her hold on Earl Tasarion, who was Nhairin's childhood companion as well as the leader of Night—and head of the Derai Alliance, in name at least. Old emotions stirred, including Nhairin's bitter conviction that the Nine Houses would never follow an Earl who had demeaned himself, and by implication the Derai, by taking an outsider consort. Sometimes I did wish her well gone, Nhairin admitted, chewing at an already ragged nail. But never dead. Despite the whispers and the Madness, she felt certain she had never wished that.

And Nerion? her misgivings answered. *What might she have whispered into your mind that you were never consciously aware of, or concealed even from yourself?* Self-doubt shook her, until Nhairin reminded herself that when the Madness took hold, Rowan Birchmoon had still been alive. And until the mysterious song roused her, she had been confined in Westwind Hold. The relief was so great she almost cried out, and afterward risked using her bow as a walking stick, so she could make her halting way to the cairn and greet Falath.

Nhairin was not sure how close the hound would let her come, or whether he would drive her off if she intruded on what he considered his territory. She stopped as soon as he stood up, taking the opportunity to rest her leg, but saw the feathery tail was beating a slow welcome. "Do you remember me?" Nhairin asked, meeting the dark eyes fixed on hers. Momentarily, gratitude for the companionship of another living creature tightened her throat, before she limped nearer. Falath whined softly in greeting, his tail continuing to wave when she rested a hand on his warm, silken head. Oh, Falath, she thought.

Someone had brought him food. Nhairin's stomach rumbled sharply when she saw the neatly cut joint, because there was still meat on the gnawed bone. She realized, too, that the Derai voices had not been a hallucination after all. Her thoughts leapt between resolving to take care and brush away her tracks, and wondering if she could persuade Falath to share the bounty, especially since the hound seemed glad of her company. His vigil, she reflected, must be as lonely as the grave he guarded, despite the visits of those bringing food.

Had it been a long one as well? Nhairin wondered, her eyes on the gray hairs about his muzzle—then shook her head, unable to recall whether she had ever noticed the hound was growing old.

Before now, she added uneasily, but made herself look past Falath to the low arch and the darkness beneath it that marked the cairn's entrance. Rowan Birchmoon's name was carved into the stone, together with the images of beasts and birds that had always been embroidered onto her clothing. So perhaps she asked to be buried here, Nhairin thought—where the small creatures of the plain come and the wind sometimes blows out of the Winter Country, rather than lying in the vaults beneath a Derai keep. She wondered, too, whether the Winter Woman had died as a result of accident or by an enemy's hand. Nhairin had certainly seen enough darkspawn sign, coming here, to make the latter feasible, even so far into the Gray Lands.

The last thought made her glance uneasily around, before studying the cairn again. The darkness within its mouth both drew and repelled her at the same time, yet Nhairin could not shake the feeling that in passing beneath the low arch she might meet herself—as she had been, not as the filthy, emaciated creature she was now—within the tomb's stillness. "But I can't go in," she whispered, clinging to Falath's warmth beneath her hand. She dared not. The darkness reminded her too much of the Madness, so that for a time she could not move at all.

"May it find you out, Nhairin, wherever you are . . . "

Nhairin jumped violently, certain the murmur had breathed out of the cairn's mouth. Shuddering, she clutched at Falath's head with one hand, while the other tightened on her bow. The hound did not move, just continued to gaze up at her, his dark eyes calm, and the whisper did not come again. Slowly, Nhairin's heart returned to a more normal rhythm. It was only then she realized that the reason her guiding thread might have vanished was because this was where it had been leading her all along.

The realization drove Nhairin back into the cave, where she remained for the rest of the day. When she finally crept out again, the stars were icicles in the blackness overhead. Watching their cold brilliance, she tried to imagine the heavens resounding with their song, but all she could hear was the music that had roused her from the Madness. Nhairin shivered—from cold, she told herself—and listened to Falath pace the hollow instead. He stopped when his patrol brought him abreast of where she sat by the seep, but uttered no sound before moving on. Afterward she crept back into the cave, eating the last scrap of food and huddling into one corner in an attempt to stay warm.

Tomorrow she would have to set snares, or try hunting the small game that could be found closer to Jaransor. Tomorrow, too, she would have to think about what being led to the cairn might mean, and whether lingering was feasible now that she knew Derai came here. Especially since they would be of Night: that seemed certain if they were feeding Falath. Nhairin's stomach grumbled, thinking about food, but although she feared hunger and cold might prevent sleep, she was just nodding off when the wolf howled.

The sound jerked her upright, her heart pounding wildly for the second time that day. A wolf *here*, in the Gray Lands, Nhairin thought, shocked because Haarth's larger predators, like their prey, rarely ventured so close to the Wall. She lay awake for a long time, tense with listening, but heard nothing more—although when sleep finally claimed her, a fiery-eyed wolf stalked through her dreams.

A nightmare, Nhairin reassured herself, waking again. Yet when she finally crawled out of her hideaway in the chill dawn, she found a pair of brush fowl dropped by the entrance, with the mark of a wolf's paw beside them in the dirt.

13

Watch and Ward

Garan thought that what the Towers of Morning priests called guest quarters was more like an entire wing of their great keep, in which he and the rest of his eight-guard rattled around like pebbles. They had been occupying it for a week now, having seen Sirit, the old Lady of Morning, and her companions safely home from the Keep of Bells. The time spent sheltering from Wall storms, together with Sirit's age, and the need to skirt wide around House of Adamant territory on their return, had made it a very slow journey. So despite Morning being one of the priestly Houses, and the Towers echoing and half-empty, the eight-guard had accepted the opportunity to rest their horses, and themselves, before setting out for the Keep of Winds.

Which I'll be glad to see again, Garan thought, checking over his sketch maps and careful notes recording their journey. Winter had barely ended when his unit had been ordered south to fetch the minstrel, Haimyr the Golden, back from the River—only to be reassigned to escort the Morning contingent as soon as they returned. Before they had even passed the Border Mark, in fact, because of a confrontation with the Adamant priests who were escorting Sirit and her company. An Adamant priest had died as a result, and their leader had promptly declared blood feud with Asantir, the Commander of Night, and abandoned his Morning charges in the middle of the Gray Lands.

Because the old Lady took our part, Garan reflected now, or the Adamant leader, Torlun, thought she had. The end result was a bad business, whichever way you looked at it. And not just because he and his unit had spent the rest of the summer shepherding—or nurse-maiding, as Innor like to put it—the Morning priests the length of the Wall. Earl Tasarion and Asantir had been trying to rebuild the Derai Alliance for years now, so the last thing they needed was another blood feud, especially with Adamant. If Torlun had just been a rank-and-file Keep of Stone priest, the business may not have amounted to much, but the Morning company had made it clear that he was First Kin to the Earl of Adamant.

One of the Morning company, Garan amended, with an inward shake of his head over the priest that Innor had nicknamed Dour Dalay—although Ter had added "humorless Dalay" beneath his breath. Garan was more sympathetic, because Dalay was Sirit's deputy, and given her age the responsibility for their journey must have weighed on him. Especially, Garan thought, when they found themselves abandoned in the middle of hostile territory and dependent on the warriors of an opposing House. He had seen how bitterly Dalay resented that dependence, and the priest's poorly con-cealed distaste when obliged to have dealings with any of the Night warriors—which because he was Sirit's deputy, was an everyday occurrence.

Garan smiled inwardly, thinking how indignant Eria would have been, on his behalf, if she had witnessed the care Dalay took to maintain physical distance, even when they consulted over the day's route or how much farther Sirit could travel. At least Garan now knew enough about the priest kind's odder sects, having served six years with Eria and her fellow initiates in the Old Keep watch, to guess that Dalay must be one of those who regarded themselves as the Nine Gods' elect. In which case, even traveling in the same company as Garan's eight-guard would have compromised the priest's religious practice, while physical contact would constitute outright pollution.

Just as well Eria isn't among the elect then, Garan reflected. Otherwise she could not have kissed him the way she had, the day he departed for the River. She and the rest of the off-duty watch had been present to see his eight-guard off, when they left via the Keep of Winds' messenger postern. Garan, who had been conferring with Asantir, was the last to reach the gate—and at the final moment Eria had come running, swinging herself up by means of his saddlebow and one foot resting on his in the stirrup, to kiss him on the mouth.

Garan, smiling over the recollection, became aware that Asha—sitting opposite him at the room's long table—was smiling, too, in an uncomfortably knowing way. Not that any of the others could have seen anything that day, having all ridden out ahead of him—except possibly Nerys, who *might* have glanced back at the critical moment. But one thing you could be sure of with Nerys was that whatever she saw, word of it was unlikely to pass her lips . . .

Still smiling, Asha's fingers tapped out a tune on the tabletop. "Doesn't this place creep you?" she asked Garan. "The only voice you hear in this whole wing, outside our rooms, is the wind."

Ter, seated at the table's far end, looked up from the arrow he was fletching. "It's practically a day's march from our quarters to their High Hall. And when you finally arrive there's no one to be seen. They're all locked away in their towers."

"Poring over paper and dabbling in ink." Asha's tone shifted from incomprehension to awe. "They have whole towers full of old books, stacks of 'em from ceiling to floor."

"No wonder they needed nursemaiding," Lawr said, from his place by the fire. "I don't think any of the old Lady's lot had been outside their towers before." He paused, frowning. "And there aren't enough of them to hold even half of this great pile, assuming they know how to do it."

Innor had been profane, over previous days, on the topic of the

Morning priests ability to defend their Towers, so Garan thought it was probably just as well she was seeing to their horses with Eanar. "And they're more vulnerable than the other priestly Houses," Ter observed, "being so far forward on the Wall."

For a moment they were all quiet, considering that anomaly, and Asha looked unusually thoughtful. "They don't seem aware of that, though. Almost as if it's not real unless it's written in one of their books." Her grin reappeared. "At least with so few of them, every scholar has a better chance of getting a tower of their own. They could stay shut away from each other for days."

"I think they already do," Ter murmured, while the others chuckled—including Nerys, who until then had appeared absorbed by the *Swarm Bestiary* that Sri, another of Sirit's company, had loaned to her. Nerys had shown it to Garan earlier, pointing silently to several entries that were of interest to both of them from six years before. Despite the fire, Garan had felt chilled by the all-too-real depiction of the Raptor of Darkness. He still felt cold, because it was only the combination of Lady Malian's fire and Commander Asantir's black spear that had finally killed the demon. But the spear had also been destroyed, and Lady Malian had died shortly afterward, in Jaransor. All of which made it hard not to wonder if everything that happened in the Old Keep, and the oath the survivors swore afterward, had all been for nothing.

Asha clicked her fingers almost under his nose. "You're wearing your brooding look again," she told him. "Which is not like you, so it's lucky we're heading home tomorrow. But how about a wager now, to cheer you up? I bet you a Sea House florin that the scholars *do* have a strategy to defend their Towers." She propped her elbows on the table. "It's obvious really. They'll bombard anything that comes through the pass with their arsenal of paper."

"The Nine know, they've enough of it," Lawr said, as Asha grinned around her shield comrades.

You know we are forbidden to fight. Garan contemplated reminding them of what Sri had cried out to Torlun at the Border Mark—but

Asha was right about his mood. "You know I'm not one to bet against a sure thing," he said, casting away the disquiet caused by the *Bestiary*.

"Ay, Garan's too canny for that—" Lawr began, but stopped as Nerys coughed, her gaze going past him to the door.

"Nine!" Ter said, but beneath his breath, and Garan groaned inwardly as he turned and saw Dalay and Sri in the doorway, with an apologetic Keron—who was supposed to have been watching the approach to their quarters—beside them.

You could at least have coughed, too, Garan thought, his eyes meeting the young guard's—but then decided he was being unfair. Keron couldn't have anticipated that his eight-leader was going to give in to stupidity at just the wrong moment. It was clear enough, too, from Dalay's stare, stiff with affront, and Sri's lowered eyes and turned-down mouth, that they must have caught most of the wager conversation. If only, Garan thought, rising to his feet, I *had* reminded Asha of Sri's words. But there was nothing to be done now, he would just have to brush through it.

"Senior Dalay, Priestess Sri." He used the titles Dalay had made clear were the only appropriate form of address from those not of Morning. "How may I assist you?"

For a moment he thought Dalay's aggravation might win out, before the senior priest jerked a nod. "It is how *we* may assist you. Mother Sirit says that you've expressed a wish to see the Towers of Watch and Ward before you leave. We're doing repairs on Ward, but I've brought the key to Watch, and Sri is willing to take you up." He paused, sending a repressive look Sri's way. "I would take you myself, but it's a long, steep climb and I have much to do."

In a keep famed for its towers, the Towers of Watch and Ward were more famous still, since they were reputed to be the tallest in any of the Derai's nine strongholds. Garan was keen to climb them for that reason alone, but also wanted to see what more their height could show him of Dread Pass. Automatically, he glanced toward Nerys, and saw that she had closed the *Bestiary* and was already on her feet—but the others shook their heads. "We've climbed stairs enough in the Keep of Winds," Ter said, speaking for them all.

Sri looked down her nose, but otherwise fell in beside Dalay without offering comment. The senior priest unlocked the tower door himself and did not give the key to Sri afterward. "Fetch me when you return and I'll see to it," he told her, then hesitated, regarding Garan and Nerys with the expression of a man weighing further speech. "We owe your commander a debt," he said abruptly. "But if she thinks that will bring Morning into Night's orbit, you may tell her she's mistaken." He paused briefly, his face still stiff, and his eyes bleak. "Whatever Mother Sirit may intend, our House acts as one or not at all. And we swore our own oath, after the Betrayal War, to never again be drawn into the fratricides of the warrior kind."

Not just the warrior kind, Garan thought. Sri's eyes were cast down again, a V drawn deep between her brows, but like Nerys, she did not speak. For a moment he was tempted to return a curt answer, before his sense of humor got the better of him. "Alas, I'm not party to the inner counsels of Earl Tasarion and his advisors, and they don't generally inform me of their thoughts. As an eight-guard leader I come and go as ordered, and do as I'm bid." Briefly, he considered apologizing for his earlier levity at Morning's expense, but decided it would probably worsen matters, rather than mending them.

"You may pass on what I said anyway," Dalay told him, but with rather less conviction than before. He only stayed to give Sri a few terse instructions, before stalking away.

The priestess raised her eyes. "It's a long climb," she said. "We'd best get started."

Garan considered himself fit, but was still sweating and short of breath when they finally reached the tower summit. Nerys and Sri were both breathing hard, too, although the priestess only paused for a moment before she began unbolting the storm shutters. All their breath steamed on the chill air. "But at least it's the calm season,"

Sri said, as Garan went to help her. "That should make your journey home quicker."

"It will," he agreed, then caught his breath again as he realized the lookout provided an eagle's eye view of terrain they had crawled through like ants when approaching the keep. The Tower of Watch looked out onto the Dread massif, and Garan could pick out deep ravines between jagged ribs of rock as the pass climbed into a brew of cloud. The Tower of Ward lay on the keep's far side, overlooking the Plain of Ash, which stretched straight and level toward the Gray Lands. Easy riding for the first part of their journey home, but Garan hardly cared about that. Whichever way he looked, all he could see was vulnerability for the badly undermanned Towers, and fear clawed at him: for Sri, with her ink-stained fingers, and the old Lady they had escorted so far; even for stiff-necked Dalay.

Frowning, he studied the pass again—and almost yelled when he turned and found Sirit watching him from the opening onto the tower stairs. After the business with the Stone Keepers at the Border Mark, Garan had decided there was more to the old Lady than met the eye, but still could not fathom how she had dragged her elderly bones up the tower's long, twisting flights. Startlement prompted him to say what was uppermost in his mind. "You need more people, a proper garrison to hold these walls, Mother." Despite Dalay's prohibition, his use of her Morning title was a reflexive echo of Commander Asantir at the Border Mark. "Sea still has numbers, and didn't a Daughter of Morning marry their Count—" At which point Garan broke off, realizing he was sticking his nose, unasked, into another House's business.

"Our daughter, Surinay: a fine scholar, whom we were sorry to lose." Sirit inclined her head to Sri, who looked almost as startled as Garan felt, before turning toward Dread Pass. Her expression was unreadable. "I appreciate your concern, but Sea will have need of their numbers when the shadows flow in on them like ocean fog."

Prophecy, Garan thought, chilled despite her everyday tone, which nonetheless managed to convey that the shadows would flow soon.

His hand moved toward the talisman Eria had pressed into his hand at the same time as she kissed him farewell, but checked the gesture as Sirit's gaze returned to him. "You have discharged your escort duty honorably, Garan, despite Morning having no claim on you or Night. Will you discharge one more commission on my behalf?"

Garan wanted to glance toward Nerys, but instead rubbed his chin, weighing caution with courtesy. "That depends on what it is," he said finally.

"Grandmother," Sri began at the same. "Dalay won't ..." Her voice trailed off as Sirit glanced her way.

"Won't like it?" The old Lady's expression did not change, but she sounded amused. "Dalay has no grounds for objection, since nothing in my commission contravenes either House of Morning policy or our oath. The fact that Dalay will not like it is neither here nor there." Sri looked away, her mouth turning down in the same way it had earlier, while Sirit's gaze met and held Garan's.

"I promise my commission will not conflict with either your duty to Night, or"—she paused—"the oath you swore six years ago, when it wakes to life."

From the corner of his eye, Garan saw Nerys stiffen. "An oath," he repeated, even more cautiously, which made the old Lady purse her lips.

"The one that binds you and half your eight-guard. I have the ability to discern the shape of such things—and that your oath *will* wake to life."

Despite everything he had experienced during the Old Keep expedition, as well as serving in the new watch with Eria and her fellow initiates since then, Garan could not prevent a flash of revulsion at such open reference to power use. But he made himself think of Eria—particularly in the moment when she had pressed half her initiate's talisman into his hand—and then refocus on Sirit, not as a priestess and power user, but as the person he had accompanied through long months of travel along the Wall. "You may be mistaken," he said slowly, "since the one we swore to died."

Sirit shook her head. "Such oaths can always waken if one knows the way to unlock their bindings. When yours does so, I ask that you pass on my gift to the opener of ways." Something in the way she said "gift" made the hair on Garan's forearms lift. "Morning owes a debt to Night for your escort," Sirit went on, her words uncannily reminiscent of Dalay's, although their import was very different, "and in all likelihood for our lives. This may count toward its repayment."

"I'll still need to see it before I agree," Garan said, as they returned to the watchroom below the lookout. He assumed he would be able to identify whatever he was shown, but instead found himself puzzling over an oblong of heavy linen. He recognized the Towers' silhouette on the cloth, but it was bordered by calligraphy he could not read, and framed within a wreath that comprised locks of hair, interspersed with drops of blood. The rectangle of linen beneath it was identical, except that the silhouette within both calligraphy and wreath looked like the great bell of Peace.

Garan stared from one to the other, trying not to show that he was at a loss. "They look like funeral wreaths," he said, sure he recognized Sirit's white hair at the apex of Morning scroll's. Mourning wreaths, which comprised locks of hair and drops of blood from a deceased's close kin, were considered old-fashioned now, but some of Night's more traditional families still followed the custom.

Sirit nodded. "We call this a rune scroll, but it is a related practice, one we've borrowed from our Sea neighbors. Their mariners frequently carry them, so if one of their number drowns, or worse, a ship goes down, the names of the lost will appear on a Sea Keep memorial. The rites of the Silent God can then be observed and the souls of the departed find their way to Hurulth's Hall."

Garan shook his head, thinking about the way Sirit had said "gift." "Is this some sort of death working, Mother?"

Sri's breath was a sharp intake, but Sirit met his eyes again, her own steady. "The scrolls are a gift for the one who wakes your oath. More than that I cannot say—except both I and my fellows in Bells will be greatly in your debt, Garan, if you discharge this commission."

Doubtless I'm a fool for even considering this, Garan thought. On the other hand, despite what he had said to Dalay, he knew the Earl and Asantir would expect even an eight-leader to play his part in building goodwill, as part of their quest to rebuild the Derai Alliance. "All right," he said reluctantly. And Sirit bowed, as gravely as if he had been an Honor Captain, before rolling both rune scrolls into a slender leather case.

"Honor on you and on your House," she said, handing it to him, "and light and safety on your road." She paused, looking from him to Nerys, and then to Sri. "May I suggest, once the storm shutters have been secured, that the three of you return to the lower halls with me? You've all proved your youth and vigor by climbing up here, but we do have a moving platform, with ropes and pulleys, on the opposite side of the tower from the stairs."

Garan, taking in Sri's flush of color, remembered the repressive look Dalay had given her, just before he specifically mentioned the long climb. Nerys looked as though her thoughts were pithy, and he was certain Sirit did not need prophetic skills to divine what had occurred. He imagined, too, that his own expression must be a study, because the look Sri darted him was a mix of apology and trepidation, but more than a little gratification as well. Garan, realizing just how completely they'd been gulled, could not help himself. He laughed out loud.

14

Crow

The daytime heat was still holding in the Aeris basin as evening fell, but later, Malian knew, the night would grow cold enough for frost. A light breeze carried dust and the scent of pine into the trading town with its ancient, ochre walls and sprawl of caravan inns and trading halls, stables and livestock yards. Malian could hear the brisk chime of harness bells from where she sat, high on the wall; a moment later she saw the mule train, making for the city gates in the last of the light. In a town like Aeris, being inside the walls could still mean pickpockets and knives down back alleys, but it also meant hot food, baths, and soft beds for those with money enough to pay.

Unfortunately, that did not include two itinerant swords-for-hire, of indeterminate origin but sporting cloth head-wrappings and the bone-and-feather fetishes favored by Lathayran mercenaries. Raven had brought both his Hill horses with him into southern Aralorn, so Malian had sold her cob in the nearest market town and abandoned the identity of Heris the scribe for that of Crow, Raven's companion hedge warrior. Birds of ill omen in appearance as well as name, she thought wryly, recalling how both innkeepers and caravan masters had eyed them askance—and sleeping rough had only added to their disreputable appearance.

The wryness deepened as Malian reflected that the journey north would already have been accomplished if she had dared use portals freely. She was strong enough to open gates of sufficient size to accommodate two horses and their riders, and extend the portals over considerable distance. Nhenir—the moon-bright helm that had once belonged to the hero Yorindesarinen and was now hers—could also cloak the power use to a degree that would fool lesser users. Or even, Malian added now, more astute adepts. But she had not forgotten the waves of power that the Swarm demon called Nindorith had blasted across Caer Argent, on the night when she and Kalan fled before him. She had to assume the demon would remain alert for any sign that she had resurfaced—and for all Nhenir's legendary ability, the helm was adamant that Nindorith would recognize its aura.

He would certainly walk right through my Shadow Band wards, Malian thought, repressing a shiver as the last light between the surrounding peaks faded from saffron to lavender. The heralds, Jehane Mor and Tarathan of Ar, had helped her thwart Nindorith's seeking by walking the goddess Imuln's Midsummer path of earth and moon, changing her essence to that of Haarth. Yet although the Darksworn—unlike the Derai—seemed aware that Haarth produced native adepts, the pattern created by regular portal use, as well as the level of power required to sustain them, was bound to attract their attention.

So rather than heading directly north using gates, Crow and Raven had pursued a zigzag course across the Southern Realms. Malian had still used portals, but kept the openings intermittent and the distance covered random, interspersing their use with stages traveled by road. Sometimes they had eaten dust for only one day, sometimes for several. This last stage, crossing from northern Emer to Aeris via the Little Pass, had taken nearly a week. All the same, Malian thought, standing up and swiping the worst of the road dust from jacket and trousers, even such restricted gate use had gained them weeks, perhaps as much as a month. And that—when she was sharply conscious that summer's end had now faded into autumn's eve, and

Kalan was traveling alone into the dangers of the Wall—counted for a great deal.

The dust motes swirled, the day's dirt and sweat and fading warmth mingling with the scent of the pines. Malian adjusted her head-wrapping against both breeze and grit, then stretched, feeling every mile of the day's painstaking journey out of the Little Pass's rough terrain. Turning away from the parapet, she looked down onto the Aeris caravan hostelry, which occupied a whole town block facing the wall. Its ground floor was a combined stable and wagon store, while the long, upstairs dormitory provided accommodation for the roughest or most impecunious travelers, with a lockup for guests' gear. The current guests included caravan guards, muleteers, and drovers, as well as herself and Raven, and one mendicant priest of Seruth.

A lamp had been lit outside the dormitory entrance, but Malian knew most of her fellow travelers would be in the nearest tavern, located close by the city gate. Descending from the wall, she saw that the tavern doors stood fully open, letting a tide of light and noise, together with the smell of hot food, spill into the street. Malian's stomach grumbled, but she waited in the shadows, assessing those who came and went. A handful of muleteers and caravan guards were sitting outside, tallying up trading runs and talking over events in Emer, particularly how safe it was for caravans heading south. "It's safe enough until Caer Argent, by all accounts," one guard said, "but there's been fighting in the Cendreward and down toward Lathayra."

An older muleteer blew foam off the top of his beer. "Skirmishing is all, from what I heard, not outright battles. The so-called champion turned rebel hasn't found much support, it seems."

"War can turn on you like a snake at any moment, though." The guard set his tankard down. "And I sign on to deal with footpads and outlaw bands at worst, not Emerian knights. I'll be seeking caravans going another way."

Those around him murmured agreement, and a woman with tattoos up her bare arms, and a caravan scout's assortment of knives, leaned forward. "I heard that the Queen of Jhaine who was visiting Emer's Duke has not gone home as expected, but is journeying on to the River lands."

Now that is news, Malian thought, as the guard shrugged. "Her road would lead south, so maybe she thinks it's too dangerous right now."

"True enough," the muleteer agreed, without much interest, while the scout nodded.

"Maybe so, especially as another rumor claimed Ser Ombrose Sondargent was behind three of her Seven dying, before he fled Caer Argent."

She had good sources, Malian reflected—although that was a scout's business when ensuring a caravan's safety, as much as establishing the best route through wild country.

"Is that right?" Curiosity stirred in the guard's face. "The way they tell it down Lathayra way, a Jhainarian queen without a full Seven is like a bird with a broken wing. Perhaps she's afraid to go back."

"Who cares, I say." The muleteer belched. "Jhaine's shunned the rest of Haarth for long enough. Let this queen deal with her own problems." The scout and the guard shrugged, but no one disagreed and the talk shifted to an upcoming cockfight. None of them seemed to notice Malian, watching and listening in the shadows, and she remained where she was until a band of drovers strode past. Attaching herself to their group, she entered the tavern's packed common room, which reeked of unwashed bodies, beer, and new food smells overlaying the old. The drovers stopped just inside the entrance, looking about for a table, and Malian slipped sideways behind their broad backs, away from the light around the door.

She found a section of wall between two windows where she could prop her back, taking stock of the crowd and looking for Raven. It was not until a cluster of caravan guards broke up that she saw him, seated on a corner bench by the rear entrance. Moths circled a lantern in the open doorway, but the corner where Raven sat was largely in shadow, although neither the gloom nor the cloth head-wrapping could disguise his taciturn demeanor. He looked well-worn, almost exactly like the hedge knight Malian had first met in the Long Pass, wearing her guise of Carick the scholar. She felt a brief regret for the uncomplicated nature of that encounter, when the hedge knight had rescued the scholar from the outlaws known as the wolfpack.

Uncomplicated on the surface anyway, she amended, since the hedge knight had turned out to be the leader of a Darksworn House that had served in the River lands for almost a thousand years, concealed behind the secret helms of the Patrol. Malian was still awed by that revelation and doubted she had fully absorbed its implications. As soon as she had recovered from her Aralorn illness, the need to reach the River and rendezvous with the Patrol had taken over, together with the day-to-day considerations of their journey. Once they made that rendezvous, they would begin the long journey north to the Wall—which, Malian thought now, should provide plenty of time for mulling over everything Raven had told her about the Swarm.

And marveling, she added, wry again, at the fate that brought a Darksworn House and the frost-fire sword from Yorindesarinen's time to Haarth, and ultimately to me. Now, however, was not the time for such reflections, or distracting herself with the way Raven said maelstrom rather than Swarm, Sworn and not Darksworn, and nation instead of House. They're just words, she told herself: what I need to focus on is a strategy for re-entering the Derai world.

"With your army," Nhenir murmured. Only the helm, of Yorindesarinen's three legendary weapons, had ever spoken, and its mindvoice was a cool-as-silver ripple across her thoughts. Adept at disguise, its appearance was currently that of a knight-for-hire's steel cap, complete with bone-and-feather decorations to match Raven's.

Malian smiled faintly, appreciating the helm's dry note. *"With the army Raven—Aravenor—has brought me. You're right, there's a satisfaction in that."* She kept her face impassive, just another traveler surveying the crowd, while wondering whether she could rely on Raven's army following her. He himself had said that they were not truly Darksworn anymore, so what if they decided to remain the Patrol?

If she closed her eyes, Malian knew she would find the memory of the solitary tower in Aralorn, with the Ara-fyr, who had once been the Derai Lost, ranged against her. Despite the tavern's close-packed warmth, she shivered, because that defiance was not unprecedented. Throughout Derai history there had been instances where Houses defied oaths and the Honor Code, abandoning an Earl or Heir's lead.

"Only in the most extreme circumstances, usually after protracted and disastrous campaigns," Nhenir pointed out. *"Night continued to follow Aikanor in the civil war, after all, although there must have been many in the Alliance who wished they had not."*

"Not all of Night." Malian felt the shadow of that old darkness stretch across the room. *"Many would say that it was the Night priesthood harboring Xeria that nearly destroyed our Alliance."*

Nhenir changed tack. *"The House of Fire has held to Aravenor's leadership all these years. Do you have reason to believe they would forsake him now?"*

"If you mean, have I foreseen it, then no, I haven't. But the rest of Fire doesn't know me. Raven will be asking them to give up everything to follow not only a stranger but a Derai, forsaking the duty they've held to for a thousand years." As soon as she said that, Malian realized she was assuming that Darksworn shared the Derai attitude to duty—and that the House of Fire had transferred theirs to the Patrol, in the same way the Lost had become Ara-fyr. The truth, she reflected, is that I'm certain of nothing, except that Kalan and I can't withstand the Swarm on our own. *"You yourself said that I would need an army,"* she reminded Nhenir. *"And you were right."*

The Malian raised to be Heir of Night was keenly aware that this particular army had been Darksworn once, an enemy in the Derai's aeons-old war—but also that Raven, who led it, had brought her Yorindesarinen's sword. Even knowing his action stemmed from a geas the sword had placed on his House, the magnitude of the gesture matched that of Tarathan and Jehane Mor, opening up the sacred path of earth and moon so she could shake Nindorith from her trail.

Both were gifts, Malian decided, and one should not compare the value of gifts. Nonetheless, even without the army he brought at his back, Raven placing Yorindesarinen's sword in her hands had outweighed the loss of the Ara-fyr.

She was conscious of the sword's latent power now, resting against her hip. The leather of both belt and scabbard were timeworn anyway, but like the helm, the frost-fire sword was well versed in disguise. Currently, it looked like any low-grade mercenary's weapon, serviceable and unpretentious, but Malian still felt a flicker of awe that the last person to carry the blade had been Yorindesarinen, ages and worlds ago. She could feel the link between the sword's power and that of the helm, and after their initial blaze of magic in Stoneford had hoped that bringing them together would enhance her ability to seek out the shield. Instead, it was as though the sword was not just containing its power, but had returned to sleep.

"The arms of Yorindesarinen are one, as well as three. To realize our full power you will need helm, sword, and shield."

Nhenir had only disclosed the first part of that statement in Stoneford, but Malian had already begun to suspect the second. Suspicion, however, was not the same as certainty—especially since Raven had told her that when Fire's scouts reached the ancient battlefield, Yorindesarinen's shield was broken. By the time the Darksworn returned in greater force, the pieces had disappeared. *"So what you're saying is that I may never fully inherit Yorindesarinen's legacy."* Malian felt a hollowness that was no longer just hunger, yet was cursed if she would accept defeat before she had even begun.

Benches scraped, snaring her attention as a group of muleteers rose. *"Still, you were remade once."* The reminder was as much for herself as Nhenir. *"And if you're one as well as three, shouldn't you know where the parts of the shield are?"*

The muleteers stopped just short of the doorway, debating where to go next. Beneath the hubbub, Nhenir's mindvoice remained cool.

"When the shield broke, the bond between us must have broken, too. I have not felt its presence from that day to this."

"So the remnants could be anywhere." I must not lose hope, Malian thought, as the drovers she had entered with occupied one end of the recently vacated table. The muleteers decided on the cockfight those outside had been discussing, and clumped out as off-duty town guards crowded in. Malian, about to start toward Raven, stayed where she was. Her eyes watched the room, but her mind returned to the frost-fire sword's bargain with Amaliannarath, the Darksworn power that had subsequently died bringing the House of Fire to Haarth. The sword's pact had bound Nhenir to silence as well—and who knew what other bargains the weapons might have made?

"I am still yours, as I was Yorindesarinen's until she bade me leave." Nhenir's mindtone was silver-edged darkness, reflecting the moon for which it was named.

But if, Malian reasoned, Yorindesarinen ordered the helm to leave when she lay dying, why not give the same command to the sword? Admittedly, the blade might lack Nhenir's ability to transport itself—except that this was the weapon that had placed a geas on a prince of the Darksworn, and through him his entire House. *"So you must have been capable of preventing your own capture. Did Yorindesarinen foresee the geas?"* she asked silently, despite knowing the frost-fire sword did not speak. *"Did she order you to allow yourself to be taken?"*

At the bar, an ale keg toppled with a crash as a patron lurched into it. Confusion followed as the man tried to regain his footing, the woman serving behind the bar moved to retrieve the keg, and those closest made valiant efforts, half serious, half sport, to roll it away. Malian took advantage of the uproar to head toward Raven's table, but felt a telltale twitch between her shoulders as soon as she moved. The sensation was still present when she seated herself. "I've caught someone's attention," she murmured. The corner location meant her back was half turned to the room, concealing the movement of her lips but increasing her reliance on Raven's vigilance.

"I thought we'd picked up a burr." He spoke around a mouthful of food to disguise the shape of his words.

About the time we came out of the pass, Malian thought, knowing he had a good instinct for such things—as did she, even without using her seeker's sense. Turning on her stool, she raised her hand for a server and took the opportunity to assess the room. "Nothing obvious," she said, once the nearest server had acknowledged her.

Raven was the one most likely to have been recognized, since the hedge knight was a persona he had used through long years of travel among the realms of Haarth. Crow, on the other hand, was as different from either Carick the River scholar or Heris the scribe as it was possible to look. Malian had even woven the hair on either side of her face into the narrow braids favored in Lathayra, working in crow feathers pulled from a hedge outside Stoneford to give color to her mercenary's name. "Could Ser Raven have old enemies here?"

"It's possible." The server finally reached their corner, and Malian ordered ale and whatever meal was being served that night. "We should see the town," Raven added, as the man departed. "There's a night fair where we can buy supplies and I've been told of a cockfight. We could make money if the bets fall right." And draw our watcher out, Malian assumed, since gambling and exploring Aeris had not formed part of their plans until now.

In fact, she had already seen most of what the town had to offer when she came here a year ago, pursuing rumors of the Lost. Now she traced patterns in the spilled ale on the tabletop, sword-for-hire fashion, and monitored the surge and clatter of the crowd. Even after their meals arrived, she still kept her seeker's sense tuned to the room—but their watcher, she decided, must be adept at concealment.

Feigning absorption with her meal, she also reflected on how much Raven had slipped back into his hedge knight persona since leaving Stoneford. Obviously that suited their current situation, but Malian wondered if he sensed that she found the old Normarch relationship more comfortable. Which I do, she conceded. Yet however much she might feel easier traveling with Raven, Malian could still see the warrior from the Cave of Sleepers—Aravenor—in his face and manner. Now she examined the latter name silently, as she had several times since learning his true identity in the Stoneford shrine, and admitted that she found it disconcerting to contemplate just how long he had lived: first sleeping through aeons in the cavern outside of time, then living a thousand years more, here on Haarth.

With you and the rest of your House concealed behind the visors of the Patrol, she thought, still concentrating on her bowl. He was not just any Patroler, though. The man sitting opposite her was both the Patrol's Lord Captain and a prince of the Darksworn who had been alive when Yorindesarinen died . . . Nonetheless, Malian's strongest recollection from her vision of the Cave of Sleepers was the weariness and grief stamped into Aravenor—Raven's—face as he lay sleeping with Yorindesarinen's sword on his breast.

With the *weight* of Yorindesarinen's sword on his breast, she amended now. In Stoneford, Raven had told her that he was the last from all three Lines of the Blood of Fire, and Malian could only imagine the burden of trying to hold an entire House together under those circumstances. She did not need to ask herself whether he had proven equal to the task—and not just because Fire had followed him into their long sleep and later a new life on the world of Haarth, or because he was still their Lord Captain. Earlier in the year, she had also seen him hold a band of beleaguered Normarchers together against a far larger force comprising were-hunts and Darksworn facestealers.

Definitely not uncomplicated, Malian reflected, scraping up the last of her meal. When she pushed the empty bowl away and looked up, Raven had his most hard-to-read expression turned to the room. I need to remain cautious, she thought, even if he did bring me the sword and I have pledged to take his Darksworn House as my own. Or perhaps, she added wryly, *because* that's what I've done.

She met Raven's eyes, keeping her expression that of Crow, a sword-for-hire of dubious repute. "How long does this night fair stay open? Or shall we try the cocking pit?"

15

✦═══✦

The Night Fair

In the end they split up, deciding that was more likely to draw the watcher out and also determine which of them had attracted the unwelcome attention. Raven joined the off-duty guards, who had decided to attend the cockfight as well, while Malian made her unhurried way toward the night fair. She stopped to look at anything that might catch a sword-for-hire's interest, from a cobbler stitching boots beneath the pool of light outside his narrow shop, to the display in an armorer's window. Even without Nhenir's invisible visor lowered, the helm's power enabled her to sift surrounding sounds: the voices of merchants who still had their doors open, calling out to passersby, and a woman humming as she closed shutters. Out of sight down a side lane, a boy was playing with a puppy, and further back along the street, someone was following carefully after her. Malian did not need to look around to know; she could hear it in the pattern of the footsteps.

A man, she thought, because there was considerable weight to the tread, however unobtrusively her follower moved. She paused outside a second armorer's and pretended to watch the smith, who was still working. Behind her, the footsteps stopped. When she moved on, the footsteps resumed, matching their pace to hers. Malian crossed diagonally to a harness maker's door, glancing casually around as she did so, but there were too many passersby to identify the follower. Cautiously, she extended her psychic awareness, but could detect no hint of power use.

If she had not known that Crow looked both dangerous and down-at-heel, Malian would have assumed her tail was a thief. As it was, every sense was alert as she turned the next corner and saw the night fair, a large two-story building that formed one side of the main square. Once Malian drew closer, she saw that people were already streaming in and out. The pattern of footfalls was still with her as she strolled into the market and surveyed the first aisles, where the goods were either displayed on planks and trestles or in booths beneath colorful awnings.

The array was far less varied than in the River cities, but Malian took her time among the stalls that offered dried food and other supplies for travelers. Aeris being a caravan town, business was brisk, but by the time she reached the last stall, Malian had narrowed her tail to one of three men. All three had emerged from the street she walked down and were lingering in the same part of the fair. One looked like a mason, with stone dust in his hair and clothes, while the second could have been any muleteer frequenting the Aeris taverns. The third man was an Aralorni archer, similar to those she had seen at the Midsummer tourney in Caer Argent.

Malian surveyed the surrounding lanes in an undecided fashion, then crossed two aisles to reach a booth displaying daggers. Most were of Ijiri make, although there were several Emerian blades and one matched pair in the Ishnapuri style. She nodded to the bootholder and bent to inspect a stiletto; by the time she straightened, the archer had arrived. He ignored the knife merchant's greeting and spoke directly to her. "You look like you know your weapons." His voice, broad with the vowels of Aralorn, was rough as gravel. "What would you recommend?"

Malian let her expression shift into a sword-for-hire's wariness. The archer might be tall, like most Aralorni, but his shoulders and forearms were thick with a swordsman's muscle, and instead of the Aralorn longbow he carried a crossbow across his back. He also had a hatchet thrust through his belt, a shortsword at his hip, and at least one dagger that she could see. His stance was relaxed, his hands resting on his belt buckle, but the eyes regarding her were hard. Just for a second Malian's truth and seeker's senses flickered, and she saw the archer's face shift, as though the eyes looked out through a mask.

Facestealer, she thought, and her stomach muscles tightened although she kept her voice neutral. "That would depend on what you're looking for."

"Well now," he said, and although his tone was casual, almost amused, the hard eyes narrowed. "I thought that was you. But you're not what I expected."

From the corner of her eye, Malian saw the booth-holder step back—as she would, too, in his place. The current of danger was palpable as the pine and dust on the night breeze. A stronger draught made the lanterns sway, and the shadows around them danced. "I?" she demanded, holding to Crow's tone, with just a hint of truculence coloring the next, logical question. "Are you hiring swords, then?"

The wind gusted again, skittering dust and litter through the market, and the facestealer's teeth bared, just a little. "My kinsman"—the rough voice paused—"my *esteemed* kinsman, does not hire swords. But he has been seeking a pair of gray-clad couriers and gave me a mark to follow. A signature, you might say." The hardness in the eyes was tempered with appraisal. "The signs became confused in Caer Argent, with the trail appearing to depart both east and south, and by the time the eastern path disappeared, the southern one had grown cold. I decided to retrace my route to the River, to which all the couriers eventually return." A smile touched his mouth but did not reach his eyes. "Then today I picked up my mark again, stronger than ever. You, though, are no courier."

Malian's mind raced, guessing that his mark must have attached itself to Jehane Mor's medallion, which the herald had given her to wear when she walked the path of earth and moon. Later, when she tried to give the medallion back, Jehane Mor had made it a permanent gift. The shift must have confused the tracking spell and drawn the facestealer to her instead of the herald. Malian resisted the urge to touch the disc, which she wore concealed beneath her shirt, and spoke with a sword-for-hire's flatness. "I don't know you or your kinsman and I've no truck with heralds of the Guild, if that's what you mean by gray-clad couriers."

Phrases like "troublemakers" and "fetch the guards" filtered to her through Nhenir, but she kept her attention on the facestealer, whose appraising gaze had narrowed. "You talk like a sword-for-hire, too—out of where, Lathayra? But your stink says native power, only with something else coiled in there that doesn't feel quite right . . . " If the archer had been a dog, or the wolf his manner suggested, Malian thought he would have sniffed at her. "A riddle, but I leave hunting out answers to others. And I don't much care for power users, outside my own kindred." He cocked his head, considering. "Or within it, come to that. Best to kill you and have done."

He drew the axe and swung in one swift, fluid movement. If Malian had not been expecting an attack, the blade would have split her skull. Yet even as he moved, her mind was burrowing into the wooden handle, splintering it to shards as the weapon cleaved the air. A voice screamed as her opponent cursed and snatched at his sword, which Malian's power told her was warded against magic. She threw the dagger from her wrist sheath, and the facestealer's smile was contemptuous as he deflected it with the sword. He was fast, she gave him that, but so was she, and his contempt slipped as she drew the frost-fire sword before he could counterstrike. The blades clashed together—and his sheared off below the hilt.

The facestealer spun clear of Malian's descending blow, a long, wickedly curved dagger appearing in his hand. This time he was more reluctant to engage and they circled, alert for weakness. Throughout the night fair the lanterns grew dim, and Malian's psychic awareness sharpened as shadows crept out from every corner.

The facestealer hesitated, as though weighing something that did not quite fit, before taking a wary step back from their conflict: "But perhaps not today, after all."

" *'Ware!*" Nhenir's alert flared simultaneously with the psychic surge that heralded a portal opening. All around the night fair the creeping shadows leapt forward like hunting spiders, at the same time as a knot of blackness fell from the roof, unfurling into a weighted net. Malian sprang aside before she was entangled and slashed at the descending mesh, which curled away from the frost-fire blade like paper disintegrating into ash. It was steel, though, she realized, and not bespelled in any way despite the surrounding shadows.

The facestealer had dived clear at the same time she did, but an edge of net had still caught him across one shoulder. "Thanir!" he spat, flinging it clear and moving back-to-back with Malian as they both edged further away. For now, she was willing to let the alliance stand, despite guessing he would abandon her as swiftly should circumstances change. The fairgoers were shouting and shoving to flee the warehouse, but a wind howled out of the shadows, snapping the doors and windows shut. Those trapped inside screamed, but Nhenir whispered in Malian's mind, showing her how to force the closures wide again. She hesitated, reluctant to play her hand too soon, and instead reached up as though securing her headwrap and lowered the helm's invisible visor.

The moment Nhenir's dawn eyes closed over hers, illusion fell away and the shadows acquired the shape of warriors in barbed armor and grotesque helmets. Yet only one, Malian thought, a tall figure in black armor that was honed to spur points at elbow and shoulder, had genuine substance. His visor was up as he stepped clear of the densest shadow, revealing a face of austere planes and sculpted angles. Around the periphery of the fair, those who had not been able to escape fell silent, huddling behind booths and beneath trestles.

"Well, well." The newcomer's voice was smooth and dark as obsidian; the language he spoke sounded like strangely accented Derai. "I thought you intended murdering the hire-sword in your usual way, Emuun. Instead it seems you truly have turned native, recruiting their mercenaries to guard your back."

Emuun grunted. "Need breeds strange alliances, Thanir." His tone was conversational, but he stayed back-to-back with Malian. "And this mercenary has an impressive sword."

"Indeed. Aranraith sent me after you, but the sword may interest him as well." Thanir did not so much as glance Malian's way, making it clear any interest did not extend to the swordbearer. At her back, Emuun snarled a curse.

"With a net? That is beyond a jest, even for Aranraith."

Thanir's expression did not change. "Aranraith does not jest, and neither does Salar, you know that. They require you to answer for your treachery in Emer."

"Treachery?" Emuun sounded as though he was testing the word. "You know better than that, Thanir, even if Aranraith does not."

"Do I?" The obsidian voice was soft. "It appears I don't. Not at all."

What now? Malian wondered. She could hear feet running and voices yelling outside the warehouse, followed by a rattle and thud as those in the square tried to force the doors. Thanir appeared indifferent to everything except Emuun, and although Malian could sense his latent power, he was not using it. The same way, she thought, the net had not been ensorcelled, despite the flexibility and strength of the steel. The reason, she imagined, was because Emuun was immune to magic. Raven had told her that in Stoneford, when he explained why Swarm agents in Emer had mistaken him for Emuun, who was also his First Kinsman.

"Our work in Emer was thwarted and at least one of those involved was immune." Thanir's voice whispered out of the wind that still buffeted the night fair. "Before they died, first Orriyn on the Northern March, then Rhike in Caer Argent, swore that immune was you. Arcolin believes you killed both of them to conceal your treachery." Thanir's barbed shoulders shrugged. "Even Nirn harbors sufficient doubt to agree that you must answer Aranraith and Salar's questions. A pity for you, of course, that they have much your own way of getting answers."

"Nirn." The single word was stone.

"He might defy Aranraith for you, but never Salar. You know that, or should." Thanir remained unmoving, but the shadows around him stretched toward Emuun. "I feel bound to invite you to come quietly."

Emuun laughed. "Now your net has failed?" The shadow warriors accompanying Thanir stepped forward as one. As though together they form a web, Malian thought, remembering her initial impression of spiders leaping out of the gloom. Emuun's tone changed, becoming conversational as he addressed her. "You realize, little crow, that he's not going to leave any witnesses behind."

I do, Malian thought. Despite Thanir's apparent focus on Emuun, she was certain he had not forgotten her for a moment. She was also aware that not leaving witnesses meant that the fairgoers trapped inside the warehouse must die—and equally sure that Emuun was only concerned about his own survival. Thanir had not stirred, but Malian sensed his power begin to build. Her grip on the frost-fire sword tightened as Emuun stooped, gathering up the net in his left hand. She had heard that arena warriors fought that way, down in Lathayra, but had never seen it done.

"If you want me, Thanir," Emuun said, "you'll have to take me blade-to-blade." Just, Malian thought, as though he had a trident or a sword for his other hand, like those arena fighters, rather than just a dagger. Yet despite the odds, she found she was not prepared to discount Emuun.

For the first time, Thanir's expression changed. He smiled. "You've stolen one face too many, if you think I've grown foolish."

As if his words were a command, the warriors accompanying him drew their swords, and whatever they might be, whether substance, shadow, or something of both, the rasp of steel was real. Cold shivered beneath it, and Malian recognized the whisper of the void: the portal that had brought Thanir here must be opening again. The shadow warriors edged closer, but were too experienced to obstruct each other by rushing in. We must take the fight to them, Malian thought, but knew Emuun would wait as long as possible, wanting either her or the attackers to create the opening he needed. Imperturbable, Thanir regarded them both—and an axe bit through the building's main doors, defying the sorcery that held them closed.

Raven, Malian thought: it has to be. Without looking away from Thanir, she countermanded his spell and flung every other door and shutter in the building wide. The trapped fairgoers scrambled for the openings as Thanir's wind roared in answer, tossing trestles and booths into the air. The axe hacked through the hinges of the main doors, preventing their being held closed again, and Raven stepped through behind the final blow, his headcloth wrapped about his face. To avoid being recognized, Malian imagined, as well as providing protection against the wind. She would have been blinded by the gale herself if Nhenir's invisible visor had not been shielding her eyes.

A small company of Aeris guards, armed with bows and halberds, fanned out to either side of Raven, only to flatten themselves against the walls as the shadow gate gaped wide. The wind, roaring back, hurled Emuun off his feet and battered him toward the portal. Malian would not have stayed upright without the power to channel the gale aside, and she saw Emuun's face shift beneath the wind's force—as though the visage he had stolen was being stripped away. Yet the face-stealer still seemed able to resist the portal's suck of power. Malian supposed his immunity must help him, despite providing no defense against the physical power of the wind. Even the shadow warriors were leaning into the blast, although their swords had acquired sub-stance now, a thicket of steel closing around Emuun.

"Pin his limbs with your blades." Malian heard Thanir's command clearly through Nhenir, despite the howl of the wind. "We want him alive, but that doesn't mean uninjured."

"What's wrong, Thanir, afraid to fight me unless I'm maimed?" Despite the taunt, Emuun sounded strained—but the last thing Malian saw, before a gust hammered into her back and she staggered, was the facestealer rolling clear of the swords and diving through the portal.

A hand grasped her arm, steadying her. "Time to leave," Raven shouted above the tumult, and she would have nodded except the wind roared again. For a moment all they could do was cling together, before the blast passed and they fought their way to the nearest doorway. Malian's counterspell was still holding every opening clear, and she wondered whether Thanir would come after her instead of Emuun, now that she had thwarted his use of power.

They're aware there are Haarth-born adepts, she reminded herself, and Emuun is his primary quarry. She had refrained, too, from counteracting either the wind or Thanir's portal, in the hopes he might decide she was no more than a native adept with limited ability. But an impressive sword, Malian added, sheathing it as she and Raven fled into the adjoining alley. Quelling her fear of drawing Nindorith's attention, she skirted piled rubbish and headed toward the square. So far she could detect no pursuit, but the wind was still howling through the building, while voices yelled orders and horns blew as the guards on the scene summoned reinforcements. Others, she guessed, would be deploying to Aeris's gates and walls, in case the night fair incident heralded a major attack.

Word of this, Malian thought, pausing to survey the confusion in the square, is going to travel like wildfire. Within a month, authorities from Ij to Ishnapur would be debating every aspect of who and what had happened in Aeris. "Something's changed," she said, and felt Nhenir's silent acquiescence. She looked over her shoulder at Raven, who was watching the way they had come. The visor allowed her to see him clearly, but the cloth still wrapped around his face prevented her from reading his expression. "We've grown used to the Darksworn operating out of the shadows. But this suggests they're done with that."

"Yes." Raven began removing the head covering. "We need to get clear of Aeris."

Malian nodded and dove into the thick of the square, using the crowd's numbers and confusion to disguise their passage. She kept Nhenir's visor down, alert for danger, but they made it through without being challenged. The furor faded once they passed into the streets beyond the square, although a squad of town guards soon overtook them, heading for the walls. A few minutes later what looked like a hastily assembled citizen reserve hurried in the opposite direction, arming themselves as they went.

The caravan house was bustling, too, with those guests who had returned from their night's entertainment gathered around the entrance to ask each other what was happening. Malian and Raven mingled with the rest but kept to the fringes of the discussion. They had reached the stable door by the time the others decided to repair to the tavern—to await more information, they agreed, walking off. Only the night hostler was left in the street, his gaze shifting between the ramparts and the departing company, and he did not look around when Raven disappeared into the stable.

Malian ascended to the deserted dormitory to collect their gear, but the boy who slept in front of the lockup had vanished, either to hide or discover what was afoot. The lockup's heavy iron padlock looked daunting, but the mechanism was straightforward—the work of a moment for Malian's Shadow Band skills. She remained alert for unexpected arrivals or the boy's return, but the building stayed quiet as she retrieved their saddlebags and travel rolls, then resecured the door.

Before leaving, she opened one bag and removed a slender lead case, unlocking it with a traced sigil. The halves clicked apart, revealing two linings: the first visible as a line of silver between the lead and an inner lining of gold bearing the Shadow Band's engraved mark. *"Fire, water, shadow."* Silently, Malian invoked the ward and slipped Jehane Mor's medallion into the case, resealing it with another traced symbol. If Swarm magic had used the disc as a marker for Emuun to follow, the case should neutralize the spell until she had time to erase it. If the medallion had been of lesser value, she would have cast it into a river or the nearest forge fire and let the elements do their work. But this was Jehane Mor's gift, and one tied to Tarathan and Imuln's path of earth and moon. So not, Malian thought, sliding the case back among her other belongings, for discarding lightly, if at all.

The hostler was still outside, seated on a cart-tail that gave him a clear view of the street in either direction. Malian wrapped herself in shadows and ghosted past him into the stables, where Raven already had the horses saddled. "We'll have to risk a portal," she said, and he nodded. They both knew the city gates would not be opened again that night and by tomorrow morning it would be too late: the Aeris guard would be looking for the sword-for-hire named Crow, who had played such a prominent part in the upheaval. Malian secured the last saddlebag and gave her mare, Hani, a pat. *Do all you can to shield us,* she said to Nhenir, and met Raven's eyes. "Ready?"

He nodded and took both horses' reins, although Malian kept one hand on Hani's neck as she opened her mind to the Aeris night: the dust from the plain, the scent of pines from the mountain slopes, and the first snow on the heights. Mentally, she retraced her journey to reach the old town a year ago, charting the main caravan route with its way stations and established campsites, before shifting to the less-used road she had taken on her return to Ar. Little more than a bridle-track in places, it looped through the foothills and mountain passes between Aeris and the wide green lands of the River.

Malian let her mind follow the secondary route, leaping over huddled villages with their sheep pens and rocky fields, to settle on a pine grove near the crest of the road's first long ascent into the foothills. She had camped a night in the dry earthy hollow beneath the trees, which grew so close together that only the very heaviest rain fell between the branches. Now, it was the best shelter she could recall along the secondary route's wild terrain. The alternative was to reach right through to the River—but even if she was confident of her ability to open a gate of sufficient size over so great a distance, the power use would resemble a comet, blazing across the Haarth night.

Not what we want, Malian thought, and gathered herself. Breathing in the resin of the pines, mingled with acrid earth, she brought the two places together in her mind, folding the distance between them. For a moment she stood poised between the quiet stable with its scents of horses and leather and hay, and the darkness beneath the pines with its thickly layered needles and scattered cones. She smelt sheep dung, too, scattered among the tree roots—and opened her portal, out of the stable and into the hollow in the foothills.

Peta, Raven's mare, tossed up her head, but he spoke a quiet word and she steadied. Hani pricked her ears forward, and then both horses followed Raven through the gate. Malian waited until the mares' tails had swished clear before following, letting the opening close as soon as she stood on the foothill side. The imprint of the stable lingered briefly against the darkness, and then there was just the pine grove, with the wind sighing down from the high peaks, bringing the chill of snow.

16

The Dark Hours

"No fire," Raven said, and Malian did not argue. Even a faint glow seen through the dense curtain of the trees would be a beacon, but it meant they were in for a cold night. She searched as unobtrusively as possible with her seeker's sense, but every indication was that they were alone in the blackness of the foothills. Regardless, she circled the hollow and set her Shadow Band trip wires, each with its own cantrip against detection.

"If you'd done that in the Long Pass," Raven observed, "the wolf-pack might not have feasted on your mule."

"Maister Carick's mule," Malian said, finally pushing up Nhenir's visor, although she kept the helm on. *You can keep my head warm, if nothing else,* she told it. "The maister was meant to draw out enemies. But for what it's worth, I do still feel badly about the mule." Raven was taking first watch, so she worked herself into a hollow between gnarled tree roots, where the pine needles were thickest, and unfolded her blanket. Even beneath the trees, the night air was already cold as iron.

Raven spoke again from the lip of the hollow, his voice quiet through the darkness: "What you did in Emer, the way you were Carick so completely, is a rare gift, one I haven't encountered for a long time."

Malian wrapped the blanket about cloak and coat. "The Band calls it illusion. It's a skill they teach all their adepts."

"Yet how many of your peers could achieve what you did in Emer, subsuming the true identity so completely beneath an outward persona?"

Despite his phrasing, it was not really a question. The truth was that Malian had been one of the Shadow Band's most gifted students in almost every respect, but no one could match her when it came to altering outward appearance and maintaining convincing disguises. First Kin to a facestealer, she thought, grimacing. Except that I create my personas, I don't murder people to acquire their faces. "You saw through most of the illusion layers," she pointed out, feeling the cold start to bite. *"I suppose,"* she added to Nhenir, *"it would be wrong of me to use my power to warm the air?"*

"For the whole night? You would run less risk of attracting unwelcome attention if you lit a fire."

"I saw through the illusions meant to convince the world you were a young man," Raven agreed. "But if Carick the scholar had been a young woman, and Malian of the Derai concealed within that disguise, detection would have been much harder, if not impossible. Even carrying the sword that is bound to both you and the helmet, I was still not sure about you for a long time."

Malian shifted, trying to get more comfortable. "But you have encountered those with similar abilities before?" Any power found among the Derai, she supposed, could also exist among the Darksworn. Her eyesight had adjusted now and she could make out his silhouette against the starlight that pricked the hollow's rim, enough to catch his glance her way.

"The gift was always rare, but we looked for it most in Night on the Derai side. Among the Sworn—" The outline of his shoulders shrugged. "We in Fire claimed it as our own, since the few with the ability among Lightning's ranks were all our kindred. As for Sun, they had facestealers, plenty of them, but Aranraith hungered for those who could assume an unshakable persona for years, or even decades. Such adepts were deadly because the assumed identity was real, its belief in itself absolute, until the moment came for the hidden personality to strike." Raven paused, and when he spoke again his voice was spiked with a chill Malian could not recall hearing before, even on the Northern March. "That is one reason Aranraith values Thanir, whom you have just met, so highly. He has many abilities, all considerable, but he is also one of only a very few facestealers who can sustain a stolen visage for prolonged periods."

Malian folded her arms, recalling Thanir's assurance from the night fair. The blanket, she decided, was doing little good against the cold. "It's true that if you don't know you are anything but the created identity, then you can't be surprised or flushed out." She shivered, thinking how important maintaining so profound a concealment would be for a Derai agent infiltrating the Darksworn. "But the inner self is always present, aware at some level and processing what it needs to know."

She did not add that it was Nhenir, building on Shadow Band skills learned from Elite Cairon, who had taught her how to weave in triggers that enabled the hidden personality to resurface at the right time and complete an assigned mission—or simply avoid being killed inadvertently, like Carick in the Long Pass. If Raven had not come along when he had, or the Normarch patrol arrived just as the wolfpack was catching them again, the Long Pass brigands would have received an unpleasant surprise when they caught their soft River scholar. But that would have destroyed her cover and created the same kind of ripples that she feared the night fair incident was going to do. So it was far better for everyone—including the outlaws, Malian reflected, conscious of the irony—that first Raven and then the Normarch patrol *had* come along.

She wondered how many of the outlaws had died later, either at The Leas or the hill fort, and supposed she could consider it recompense for her mule if they had. Except that during her time away from the Wall of Night she had learned that sometimes it was circumstance and weakness, as much as outright evil, that made outlaws. Her father, that stern unbending man, had taught her that justice must be served, but that cruelty and the desire for revenge should never guide it. *Something the wider Derai Alliance forgets too often,* she thought, remembering the stories about her grandfather, as well as the fate that had befallen her mother in the House of Adamant.

The Patrol, on the other hand, had served justice and kept the peace of road and river in the River lands for close on a thousand years.

"It was more than that," Nhenir said softy. *"They* made *peace in the River lands."* And momentarily, Malian heard the echo of Yorindesarinen in the voice that was both bright and dark.

Yes, she acknowledged silently. For with road and river kept safe and people able to travel freely, she could see how peace and justice would flourish more readily in the cities. Reflecting on what she knew of Raven from Normarch and Caer Argent, Malian thought he and her father might well understand each other if they were ever to meet. Except one was Derai and the other Darksworn, the latter a term that also encompassed Emuun and Thanir, Nirn and Arcolin, as well as the demon Nindorith. *And potentially my mother,* Malian thought, remembering a long-ago conversation with her father. She could still hear his voice when he had revealed that possibility—and added that if it were true, the gods only knew what sort of twisted creature Nerion would have become.

Yet Raven was not twisted, and Nherenor had not seemed so either, before he fell to his death. Even the facestealer, Malisande, in Normarch . . . *Ruthless yes,* Malian thought now, *and deadly, too, but I'm not sure I would have called her twisted. Yet Maister Gervon had been.* Malian's lips compressed, too, as she remembered the runes painted onto Arcolin's arms with poison and the death cup he had sent to Ghiselaine. *I have also killed,* she reminded herself: *on rooftops and battlements and far down in the darkness of Night's Old Keep. Maister Carick's hands might have been clean of blood, but Malian of Night's were not. Kalan's weren't either, or Tarathan's,* Malian thought, remembering them both as they had been at the hill fort, and then again in Imuln's dome at midsummer, splashed with blood that was not their own.

"Do we need to lose Crow and Raven?" she asked, changing the subject. "How likely is it that either Emuun or this Thanir will come after us?"

"That depends." Raven was thoughtful. "Initially on how the conflict between them resolves, then on how badly they want us. Although Emuun followed you earlier, which suggests he didn't recognize me. The hedge knight," he concluded softly, "does not much resemble the long-ago prince of the Sworn."

People also see what they expect to, Malian thought, even Darksworn hunters. "He thought I was Jehane Mor." Briefly, she related what Emuun had said to her. "But now he knows I'm not . . ."

Raven nodded. "Unfortunately, you never could tell which way Emuun would jump, and I doubt he's changed. As for Thanir— Arcolin, Nirn, or Aranraith would all want to stamp out anyone or anything that countered their magic, almost as a matter of principle. Thanir, however, will be intrigued. But his interest is every bit as dangerous as their vindictiveness."

Like Nindorith, Malian thought, remembering the demon's surprise when she countered his power in Caer Argent. *Who are you? What?* he had asked, speaking directly into her mind. And having caught his attention, she had barely escaped.

"It's probably wisest to change identity," Raven continued. "The Patrol, once we make our rendezvous, has cadres of adepts whose job is to turn aside unwelcome attention, exactly as happened in Ij last spring. But we don't want to blaze a trail from Aeris to the Patrol's door."

"No." Malian hoped there would be less chance of that now she had the medallion quarantined. Yawning, she shifted position again, but her mind was still wide-awake as she mulled over events at the night fair. She imagined that Emuun's challenge to Crow would be put down to the usual rivalries between itinerant mercenaries, which frequently began or ended in fighting. Thanir, on the other hand, had not only stepped clear of the Darksworn's traditional shadows; he had used magic and opened a portal in the most public way possible, practically inviting the furor the night fair incident would generate. Something's changed, Malian thought again. The warrior-adept had not seemed troubled by his failure to net Emuun either. Playing a deep game, perhaps . . .

Malian realized she was gnawing her lower lip and stopped, although her frown did not lessen. The Swarm had been operating relatively freely, if not unchecked, in Ij and Emer, and now they had just created a major incident in Aeris. For all she knew, they could be as active in other places—while all this time the Derai had seen the Wall as a bastion, holding the Swarm back from the rest of Haarth. "Zharaan and Kiyan," she murmured, and saw the shadow of Raven's head turn.

"The Queen of Jhaine and her First? That's an old story."

"Yet even in the early years following our arrival," she said softly, "Swarm agents were able to attack the priestess-queens in Jhaine, until Zharaan and Kiyan's blood magic shut them out."

"Salar's children at work," Raven replied. "Mostly they comprise those who ride the Wall storms, but some are adept at slipping through fissures in the fabric of reality, whether singly or in pairs, to wreak their havoc. But that doesn't equate to a Swarm breakout."

Malian knew from what he had told her in Stoneford that Salar was one of what the Darksworn called Ascendants, as Nindorith was also, and Amaliannarath had been. "But they're breaking out now, aren't they?"

"They'll have to, if the maelstrom is rising." Raven was matter-of-fact. "The Sworn are the vanguard. Always, they flee ahead of the storm, partly to open up a path for what follows, but to stay alive as well." He paused to survey the night beyond their hollow, before continuing. "Even without the Golden Fire, the roots of the Wall go very deep. And despite some wavering, the Nine Houses have kept to their watch. That's why this has been so long in coming. Still, it's questionable whether the Wall is capable of withstanding a sustained assault anymore."

Malian stared, not at him but into darkness, her heart hammering as she recognized the old fear from her earliest childhood: that without the Golden Fire, the Derai would fall as soon as the Swarm rose again. Beneath the blanket, her hands were fists, because even if she could bring Yorindesarinen's weapons of power together, she knew it would not prevent what was coming. The weapons might have been made by the gods, but Yorindesarinen still had not prevailed against the Chaos Worm—and the Swarm was so much more powerful than any one monster it created, however great.

According to Raven, the Darksworn called the Swarm the maelstrom because it was raw power, which either absorbed or reshaped everything that came within its ambit. As for the minions, or demons, that the Derai also thought of as the Swarm, apparently they were born out of the wave edge of the maelstrom's advance, although Raven was not sure how. "They were not the kinds of questions I concerned myself with when young," he had said in Stoneford, with a certain grim humor. "Until, that is, I no longer had the opportunity to ask them."

And I still have too few answers, Malian reflected. What she had learned from Raven was hardly comforting. The Darksworn claimed there was an awareness driving the maelstrom, but once it rose and expanded outward the surge of power was indiscriminate, unable to distinguish between friend and foe. In the past, Salar, Nindorith, and Amaliannarath had shielded the Darksworn Houses, but could only do so to a limited extent—so to survive, the remaining Darksworn *had* to break through the Wall's containment.

Surely, Malian thought, there must be *some* way to defeat the maelstrom once and for all. She was grimly aware that was supposed to be her destiny, as Chosen of Mhaelanar, but the inevitable conclusion from her Stoneford discussions with Raven was that the Derai had never come close to doing so, not even when at their strongest. While now, with the Alliance fractured and the Golden Fire gone, Derai power was at its lowest ebb.

One secret Malian had not shared with Raven was that Hylcarian, the one-time Golden Fire of the Keep of Winds, lived on in the heart of the Old Keep. Yet his power was only a remnant of what it had been when the entire Wall of Night blazed with golden light—a fact Malian recalled every time she jolted awake in the dark hours, reliving the nightmare of Nindorith's pursuit through Caer Argent. She and Kalan might embody the greatest powers born to the Derai in many generations, but even together they had barely escaped the Darksworn Ascendant. So although the Wall of Night might continue to hold for now, everything Raven could tell her only confirmed Derai history: that the dark tide of the maelstrom—or Swarm—would rise again, and when it did . . .

The Wall will fall, Malian thought, the certainty tight as a fist, clenching in her gut. Unless, even if I can't destroy the maelstrom outright, I somehow find a way to hold it back, buying time until I can search out a means to defeat it.

The same way, she countered silently—the fist tightening further around her doubt—that Yorindesarinen bought time when she stood alone against the Chaos Worm? And my starting position is so much weaker than hers was then.

Malian shivered, her breath misting against the night's deepening cold. The horses were standing close together for warmth, and she knew Raven's regular circuit about the hollow was as much about counteracting the cold as keeping watch. I need to sleep, she thought. But the cold clawed through blanket and cloak and coat, and her mind kept returning to Thanir and whether he would involve Nindorith in his hunt. In the end she gave in and extended her seeker's sense again, searching for any hint of pursuit.

Given Raven's ability to detect power use, she was not surprised when he looked her way. "For the moment," he said, "I think we've gotten clear."

For the moment, Malian repeated silently. She had not forgotten that Emuun, like his First Kinsman, was immune—or that she had not known Raven was present, watching her encounter with the Arafyr. She stood up, stretching stiff limbs and flexing her gloved hands.

"I eluded Nindorith in Caer Argent, but only just. Now the night fair incident seems certain to attract his attention."

"Except Nindorith holds to Lightning, not Sun, so neither Thanir nor Emuun will solicit his aid, except as a last resort." Raven paused. "So far, too, your measures to counteract Nindorith's seeking appear to be working."

Malian nodded, before realizing that he would not see the gesture. Again, she re-examined her memory of Nindorith's power blasting through the midsummer dark. "Nhenir told me that if I looked in the earliest annals of the Derai Alliance, I would find the demon there." She stopped, silently cursing her tiredness. "I'm sorry. I should say Ascendant."

"It's probably best." Raven's silhouette continued to face the hillside, and humor, rather than offense, colored his tone. "Otherwise, to be consistent, you'll have to refer to every Golden Fire in the same way."

Malian's truthsaying, seeking, and seer's sense all quickened, telling her this apparently throwaway remark mattered. Perhaps she made a sound, because Raven's head turned as though she had spoken, and she sensed his scrutiny through the darkness.

"I assumed you knew," he said slowly. She had never seen him taken aback, but thought he sounded close to it now. "It never occurred to me that the Derai could have allowed themselves to forget anything so fundamental." They had both been keeping their voices low, aware of how far sound could carry in the isolated terrain, but now he spoke more quietly still: "Amaliannarath and Fire, Nindorith and Lightning, Salar and Sun—and one Ascendant, too, for each of the Derai's Nine Houses."

The room at the heart of the Old Keep of Winds had twelve doors, and the table at its center was divided into twelve parts, not nine ... Recalling that, Malian felt the same hollow sensation as when Nhenir had said she would need all three of Yorindesarinen's weapons to fully access their power. She was also remembering that although Nindorith had subsequently taken the form of a unicorn, his initial manifestation in Caer Argent had been as fire. Later, she had guessed Nindorith must be the unicorn on Lightning's insignia, but her mind had not leapt to the winged horse device of Night as it did now. Yet surely the winged horse *was* just a device, because flame had always—*always*—been the only form taken by the Golden Fire: either as the individual entities that once infused the heart of the Derai's nine strongholds, or in its collective aspect.

I need to say something, Malian thought. "I didn't know," she said. "I don't. Even the term Darksworn is almost forgotten among the Derai. I learned it from Kalan, and the old priest who told him the secret said the Alliance could shatter if we discovered that our own kind were also the Swarm's foremost adherents." She did not add that she had not fully accepted that truth until midsummer, when she had seen her own face reflected in Nherenor's features.

Raven's silhouette studied the dark hillside again before turning back to her. "If I were being true to my Sworn heritage, I would say that I'm not surprised the Derai want to forget. But you are Heir to the House that leads the Derai. I believe you need to know."

Life is a risk, Malian thought, despite the hollowness at her core. And Asantir had always said she needed to know as much about her allies as her enemies, a philosophy that had tallied with Elite Cairon's Shadow Band tutelage. She stamped her feet, silent on the pine needles, and drew the blanket closer. "I'm listening," she said.

17

Faces of the Moon

Through the link between them, Malian was aware that Nhenir was listening, too. How much of this do you know? she wondered. But Raven was already speaking, his voice acquiring a storyteller's rhythm. *"Sworn or Darksworn, demons or Ascendants, the distinction in names drives to the heart of the original conflict that sundered the Sworn from the Derai."*

She guessed that was how he had first heard the account, much as fireside tales had introduced a young Malian to the traditions of the Derai. It might also seem an easier way to recount a difficult history. Which, she reflected, I may be the first among the Alliance to have heard told—in how long, aeons?

"What the Sworn call Ascendants," Raven went on, *"took the form of rare beings, distinct in kind but close in friendship with what were once twelve allied peoples. When the maelstrom first rose, the friendship had endured for as long as anyone among the nations could remember, perhaps since the dawn of time. The twelve became aware of the maelstrom shortly after it appeared in the space between worlds, but the expedition they dispatched to learn more was sucked into the maelstrom's maw and came close to perishing. All would have been lost if the Ascendants present had*

not joined with the strongest of the expedition's adepts and pulled the survivors out.

"Nonetheless, despite all that went wrong, some felt they had begun to communicate with an intelligence at the maelstrom's heart. They argued for persevering with communication, while others, led by Salar, highlighted the potential to harness the maelstrom's power for the twelve's benefit. But the majority who returned were adamant that the maelstrom threatened all life and must be destroyed before it expanded beyond their ability to contain, if it had not already done so. Eventually those differences hardened into divisions between the twelve peoples."

They would, Malian thought, reflecting dryly on what she knew of both Derai and Haarth history. She flexed her hands to warm them, while Raven checked their perimeter before resuming. *"As the maelstrom expanded with increasing rapidity, consuming everything around it, the divisions fractured further. Those who saw it as an opportunity dwindled, while the ranks of those who argued for destruction swelled. Increasingly, they sought a weapon strong enough to counteract the maelstrom's power and eventually focused on the twelve Ascendants. Only their strength, it was argued, could withstand the maelstrom. Absolute unity would be essential, too. Individual Ascendants could not be permitted to withdraw unilaterally, while the whole must be able to compensate if a component part was wounded or destroyed. To increase the likelihood of success, the twelve's greatest adepts would act in concert with, and where necessary direct, the enhanced entity—or weapon, as in fact it was."*

Malian's mind flew to the serpent of power, the conjoined force of the priestess-queens of Jhaine, that she had confronted when walking the path of earth and moon. She was also beginning to perceive how this must end. Waiting for Raven to confirm it was like watching the executioner's blade begin to fall—but Malian did not think she could have spoken, even if she wanted to.

"The plan's adherents argued that binding the Ascendants was the price of preserving life itself: a necessary evil, but of short duration. Those who opposed them called it enslavement, the betrayal of

free beings that were also friends, and swore never to accede to such a deed." Raven paused. *"Then the first of the twelve's home worlds was consumed by the maelstrom."*

Now the blade was falling, and Malian wanted to hasten the end by whispering, *And?* But her lips refused to open.

"And," Raven said, as if she *had* spoken, *"all those who had argued for the binding of the Ascendants decided that the time for discussion was over. They enacted a great working to achieve their end, and drew on the power of the Nine Gods themselves to create the binding. Those who had vowed to defend the Ascendants' independence—calling their faction the Sworn—became aware of the working in time to flee before it could take hold. But they were outcast, devastated, and betrayed, as well as vulnerable to the Derai Alliance and the newly forged power of the Golden Fire. So although the Sworn did not immediately join the maelstrom, it was inevitable that they would be drawn into the only alliance powerful enough to counter not just the Derai and the Golden Fire, but what they saw as abandonment by the gods themselves."*

The Golden Fire: Malian's truth sense was raw edged, jangling that this was *true, true, true* . . . She felt as though she had just stepped off a precipice into deep water, with the cold and the dark closing over her head. She was falling, drowning, lost—while all that she had held as certain, and believed the Derai to be, was flotsam, whirling away. The need to be alone seized her, to get away from whatever judgment or condemnation, or careful lack of both, might follow Raven's tale, and *think* . . . But every Shadow Band instinct warned against showing weakness, so she spoke calmly as she laid the blanket aside. "You were right, I did need to know that." Rising, she moved to the opposite side of the hollow. "I'll cast a wider circuit before standing watch, double-check we're really alone out here."

Raven said something that Malian did not catch because she was already gone, slipping between the pines and her own trip wires. Beneath the surface calm, her heart was racing. If possible she would have folded the blackness around her like a second cloak, shutting out every word of Raven's story. This *truth*, she thought, curled like a worm at the heart of the Derai Alliance.

Survival breeds necessity; necessity drives hard decisions: Malian repeated the Shadow Band adage to herself. But this— If the Golden Fire really had been forged out of a compulsion wrought from the power of the gods themselves, then that act went against every tenet the Derai held sacred. The sanctity of friendship, she thought, doggedly combating the sensation of falling—and keeping faith with comrades, as well as Earl, Heir, and House. Not least, the taboo against slavery.

Yet the binding Raven had described *was* a form of enslavement, in fact if not name.

"That is how the Sworn tell the story, at any rate." Nhenir was calm as moonlight.

Malian frowned, her eyes fixed on the starry horizon and the mass of shadowed ridges below it, rolling into a distance that would eventually become the River. *"Have you heard it told differently?"*

Uncharacteristically, the helm conveyed hesitation. *"I know Yorindesarinen held that truths may not always be as they first appear."*

"Did she know of this?"

"She found out. And vowed to set it right, except death intervened."

Is that when the Derai buried knowledge of the Sundering? Malian asked herself. Is it possible that's *why* we buried it? This time, she looked south rather than north, as though she could see across time and physical distance to the Aralorn tower where she had refused to compel the Ara-fyr back into the Derai Alliance. Yorindesarinen's influence had shaped that choice, since the dead hero did not seem to believe that sacrificing anyone or anything to the Derai cause was what it meant to be the Chosen of Mhaelanar, champion of a god.

Yet if the gods themselves had loaned their power to the compulsion that transformed nine Ascendants into the Golden Fire, bound to the Derai keeps and the Blood of the Nine Houses ... Malian shook her head, deciding that the world, already far from straightforward, had just grown considerably murkier.

"It was largely because of your decision not to compel the Ara-fyr," Nhenir reminded her, *"that Raven revealed himself and returned the sword. Do not forget that you are also part of what the Derai are."*

And the moon turned both dark and light faces to the world: Tarathan had told her that on Imuln's blessed isle. *"I suppose you're right."*

Jehane Mor, too, had spoken words of reassurance when telling Malian and Kalan of the cataclysm that the Derai's arrival had wreaked on Haarth. *"It was a long time ago, and it was not the two of you, or any of the Derai who live now, who destroyed Jaransor."* Malian repeated the herald's words, her mindtone thoughtful. *"If Jehane were here now, she would say the same about the Sundering."*

"She is wise." Nhenir paused. *"They both are."*

Malian suspected the hesitation arose from the need to include Tarathan in that wisdom, since the helm had been swift to tell her, after Imuln's Isle, that he was not for her. Briefly, she felt the fire from the path of earth and moon reignite along her veins . . . But her heart tugged toward her seer's memory of the Gate of Winds, breaching mist and darkness with the vast body of the Derai world concealed behind it. Until the civil war, that world had included the Golden Fire, the core of the Derai's Alliance and their bulwark against the Swarm—a lost legacy she had been raised to honor. Setting Raven's account against it was painful, a blade that struck to the heart.

The moon has two faces. Malian repeated the adage to herself, but knew she could no longer assign the light face to the Derai while naming the other as Darksworn. Yet when Hylcarian had aided her, six years before, he had said that he and his fellows were the Derai's long allies and their friends in the age-old war against the Swarm. When she left the Keep of Winds, he had also said that he would be waiting on her return. *"Perhaps Yorindesarinen was right. The truth, like the moon, may wear more than one face."*

"She, too, was wise."

And kind, Malian thought—although neither attribute saved her. That thought, too, was a blade, companion to the realization that despite a history that seemed little more than one long unraveling of betrayal and death, she still yearned to return to the Derai. *"Are you still there?"* She cast the mindwhisper toward her last memory of Hylcarian, a slender bridge across the leagues of darkness between Aeris and the Derai Wall. Yet the only answer was the night breeze, speaking of emptiness and distance as it had throughout her exile.

Time to focus on the present, Malian thought, and my immediate responsibilities. The pines, stark against the stars, made retracing her path easy; when she reached the hollow, Raven was still on its far side. She saw his head turn her way, but spoke first, deliberately adopting Crow's sword-for-hire manner. "All's clear out there. And now it's my watch." Picking up her blanket, she held it out. "I doubt it'll make much difference, but one of us might as well try and be warm."

"I should have thought of that myself." Raven's voice matched hers for matter-of-factness as he took the blanket.

Malian repressed a sigh of relief. "If I'd thought of it sooner, I would have asked for yours." She kept her tone light as she settled into a vantage point on the lip of the hollow and studied the pattern of slope and shadow beyond. Soon, her attention was absorbed by the need to both stay awake and keep warm. She had heard the Aeris winter was hard and could imagine how bitter it must be once snow lay low on the hills. It would be difficult then, if not impossible, to survive a night in the open without a fire. Now, Malian used activity to combat cold as the night crawled by, changing position as Raven had and rechecking her trip wires and Band wards—although at one point she thought the first gray light might never come. When it did, she moved to a tree that looked south rather than east, so the rising sun would not dazzle her. But the lightening of the world was slow, the cold still iron.

Her seer's vision came with the first line of gold on the far side of the Aeris basin. The color split the grayness above from the darkness of the world below, as an answering fire arced across Malian's inner sight. Part of her remained aware of the pine hollow and surrounding hillside, while the seer within stood on a pebbled plain. In the vision, sheer mountains rose on either side, and a high massif loomed ahead. A thin wind shrilled, and the entire scene filled Malian with foreboding.

"Dread Pass," Kalan's voice whispered, as though he were standing beside her. Somewhere in Haarth, she knew his dream must be overlapping her vision.

Dread Pass, Malian repeated. The wind whipped the grit into clouds, blinding her, and when she shaded her eyes and looked again, the plain was covered in low-lying cloud. Armies fought through it, first one side and then the other reeling forward and then back, all within an utter silence that belonged to the seer's vision. Is this a battle yet to come, she wondered, whether in my or the Derai's future—or the glimpse of some long ago past, a clash during the civil war or on some distant world? Horses charged, a thunder across the plain that she felt as a reverberation through her body, and she forced her seer's sight to focus on the combatants. Gonfalons hung heavy in the fog, but she recognized Swarm fighters: fell lizards hurtled forward as a were-hunt brought down riders. A warrior rose in his stirrups, rallying those about him, and she saw the blazon on his shield as he led a counterattack that drove the Swarm assault back.

More cloud rolled in and the grayness thickened until clinging damp displaced the Aeris cold. For a long time the brume remained dense—then swiftly lifted to reveal low, rounded hills and outcrops of jagged rock. A double column of warriors traversed a narrow defile beneath discolored sky, and Malian felt a shock of recognition, knowing she had seen this once before, when she looked into Yorindesarinen's fire in the glade between worlds.

The seer's vision might be an uncertain art, but she waited with a sense of inevitability until the attackers rose, seemingly out of the ground, to hack and slay. Swords rose and fell, only this time Malian could hear the wounded crying out and horses screaming as they fell. The riders sought to rally about their leader, holding a path for his escape, but there were too many attackers. One by one the defenders fell, until the leader alone was left and his assailants closed in. At the last moment, exactly as in her first vision, the leader vanished, winking out from beneath his assailants' blades while they howled rage and frustration to the bruised sky.

"I could only save one." The mindvoice spoke out of Malian's memory of a cavern ringed with crystal torches and filled with an army of sleeping warriors. *"Time and the blades of the murderers pressed, so I had to act swiftly or lose all three Lines. Cruel,"* the mindvoice whispered. *"Bitter. But I had to choose."*

The vision swirled again: sky, hills, the narrow defile and the ambush; the assailants closing in on the last rider, screaming death and bloodlust as they reached out to drag him beneath their blades. Fire roared across Malian's vision, but the screaming and clamor of battle went on. When the fire cleared, the sky was still discolored, this time by smoke from the fires that burned both within and outside the River city of Ar. As she watched, catapults hurled rocks and more fire while siege engines lumbered toward the soaring walls.

Malian did not cry out—they had trained that out of her in the Shadow Band—but she swallowed hard against bile. She was aware that the dawn sky above Aeris was fading from fire to rose—but the vision persisted, wrapping her in the darkness of another plain that was scored by a multitude of smoldering brushfires. Their glow outlined a small hill, but it was not until Malian drew closer that she realized the mound was the ruined bulk of some giant beast, dead upon the plain. She stepped back, stumbling over metal shards, and when she looked down saw the shattered remains of a shield. A warrior's body lay beyond it, sprawled not far from the dead beast, with one gauntleted hand still resting on the hilt of an unsheathed sword.

"I know who you are," Malian whispered, "where this is." But the hacked and bloodied figure did not sit up, the riven armor shimmering back into unbroken silver as it had in the glade between worlds, with Yorindesarinen's smile glinting like the stars in her hair.

We did for each other, that Worm and I. This is the reality, Malian thought: bodies that stay dead in the middle of a devastated plain. In the distance a hound howled, a long, drawn-out cry that spoke of disaster and war. The plain stretched, becoming an impassable expanse that separated Malian from the dead, both Worm and hero. Slowly, the fire glow dwindled and the plain, like her vision, faded away.

18

The Wayhouse

The first blue was creeping into the sky, and somewhere a dog really was barking. Malian shook off the last shadows from the seer's vision and scrutinized the hillside. Behind her, she was aware that Raven was on his feet, hand on sword hilt, but she shook her head without looking around. "That dog's not hunting. And I can't detect anything out of place." Noises often sounded close in such empty country, and she knew from last year's journey that there were farmsteads scattered throughout these hills. The dog was probably some shepherd's companion, beginning work, or a farmer's hound greeting the day.

"Sound carries," Raven said, echoing her thought, but he studied the surrounding terrain as carefully as she had, even after the dog fell silent. Eventually he turned that careful look on her. "Still, it could be wisest not to linger."

"Another gate will give us more distance." She shivered in the aftermath of her visions and the night's cold, weighing risk. "It's worth it, since there's no sign of pursuit."

They erased any obvious evidence of their presence beneath the pines before Malian opened the gate, bringing them out a good half day's journey farther west. Her locus point was a crumbling wayhouse with a straggle of orchard on one side and a field of wild fennel on the other. She had found, when she practiced using gates during her River years, that the farther apart the entrance and exit were geographically, the more likely the time of day would have altered when quitting the gate. But she had deliberately kept this distance small, to minimize any disturbance caused by the portal, and they arrived in the clarity of the same postdawn hour.

The only signs of life were a flock of goats, their tuft tails disappearing into the fennel, and a blackbird calling from among the fruit trees. Malian could detect no evidence that their passage had attracted attention, an impression Nhenir affirmed, so decided it should be safe to eat before continuing on. In hopes of dispelling the shivery aftereffects of so powerful a series of visions, as well as thawing out, she settled into a patch of sun against the wayhouse wall and did not object when Raven lit a small fire to cook their breakfast. By daylight, the glow would not betray them, and the fuel was so dry that the smoke was little more than a shimmer against the air, one that soon dissipated. Her eyes grew heavy, but rather than dozing she re-examined the visions, particularly the one of Yorindesarinen's shield. Both Nhenir and Raven had said that it was broken, but she had imagined that meant riven into two or three parts, not shattered into fragments.

Not just broken, Malian thought now, but destroyed—which would explain why Nhenir has not detected the shield's presence since that time. She welcomed the distraction provided by hot food, and once it was ballast in her stomach she sat back, her eyelids sinking again, while Raven brewed a hot drink. When he spoke, she was hovering close to sleep: "Malian."

It was the first time, she realized, forcing her eyes open, that he had spoken her Derai name without the honorific "of Night." Raven was concentrating on the small, dented pan over the fire, so she could not read his expression—but whatever he was brewing smelled remarkably good. Malian inhaled deeply, trying to decide what it was as he looked up, his level gaze meeting hers. "Seeing your strength," he said quietly, "but also knowing your Derai upbringing and Shadow Band training, it's easy for me to forget how young you are."

I suppose I am, she thought. And then, with a spark of humor: although anyone would be, compared with you.

"Also to overlook other things," he went on, still in that quiet voice. "Like the way the Band see themselves as champions, despite being Dancers of Kan."

"Because of Kelmé," Malian said, then wondered why, when he must know the story better than she did. Besides, she knew what he was trying to say.

"Because of Kelmé," he agreed. His expression remained steady, but she heard a smile in his voice.

"It's all right," she said. And then, because something more seemed required, "I understand." That you weren't attacking me with your explanation of the Sundering, she added silently, or not intentionally, anyway. She could see, too, how he would have assumed that a story so integral to the Sworn would also be remembered by the Derai. "But you're right about the Shadow Band. As well as what you do not say," she added. "That we Derai also like to think of ourselves as champions."

Heroes, she thought sadly, as she recalled Yorindesarinen, dead on the plain. Despite every unpalatable implication of the shield's loss, that was still what caught at her throat. She lifted her face to the sun, thinking how it never shone on the Wall of Night. The first time she had experienced anything but leaden skies and pale daylight had been in Jaransor. Her Derai teachers had said the invisible sun was just another star, one of the many the Derai had encountered in their long conflict with the Swarm—a vast history that now seemed to dwindle to this one moment, as small as a campfire in the back country of Haarth.

The contents of the pan bubbled and Raven lifted it clear of the flames, pouring hot liquid into their tin cups. "I do understand," Malian repeated, taking the one he held out. "And we've forgotten so much, or suppressed the knowledge, that I need you to share what you know, however difficult I may find it." She paused, sniffing, then peered at her drink. "Is this Ishnapuri chocolate?"

"It is." He lifted his cup in salute. "Hedge knights are good at foraging."

"I think," Malian said, very dryly, "that unless you paid out the gold needed to buy it in Emer, having Ishnapuri chocolate might count as looting."

He smiled slightly. "Foraging, looting ... Either way, I thought we both needed something to counter last night's cold. And when we heard the dog barking, you looked like you'd seen a ghost."

Several, Malian thought bleakly, but kept both voice and expression light. "If it gets me chocolate, I'll see wraiths more often." She blew on the chocolate's surface to cool it, before taking a long sip. "Or perhaps whole legions of them, this is that good." Immediately, Malian remembered the armies in her vision and wished she had chosen a better jest. Curling her hands around the cup's warmth, she watched him over the rim. "I saw you," she said, "in my seer's vision. I'm almost sure it was you, anyway."

Raven raised his eyebrows, which she took as sufficient invitation to describe the ambush beneath a bruised sky. "I've *seen* it once before," she finished, "only some years ago now, before I met you." He was right last night, she decided: the young man on the horse had looked very different from the one sitting opposite her now. "This time I heard Amaliannarath's voice, saying that she could only save one. And in Stoneford, you said that you were the last from all three Lines of the Blood of Fire."

His expression had grown shuttered. "Yes," he said at last. "If that was your vision, then it was indeed me that you saw, on the day Amaliannarath snatched me from beneath the swords of Aranraith's killers."

Malian hesitated, because his expression was not inviting. But if she was truly to take the House of Fire as her own, she needed to know what she was dealing with. "Was it because of the sword?"

"It was." Malian thought that might be all he was going to say, but then Raven set his cup down. The metal clinked sharply against a stone. "There is always a price," he continued quietly, and Malian's heart jumped, because they were the words from her fever dream in Stoneford, the ones whispered out of Rowan Birchmoon's cairn. "What we can never know is how that price will be exacted. Khelor took the sword and triggered the geas it laid on him, and through him, on us all. Yet possession of such a weapon, and so great a secret, are difficult to conceal."

He paused as the blackbird sang again from the orchard, although she guessed he was not listening to its song, but gazing back down the tunnel of years to those long ago events. "Sun is by far the largest of the three nations of the Sworn, and Aranraith has been its prince for a very long time. He wanted the hero's arms for himself, but the helm had vanished before we reached the battlefield. By the time Khelor recovered sufficiently from dealing with the sword to take thought for the shield, its shards, too, were gone. Aranraith was furious, and it was inevitable his wrath would fall on Fire, believing we had appropriated all three weapons. For that reason alone, Amaliannarath said that we would have to flee."

"But Aranraith struck first?"

Raven nodded, his face obscured as he refilled her cup, so Malian watched the movement of his hands and the tattoos that circled his wrists, the lines blue in the early light. "Salar, Sun's Ascendant, is subtle, although some would just say cunning. Between the two of them, they left nothing to chance." Raven's voice remained as steady as his hands, although he had glanced toward the sun, so Malian still could not see his expression.

"They asked Amaliannarath to undertake a deep seeing for all the Sworn, tying her power up in that, but Salar must have been blocking her, in any case. It was only the first deaths that broke his working. By then the worst was already done, because Aranraith's forces had fallen on all three Lines of our Blood at once. Everyone died: Khelor of the First Line and Iriseult of the Second, with all their kin—and my extended family as well." He set the pan down again, and now

Malian wished she could look away from the bleakness in his face. "I was riding to my betrothal with a few close friends, our retainers and honor guards. You saw what happened, how they all died. I would have, too, except Amaliannarath snatched me away at the last."

Raven paused, his bleakness shifting into the stern lines Malian recognized from the Cave of Sleepers. "She only had an instant, from becoming aware of the attacks to deciding how to act. Afterward, I raged against her for saving me and not Iriseult or Khelor, but she would only say that it was already too late for them and she very nearly could not save me." If my vision was accurate, Malian thought, she was right. "Later, I was sorry for the recriminations I hurled at her. But at the time I was beside myself with grief, shock, and fury."

Amaliannarath would have understood that—although Malian wondered if the Ascendant might not have been suffering from shock as well. The whole story had a similar ring to that of the Derai and the Night of Death, and despite the sun's warmth, she wanted to shiver. "So it wasn't just that you were sick of war," she murmured, recalling Stoneford. "That you fled to Haarth, I mean."

Raven's smile was grim. "War-weariness was why we were apt to the sword's influence. The reason we fled so far was survival. Fire had always been the smallest of the Sworn's three nations, and we were reeling from the loss of almost all our Blood. We didn't know whether Lightning had been part of Sun's scheme either and we couldn't wait to find out, not with Aranraith pressing his advantage." The grimness faded. "But the reason we came here, in particular, was Amaliannarath's decision, part of her foreseeing. From what you've said, it may also have been driven by her private bargain with the sword. And she said that she would take us all, that she was capable of the feat."

Malian heard the grief, raw still after all this time, beneath his level tone. "'*I died a long time ago, so that they might live.*'" Softly, she quoted the words from her conversation with the ghost in the Cave of Sleepers. "But what she did . . . She must have opened a Great

Gate long before the Derai did, crossing time as well as worlds to bring you all here. And she did it on her own."

Raven nodded. "Largely on her own, because as with the Derai, our Blood provided our greatest adepts." The familiar sardonic edge touched his voice. "Aranraith's efforts in that respect left us with a disproportionate number of immunes, which has been useful to us as the Patrol. But it did not help Amaliannarath."

No, Malian thought. She half closed her eyes, studying the sun dots against her lids and recalling the Emerian folklore that whispered that the Patrol were demons, hiding their true nature behind masked helms. Once, if she had known they were Darksworn, she would have said that was true ... Lifting her gaze, she met Raven's again across the dwindling flames. "I *am* young, so perhaps that's why I find it hard to comprehend just how long you've lived—that you were alive when Yorindesarinen died." She drank the last of the chocolate, while the blackbird called again from further down the hill. "I know you crossed time with Amaliannarath and slept in the cave, but it's not *just* you and Fire. Emuun and Thanir and Aranraith, they were all alive then, too." Hylcarian had also warned her against Nirn in the Old Keep, which meant the sorcerer had to be at least five hundred years old. Malian guessed it was a lot more than that, though. "We thought the Golden Fire was immortal, or close to it, although the Derai never were ... " Briefly, she wrestled with the enormity of it all. "Are you immortal now? Was that part of your bargain with the maelstrom?"

"One does not bargain with the maelstrom." Raven had begun cleaning out the pan. "But one outcome of prolonged exposure to its power turned out to be greatly extended life. We can be killed, but none of us have died of old age for a very long time. Whether we are immortal or not remains to be seen." He paused. "As our life spans extended, all three nations of the Sworn had fewer and fewer children; I was born into almost our last generation. And no children have been born to Fire since we came to Haarth, despite being separated from the maelstrom for so long."

No children at all, Malian thought, shocked. There had been few enough in Night, compared with the River or Emer, and she wondered if that could be because her House stood farthest forward on the Wall of Night, closest to the maelstrom. Finally, she found her voice. "But Nherenor, the Darksworn envoy in Caer Argent, was young. I'm sure he was no older than me, if that."

"True enough." Raven finished with the pan and began packing away their food. "Yet I doubt he had many siblings or playmates growing up, if any."

Nor did I, Malian thought—but she was beginning to appreciate just how hard Nherenor's death would have struck Lightning. She frowned, recalling that misty dawn in Caer Argent and the Sworn youth laughing as he leapt to confront her. "Did you know Nherenor was Ilkerineth's son?"

Raven nodded. "Nindorith's presence in Caer Argent, and before that outside Tenneward Lodge, meant Ilkerineth had a hand in the game. When I saw the Lightning knights with their young lord at the tourney ground, I guessed the rest."

Malian studied their small fire, still thinking of Nherenor as she had last seen him, one moment laughing and alive, the next dead on the cobbles of a narrow alley. No children, she repeated, and wondered how many in Haarth, and probably among the Derai as well, would think prolonged life worth that price. Raven shook his head when she said so.

"They might reconsider when all whom they call friend, or come to love, live far shorter lives. After a time, they would find themselves drawing back from a world in which nothing else endures as they do, and in which they alone do not alter. Among the Sworn, there have been many whose minds have darkened and their hearts cooled, losing sight of friendship and love as they saw failure, savagery, and destruction endlessly repeated." He had not looked away from Malian in Stoneford, when he placed Yorindesarinen's sword in her hands, and he held her gaze now. "Some seek feeling at second hand. Sun's way, in particular, has been by inflicting pain. Others retreat into themselves or interact only within a small, closed circle. Some take their own lives."

Malian was silent, thinking that no one seemed less isolated and more alive than he did. "Even among the Patrol?" she asked.

"One reason we took up that service," he replied, "was to stay as close to the cycle of life and renewal, growth and change, as we could. The other was to earn our place in this world through serving it." Momentarily, his eyes dipped to the saddlebag he was opening, before meeting hers again. "Amaliannarath's argument was that children are part of life's cycle of renewal and change—and so, too, is death. Even before the sword, she felt that our alignment with the maelstrom had trapped us in stasis, which would end being worse than dying. *'I died a long time ago, so that they might live.'*" Raven repeated the quote. "She has already shared what lies at the heart of why we were apt to the sword's will, as well as her sacrifice."

He extracted a whetstone from the saddlebag and began to hone his sword. A swallow darted overhead, and Malian watched it for several seconds before turning back to Raven. "Given the current state of the Alliance, it's hard to see how rejoining the Derai will deliver either hope or life."

She caught the ghost of a smile as Raven sighted along the blade. "Whatever their flaws, the Derai have been proven right on one point: what the Alliance fights for is life itself. However stubborn and unbending, they remain part of that cycle, whereas the Sworn—" He paused as a second swallow joined the first, flitting from beneath the wayhouse eaves. "Fire's choice has never been between the Sworn and the Derai. It's between atrophy and life. That aside"—now the ghost smile became the hedge knight's twist of the mouth—"Amaliannarath foresaw hope if we allied ourselves with you, Malian. I would not go so far as to say that we're rejoining the Derai."

She smiled and raised a hand in a River fencer's gesture, acknowledging the humor, then almost immediately sobered as the swallows darted again. Soon, she reflected, they too will be leaving, fleeing south ahead of winter while I journey north.

Raven resheathed the sword and put the whetstone away. "Time we moved on," he said, and began extinguishing the fire.

Malian nodded and rose, stretching away the last of the night's stiffness before retrieving the horses. Hani snuffled against her coat, hoping for treats, and despite the previous night's violence, flight, and cold, as well as the darkness of her visions, Malian smiled. She also pushed the mare's questing nose away. "Perhaps tonight," she murmured, "if we can find a decent inn." She looked around to find Raven watching her from beside Peta. Momentarily, her smile included him, before fading as she considered what lay ahead.

They were to rendezvous with the rest of Fire near the trading post at Hedeld, on the Telimbras, country that was almost far enough north to count as the Wild Lands rather than the River. The Patrol had a fort and training grounds there, ideal for a large muster—and apart from the main road through the Barren Hills, the Telimbras offered the clearest route north. Malian knew the country from her years in Ar, but now her thoughts returned to Amaliannarath's whisper, ghosting through the Cave of Sleepers: *I died a long time ago, so that they might live.*

The dead Ascendant may have thought alliance with her would offer Fire hope and the potential for renewal, but events in Aeris, together with her visions, had deepened Malian's doubt over what lay ahead. The Shadow Band adept had learned to keep her own counsel, but the Heir of Night, raised between her father's scrupulous justice and the flame of Asantir's valor, felt that in this case honor compelled honesty. "The Shield of Stars was broken." Malian relived *seeing* the metal fragments underfoot as Raven swung into the saddle. "The Derai Alliance can no longer rely on the Golden Fire. And Amaliannarath, whatever hope she may have foreseen, is dead." Death down every road: Malian felt the chill touch of fear although she kept her voice level. "Whoever stands with me will bear the brunt of the conflict that is coming, and despite your longevity you can still be killed. So riding in my shadow may not bring hope but the extinction of your House."

Raven was motionless as a statue on Peta's back, his expression unreadable. "What do you propose?"

Malian frowned up at him. "The Patrol has kept the road and river safe for a millennium, so taking it out of the River lands would be the same as taking the Ara-fyr away from the Aralorn-Jhaine border." She resisted folding her arms in the face of his continued silence. "I'm not being altruistic. The peace of the River, even more than that of Emer and the rest of the Southern Realms, is vital to our supply. Disrupting that successfully, let alone militarizing the River against us, could well win the war for the Swarm."

Raven was regarding her as closely as she had seen him study unknown terrain. "So you think the Patrol should stay on the River?"

"Yes." Strategically, he can't disagree, Malian thought. Unless taking the Patrol to the Wall will defeat the Swarm quickly—but we both know that's not going to happen.

"I think you are being altruistic." Raven, too, was level. "The River argument has merit, but the counter is that even if Fire won't turn the tide of the war, having an armed force to command may open up opportunities you can't foresee or won't be able to exploit on your own."

He's right, Malian acknowledged silently. Sooner or later—probably sooner—I'll need Fire. Yet the moment she thought it, the vision of Ar assailed by war rose before her, together with the aftermath of Yorindesarinen's battle with the Chaos Worm. Foreseeing might never be certain, but both visions had been very clear.

"I'm the Chosen of Mhaelanar as well as the Heir of the Derai." This time Malian did fold her arms. "If the prophecy of the One is going to work out in my favor, then arguably it will do so regardless of armies and powers. If it isn't"—if prophecy is going to fail me as it did Yorindesarinen, she added silently—"then having the House of Fire with me isn't going to change that outcome either."

"You left out being a Dancer of Kan, a scholar, a sometime bargee, and a priestess-queen of Jhaine." Peta tossed her head at the same time as Raven spoke, momentarily distracting Malian from the fact that he was smiling at her: not with the hedge knight's sardonic expression, or Aravenor's graver smile from the Stoneford chapel, but an easing into light and warmth. The smile reminded her of Nherenor—and she wondered if she was catching a glimpse of another young prince of the Sworn, before war and betrayal, long years and bitter loss, transformed him into someone that even Emuun, a close kinsman, did not recognize.

I'm staring, Malian thought. But then Raven spoke again, with the hedge knight's familiar intonation, and the moment, like the smile, had passed. "I think we both know that prophecy doesn't work that way. Fortunately, Amaliannarath was farsighted and gave us the means to hedge against exactly the concerns you raise. Fire *will* march, but the Patrol will not leave the River."

Now it was Malian's turn to remain unmoving, keeping her arms folded and her regard cool while she traversed her first recollection of the Cave of Sleepers, from the moment of her arrival until she spoke with Amaliannarath's ghost. The cavern had been immense and entirely filled by Fire's sleeping warriors. Yet when she had returned during the Midsummer rite, while walking the path of earth and moon, the cave had been empty, even its ghost presence departed. Reality or illusion, Malian wondered now, knowing that in the realms beyond the Gate of Dreams the dead were always more powerful than the living. Illusion, though, was the only solution that matched Raven's riddle. "The Patrol isn't all of you," she said. "Some of Fire never woke from sleep."

His answering look was grimly appreciative. "Initially we all woke, but it was part of Amaliannarath's spell that we could sleep again at will. A few have stayed awake throughout, but the rest have taken turns through the long years, serving with the Patrol and then sleeping again, while dreaming the passage of events." The appreciative look grew rueful. "I intended discussing all of this once we reached Hedeld, but I should have known you would be thinking well ahead."

Not far enough, Malian thought, to have decided on a strategy for when I reach the Wall. Afraid Raven would read that truth in her face, she shifted her gaze to the swallows, chasing each other through the bright air—and her seer's power coiled around her again, swifter than the snake that the Aeris caravan guard had called war. Only this time, Malian's inner sight opened into the oak forest that was the Emerian portal into the Gate of Dreams.

Drifts of mist lay between black trunks, and a russet fox slipped out of the undergrowth, stopping with one paw raised to gaze at her from eyes she knew would be the color of barley ale. Above its head, a knot in an oak trunk twisted into a fox's mask, before shifting into the face of Lord Falk, Castellan of Normarch and leader of the Emerian Oakward. The russet fox slipped away.

"Ah," Lord Falk's expression was as inscrutable as any Raven could muster. "I wondered when you would come calling on me again."

"I believe we need to talk," Malian told him. "Keep the horses close," she added to Raven, as the blackbird trilled again from the abandoned orchard—and she opened up a portal through the medium of her vision, stepping out of the daylight world and into the Gate of Dreams.

19

Rift

The far side of Thanir's portal was hot, the air dry enough to suck the moisture out of every breath. Yet despite his armor, he showed no sign of being affected by the heat. Instead he waited, one hand resting on the pommel of his curved sword as he studied this particular pocket universe within the Gate of Dreams. Ahead of him, dunes climbed ochre and tawny through layers of heat, their crests wavering toward the baleful glare of a molten sun. He turned, the shield on his arm flashing, and took in a wide, dry riverbed, dotted with spines of thorn brush, and low brown hills beyond. Nothing moved, but he could hear a steady insect drone nearby.

The body was staked over mounded earth on the far side of a thornbush. The drone was from flies clotted on the wounds where eyes and nose, lips and ears and genitals had once been. A pattern Thanir recognized as runes had been carved into the victim's skin, and he could see the red lines where the blood had run, despite the skin having burned raw in the sun. His gaze swept the surrounding terrain again but it remained empty, motionless except for the layered heat. Returning his attention to the corpse, he placed his shield against the thornbush, snaring the sun's reflection in its burnished surface. Yet neither Thanir nor the shield cast any shadow across the arid ground as he stepped away from the body. When he spoke, his tone was conversational. "It's always surprised me that you and Aranraith don't get along better. You have the same appetite for pain and death."

The sun in the shield wavered, its zenith and nadir extending into a line around which all other light bent. Slowly, the line wavered toward Thanir, and although he did not look toward the shield's surface, he smiled as though at some secret jest. Keeping his eyes on the heat shimmer between the staked out body and the dunes, he spoke a single, grating word—and the shimmer parted around a flaw in the air that matched the image in the shield.

"The difference," Emuun's voice said, out of the rift, "is that Aranraith perpetrates his cruelties because he loves them, whereas my object is to terrorize and so weaken my enemies." As he spoke, the fissure spat a small cloud of grit toward the shield, but it exploded in midair, well clear of the burnished gleam.

"An observer might be forgiven for mistaking professional pride for pleasure, since the end result is the same." Thanir did not appear to expect a reply, for he added, "I'd forgotten your anteroom into Haarth's deserts, until I realized the only way you could have escaped my portal was via another that opened inside it." His tone grew dry as the heat. "I imagine your allies did that for you, since your abilities, however impressive, don't include gates."

The air within the rift swirled, momentarily assuming the form of a man. "My dealings with the great djinn are founded on mutual aid. Having such dealings does not make me a traitor."

"You won't be the first, on either side of our conflict, who's turned native." Thanir was dispassionate. "But you've been using our runes to feed them blood and magic."

"They have a taste for it, and once sated, offer gifts in return. If benefiting from that equates with turning native, then I'm guilty."

"Yet still deny the treachery." Thanir studied the bulge of light and shadow around the rift. "Why not come with me, then, and defend yourself to Aranraith and Salar?"

Emuun's laugh rasped through the heat. The line within the shield had stopped moving but continued to ripple, bulging out and in like the split in the air. "As you yourself said in the night fair, their way of asking questions is too similar to my own. You've nerve coming here, though, even with Aranraith driving the hunt. Not," the face-stealer added, "that you are precisely here, are you?" His laugh rasped again: "Wise."

Thanir shrugged. "We all know your liking for sending unambig-uous messages to your enemies, as you have done with the Ishnapuri magi through torturing their adepts." He paused. "That seemed as good a reason as any for me to mindwalk, rather than coming here in my physical body once I decided to speak with you privately."

The flaw in the air hung motionless—but within the shield its mirror image began drifting toward Thanir again. When he spoke another word in the grating language of stone, the fissure wavered first one way and then the other as though caught in contrary winds. Finally it split apart to reveal Emuun, who made a show of applauding his adversary.

"You know your runes. And how to manipulate the Gate of Dreams. But if you want to talk rather than bringing your shadow hunt after me, something must have changed ..." He frowned. "Surely you're not concerned by a sword-for-hire with a few adept's skills thrown in? You know how common that is here. Most of them are barely aware they have power, let alone knowing what to do with it. Easy meat," he added, a feral grin displacing the frown.

"Your crow warrior had a very interesting sword." Thanir was measured. "She also countermanded my spell holding the exits from the building closed."

Emuun grunted, his frown returning. "I agree, that does go beyond a few adept's skills. But it doesn't explain why you're suddenly inter-ested in talking. You could hunt her down yourself, if you wanted to." His hard eyes narrowed, considering possibilities. "Something you saw but I didn't, beyond the hedge adept and our little conflict."

"The crow warrior countered my closing spell." Thanir spoke

softly. "But *before* that, someone else put an axe through the main doors."

A ripple shivered across Emuun's stolen face and as instantly stilled. His eyes remained old and dark, twin pits focused on Thanir. "Another immune—and in Aeris. You're right, that is interesting."

Thanir's smile did not reach his eyes. "An immune was involved in foiling our coteries in Emer as well."

Emuun bared his teeth. "So now that doubt has been sown in your mind, perhaps you'd best see where the trail leads."

This time, genuine humor touched Thanir's expression. "You know that's not how this works. You're the one Aranraith wants, whatever the truth of events in Emer. But if you find the Aeris pair and learn exactly who they are—" The barbed shoulders shrugged again. "If you can prove there is at least one other immune operating in Haarth, that should persuade Nirn and Salar. Nothing will sway Aranraith in your favor, but if you were to bring him the sword and both heads, a native immune and an adept for his trophy wall, he may be appeased. So long as I know you're on that trail, I'm willing to suspend the hunt."

"Hunting is one thing, bringing down the prey another." Emuun's gaze rested on the mutilated corpse, his tone more thoughtful than aggressive. "You obviously think this Aeris business is important, so why not pursue it yourself? Why make bargains with me?"

"The Aeris pair intrigue me, but I have more pressing business to resume in the north." Thanir rubbed one gauntleted thumb against the pommel of his longsword. "While your only hope is to deflect Aranraith's wrath. Even you, Emuun, won't be able to elude his hunters forever."

Emuun scowled. "Not if he calls on Salar. I do know that. But why is the great Lord Thanir suddenly so concerned for my well-being?" Sand eddied around him, although there was no wind, and the flies rose, too, replicating the spiral of sand. The outlines of both warriors blurred as the facestealer's gaze quartered the horizon, from the crest of the dunes to the rim of the low hills. "This place is starting to disintegrate." Slowly, both sand and flies resettled, and his eyes narrowed. "That had better not be your doing."

"You know what this is, or should. It's the same reason I prefer not to lose one of our most experienced and ruthless agents—so long as we can be sure you're not behind recent setbacks in the River and Emer."

"The maelstrom," Emuun said slowly. "Nirn has hinted, but you know he's no longer what he once was."

Thanir said nothing. In the mirror, a shadow darkened the reflected dunes, although no cloud marred the sky overhead. Emuun studied it, his expression set. "Aranraith likes playthings," he observed, "as does Salar. Perhaps they might prefer the Aeris pair alive—if I accept your offer."

Thanir's image was fading. "Do as you will, Emuun. But there is no more time: you must decide whether you are for us or against us. If you are with us, then you must prove it, or flee fast and far." His waning gaze rested on the mutilated corpse. "And cease feeding Nirn's assassin agents, but more importantly, the taste of his magic, to your djinn allies. The recoil of this one's death was felt by his acolytes in Grayharbor, and although they thought it was weather-worker magic, I suspect Nirn knew better. And if word were to come to Salar—" Thanir left the sentence hanging, like the threat, as his form vanished from the portal. A moment later his shield, too, disappeared.

Emuun cursed, a pithy necklace of expletives, while the sun's eye blazed and the air roared like a furnace. "If the fates are kind, they'll give me *him* beneath my knife, before I'm done." He spat on the corpse. "Assassins, adepts, the high-and-mighty Blood of the Sworn: they all think they're strong, but every one of them screams and begs in the end." He kicked the corpse and the flies stirred, but did not rise. Drawing a dagger, Emuun scored the tip across his palm, dripping blood along the lines carved into the assassin's flesh. "At least I put his death to better use than Nirn was making of his life."

"Your enemy was too cunning for you." The voice sighed out of the air, a susurration of wind through sand. "A spirit sending is far more difficult to ensnare than a physical form, and he used the shield as a mirror to prevent me manifesting and springing your trap."

Emuun grunted. "He's clever, no question. And knows too cursed much about what we're about, Amaliannarath take him." He paused, watching the careful drip of blood slow. "He's right, though. If the maelstrom is rising, even vengeance will have to wait."

"You promised us blood and magic, as well as your enemies' deaths to feed our power."

"I have given you both many times over since we made our bargain." Emuun licked at the last drip, lingering over blood and salt and sweat. "Thanir is doubly right, curse him. I need Aranraith off my back, else I'll be dead and there'll be no more of this brew for you. And we'll all be dead if the maelstrom rises and we let the wave edge overtake us."

"So you say." The murmur rustled from all sides.

Emuun shrugged. "You felt what touched this place before; the way the whole construct shivered. Believe in that if you don't believe me." He knelt, his forefinger tracing fresh blood over the section of pattern where the drips had fallen. "But you've had your magic and death, and now I've given my own blood to fuel this hunt, in lieu of what you hoped for. It's time for your side of the bargain."

"A bargain is a bargain," the voice of sand and wind agreed, "even if we did not taste the greater death you held out to us."

Slowly, other voices whispered through the first, rustling together like flames in a grate. *We will aid your hunt. A bargain made must indeed be kept, and the greater death was not a promise, only a possibility. Besides, given what rides on your hunter's back, the trap may well have turned and bitten us.*

Emuun rose and began using swift, bold gestures to draw the same pattern as the freshly blooded runes onto the air. Wisps of steam curled around the invisible inscriptions left by his hand, and if he heard the whispered observation, he did not respond.

PART IV

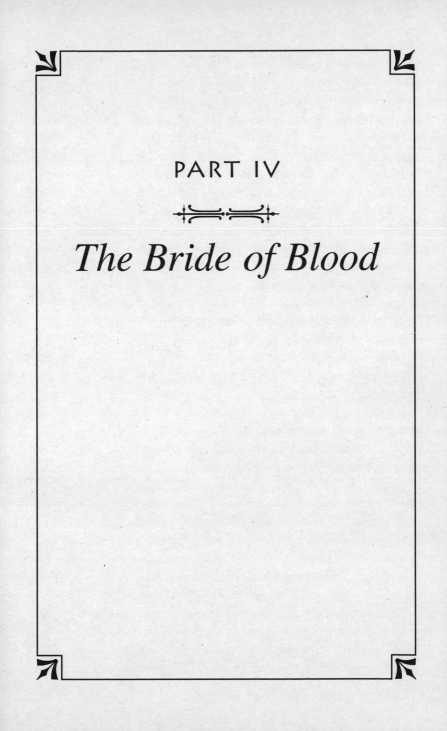

The Bride of Blood

20

Emissaries of Night

Myr's head ached from the weight of her hair, coiled and pinned tight beneath an even heavier jeweled headdress. The gauze veil, also a-glimmer with jewels, stood out stiffly to either side of her face and made it difficult to see without fully turning her head. And if I do that, Myr thought, I might swipe one of the stewards as they bend to serve us. Terror of so public a display of maladroitness turned her first hot, then cold—so she kept the painted mask that was her face turned rigidly forward.

She had protested when Ilai, a new attendant seconded from Liankhara's household, had insisted on applying the elaborate formal makeup, but was glad, now, that the watchful gathering would only see an archetypal Daughter of Blood. No one, she felt certain, could detect any sort of personality, let alone Myrathis the Mouse, beneath what felt like a porcelain glaze over her true features. At the same time, Myr knew that few of those seated in the banqueting hall would care whether a personality existed beneath the mask. She was a figurehead, that was all, a piece to be played in Blood's bid for Derai power, where only strategic gain mattered and Earl and Heir alone were not considered expendable players. Myr's reflections heightened her awareness of her father's impassive presence, seated beside her in his great chair, but she resisted the impulse to try and read his face since that would mean turning her head. As for her siblings, she did not need to look around to know where they were.

Myr had been told that the House of Night still maintained the old Derai custom whereby Heir and Earl sat apart, but Kharalthor was seated at their father's right hand, in what Blood regarded as the Heir's place. Her own elevation to a place on the Earl's left reflected her new status as Bride, displacing Hatha to one end of the high table while Huern sat at the other. The rest of Myr's siblings were also at the Earl's table, interspersed with their leading Blood guests and the Earl of Night's emissaries. Only Liankhara was absent, but Myr knew she would be secreted somewhere close by, observing the play of events.

Besides, although Ilai had been seconded to the Bride's household, Myr felt sure that she still reported to Liankhara. Her other siblings, too, would doubtless have their agents in place, to keep them informed of the Bride's business ... Myr kept her eyes lowered but was aware of Sardonya's cool gaze from several places away, while Parannis lounged directly opposite. Her half-brother exuded such sleek satisfaction that Myr suspected the whispers must be correct and he had been calling out those he considered enemies, killing or maiming them in secret duels.

He's cruel, she thought, and repressed a shiver, certain the supposed enmity was just a pretext—and because she had learned young that Parannis was the brother to most actively avoid. She also wondered if he was deliberately defying their father. Shortly before the Night marriage was first raised, the Earl had forbidden Parannis's duels, saying no House could afford to alienate so many retainers. Yet Myr suspected that Parannis disdained such considerations, just as he derided the Honor Code as outmoded.

Right now, he was also ignoring the Night and Blood guests seated to either side of him. At least Anvin and Sardonya were maintaining a semblance of courtesy, even if they, too, disdained this marriage and believed Blood should lead the Nine Houses as of right. Even

Sarein, who was actively establishing herself in the so-called New Blood faction, with its Haarth ambitions for the Derai Alliance, was nodding at whatever her dinner partners said.

All the same, Sarein's small smile scraped at Myr's nerves, in much the same way as one of the hairpins, inserted at too sharp an angle, was a line of pain along her scalp. Her half-sister had been wearing an identical smile when the ruling kin left the High Hall in formal procession—and she managed to step on the heavy train that trailed from Myr's shoulders. If it had been Sardonya, Myr might have accepted the misstep as accidental, but she knew Sarein's action was a deliberate attempt to humiliate her before the vast gathering of Blood. It might have worked, too, except that Myr had guessed she would be made to suffer for walking ahead of all her siblings, except Kharalthor, in the formal ceremonies. Her elevation might be dictated by tradition, reinforced by the Earl's command, but Sarein, like her twin, would not care. If she perceived a slight, sooner or later someone would have to pay.

Myr had not expected the retribution to come so publicly, though, especially when it was the House of Blood's prestige at stake, not just her own. Despite her wariness, she would have stumbled, perhaps even fallen outright, except her new attendants had been walking to either side and Ilai—under the pretext of adjusting Myr's veil—had seized her arm, counteracting the abrupt jerk on her shoulders. The attendant might be Liankhara's agent, but Myr had still been grateful for both her supporting hand and presence of mind as Ilai signaled the other attendants to gather up the sweeping train. Otherwise only Huern had appeared to notice anything amiss, first studying Ilai and the train with his most inscrutable expression, before shifting the same enigmatic look past them to Sarein.

Huern was wearing the same expression now as he listened to the dinner guests on either side. Myr had always found him difficult to read, but thought his incalculable demeanor had grown more pronounced since the Night contract was proposed. As if Myr's thoughts had drawn his attention, Huern turned her way, so she concentrated on making a show of eating, although everything tasted like sawdust. But between Huern's scrutiny, Sarein's smile, and Parannis lounging opposite, she had to grip the utensils fiercely to prevent her fingers trembling. When she did finally look up, Sarein's smile had been redirected toward the Night guest on Kharalthor's right. Teron of Cloud Hold: Myr repeated the name from the list she had committed to memory. He was strikingly handsome, and Sarein's look had grown almost avaricious. Sardonya, too, was smiling as she studied the young Night warrior and Myr found herself hoping that Teron of Cloud Hold had well-honed survival skills.

"Are you looking forward to judging the contest in your honor, Lady Myrathis?" the guest to her left asked.

Asantir, Commander of Night, Myr told herself, although she had not needed a list to identify the quiet, keen-faced warrior who led Night's emissaries into the High Hall. The Commander was known by reputation in the Red Keep, chiefly as the Earl of Night's sure right hand and foremost envoy in his endeavors to reunite the Nine Houses. She was also said to be a priest lover, an apostate who bent the terms of the Derai Alliance's Blood Oath even if she never—quite—broke them. Since the betrothal was confirmed, Anvin and Parannis had both informed Myr that the Commander and the Earl were so close they must have been lovers in the past, if not now. Myr was far more interested in the rumor that the Commander of Night had once slain a siren worm with a black blade, but knew Anvin and Parannis would say that Night generated such tales to shore up its failing leadership. Siren worms, after all, belonged in fireside stories, the sort used to frighten children into good behavior.

Narn of Bronze Hold, on the Commander's far side, had kept Asantir engaged in discussion since they sat down, canvassing weapons and armor before he expanded on boundary patrols and tactics. But now I have to make conversation, Myr thought, conscious of the lengthening pause. Her lips parted, but before she could force words out, Kharalthor leaned forward. "My young sister will sit with us, Commander Asantir, but you'll find the judging falls to our lot."

Myr's gaze slid sideways in time to catch the elegant lift of her neighbor's brows. "Indeed?" The Commander's nod acknowledged Kharalthor before she turned back to Myr. "Is that because you feel it's important you show no favoritism?"

Myr felt transfixed, aware that almost every face in the banqueting hall, not just those around the Earl's table, was focused on her—but Kharalthor's frown warned that it was time to pull herself together. "No," Myr whispered, before swallowing in an effort to strengthen her voice. "The contest must be completely open, that is one of our oldest traditions. But I have no familiarity with war as you have, or my lord brother, our Battlemaster." Her voice still felt faint against the weight of the banqueters' attention. "I judge it best to be guided by your experience."

Kharalthor's frown vanished as he nodded. Instinctively, Myr looked toward the Earl but saw no visible change in his expression, although Hatha grinned at her from the far end of the table. Parannis was smiling, too, as he studied Asantir. "Mind you," he said loudly, "given the record of Night's honor guards these days, even our youngest sister might well prove a sounder judge of warriors than their former captain."

If the hall had been quiet before, waiting for Myr to speak, the silence now was absolute as every stare switched to the Commander of Night. Teron of Cloud Hold's hands clenched and the muscles in his neck were rigid, although however much he might want to, he did not rise from his chair. Still Myr could almost feel the strain in him from three places away, while beside her, Commander Asantir appeared unruffled. Yet surely, Myr thought, *surely* she must answer or Night's honor be forsworn.

At the same time, she saw the dilemma, for how could a guest call out the Earl of Blood's son in the Red Keep's own banquet hall? Although if the Commander of Night did not— If she doesn't, Myr told herself, she will be held a coward anyway. And if she does, then both she and this new treaty with Night may be equally dead. So Father has to intervene: as Earl, he must be seen to act. He *has* to, Myr repeated, unable to shut out the stares, most appraising or carefully neutral, but a significant number openly malicious as the silence stretched—until finally, Earl Sardon spoke.

"Doubtless, my son, it was your zeal to support the Bride's role as judge that led you to misspeak our guest. Inadvertently, I am sure," her father said levelly. "Nonetheless, you will withdraw your remarks and apologize."

Many of those watching exchanged glances, or openly sat back. Myr held her breath, because she could see the gleam in Parannis's eyes, but the Commander of Night spoke before he could respond. "The Son of Blood's championship of his sister's judgment does him credit, Earl Sardon," she said, in her quiet way. "I also applaud your concern, Lord Parannis, for the record of those who will guard Lady Myrathis once she is Countess of Night. Although I am sure that you are not questioning the searching inquiries your Lord Father"—here she inclined her head to the Earl—"made on the same matter before setting his seal to the marriage treaty."

More glances were exchanged and several surreptitious looks directed toward the Earl, but Commander Asantir was still speaking. "If it will ease your fears, Lord Parannis, I'm happy to give both you and Lady Myrathis the same assurance now that I have already made to your father. The former Honor Captain, the one who made the guard selections that so rightly concern you, has since made the full restitution that both the Earl and House of Night, and his personal honor, required."

Myr shivered, because full restitution could mean execution or the invitation to commit suicide, both traditional Derai remedies in such cases. But the murmur that ran around the room suggested approval, and although some might still doubt Commander Asantir's courage in private, it would not be possible to speak publicly without appearing to doubt Earl Sardon as well. Myr wondered if that was what Parannis wanted, or whether he had simply overreached himself.

"Your words, Commander, honor both Blood and Night." Myr did not need to look to know that her father's face, like his voice, would give nothing away. She avoided meeting Parannis's gaze, but his exaggerated earnestness jangled her nerve endings as badly as Sarein's smile.

"I assure you, sir, I am fully aware that the Commander stands as proxy for the Earl of Night in these ceremonies. And you know that I would never insult my sister's future husband."

No, Myr thought, but I'm your *half*-sister. She wondered how many present knew that Parannis was always careful to observe that distinction. When she slanted a look at Commander Asantir, trying to discern her reaction, the Night warrior's expression was as impassive as Huern's, watching from the far end of the table.

"Your motivation, my son, is well understood." Earl Sardon, too, was imperturbable. "Nonetheless, the honor of House and keep require that you apologize to the Commander."

Myr, watching covertly, thought Parannis's mouth tightened, but the movement was too small to be sure. Graceful as an uncoiling snake, he rose and bowed to Asantir. "I apologize for any inadvertent insult," he said smoothly. "As redress for my error, I shall withdraw."

Myr could not help admiring the way his words said one thing on the surface and quite another if you listened to them another way. But Parannis was already pacing from the hall, acknowledging those along his route with a smile to one side, a lift of his eyebrows to the other. Myr wondered if some present might rise and follow him, but apparently even his New Blood adherents dared not go so far. Or perhaps the weight of their oaths to Earl and Heir still restrained them, no matter what they might think of the House of Night, its Earl, and the apostate Commander who sat, outwardly unperturbed, in their midst.

What is she thinking, though? Myr thought: she can't have missed that Parannis really made no apology at all. If Myr were in the Commander's place, one of only a small group of emissaries in the heart of another House, she would be terrified—and immediately realized she could well find herself in exactly that situation when her Blood retinue departed the Keep of Winds. Momentarily, her hands shook, but she made herself focus on Sarein, who was leaning forward.

"You must forgive my poor brother, Commander." Sarein turned the full sweetness of her smile onto Asantir. "He can be *so* careless in his speech, but I assure you he is very conscious, indeed we all are, that you are said to have hunted down Night's miscreant guards and slain them with your own hands." Her widened eyes gazed around the table. "I am sure we all applaud such loyalty and dedication."

Only Sarein, Myr thought, staring at the food congealing on her plate, could manage that innocuous tone while implying the Commander might have been silencing the traitorous guards, rather than meting out justice. Yet the same possibility had occurred to Myr when she first heard the story ... She stole another glance at the Commander of Night, but if Asantir felt Sarein's barbs, any flinch was well concealed. "I strive to serve Earl and House to the best of my ability, Lady Sarein. If I succeed, that is applause enough for any warrior."

She sounded exactly like one of Earl Sardon's life-sworn warriors, and Myr was conscious of a flash of disappointment—until Asantir smiled, an expression reminiscent of the slender blade Taly carried in her boot. "Although the forsworn guards were as much a murder weapon as the arrows they loosed. The hunt for those who forged the weapon, and directed it, is not yet done. And won't be, until they are all dead."

Myr was still thinking about the Commander's words when she finally sat in her dressing room and let Ilai lift the headdress and veil clear. Many in the banquet chamber had applauded the sentiment, while Sarein sat back, balked of her prey. But Myr, her eyes darting along the table, had seen the faint narrowing of Huern's eyes and suspected that he, too, had caught the implication that Commander Asantir might be hunting here, in the Red Keep.

How my head aches, Myr thought—only now it was not just from tension and the weight of the headdress. Kharalthor had expressed surprise that the murder of Earl Tasarion's former consort could be more than just an isolated incident, the perpetrators rotten wood that needed cutting out of Night's Honor Guard. Myr, though, had only been surprised at how little shock she felt that Asantir believed the matter went further. She stared into the mirror as Ilai began unpinning her hair, and thought her eyes looked haunted: by how much her father and elder siblings wanted the Night marriage, and fear of what might have been done to bring it about.

I doubt my own family, she thought, and would have shivered if Ilai had not been there.

"Completely unsuitable, of course." A voice spoke from the adjoining dayroom, and Myr recognized the speaker as Kylin, another of her new attendants. A smothered laugh followed before Vela, a second newcomer, murmured back. Her words were indistinct, but despite the new, much larger suite of rooms allocated to Myr as Bride of Blood, both must know that the door between the dressing room and the dayroom was open, so there was a good chance Myr would overhear.

Kylin is like Kolthis, Myr thought. She may not actively intend me to hear, but she doesn't care if I do. Behind her, Ilai's hands had stilled briefly, but now she laid the hairpins aside as a man's voice joined the dayroom conversation. "I'd say that suit of armor is proof Night's intelligence network is no patch on Lady Liankhara's."

One of the new guards, Myr thought. She had not yet learned all their voices, or the names that went with them. Both the maids tittered, although Myr knew their mirth was directed as much at Night this time, as at her. Besides, she could hardly be angry with her attendants when Kharalthor had sat with his hand concealing his lower face while the Night armor was presented as her betrothal gift. Myr closed her eyes against the memory, but pretended it was because Ilai had begun to wipe away the makeup mask.

"Your troth bracelet is a noble gift, Lady Myrathis." Ilai spoke softly, but Myr almost opened her eyes again, she was so surprised. Does Liankhara's agent feel sorry for me? she wondered, curious behind her shut lids.

"Yes," she replied, because the bracelet—interlocking yellow- and white-gold bands in the form of a warrior's vambrace, with a spinel as its centerpiece—was a marvel of the goldsmith's art. Yet whatever gifts Aralth, her father's chamberlain, had selected for the Earl of Night could hardly be less appropriate than a suit of armor and a vambrace bracelet were for her. Clearly, Myr thought, the Earl of Night still believes he's getting a true Daughter of Blood as his wife. She smiled a little ruefully as Ilai's light eyes met hers in the mirror.

"You're amused, Lady Myrathis?" The attendant wore her hair concealed beneath a dark, close-wrapped hood, a practice still followed by widows from the traditionalist holds.

I must ask about her husband once I know her better, Myr thought, even if she does report back to Liankhara. Especially, she added wryly, as a large part of the keep does that. "By the armor, yes," she replied. She dared a grimace for the first time since Ilai had applied the makeup, long hours before, knowing Taly would say that she could make the gift meaningful by learning to use the armor effectively. "Although it could hardly weigh less than today's regalia, so perhaps I should wear it to the contest of arms tomorrow."

Ilai appeared to consider the idea. "If it were Blood armor, Lady Myrathis, then yes. But since it's not—" Her shrug made it clear that wearing Night armor was not an option. "A pity, since you will have to be sewn into tomorrow's robes. So why not go encased in armor instead?"

Is she sharing a joke with me? Myr wondered, but Ilai was already busy pouring fresh water into a basin. By the time she finished, the moment had passed, and they both remained silent as the attendant completed her work. Almost, Myr reflected, as though we're frightened by what a simple jest between us might mean. But the hint of shared humor gave her the courage to have Ilai dismiss all those waiting in the dayroom, while she retreated into her bedchamber.

Alone at last, Myr thought, leaning back against the closed door. Such moments would be rare during the coming week, since the Bride must attend all stages of the Honor Contest. To preside over the competition with Kharalthor and Commander Asantir, she reminded herself—and would have laughed out loud except that someone might still be listening. All the same, Myr knew she would need to pay attention out of respect for the competitors, even if Kharalthor did not expect her to contribute to the selection process.

The Bride must also attend the banquet on the second night, held to honor the contestants who had excelled in the individual competitions and were proceeding to the two days of group contests. A rest day would follow before the final grand melee, but Myr's time would be taken up by formal receptions for Blood's hold and clan leaders, as well as any representatives from other Houses. The Honor Captain and Guard would be named on the fifth day of competition, following the melee, with one final night of feasting for the successful candidates and the gathered House.

As if all that were not enough, Myr would have to wear two different costumes on the days when there were both contests and feasting, and possibly change a third time for the formal receptions. Aralth, as well as Ise and various of Myr's siblings, had emphasized that each successive costume must be more elaborate than the last, because what the Bride wore reflected on Blood's prestige. Consequently, Myr had spent long hours being draped in linen and sumptuous velvets from the River cities, together with the silks and frail gauzes of Ishnapur. An Heir's ransom in fabric and jewels, she reflected now. She suspected that the cost of her wardrobe for these ceremonies, together with the wedding clothes she would take to the Keep of Winds, would keep Blood's army in uniforms for a year. And Blood was the largest House in the Derai Alliance—larger even than Night, Myr thought, pulling on her nightdress and climbing into bed.

After the initial relief of resting her aching head on the pillow, she kept returning to Sarein's smile and Parannis's false earnestness, and the way her father had let them play their games unchecked. Myr tried to reassure herself that Night's emissaries had been welcomed formally, but knew it would not be the first time that the laws of Derai hospitality had been broken by a blade in the dark. It could not be open murder, though, not if her father wanted this marriage and the potential path to leadership of the Derai Alliance. But if the Commander of Night were to fall as a result of more subtle means—well, that would be a blow Earl Tasarion would need time to recover from, undermining his attempt to rebuild the Derai Alliance while Blood consolidated its own leadership claims.

Seen in that light, I'm not so much a bride, Myr decided, as a dagger poised against the Earl of Night's throat. Surely he must know that . . . Although perhaps he saw no choice, since he needed a wife recognized by the Alliance and an Heir for his House. After all, despite Derai custom, none of his marriage emissaries were drawn from Night's ruling line. Because Earl Tasarion, Myr thought, has no blood kin to send.

If Night falls, all fall. Reflexively, she repeated the old warning and wondered if the Earl of Night and his House truly believed it anymore, since Blood—almost openly—did not. And what about Commander Asantir? she asked herself. What will she do, what *can* she do, if the trail from the murder of her Earl's consort does lead back to Blood? Appeal to my father, I suppose . . . Myr would not let herself consider that the trail might lead to the Earl himself and what that might mean. Unable to lie still, she flung back the covers and ghosted through her dressing room, easing the door into the dayroom ajar. The lamps had been turned down but their muted glow illuminated the black armor on its stand, with Night's winged horse emblem glittering on the breastplate. Myr hesitated, checking for loiterers, before crossing to study the armor more closely.

The craftsmanship was easily as good as the best work done by Blood's armorers. White gold gleamed on gorget, vambraces, and greaves, while diamonds glittered on the winged horse device and around the elaborate belt buckle. If the Bride's clothes and jewelry added up to an Heir's ransom, this armor would fetch a royal price in the Derai's trade with Haarth. An apt counter to her own House's display of wealth and power, Myr supposed, tracing the winged horse insignia with a fingertip. "Armor fit for a warrior queen," she murmured. "But that's not me."

"You could make it your own." Myr whirled to face Taly, who had appeared in the entrance to the adjoining reception suite. The ensign frowned around the dayroom. "There should be a guard on either side of this door."

"I sent them away. Surely," Myr protested, seeing Taly's expression, "guards on the suite's outer doors are enough?"

The ensign shook her head. "Not when the keep's overflowing with warriors we've never met. Plus a Sea House envoy's here already, to witness the contest and travel on to your wedding."

"We're friendly with Sea." Myr had seen the Sea House colors among those gathered in the High Hall, although the subsequent banquet had been for the leaders of Blood and their Night guests only. "You can't think their envoy poses a threat?"

"It's a tepid friendliness at best. And they, like most of the Alliance, won't favor this marriage." Taly's gaze swept the room again. "I'm sure Mistress Ise has explained how it will alter the balance of power between the Houses."

"I didn't need Ise to tell me." With any other guard, Myr would have rolled her eyes, at least inwardly. "But if you're afraid of assassins, our enemies will know there are other Daughters of Blood if anything happens to me."

"Two of whom have publicly denigrated the marriage." The ensign's voice was flat. "My orders are for guards on both sides of the inner as well as the outer doors, excepting only your bedchamber—unless we're really worried."

"Then I'd never sleep." Myr folded her arms. "I already can't. And my head aches."

"Too many dress fittings and not enough training." Taly grinned at Myr's grimace of denial. "If you're physically tired enough, you will sleep, Lady Mouse." Her gesture took in the grand new suite and tomorrow's robes already draped on a stand facing the armor. "Training would get you away from all this. You have only to send for me, or Dab, when you want to escape. You could say you need to accustom yourself to wearing Night's gift."

"Except you'll really make me wear it," Myr muttered. "And I knew you'd say I have to make it my own."

"Well, don't you?" Taly moved closer. "It would be tactful to wear it for your formal entry into the Keep of Winds, so you'll want to be confident of its weight and balance. We'll have to adjust the fit, too."

"So I look the part, even if it's a sham?"

"That's up to you," Taly replied, exactly as Myr had known she would.

"I thought your watch was done," she said, changing the subject.

"This is my last round before going off duty." Taly paused. "I'm sorry, Lady Mouse, but I must ensure guards are stationed in here before I go."

Of course, Myr thought. Dab she might have talked around, but never Taly. She frowned at the winged horse: Night's emblem, which would soon be hers—at least for the next seven years. "You and Dab," she ventured. "Hatha showed me the list of contestants today, but your names weren't on it."

Immediately, she wished the words back, because Taly took her time replying. "Do you want us to enter?" she asked finally.

"I would like to see some familiar faces in my Honor Guard." Myr could not say friends, not after Taly's delay.

"If it's your wish, we'll compete for a place." Taly hesitated again, her expression guarded. "You realize that your father and siblings may have their preferred candidates?"

Very likely, Myr thought, but still . . . She repeated what she had told Commander Asantir at the banquet. "Kharalthor has assured me that the selection must be completely open, that it's one of our oldest traditions."

"And if we're not in the contest we can't be selected." The ensign remained guarded. "Only the very best should be in a Bride's Honor Guard, Lady Mouse. That may not be us."

You're all I've got, Myr responded silently. "Hatha says you're good, very good even, both of you."

"Captain-Lady Hatha honors us," Taly replied formally. She

saluted. "I'll send those guards in, then find Dab. We'll need to pre-pare if we're to do you credit in the competition."

Myr bowed as the ensign withdrew, both to answer the salute and avoid meeting Taly's eyes again before the door clicked shut. Afterward she stared at the closed door and wondered if Taly and Dab would prefer to be free of her service. She felt sure they were not afraid of competing. And serving in a Bride's Honor Guard meant automatic advancement once the escort returned to Blood, which only made it more inexplicable that Taly and Dab had not entered the contest voluntarily.

Myr frowned, hurt and puzzled at the same time, until boots trod heavily in the outer room and she whisked back into her bedroom ahead of the guards' arrival.

Exactly like the mouse of my nickname, she thought—so perhaps it's little wonder if Taly and Dab are secretly ashamed of serving me, since a true Daughter of Blood should stand tall, like Kharalth of the Battles. But even if they were selected for her escort, Myr knew she was only putting off the inevitable. Once the marriage ceremony in the Keep of Winds was over, they and the rest of the Honor Guard would ride home, leaving her alone in a keep of strangers.

21

The Field of Blood

Noise broke over Myr like a physical wave as she approached the arena known as the Field of Blood. She stopped, almost reeling from its force, while the curtains to the Earl's box stirred before her. Kharalthor's retinue and Blood's guests would be waiting on the other side—and from the roar of sound, every tier that ringed the great amphitheater must be full. Myr took a deep breath, summoning resolve, while her attendants whispered and the guards stood like statues, blank faced.

A Daughter of Blood must not show fear, Myr told herself. She did not want to shame her Rose heritage, or Ise's tutelage either. The old Rose woman had risen early to see her dressed, but Earl Sardon had made it clear he wanted no breath of doubt to cloud his youngest daughter's status as a true Daughter of Blood. So Ilai, not Ise, led the retinue of attendants, and even Myr's hair, the betraying black she had inherited from her mother, must be concealed by another jeweled net rather than braided or worn loose.

Myr took another deep breath, then pushed the curtain aside to meet the crowd's thunder, swelling to acclaim the Bride of Blood. "Smile, little sister," Kharalthor said, and Myr did, bending to right and left while Ilai and Vela adjusted her train and the fall of her jewel-embroidered sleeves. The galleries that circled the amphi-theater, rise on rise of them, were not just full, they were packed, while the arena below glittered with the massed ranks of Blood contestants. All here, Myr thought, dizzied by the magnitude of it all, to contest for a place in my Honor Guard.

No, she amended immediately, a Bride of Blood's Honor Guard—although there was more to it even than that. The array of colors knotted around the warriors' arms reflected those draped around the tiered galleries: hold and clan, sept or warrior society, the diversity of warrior allegiances and the sheer numbers Blood could muster were both on display. We're not just showing our strength, Myr reflected, but underlining our readiness to take what we see as our rightful place in the Alliance. When she slid a glance toward the Night emissaries, Asantir was studying the mustered warriors keenly. The Sea House delegation was seated in the adjoining box, and Myr had to stop her-self staring, fascinated by their cabled hair, the rings in their ears, and the rich colors—sea green and royal blue and violet—of their clothes.

Ilai and Vela finished settling her robe and stepped back, allowing Myr to take her place at last. Kharalthor, as Battlemaster, was to pre-side over the contest, and Hatha was seated to his right, surveying the field as closely as Asantir. So far, she was the only other Daughter of Blood present. Parannis was also absent, but Anvin was sitting beside Teron and the two appeared to be enjoying each other's company. The Night warrior was leaning forward to see better and plying Anvin with questions. Myr saw the scene again through his reaction to it: not just the densely packed arena and crowded galleries, but the rock walls of the amphitheater that was hollowed from the mountains—so significant a natural feature that Blood had built their keep around it.

When Myr studied the arena again, she realized that the colors and devices on display included some she had never seen before, even on the lists both Ise and Hatha had insisted she memorize. "Splinter septs," her sister explained, when Myr asked. "They're hard to keep track of, especially since some of the more remote holds are little better than redoubts."

"How do we know they're truly ours?" Myr asked, recalling Taly's security concerns. "Couldn't they be enemies in disguise?"

Huern, who was seated behind Kharalthor, raised his eyebrows, while Hatha nodded. "A good question, little sister. But no one passes the Blood Gate unchallenged, and we have wyr hounds, as well as guards, at every entrance."

Liankhara had her spies as well, Myr supposed—but one of the Sea delegation must have made a jest, because they all laughed. She was startled, but tried not to show it. Blood warriors seldom laughed out loud, and Ise, too, believed open mirth was undignified. Myr thought the Sea Keepers did not look as if they would care, although their apparent ease might also be a way of defying Blood's display of might. She scrutinized the competitors for Taly and Dab, but without success. The front row stood some distance from the Earl's box, and many contestants were already wearing helmets.

Beside her, Kharalthor rose to take the oath, and the gathered warriors turned toward the huge statue of Kharalth that dominated the northern end of the arena. Like the amphitheater, the goddess of battle and war was hewn from the mountainside itself. Her great shield was slung upon her back, but a spear was raised high in her right hand and her left dangled skulls, the fingers crooked into eye sockets or hooked around jawbones. A red wash stained the goddess's arms and was splashed across chest and face, depicting the gore of conflict, but did not obscure the fierce exultation of her expression. "Kharalth!" The competitors' spears clashed down onto their shields. "Kharalth! Kharalth! Kharalth!"

"Kharalth!" Myr chanted with the crowd. For a moment, caught up in the surge of voices, she shared their exhilaration as the contestants turned back to face the Earl's box and their spears clashed again.

"Myrathis! Myrathis! Myrathis!" Momentarily transfixed, Myr stumbled upright as Kharalthor seized her arm, raising it high in acknowledgment. His sideways grin was fierce.

"See, little sister. Your House loves you."

No, they don't, Myr thought, although she bowed to right and left again and smiled until she thought her makeup might fracture. She knew the warriors would shout for Sardonya just as loudly, or for Sarein, if either of them stood in her place—which might be the reason her sisters were absent, since neither liked being overshadowed, least of all by Myr. The Night contingent also wore smiles, but when Myr met their Commander's dark gaze she found it measuring. As though I'm a doubtful recruit, Myr thought, nettled. Or, she added, the annoyance fading, an unknown quantity at the very least, which I suppose I am.

Kharalthor finally released her arm and they both sat down as the competitors dispersed to the four marked-out combat grounds: two close to where Myr sat, and two on the far side of the amphitheater. A team of Blood provosts and their sarjeants would oversee each arena, while pages relayed results to the marshals, seated in a stern row below the Earl's box. Myr did not need the shouted announcement from the senior marshal to understand the order of contests; Taly, Dab, and Hatha had described the process at length once she became the Bride. A point all three agreed upon was that Blood was not trying to discover who was best with any individual weapon. The first two days of competition aimed to identify warriors who excelled with a range of arms and could also fight on effectively if their weapons failed.

The unarmed form of the Derai-dan, the combat system reputed to be as old as the Derai Alliance, had fallen out of favor in Blood, although most warriors still knew parts of it. But whether armed or unarmed, the opening days would focus on individual strength and skill, with contestants on foot the first day and mounted the second. All around her, Myr felt expectancy soar as the marshal fell silent and the provosts raised their batons in unison. Kharalthor grinned at Asantir: "Now, Commander, we shall see some fun."

Myr was less sure that she was going to enjoy herself, but focused her attention on the four combat grounds. The archery trials on the far side of the field involved the competitors shooting at fixed and moving targets respectively, while the squares closer to the Earl's box were for armed combat. The combatants could bring any weapon into the ring, and also continue to pursue an opponent unfortunate enough to be disarmed. The contests tended to be swift and brutal, but Myr was enough Hatha's student to admire the skill of the warrior who held a glaive wielder at bay with sword and dagger, and the fierceness and dexterity with which another plied his war-axe.

"Impressive," Teron said, as eager as any Blood warrior. Myr thought his grin held more than a hint of the axe warrior's ferocity, but she applauded with the rest as Kharalthor clapped Hatha on the shoulder. When two combatants ended up hammering at each other immediately below the Earl's box, she was as enthralled as any of her companions—and gasped with the crowd as well, her hands flying to her mouth, when one contender's sword shattered. The contestant hurled it aside as his adversary raised his sword, as if intending to strike head from body. Rather than retreating, the disarmed combatant advanced, and in a movement too blurred for Myr to follow twisted the blade clear and threw the swordsman over his hip. In the rapt silence from the galleries, Myr heard the snap of breaking bone.

"Well fought," Kharalthor roared, applauding, and as though released from a spell, the surrounding tiers clapped, stamped, and cheered. Kharalthor's right, Myr thought, the victor's counter was superb. She kept applauding even when the winner raised his visor to salute them and she realized it was Kolthis. Of course, she told herself, her smile grown stiff: he wants the advancement and need only suffer my service again for a short time to achieve it. And because Kolthis served Huern now, that almost certainly made him one of her brother's candidates, not just for a place in the guard, but for Honor Captain.

Huern's expression gave nothing away, but in the subsequent combat rounds Myr recognized two of Kolthis's sworn companions by their colors. The first was Ralth, a warrior recruited from the Red Keep's ranks, while the second, Rhisart, had joined the keep garrison from Bane, a New Blood Hold. The jolt of realizing that Kolthis and his cronies were competing took the dazzle off the skill and strength displayed by other contestants. Instead the savagery of the assaults began to dominate Myr's perception, and she found herself counting the wounds and broken bones incurred, despite the combatants supposedly using blunted weapons.

"They are determined to enter your service," Kharalthor observed, as war horns ended the first half-day of eliminations. His hand checked before clapping Myr on the shoulder, the way he did with Hatha, but the subsequent squeeze, together with the tally of injured being helped or carried from the field, still made her wince inwardly.

"Your Dabnor did well in the archery," Hatha said cheerfully, as a steward announced that lunch was waiting in the adjoining chamber. "Did you see him?" Myr shook her head as they all rose, aware of Kharalthor's frown and that Huern was also listening. "Taly was more than holding her own, too, from what I saw." Hatha stood aside to let Myr pass through the heavy curtain ahead of everyone except Kharalthor. "I think they'll both make it into the group contests."

Nine willing, Myr thought, but was distracted by Anvin's arrival with Teron of Cloud Hold. "The Storm Spear fought well," her brother said to Hatha. "Did you mark him?"

"I did." Methodically, Hatha began piling food onto a plate. "He's not overly tall, but he's built like a mountain wall. And I liked the way he countered Bajan of Bronze's glaive with the sword and dagger."

Huern turned away from the table. "I didn't think Blood had Storm Spears anymore."

"Nor did I." Hatha licked her fingers, unconcerned by their company. "It seems we thought wrong."

"A Storm Spear?" Teron looked puzzled.

"One of our elite warrior societies," Anvin explained: "From the old days."

"Possibly the greatest of them," Hatha observed, which made Myr look up, because if it was anything at all to do with Blood's warrior heritage, Hatha would know. Huern must have thought so, too, because he regarded her thoughtfully.

Anvin, however, dismissed history with a shrug. "We still have a few warrior societies left, but the Storm Spears were supposed to have died out forever ago, maybe in the passage to Haarth."

"It was after the Betrayal War," Hatha said. "They were always religious, you see, as well as being obsessed with war and honor. 'I keep faith,' " she added, "was their motto."

Does she mean they were warrior-priests? Myr wondered. Ise had taught her that such orders existed, even in the warrior Houses, before the civil war.

"Warrior-priests?" Teron sounded as affronted as any Blood-born warrior at the idea. "Surely there's no such thing."

Hatha shook her head. "The Storm Spears weren't priests, they just took service to Kharalth, Mhaelanar, and Tawr very seriously. They were also famous for being reclusive."

"Secretive," Huern said, as she paused to help herself to a plateful of cakes.

"Reclusive, secretive . . . " Hatha shrugged. "But a small number could well have survived when we thought them gone."

Anvin, Myr saw, was looking bored. "Well, this one can certainly fight," he said, "which is what he's here for. Although if they're as religious as you say, they probably believe the same fireside—" He broke off as Hatha's move to take another cake jostled his plate. "Careful, Hath!"

"Sorry." Hatha blinked at him amiably, while Huern looked amused. Teron, Myr decided, was completely oblivious to the byplay. "Does it matter what they believe?" Hatha bit into another cake. "It's their fighting ability that counts."

Myr almost smiled when she saw Anvin and Teron exchange an identical glance, before both nodded. Huern still looked thoughtful, but turned as Anvin smiled past him. Myr, turning too, saw Sardonya posed in the doorway. Her sister waited a moment longer before sweeping into the room and smiling brilliantly on Teron. The young Night warrior looked suitably dazzled—and once they returned to the arena, he seated himself beside Sardonya. I don't suppose he'd believe me, Myr thought, listening to her sister's honeyed tones, if

I told him she shouted down Kharalthor several times during the marriage arguments.

She was aware that her sister's flow of conversation showed up her own reserve, but returned her attention to the arena when she realized that both Huern and Asantir were watching her. Hatha lingered to point out Dab, competing to some effect with sword and buckler, then Taly's distant figure among the longbow archers. "Which is the Storm Spear?" Myr asked, because there was something intriguing about a warrior who belonged to a reclusive—or secretive—order that her family had believed vanished.

Hatha pointed toward the archers' line. "There, three places down from Taly. Look for the broad shoulders," she added, and chuckled. The warrior she indicated did have very broad shoulders, but he was only of average height. "Disappointed?" Hatha asked.

Myr nodded. "He doesn't seem any different from the others."

Her sister grinned. "Ay, with a Storm Spear we all expect a warrior seven feet tall at least." She narrowed her eyes toward the far side of the arena. "His shooting is well above the ordinary, though, as is your Taly's."

Myr wished Hatha would not say "your" quite so persistently—but she applauded until her hands ached when Taly's and Dab's names were among those announced by the marshals when the day concluded. Kolthis and his cronies were advancing, too, and so was the Storm Spear.

"A long list still, but that's as it should be," Kharalthor observed to Asantir. "We've seen their capabilities on foot. Now we need to see 'em on horseback before making the real cull."

Taly's an excellent rider, Myr thought, so she'll have a good chance tomorrow. And Dab's at least good enough to be in the running. Yet she still lay awake that night, thinking about the contest injuries and how she had heard bone snap when Kolthis threw his opponent—and prayed nothing similar would befall Taly or Dab. Warriors could as easily die or be wounded on border patrols, let alone in war, but these injuries *seemed* worse because the contest was only partly to select an elite guard. The rest was spectacle, designed to enhance the prestige of Blood.

In our own eyes at least, Myr reflected, recalling Commander Asantir's cool, impassive countenance and the laughter of the Sea Keepers. As Bride, she could not absent herself from the contest, but she would ask Ise to visit the infirmary on her behalf. By the standards of Blood, injured warriors were held to have failed in the contest, but they had still competed in Myr's name. Ise would know what to do for them and advise her on whether more was required . . .

Yawning, Myr settled deeper into the bed. Even the Red Keep, filled to capacity with contestants and those gathered to watch them compete, grew quiet in the late watches, so she heard the hound when it howled. She shivered beneath the warm covers, but despite waiting, wide-eyed in the darkness, the howl did not come again. Later, though, her dreams were full of blood-eyed hounds pursuing a milk-white hind that twisted and turned and doubled back, but could not escape.

22

Honor Contest

On the Field of Blood, the Storm Spear galloped his bay charger down a row of targets and shot an arrow dead-center into them all. "Impressive," Asantir said, as the crowd stamped and applauded. In the adjoining box the Sea Keepers stood right up, cheering and whistling, and Myr wished she could do the same. But that would be unbecoming conduct for a Bride of Blood *and* show favoritism.

Beside her, Kharalthor's narrowed gaze dismissed the Sea Keepers before returning to the field. "Ay. None of our Wall horses can match his pair for size or martial training."

Conscious of his reserved tone, Myr was careful not to clap too long. Her spirits had lifted from the first moment the competitors entered the arena, the horses' crests arched and both coats and harness gleaming. She loved the speed and power as opponents thundered toward each other, or shot accurately from a gallop as the Storm Spear had just done—and longed again for the Sea Keepers' freedom or to be an arena page, yelling for her favorites and placing bets.

"It's not just their size." Huern, too, was intent on the Storm Spear as the bay walked back to the muster point. "Both his roan and the bay are neat on their feet as cats."

"They're Emerian great horses." Teron sounded both admiring

and grudging. "But however well they do in the arena, they'd be useless in Wall terrain."

"Among the passes, yes," Asantir replied. "In more open country they could be a battle winner."

"Heavy cavalry, ay," Kharalthor agreed, which sparked discussion on how such a force might be countered. Asantir nodded at times, but kept her eyes on the field, and Huern, too, remained silent. Myr only realized that Hatha was also paying more attention to the contests when her sister leaned forward. "Another clean round," she said, clapping, and Myr saw that the successful archer was Taly.

Despite Hatha's exclamation, Myr thought her brothers' applause was perfunctory. They did not seem enthusiastic when Dab bested Ralth either, after a fierce, knee-to-knee flurry of blows. Later in the morning, Rhisart bore down on the Storm Spear—who had switched to his roan destrier—with a war-axe. But the warhorse shouldered the Bane Holder's mount off line, before bringing his rider in close enough to knock the axe clear of Rhisart's grasp.

"Who should we put in the Honor Guard, though?" Kharalthor drawled, as the cheers died away. "The rider—or the horse?"

Hatha slapped her thigh in appreciation, but Myr was not convinced her brother had been joking. She herself felt far less enthusiasm for both the warrior and his destrier during the afternoon, once he and Taly fought. The ensign held the Storm Spear at bay for some time, demonstrating considerable skill with her sword and using her horse more effectively than Rhisart had done, until the cat-footed roan switched direction unexpectedly. The maneuver allowed the Storm Spear to catch Taly off-balance and hook a leg beneath her knee, heaving her half out of the saddle. Taly's horse leapt away, but she clung to its neck with one leg still clamped across the saddle and quickly retrieved her seat. Seeing daylight between rider and saddle was still a defeat, though, and the provosts pointed their batons toward the Storm Spear.

Or his horse, Myr thought, echoing Kharalthor's sentiment despite knowing she was being unfair. The Battlemaster buffeted Hatha's shoulder. "Your protégée will have a hard job coming back from that."

He's right, Myr thought, her hands balled inside her sleeves. In that moment she hated the Storm Spear almost as much as she resented Kharalthor's good humor and Huern's indifference. Hatha just shrugged. "The day's not over yet and the final selection will be on overall points, not one win or loss."

She's right, too, Myr reminded herself. Her sister was being very open about supporting Taly, but Hatha had always liked the ensign and was not an official selector, so could afford to show partiality. Myr could not, but remained acutely aware that Kolthis was among those who were currently undefeated. He was skilled, too. She had to concede that as he won again.

"What do you think, Commander?" Kharalthor spoke across Myr to Asantir. "Going into this, we felt Kolthis was a promising candidate for the captaincy."

So they *had* decided. Myr's nails bit into her palms but she kept her face turned blindly toward the field. Sardonya or Sarein would probably seize the moment to argue for an alternative candidate, but Myr doubted she could force even a whisper out.

"I agree he shows promise," Commander Asantir replied. "A number of other candidates do, too, which is heartening so early in the contest. But it's the group competitions that will show us their ability to work effectively with others, plus the tactical leadership we've agreed is vital for the Guard's officers." She paused. "Although perhaps you have a preference, Lady Myrathis?"

Myr caught Kharalthor's headshake as Sardonya and Anvin broke off their conversation to listen. She was aware that Huern, too, was watching, and guessed they would see her hesitation purely as timidity—but wanting Taly and Dab in her guard did not necessarily mean she believed either one should be Honor Captain. Like the Commander, Myr considered it was too early for that discussion, but knew saying she had no preference would reinforce Kharalthor's determination to choose for her. On the other hand, insisting she didn't want Kolthis would only provoke her brother, not persuade him. And if word got back to Kolthis, his dislike might harden into enmity . . .

I must just say that Commander Asantir's words have persuaded me I should wait until after the group contests and the melee before finally deciding, Myr thought: that way I shouldn't offend Kharalthor, or the Commander either. She swallowed, knowing her silence had become awkward. "I," she began—but was drowned out by the crowd's groan.

A horse and rider were down, Myr realized, turning with the rest. When the dust settled, she saw the rider's leg was trapped beneath his mount and several serjeants, a farrier, and two field surgeons were conferring. Eventually, the horse was helped to rise, but seemed unable to place its right fore-hoof down. Myr watched the farrier shake his head, but also saw how the rider's leg was twisted unnaturally. A moment later one of the field surgeons touched it, and the fallen rider screamed.

"A bad business," Hatha said heavily, and even Kharalthor nodded. Instinctively, Myr glanced toward the Sea Keepers, but they, too, looked grave, and one of their number, who was craning to see better, looked particularly grim. The horse was led off, limping on three legs, and Myr guessed from the farrier's reaction that it would be put down. The surgeons took longer to remove the warrior. He did not scream again, even when lifted onto a stretcher, but his agony was palpable.

"His warrior days are done," Teron muttered. The crowd, too, was somber, and the applause more subdued once the contests resumed. But the feast tonight will still be held, Myr thought, to celebrate those who will go forward for another three days of this. For the first time, having seen the wreckage of the fallen warrior's leg and heard him scream, she hoped Taly and Dab would be eliminated after all. She was still feeling that way during the last round of combats—until she turned away from Ilai's murmured suggestion that they leave early to prepare for the feast and saw Taly ride straight at Kolthis in the middle of the field. A flurry of sword strokes followed, but the dust around the trampling horses made it hard to discern what was happening.

The horses wheeled again, and this time Myr saw Taly clearly, pressing in close behind another rain of blows. Kolthis was blocking and trying to bring his horse around, but Taly kneed her mount forward and drove her shield into his visor. Myr saw Kolthis's head go back and steel flash in the ensign's hand, low toward the horse's belly. Not the horse, Myr thought, her hands flying to her mouth: Taly wouldn't—then she blinked as Kolthis and his saddle slid to the ground together, raising another swirl of dust. For a moment he lay still, before rolling clear of the trampling hooves.

"She sliced the girth!" Hatha was slapping her thigh again. "I taught her that trick," she added, and punched Kharalthor's arm. "He doesn't look much like an Honor Captain now, on his arse in the dirt."

Kharalthor's expression darkened, but Hatha continued to grin at him. "I told you the day was not over, brother." She leaned toward Asantir. "I think Ensign Taly's just proven she's Honor Guard material, don't you agree, Commander?"

Myr blinked again, wondering if Hatha could really like Taly enough to box in Kharalthor so publicly. But if Asantir agreed that Taly was a worthy candidate . . . Myr held her breath.

The Commander of Night smiled slightly. "I'll reserve all decisions until after the group contests and the melee." She glanced back to the field. "But the ensign—Taly, did you say?—has been a consistent contender, and that unhorsing was outstanding."

Outstanding, Myr repeated silently, and dared not look at Kharalthor as the last contestants quit the arena. Behind her, Ilai stepped forward again. "We really should go, Lady Myrathis, if you're to make the feast on time. Your father is to preside, remember, so you can't be late."

Lateness would insult the finalists, too, since the feast was in their honor. Yet despite having wished, so short a time before, that Taly and Dab would not be selected, now Myr fervently hoped they would. Taly had been wonderful—and throughout the walk back to her apartments Myr kept reliving the moment when Kolthis had landed on the ground. If not for her attendants and escort she would have clapped her hands and laughed out loud. Like the Sea Keepers, she thought, and wondered what that would feel like.

Instead she allowed herself a small private smile, and was still smiling inwardly while Vela and Kylin fussed over her evening gown. She barely noticed the weight of the hydra headdress and waited patiently as Ilai prepared to reapply her makeup. "After which," the attendant murmured, "there can be no more smiles."

She smiled, though, saying that—but before Myr could think of a witty reply, a page arrived carrying a rolled parchment. "Compliments of the Commander of Night," she said, bowing and extending the scroll simultaneously, "and here's the list of those who've made the finals in your Honor Contest."

Taly and Dab's names were on it, Myr saw, trembling as she studied the sheet. So was the Storm Spear, whose name was listed as Khar, and Bajan of Bronze Hold. Kolthis was there, too, as she had known he would be despite his fall, and Rhisart—but not Ralth. Scanning the list again, just to be sure, Myr felt as though the goddess Ornorith had smiled. Until, that is, she remembered the fallen rider screaming as the surgeon touched his broken leg, and the horse that had probably been put down. The rider would be in the infirmary, she supposed—and remembered that she had not seen Ise to ask how her visit there had gone.

I'll talk to her after the feast, Myr decided, or early tomorrow since it's the rest day; I should have time to do whatever's needed, too, between the receptions. Slowly, she rerolled the scroll and met Ilai's eyes in the glass. "Make me look the part," she said, and to her surprise, the attendant bowed before picking up the cosmetics tray.

Even after the eliminations, the number of contestants going forward remained a formidable company, and the banquet hall was so full of unknown faces and busy servers that Myr still had not picked out

Taly and Dab when the meal ended. A long round of toasts followed, led by her father's salute to the successful contenders and the clans and holds they represented. The clan and hold leaders then replied in turn, praising the valor of Blood and the honor of Earl and Heir.

So much spectacle, Myr reflected, as she had the previous night—although at least the speeches held the warriors still enough to survey their faces over the rim of her goblet. The servers remained active, refilling cups and sweetmeat platters, but Myr finally located Taly and Dab at the far end of the hall. The Storm Spear was seated close by, and all three had their eyes lowered as Lord Fray recounted highlights from the past two days, emphasizing the prowess of his Bane Hold warriors. Rhisart's name was mentioned several times, despite serving in the Red Keep now, and the accompanying stir helped Myr pick out Kolthis, halfway around the hall. Rhisart was seated on his right, and a warrior she did not recognize to his left, where Ralth would have been if selected.

Despite the loss of one adherent, Kolthis's manner remained assured, in stark contrast to many of the warriors from outlying areas who stared openly: at the room and their fellow warriors, but mainly at Earl Sardon, Kharalthor, and herself, the Bride of Blood. Their stares, together with Kothis's bold, dismissive glance, made Myr thankful for both her masking makeup and the hydra headdress, its nine raised heads shadowing her upper face. Lifting her goblet again, she debated how soon she might withdraw. Lord Fray had sat down at last, and Paran of Oath risen in the final place, which reflected his hold's standing as Blood's oldest satellite fort. He was also Parannis and Sarein's maternal grandfather, a fact that underlined their continuing absence when even Liankhara was seated at the Earl's table. Currently, she had her head inclined toward Lord Paran, apparently absorbed by his enumeration of Oath's lineage and achievements.

When she must have heard it a hundred times before, Myr thought. Huern was looking particularly saturnine, an expression that grew more pronounced when Lord Paran promised his own gleeman would sing the contestants' praise. Myr sipped her wine as the Oath lord finally sat down and the banquet noise resumed. Her gaze returned to Taly and Dab, before shifting to the Storm Spear—at which point she became aware that someone was scrutinizing her in return.

Startled, Myr looked more closely and saw there was a page standing behind the Storm Spear's chair. The boy was small, which made it hard to see him behind the warrior's broad shoulders and the chair's back, but he was definitely watching her, apparently as fascinated by her remote, elaborate appearance as she had been by the colorfulness of the Sea Keepers. Myr thought he looked a little like a Sea Keeper himself, with his hair fastened into numerous tiny braids that were shorn off level with his chin. Yet that style was also favored by Ward Hold warriors, and the boy's copper-and-bronze coloring was all Blood. And if he's with the Storm Spear, Myr decided, he must be in service to their order. But the Bride must not be seen staring, so she let her gaze drift away. By the time it drifted back, the page was staring through the hall's open doorway, his expression bored.

The Earl's voice recalled Myr's attention, saying he would escort her back to her apartments. He can't want to hear the Oath gleeman either, she thought—and since his wording did not permit a refusal, she bowed her head and stood up. The entire gathering rose, too, and remained standing as they left, with her father's guards leading and Myr's retinue walking behind. She glimpsed the page again as they approached the doors, only this time he was staring at her father and the bored look was gone. Myr tried to catch Taly's and Dab's attention, but their straight-ahead focus eluded her—and then she was through the doorway, with the Earl's squires hurrying to clear the way ahead.

Leaving together was another gesture, Myr understood that: a sign to Blood's elite that she stood high in her father's favor. Their journey was largely completed in silence, but at the entrance to her apartments the Earl's right hand closed over hers before she could turn away. With the left, he waved both retinues far enough back that his speech would not be overheard. "You are conducting yourself well, Myrathis." His look, beneath heavy lids, was narrowly assessing.

"But never forget what this marriage means to me and to Blood. Or that it is your chance, in the eyes of your House, to put the Half-Blood slur behind you. The gold, jewels, and mining revenue I offered your sisters shall be yours, seven years' hence. But for now—" He broke off, the hooded look grown brooding before he spoke again. "If you continue to do your duty without complaint and do not shame me before the House, then when this contest is done you may ask me for a boon."

Reaching out, Earl Sardon tapped two heavy fingers against her cheek. "Any request within reason, Myrathis." He paused again, while the stone hydra above the apartment entrance stared straight ahead and Myr felt equally frozen in place. "Make sure you ask wisely, my daughter. I would not wish to be disappointed in you."

23

The Midnight Keep

I would not wish to be disappointed in you. Her father's words continued to haunt Myr long after her attendants had left. Any request within reason, she thought, but what would he consider reasonable? Or wise? Suspicion it might be a test made her huddle the covers closer, especially as her father had as good as said her Rose heritage *was* a shortcoming. In which case, Myr reflected, why marry me into Night? The only reason she could think of was that somehow, through her, that would bind the House of the Rose into Blood's power play, although she could not see how.

So it must just be that I'm the default choice, she decided finally, because my father had no other alternative ... Myr pulled a face, wishing she was back in her old rooms where she could consult Ise without worrying so much about hidden listeners. In the new suite, every room almost certainly had a listening post for Liankhara's eyes-and-ears, and Myr could not rule out her household eavesdropping either—if Ise had been here to ask. But she and Meya, her longtime attendant, had gone to keep an all-night vigil in the chapel of Thiandriath.

Myr shivered, because the vast, echoing spaces and deserted hallows of the near-abandoned Temple quarter always made her nervous—although that could be because Parannis and Sarein had chased her in there when she was small. They had almost trapped her, too, except that Ise had been in Thiandriath's chapel that day as well and heard the twins about their hunt. The old Rose woman might be diminutive, and the twins full of jeers, but when Ise drove her walking stick onto the paving, exactly like a warrior grounding a staff, Sarein and Parannis had fled. They had been children then, too, of course, but Myr knew their natures had not changed.

So at least one positive aspect of the Night marriage, she reflected now, is that I won't have to take pains to avoid them anymore. And even if there were similar personalities in the Keep of Winds, they would not be her half siblings. She would also be Countess of Night and able to deal with those who troubled her on different terms. *Unless one of them is the Earl of Night.* The thought was chill as a draught, but Myr would not allow herself to dwell on it. I'll go to the chapel of Thiandriath myself, she decided: it's not too late yet and I can at least find out about Ise's infirmary visit.

Besides, doing something had to be better than lying awake, worrying over her father's expectations and the unknown future. Quiet as the mouse of her nickname, Myr pulled on everyday clothes: the plain kirtle and jacket, and soft, heel-less boots that had been her preferred garb before becoming Bride of Blood. She bundled her betraying hair into a cap as she crossed to the dayroom door, chinking it open as she had the previous night. Again, the gift armor glittered on its stand, facing her next day's costume, only this time guards were present as well, stationed at the doors into both the reception room and the main hallway.

Myr could imagine their expressions if she told them she wanted to go out again at this hour, especially down to the Temple quarter. They had been noncommittal enough when relaying where Ise had gone, because although Earl Sardon and the Heir might chart a middle course between more traditional elements and the New Blood, only the rites of Kharalth were still observed in the Red Keep. Worse, Thiandriath was not even one of the warrior gods. So if she openly followed Ise to the Lawgiver's chapel, all the Half-Blood whispers might spring up again.

Grimacing, Myr eased the door shut and went to the service door on the far side of Ise's rooms. It opened onto a short walkway, which in turn led to a series of back stairs and narrow corridors used by servants and the keep's pages. A sentry was stationed where the walkway joined the main corridor, but most of the new guards did not know her, so if she carried Ise's empty supper tray . . .

Then together with my old clothes, Myr thought, I should pass unchallenged. She experienced a moment's light-headedness at her own daring, but also decided to leave a note for Ise. Because if the Rose woman felt she was too old to keep the all-night vigil and found Myr gone, she would rouse the keep.

The night lamp in Ise's sitting room was turned down, and Myr tripped against a low table in the dimness. Her heart pounded as she crouched down, steadying the antique silver tray on its stand. Each leg was carved into the shape of a dragon, with the tray held between their open jaws. When Myr was very small she had liked to rub the snarling heads and trace the moon-and-star patterns incised into the tray. Ise had brought the table with her from the House of the Rose and always used it for their court's rituals of calligraphy and taking tisane. Now Myr left her note there, inscribed in bold letters so Ise's old eyes would not miss it.

Picking up the supper tray, she returned to the service door and boldly opened it. The guard on the walkway scrutinized her carefully, but did not speak or acknowledge Myr's head bob as she crossed to the service stair. She left the tray in an alcove off the first landing before continuing on. As much as possible she kept to the shadows, and concealed herself several times on hearing voices or approaching footsteps. Each time, however, the footsteps went another way and Myr crept on. Once, she thought she heard the hound again, its drawn-out howl rising in the distance. But when she stopped there was only silence and the wind's low whine. Stop jumping at shadows, she told herself.

The Temple quarter seemed further than she remembered, so perhaps the back ways were more roundabout, or maybe it only felt that way because she was alone in the midnight keep. She hesitated over two staircases that led away from another landing, trying to decide which would emerge closest to the Temple quarter. In the end she chose the narrower, spiral stair, her shadow stretching ahead—and was almost at the bottom when another shadow loomed, leaping up and across the wall as though to devour hers. Every Wallspawn story Myr had ever heard rushed into her mind as the shadow billowed, a giant's shape of terror cast across stone—until a warrior in Blood armor appeared below her, his gaze sweeping the stairs. "I thought I heard someone," he said.

Myr's relief was so great that she sat down, hugging her arms around her knees to stop herself shaking. Her mind focused on disjointed facts: that the warrior wasn't tall, after all, although his shoulders filled the narrow stairwell, and that his expression was concerned as he regarded her. "Are you all right?" he asked.

A Daughter of Blood, Myr reminded herself, does not admit to fear. For those few seconds, though, she had been petrified, and her heart was still galloping like a runaway horse. Her terror must have been obvious, too, which was doubly shameful. To make matters worse, the warrior before her was not keep garrison and wore no recognizable hold insignia, which meant he must be from one of Hatha's splinter septs. And so, Myr concluded slowly, should not be here. She knew Hatha or Taly would demand an explanation, but she was Myrathis the Mouse . . . Besides, she still did not trust her voice. So she said nothing, just continued to stare.

"I didn't mean to alarm you." The warrior spoke gravely, but he looked like a person who smiled easily, the way Dab did. "We've taken a wrong turn and I hoped you might set us right."

We, Myr thought, as light and shadow leapt again and a page with a lantern peered around the warrior. She guessed he must have swung the lantern to illuminate the stairwell for his companion, which was why the warrior's shadow had jumped in so terrifying a fashion. The same realization was in the warrior's face as the shadows settled again. He grinned at her, clearly intending to reassure. "I can see why we surprised you."

Myr could discern details now, past the lantern's beam, and recognized the page from the banquet chamber. Of course, she thought, remembering the Storm Spear's breadth of shoulder from the arena. He was younger than she had expected, though. When his grin faded to a quizzical expression, Myr realized she still had not spoken, and that to stare so long might be considered rude. "You're the Storm Spear." Khar, she thought, was the name on Commander Asantir's list. Her voice was a whisper, and she swallowed, willing it to strengthen. "You've fought well so far; everyone says so."

Pride flashed in the page's face, although for a moment, when she said Storm Spear, Myr thought Khar was about to demur. Instead he looked quizzical again and mimicked a swordsman's salute. He's too casual, Myr thought, puzzled—then realized that like the sentry guarding the service walkway, he would not recognize her. "You shouldn't be here," she said, pushing to her feet but keeping one hand against the wall. "Not in this part of the keep." She felt calmer now, and for the first time registered that the Storm Spear was close to fully armed, even if he went bareheaded. Her caution reasserted itself. "You've armed yourself since the feast."

"Were you there, too?" Khar studied her more closely. "A keep guard brought a summons from Lord Huern to my billet, asking me to attend him in the small council chamber. The guard said it was in this quarter of the keep." He made a slight gesture toward his armed state. "And, 'When summoned by a Scion of Blood, a warrior must assume that deeds of arms may be required.'"

Myr nodded, recognizing the quote, which was engraved above the gates leading from the barracks into the High Hall, but frowned at the same time. "A guard brought the summons, not a page?"

He was still watching her closely. "Do you think it's a ruse? I did wonder, but I can't refuse a summons from a Son of Blood."

No, Myr thought. She was thinking of the barracks' tales she had heard over the years: of warriors concealing opponents' arms to prevent them from competing in similar contests, or ambushing a rival they disliked. But there *was* a small council chamber attached to the training halls—those reserved for the ruling kin and their households—that adjoined the Temple quarter on this side of the keep. The muster ground for the Field of Blood lay on the quarter's far side, so it made sense for the Storm Spear to have come this way. And despite the late hour and the feast, Huern might still be working, so Khar *had* to check the small chamber. Ambush remained a possibility, though. The Honor Contest was sacred to Kharalth, and competitors were meant to be sacrosanct, but Myr doubted the old rites would restrain the New Blood's adherents if someone decided the Storm Spear was an unsuitable candidate for her Honor Guard.

Myr frowned, conscious of how much she had hated him when he defeated Taly that afternoon. Now, with Taly and Dab both in the finals, she could find nothing about the Storm Spear to dislike. "I'll show you the way," she said, because surely, if an ambush was planned, her presence must put a stop to it. *Surely*, Myr repeated to herself, but wished she felt more confident.

The Storm Spear regarded her a moment longer, then nodded. "It might help." He and his page retreated as she started down the stair. "The keep's hard for a stranger to navigate."

"It's not far," Myr said, as they reached the lower hall, but when she tried to think of something more to say, nothing occurred to her. With her mind focused on ambush, her heart lurched when the light flickered, but it was just the boy swinging his lantern in a wider arc. A Daughter of Blood does not show fear, Myr reminded herself. Still, she was relieved when they reached the small council chamber and found it empty. No Huern, she thought—but more importantly, no ambush. Nonetheless, the Storm Spear had been sent on a fool's errand, possibly to tire him, or to draw him away from his billet and sabotage his equipage. He would have the rest day to try and repair damage, but still . . .

"Played for a fool," Khar said grimly, "and it's a long walk back to the stables." Myr's confusion must have shown, because he explained. "The barracks and guest quarters are overflowing, so the best billet I could manage was a corner in the stables. Straw makes comfortable enough bedding," he added, correctly reading her dismay, "and I'm close to my horses." His smile was grim, too. "I wasn't such a fool as to leave my gear unattended. It's stowed with one of my warhorses, and Madder won't take kindly to anyone but me or Faro here coming near."

The page grinned, a distinctly fierce expression, but said nothing. He had not spoken at all since they met, and Myr wondered if he might be mute. "All the same," the Storm Spear added, "I shouldn't delay getting back. I don't want Madder killing anyone, or sustaining an injury if someone thinks to search his stall."

The keep's stables, armories, and storage crypts adjoined the muster ground. "So your quickest way back," Myr said, thinking aloud, "is the same way you came, through the Temple quarter." She hesitated. "I'm going as far as Thiandriath's chapel and can give you directions from there."

Khar's answering look was curious. "Thank you. But I thought all the chapels except Kharalth's had been deconsecrated?"

"You can still use them." Ise always said that you didn't need a sacred image or the votive flame to serve the Nine, but the divisions between the Old and New Blood made such discussions risky, so Myr lapsed into silence. Their footsteps echoed and she appreciated the lantern once they entered the Temple quarter, where the lights were dim and widely spaced. It even smells abandoned, Myr thought, wrinkling her nose at the dankness. The page, Faro, swung the lantern toward the first dark, gaping entrance and shrank closer to Khar.

She wanted to reassure the boy, but Khar had stopped, his hand on his sword. Myr halted, too, but could hear nothing except the hound howling again, remote with distance. She wished it would stop—and simultaneously heard the slap of footsteps, racing their way. A moment later a page hurtled around the corner and would have cannoned into Khar, except that he sidestepped, preventing the girl's headlong trip by the simple expedient of sweeping her up and around in a circle, half laughing as he set her safely back on her feet. He's like the Sea Keepers, Myr thought—but she recognized the girl as the page who had brought her the finalists' list, and that she was gasping from distress as well as haste.

"Ambush," the page wheezed out, after one deep tearing breath. She grabbed Khar's sword arm, trying to drag him in the direction she had come. "You have to help!"

Myr thought the Storm Spear might push the girl away, but he allowed the imperative grasp. "I'm coming. But best leave my arm free, if you really want help."

The girl dropped his arm and started running back, simultaneously gabbling about ambuscade and the purity of the Honor Contest. Khar's armor rang as he jogged to keep up, while Faro ran alongside, the lanternlight bobbing. Myr's natural instinct was to creep away and hide, but she did not want to appear a coward in the Storm Spear's eyes. Her heart hammered, though, when she heard the first snarl of voices and crack of splintering wood.

Khar extended his arm, stopping her much as Taly had done on the tower, the day Myr learned she was to be the Bride of Blood. "You're not armed, so best stay back. You, too, Faro," he added, flattening himself to one side of the next corner. The girl was already pressed against the opposite wall, and Myr and Faro exchanged one look before creeping forward to join her. Khar ignored their rebellion, concentrating on the fighting as more timber splintered and a bellow of pain and fury rose above the din. Cautiously, Myr peered around the corner.

The concourse beyond was a melee of writhing shadows and trampling, heaving bodies. The splintering had come from a door, which someone—or several someones—had clearly been thrown through. Rotten, Myr thought, seeing the remains, then shrank back as a body hurtled her way. When she dared look again, a warrior was pushing himself onto his hands and knees with blood pouring from his nose. But it was only when he staggered up and the dim light caught him that she recognized Ralth.

Myr stared, understanding why the page had babbled about the purity of the rite. Not only were competitors sacrosanct, they were also bound not to fight beyond the confines of the arena until the Honor Guard was selected. So the fighting before her was sacrilege, the penalty for it death. Even for eliminated contestants, Myr thought, watching Ralth reel back into the furor.

If the Storm Spears were as religious as Hatha believed, then Khar would not want to intervene, even if doing so did not risk execution. He might also agree with another of Hatha's favorite observations: that sometimes the best way to settle differences was to let warriors have their bloodletting out. Sometimes, too, intervention only resulted in everyone turning on the newcomer. Glancing Khar's way, Myr thought he might be weighing similar considerations.

Another attacker staggered backward, doubled up over her stomach, and Myr finally saw the three beleaguered fighters at the center of the melee. Her hands flew to her mouth as she recognized Taly and Dab fighting shoulder-to-shoulder with Bajan of Bronze Hold, their backs to the wall. They were outnumbered three or four to one, and as Myr watched, more assailants pushed forward. A mailed fist jabbed toward Dab's head, and he ducked and struck back, knocking the attacker down. Several more retreated before Taly's hammering of high and low blows, but again, fresh opponents piled in. One landed a hit that made Taly reel, before she recovered and took her attacker out with a low, savage kick through the knee.

Dab and Bajan were both hard-pressed as well, and Myr stifled a cry as the Bronze Holder collapsed to one knee. Dab drove the assailants back, headbutting one and shoving an elbow into the other's throat as Bajan staggered up. The page turned a white imploring face on Khar. "You have to help," she said, "or they'll kill my master and the other two. And we'll all hang if the provosts come."

So she's Bajan's page, Myr thought, even as her fear churned at the girl's words—and because she saw steel gleam as Ralth circled closer to the combatants. "Blade!" Her warning was a strangled whisper, but Khar must have heard it beneath the fracas because he looked her way. He still did not draw his sword, though. Myr closed her eyes, sure that at any moment one of the three would be stabbed—then jumped violently as a whistle pierced her ears. Her eyes flew open as the Storm Spear whistled again and stepped forward.

"Provosts coming!" he yelled. Those on the periphery of the assault looked around and began calling to the others to break away. "Hurry!" Khar yelled. "They're almost on us!" He threw a look behind him, as though sighting provosts—and the attackers broke off and fled down the opposite corridor. Ralth lurched into Dab as he passed and a flurry ensued, before Dab shoved Ralth clear and another straggler hauled him away.

Both Taly and Bajan were breathing heavily but looked ready to fly, too, until the Bronze Holder saw his page. "Was that a ruse?" he demanded, between gasps, while Dab leaned against the wall.

"It was," Khar replied, "but someone will have heard the clamor. We should make ourselves scarce before the provosts do turn up."

"Or the others come back." Taly's breath was already steadying.

Bajan nodded, but took a moment to rumple his page's hair. "Well done, Liy." He held out his other hand to Khar. "That was sound strategy, Storm Spear."

"We need to clean ourselves up." Taly was terse. "Otherwise our appearance'll give us away—" She broke off, swinging around as Dab slumped to his knees. Myr saw the bloom of blood across his tunic's right side and ran forward, but although Taly had an arm about him, Dab could not stand. "He's been knifed," the ensign said, as Khar knelt on Dab's other side.

"We need to get him someplace safe, where we can see to his wound." Khar spoke quietly. "And you two can set yourself to rights."

Taly nodded, the line of her mouth tight, as Myr made herself look away from Dab's wound and meet Khar's eyes. A corner of her mind noted that they were gray, rayed with gold, and that the gold gleamed in the lanternlight—but the light was gleaming on Dab's blood as well. "My old rooms are only a floor above the training halls." Myr's voice was strained, but better than a whisper. "They're empty, so we can go there."

"Lady Myrathis!" Taly's head snapped around. "What by all Nine Gods are you doing here?"

"It *is* her," Liy whispered, as the others stared, although Khar's look was fleeting before he slipped an arm beneath Dab's shoulders. Despite the blood and Dab's gray-white pallor, Myr's voice must have reached through to him, because the guard's eyes opened.

"Lead on, Lady Mouse." He managed a ghost of his familiar grin. "We all need to scamper now, before bad turns worse."

24

A Chosen Band

Their flight did feel like scampering as they moved from shadow to shadow, dispensing with Faro's lantern in favor of stealth. Myr led the way, but was not the only one to keep glancing over her shoulder as though pursuers might appear at any moment. Bride of Blood or not, Myr knew she could not save them if that happened. The New Blood might only pay lip service to Kharalth, but many holds still clung to the old ways and would demand that the purity of the Honor Contest be upheld. And because it touched on honor, many of the New Blood would be of the same mind.

Hurry, hurry, Myr's nerves whispered—but they could not hurry Dab. Khar and Taly were practically carrying him, his arms draped over their shoulders and his eyes closed. Taly had wadded her jacket inside his, and Bajan and Liy followed, the page using her undershirt to wipe up any drops of blood. *Hurry*, Myr's heart drummed, but she kept her pace slow as they skirted the training halls. Blood's nine-headed hydra reared above the entrance onto the stair where she had met Khar, and Myr felt as though every stone eye was boring into her. As if it, too, saw her as the Half-Blood, corrupting her House's heritage.

But if Ralth and the New Blood can pick and choose among Derai traditions, Myr thought, including the rites that govern an Honor

Contest, then so can I. She would always choose Taly and Dab, too; no matter what rule said an Honor contestant must not fight outside the arena. Besides—she addressed the hydra's stone stare in her mind—they were ambushed, so if they hadn't defended themselves and Bajan come to their aid, they would have been killed. Where's the purity in that? Shivering, she glanced back again and saw the Storm Spear, his face set, carrying Dab across his shoulders while Taly followed them up the narrow spiral.

Not overly tall, but built like a mountain wall. Myr acknowledged the accuracy of Hatha's observation now, although she thought Khar was glad to put Dab down once he reached the top. She hoped Dab might make a joke, but his eyes stayed closed, as though staying conscious was taking all his strength.

"We're close now." Taly was supporting Dab's other side again, but Myr was not sure whether the ensign was speaking to him or Khar. This time she did hurry ahead, so she had the door into her old apartments unlocked—despite dropping the key because her hands were shaking—by the time the others arrived. She locked the doors behind them again and prayed Liankhara's eyes-and-ears were too busy to monitor empty rooms. "We'll put him on your bed, Lady Myr." Taly was already moving toward the bedchamber door, and Myr signed to Faro to open it. Bajan stayed by the main entrance and sent Liy to keep watch over Ise's former rooms.

"There's water there," Myr told the page, and described how to find it, before taking a taper and lighting the lamps around her former dayroom. The space felt small after the Bride's great suite, but achingly familiar. All the old furnishings were still in place, and when Myr entered the bedchamber she found her bed had been left made up. She frowned as lamplight flickered over a tapestry that had belonged to her mother and gleamed on the shield opposite, which served as a mirror after the fashion of an earlier age. The chamberlain had promised to have both packed in preparation for her journey to the Keep of Winds—but Myr dismissed Aralth's failings as Taly and Khar lowered Dab onto the bed.

"It's not as deep as I feared." Khar kept his voice low as he re-examined the wound. "And it's low and to the side, so there's a good chance the blade missed vital spots. A healer should still clean and stitch it, though."

Taly looked as haggard as if she were the one injured. "We can't go to the infirmary or the field surgeons, because no one will believe it's a training accident if they find evidence of the fight. And once questions are asked, Ralth's lot will be prime witnesses against us. He's like that," she added contemptuously.

I don't like him either, Myr thought, still surprised he had acted independently of Kolthis and his other cronies. She remembered him as surly and aggressive, but not particularly clever. The memories made her shiver, a reminder to light the fire that had been left laid in the grate.

"Is there no one you can trust?" Khar asked Taly. "The Sea envoy has a healer with him, but knocking on their door, especially at this hour, would bring any hunters down on us."

Myr straightened from lighting the fire to meet the question in Taly's eyes. No! she thought. Ise might have taught her drug lore and how to stitch household wounds, but doing so herself was very different from helping her Rose preceptress. Although perhaps if she were to fetch Ise from Thiandriath's chapel—except Meya was there, too, which meant any secrecy would be lost. Myr knew, too, that fetching Ise would be almost as slow as getting Dab back here . . .

Taly's steady hazel gaze still held hers. "You have to do it, Lady Myr, for Dab's sake. Mistress Ise says that you have an aptitude: that if you'd been born into the Rose, you would have been sent to learn from the healers of Meraun. And she never says what she doesn't mean."

Myr still wanted to protest that household injuries were not the same as those sustained in battle—although, in fact, Dab's wound did not look significantly worse than some of the injuries from the keep's stables, smithies, and kitchens that she had helped Ise treat. Ise had left the bulk of her healing supplies stored here as well, again ahead of transportation to the Keep of Winds. Not the expensive and dangerous medicines, of course. But many of the commoner herbs, as well as salves, linen, and reserves of needles and bandages, were all still in the storeroom.

"I'll need boiling water," Myr said, gathering her resolve, and went to find what she needed. When she returned, Khar had hooked up Faro's lantern to cast a better light over the bed. Nervous now, Myr washed her hands and arms before finally turning to Dab. She had hoped he might be unconscious, because Ise had left none of the precious drugs that brought that state, but found his eyes fixed on her.

"You can do it, Lady Mouse," he said. Again, the ghost of his grin flickered. "And they breed us tough in Froward Hold." Myr summoned a smile at the old joke, because it was really Forward Hold, but Dab always said "froward" because Sardonya had complained that his levity was disrespectful. It was why he had been transferred from Anvin's household guard to Myr's: a demotion for him, but one that had worked out for her. "Heart up," he whispered, as she hesitated.

"Tough or not, bite on this," Khar said, and Myr saw that he had taken off his sword belt, wiping the heavy leather band clean before placing it between Dab's teeth. After that, she shut out everything except the wound and what her hands were doing. Dab passed out while she worked, and by the time she was done, Myr felt as white and wrung-out as his unconscious face.

"I'm sorry," she murmured to him, then straightened, stretching out the tension in neck and spine. Her handiwork looked all right, she thought: perhaps not as neat as what Ise would have managed, despite her age, but competent enough. She had cleaned the wound thoroughly, too, and Dab was young and strong, so with luck infection would not set in. If Ornorith smiles, Myr told herself, washing her hands again. "Although once, if what Ise says is true, we would have had the Golden Fire to call on for healing, rather than relying on luck."

Myr only realized she had spoken aloud when Khar raised his eyebrows. Immediately, other sounds reasserted themselves: the rustle of the fire in the grate, the *thunk* as Faro put another log on the blaze, and the murmur of Bajan's and Taly's voices from the dayroom, talking while they cleaned themselves up. At least that meant only the Storm Spear and his page had heard her blunder. "Of course," she added hastily, "I know that's all just fireside tales."

"Do you?" Khar looked interested rather than contemptuous. "But you've done a good job here, Lady Myrathis, even without Golden Fire."

Myr flushed, with pride as much as embarrassment, and could not think how to reply. "A very good job," Taly echoed, returning. She studied Dab's unconscious face. "We may even get him down to the training halls before the keep rouses tomorrow. Then we can simulate a training accident before anyone is around to know otherwise."

She and Bajan, it seemed, had already deliberated on ways and means, and Taly continued to discuss the mechanics of the plan with Khar while Myr tidied Ise's materials away. Once she rejoined their conversation, the ensign insisted that Myr explain her presence in the midnight keep. Her eyes narrowed when Myr mentioned the service entrance, but however much Taly might frown over the rest, she remained focused on their plan to save Dab. "You're the key to making it work," she told Myr. "We need Mistress Ise to say that she was returning that way and tended the wound herself. You'll have to join her at the chapel as you originally planned and find a reason to send Meya on ahead, but that shouldn't be too difficult."

No, Myr thought, because Meya was goodhearted and accepted events at face value. "Then I can say any supplies Ise needed came from here." But the whole plan relied on too many variables: on Dab being able to play his part, on getting to the training hall ahead of anyone else, and on not encountering others along the way. Most of all, they would be relying on Ise being willing to create a false impression for Myr's sake. She'll probably do it, Myr decided, but she won't like it. And the whole construct, she felt uncomfortably certain, wouldn't stand up to close scrutiny.

Khar's expression suggested that his reservations matched hers, and Taly must have read their doubt because her mouth tightened. "We can't just tell the truth and think we'll be excused." The ensign looked older, her expression harder than Myr had ever seen it. Her stare challenged them all as Bajan came to stand in the bedroom door. "That ambush wasn't a disgruntled few acting on drink and spleen. And Lord Kharalthor giving a speech doesn't make the Honor Contest open. As soon as it was announced, word came down that entrants from the keep garrison would be preselected. A chosen band," she said, cool now. "Everyone else was to keep their noses out."

And then I practically ordered you and Dab to enter, Myr thought. She felt bleaker still, recalling how Kharalthor had identified Kolthis as a potential Honor Captain—before Taly unhorsed him and Hatha got Commander Asantir to agree the ensign was Honor Guard material. A situation, Myr supposed, that someone must have decided to remedy before the contest resumed.

The Storm Spear looked doubtful. "The contest comprises warriors from every hold and outlying post of Blood, as well as the keep garrison. Given that sort of mix, no one could hope to control who makes the Honor Guard."

Taly shrugged. "My guess is that it's more about ensuring those selected won't be personally loyal to Lady Myrathis. That risk is much lower with holders who won't know her anyway, especially as Lord Kharalthor can nominate the captain, who then selects the other officers. The suggestion," she added, "not that anything was ever said right out, was that any other situation would be too dangerous. Especially with you, Lady Myr, being so young and untried."

Myr thought it more likely her Rose lineage meant she was not seen as a true Daughter of Blood, but one who might abandon duty and honor under pressure. Khar shook his head. "That implies a Bride might lead in the field, which would be unusual." He studied Myr, his expression reminiscent of Commander Asantir's on the first morning of the contests, an officer weighing an unknown recruit. "And surely the Earl will send advisors with you anyway?"

Myr felt grateful for all Ise's lessons in schooling her expression, since no one had mentioned advisors accompanying her. Yet now it seemed obvious that just as Night emissaries were currently in the Red Keep, Blood officials would accompany her to the Keep of Winds. Possibly it was too early for that, just as nothing here had been packed, but it did seem odd . . .

Taly's face was still hard. "Who knows the true reasons? But once we defied the word that came down and entered the competition . . . " She shrugged. "We knew it wasn't a question of whether retribution would come, only when."

"But this is an Honor Contest. And what you're saying, this deceit—" Bajan broke off, shaking his head. "It profanes one of our oldest and most sacred traditions. When Lord Narn finds out—"

"You mustn't tell him." Myr surprised herself, her voice was so steady. She felt as though she were gazing at one of the puzzle games she had played as a child, with all the pieces fitting together. Even Hatha's championship of Taly, and her insistence that the ensign and Dab were Myr's candidates, could now be seen as drawing attention to what otherwise might have been overlooked. While Ralth, however surly and aggressive, would never have acted on his own initiative.

Not without orders, Myr thought, equally sure that no direct order would have been given. Nonetheless, Ralth and his fellow ambushers would have been led to believe that they served the ruling kin's will. No doubt, too, it would have been implied—without ever being said outright—that the ambushers' advancement would be guaranteed if they only resolved this little problem of Taly and Dab. Well, Dab was out of it now. "And you," Myr told Taly, "must withdraw."

"Why?" Taly asked, blunt as a practice sword.

Myr blinked, because although she might see the pattern of events, she had no proof, and to speak would cast doubt on her family's honor. Possibly even my father's, she thought, recalling his words after the banquet. Myr shook her head, knowing she would never dare voice that doubt, and chose what she did say with care. "Because it's the group contests next and I don't want anyone else to get hurt because of me." She felt certain that if Taly, or any other unwelcome contender, could be dispatched in the mock battles without open dishonor, then Kharalthor would let the deed pass. "I couldn't bear if anything happened to you just because I wanted familiar faces in my Honor Guard." Not *you*, Taly, Myr added silently, while the three warriors exchanged glances she found impossible to read.

"Lady Myr—" Taly began, then stopped.

"You have a right to ask those who serve you to compete on your behalf," Bajan said. "Any fault in this doesn't lie with you, Lady Myrathis."

"We knew the risk, Dab and I." Taly spoke again, her look steady. "Having entered the Honor Contest, I can't withdraw without dishonor. Especially now, when it would mean letting Dab down, as well as myself."

And now you're a contestant, I can't order you to do so, Myr thought bitterly. Only Kharalthor, the Battlemaster and presiding judge, can do that.

"No one may come between a warrior and his or her own honor, Lady Myrathis." Myr could see Khar would not be moved on that point, any more than Taly would—or Bajan either, she acknowledged, glancing toward the Bronze warrior. "To persist in asking," the Storm Spear continued, "will wrong Taly, since more than any of us now, she carries your honor in this contest."

Myr bowed her head, feeling the weight of all their eyes, but she knew Khar was right. "It'll be all right, Lady." She was not sure when Liy had joined Bajan, but the page's young face was full of confidence. "You'll see. My master will have your guard's back, just like he did tonight. The Storm Spear will, too, and they're the three best fighters in this contest."

"Hearken to the sage," Bajan said, grinning. Faro leapt up to enact some page's ritual of affirmation with Liy, which from what Myr could see mainly involved punching each other, and the tension dissolved. Khar grinned, too, before saying he would take the first watch and sending everyone else to get what sleep they could.

Myr curled up in the bedchamber's deep armchair with a blanket, so she could watch over Dab, while Faro lay down by the hearth. He fell asleep almost at once, burrowed into his coat, and Myr went to fetch another rug to place over him. Khar had taken up Bajan's former station by the outer door, and although he nodded to her, neither of them spoke. Returning to the bedroom, Myr blew out all but one lamp, which she turned down low. Her face, glimpsed in the shadowed metal of the mirror, looked wan and tired. Bedraggled even, she thought ruefully—although at least the fire's light was comforting, casting its glow across both mirror and wall hanging.

The Lovers: Myr repeated the name of the tapestry to herself as she retreated to the chair and her blanket. Like the patterns incised into Ise's table, she knew the scene it depicted by heart: the dark warrior and the fair maid who stood on the summit of a hill with their hands clasped, while a circle of milk-white hounds formed a border around the web. A hind as white as the hounds lay at the lovers' feet, and a crow perched on the vine above their heads. The latter always seemed out of place to Myr, because in the poems and songs of the Rose that Ise had taught her, tradition always placed a singing bird in the garden where the lovers met.

The *young* lovers, she amended, remembering how Sarein and Sardonya had both insisted that the Earl of Night was old. Now she debated whether they meant old as in their father's age, or older still—although surely they could not have meant old like Ise, who relied on her cane and could never walk very far, or fast, even when she had it. Myr wondered about Commander Asantir, too, in light of Anvin and Parannis's claim that she and Earl Tasarion had been, or were, lovers. She doubted the Commander was even as old as Kharalthor, but it didn't follow that the Earl must therefore be a similar age. Better not to think about it, she decided, and studied the vine above the lovers instead. Ise said it was a rose, which in some versions of The Lovers bore flowers as well as leaves, the rare blooms that were now only found on the one remaining vine in the Court of the Rose.

One day, Myr promised herself, I will see that remnant for myself, perhaps when my seven years in Night are up. She tried not to let mournfulness color that thought, even when the far-off hound cried on a sustained, eerie note. This time another beast answered it, baying as though somewhere in the keep the hunt was up. For us? Myr wondered, alarmed: would they use wyr hounds? She reminded herself that often the keep's wyr pack howled to warn of a new storm building, but she could detect no change in the wind's low whine. Possibly the beasts were simply on edge with so many strangers crowded into the keep. I can understand that, Myr thought, but was still glad when the howls subsided. Drowsily, she watched the play of light and shadow across the mirror, as though clouds moved in the metal depths—although after a time she fancied the shapes became people, moving to and fro.

"Fro and froward," she murmured, "like Dab." She felt as though she were looking into the room from outside, watching herself in the chair and Faro before the fire, while Dab lay in her old bed and tendrils of mist crept out of the mirror toward the three of them . . .

Footsteps crossed the outer room, and the tendrils fled back into the mirror. By the time Khar's broad shoulders filled the doorway, it was just a metal oval again and the shadows tarnish, rather than clouds or people moving below the shield's surface. Myr blinked fully awake as the Storm Spear's gaze swept the room. Eventually his frown rested on the tapestry and the lovers, standing within the circle of milk-white hounds.

"The web's called The Lovers," Myr said, mostly for something to say as she rose to build up the fire. "But I've always thought the crow seems out of place." She waited until the flames leapt higher before looking around, to find Khar still studying the web.

"It's not," he said finally.

Myr frowned in her turn, puzzled by his certainty. "Who are you?" She spoke softly, and was surprised at the way his eyes widened as he turned toward her—as if she had startled him. "How would a Storm Spear know what elements belong in a Rose tapestry?"

She must have imagined the startlement, because Khar's reply was matter-of-fact. "This particular depiction may have come from the Rose, but I doubt that's where it originated. As for the crow, it's nothing to do with my being a Storm Spear. I've seen it before, that's all."

He didn't really answer my question, Myr thought. She was about to ask whether the Storm Spears had the same tapestry, or what they knew of the background story, when the hounds howled again: not just one or two this time, but a full pack belling. She jumped, but they still sounded distant. "I've never heard them like this before," she said, feeling she needed to excuse the jump.

Khar frowned, his head tilted as though listening more intently. "They're not hunting," he said finally. "Sleep if you can, Lady Myrathis. Your part in the plan will be critical if we're to save Dab."

As if, Myr thought, listening to his retreating footsteps, I'm ever going to sleep after hearing that.

25

Guest Friendship

S he slept almost at once, sliding down into darkness, and it was still profoundly dark when Taly woke her. "It's time, Lady Myr."

As soon as Myr moved, she found her neck was stiff, but she straightened her rumpled clothes and tucked stray hair beneath her cap, trying to look more like a Daughter of Blood. She paused momentarily, her eyes fixed on those of the shadow girl in the mirror, before turning when she saw Khar and Taly getting Dab to his feet. His color had improved, but his mouth was shut hard and his breath came in harsh gasps. You can do it, Myr willed him: you have to.

He did do it, but their progress was almost as slow as it had been just a handful of hours before. Faro and Liy were charged with scouting ahead, while Bajan led the rest of their small party. Khar and Taly followed with Dab, and Myr brought up the rear. She was about to propose they take the wider of the two stairs when Taly made the same suggestion, and the rest of their painstaking descent to the training hall level was completed in silence. "It's probably best if I go for Mistress Ise," Taly said then. "She might argue with you about what's best, Lady Myr, but she'll come at once if I say you need her."

She had barely departed when Liy came flying back. "Someone's in the hall," the page whispered. "Faro's still there, on lookout, but we couldn't identify 'em in the dark."

Bajan looked at Khar. "Lady Myrathis is the most likely to know them, since this area's restricted." The Bronze warrior's nod acknow-ledged Myr. "If you go ahead with Khar, Lady Myrathis, Liy and I'll take care of Dabnor."

I might not recognize them either, Myr thought—but she followed Khar along the still-dark corridor without argument, leaving Bajan and a plainly disappointed Liy to ease Dab down onto the stairs. Khar appeared relaxed, but after the first few paces he moved further out into the corridor, indicating Myr should walk between him and the wall, and his hands stayed close to his weapons.

They found Faro waiting outside the upper entrance to the small-est training hall, his face shifting from uneasiness to relief as Khar appeared. The main door lay around the next corner and down another flight of stairs, but Taly had suggested the pages use this one, which opened onto a gallery that allowed a watcher to observe the hall without necessarily being seen from below. Myr crouched low anyway as she slipped inside, kneeling to peer through the bal-ustrade's fretwork. The hall was dimmer than the corridor outside, with only one glim burning by the main doors. It barely illuminated the training floor, and the area beneath the balcony was darker still, but Myr could see someone moving. Curious, she waited for her eyes to adapt to the darkness, while Khar settled onto his heels beside her, leaving Faro to keep watch outside.

After several intent moments, the movement below resolved into a single figure with two swords, although Myr thought there were others present, concealed beneath the gallery. Shortly afterward, as the warrior flowed seamlessly from one form into another, Myr realized she was seeing a variant of the Derai-dan. Patterns at ground level spun into airborne, acrobatic leaps, and she barely breathed as the blades continued to inscribe their flawless, fatal parabolas around the warrior at the heart of the gyre. This is the true Derai-dan, she thought, not the flashes of it we've seen in the arena, or the fragments incorporated into Blood's drills. Kolthis's counter, she admitted grudgingly, probably came closest, but seemed like a journeyman's technique now, when set against a master's work. Khar, too, looked absorbed—but what struck Myr was the way he leaned forward and the angle of his head, which suggested that he knew who this was.

Below them, the flow of the Derai-dan slowed and then ceased altogether. Myr held her breath and waited: for someone to move or strike a brighter light, or for the warrior's face to lift and turn so she could put a name to it. Instead applause sounded, a slow mocking handclap that fragmented the silence, and she pressed back panic as Parannis stepped through the main doorway.

The glim cast a halo around her brother's tightly braided hair, and Myr saw that he was wearing his swords, as well as the light mail he preferred for dueling. Household warriors filed in behind him, several carrying lanterns that illuminated their lord's sleek, predatory expression. Two warriors stepped from beneath the gallery to intercept them, and the lanternlight glittered on the winged horse device on their breastplates. Night honor guards, Myr thought, and knew who the warrior in the center of the floor must be.

"Commander of Night." Parannis was almost purring with satisfaction. "I hoped I would find you here."

"Lord Parannis." Asantir remained poised between darkness and shadow, her voice impossible to interpret.

"You dance a pretty dance." Parannis was smiling now. "You also tried to deflect me with pretty words at the welcome banquet. But I'm not so easily diverted." When Asantir remained silent, his tongue traveled slowly across his lips. "I thought I had offered sufficient provocation to bring you down from your envoy's pedestal. Alas, I was wrong." Parannis tilted his head. "Or rather, I was proven right about how far Night has fallen from its greatness. Unfit to lead." His smile twisted. "But it hardly matters. If you are too craven to answer me, even to defend your warrior's honor, then I must challenge you directly."

If such words had been spoken within the clans of Blood, Myr thought, the fight would already be joined. But the two Night guards remained unmoving as stone warriors and their Commander's voice was dispassionate. "I am your father's guest and the Earl of Night's emissary in his marriage to your sister."

"Half-sister," Parannis spat, then collected himself, the smile settling back into place.

"The degree of kinship does not matter, Lord Parannis. Oaths, honor, and law all prevent my fighting you. You should know that."

Parannis's teeth gleamed. "What I *know*, Commander, is that my father has not sworn guest friendship with you. Or had you not noticed that?"

He's right, Myr thought. The Night emissaries might be Earl Sardon and Blood's guests, but her father had not made them guest friends. She was forced to admit that allowed leeway for Parannis's challenge—and possibly a sanction for it as well—and closed her eyes, her ears filled with a roaring that would have done credit to a Wall storm. Parannis's laugh cut through her turmoil. "Perhaps, Commander, because your degenerate indulgence of Night's priest-kind insults Blood. As for my half-sister, she may be the least of our line but this marriage sullies even her. And through her, all the ruling kin."

The Night guards were rigid, but their Commander's voice remained thoughtful. "I am sorry you feel that way, Lord Parannis."

How can she stay so cool? Myr wondered—then immediately realized that if Asantir was anything but measured, she and her company might all die, and sooner rather than later. Like Tasian of Stars and his Honor Guard at the start of the Betrayal War, Myr thought, as Asantir continued speaking. "But that doesn't change my situation or yours, not with a Daughter of Blood pledged to Night's Earl and the contracts between our two Houses signed."

Parannis sneered. "I don't give a storm's leavings for any of that. The whole Alliance knows you have no honor, thinking you can bring the tainted back into our ranks. As for your Earl—" Contempt twisted his face again. "If he thinks he can use marriage to bind Blood's greatness and trammel our destiny, holding us to the Wall with fireside tales when all of Haarth waits to be taken, then he's mistaken. But you, Commander—you I intend to see dead by my own hand."

No, Myr thought. Her thoughts scurried, imitating the mouse of her nickname, but could find no alternative. Somehow, *she* must stop this. "No," she repeated, aloud this time, and stood up. Parannis whipped around, and the lead weight of dread became faintness as she met his scowl.

"No, did you say, little Myr? How do you intend to stop me?"

I am a Daughter of Blood and First Kin to the Count of the Rose, Myr reminded herself—but was still astonished when she managed to imitate Asantir's calm and speak without a tremor. "I am the Bride of Blood, Parannis, and the Commander and all her company are therefore my guests as well as our father's." From the corner of her eye, she registered Khar easing upright and withdrawing into the background: correct behavior for a warrior in a conversation, let alone confrontation, between members of the ruling kin. Myr tightened her grip on the balustrade until she thought either her fingers or the timber might crack. She also tried to remember everything Ise had taught her about pitching her voice to carry. "So *I* name them as my guest friends and bring them within the bond of First Kinship and blood that will be formalized by my marriage."

For a moment Parannis's expression was pure snarl, and fury stripped his face of color. His eyes looked almost black by contrast, and Myr's fragile courage wilted. If she had not been clinging to the balustrade, she thought her legs might have given way, just as they had the previous night.

"So the mouse can squeak after all. We thought you ambitionless, with water not blood in your half-caste veins, but it seems you *desire* to be Countess of Night." Parannis's lip curled as he emphasized "desire," his hand hovering near his sword. Myr swallowed, knowing the least move or wrong word would trigger violence. For the first time, too, she registered that Asantir had not sheathed her blades, and her breath caught as the moment stretched taut. No one moved or spoke—until Parannis laughed.

"Quite badly, it seems." His smile was feral, his words belying his conversational tone. "You will pay in full for your interference, Sister Mouse, but for now I fear you have overreached yourself." His flourish parodied respect. "Although I'll concede I'm entertained that you thought you could thwart me, when I would challenge Kharalthor himself—brother of my father's blood, Heir and Battlemaster of our House—if I thought him tainted by the same apostasy and coward-ice as Night's Earl and his leman Commander, who whores for him along the Wall."

Both Night guards started forward, their eyes blazing, but froze at Asantir's spiked, "Hold!" She waited a moment longer, then bowed to Myr. "We honor your guest friendship, Lady Myrathis, but insults of this order to our Earl and House must be answered."

"Yes," Parannis agreed merrily, "indeed they must."

Asantir ignored him. "Within," she continued, each word precise, "the bounds prescribed by the Honor Code."

The Honor Code: of course, Myr thought, as her brother's guards smirked. Desperately, she thrust the darkness hovering around her vision back and recalled Hatha's many lectures on the Code's origin and strictures. "Yes," she whispered, before moistening her lips and gathering her voice. "But not by you, Commander, or any of those I have named guest friends, for the reasons you yourself have given." She paused again, praying that she had the next part right: "However grievous the insult offered, First Kin or guest friends may not fight directly. But the one insulted may call on a champion from outside those sacred bonds, to fight in his or her name."

Parannis's guards exchanged covert glances, but he looked con-temptuous. "What would Myr the Mouse know of the Honor Code? *This* for your talk of champions," he said, and spat.

"Actually, she's quite right." The Commander of Night remained cool, although she still had not sheathed her swords. "Both Code and law require that the sanctity of blood kinship and guest friendship, which help bind the Alliance together, may not be undermined."

Parannis hesitated, and Myr could see he was poised between precipitating a combat here and now, and suspicion his own life might be forfeit if he did so. He could not, she knew, feel confident that Kharalthor would not demand it, if the circumstances allowed. One of his guards leaned in, whispering, and Parannis's expression darkened, then as quickly transformed into a brilliant, savage smile. "You have frustrated your own purpose by including all Night's company within your guest friendship, Sister Mouse. If no one from Night may defend Earl and Commander, then someone from Blood must champion them—and your guest friendship. Yet who," he mused, "will be willing, do you think, if it means standing against me for a Half-Blood and Night's apostate Commander? I suspect even your pet guards will balk." His headshake was exaggerated. "Yet without a champion the Commander here will still be forsworn. As will you, little Myr."

At least he didn't know about Dab, but otherwise Myr felt numb because Parannis was correct: this would now be as much about her as Night's Commander. Her brother never lost either, so if Taly took on the championship for Myr's sake, it would be as good as signing her own death warrant—and also expose the ensign's family to Parannis and Sarein's enmity. Anyone, Myr thought, would rightly balk at that.

"What, nothing to say?" Parannis's smile mocked her now. "Of course, you could always rescind your guest friendship for another of the Night lot." He looked from one Night guard to the other. "Which one of you wants to be killed in your Commander's stead?"

"No one will be killed in my stead," Asantir said quietly.

Myr saw exultation and eagerness flash in her brother's face, but before he could respond, Khar spoke from behind her. "Only a warrior of Blood may champion the Bride, or so we were told on entering the contest." The Storm Spear resumed his place at Myr's side. "And once pledged, it would dishonor Earl and House for a guest friendship to be taken back." He was so composed that Myr felt sure he could not know Parannis's reputation, however respectful his salute. "Son of Blood, I would be honored to meet you on behalf of Lady Myrathis and the Commander of Night."

Parannis's eyes had narrowed to a dangerous glitter, yet Myr was the one who felt off-balance. While she hesitated, wondering what to say or do next, Asantir sheathed first one sword, then the other. The deliberate action drew all eyes as the Commander turned away from Parannis—although without turning her back—and bowed to Myr. "Lady Myrathis, I accept your guest friendship and pledge my own friendship in return." She bowed again to Khar. "I also accept your offer to stand as champion, Storm Spear, and will uphold the bond that establishes."

Myr could not recall Hatha mentioning a bond, but the gap in her knowledge would have to be remedied later. A murmur of voices and creak from the door behind her suggested that the others had arrived at last, and she hoped fervently that they would not just crowd in. Of course they'll check, she thought, hearing a boot's scuff, followed by silence. Taly and Dab had never been stupid, and if Ise was with them— But the current circumstances could not be less conducive to their plan, and very soon now the entire keep would be stirring.

Parannis looked disdainful as Khar bowed in response to Asantir's words. "So you're the dregs that's resurfaced when we thought all your kind well gone. This could prove entertaining after all." The look he turned on Myr promised an early reckoning, before he made a show of looking past her. "No attendants or escort, I see—except for your newfound champion. I wonder what your guest friends will make of that when they report to your future husband?"

Myr comprehended the implication but could only blink at him, she was so astonished by it. Yet as if on cue, Taly opened the door behind her wide enough to lean through. "Mistress Ise says she's ready to continue now, Lady Myrathis— Oh!" Taly made a show of surprise, saluting first Parannis, then Asantir. "I didn't realize you were engaged. We'll wait on your convenience."

She must have been holding the door just wide enough to hear what was going on, Myr thought, with a stab of pleasure for Parannis's discomfiture. Her brother's expression, however, was already a blend of calculation and malice. "So you did bring the Rose harridan with you. And your tediously correct ensign, who will not under any circumstance be suborned from her duty." His smile reasserted itself as Khar glanced toward the main doors. "Looking for escape, Storm Spear? I don't think I can allow that, not when the Forward Holder is doubtless lurking as well." He clicked his fingers as though trying to recall Dab's name, before abandoning the attempt. "You've said you'll champion the Mouse's cause, and now her pet guards step forward: seconds made to order. So we can settle this here and now. What," he demanded, "could be better?"

"An explanation," Earl Sardon said, appearing in the main doorway, "would be desirable."

You had to admire Parannis's nerve, Myr conceded, because he kept his expression smooth and turned with his customary grace. "My father and Earl." He bowed, his sword hand over his heart, as their father stepped forward with Banath, his Honor Captain, beside him. Myr could see a strong contingent of guards outside the door, and Liankhara was there as well, with Ilai hovering in the background.

She's Liankhara's agent, Myr reminded herself, you've always known that. She wondered if the attendant had arrived early and found the note left for Ise, or whether her father's arrival now was because Liankhara's other eyes-and-ears had been about their business. Whatever the reason, Myr was grateful if it meant he would finally put an end to Parannis's games.

"One," Earl Sardon continued, his gaze traveling from Parannis to Myr on the balcony, "that I might be willing to accept."

Myr's thoughts whirled, wondering what she should say and what Parannis might allege, whether the Commander could or would intervene, and if her father might forbid the duel. But before she or anyone else could speak, Kharalthor strode in with Hatha and Huern—and the morning disintegrated into another of her family's battlegrounds.

26

Service and Duty

The only benefit to the furor, Myr decided, when she was finally back in the Bride's suite, was that no one had been interested in summoning the rest of her companions into the training hall. They had all been dismissed out of hand, and Myr felt confident Taly would make certain the training accident explanation for Dab's wounding passed unremarked as the keep buzzed over challenge and champion. And there had been enough shouting among her siblings, first in the training hall and afterward in her father's war room, to ensure the keep hummed with conjecture for days.

Or even weeks, Myr reflected, leaning back against her bedchamber door, which she had shut in her attendants' faces. The nightmare hour within the war room's walls had been filled with charge and counter-accusation, chiefly between Kharalthor and Parannis. Enough of the storm had still fallen on Myr's head, though: for being where she should not, and daring to pledge guest friendship on her own—and by implication Blood's—behalf. She still felt physically battered by the assault of words, every muscle locked tight with tension from withstanding the pressure to rescind her guest friendship, and was only surprised she had not been blinded by a headache.

But Khar was right, she thought now. Once pledged, guest

friendship cannot be withdrawn without dishonor. Similarly, Myr was sure that even if she did retract her pledge, Parannis could—and would—insist on the duel still being fought, now that the Storm Spear had accepted his challenge. So all she would achieve by withdrawing guest friendship, the same conclusion she had clung to throughout the war room storm, would be to compound her dishonor by abandoning her champion. She had hoped her father might forbid the duel, but he had shaken his head when Hatha suggested it, while simultaneously ruling out Sarein's riposte that he overturn Myr's guest friendship instead.

"Even an Earl," he had said, "may not instruct another in matters of her or his personal honor. And offers of guest friendship and challenges between warriors are both matters of honor under our Derai Code. My hands are tied."

Myr could detect no regret for that fact in either his face or voice. A moment later, Kharalthor's fingers had drummed on the tabletop. "The Storm Spear can't remain in the Honor Contest now that he's assumed the champion's role. We can't have the duel decided by default if he were to be injured in the group combats."

Yet only those who completed the contest were eligible for the Honor Guard. So with Dab wounded, Taly would be further isolated among those who wished her ill. Except, Myr reminded herself, I'm forgetting: I have Liy's assurance that Bajan will watch her back. Despite exhaustion and worry, the memory brought a smile. It faded, though, as she considered Khar's situation. The dangers of the Honor Contest were real, but Parannis had never lost a duel. So by intervening to save the Commander of Night, all Myr had achieved was to condemn Khar. Even if the impossible happened and the Storm Spear prevailed, he would have killed a Son of Blood, and whatever the Earl might rule, neither Sarein nor her Oath Hold kin would rest until he was dead.

But it was not only that. If Khar won, then the Bride's champion would have slain her own half-brother ... Myr closed her eyes against that thought, because she knew all those who held to the old ways of Blood, and many who purported to support the New, would regard that as little better than fratricide. They will say, she thought, that both Bride and marriage must be cursed with ill-luck—and the rumors of that will not stay in Blood; they will fly ahead of me to the Keep of Winds. She had felt afraid before, guessing most in Night would regard her as Blood's agent, insinuated into their midst, but if they thought her accursed as well . . . I'll be alone, Myr thought, in a House where honor guards murdered their Earl's consort.

But I mustn't dwell on that, she added quickly. I can't, or I'll go mad. Straightening, she kneaded her stiff neck and reminded herself that she had known from the outset that the combat would be to the death. Duels always were when Parannis fought. He had practically boasted of it when asked to withdraw his challenge. "Withdraw? I?" His brows had lifted with Sardonya's hauteur. "Never! I am looking forward to sending the Storm Spear the same way our forebears sent the rest of his kind."

Which suggests, Myr thought, that he knows something I don't about Blood history. Slowly, she circled her chamber, picking up and replacing objects at random while recalling her father's contemplative look and the mix of shrugs and blank stares among her siblings. You could never be sure with Parannis—and Hatha, who knew about the Storm Spears, had been absorbed in cleaning her nails while the arguments eddied about her. "This is a matter of the Bride's honor as well as my son's," the Earl had said finally, summoning his Honor Captain forward. "So you had best see to her champion, Banath. He'll need separate quarters until the duel is fought."

Huern's brows had lifted. "I doubt there's any spare room to be had."

"Put a minor Holder out." Kharalthor replied brusquely.

"My old quarters are empty," Myr had begun, before stopping in the face of Sardonya and Sarein's identical expressions of incredulity.

Sardonya's foot had tapped. "One of the ruling kin's quarters, for an outdweller—"

"Who'll be dead soon anyway," Parannis murmured.

But the Earl had nodded. "A good suggestion, Myrathis. And Banath, oversee the watch on him yourself."

Myr stopped by a gilt-edged mirror that reflected the entrance into her dressing room, and frowned at the hydra emblem worked into the frame. At one level, the Storm Spear was effectively being taken into custody. At another, Banath's involvement sent a message that harassment of her champion ahead of the duel would not be tolerated. A warning most likely aimed at Sarein, she decided, because Parannis would not do anything that might cheapen his kill in the arena. Myr's mouth pinched, because in a duel to the death, wishing for her champion's life was the same as desiring her brother's death. Knowing what Parannis was, it would be easy to hope for that—but he was still her brother. Only a full sibling would have more claim on her in terms of duty and honor.

Even, Myr added silently, if Parannis does not see it that way. But then, his allegiance was to the New Blood, who thought they could pick what they liked from Derai traditions and ignore the rest. Slowly, she reached out and touched the gilded hydra—then froze as the reflected door between her dressing room and the dayroom clicked open. Taly's frown over the service entrance, and Parannis's threat of early retribution, both leapt into her mind. Call out, Myr told herself: summon the guards. But her voice was frozen, too. The door edged a little wider before a gamine face peered around it—and Myr released her breath as Liy came right into the dressing room and closed the door. "Liy, what are you doing here? I told the guards I wasn't to be disturbed."

The page sniffed. "I know. They sent me away. But I've a message for you from the Storm Spear and I thought you'd want it. Everyone's talking about the challenge, so I just waited until your guards went back to doing that, too." Liy grinned, clearly pleased with herself. "Pages are everywhere, and folk assume you'll go once they've dismissed you. And I heard what you told Ensign Taly about the service door last night." She shrugged. "Faro slipped me a note. They had to bring him down to the stables, you see, when no one else could manage those great horses." Liy smirked. "It was funny, seeing all those guards and grooms hang back."

Khar's horses, Myr thought, had obviously justified his confidence in their ability to safeguard his gear. She beckoned Liy through into the bedchamber and took the note the page worked free of her cuff. The cursive script was to the point. "Khar wants an audience."

"Course," said Liy, craning to read over her shoulder. "He's your champion. He's entitled to look to you to settle his affairs—" She paused, her face grown troubled.

Of course, Myr repeated silently. She could receive Khar here, in the reception chamber, but that would mean a meeting stiff with formality, the room lined with guards and attendants. She fingered the paper, wondering why the request had come by such circuitous means, if Khar was entitled to make it. The manner of delivery might simply be the pages being mysterious and important, but—

"I'll go now," Myr said, and picked up one of her new mantles, a fine scarlet wool lined with fire-orange silk, as Liy ran to open the dayroom door. Ise was sleeping after her vigil, and the attendants would not return until it was time to dress Myr for the afternoon's receptions, but the guards—caught out talking through the open door to their comrades in the hallway—sprang hurriedly to attention. Taly, Myr thought, would not tolerate such laxness. Then again, the ensign would probably frown over what she intended doing now as well. "I'm going to my old quarters." She was pleased with the sureness of her voice. "Liy will accompany me and two of you may provide my escort. When Mistress Ise wakes, please tell her where I am."

Once the guards recovered, they would probably rouse Ise or summon her attendants, but for now they were caught wrong-footed. Liy advanced on the main door, and the nearest guard stepped aside, his eyes fixed straight ahead. Myr draped the mantle about her shoulders and swept past the guards in the hallway as well. She did not look around, but her heart thumped until she heard two of them fall in behind. Liy, grinning widely, darted ahead.

*

Banath had stationed an eight-unit from the Earl's Honor Guard out-side Myr's old rooms, and the guards on the door saluted respectfully when she arrived. Nalin, the sergeant-in-charge, made no objection to Myr entering, but asked that Liy wait outside with the escort guards while two of the eight-unit accompanied Myr inside.

Despite having seen her old quarters the previous night, Myr thought the main room looked shabby in the Wall's gray daylight. She also found it strange seeing a warrior's armor and weapons there—the equipment, she assumed, that Banath's guards had needed Faro's help to retrieve from the stables. The arms looked serviceable rather than fine, but from what she could recall of Ise's lessons, some of the old military orders had deliberately shunned ostentation and any outward display of power. Behind her, Nalin's guards closed the door and took up position to either side.

Khar and Faro had both risen as Myr entered, and made their bow together. She bowed in answer, while pondering last night's unanswered question: who are you? She knew Ise would caution her that the Storm Spears were an unknown quantity, having been absent from Blood for half a millennium, and that Khar would not be the first enemy to insinuate himself in the guise of an ally. Or a cham-pion, Myr added silently. She did not believe Khar was an enemy, but knew she must remain on her guard.

"You wanted to see me?" she asked, and made herself look at him directly, rather than past his shoulder or even at the floor. His eyes were gray as the day, but she could see the gold flecks in them as he studied her in return. Measuring me again, Myr thought. "I am grateful," she continued, "for your defense of my guest friendship, even in the face of my brother's challenge."

Faro glanced up at Khar, hero worship in his expression, but the Storm Spear was matter-of-fact. "I vowed to uphold your honor and defend your cause as Bride when I entered the contest, as did every other contender on the Field of Blood. Any one of them would have done the same if they had been in my place."

Myr thought of Kolthis and wished she could share his conviction.

"I suspect many would consider that being obliged to fight a duel"—she would not say, *to the death*—"with a Son of Blood goes beyond the service encompassed by that oath."

Khar shook his head. "With respect, Lady Myrathis, we entered the contest to serve you until your marriage. Having done so, we cannot expect to pick and choose what that service entails."

I suppose not, Myr thought. "My sister Hatha," she said carefully, "says the Honor Code requires that I make you a gift, as my champion." Faro's slantwise glance was startlingly close to a scowl, enough for Myr to check before carrying on. "She also says there'll be some Storm Spear equipage from past times in the lumber rooms, which she'll have Aralth hunt out for you." She stopped, because that seemed far more like Hatha's gift than hers. And he would not have sought an audience to discuss whatever lay forgotten in the Red Keep's vast undercroft.

"I am grateful for Captain-Lady Hatha's interest, and for your time, Lady Myrathis. I would have come to you, as is more correct, except for the ... er ... protective custody."

I suppose that's exactly what this is, Myr thought, conscious of Nalin's guards behind her. "I was pleased to come," she said, and bowed again. As she straightened, the distant hound, which had been quiet since the previous night, howled again. Myr almost jumped, but held herself still as Khar placed his hand on Faro's shoulder.

"I do not require a gift, Lady Myrathis, for fulfilling oaths and honor. But as your champion, may I request a boon?"

"You may." Myr waited as courtesy demanded, despite the hand on Faro's shoulder having told her what the boon would be. She did not think that the page realized, though.

"I would be grateful, Lady, if you could personally escort Faro to Lord Nimor, the Sea envoy, and commend him into his care."

Faro tried to wrench away from Khar's hand, his expression burning with indignation and reproach. Myr thought the request an unusual one, coming from a warrior of Blood—until she ran her family under mental review and decided Khar was right to assume their enmity would extend to his page. Since she could not protect either of them, much as she might wish to, that meant there would be no succor for the boy in Blood. "Of course," she said, and was rewarded by Khar's smile.

Faro shook his head violently, but Khar checked him. "You were warned, when I took you as my page, that you had become mine to do with as I will, subject to the laws of the Derai. Including disposing of you as I wish—without question," he added, when the boy's mouth opened. Faro subsided, although his expression remained a mix of desperation and denial as Khar turned back to Myr. "I also have two letters. The first is for Lord Nimor and includes my will. In the event of my death, my arms and the bay warhorse, Tercel, are to go to Faro, as well as any money remaining after his and the horses' care."

Faro, Myr saw, was rigid. She could only imagine how frightening it must be for him, not only being placed in the custody of a stranger while in the heart of a hostile keep, but forced to face that the master he hero-worshipped might soon be dead. Yet Khar is right, she thought, to make provision for the boy now.

"The second letter," Khar said, "is for the navigator of the ship that brought me back to the Wall. Both Faro and the roan, Madder, are to be conveyed into her charge."

Her, Myr thought, taking the folds of sealed paper and repeating the inscriptions to herself: Lord Nimor—and Che'Ryl-g-Raham. She wondered what Khar had been to the unknown Sea House navigator, that she would be willing to take custody of his warhorse and a House of Blood page. But it was not a question she could ask, so Myr put the letters in her pocket and turned to Faro. "We should go," she told him, because she had not missed the unspoken "now" in Khar's request. And she, too, was keen to circumvent any hidden listeners who might take steps to acquire Faro as leverage.

The page's gaze was fixed on Khar, his eyes imploring, but the Storm Spear shook his head. "Go with Lady Myrathis and do as she and Lord Nimor tell you, exactly as if I were the one commanding it. Do not speak," he added, swift and stern. "It will do you no good."

That must mean he can speak, after all, Myr thought. Her heart went out to Faro's look of desolation, because she also knew what it meant to face being sent away, her fate given over to strangers. "Faro." Myr spoke quietly, and after a grudging pause the page turned her way. She doubted he was really listening, but tried to reach him anyway. "When I was growing up in these rooms, my governess told me that service and duty must govern all that I am, and do. They are hard lessons, but lie at the heart of what it means to be Derai." She paused, hearing the echo of Ise's voice weave through her own. "It is the same for a governess as for a warrior, a page as a Daughter of Blood."

Faro had stiffened, and Myr wondered if he was going to flare into defiance, but she continued to meet his mutinous gaze as steadily as Ise had always held hers—and finally the page frowned and jerked a nod. The mutiny and the frown made Myr think he had probably heard the stricture before, even if he did not fully accept it. Khar's hand still rested on his page's shoulder, and now Faro seized it between his own. Turning, he knelt and pressed his lips to the Storm Spear's black-pearl ring.

"Faro—" Khar began, but the boy shook his braided head and stood up, crossing to Myr's side without raising his eyes. She resisted the temptation to lay her hand on his shoulder as Khar had done, suspecting it would only be thrown off—or worse, suffered because of who she was. He did not look at Khar again, and Myr found that she, too, had to withstand the urge to look back as the nearest honor guard opened the door.

Nalin, who was waiting outside, turned to instruct Myr's escort while Faro stared straight ahead with a stoniness that would have done Earl Sardon credit. Yet at least we both get to walk away, Myr thought, acutely aware of Khar's presence through the still-open door. For all Banath and Nalin's Honor Guard correctness, in every practical sense he was a prisoner, one who would be given no opportunity to escape the duel to the death.

To the death, Myr repeated silently—and the ghost howl rose again, a scrape along already raw nerves. "Nalin," she said, checking the sergeant's move to close the door, "has the Earl ordered that my champion be confined?"

Nalin paused, her headshake as cautious as her expression. "No, Daughter of Blood. 'Kept safe' is the order."

Myr nodded. "Then unless the Earl instructs otherwise, please ensure that he is suitably escorted at all times, but not prevented from coming and going."

Nalin saluted. "As you command, Daughter of Blood."

I do command it, Myr thought, and felt a little less like a coward, abandoning her champion to his fate, as she turned toward Liy and her escort. The hound howled again, a bereft, drawn-out cry, and she stopped. "I wish someone would find out what's wrong with that hound. Nalin, is that something you could see to?"

The sergeant looked blank, and Liy troubled. "It's only the wind, Lady Myrathis."

"Probably whining through a storm shutter that's looser than it should be," Nalin agreed. "I don't hear anything, but we're used to all sorts of wind noise from battlement duty. The only howling today's been the wyr pack just after dawn. You might not have heard them, Lady Myrathis," she added, "because of being in your father's war room."

Because of all the shouting, you mean, Myr thought, admiring her tact.

"Or maybe you did catch something, but just didn't realize it," the sergeant continued. "It does stick in your head when the wyr pack gives voice like that."

"Why—" Myr began, then stopped at the look on Liy's face. "What happened?"

Liy shifted feet. "The contestant whose leg broke yesterday—" She stopped, looking to Nalin.

"He was in a fever, Daughter of Blood, but came out of it this morning, long enough to take in what had happened to his leg. He killed himself. That's why the wyr pack howled. They always do when it's a suicide."

I didn't know that, Myr thought numbly. I didn't know. Even Faro was watching her now, drawn out of his introspection as one of her escort spoke, his voice heartening. "That'll be it, Lady Myrathis. Just the wind and recollection of the wyr pack, like Sergeant Nalin says."

Could I be that mistaken? Myr wondered. Instinct made her look toward Khar, who was standing just inside the doorway, although he made no attempt to step through. He wiped his expression clear at once, but she felt certain that whatever hound she was hearing, the Storm Spear could hear it, too.

27

The Turnings of Fate

A snarl of shadows writhed through Kalan's dream, twisting over and around each other like a pit full of snakes. He heard panicked sobs, then Faro gasping out something about lightning, black magic, and secrets, before the shadows smothered the boy's voice with a murmurous whispering. When Kalan pursued the sound, he found himself hemmed in by his own wards while the greater part of the Gate of Dreams flowed around him: partially visible and audible, but impossible to touch. Until the wards were lifted he would have to follow the Oakward's path and wait for what the Gate showed him, rather than imposing his will on it as Nhenir had advised in Emer.

The whispering slipped away and Kalan turned back toward sleep—but the dream transformed into a heaving mass of water. Overhead, lightning tore the heavens apart, while thunder, wind, and ocean battered at each other. Have I crossed into one of Yelusin's memories? he wondered, recalling the Sea mariners' accounts of deep ocean storms. The vision rolled, hurling him onto the back of a mountainous wave. For a moment he rode above the abyss, lightning spearing around him, before the crest collapsed. An avalanche of water crashed into his side, and he veered wildly off true. Voices screamed as a snapped mast thudded down, and he was running blind, every fiber stretched to breaking point as he strained to climb the next towering wave.

Lightning exploded again and the black clouds boiled as a behemoth plunged through them, trailing streamers of fire. Kalan felt as though he might splinter apart at any moment but clung to the dream, striving to understand what the Gate—or the fragment of Yelusin contained within his mind—was showing him. *"Too soon."* The whisper burned in his mind like one of the streamers of fire. *"Too soon . . . But I burn. I cannot hold—"*

"We're tearing apart!" The man's shout was raw with urgency, although Kalan could see nothing but black rushing water and the lurid glow overhead. *"She'll never hold unless—"*

Unless what? Kalan wondered, as the clouds overhead snapped closed and the behemoth disappeared. The tempest continued to batter at him, but the wind's fury was dying. The next time cloud and water swirled, the funnel around him was gray, not black. Finally, the storm dissipated altogether, transforming into clear dawn above a long gray firth.

Grayharbor—but Kalan's dream funneled again and hounds bayed beneath a shadowed moon. His feet crunched on frosted ground, climbing a slope that rose almost as steeply as the storm's waves. Just below the crest, he lowered himself prone and snaked through thorn brush, the spines tearing at his clothes. The terrain below was spectral as the moon, and narrow pennants hung motionless above an encampment of circled wagons. A ghost caravan, Kalan thought, seeing no people, or animals, or fires: no movement at all within the camp or on the surrounding plain. The only sound was the hounds, baying out their paean of blood and death.

Kalan was aware, with one part of his dreaming mind, that he was turning over in the same bed that Dab had lain on the night before. A fire burned in the grate and he re-experienced the previous night's shock of recognition as Lady Myrathis turned toward him, the firelight playing across her shy, fragile face. *"Who are you?"* she asked now, as she had then, so that he finally recognized her from his

Grayharbor dream. She could hear the Hunt of Mayanne, too, which should not even be possible.

So who is *she*? Kalan thought, prowling the perimeter of dream and wards like a wolf: Earl Sardon's ninth and youngest child, who was also the daughter of Lady Mayaraní of the Rose, and now the Bride of Blood, but who had grown up with a depiction of the Hunt on her wall. In his dream, Kalan stared at the circle of milk-white hounds. Is that why she can hear you? he mused. Has your presence here caused the veil between the Red Keep and the Gate of Dreams to grow thin? Or perhaps it was his presence—with the ring on his hand and in such close proximity to the web—that allowed the Hunt to draw near.

The hind's head was tilted to gaze up at him, while the crow above the lovers' heads gazed down with a searching, corvid's eye that also seemed to ask the Daughter of Blood's question: *Who are you?* Strange, Kalan thought, that Lady Myrathis questions your presence, when for me you will always belong with both Huntmaster and Hunt. "But you," he said to the hind, "I do not know. Where do you fit?"

"What is his lineage?" A new voice, somber and disturbed, whispered beneath the baying of the Hunt. *"Who are his clan and kin?"* Kelyr's words from the *Che'Ryl-g-Raham*, Kalan thought, but not his voice.

"We know who he is." This was the Luck's answer, but Yelusin's voice, sunlight reflecting on the surface of the sea.

Slowly, the baying died away, and a man spoke in its place. "Cap'n wants to see you."

Another man groaned. "What about a meal? Or better still, a bath." Kalan knew he had heard that weary voice with the underlying humor in another dream. Dust prickled his nostrils, as though gauntlets had been swatted against a tunic stiff with dirt. "We've been shuttling the length of the Wall for an entire season now, on top of the journey to the River."

"Nursemaiding priest-kind," a woman added. She, too, had spoken in the earlier dream. "Have a heart, Sarus, we've only just ridden in."

"Not you, Innor," Sarus said. "Just Garan and Nerys. Straightaway, the Captain said—and given the way you lot stink, another hour without washing's hardly going to matter."

"You know what it's like out there." A third man spoke without rancor. "You wouldn't linger over ablutions either, not with dark-spawn every other place you look."

Kalan sensed Sarus's shrug. "It doesn't change the fact that you lot stink. Or that Garan and Nerys's first stop is the Captain's rooms."

The third man lowered his voice. "Why can't Blood just *appoint* an Honor Guard for their Bride, like a House of sense? Why does our Commander have to waste time over their cursed selections, when everyone knows it's the Battlemaster who'll make the final cut?"

"You know why, Ter." Garan's voice was half a sigh. "It's so Night bears some culpability if anything goes wrong, all under the guise of elite selection and open opportunity."

" '*A Battlemaster's star in every Blood warrior's kit.*' " Ter quoted the Blood saying softly. Quiet chuckles answered his subsequent snort.

"Eyes-and-ears," Sarus warned. "Remember where we are."

"Let's get this done." Garan ended the brief silence that followed. "You ready, Nerys?"

Silent Nerys. Even in his dream, Kalan remembered her, just as he could still dredge Garan and Sarus, Innor and Ter, out of his six-year-old memories of the Old Keep of Winds. Gauntlets slapped again, only this time the scent in his nostrils was woodsmoke, leather, windchill—and the face he saw was Malian's, gazing into a campfire. But when she leaned forward he recoiled, because the eyes that met his were Ser Raven's: a stare so darkly blue that it was almost black.

"*A child of my blood,*" the knight's voice said, speaking out of Malian's mouth, "*driven like a deathstake into the heart of the Derai Alliance.*" Ser Raven's tone was as hard as any Kalan had heard him use in Emer, but he wondered why his dream would juxtapose the Haarth hedge knight with Malian and the Derai Alliance. Yet when the firelight wavered, then steadied again, the cool, measuring gaze was Malian's own.

"*I am to fight a duel to the death,*" he told her through the medium of fire and dream. *"Regardless of the outcome, I have failed you in terms of my purpose in coming here."*

Flames danced across Malian's eyes, but she made no reply. Kalan stirred, close to the surface of both dream and sleep, and heard the somber uneasy murmur again: *"Kalan-hamar."*

"Yelusin?" he queried, but the spark of her Fire remained quiet within his mind.

"Kalan-hamar," the voice said again, on a deeper note—before, like the dream, it disintegrated into a fist pounding on timber.

"Khar! Storm Spear!" Time to wake, Kalan thought, and opened his eyes to evening shadows in every corner and a dying fire in the grate.

"Khar!" The fist pounded again, and Kalan recognized the voice as Jad, the eight-guard leader who had relieved Nalin when the watch changed.

"Coming!" he shouted, but took a moment to orient himself before standing up. He had not needed his dream of a snakepit, or Sarus's caution regarding eyes-and-ears, to warn him how perilous his situation was, and so had lain down in his clothes, with his weapons close to hand. Buckling on his sword, he went to the main door and listened intently, but the sounds from the corridor conveyed no hint of danger.

Jad saluted as soon as the door opened. The Earl's honor guards were being nothing if not correct. Another honor guard in Night armor, with the winged horse device on his breast, bowed as Jad saluted. Kalan recognized the youthful warrior as one of the pair who had been in the training hall with Asantir. "I am Morin," the Night guard said. "The Battlemaster has approached Commander Asantir, as the one whose honor you primarily defend, to formalize arrangements for the duel. She is leaving tonight's banquet early and requests that you meet with her."

Kalan's thoughts raced, wondering how great a risk it would be for him to meet Asantir in person. He had still been a boy when they met briefly in the Keep of Winds, and now he was a grown man who looked his part of a Blood warrior, complete to the Storm Spear insignia engraved onto his armor by the *Che'Ryl-g-Raham*'s armorer. Yet the Asantir he remembered had been astute, and he would have preferred to conduct their business at a distance. His best hope of that was Jad objecting, since a refusal on his own part would raise unwelcome questions, but the eight-guard leader only said that Blood guards would have to accompany him. "No disrespect intended," he added to Morin.

"None taken," Morin murmured, so there was nothing for Kalan to do but arm himself formally, then fall into step beside the Night guard. Jad and another three of his eight-unit went with them— taking no chances, Kalan thought. He rotated his shoulders, easing the ache from the previous two days of both receiving and dealing body-jarring blows. At least, having slept away last night's tiredness, he felt better prepared to face what lay ahead.

I might well die, Kalan told himself, evaluating that prospect as coolly as he could. The part of him that had been raised in the Keep of Winds' Temple quarter understood that no one ever truly expected that outcome for themselves: it was always another's blood that would stain the arena sand. Yet he also knew that death was part of the warrior life and could come at any time, not least from the sort of misadventure that had caused the warrior with the broken leg to take his own life.

"*'Life and death, death and life.'*" The saying belonged to the Winter People, but Kalan had found its echo among the fractious wards, marks, and marches of Emer. His only real regret was that regardless of whether he won or lost, he had failed Malian, since he was meant to have won a place in the Bride's Honor Guard and so gain unremarked entry into Night. He would fail Yelusin, as well, if he did not carry the spark of her former Fire to rejoin with Hylcarian in the Keep of Winds. Seen from that perspective, perhaps he should have let the business between Lord Parannis, Asantir, and Lady Myrathis play out. Especially, he reflected, since the Daughter of Blood was right: many of his fellow competitors would not have felt their contest vow obliged them to defend her pledge of guest friendship.

Her courageous pledge, Kalan amended. Lord Parannis had called his half-sister a mouse, intending insult, but Kalan saw a more favorable analogy in Lady Myr's liking for back stairs and staying out of sight. She had seemed very like a mouse in the training hall, too: outmatched but still defying the predator that was her brother. And although born Derai, Kalan had also been raised on Emer's dangerous Northern March, where courage and resolution were among the qualities that kept barbarism at bay. No matter the scope of the Honor Contest vow, he could not have let Lady Myr stand alone against her half-brother and still called himself a knight of Emer and Falk of Normarch's foster son.

Besides, it was Asantir who had brought about his and Malian's escape from the Keep of Winds, and Kalan had always been aware that she could have saved the Heir of Night and left him to his fate. I owe her a debt, he thought, just as I do Rowan Birchmoon and all those who helped us both. Not that he was convinced the Commander of Night needed his help. His instincts told him she was more than capable of extracting herself, no matter how tight a corner might appear. Lady Myr, though— Kalan pursed his lips, because from what he knew of her family, she had dire need of a champion, and not just for this duel with her half-brother.

And after she reaches the Keep of Winds? he asked himself. He had only caught a glimpse of the Earl of Night six years ago, but recalled a stern, remote man. Rowan Birchmoon loved him, Kalan thought—and he her, from what Malian had said. Still, he found it difficult to imagine Lady Myrathis and Earl Tasarion being well matched. On the other hand, champion or not, that was hardly his business, especially since it was really a marriage between two Houses, rather than two individuals. Strategic marriages happened all the time, both on the Wall and in Emer, although Derai contracts had a time limit on them—seven years in this case—after which it was up to the parties and their respective Houses whether or not the union continued.

The gossip among the contestants, low-toned but usually with a wink thrown in, was that for all her beauty, Swords had been all too ready to send Lady Sardonya home. Kalan was still suppressing a grin over that recollection when they reached the wing reserved for guests from other Houses. Two guards with wyr hounds were stationed at the gate, the first time he had encountered the beasts since passing the Red Keep's Blood Gate with the Sea embassy.

"You carry Yelusin's spark now," the ships had assured him, before he departed the Sea Keep, *"and wyr hounds were bred to recognize every aspect of the Fire as friend and ally, as well as to detect Swarm influence."* Kalan had been less reassured by this than the ships intended when he reflected on the five hundred years in which wyr hounds had been retrained to hunt Derai with the old powers. Yet whether because his wards were strong enough, or due to the spark of Yelusin he carried, or even the shortcomings of Blood's pack—on which subject the Sea Keepers had been eloquent—the wyr hounds at the Blood Gate had shown no interest. One hound had come close to sniff at Faro, but turned away almost at once.

Although neither so large nor as terrifying as Kalan's memories of the Hunt of Mayanne, the beasts at the entrance to the Envoys' Quarter were tall, with sleek narrow heads, and his muscles tightened as the pale, phosphorescent eyes turned his way. The sentries' eyes followed those of their hounds, and one of them cleared his throat. "Seems they recognize a Storm Spear. Old Alth said they would."

"Alth's our senior wyr handler," Jad explained, as the other sentry shifted stance.

"When the Storm Spears ride in, trouble rides with them." The sentry's comment sounded like a quote, although several contestants had muttered similar opinions within Kalan's hearing. He decided again that he knew far too little about the society whose name he bore, but despite the guard's veiled challenge, the wyr hounds remained quiet.

Jad frowned. "Have done, lads. You know who we are." The second sentry looked inclined to argue, but the first waved them through into a much wider hallway that was hung with rich tapestries, all depicting Blood victories over massed foes. Kalan noted that while the older hangings featured a range of monsters from the *Swarm Bestiary*, the newer tapestries depicted solely warrior armies. Only one, which was also the most frayed, showed the Golden Fire. The keep in the tapestry was ablaze with it, the conflagration rising in long necks and curling heads of flame as light surged from the walls to push back a shadow host. A giant figure loomed above the main gate, wreathed in golden flame and casting lightning bolts into the besiegers.

Blood called such legends fireside tales now: Kalan rotated his shoulders again and contemplated the folly of that as they reached the area allocated to Night. Two of Morin's comrades were posted outside their Commander's quarters, and when they insisted that those who entered both surrender their arms and allow a check for concealed weapons, Jad and his escort opted to wait outside. Once allowed through into Night's anteroom, Kalan found the Commander's door shut, although voices filtered through. "Garan's lot have turned up," the guard on the inner door told Morin. "You'll have to wait."

Morin looked surprised, but waved Kalan to one of several armchairs. "Who else is in there, Aeln, besides the Commander and Garan?"

"Nerys"—Aeln's tone implied an, *of course*, as Morin nodded—"and Lieutenant Teron."

Teron of Cloud Hold had been the Earl of Night's squire six years ago and was now an envoy for his marriage. Kalan pursed his lips again at the turnings of fate, taking note of the ubiquitous Blood hydra above the anteroom's unlit hearth before he sat back in the chair and closed his eyes. His hearing was sufficiently acute that after a very brief adjustment he began to distinguish individual speakers among the rise and fall of voices in the adjoining room. Asantir was the easiest to identify because he had heard her speak only that morning. She also asked the majority of the questions. The person who replied most frequently was Garan; Kalan recognized his voice from the dream. The second man, whose intonation occasionally indicated a question, but was more often observation, must be Teron, while Nerys was living up to her epithet and not speaking.

' "Would you like something to eat or drink while you're waiting?" Morin asked.

Kalan opened his eyes, but shook his head. He made a show of studying the hydra, but let his ear re-attune to each speaker and gradually discerned meaning.

"... where exactly did you find the messenger?" Asantir asked.

"On the boundaries of Adamant territory." Kalan thought Garan sounded bone weary. "He managed to tell us that he was on his way here. His escorts were dead, but the Sword warriors present claimed their arrival prevented the 'spawn ambushers from finishing him off." He paused, and Kalan, his curiosity rising, felt the hesitation's weight. "Our scouts, Asha and Lawr, say they cannot be sure but thought the Sword warriors were looting the bodies when first sighted. We checked the whole area afterward, too, but could find no 'spawn sign."

"Derai outlaws?" Teron exclaimed. "That's not possible!"

"It may not happen often," Asantir observed, matter-of-fact, "but our own have turned renegade before, and there are enough deserted watchtowers and redoubts in that part of the Wall to give them a base. How did the Sword band account for themselves?"

"They said they were returning to the Keep of Swords on a Matter of Kin and Blood. But they didn't seem to be hurrying."

Orth's lot, Kalan thought, and decided he would not put it past them to prey on fellow travelers if opportunity arose.

"They may have learned that their news has already reached the Keep of Swords." Asantir sounded thoughtful. "A messenger arrived here from the Sword Earl the day before the contest began. A letter had come from the Guild House in Terebanth, via Sword's factor in Grayharbor, saying his nephew had been lost, believed dead, in Ij. Ostensibly, that's why no Sword envoys are here, although the apology said they would attend the wedding."

Tarathan and Jehane Mor must have sent that message, Kalan supposed, or caused it to be sent, since they had learned of the Sword captain's disappearance when in Caer Argent—but he found he had lost track of the conversation and refocused.

" . . . so I set Ter and Innor to trail them. Their sign left the main route not far beyond the ambush site."

"They're certainly not traveling by the direct route." Asantir was dry. "I'll let our Blood hosts know, so their patrols can sweep those old redoubts before the bridal caravan passes through."

A bridal caravan would be too large for outright attack, but Kalan knew from Emerian experience how a small, determined group could prey on the fringes of even well-armed merchant trains. Wherever such groups operated, any stragglers were as good as dead. He shifted uneasily, remembering his dream of the ghost caravan, before reminding himself what Tarathan had said about the paths of fore-seeing. A chair scraped in the other room—someone moving, Kalan guessed—and he lost most of the next words.

" . . . dispatch pouch," Garan said. "I know our orders were to return home once we'd seen the old Lady and her company back to their Towers, but once we saw the urgent seal and that it was for you . . . " Again the scrape sounded. " . . . bring it here."

During the subsequent pause, it occurred to Kalan that he was listening to a conversation not meant for him. Yet since his whole purpose in being here was to further Malian's cause, he would be foolish not to use the opportunity presented. Nonetheless, the part of him that was a knight of Emer felt uncomfortable at the whole notion of eavesdropping, let alone spying—although he supposed calling it intelligence gathering gave the business a fairer face. "You judged rightly," Asantir said finally.

In the anteroom, Morin spoke to Aeln in a clan dialect of Night. "Should we knock, do you think? Let her know the Storm Spear's here?"

Aeln replied using the same dialect, but the glance he threw Kalan was dismissive. "He can wait."

They could not know, Kalan thought, amused, that he had spent seven years in Night. Besides, Aeln was right. For now, he could wait.

28

━┿━━┿━

Field of Play

"S o how," Asantir said, on the other side of the door, "did the rest of your mission go?"

"Slowly, because the old Lady tired so easily." Garan sounded rueful. "Still, that gave us time to scout more thoroughly, as you ordered."

"And?" Asantir asked.

"Not good." Kalan grimaced inwardly as Garan recounted the prevalence of darkspawn sign, not just around the Wall's main passes but well into the Gray Lands. House of Adamant hostility was also mentioned, because it had forced the Night escort to take their charges—who, Kalan realized with considerable interest, comprised a party of Morning priests—farther out into the Gray Lands than originally intended. "The Keep of Bells territory is reasonably well protected by Swords, but Morning's wide open. Their Towers are defensible enough, but they sit a lot farther forward on the Wall than the other priestly Houses and they've no warriors at all to garrison their walls. Precious few priests either, from what we could see. But it's not just that."

Kalan concentrated fiercely as Garan's steady, weary voice described the terrain: the surrounding mountains that provided protection against assault but were also an impassable barrier between Morning and their nearest Derai neighbors, and the Towers' location adjoining a long, narrow pass through the Wall. "Dread Pass," Garan said.

Of course, Kalan thought, because the spoken account matched the landscape from his Grayharbor dream, when he had heard Garan and Innor discussing the mission the Night guard was reporting on now. "If a Swarm force did come through the pass and take the Towers," Garan continued, "they would not only have a strong foothold on the Haarth side of the Wall, but a clear route through the Plain of Ash and into the Gray Lands." He paused. "Here, Commander, I've drawn it as best I could."

"Surely this is the priest House's problem, though?" Teron sounded both puzzled and impatient. "Let them look to their allies rather than whining to Night for help."

Typical, Kalan thought, recalling Cloud Hold's reputation for rigid adherence to the Oath that separated priest and warrior kind. But Teron spoke again, as though studying Garan's map at the same time. "The Sea Keep's vital, of course, but it's protected from Dread Pass by the Impassable Range." Reluctance entered his tone. "I suppose Garan's right. An enemy that occupied the Towers would be almost impossible to dislodge, and would have untrammeled access to the Gray Lands as well. But it's still Morning's responsibility, and their allies', to guard against such attack."

Kalan closed his eyes again, trying to visualize the territory under discussion as Asantir asked the question he also considered obvious: "But if they can't—and their allies don't, or won't?"

In the anteroom, Morin cleared his throat, obliging Kalan to open his eyes. "It's been too long. I *should* let the Commander know you're here." An edge crept into his tone as he met Aeln's gaze. "We shouldn't rule out foul play either."

Aeln snorted, but did not stop the younger guard from knocking. When Asantir called out permission, Morin opened the door. "The Storm Spear's here, Commander."

Garan spoke at once. "Nerys and I can wait outside, or return later as best suits."

"I think we've done all we can for now," Asantir replied. "Get some rest and we'll talk again before tomorrow's contests. Khar of the Storm Spears," she added, rising as Kalan joined Morin: "Come in—and my apologies for keeping you waiting."

Entering as bidden, Kalan saw Garan and Nerys salute crisply despite their dirt. They were both worn to leanness and shadowed eyes, but nodded in courtesy to Kalan as they left. Teron stayed seated, his arms folded across his chest, although his scowl faded as Asantir made the formal introductions. Kalan bowed, murmuring a polite response, and decided the former Honor Captain looked much as she had six years before. Her Commander's black mail might be washed with gold, but the dagger hilts at her belt were still well-worn and her dark gaze was as keen as he remembered.

Let's hope, he thought, that she only sees what she expects to, all the same. Taking the chair offered, he saw the tabletop was layered with papers and maps, dispatch pouches, and scroll cylinders. The pouch closest to Asantir's chair was crusted with dried blood, and he guessed it must be the one Garan had retrieved from the dying messenger. A pair of swords graced a weapons' stand on the wall—Asantir's, Kalan assumed, since she currently wore none, before his eyes were drawn to the traveling chess set on top of a battered chest, where a game had been left partway through. Each small figure was carved into a representation of the Derai world, from Earl and Heir to household warrior. "Do you play?" Asantir asked, following his gaze.

Kalan nodded. "A little."

"He won't know that you always win," Teron said to Asantir, with a flash of humor, "so might be willing to give you a game."

If I live, Kalan thought, seeing Teron's look grow conscious, although Asantir's expression did not change. "Perhaps," she murmured, then bowed to Kalan, a sword exponent's salute with her right hand placed above her heart. "I thank you, Khar, for upholding Lady Myrathis's guest friendship and standing as her champion and mine in the duel forced by Lord Parannis." Teron stirred at that, but did not speak. "The Battlemaster approached me earlier to discuss the time and terms of the combat. Needless to say, he's not happy with any aspect of the business."

Kalan could see why. For Lord Parannis to challenge the Earl of Night's emissary, who was also the Battlemaster's fellow judge, was irregular in the extreme. To persist in his challenge once the Bride had made the Night envoys her guest friends tested Derai tradition and the Honor Code to their limits. Yet whatever the Battlemaster might say, Earl Sardon had effectively allowed this train of events: by not extending guest friendship to the Night envoys from the outset, by failing to rein Lord Parannis in, and then by not forbidding the duel.

Earlier that day, Kalan had overheard Banath informing Nalin's watch of the official line: that with the challenge given and accepted, the Earl's hands were now tied. Kalan, however, had spent seven years in Night's Temple quarter, where Brother Selmor's study had been history and Sister Korriya's the law. He knew how rarely an Earl's hands were ever truly tied. *"Failure to act is still an action."* Kalan repeated the axiom, one of Lord Falk's favorites, to himself, and considered its implication: that Lord Parannis was behaving as he did, and the duel going ahead, because Earl Sardon wanted both those outcomes. One possible reason was that the marriage had never been more than a pretext for Blood to strike against Night, through its Commander. Despite the duel now taking matters along a different course, it was still a convenient way to remove an unwelcome contestant, or even—and here Kalan frowned—dispose of a son who was becoming a liability.

The Earl of Blood, after all, had eight other children.

Kalan saw Asantir take note of the frown before she spoke again. "The Battlemaster asked me to say that he interceded with Lord Parannis, who refused to withdraw, while Lady Myrathis also maintains her guest friendship."

Despite considerable pressure, I'm sure, Kalan thought: bravely done, Lady Mouse. "Lord Kharalthor," Asantir continued, "requested I point out that you also have the option of withdrawal."

Kalan's eyes met hers, but the dark gaze was as neutral as her voice. She had to honor Lord Kharalthor's request, he supposed, just as the Battlemaster had to go through Asantir or Lady Myrathis rather than approaching their champion directly. Doubtless, too, Lord Kharalthor had to be seen trying to avert the combat, even if Taly's view suggested it furthered his interests. "I regret that's impossible," Kalan said.

The Commander inclined her head. "In that case, the Battlemaster has advised that the duel will conclude the final day of contests." A grand finale, Kalan thought ironically. "Since Lord Parannis issued the challenge, the choice of weapons is yours."

That, at least, was easy: "Swords."

Teron stirred again. "Lord Parannis is said to excel with the sword, Storm Spear. You'll be playing to his strength."

"The sword is also my weapon," Kalan replied quietly.

The Cloud Holder looked resigned, but his scowl returned as Asantir spoke. "Given the open nature of the Honor Contest, the Battlemaster prefers that the duel also be public."

"To maximize Night's humiliation should our champion lose." Now Teron sounded bitter. "I'm starting to wonder whether Blood wants this marriage to go ahead."

Only "starting to," Kalan thought, with a touch of humor, but Asantir shook her head. "The contracts have been signed since the spring, Teron. For Blood to withdraw now would contravene both convention and law, and entitle Night to considerable reparations. Your speculation," she added, "also impugns the honor of Earl Sardon and his House, so please don't repeat it elsewhere."

The warning conveyed the danger of repeating Teron's doubt, without denying its import—which Kalan decided was interesting, given the likelihood of eyes-and-ears. He eyed the Commander of Night and decided she played a hazardous game. "You *have* to admit though—" Teron began, then broke off as Asantir's eyebrows lifted. She continued to regard him a moment longer, before turning back to Kalan.

"Forgive me," she said, "but I must ask. Should the worst happen, do you have kin or a liege to whom I should send word, together with your possessions?"

Kalan's thoughts flew to Malian, then Lord Falk and his Normarch friends—and Jarna as he had last seen her, with her face turned away from him, toward the wall. Yet he could mention none of them, let alone the family that had exiled him, so shook his head. "Thank you, but I have asked Envoy Nimor to see to all such matters. Lady Myrathis conveyed the necessary letters to him."

The letter to Che'Ryl-g-Raham asked that she do all within her power to ensure Madder's safe return to Jarna. That in itself would serve as news of his fate for all those he had left behind in Emer, but his letter to the navigator also enclosed another to Falk of Normarch. In it, Kalan asked that the Lord Castellan accept Faro as foster-son in his own place. He felt confident Che'Ryl-g-Raham would ensure both her charges reached their destination, and Faro would then be as well provided for as an uncertain world allowed. If only, that is, he heeded Kalan's caution not to betray his atrocious Grayharbor accent, and himself, while still in Blood territory.

Asantir nodded. "I will let Envoy Nimor know that Night will render any assistance the Sea House may require."

Teron's expression was curious. "Anvin said that you sent your page to Nimor as well. To conduct back to your order, he supposed?"

Did he now? Kalan thought. Clearly, the contest talk that claimed Teron stood on easy terms with Lord Anvin was correct. Still, the speculation was close enough to the truth—even if the order in question was the Oakward and not the Storm Spears—that Kalan nodded, aiming to satisfy curiosity without actually confirming it. At the same time, it occurred to him that Blood might trail Faro and the horses in order to locate the Storm Spears' base. Let them waste their time, he decided. He was confident of the Oakward's ability to deal with Blood spies, and the subsequent puzzle might give the ruling kin pause.

Asantir interrupted this train of thought. "Tradition requires that the one whose honor is at stake should make the champion that defends it a gift."

Captain-Lady Hatha, Kalan recalled, had told Lady Myrathis the same thing. Teron looked surprised. "I didn't know that," he said.

"The tradition is old—as old as the Derai Alliance, I believe." Asantir moved to the sword stand. "Should you visit Night, Khar, I will make you a more permanent gift. But now, since you fight in my name as well as the Bride's, I would be honored if you used my swords." She paused. "For this combat, and given Lord Parannis's resources, you will need weapons of their caliber."

She was right, Kalan knew. A Son of Blood could command the finest armor and weapons, and his own, while serviceable, were hardly of the same order. His mind flashed to the contestants' gossip again, and the rumor that the Commander of Night's swords were black blades. A confused account of a Gray Lands' confrontation involving Night warriors and Stone Keep priests had been part of the mix as well. All Honor Contest speculation—except that Kalan knew Asantir *had* brought a black spear into the Old Keep six years before and used it to slay a Raptor of Darkness.

"Of death my song ... " His skin lifted into gooseflesh, reliving the moment when the spear, wreathed in golden fire, had carried the Raptor with it into the void. The memory bore out the legend that went with the ancient rhyme, which claimed that even the slightest nick or scratch from such a weapon meant death. Although according to Brother Belan, his mind wandering between ancient lore and more accurate histories, a blade's potency had always been controlled by the wielder's intention. The old priest had also claimed that the ruling kindreds, possibly through their bond to the Golden Fire, possessed some resistance to the black blades' power. Limitations or not, such weapons would certainly give anyone who wielded them an edge, as Asantir's use of the black spear had proven. But as Kalan recalled matters, the spear had been a legacy of Night's Honor Captains, so Asantir's possession of more heirloom weapons would be unlikely at best.

"Perhaps you're not familiar with twin blades?" Teron suggested, misinterpreting his hesitation.

"No, I've learned them." It was unnecessary, Kalan decided, to explain that Normarch instruction had focused on the Lathayran and Jhainarian styles for such weapons, not the Derai.

Humor gleamed in Asantir's expression. "He fought the glaive wielder with a sword and dagger, Teron. If I may?" she added, and lifted the longer of the two swords from its stand. Accepting it from her, Kalan drew the blade clear of its sheath. The steel was black with a blue sheen, but he could not detect any echo of the hornet song that had characterized the black spear six years before. Returning the blade to its scabbard, he exchanged it for the shorter weapon.

"A champion's blades," the Night Commander said quietly, and Kalan nodded, because the workmanship, weight, and balance of both swords were superb. Carrying them, he would meet the Son of Blood on equal terms, at least when it came to weapons.

Asantir replaced the longsword on the stand, her expression reflective. "I acquired this pair when I journeyed into the River lands with Earl Tasarion, before he became Night's Heir. I had taken cover from a spring downpour in a dark, narrow little shop in Terebanth." She paused. "I learned later that the trader, Gray Taan, was famous. As soon as I entered, he said that he had something that might interest me."

"Did he know the swords' history?" Kalan asked, curious now.

She shook her head. "Only how they came into his hands, amidst an array of weapons of dubious provenance—his words—in a tinker's wagon. Too rich and too foreign for easy sale, the tinker had told him; apparently he had been thinking of melting them down."

Teron's inward suck of breath matched Kalan's, although if these *were* black blades, the tinker might have had difficulty melting them down. What were you doing in a River tinker's cart, so far from home? Kalan asked silently, appreciating the wave-sheen of the shortsword's blade.

"So I purchased them," Asantir said, "and for more than I wanted to spend, although Gray Taan maintained they were cheap at the price, which was true enough."

Whatever the swords' more immediate provenance, Kalan

reflected, turning the steel so the light played across it, they were both Derai and old. "I thought," he said slowly, "that Tasarion of Night's visit to the River was meant to be the Derai's first venture south of Grayharbor."

Teron looked puzzled, but Asantir shrugged. "So far as we know, although rumors of our lost priest-kind persist. Fifteen hundred years is a long time, even by our standards, so it's possible not all expeditions were recorded, especially in the period following the Betrayal." Her keen gaze studied him. "You came via the Sea Keep, so you will know that not all their ships return safely."

Flotsam from wrecked ships could drift, Kalan supposed, and good quality metal might not be ruined by salt water . . . He handed back the sword. "Even the use of these weapons is a lordly gift, Commander, and I am no lord."

"Tradition specifies a gift, but not its value, and you will be fighting for both my honor and the Bride's. As well as for your life," she added coolly, "all matters I consider valuable. I will not diminish myself, or my honor, by stinting on my gift."

"Besides," Teron observed, "to refuse would be churlish."

The Cloud Holder was right; Kalan knew his surprise at that was churlish as well, or at least ungenerous. He bowed his head, catching the glimmer of Yelusin's humor deep within his mind. "I would not presume," he said, trying not to sound stiff, "to instruct the Commander of Night in matters of her own honor. Or wish," he added, humor reasserting itself, "to be thought a churl. I accept, with gratitude."

Asantir inclined her head. "You will need to familiarize yourself with them before you fight. Under other circumstances I would give them to you now, but we must not risk their loss ahead of this duel." Kalan nodded, ashamed, as one born to the House of Blood, that he could not argue against her inference. "I must preside over the remaining contests, but Garan and his eight-guard know the twin-blade style. They can bring the swords with them to train with you."

Another risk, Kalan thought, because Garan and many of his

eight-guard had also been part of the Old Keep expedition—and it was Garan and Nerys who had taken him from the Temple quarter the night he and Malian fled the Wall. I've changed a great deal in six years, he reminded himself, as Asantir spoke again. "But I shall personally ensure that you have the swords for the duel."

Teron, rising to second Asantir's salute, bumped the desk. A scroll cylinder rolled toward the edge and the Cloud Holder grabbed for it, knocking a sheaf of papers to the floor. Kalan bent to retrieve a sheet that fluttered to his feet and saw *Dread Pass* written in cramped letters across the top. He handed the page back, and Teron peered from it to the papers he had recovered. "Garan's jottings." He shot a look at Asantir, but addressed Kalan. "What would you say, Storm Spear, to a priest-kind rabble that left their borders undefended?"

Kalan assumed a perplexed air and waited for Asantir to close the conversation down. Instead she seated herself on a corner of the desk, her expression bland. "You'll need to give him more information, Teron." Her gesture invited the Cloud Holder to hand the pages to Kalan.

Teron hesitated, looking as though he regretted his impulse, before passing the sheaf across. Kalan's mind raced as he laid the maps on the desk, wondering why Asantir wanted him to see them. "These show the Towers of Morning country," he said finally, and glanced at Teron. "Is that what you meant by undefended borders?"

The Cloud Holder nodded. "They're wide-open to attack, but it's their responsibility to rectify that, I say!" He shot another look toward Asantir, but she appeared absorbed by the swing of one booted foot.

"What if they can't, though?" Kalan repeated a variant of the Commander's earlier question. "Morning was decimated in the civil war and hard hit again in the plague years." In the face of Teron's silence, he changed tack. "Traditionally, the Swarm have focused their assaults on our Alliance. So in effect we've always fought each other and rolled over anyone else who got in the way. But prior to the last five hundred years, the Alliance never depended on others for resources the way we do now."

Because we've lost the Golden Fire, he added silently: at least as
it was before the Betrayal. The resource implications of the Fire's
loss had been one of Brother Selmor's pet themes, but Kalan had
never seen its consequences illustrated as clearly as he did now,
studying Garan's maps. "So if an enemy force did take the Towers,"
he continued, as Teron shifted his weight, "they might not necessarily attack the Houses on Morning's flanks next. Instead, they might
push through into the Gray Lands, cutting the rest of the Alliance
off from both the Sea Keep and the route through the Barren Hills."
Ostensibly he spoke to Teron, but his eyes went to Asantir, and this
time she looked back, her gaze steady. Of course she sees it, he
thought. "The Alliance's maritime and landward supply routes would
both be severed."

Teron practically shoved Kalan aside to stare down at the maps.
"And," Kalan said, still looking at Asantir, "once they got that far
they could just sweep on south and into Haarth. There's nothing
between the Border Mark and Grayharbor to stop them." Mentally, he
flinched away from the vision of the Swarm pouring into the peaceful
country he had seen as the *Halcyon* sailed from Ij to Grayharbor. But
if Morning and its Towers were as vulnerable as Garan's maps suggested, and the Alliance remained divided—or asleep, he thought,
with inward despair over Blood's insistence the Swarm was a fireside
tale—then it might not be possible to prevent it.

"We would be starved of resources." Teron's hand clenched, crumpling paper, then as hastily smoothed the sheet open again. His tone,
however, matched the violence of his initial gesture. "*We* should take
the southern lands first and make sure of what we need."

He sounded, Kalan thought, like someone who had been listening to Lord Anvin and Lady Sardonya, who were both New Blood
adherents. Asantir shook her head. "Shoring up the Wall's defenses
would be more prudent. They are still considerable and our forces
insufficient, even if the Alliance truly stood as one, to wage war on
two such widely disparate fronts."

Teron grunted, but he was preoccupied with the maps again, so

Kalan was not sure he fully took in the Commander's point. He was debating whether to point out that the Wall itself was the source of resources that ensured the Alliance's favorable trade with the rest of Haarth, when a knock sounded and Aeln looked in. "The Blood guards are asking if you'll keep the Storm Spear much longer, Commander?"

They had been closeted some time, Kalan supposed. He took his formal leave when Asantir excused him, although he had to wait in the anteroom while Morin retrieved his weapons. Teron departed a few moments later, leaving the office door wide enough for Kalan to see Asantir, still seated on the desk. She was looking toward the chessboard, her expression deeply thoughtful, but turned as Aeln reached for the latch. The Commander nodded as she met Kalan's gaze, although it was clear her mind was elsewhere.

Even after Morin returned with the weapons and he rejoined Jad's escort, Kalan's own focus remained on the business with the maps. The reason Asantir had encouraged the discussion, he realized finally, had to have been for the benefit of Liankhara's listeners in their spyholes, while also being aimed—through Teron—at others within the ruling kin. The Cloud Holder would doubtless believe he was being close-lipped, but Kalan felt sure Asantir was relying on him revealing more than he intended, presumably to try and get Blood to rethink where their focus on the Southern Realms could lead. Especially, he reflected, as they passed the wyr hounds and sentries again, with passes like Dread leveled like a weapon at the collective Derai throat.

Yet the Commander of Night's game was fraught with risk, since as with Teron's initial reaction, the vulnerability she had highlighted might simply reinforce Blood's Haarth ambitions. Alternatively, the warrior House might decide to take pre-emptive action in support of its larger goals and march on Morning, as it had once before during the Betrayal conflict.

Struck by the force of this possibility, Kalan almost stopped short—because if Blood did pursue the latter course, it would almost certainly reignite the still-smoldering embers of the Derai's five-hundred-year-old civil war.

After the door closed, Asantir turned away from the chessboard and picked up the dispatch pouch Garan and Nerys had brought her. The messenger's blood had dried in a thick clot above the seal, but she prised it open. She expected to see Earl Tasarion's hand on the folded paper within, but instead found Haimyr's flowing script. As she read, her expression grew somber, and she sat for some time afterward, her gaze on the wall.

Nhairin, she thought: *Nhairin*—and swung back to the chessboard. Black's line straggled across the field of play, while white maintained several strategic groupings. The largest of these dominated the center of the board, although several lesser pieces had been removed, opening up gaps. Asantir considered these before returning to the scattered line of black. The Earl piece—what her long ago Terebanth opponents would have termed the king—was located well back, with the powerful and versatile Heir strategically placed to both defend the Earl and support black's forward line.

Slowly, Asantir extended a hand toward a black pawn, out on its own to one side, then paused, considering the two black pieces that had reached white's end of the board. One was still a pawn, but its former companion had been replaced by a black Honor Captain, what both Haimyr and the Terebanthans called a knight. White's Heir stood close by both, but currently offered no overt threat to either.

Asantir continued to study the pieces intently, before the ghost of a smile touched her face. "There you are." The fire in the grate flared, as though answering her reflective murmur, and firelight washed the new Honor Captain with vermilion before the flames steadied and the red glow faded, restoring the piece to Night's black. Gently, Asantir reached out and tapped the Honor Captain's horsehead crest. "After all these years, here you are again."

29

Risk

Kalan kept walking, turning when his escort did and automatically marking the detail of corridors, adjoining halls, and separate wings branching off, as well as units of guards on their regular patrols, and guests returning from the banquet. The expressions directed his way included curiosity, doubt, and outright hostility, but he ignored them, still intent on the implications of the Dread Pass maps and subsequent conversation in Asantir's office. High stakes, high risk, he reflected—but that was no different than the game he and Malian were playing, with the fate of a world, not just the Derai Alliance, hanging in the balance.

Although to continue playing, he would have to win the duel against Lord Parannis. That, by implication, meant killing a Son of Blood before his kin and gathered House—which will only create a fresh Wall storm of problems, not end them, Kalan reflected grimly, as they passed the great arch into the muster ground. The gates were locked and the hydra above the arch unlit, but he still felt as though every shadowed eye was marking him. He might jeer at himself for shying from a representation carved in stone, one of hundreds throughout the Red Keep—but it was at that moment the first sense of being followed crawled across his shoulder blades.

They were turning into the adjoining Temple quarter when he heard footsteps jogging to catch up. Two warriors, Kalan decided, as one of the Blood guards turned his head, listening too. "What's the odds that's for us?" the guard said, with a less-than-friendly glance Kalan's way.

Jad just grunted, but stopped to wait. A few seconds later Morin caught up to them, accompanied by another Night guard. "Two separate messengers came looking for you," Morin told Kalan. "Apparently there's trouble with your horses again, and the Sea envoy says your page has gone missing."

"We're close to the stables," Jad said, before Kalan could respond. "We can deal with whatever those devils you call horses are about, then talk about looking for your page. If you don't think he's just playing truant." His tone said he thought this likely.

Kalan thought it likely, too, but whether Faro had gone adventuring with Liy or was trying to rejoin him was another matter. With any luck, by the time he settled the horses, the boy would have turned up. "What's the quickest way there?" he asked.

Another of the Blood guards pointed to a small chapel adjoining the darkened Hallows of Tawr. "Through there. The rear door opens onto the main service stair for this part of the keep."

"You lead, Dain." Jad waved the guard forward while he remained beside Kalan, and the Night guards fell in behind them.

"The Commander," Morin explained to Kalan, "ordered us to assist you as required."

Jad compressed his lips, and Kalan wondered if he would order the Night guards away on principle. Instead the eight-leader asked Morin to light a torch from one of the corridor lanterns. "So we don't fall over each other, getting through the mausoleum."

Kalan felt unease prickle again as he turned toward the entrance with the rest, which suggested that whatever he had sensed following them could not have been the Night guards. Alert for danger, he paused before stepping through the unlit door into what Jad had called a mausoleum. "Although it's more of a memorial," the eight-leader explained, as Morin's torch illuminated the interior. A sequence of faded banners hung to their right, facing the bas-relief of a young, stern-faced warrior in full Blood panoply.

"Ammaran," Kalan said, reading the inscription beneath the warrior's mailed feet.

Jad nodded. "He was the last Heir of the old line of Earls. The family died out shortly after the Betrayal War, when he and his Honor Guard escort were lost."

"There's no flame," Morin said, his voice hushed against the silence. Kalan knew what he meant. If this was a memorial, a votive flame should be kept lit in a niche to Hurulth, the Silent God.

"The House of Adamant, who are Blood's enemy, follow Hurulth first amongst the Nine." Jad's voice was colorless as Dain headed toward the rear door. "We follow Kharalth of the Battles, and the only flame kept burning is in her sanctuary."

Morin said nothing, but Kalan sensed his shock. Traditionally, all Derai believed that the Silent God kept his hall for their dead. In order for the souls of the fallen to enter, the vigil of Hurulth must be kept and the rites for the dead spoken. Failure to do so risked the spirits of the dead remaining trapped, hungry ghosts clinging to the fringes of the living world until their essence either dissipated, or worse, was consumed by the Swarm.

"Here in the Red Keep, anyway," Dain said. "Most of the holds still follow all Nine Gods in the old way." He glanced back as he reached the side door and shrugged at Jad's frown.

That tallied, Kalan thought, with what he had gleaned from the Sea Keepers' conversation on the road here. They had not said why all the Red Keep temples except Kharalth's had been desanctified, but he assumed part of Blood's motivation was to minimize priest-kind numbers. The Emerians, he reflected, would say mourning rites were not essential anyway, because everyone came to Imuln in the end. They held, too, that the goddess was great enough to find every soul, no matter how far from home a body might fall. Yet the essence of what it meant to be Derai derived from the ancient powers that flowed from the Nine Gods, together with the bond to the Golden Fire and the commitment to withstand the Swarm.

Still, Kalan could see the path Blood had taken. Having lost the Golden Fire and turned against those with old powers, then consigned the Swarm to fireside tales, the next logical step was to abandon the Nine as well and trust solely to armed strength. Kalan wanted to shake his head as Dain finally persuaded the rear door to open, because he had spoken with two surviving aspects of the Golden Fire now: Hylcarian in the Old Keep of Winds, and the remnant of Yelusin housed in the Sea Keep fleet. He had also passed the Gate of Dreams and met both the dead hero, Yorindesarinen, and the power known as the Huntmaster. He had fought Swarm demons and the Darksworn as well, not just the low-level minions the House of Blood now termed Wallspawn.

Fools, Kalan thought. Unfortunately, they were also dangerous fools, given their numbers, wealth, and ambition—and the fact that the Derai Alliance relied on Blood's strength as the rearguard, anchoring their battle line of keeps and holds.

Dain waited until everyone had cleared the memorial before turning onto the service stair, which plunged downward in a series of narrow flights. Despite the need to concentrate on his footing, Kalan still felt the prickling awareness of pursuit and regretted the suppressed shield sense that would have told him whether the pursuit was physical or psychic in nature. Nonetheless, they reached the stables without incident. Another hydra reared its nine heads above the gate, the stone eyes fierce and each fanged mouth snapping in a different direction. The complex beyond was vast, with row on row of stalls and loose boxes interspersed by tack rooms and grain stores. Even before he entered, Kalan could hear the commotion from the far side of the complex where Tercel and Madder were stabled. His stride quickening, he sifted the thud of a horse's hooves against wood, and the simultaneous crack of timber, from a mutter of voices: ". . . attacked . . . Oathers . . . let out . . . did anyone see . . . killer . . . I'm not going near . . ."

When Kalan and his escort emerged from a long line of stalls, they found a small knot of grooms watching Madder from a safe distance. The door into the loose box adjoining Tercel's stood wide, and a trail of splintered wood led to the roan destrier, standing his ground in the entrance to a narrow alley that ended in an open storeroom door. Madder's ears were flat against his skull and he struck a hoof against the flagstones as the newcomers approached. Kalan's gut tightened as he saw gore on the destrier's metal shoes, and a swift glance along the alley revealed at least two bodies. "What happened?" he asked the grooms.

"I heard a noise," one of the grooms began, "like people creeping—"

"There's another body in here." Straw rustled as Jad entered the loose box. "An Oath Holder, by his badge. His skull's broken and his ribcage crushed."

Oath, Kalan recalled, was the hold of Lord Parannis and Lady Sarein's maternal kin, but another groom spoke before he could reply. "That horse's a killer." When she took a step close Madder pawed the flagstones in answer. Snaking his head forward, he bared long yellow teeth.

"Stay back," Kalan commanded, although he kept his voice calm. "In this state he won't let anyone but me near him."

"Put the brute down," another groom muttered, but Kalan ignored him, beginning a deliberate, unhurried approach toward the roan destrier.

"Let him work," Jad said, just as quiet, and the watchers fell silent. Kalan took another slow step forward, gradually extending his arms wide and speaking to Madder in Emerian, adopting the same soothing drone he had used in the *Che'Ryl-g-Raham*'s hold.

"That's right, Madder, you know me, don't you? Easy boy, gently there." The destrier rolled the whites of his eyes and stamped, but eventually first one and then both ears lifted, swiveling toward Kalan's voice. "Easy, Madder, easy. Softly, my braveheart." Slowly, Kalan reached out, and although the destrier snorted, he let Kalan put a hand to his halter and lead him away from the alley.

"Was that some Storm Spear tongue?" a groom asked, and Kalan answered in Derai, using the same soothing tone for Madder's benefit.

"No, it's Emerian. These are great horses out of Emer, and at times like this it's best to use the language they know best."

The grooms' reaction suggested they saw the sense in that. "Although I still say he's a killer," the woman reiterated.

"They are both warhorses and trained to kill. Especially," Kalan added, "if they're attacked. Now I need to secure him in another stall, somewhere quiet and away from the scent of blood."

In the end he moved both horses, judging Madder would be calmer with Tercel's familiar presence. When he returned to the body in the stall, the duty groom was telling Jad about the intrusion. "I heard something odd and then the ruckus broke loose. By the time I got here the box door was open, and the intruders fleeing with the horse after them like a Swar— Wall demon."

"And there's this." Jad picked up a sickle blade from beside the dead Oath Holder. "I'd say they intended to either kill or maim the horse."

Kalan saw two of the Blood guards exchange significant glances. "It would be of service to me now," he said to Morin, "if you could bring the Sea envoy here."

Jad frowned and turned to the guard whose manner had suggested he saw Kalan as trouble. "Rhanar, if we're to have envoys here, you'd best get Captain Banath."

The eight-leader's expression remained tight after Rhanar left, although he still joined Kalan beside the first of the alleyway dead. The body, which had once been a man, was pounded to pulp and splinters. The corpse a few paces further on was untrampled, the Oath Hold insignia on the tunic clear, but the victim was also smaller. A squire, Kalan guessed from his age and garb, and killed by a blade through the throat. "A page's dagger," Jad said, and Kalan guessed they were both thinking of Faro, missing from the Sea envoy's accommodation. "This reads like the Oath Holders entered the stall, doubtless to kill or cripple your horse, and found they'd taken on more than they could handle. But they also surprised someone else there."

"It could have been Faro. He liked to sleep in my horses' stalls." Kalan's eyes went from the squire's bloody knife, lying just clear of his hand, to the blood drops leading into the storeroom. "Is there another way out of there?" he asked the duty groom.

"Only an air well," the man replied. "The vents open into both kennels and stables."

If the fugitive was Faro, then he would find that air well—so long, Kalan thought, his eyes on the blood, as he can still move. "I'll check in here. But we should send guards to the kennels' side, in case I flush out something other than my page." Several of the grooms nodded. Many of their number were guards who had been discharged because of injury, but their old instincts, whether for 'spawn or enemy agents, would still hold good.

"Dain and Palla," Jad said curtly, "see to it."

Kalan flattened himself to one side of the storeroom door, clear of an arrow or spear's trajectory but where he could slant a look inside. Nothing moved, and the only scents were timber and grain, cool air and dust. Gradually, he shut out the stable's background noise and isolated the storeroom's smaller sounds: the skitter of a mouse, the draft out of the air shaft—and finally, the shallow, suppressed breath of a hunted creature. Kalan could almost feel it, crouched down in darkness and listening, as he was listening.

He debated calling out, but if it was not Faro in there he would only spook the quarry. Instead, he signaled Jad to take the nearest lantern away, to avoid being silhouetted against its light—then kicked the door wide, dropping low and rolling behind a feed bin. Still nothing moved, except when Jad took his place outside the door. *Wait*, Kalan signed, and eased into a crouch, patient as the concealing bin. Finally, he stood up and began to close in on the breathing, setting each footstep soundlessly down. He heard Jad enter the storeroom behind him but did not look back.

The blood trail ended between stacked grain sacks, and Kalan could see where Faro, or a creature of similar size, had tunneled through them. Into the air well, he wondered, or some other hiding place—but paused as exclamations and stifled curses sounded from the stable, followed by a *click-click* over the flagstones. Not an attacker, he decided, reluctant to look away from the area where the blood spots led, and aware that Jad had not moved.

Click-click: the sound paused on the storeroom threshold, then resumed, and despite Jad having allowed the intrusion, Kalan almost yelled as a waist-high body brushed past. A second wyr hound stopped beside him, while the first used its head and powerful shoulders to push the disturbed sacks further apart, revealing a cavity in the wall with a small form curled inside. Faro, Kalan saw, as the wyr hound sniffed at the balled figure before settling down, its lean dark body curved around the boy, and stared back at him out of ghostly eyes. Jad, who had followed the hounds in, swore beneath his breath.

A way with wyr hounds as well as warhorses, Kalan thought, but realized that Faro must be unconscious, or near to it, since he did not stir. The wyr hounds looked like the pair from the guest quarter's gate, although they seemed to have dispensed with their handlers. Kalan guessed that they had been his unseen followers as well and recalled how one of the beasts on the Blood Gate had shown interest in Faro before turning away. Except these hounds had not followed Faro here; they had followed him.

Kalan dismissed the unease that thought brought, because right now he needed to determine the extent of the boy's injuries. The hound lying beside Faro yawned, its tongue lolling over wicked teeth. "Easy," Jad breathed, as Kalan stepped forward and settled onto his heels, extending his gauntleted fist for the beast to sniff. When seen this close, its array of teeth looked more like daggers, and its jaw capable of doing considerable damage, even to a closed fist. Kalan's pulse quickened and he wanted to wipe his palms dry, but forced himself to remain still—until the hound before him whined, deep in its throat, and the second beast rested its great head on his shoulder.

"Well, I'll be cursed," Jad whispered.

Faro, rousing, struck at Kalan's arm. "I won't let you hurt me." His tunic was torn, but the blood came from a gash along his forearm, and a cut above a bruised and swollen eye. He swiped at Kalan a second time and scrabbled back against the hound. The next time the boy's fist jabbed, his table dagger was clutched in it. The blood on the blade, Kalan thought, disarming him, suggested he had used it to better effect against the Oath squire. Deflecting a fierce but unscientific counterpunch, he kept a cautious watch on both wyr hounds. The beast curled around the boy whined again but did not move, even when Faro lunged for the dagger and Kalan fended him off once more.

"Faro, you little fool. It's me, Khar."

The boy's breath was coming in shallow, rapid pants, but gradually his good eye focused on Kalan. "You gave me to the stealers," he mumbled. "But I knew Madder and Tercel wouldn't abandon me. *They* keep faith."

"Madder certainly championed your cause to good effect." Kalan kept his tone easy, but although Faro's whisper was currently hoarse enough to disguise his accent, he needed to reinforce the caution against him speaking. "Try not to talk, Faro. Right now we need to get those gashes seen to."

He moved to help the boy clear of his bolt-hole, but Faro flailed at him again. "I won't let anyone hurt me, not ever again."

"It's all right. No one here's going to hurt you." Kalan let him crawl out himself, since he seemed to be managing—only to turn as a woman spoke from the doorway, her voice dripping sweetness and menace.

"I wouldn't be so sure about that, Storm Spear."

30

Pledge of Faith

The hair beneath the lady's hood was bright as a torch flame, her eyes pools of shadow as she regarded Kalan. "Do you really think you can save anyone, Storm Spear, even yourself? Or that your pet would be safe just because you gave him to the mariners? In *our* keep?"

"Our keep," Kalan thought, as the wyr hounds howled and what sounded like the entire Red Keep pack answered from the nearby kennels. Jad was standing rigidly to attention, his face devoid of any expression as he spoke above their din. "Daughter of Blood, you need to stand back. I have my orders." So now Kalan knew who the woman in the doorway must be. Lady Sarein was the only one of the five Daughters of Blood whom he had not yet seen, either in the Earl's gallery above the Field of Blood or in the banquet hall. Even the secretive Lady Liankhara had been with the Earl that morning in the small training hall, so this had to be Lord Parannis's twin.

Now her full mouth thinned as the wyr pair howled a second time, and the pack answered with a prolonged paean to *fear* and *danger*. "If someone," she said over her shoulder, "does not silence those Nine-cursed beasts, then I will see you all hang. With these two," she added, swinging back to the storeroom, "strung up beside you."

Ostensibly she meant the wyr hounds, but Kalan guessed her meaning was deliberately open. Faro must have felt her menace even if he missed the double meaning, because he shrank behind Kalan as both the hounds with them fell silent. The first rose and rejoined its companion, their glowing eyes fixed on the Daughter of Blood. "That's better." Lady Sarein was smiling again, despite the kennel pack's continued howls. Her gaze rested on Jad. "What if I'm here to bring you new orders—Jad, isn't it?"

Kalan could almost feel Jad's inward flinch at her knowing his name, although his demeanor did not change. "All orders in respect of the Storm Spear must be received from Captain Banath, unless Earl Sardon or the Battlemaster issue them in person. And other than the Bride, whom he champions, none of the ruling kin are to approach the Storm Spear without express permission."

"So punctilious," Lady Sarein murmured, but remained where she was. Her gaze dismissed Jad and returned to Kalan. "Where had we got to, Storm Spear? Ah, yes. We were discussing whether you could save anybody, let alone that misbegotten brat who thinks I might overlook him, cowering at your back." Her smile showed the tips of white teeth. "What if an allegation were to be made that he's tainted with old power? The Sea envoy could do nothing, since the boy is of Blood, and once made the claim would have to be investigated. *Thoroughly* investigated." She ran her tongue along her upper lip. "What will you do then, Storm Spear? What can you do, when two nights from now you'll be dead?"

Kalan schooled his features into calmness. "I take it you're here on your brother's business, Lady Sarein?"

"I? I am always about my own business, Storm Spear. Although I try never to interfere with Parannis's pleasures—and since you thwarted him of his preferred prey, he does appear very set on carving you into small pieces on the Field of Blood." She paused, still smiling, but shrugged when he made no reply. "I suppose there *is* nothing you can say to that. Or perhaps you are thinking that it was our dear little Myrathis who thwarted Parannis of his prey. *Not* a sisterly act, even if she has taken a fancy to being Countess of Night. Ah, you smile." Her lips pursed as she regarded him. "It *is* amusing when one considers the Mouse, I'll grant you that."

Kalan continued to smile. "What I was thinking, Lady Sarein, is that the Bride did your lord brother a kindness. The Commander of Night would eat him up and still sit down to her breakfast."

Sarein's eyes narrowed. For a moment, Kalan thought she might spit like one of the hooded snakes found in Ishnapur—but then she clapped her hands. "Oh, very good. I must share the jest with my twin. But as for doing him a kindness, I hardly think so." Again, she ran her tongue over her lips. "In due course, too, we will square our reckoning with the Half-Blood for her interference."

"As you tried to square your reckoning with me by sending your Oath Hold kindred after my horses?" Kalan kept his tone level, but Lady Sarein's smile did not falter.

"The account my grandfather's Oath Hold retainers brought me was that they heard a disturbance. When they investigated, your killer horse slew two of their number, and your page another." She shook her head. "Restitution will need to be made: blood debt paid in full or else blood feud declared."

"Against a horse and a page?" Kalan inquired, matching her tone. "Seeing as I'm to be chopped into mincemeat by your lord brother."

She raised one shoulder delicately, then dropped it again. "Blood demands blood. And it was your page, after all, that brought a sickle blade into your horse's stall."

Kalan felt Faro's jerk of protest as the wyr hounds growled, a low vibration of warning. Sarein bared her teeth in reply. "The beasts take your part, Storm Spear, against their ruling kin. Perhaps they are becoming mad, as well as increasingly unreliable. Many say so, but until now their madness has never been turned against *us*." She tapped a fingertip against her lips. "Perhaps I should see these two hang, after all: make an example to the rest of their hideous pack."

"I don't believe," Kalan observed, very dryly, "that hounds of any kind are capable of absorbing that sort of lesson."

"You may be right, Storm Spear. But a butcher's hook through this pair's slavering jaws could be entertaining." Kalan saw distaste flicker in Jad's eyes, while Faro suppressed a whimper. He kept his own features immobile, knowing Sarein was trying to goad a reaction. "Parannis and I like executions," she continued, "especially hangings. We enjoy seeing the bodies drop and listening to the necks snap. Hangings of the tainted are better still, because no one cares if we amuse ourselves with the formula." She paused, growing reflective. "Parannis likes watching them dance on air, but a hanging that ends in decapitation is best of all. We're agreed on that."

Despite understanding her game, Kalan had difficulty containing his revulsion. If even part of what she had said was true, then everyone in the Red Keep must realize, at some level, that those with old powers were being hung. They might try and suppress the knowledge, looking the other way, but he was certain they would know something. Including Lady Myrathis? he asked himself—and felt sick and old as the wyr hounds whined, and a new shadow fell across the doorway.

"Is that so, Sarein?" The shadow's voice was dark, as well as smooth. "I believe the dealings of your Oath Hold kin may require closer scrutiny. The last time I consulted Derai law it stated that the tainted may be exiled, but not executed. Or tortured."

Lady Sarein's mouth pinched. "Huern. And with dear Lord Narn in tow. As for Derai law—" She shrugged. "In the New Blood we make our own rules."

"Do you?" Lord Huern's tone was all polite interest. "You must expound that view to our father, since exile, not execution, is also his ruling."

"We Derai do not kill our own clan and kin for an accident of birth, even the taint." The second speaker was gruff, and Kalan guessed this was Bajan's liege, the head of Bronze Hold. "We must breed the defect out of our ranks, Lady, not violate the ties of kin and blood."

"Ways change, Lord Narn." Lady Sarein was smiling again, but her tone suggested she did not care for the holder's admonition. "But I was only making sport of the Storm Spear, brother. You know I—and my Oath kindred—would never contravene our father's rule."

In the lull that followed her words, Kalan distinguished Dain's voice, saying Palla's name. The rest of the honor guard's comment was too muted to catch, but the pair's presence suggested that they must have found the two lords at, or on their way to, the kennels. "Stay here," he told Faro, keeping his voice low as the wyr pack, too, finally stopped howling. "If I signal, flee into the air well, but don't stay there." He would not, he reflected, rule out Lady Sarein having it walled up. "It should bring you out in the kennels." The boy nodded but said nothing, retreating into the shadows as Kalan moved toward the door.

"Do I know that?" Lord Huern spoke again. "I find I cannot entirely dispel my doubt. Putting that aside, your kindred's retainers have come to grief here. Hardly the time for making sport."

"Deaths," Lady Sarein countered, "that were precipitated by the Storm Spear's page bringing a sickle blade into the roan's stall. Bent on revenge, no doubt, for being passed on to the Sea Keepers now that"—she paused delicately—"the Storm Spear's use for him is past." She paused again, angling her body to keep Kalan in sight while effectively blocking his exit. Jad met his eye but made no move to intervene, and Kalan could not blame him. Staying clear of the verbal fencing between the Son and Daughter of Blood was undoubtedly the prudent course.

Kalan, though, did not feel inclined toward prudence, especially hearing Lady Sarein reiterate her version of events, in which the Oath retainers went to investigate and Madder—presumably already enraged by Faro—turned on them. In Emer, both upholding and speaking the truth formed part of a knight's oath to the god Serrut. And lies, Kalan reminded himself, are anathema to the Nine Gods as well.

"You surprise me about the page," Lord Huern said. "I thought the sickle blade and the horse's head delivered as a gift was your trick."

"Do you take his part—" Sarein began, but Lord Narn spoke at the same time.

"Is *that* why Valan of Ward Hold withdrew his suit to Lady Sardonya? We knew something went awry with his gift, but he will never speak of it."

"He probably does not dare." Irony tinged Lord Huern's tone. "Having received so clear a message that he proffered his suit to the wrong sister, I imagine Valan was—and is—keen not to go the same way as his intended troth gift."

Jad's expression was so wooden that Kalan guessed the story must be mostly true. Rather than denying it, Lady Sarein shrugged. As if it were of no consequence, Kalan thought, as appalled by that as by her series of lies. "Speaking of the Storm Spear," Lord Huern continued, "perhaps you could step away from the door so he and the honor guard can leave without actually setting hands to your person. Unless that's what you're hoping for, of course."

However true that might be, Kalan knew that Audin, who was nephew to the Duke of Emer, would say it was highly irregular as well as unchivalrous to cast the slur in public. Not, he reflected, that there seemed to be anything resembling Emerian chivalry, or the exemplary behavior extolled by the Derai Honor Code, among Blood's ruling kin—although Lord Narn's tongue click suggested discomfort. Lady Sarein's gaze glittered, but she moved clear of the door, and Kalan reached the threshold as she stopped beside Lord Huern. "You will pay for this, brother." Her smile did not waver for an instant. "Be sure of that."

Kalan was probably the only person outside the two half siblings who could distinguish her murmur. In any case, voices sounded from the stable entrance as she spoke, and most of those present glanced that way. The newcomers' accents told Kalan that the Sea envoy had arrived at last, and he spoke over his shoulder to Faro. "You can come out now." But it was the wyr hounds that padded out first, their nails *click-clicking* over the flagstones.

Lord Huern looked intrigued. "I thought it was only you and

Parannis they liked to haunt, Sarein." The gleam in his eyes suggested appreciation of some hidden joke, but not one derived from either kindness or warmth. The wyr hounds bared their teeth, growling and stiff-legged, before settling between Kalan and the ruling kin, their pale eyes intent on both brother and sister. Eventually, Faro crept out, too, but clung to Kalan's shadow, his eyes fixed on the floor. From what Kalan could glimpse of the boy's frozen expression, there was no need to worry about his accent giving him away. He looked incapable of speech.

Lord Nimor and his companions came into view on the far side of an avenue of stalls, at the same time as Jad emerged and saluted both Lord Huern and Lady Sarein in turn. But—exactly like the wyr hounds—the eight-leader then took up position between Kalan and the ruling kin. "He has orders, brother." Lady Sarein continued to smile, but her gaze was hooded.

"I'm aware of his orders," Huern returned. "They're to ensure the duel takes its course without interference. That includes not harassing the Bride's champion by means of his horses or his page."

"Quite right," Lord Narn agreed. "The Code requires it." Kalan had seen the gray-haired hold commander before, but only from a distance. Up close, he smelt of sweat and hounds. His face was so deeply lined it gave him a permanently worried air, but Kalan thought he must have considerable courage to even imply criticism of Lady Sarein.

"But he's not really the Bride's champion, is he?" the Daughter of Blood retorted. "Primarily, he's defending the Commander of Night's honor—when the apostate can have no honor, we all know that. Having to fight such a contest sullies Parannis and diminishes us all."

Narn looked uneasy, but Lord Huern's irony glinted. "Still playing your tricks, Sarein? Parannis forced the duel, remember. All he's concerned about is not being thwarted of a kill."

"So best, perhaps," Narn put in, "to let matters here lie as they've fallen."

Kalan studied him carefully, but could detect neither irony nor humor, however dark, in the hold lord's expression. He could not imagine Lady Sarein agreeing, given the Oath Hold dead, but was willing to add a supporting argument as Lord Nimor and his company finally reached them. "Since the duel is to the death, any blood debt here could be added to Lord Parannis's cause."

Lord Huern's brows rose, but Sarein showed her teeth again. "You're already a dead man, Storm Spear, and your page has transgressed against House Blood. *He* must pay in full."

"I'm afraid it's no longer that simple," Kalan said. He rested his hand on Faro's shoulder, keeping him close. "Earlier today, Envoy Nimor not only took my page into his care, he confirmed the Sea Keep's wardship once the boy, and the required papers, were conveyed into his charge."

At the far end of the alley, Nimor bowed, his cabled hair a brindle of gray and black; the rings in his ears gleamed in the lanternlight. Lady Sarein's eyes blazed, and Faro shrank closer to Kalan, but Lord Huern inclined his head to the envoy. "Lord Nimor. Is this correct?"

"It is." The envoy bowed. "With respect, Daughter of Blood, I believe your understanding of my ward's part in events may be mistaken. Khar of the Storm Spears' will not only transfers ownership of the bay warhorse to Faro, but in the event of Khar's death the roan also passes into Sea House custody."

Conjecture buzzed among the Blood retainers, but it was Lord Huern who spoke. "In view of the wealth these horses represent, the boy would be as likely to cut his own throat."

Lord Nimor nodded. "If you question your witnesses again, Lady Sarein, you may find their initial account was muddied by confusion and the speed of events."

Huern's smile was mocking. "Yes, do question them again, Sarein. Or my father may wish to do so, since his hand is over the Storm Spear until the duel is concluded." The Son of Blood leaned close to his half sister. "Admit it, you've been outplayed. The boy and the horses have gone beyond your reach, and pressing matters further will create a confrontation with Sea. I doubt even your New Blood adherents are ready for that, and no one else will support you. Take consolation from the duel and withdraw now with whatever grace you can muster."

Not a great deal, Kalan thought, watching Lady Sarein stiffen. And while Lord Huern might sketch him a duelist's salute, the Son of Blood's expression remained cool, the look of one who has just seen a new opponent step onto the field. Kalan inclined his head in acknowledgment of the salute, before turning to Faro. "You must go with Lord Nimor now," he said, as the boy tried to remain concealed behind him. "And as a Sea House ward you must not leave the envoy's company for any reason, except by his express order. Heart up," he added, adopting Dab's phrase.

The wyr hounds stretched and got to their feet, swinging their great heads toward the Sea company. The duty groom, apparently deciding the crisis was over, began to light more lamps, but Faro did not move. "Marching orders," Kalan said, and steered him forward.

"Death," Lady Sarein said, so softly she might have been speaking to herself, "demands death." Steel gleamed in her hand—and then hers was the only movement, the blade continuing to rise while the rest of the world—stables, people—remained frozen and the hounds in particular appeared to simply wait. A split second later both Lord Narn and a Sea Keeper shouted, and Jad stepped between Faro and the blade. But Kalan had already registered that the boy was not the intended target and spun him around, pressing Faro's face into his tunic as Sarein of Blood seized the first hound's head and severed its throat.

The wyr pack howled from the kennels on a prolonged mournful note as Sarein threw the dead hound from her. Blood stained the blade, and was splashed across her hands and arm, as she turned upon the second hound—but Jad had already shoved the beast away. "With respect, Lady Sarein," he said, blocking the knife stroke as she rounded on him instead, "the wyr hounds have not wronged you."

"But you have, Honor Guard, daring to raise your hand to a

Daughter of Blood." Sarein's eyes might burn, but when she spoke again her voice was silken. "I think all here would agree that you have exceeded your orders, and for what?" She spurned the first hound's still-convulsing body with her foot as the pack's clamor fell away, then rose again. "A flea-ridden cur. Take it away," she added. Her left hand summoned the grooms forward, although she had to raise her voice to be heard above the pack. "Hang the carcass above the Blood Gate to remind this House what becomes of those who thwart my will."

The look Sarein darted at Jad made it clear the last remark was for him, and the guard paled, although he stood his ground. The grooms looked toward Huern, who nodded, his expression unreadable. "You have your orders. Clear away the Oath Holder dead at the same time."

As if, Kalan thought, such events were an everyday occurrence— although many of the Blood retainers looked strained and Lord Narn was openly shocked. Faro was rigid, his face still pressed into Kalan's tunic. Jad's glance toward them both kept Sarein and the knife within his peripheral vision.

"We'll leave when you're ready, Storm Spear."

The Daughter of Blood turned on him like a viper. "Don't think I'll forget your transgression, Honor Guard." Every word was shaped into another dagger thrust. "I shall have recompense in full for your presumption."

Jad was watching her, so Kalan could no longer see his face, but he saw Dain and Palla's dismay. And Lord Huern's demeanor made it clear he had no intention of intervening. "Lady Sarein." Kalan shifted Faro to one side and bowed, just low enough to avoid disrespect, and had the satisfaction of seeing her stare fix on him as he bowed again to her brother. "Lord Huern. Lord Narn." The grooms were removing the hound's corpse and the bodies from the alley. The second beast had disappeared, although the pack's dirge continued to rise and fall as Kalan placed his hand on Faro's shoulder. "Make your bow to the Children of Blood so we may take our leave."

Faro kept his gaze averted but bobbed his head as bidden, and

Kalan concentrated on staying between the boy and Lady Sarein's unsheathed blade as they started forward. A much younger Kalan, kicking at the confines of his life in the Keep of Winds' Temple quarter, would have hated the Daughter of Blood for the small, complacent smile that curved her mouth, as much as he despised Lord Huern for his indifference. But the warrior whom Yelusin had named Kalan-hamar observed both with dispassion.

"Keep him close," he said to Lord Nimor, as he and Faro reached the Sea envoy. On impulse, he replicated the ancient salute used by the *Che'Ryl-g-Raham*'s Luck.

The envoy returned it. "I will," he promised. "Honor on you, Storm Spear. Light and safety on your path, until its end."

"And on yours," Kalan replied. "Honor on you and on the Sea House." He touched Faro's hair one last time. "I'm sorry," he said, as the boy's features contorted. He meant it, too, but still turned away, nodding to Morin and his companion as they rejoined Jad's escort. Although conscious of the eyes at his back, both hostile and well disposed, he put them out of his mind. He had a duel to the death to prepare for—and although Kalan had been willing to fight before, for the debt he owed Asantir, and to uphold Lady Myrathis's pledge, now his sense of what was at stake cut deeper.

It's about Blood, he thought, stopping beneath the stony, nine-headed gaze of the hydra over the stable's main door: what this House once was and could still be again. The others halted, too, and Kalan was aware of their confusion as he bowed to the hydra with the fingers of his right hand above his heart. I keep faith, he told it silently: with Malian of Night and with Asantir, with Faro and Lady Myrathis—and with all you once represented, the emblem of this House since the beginning.

Taking his time, Kalan bowed again, and felt his heart grow still, calm, sure. So be it, he thought, as if the matter had ever been in doubt. I also keep faith with myself: I fight.

And still the wyr pack howled.

31

Oriflamme

Lady Myrathis's former apartments were both dark and cold when Kalan reached them, so the first thing he did was hunt out fresh oil for the lamps. He found the suite's storeroom off the short passage between Myr's rooms and her onetime governess's, the small space aromatic with stored herbs and beeswax candles, the latter in a box bearing an Ijiri chandler's stamp. The lamps took some time to refill, but the subsequent glow was friendly, as was the warmth of the fires once he got them started in both the sleeping chamber and dayroom grates.

Kalan stayed on his heels in front of the dayroom blaze for some time, listening to the wyr pack's distant howls. With the benefit of hindsight, he was increasingly convinced that the slain wyr hound had *let* Lady Sarein kill it. Even if the beast had been taken by surprise, it should have done more than just stand there as though waiting for the blade. The only rationale for such behavior that Kalan could fathom was Sarein being one of the ruling kin, whom the wyr hounds were bred to defend and obey. Yet since Red Keep opinion held that all wyr hounds were erratic, and most at least half mad, perhaps he should look beyond logical explanations . . .

Kalan shook his head, recalling the weight of the second hound's head on his shoulder and Jad's exclamation of surprise. On the road here, his Sea House companions had alluded to shortcomings in the Red Keep wyr hounds several times, comparing them unfavorably to the Sea Keep pack, which was trained by Temple seekers to detect Swarm incursion. "Handlers," one marine had said, shrugging, "with the skill to actually recognize 'spawn." She had changed the subject when she saw Kalan listening, and it was only now he appreciated her implication: that wyrs, like any other hound, had to be *taught* to recognize their quarry. Yet a House that consigned the Swarm to the realm of fireside tales and had exiled or—if what Sarein suggested was true—murdered most of its own with power, must have very few left who could teach their wyr hounds to recognize magic's so-called taint.

Kalan pursed his lips in a silent whistle, because he could see why the Sea Keepers might not want a Blood warrior pursuing that train of thought. The obvious consequence, if Blood's wyr packs only recognized the forms of power their handlers were familiar with, was that the more Blood culled power users from their ranks, the narrower the hounds' range was likely to become. And begs the question, Kalan thought, as to whether they would recognize the rarer aptitudes at all, let alone those with power unique to other Houses— like weatherworkers. It could also explain why the wyr hound at the Blood Gate had sniffed at Faro but turned away. If the boy's ability to play least-in-sight derived primarily from Haarth, or from another Derai House, then the hound might well have detected power, just not the sort it was trained to expose.

How much, Kalan asked himself, do the other Houses—besides Sea—suspect? And what about the ability of Blood's wyr packs to detect Swarm intrusion? Their handlers should know the common forms of what they called Wallspawn and train the hounds accordingly, but beyond that ... Kalan felt cold, despite the fire, when he remembered his encounters with Darksworn facestealers in Emer, let alone how he and Malian had been forced to flee from the demon, Nindorith. Potentially, anyone in the Red Keep could be a Darksworn agent and no one the wiser if the wyr pack did not know to sound the alarm—a situation that would also leave Blood dangerously vulnerable to surprise assault, like the one made on Night six years ago.

Kalan shuddered, remembering that night of death, although in view of the Red Keep's rearguard location, he thought facestealers a more likely option. He was tempted to suspect Lady Sarein of being a facestealer, but knew that was too easy—as if her cruelty and bloodlust were not part of the Derai's heritage, when the unpalatable truth was that they always had been. The Derai might not betray their sworn allies or their oaths, but blood feud and assassination, massacre and torture, had all been present in Brother Selmor's histories. Nor had they been restricted to the Alliance's dealings with the Swarm.

Six years before, Rowan Birchmoon had opened Kalan's eyes to the way in which the Derai had always used others' worlds as bases in their long war with the Swarm, but made no compacts with the inhabitants. *So we could abandon them without compunction as soon as the struggle required it,* he thought, frowning at the flames. From what he had seen of both Sarein and Huern tonight, as well as Parannis earlier, they would not hesitate to pursue such behavior again—although the Derai could no longer muster the power required to open another Great Gate. And not only because the Golden Fire had been the prime mover for such massive acts of power; the memorial in the Sea Keep was testament to the vital part required of others within the Derai Alliance.

Grimly, Kalan pulled his thoughts back to the present, because both the Golden Fire and the Derai Alliance as they had been *were* no more than fireside tales now. A more pertinent consideration was whether what was left of the Derai would last long enough to resist the Swarm—and if the Houses descended into civil war again they might well exterminate themselves, leaving their enemy to walk into empty keeps.

If I were leading the Swarm, Kalan concluded, *I would do all I could to set the Derai on that course.* He knew, too, that if Darksworn agents had already infiltrated the Red Keep, the ruling kin would not be alone in viewing the return of a Storm Spear as an unwanted complication. The Darksworn, too, would want him dead.

The wyr pack continued to howl all that night and through the following day, a mournful cacophony that could be heard throughout the keep. Kalan gleaned this information from the conversation of the guards outside his door, as well as the intelligence that no one could recall such an occurrence before. The stewards and pages were openly shaken, and the longer the howling continued, the more restless the guards became. Successive sergeants on duty were quick to squash any talk of ill luck, but the uneasy atmosphere remained.

The Night honor guards commented on it, too, when Kalan met with them to familiarize himself with Asantir's blades. None of them appeared to recognize him, and he hoped the Red Keep's strained atmosphere, together with the weapons practice, would keep their minds off events six years in the past. Garan certainly worked him hard, testing his command of the blades with a variety of armaments and attacks. The twin swords also justified their reputation as fine weapons, but Kalan could detect no hint of their reputation for arcane power.

Nalin was on duty again when he returned to his quarters, but when he asked after Jad, she would only say that he and his eight-guard had been reassigned. She was reticent, too, about the day's contests. The group combats had gone well, she said, with no serious injuries, but she did not know which companies, or individuals within them, had excelled. "Oh," she added, checking as she started to leave, "I almost forgot. A steward left this, with the compliments of the Bride and Captain-Lady Hatha." She handed him a pouch of oiled silk, the flap sealed by wax that had been stamped with the elder Daughter of Blood's insignia. "I'm also to say that the pavilion that goes with it will be set up for you on the Field of Blood tomorrow."

That must be the same pavilion Lady Myr had mentioned, Kalan supposed. When he slit the wax open, he found a crimson pennant inside. The Storm Spears' device of crossed war spears, with a twelve-pointed star above their conjunction, was blazoned on it in gold thread. "The oriflamme of your order," Nalin said, as Kalan let the heavy silk unfurl. "The Captain-Lady must have dug deep to hunt that out." Her tone said that she wondered why the Daughter of Blood had gone to so much trouble, which mirrored Kalan's thought—but at that moment the wyr pack fell silent.

"Eerie," Nalin said, after they had both listened to the ensuing quiet. The pack had cried for a night through until the next day's dusk, Kalan realized, exactly the length of time prescribed for the rites of Hurulth. He wondered whether he dared put that down to coincidence. "Fireside tales," the sergeant muttered, as if she were holding a similar, internal conversation, then took her leave.

Kalan draped the oriflamme from a hook on the sleeping room wall, where it hung down like a tongue of flame. When he lay on the bed, he could see the crossed spears and star reflected in the shield-mirror opposite, where the play of firelight created an impression of shadows clustered around the bright insignia. His gaze shifted to the white hind in the tapestry, haloed with rose and gold by the fireglow. Where do you fit? he inquired silently, but unsurprisingly the hind made no answer, just continued to gaze at him with limpid, trusting eyes. Like Lady Myrathis, he thought, trusting in me to fight a duel to the death in her name.

And this time tomorrow, either he or Lord Parannis would be dead.

Contemplating that prospect, Kalan let his focus center on the moment when he would enter the duelist's circle on the Field of Blood. After that there would only be himself and Parannis. Everything else—honor or dishonor, success or failure, life or death—would fall to either side of the honed blade that was the warrior's path through life. My chosen path, Kalan thought, and however many shadows might gather around the Storm Spear's oriflamme, in that moment he was content.

*

Kalan slept deeply, without hearing the wyr pack again or any echo of the Hunt of Mayanne. All he could recall on waking was the play of firelight across The Lovers, in which sometimes the young woman looked like Myrathis, and sometimes like a Sea Keep mariner, with cabled hair and features lost in shadow. Sometimes, too, her dream face had reminded him of Yorindesarinen, illuminated by fire in the glade between worlds. The dream face of the man had alternated between that of Ammaran, from the memorial in the Temple quarter, and an older, harder visage that Kalan could not recall seeing before.

But today was not a day for being concerned about the significance of dreams. Today, Kalan thought, rising and beginning a series of stretches, is for the edge of the blade.

Later, after he had washed and eaten, he went over his armor piece by piece, before taking out his whetstone and ensuring every weapon was honed to a killing edge. On the Field of Blood, the final phase of the Honor Contest would be playing out, the watching crowd absorbed. Yet even a grand melee and the selection of a new Honor Captain paled beside the prospect of a duel to the death between a Son of Blood and a Storm Spear. So the gathered House, Kalan guessed, would be reserving their full fervor for the ultimate event.

He put the whetstone and the last slender dagger—one of a pair that would slide into sheaths inside his boots—to one side, then laid out the full array of his weapons and armor. His fingers lingered over the Storm Spear device on the cuirass, which the *Che'Ryl-g-Raham*'s armorer had superimposed over the earlier, expunged insignia, before he dismissed the mystery of that erasure. Whoever the former owner had been, his or her memory had been obliterated with the device, and Kalan would never know what warrior of Blood carried the arms south into Haarth. It did not matter, he realized. All that mattered was that he bore himself, and the arms, with honor.

Kalan surveyed the full armament one more time, before composing himself into the vigil of an Emerian knight. He had never observed it in full at the festival of Summer's Eve, seeing out the cycle from one day's dawn to the next in Serrut's chapel, because he and all his fellow knights-in-waiting had been called away to rescue Ghiselaine of Ormond. By the time the festival had passed, many of those who had begun the vigil with him were dead, slain before they gained their knighthood. Kalan took time now to remember them all, as well as the Normarch damosels and the guards who had also died at Summer's Eve, before sinking deeper into the vigil's trance.

Kalan-hamar-khar. The whisper sifted through the layers of stillness, brushing at his awareness with phantom wings: *Storm Spear.* Kalan held both mind and body quiet, tracking its flutter. Other fragments spiraled into his consciousness: the tramp of guards' feet, a roar of acclamation from the Field of Blood, and the perpetual Wall wind, prying at shutter and stone for entry as the phantom circled his stillness again. *A champion, after all this time.* The ghost touch feathered across his suppressed wards—and startled away, dissipating into footsteps, voices, and the hungry wind, crying to be allowed in.

The tramp of feet reached the corridor outside his rooms as Kalan withdrew from the vigil. He stretched again to the crisp accompaniment of challenge and response between his current guards and the new arrivals. When the knock came and he lifted the bar clear, his hands were as steady as its steel-banded oak—and remained so, even when he saw Taly on the far side with Jad beside her. Both warriors wore white surcotes rather than the customary Blood red, their faces unreadable as the surrounding stone, while every other guard in the corridor looked straight ahead with no expression at all. "By the Earl's will and the Battlemaster's command," Taly said, "we are to serve as your seconds."

Kalan guessed the secondment was a public sign of disfavor, rather than an honor, since it would have disqualified her from further participation in the Honor Contest. Yet even if this had been the time and place for questions, Taly and Jad's reserve forbade it. So he stood aside to let them enter, while the escort, which Kalan assumed was to see him to the Field of Blood, remained drawn up in the hallway.

Initially, the arming was a silent affair on both sides as Taly and Jad ensured that every lace was tight, every strap and buckle secure, with no gaps or looseness for Lord Parannis's weapons to exploit. Finally, the two Blood guards handed Kalan each set of weapons in turn: first the boot knives, then those for his belt, and lastly his sword. He had no doubt Asantir would have her twin swords ready for him, but still buckled on his own blade for the journey to the arena. Once the weapons were secure, Kalan tucked his gauntlets into his belt. He would only don them on entering the arena, just as Taly would retain the shield, and Jad his helmet, until the time came to fight.

Taly cleared her throat. "I've seen Lord Parannis fight. He'll take the offensive, coming in hard and fast to get you on the back foot. He's strong, too, and very fit, so you can't expect to wear him down easily." She looked at Jad.

"The Son of Blood likes to display his virtuosity." The honor guard spoke stiffly, as though his sworn duty to Blood and its ruling kin was warring with the command of Heir and Earl that he act as second. Yet since it was a second's duty to advise the duelist, honor and loyalty also required that he discharge it fully. "Defeat alone isn't sufficient, he wants to display mastery over his opponents." Jad's eyes narrowed as though reviewing Parannis's duels. "His repertoire is considerable, and he's ambidextrous. Far more than with most opponents, you must expect the unexpected."

"He also likes to wound first, so that his opponent's strength bleeds out." Taly rubbed at the shield's gleaming face. "And he always maims before he kills."

Jad hesitated, then spoke very quietly. "I've heard he may use poison on his blades; that some opponents have done well against him until he draws blood."

Taly stared, her reserve banished by shock. "Surely that's because of the blood loss, otherwise—" Her voice trailed off. A duelist who used poison was considered lost to honor under the Derai Code, but when Kalan remembered Lady Sarein's behavior in the stables, and the way Parannis had pursued his challenge, he was not prepared to dismiss Jad's warning.

"I don't say that it's true," the honor guard said, "only that I've heard it whispered. Apparently the subsequent weakening always happens too fast for bleeding out, especially when the wound is shallow." Jad met Kalan's eyes, shame in his own. "He still always wins, even when those he fights aren't wounded ahead of the killing blow."

The shame, Kalan thought, could be at having to stand as second to a Blood outsider, or have its source in Parannis's dishonor—or arise because the honor guard had been ordered to pass on that last message, in hopes of unsettling him ahead of the duel. Taly's fist rapped against the shield, her expression grown hard. "There's always a first time." She turned away from Jad's shrug, visibly rechecking that every detail of Kalan's weapons and armor was in order.

"Time," Kalan said, "to go."

The ensign hesitated, then drew herself up. "I would not have withdrawn from the contest except by the direct order of Earl and Battlemaster. Nonetheless, I am honored to serve as your second." Surprise fleeted across her face, as though having spoken the words formality required, she realized that she meant them. "The Nine keep you, Storm Spear."

"And you," he replied. "I am honored to have you both as my seconds."

The warriors nodded, acknowledging that, before Jad moved to open the door while Taly stepped back, waiting as Kalan retrieved the oriflamme and folded it across his arm. He looked toward the tapestry one last time, taking in the detail of the lovers and the crow, caught within the hounds' eternal circle. But the element that stayed with him was the trust in the hind's eyes as she watched him go.

32

Death Name

Kalan and his seconds were as quiet on the walk to the Field of Blood as they had been during the initial arming, and the escort also kept silence. The surge of the crowd as they reached the muster ground reminded Kalan of the ocean, booming into the outer walls of the Sea Keep during his brief time there. "The beast is hungry," Jad said, as they passed beneath the hydra gate.

"For blood and death," Taly muttered.

Kalan clasped her mailed forearm, exactly as he would have done with any of his Normarch friends. "Whatever the circumstances, we all come to this in the end." He had almost said that everyone came to Imuln in the end, but checked the Emerian reference in time.

Taly nodded, although her face remained set as they approached the heavy curtain that marked their designated entrance into the arena, with the Storm Spears' device worked in gold on the garnet cloth. Jad's gaze fixed on it, his expression hard to read. "If you give me the oriflamme," he said finally, "I'll see it's raised above the field." His voice, too, was unrevealing, but he folded the pennant carefully before turning away.

The escort took up position to either side of the entrance, so only Taly followed Kalan inside. The crowd's noise increased immediately, because the body of the tent was pitched on the Field of Blood. At present, the entrance onto the arena was still tied shut, but Captain-Lady Hatha sat at a trestle table beside it, with Garan and Nerys standing to her right, and two dour-faced Blood warriors on her left. A black cloth covered two long narrow shapes placed in the center of the table—Asantir's swords, Kalan thought automatically—with a rolled scroll to one side, and food and drink set further down the board.

Outside, the crowd's background surge swelled into a roar. "That'll be Parannis's colors going up," Hatha observed, "or your oriflamme." She was seated at her ease, with one booted ankle crossed over the opposite knee. A lazy gesture invited Kalan to partake of the food and drink.

He contented himself with a cup of water, for courtesy's sake, and regarded Earl Sardon's eldest daughter across its rim. "Why are you here?" he asked, careful to keep his tone respectful.

Hatha grinned. "Don't hide your teeth, Storm Spear. What in the name of all the Nine am I doing here, is what you really mean." She eyed him, her gaze shrewder than her reputation in the muster grounds would credit. "Anvin will be standing with Parannis on the other side of the field, and the Battlemaster and I felt the ruling kin must be seen to honor the Bride's champion as well. The House needs to see that we value such service, especially after the business in the stables."

Kalan interpreted that as meaning that the unease caused by the wyr pack's howling must have been widespread, but inclined his head as Hatha nodded toward the Night guards. "The Commander of Night also honors you. And you have worthy seconds." She paused, studying Taly's rigid, straight-ahead expression, before the broad mailed shoulders shrugged. "Although you," she added, addressing Jad as he ducked inside, "*have* been unlucky."

Jad saluted, conveying irony without a noticeable change in expression. The Captain-Lady chuckled and waved Garan forward. "Discharge your duty, Honor Guard."

Garan bowed, first to her, then to Kalan, before lifting the black cloth clear of Asantir's blades. "Asantir, Commander of Night, pledged you the use of her swords." The Night guard spoke as formally as if he had not spent hours training with Kalan the day before. "She asked me to say that she is honored to fulfill her commitment today."

Soberly, Kalan took up the blades, clicking each sword clear of its sheath in turn. As expected, both had been honed to the same killing edge as his own weapons. His bow to Garan was deep, acknowledging the magnitude of the gift. "Thank the Commander of Night in my name, and tell her that I am proud to bear her swords and champion her honor."

The noise from the crowd intensified again, and Kalan guessed that the serjeants must have completed preparing the duelists' circle. Hatha cocked her head, listening too, but pushed the scroll forward. "This is from the Sea envoy."

Twinned cords of indigo and sea green bound the parchment, their ends weighted with silver seals. One seal was stamped with a ship, the other with a mer-dragon. Once unrolled, the scroll depicted another mer-dragon, this time curled around a shrine that Kalan recognized as the Great Gate memorial within the Sea Keep. Characters were brushed down the left and right sides of the page in flowing curves of sea green and charcoal, indigo and silver. Only the final character looked blotched, as though the hand that drew it had wavered, or the ink had run.

Kalan's gaze lingered on it before he let the scroll roll closed. Beyond the enclosed world of the pavilion, the crowd's ocean voice swelled again, and he could visualize the provosts moving to their places across the swept-smooth sands. Setting the scroll down, Kalan drew the black-pearl ring from his finger and threaded it onto the cord with the ship seal. He took care over retying the cords into their original, intricate knot, then placed both the scroll and ring inside his jupon. His heart was beating out his pulse in hammerstrokes, as it had since he unrolled the parchment, but he took care to keep his face as steady as his hands.

"What is it?" Taly asked finally. "Could you read those strange characters?"

As it happened, Kalan could, because Brother Belan had taught him the rune-script once learned by all those born with the Derai powers. "I know what it is," he temporized. "The Sea mariners carry such scrolls with them when they venture the deep ocean." He paused, then added quietly, "It will contain my death name."

Hatha's brows rose almost to her hairline, and both Taly and Jad looked shocked. Garan and Nerys also exchanged a look, although it was harder to interpret. "It's a gift," Kalan reassured them all. Che'Ryl-g-Raham had explained the practice when she showed him the Great Gate memorial, saying it had begun with the navigators the shrine commemorated. Now the Sea mariners regularly carried either scrolls or cloth banners, inscribed with a rune name that connected their essence to the memorial, so if a ship foundered or a mariner's body was lost, the soul would still find its way to Hurulth. So, too, if Kalan died today and Blood discarded his body without even their new observance of Kharalth, as they well might, his name would appear on the Sea Keep memorial and his spirit pass to the Silent God.

A great gift, Kalan thought—but outside, the voice of the crowd had subsided. The provosts would all be in their places, and the beast in the galleries waiting to have its thirst for blood sated. Employing the same deliberation with which he had retied the scroll, Kalan unbuckled his belt and set his own sword down on the table, before replacing it with Asantir's blades. Only then did he meet Hatha's speculative stare. "I'm ready," he told her.

Lord Parannis's visor was shaped into a smiling mask of his own face, cast in crimson and black. He came in hard as soon as the provost's baton fell, shifting fluidly through a series of attacks that moved from high to low, left to right, with a speed many opponents would have found overwhelming. The Son of Blood was also as strong as Taly had suggested, his battery of blows designed to break Kalan's guard from the outset, pushing him onto the back foot.

But Kalan, too, was strong, his physique hardened from years training for war in the heavy armor of the Emerian knights, and Asantir's longsword gleamed as he answered Parannis's whirlwind assault with a blur of counter and riposte. The fine sand the serjeants had laid down was even beneath his boots, the crowd's roar banished to a background murmur by the surge of his blood and the cut and thrust of the weapon in his hand. His vision was narrow, concentrated on the lethal figure in crimson and black, the smiling visor, and the blade that rang against his own and drove forward, seeking an opening.

Parannis's eyes were little more than gleams seen through his visor's eye slot, but Kalan could read the story his body told, particularly the telltale carriage of head and neck that heralded intention as surely as an opponent's eyes. He caught the minute change that signaled the Son of Blood's feint to his right, ahead of a two-handed sweep toward the knees. The blow would have broken Kalan's stance if not his armor, if he had not blocked hard and forced the blade away. His reverse cut drove toward Parannis's neck—and now it was the Son of Blood who leapt clear, before recovering and prowling around to Kalan's left.

Kalan steadied his breathing, his concentration stretched tight as he and Parannis revolved about each other. Friction burned along the edge of his wards, and when Parannis sprang forward, assailing him with another succession of lightning-fast strikes, a torrent of fear surged behind every blow, battering at Kalan's will to resist.

The Son of Blood was using the old Derai power. Kalan could sense the spate of terror building every time their blades crossed. Parannis's blows also felt increasingly powerful, as though he were drawing strength out of the earth underfoot—exactly as Kalan had reinforced Audin's failing strength in Emer, when Orth came close to killing him in the sword ring. Now he retreated before the barrage, parrying for time as he absorbed the true source of the Son of Blood's undefeated record. The battery of old power matched the accounts of Parannis sapping his opponents' strength—although

Kalan, retreating again, remained wary of poison on swordtip or blade's edge.

Despite the wards muting Kalan's psychic sense, Parannis's onslaught screamed of an instinctive use of old power, rather than a conscious one. The Son of Blood, raised amid the Red Keep's prevailing ignorance, probably considered the power a reserve of natural strength, one he drew on automatically when challenged by another's forcefulness or skill. And no one the wiser, Kalan's pulse hammered: no one the wiser, despite the swathe of power he unleashes. Kalan might have appreciated the irony, given Sarein's revelations, if every reserve of sinew and will had not been deployed, fending off a renewed assault.

Parannis's blade blurred, cleaving to sheer through armor and neck. Kalan twisted aside just in time, deflecting the strike off the rim of his buckler. If the blade had hit square, the sheer force behind it could have split the shield; as it was, the impetus drove him back. The Son of Blood's laugh was euphoric with power and anticipation of the kill. The enhanced strength of his attacks was already an ache up Kalan's arms and into his shoulders, and together with the psychic offensive's drag on his physical strength, he was tiring fast. Grimly, he fought down panic and beat aside another strike, his own blow designed to jar—then whipped his swordtip back toward the eye slot in the smiling visor.

Parannis's recoil was slight, but allowed Kalan to break off and circle again. The roar of blood and breath thundered at him to abandon his wards and shield out Parannis's psychic offensive—but if he ripped out the interwoven layers of suppression and concealment, he might not be able to control the ensuing spike of released power. And he would betray himself to his enemies.

Kalan evaded again as the Son of Blood sought to close, and Parannis reversed direction, aiming a strike that could have scored either throat or eye if Kalan had not managed to spin clear. But his whole body was pain now, and darkness flecked his vision.

"Black blades." The moth's spiral from his vigil was a phantom

whisper as Parannis stalked forward, power and terror billowing ahead of him like a Wall storm. Kalan drew a deep, tearing breath and prepared to cut his wards loose—but the moth flutter brushed his mind again: *"Black blades; paired blades. Darkness draws darkness, Kalan-hamar-khar."*

Darkness draws darkness. Parannis laughed a second time as he lifted his blade, intent on making an end.

Black blades; paired blades. Kalan hurled his shield into the face of Parannis's advance, drew Asantir's second sword and closed again with the Son of Blood.

Myr gasped with everyone else as Khar of the Storm Spears cast his shield at Parannis and drew his second sword. He fought Bajan's glaive with a sword and dagger, she reminded herself, and a glaive has far greater reach than a sword. So Khar dispensing with his shield was not necessarily the act of desperation it might appear at face value, although Myr was as aware as any of the surrounding warriors that after an initially promising start, the Storm Spear had been giving way before her brother's assault.

However much she might know that Parannis always won, it did not make watching her champion's defeat any easier to bear. She could not look away, though, not even to glance to her right where she knew Sarein would be wearing the same sleek, satisfied look as her twin when he made a kill. Myr did not want to look left either, to the next gallery along where Faro sat, white faced and rigid, among the Sea emissaries. They should not have brought him: that had been her immediate reaction when the Sea contingent entered—only to ask herself how she would feel, knowing someone she cared about was fighting for his life on the Field of Blood. She would want to bear witness, too, not pace and wait, caught between dread and hope until someone else, whether friend or stranger, finally brought word of the outcome.

Now, as the spectacle unfolded, Myr was forced to admit that someone she cared about *was* fighting for his life in the arena below—and so gasped with the rest as Khar's shield went spinning into Parannis's path and a second, shorter blade flashed in his left hand. Rather than evading again, as Myr felt sure Parannis must have expected after their recent encounters, the Storm Spear was taking the fight to her brother.

"Two swords, eh," Kharalthor said, very much at his ease. "Now we shall find out if there's more to him than we've seen so far."

As if it's all sport, Myr thought, still unable to look away as the two figures in the center of the field clashed. She was conscious, too, of her father's impassivity, his demeanor more that of image cast in stone than a flesh-and-blood Earl. Does it mean nothing at all to him, she wondered, that one of those whose life is at stake is his son? Parannis might never have lost before, but Blood was a warrior House: they all knew no combat was ever certain.

The adversaries were locked in a tight, trampling wheel of cut and thrust that made it impossible to decide who was winning or losing now, although Khar's use of the two blades did appear to have counteracted Parannis's previous dominance. Soon, Myr thought her brother might be starting to give ground as often as he pressed an attack. Kharalthor leaned forward. "It looks," he observed, "as if we have a fight on our hands, after all. Better," he added, speaking past her to Asantir, "than the pallid fare we've endured these past few days, eh, Commander?"

Myr did look around then, an involuntary sideways glance at the warrior seated, cool as a shadow, on her left. The Commander of Night inclined her head, acknowledging the remark, but the gesture could have meant anything at all. Myr did not understand how Kharalthor could address his fellow judge so lightly, knowing it was her honor at stake, not to mention a man's life. And my prestige, Myr supposed, although that was of little account when set against a life.

Commander Asantir had given Khar the use of her swords; that alone suggested she was fully aware of what was at stake. Myr stole another glance the Commander's way and thought her face, gazing down into the arena, was as inscrutable as the visage masks in Ise's stories, the ones worn by the ancient lords of the Derai. Myr shivered at both the image and the savagery of the combat, as Huern spoke for the first time since the duel began.

"A fight indeed, my brother," he said, in his smooth, dark way. "I think Myrathis's champion may actually be going to win."

Darkness draws darkness . . . Wielded together, the black blades were absorbing the bulk of Parannis's power and deflecting the remainder to either side of Kalan. The effect felt like fighting inside a cocoon of clear air while the storm crackled outside its perimeter. When Kalan had trained against the Night honor guards, with no challenge of power to answer, the swords' power must have lain dormant. But with his life threatened by an opponent wielding old power, the magic concealed within them had flared into life as soon as Kalan drew the second blade.

Steel clashed against steel again as Parannis hammered his way forward. For a split second, Kalan's counterattack locked the Son of Blood's blade, his eyes boring into the narrow eye slot—and he felt Parannis's momentum falter as the buffer of power was leached away. An instant later the Son of Blood wrenched the trapped blade free, recovering his equilibrium. Even without his reserve of old power, he remained a strong and agile swordsman. But Kalan had fought agile and strong opponents before and flowed back into the rhythm of blade and body, breath and mind, a gyre of life and death in which the paired blades forced Parannis to keep his shield in play. Steadily, inexorably, he drove his opponent into a defensive pattern.

The Son of Blood was not used to losing the offensive; Kalan perceived that through the way his swordplay tightened. Mentally, as well as physically, Parannis was being driven onto the back foot. His counterattacks became more ragged, and his attempts to regain the initiative wilder. The jerk of his head was more noticeable this time, signaling the same feint and sweep toward Kalan's knees that he had attempted earlier—only this time it was a double feint, with Parannis poised to flow into a counterstroke. Spinning to meet it, Kalan blocked Parannis's cut with Asantir's longsword. Simultaneously, he extended the shorter weapon in a stop thrust to the throat. The blade slipped between Parannis's body and his shield, now too far offline, and although the Son of Blood leapt back it was too late. Kalan's swordtip scored his gorget and tore mail.

Parannis landed badly, collapsing over his right ankle, then staggered sideways, trying to recover his stance and interpose his shield as Kalan advanced. Another blow sent the Son of Blood reeling back, and this time he could not regain his balance when the ankle collapsed again. He attempted to roll left instead and force himself up using his shield and good foot, but Kalan was faster. His kick sent Parannis sprawling back, and the smiling visor cried out as Kalan stamped down on his sword hand. Turning the longsword against the inside of the Son of Blood's shield arm to prevent any counter blow, he slid the shortsword through the rent in the coif, checking the tip just clear of Parannis's throat.

In an Emerian tournament, the victorious knight would now call on his opponent to yield. But this was the Derai Wall and the duel was to the death. Kalan's body was one heaving breath, his vision dark as he stared down at Parannis of Blood. How many have you dispatched without compunction, he wondered, not to mention the cruelties visited on the so-called tainted, if Lady Sarein's taunts are true?

The Son of Blood was tainted himself, although he probably did not know it, but that did not absolve him of the many lives that stained his hands. If the stop-thrust had gone home, Kalan would have spared little regret for his death. But to deliver the same blow once the combat was over, and mind and vision already shifting out of battle focus—that, Kalan found now, was another matter. And he had promised the hydra symbol of his House that he would keep faith, not least with himself.

Kalan might not be absolutely sure what Malian would do in the same situation, but he knew what Lord Falk would advise. And Yorindesarinen also, he suspected, recalling the glade between worlds. "I choose mercy," he said, his voice still thick and a little fast. He kept his blades in place, though, because he did not trust Parannis of Blood.

"A champion, after all this time." The ghost whisper was so soft, and the thunder of his pulse still so loud, that Kalan thought he might have imagined it. The senior provost stepped into his line of sight, and the voice of the crowd began to intrude again, but he kept his eyes on Parannis.

"Weak," the Son of Blood said—a whisper, since he still had a sword at his throat. Kalan, conscious of Brother Belan's tales, took care not to let steel touch flesh, but he felt the hunger in the blades, as if they sensed the proximity of an enemy's lifeblood. And his power? Kalan wondered, recalling how the swords had absorbed the psychic assault. This close, too, he could see his opponent's eyes clearly, despite the visor, and read their blaze of hate as Paranis spoke again. "The old Earls should have done a better job of stamping out your kind."

"Maybe so," Kalan replied, and let humor glimmer. "But I don't see you driving your throat onto my blade." He pitched his next words to carry beyond the approaching provosts to those crowded into the galleries, denying them their finale of life's blood and death. "I give you back your life, Parannis of House Blood, which is forfeit to me." A collective exhalation and low uncertain grumble answered from the stands: the beast, it seemed, did not know what to make of this. Kalan let the sound roll over him before speaking again. "But I leave you this, as a reminder, ever after, of my kind—and that your life is a gift."

And sheathing the longsword in order to better contain the black blades' power, he turned the tip of the shorter weapon, scoring a fine line of blood across Parannis's throat.

33

The Custom of Blood

For a moment Myr thought Khar had slain Parannis after all—and guessed, from a fleeting glance at Sarein's frozen profile, that she thought so, too. But then Khar stepped back, and the provosts surrounded both contestants in a loose circle. To her right, Kharalthor was talking with Banath, who said he thought Parannis's ankle might have broken. On the field, Khar took another step away, clearly allowing his opponent room to rise. Myr dared not look at Sarein again, but she did glance toward the Sea company and Faro's face, white with tension and exultation.

He thinks it's over, she thought, pitying the boy, because the provosts' circle had already told her it was not. Most of those around her, as well as those in the nearby stands—the ones who were not still watching the field—were either openly or covertly eyeing the triumvirate comprised of her father, Kharalthor, and Huern. Teron was speaking to Asantir, his voice very low, but Myr could see he had relaxed and that, like Faro, he thought the matter settled. His attention, she suspected, might have already shifted to the road home, because once her Honor Guard and its new captain were named, Night's business in the Red Keep would be done.

In the dueling circle, Khar was wiping his unsheathed blade clean.

Her father, Myr saw, was studying him with the same hooded look he had given the oriflamme when it rose above the Storm Spear's pavilion. The Earl looked away as Khar sheathed the sword, his gaze traveling from Hatha to Anvin as they and the respective seconds approached from either end of the field. Myr's eyes went immediately to Taly, walking on Hatha's left. The first day of the group trials had been almost over before she realized that Taly was no longer competing. When she ventured a question, Kharalthor had shrugged and said it was the Earl's decision. "It's fitting that the best of your household guards should support your champion as seconds. And a signal honor. When our father learned of your Dabnor's training injury, he nominated one of his own Honor Guard in his place."

The same guard who had offended Sarein, if rumor was correct, which Myr thought illuminated how much was honor, and the rest her family finding a way to remove Taly from the Honor Contest. Currently, Huern was leaning on the back of Kharalthor's chair, where he could speak to either the Earl or Battlemaster without being overheard. When he looked around and found Myr watching him, his gaze was so dispassionate she felt as though she were meeting a stranger's stare. Mesmerized, she gazed back, her discomfort sharpening when the curtain into the gallery was lifted aside and Kolthis stepped through.

So it's certain, Myr thought, watching his progress to Huern's side. They will make him Honor Captain as they always intended, no matter what I may wish. Kolthis did not so much as glance her way, but the smile he directed at the field was a small, tight curve comprising equal parts malice and satisfaction. The thought of crossing wild country with a Guard captained by him made Myr's stomach churn. Blindly, she stared down at the arena—and remembered that her father had promised her a boon.

Perhaps she *should* ask for a captain of her own choosing, since it was a request her father could reasonably grant, especially if she asked before Kharalthor made his wishes known ... Myr almost stopped breathing as she realized that once her father ruled on the matter, it would do her siblings no good to rage. Even if they raged anyway, the matter would be settled, so she wouldn't have to listen—a thought so startling that Myr blinked and sat up straighter, bringing events on the field into focus again.

Hatha and Anvin were in conversation with the provosts, as Parannis's seconds helped him to his feet. In the gallery, Huern turned to Earl Sardon, speaking so all those nearby could hear. "Arguably, since the duel was to the death, the Storm Spear's life is forfeit for defying both its terms and your will in approving them." He did not so much as glance Myr's way. "And since the role of the seconds is to guide their principal, they must share in his punishment."

Not Taly. Myr thought, unable to move. Please, she begged silently, of any of the Nine that might be listening: not Taly. Not anyone, she added a moment later, and her hands, concealed within the folds of her robe, clenched until the fingernails cut into her palms.

"Is that the custom of Blood?" Commander Asantir was politely inquiring. "My understanding of the Code is that even in a duel to the death the victor may grant clemency."

"Death means death," Kharalthor said flatly, "or should do so."

"There is no place in Blood, whether keep or hold, for those who set their will against the Earl's. Always," Huern added, "a failing of the Storm Spears, I believe."

"Parannis is also our brother," Myr tried to say, but her voice was a whisper and she did not think anyone heard as her father raised his hand. Slowly, the arena grew quiet, the silence widening out from the Earl's chair.

"The matter must be adjudicated." Earl Sardon turned to Banath. "Parannis and his party are to leave the field. Hatha and the provosts will escort the Storm Spear and his seconds here. Convey my instructions personally, Banath."

It could only have been a few minutes, Myr supposed, from the time Banath strode onto the field, until the moment Khar and his escort started toward the gallery. Yet it felt like an eternity, especially listening to the crowd shift, although the overall quiet persisted. She thought Parannis must have argued at first, judging by the way Anvin grasped his arm and spoke close to his ear. Parannis jerked his arm away, but allowed his seconds to help him toward his pavilion, a splendor in crimson and black that dwarfed the Storm Spear's tent.

Now that she dared really look around, Myr saw that many sections of the crowd were sporting crimson and black as well. Showing their support for the New Blood, she supposed, although it also occurred to her, with a tiny glance at her father's impassive profile and Huern's inscrutable one, that the duel had drawn them out into the open. Regardless, she suspected there would be many in the galleries, especially those who had lost kin or comrades to Parannis's dueling, who would be wishing the Storm Spear had killed him.

Myr could appreciate their point of view, but she also hoped her father realized that the death of the Bride's half-brother at her champion's hands, on the field consecrated to her honor, would shroud Myr's name with ill luck and blight the Night marriage. We should be grateful to Khar for his forbearance, she thought, not proposing to execute him—and her hidden hands opened and shut hard again as the Storm Spear and his companions stopped below the Earl's seat.

Khar had removed his helmet, so Myr could see his face as he gazed up at Blood's Earl and ruling kin, all frowning down on him. Sweat had darkened his hair and still gleamed on his skin, although his breathing was steady. Myr thought the gaze he directed toward Asantir was as searching as one of the Night Commander's own, but when his eyes found hers he inclined his head. How can he be so composed? she wondered, then gasped as he drew the longer of his two swords and all the honor guards present stepped forward as one.

Myr thought Khar's quickly suppressed expression might be a smile, but he was already raising the sword in a salute to her father, before acknowledging Kharalthor as Heir and Battlemaster, as was only right. The third time Khar's blade rose and swept down again, the deep and deliberate courtesy was for Myr. Finally, he saluted Asantir, a very public reminder that his victory was for both of them.

His victory and his clemency as well; momentarily, Myr felt faint, but steadied herself.

Beside her, Asantir rose and answered Khar's salute, placing the tips of her fingers above her heart and inclining her head in formal recognition. A chair scraped as Kharalthor stood, too, echoing Asantir's tribute. Of course, Myr thought. Khar's just made the victor's salute to the ruling kin, and Kharalthor's the Battlemaster so he has to acknowledge it—which also means acknowledging Khar. It was *all* spectacle: the whole contest, including the duel, was as much about pageant as the practical exercise of choosing an Honor Guard. Clearly, Khar understood that. He had fought a combat to the death and won, and now he was dueling again. No matter the weight of power arrayed in the gallery above him, he hadn't given up—which made Myr want to cry now, rather than faint. Instead she looked past the Storm Spear to Taly.

She'll know what's at stake, too, Myr thought. Oh, Taly ... But Khar was turning toward the Sea contingent as Kharalthor and Asantir sat down, sheathing his sword before raising a hand to acknowledge Faro. The boy flushed, his hand half rising before he snatched it back, frowning and looking away in a gesture that said he was not so easily appeased. Myr would have smiled, if not for her makeup mask—and because her father was speaking.

"You have fought well, Storm Spear, both today and during the early part of the Honor Contest." The surrounding galleries rustled, the weathervane of the House veering before its Earl's praise. "Still, the terms of the duel were clear. The combat was to the death."

Khar's manner was courteous. "I was not consulted over the terms of the duel, although arguably, as the challenged party, I should have been. But as the victor, it is my right to choose whether I deal death or grant life. I have chosen mercy, Earl of Blood."

Mercy—mercy—mercy. The word rippled around the galleries, the initial murmur building like the onset of a storm until the Earl held up his hand and the sound died away. "You were not consulted because I approved the terms of the contest." The look he directed at Khar was heavy. "So in effect, Storm Spear, you have defied me."

"Lord Parannis is your son." Khar spoke quietly, but because the crowd had settled his voice carried. Another flurry of whispers disturbed the galleries, to as quickly fade. Myr, who had turned so she could see both Khar's face and her father's, caught Kharalthor's frown at this reminder. Huern remained unrevealing.

The Earl smiled, an expression that did not reach his eyes. "I am aware whose son he is. So, having returned his life to me you feel I should be grateful, is that it?" He paused. "On one hand, you leave me with a contest to the death where a life remains forfeit. On the other, our guest, the Commander of Night, agrees that it is your right to show mercy." He leaned back, surveying Khar beneath half-closed lids. The way Sarein would, Myr thought, repressing a shiver. A hush waited on her father's next words, revealing that he, no less than the Storm Spear, understood grand spectacle. "Yet my son Huern assures me that your life, and that of your seconds for not instructing you better, is forfeit for defying both the terms of the duel and my will in approving them."

The amphitheater was completely silent, and Myr had no idea what Khar was thinking behind his impassive expression. Taly and her fellow second's faces were also masks, but the ensign's bearing persuaded Myr that she at least was not surprised. Sarein was smiling again, and when she spoke her voice was honeyed. "I need not remind you, my father and my Earl, that one of the seconds is an honor guard, so any failure on his part must also fall on those who serve most closely with him. Since"—and here she lifted her eyes—"it is as much their duty to counsel him, as it became his to guide the champion."

Myr's swift glance from Banath's face to Kharalthor's suggested that Sarein must be correct. Yet if Khar was within his rights, according to the Honor Code, then his seconds and these other guards must also be absolved. Myr looked toward Asantir, hoping she might intervene, and found the Night Commander studying her. For once, she knew exactly what Asantir was thinking. Now was the moment when she, Myr, must be a Daughter of Blood in truth and keep faith with her champion. *She* must defend Khar's cause, as he had fought for hers.

No one will listen, Myr thought, not to me. At the same time, she knew Asantir was right: she must play her part in this spectacle. Now, Myr told herself, before the pause drags out too long. Her heartbeat felt erratic, but despite the deadweight of her limbs she *was* standing, using the chair's curved arms to push herself upright.

As slowly as if this were a dream, her father and those around him—Kharalthor and Huern, with Kolthis beside him; Sarein and Sardonya, her brows arched high; and Banath, with a blur of other faces beyond—all turned her way. Myr longed to keep hold of the chair for support, but made herself step away. A corner of her mind was aware of the buzz of speculation from every gallery, but she had to concentrate on her own part: sinking down and down in the deep obeisance, not just of a Daughter of Blood before her Earl, but of a supplicant kneeling to the head of her House.

"My Earl and my father." Myr used the same formal phrasing as Sarein, but her voice was too faint and she had an inkling of how Parannis's might have felt with a sword against his throat. Yet she knew the formal phrases, as well as the ritual gestures, because intercession was part of the legacy of the Rose, which Ise had been teaching her since she was small. She knew, too, that her words had to carry beyond their immediate circle, even if most in the arena would have to rely on the mime of her gestures for understanding. Myr could almost hear Ise's injunction to project her voice, and when she spoke again she felt as if she were shouting. "You have pledged me a boon."

"Any request within reason." Her father did not appear to raise his voice, but his words rang clear. "I have not forgotten."

Myr's legs started to shake and she prayed for the strength to hold the curtsey. "Khar of the Storm Spears has fought well and honorably, as you have acknowledged. Even if he erred against our custom in showing mercy, I am grateful, because Lord Parannis is my brother as well as your son."

"*Half* brother," Sarein hissed, as another murmur ran around the crowded arena. Myr forced herself to ignore the interruption and resisted bowing her head.

"Marking the end of my Honor Contest with the death of my brother and your son would have been a grief to me. It would also have cast a pall over my wedding journey." Myr paused, because she knew the next words had to ring true. "Ending with three executions, or ten as Sarein suggests, will also cast a long shadow. For the sake of all we hope from this marriage, I ask you to spare the lives and freedom of Khar of the Storm Spears, his seconds—and by extension, your affected honor guards—as my boon."

Any request within reason, he had said, and surely this must meet that test. My choice, Myr told herself, even if it does mean having Kolthis for my Honor Captain. Both her father's silence and the hush in the arena stretched again, and she tried to ignore the tremor in her legs and the stiffness in her neck, locked into her formal upward stare.

Kharalthor leaned close to their father. "She may have a point about the marriage. A good one, even, by Kharalth."

"I agree." The Earl raised Myr to her feet, kissing her formally on both cheeks. "Your points are well made and we are also mindful of the Commander of Night's counsel." Still formal, he turned toward Khar and his seconds, favoring them with the very slight nod of the Earl of Blood to warriors in the ranks. "By the grace of the Bride and her guest, and in recompense for the life of my son, I will overlook the slight to our custom and my will. I grant you your lives and your freedom to leave this field in honor."

The company below the Earl's gallery all saluted him as the crowd cheered, although Myr detected uncertainty beneath the acclamation. She looked away and caught both Huern and Kolthis watching her: her brother with reserve, while Kolthis's lip curled. Yet her father had not dismissed the three before him, and when Myr looked back his eyes were hooded again.

"Nonetheless," Earl Sardon said, once the crowd realized there was more to come and grew quiet, "a transgression against our custom and my will may not be completely overlooked. I grant you your lives and your freedom, but you may no longer pursue them within this keep, or any of the holds and territory that belong to Blood. In Kharalth's name and my own, I banish you all: Khar of the Storm Spears; Ensign Taly, formerly of my daughter Myrathis's household; and Jad and his eight-unit, formerly of my Honor Guard. You have until tomorrow's dawn to leave this keep, and until dawn three days from now to be clear of Blood's territory. After that time your lives will be forfeit to any with the ability to claim them, without fear of Derai law or blood debt."

The crowd clamored, a sound half mournful, half hungry, that reminded Myr of the wyr pack. Exile from House and keep was as good as a death sentence on the Derai Wall, all there knew it. Faro cried out, a hoarse ugly sound, and the Sea Keepers had to haul him back from the lip of the balcony as he tried to reach Khar. Myr wanted to cry out, too, against the knowledge that she had failed. She had played her part in the pageant as Ise had taught her, but it had not turned out like the hero tales.

Khar's face, when she dared look his way, was a stone mask that matched her father's. She could not bring herself to look at Taly or the other second, the honor guard her father had called Jad, whose eight-unit would share his fate because he had thwarted Sarein of a kill. Contemplating that injustice, Myr felt like flotsam, marooned by the floodtide of her family's maneuvering. She had never been more glad of Ilai's elaborate makeup, concealing her expression—and was even more thankful for it when her father turned and kissed her formally, first on one cheek and then the other.

"I told you to ask wisely," he said, close by her right ear. "You could have asked for the armies of Blood to march on your command, but instead you fritter my grace on this ragtag band." Both eyes and face shuttered, he leaned forward on her left: "I am disappointed in you, Myrathis."

Myr thought her legs might give way then, despite the shame of a collapse before the gathered House, except for two circumstances.

The first was that Commander Asantir stood up to salute the Earl and put out a hand to steady her. Like Ilai, Myr thought, holding me up when Sarein stood on my train. The second reason was because—in the moment Asantir steadied her—she looked past her father and met Khar's gaze, watching from the arena below. When he caught her eye he bowed, not a salute with the sword this time, but the same bow that Asantir had made to him, with the fingertips of the right hand resting against the heart.

He was saying something, although it was hard to hear because of the crowd. Myr frowned in concentration as Taly and Jad bowed, too, echoing his gesture, and barely noticed Asantir's hand being withdrawn, or her father and the others turning as Khar straightened out of his bow. But in the lull that followed she heard his next words clearly. "Lady of Grace," he said, using the salutation associated with heroines like Emeriath and Errianthar, out of the oldest stories. "Lady of Grace, I keep faith."

I keep faith. It was the motto Hatha had quoted as belonging to the Storm Spears, and Myr's heart beat fast as she curtseyed again in acknowledgment. An answering sigh ran through the crowd, but it was not just for the salute or the pledge, she realized, looking beyond their small tableau as she rose. For even as Khar spoke his order's ancient words, and before he and his seconds had departed the Field of Blood, the oriflamme above the Storm Spear's pavilion was coming down.

34

A Long Road

Kalan heard a hound give voice as he strode from the arena, and by the time he pushed into the Storm Spear's garnet-and-gold tent what sounded like every beast in the Red Keep had joined in. The honor guards who had escorted him there were gone, but Garan and Nerys were watching the muster ground entrance. Waiting to retrieve Asantir's swords, Kalan supposed—then saw that Dab was there, too, with a staff supporting him on one side and Liy on the other. "You can't delay," the guard said. "You have to leave at once."

"The Earl's guards have gone from outside as well," Garan said, and Kalan did not need to ask what he meant. The protection that had been extended to him until the duel was fought had been withdrawn.

"They're gone from Lady Mouse's old rooms, too." Dab grimaced. "I started thinking what would happen if you won, so I sent Liy out to scout. She found the rooms unprotected."

"And unlocked," Liy added, managing to sound frightened, excited, and important at the same time. "Lucky you don't have much gear, so I brought it down to your horses, like Dab told me."

"Thank you." Kalan smiled at her, before he looked from Taly to Jad. "This needn't mean death, not if you come with me." Exiled from Blood twice over in my case, he thought wryly, but at least he knew it was possible to survive, even on the Wall. Taly's face was bleak—still trying to absorb what had just happened, he suspected, and Jad looked equally confounded. When they remained silent, Garan spoke again.

"I and my eight-guard are leaving now, by the Commander's order. You can ride with us to the boundary of Blood's territory, or as far as our roads lie together."

Briefly, Kalan wondered whether Asantir had anticipated this, too, just as she had known he would need her swords against Parannis. A gift that countered the Son of Blood's use of old power seemed too neat for chance. But Dab was right, he could not delay for that now. Their enemies, starting with Sarein and Parannis among the ruling kin, would be unlikely to wait for tomorrow's dawn. They might not come at the exiles directly, but retainers who sought favor would already be sharpening weapons that could be hidden in boot, glove, or sleeve. "Liy can fetch your eight-guard," he told Jad. "We need to gather supplies and gear together quickly, then get out."

"Our possessions are forfeit anyway," Jad said, visibly pulling himself together. "My unit will have been watching the duel, so they'll probably head for a place we meet when we've matters to discuss that aren't for the rest of the barracks." He looked at Liy. "I'll go after them, but maybe if you check the barracks, just in case. And if it's safe, grab what you can of our gear."

"We'll need food—" Taly began, but Dab shook his head at her.

"Already taken care of, Tal, together with your personal gear." He pulled a rueful face. "When you're lying flat on your bunk there's nothing to do *but* think, and fortunately Liy came by to see how I was doing, so the rest was easy. Everything's with Khar's horses," he added, "so you just need to get to them and out the Blood Gate."

"Just," Kalan thought. "Meet us at the stables," he told Jad, "or failing that, the Blood Gate." Once the honor guard and Liy had gone, he turned to Dab. "Can you get clear before any hunters arrive?"

The guard shook his head. "Forget about me. You have to go *now*."

"I'll see him clear, Storm Spear." Bajan ducked through the

muster-ground flap. He was carrying his glaive with the blade reversed, but Garan and Nerys automatically adjusted position to take account of its reach as the Bronze Holder tossed Kalan the oriflamme. "Two of Kolthis's cronies seemed to think they had some claim to this, but I disabused 'em of the notion. I relieved them of the crossbows they had trained on the tent entrance at the same time," he added, with a grim smile. "Jad's taken both bows with him and Liy's keeping watch until we leave. She'll head to the barracks after that."

"We'll go now." Kalan stuffed the oriflamme inside his jupon, alongside the scroll and ring, and joined Bajan at the entrance.

"The announcement of the Honor Guard and its captain should keep the muster ground clear for some time yet," the Bronze Holder said. "Even so, I'd take the horse tunnel to the stable, not go via the main gate. There're too many supporters gathered there, waiting to cheer the successful candidates. You can lose yourself among 'em, though," he told Dab. "It's close enough, even with your wound, especially as I can help you get that far."

Of course, Kalan thought: Bajan was still a contender for the new Honor Guard so couldn't pass beyond the gate until the announcement was made. He chinked the flap wide enough to survey the muster ground, then recalled Asantir's blades. "Will you return the swords to your Commander?" he asked Garan.

"You're to keep them," the Night guard said. For once, his normally expressive countenance was unrevealing. "Until you reach Night, she said."

So Asantir did anticipate this, Kalan thought, while Taly focused on the more obvious implication of Garan's message. "Will we be permitted to enter Night?"

Garan nodded. "My eight's new mission doesn't lie that way, but once you reach our borders you'll have safe conduct."

There's a long road there yet, Kalan thought, knowing the paired swords would be invaluable for a party of fugitives daring the Wall's dangerous terrain. Taly's expression indicated that she understood the difficulties ahead, but a little of her bleakness had eased. "Thank the Commander for me," Kalan said, but Nerys checked him before he could step outside.

"Let us go first," Garan said. "For the service you have done the Commander and Night."

The Night guards had quit the tent before Kalan could muster an argument, and a few moments later Nerys whistled the all-clear. When he joined them, Kalan saw Liy crouched on a vantage point above one of the muster ground's many gates into the arena. She waved as Taly led the way toward the horse tunnel, and Kalan sketched a salute back. He received a gamine grin in reply, at the same time as Taly and the Night guards disappeared from view. Once inside the tunnel, they all ran, the low stone roof and their pounding boots muffling the somber chorus of the hounds.

"Although," Taly said, as they entered the stable, "none of us actually own our horses. They're all the property of the Red Keep. As guards we only have the use of them."

Kalan knew he should have remembered that, because it had been the same in Night, but he still sustained an Emerian knight's shock at such an unnatural circumstance. "The Commander's company have spare mounts," Garan told them. "You can return them to the Keep of Winds with the swords. I'll give you a note-of-hand," he added, "so you won't be accused of theft."

"Thank you." Taly spoke stiffly, standing very straight. Kalan guessed the gall to her pride would only rub more because without horses the chance of surviving at all, let alone meeting Earl Sardon's time frame, would be close to impossible.

"You're not returning to the Keep of Winds yourselves?" he queried.

"No." Garan was rueful. "As reward for our exemplary nursemaiding of a flock of Morning priests from the Border Mark to the Keep of Bells, then back to Morning, we are now to search the vastness of the Gray Lands for a stray from Westwind Hold. The woman's mazed, but still managed to slip her watchers and Night territory." His ruefulness became pity. "If we find her at all in that country, most likely she'll be dead. Nonetheless, we have our orders."

When the Night guards turned away to fetch their horses, Taly accompanied them. Kalan saddled Tercel and Madder, strapping on the equipment and supplies that Liy had stashed inside Tercel's loose box. Bajan's page was full of resource as well as pluck, he decided, lifting the concealed items clear. The hounds' clamor was much louder here, being so close to the kennels, and Kalan, his hands busy with straps and buckles, wondered what had set them off this time and how long they would continue before falling silent.

By the time he finished, Garan and his unit were at the stable entrance. Kalan's eyebrows rose when he saw that all eight were leading messenger horses, although the mounts allocated to the Blood exiles were regular troopers.

"Garan's company will go to the Blood Gate by the main route and take all the horses through with them, including yours if they can be led," Taly told him. "They're distinctive, but may be less so among the rest of the string. The gate guards are unlikely to prevent a Night company leaving, in any case." She shrugged. "Horses are one thing, but Night can't openly undermine Earl Sardon's ruling, so best if we take a separate route to the Blood Gate. There's a back way that runs behind both kennels and mews, and if the gate seems chancy there's also a sally port we can try." Unhappiness crept into Taly's voice. "Although that would mean leaving the port unsecured behind us."

Kalan understood her reluctance. "Let's hope we don't have to," he said, and handed his horses' reins to Garan. "They'll accept being led but don't try and ride them, especially Madder."

The back way was a zigzag of lanes and alleys, all currently unused with the Red Keep still focused on the Field of Blood. Kalan stayed alert for pursuit beneath the hounds' cacophony, while his thoughts returned to the final events in the arena and particularly his salute to Lady Myr. He had not intended to use the term Lady of Grace, or to couple it with the Storm Spears' motto, but the words had burned themselves out of his mouth when he overheard Earl Sardon rebuke his daughter for interceding.

Lady of Grace. Kalan repeated the epithet to himself and decided that if Earl Sardon could not see his youngest daughter's courage and integrity, then he might be adept in games of power but was far from wise. He was still thinking about that when Taly turned into another tunnel that curved gently down, and the hounds fell silent as abruptly as they had begun to howl.

Kalan caught the first reverberation of boots off stone at once, interspersed with voices and the clink of armor. Listening intently, he decided there were between four to six warriors behind them, approaching at a pace that would see them catch up shortly. A few seconds later Taly glanced behind, but shook her head when he asked how far to the gate. "Too far, even if we run, and there's nowhere to hide either." She glanced back again: "Best to confront them."

But keep an eye to our backs as well, Kalan thought, as they faced the way they had come. Beside him, Taly could have been his mirror image, prepared but not overtly threatening. The boots were louder now, ringing in the confined space, and soon Kolthis rounded the corner, with Rhisart and Ralth to either side—the latter sporting a heavily bruised face and what looked like a broken nose. Three more warriors followed a pace behind them. "Ah," Kolthis said, stopping. "I feared you would escape my grasp."

"What's actually escaped you is Earl Sardon's deadline," Kalan replied. "We have until tomorrow's dawn to quit the keep."

"If you survive to do so," Kolthis returned softly. "I'm sure you already know that no one's going to ask questions if you and the ensign here vanish. Even the Mouse will assume you've left as ordered."

Taly's head was up in a way that reminded Kalan of Girvase at his most dangerous. "I thought you would be on the Field of Blood, Kolthis, receiving your preordained captaincy. Or is this last piece of dirty work what's required to secure it?"

Kolthis shrugged. "Poor Taly, you must have known it was never going to be you." His look grew reflective. "How did Lord Huern put it? That the Battlemaster might tolerate one of your line's get in the keep garrison, but never in any of Blood's elite corps. Not even the Half-Blood's Honor Guard, apparently." As if on cue, his companions smirked. "Of course, we're here to ensure he no longer needs to tolerate you at all."

"Besides," Rhisart added, "they've decided to announce the Honor Guard and the captaincy at tonight's feast."

"In order to safeguard the purity of the contest from your disgrace." Kolthis took the Bane Holder up smoothly, although Kalan detected an initial flash of irritation. "And the Bride's folly. Naturally, as captain, it will be my privilege to ensure such folly ceases. Starting," Kolthis ended, "with removing its current source."

The rasp of steel clearing scabbards echoed along the tunnel. Taly's blade was a gleam in Kalan's peripheral vision as he drew Asantir's longsword. "If we do this, you know there's no guarantee you'll live to accept that captaincy."

Kolthis smiled. "You may be good, Storm Spear, but even with Taly to back you, the odds favor us."

If Girvase were here, he would say that two against six was close enough to be called even—but before Kalan could move, a deep growl sounded from behind him. "Khar," Taly said, very quietly, at the same time as a large form brushed between them and Kolthis's eyes widened. More bodies followed, but even before Kalan saw the sleek heads and glowing eyes, the beasts' size had told him they were wyr hounds. When a head bumped against his hip, he risked a swift glance down, sufficient to recognize the hound that had survived the stables.

"Scion of Tavaral: Kalan-hamar-khar." The moth whisper brushed his mind again, but this time Kalan heard a deeper, more sonorous note beneath it. The narrow head swung back toward Kolthis, the pale eyes as incandescent as the Night Mare's had been in Jaransor, six years before. When the hound growled and took another step forward, the rest of the beasts advanced in unison. Kalan counted thirteen of them altogether, their hackles raised and ears flattened, standing between him and Kolthis. "Kol." Rhisart sounded uneasy. "They're wyr hounds . . ." His voice trailed away.

"I know what they are!" Kolthis snapped. "What I *want* to know is what by the storm-cursed Wall they're doing here!"

"Upholding our cause, it seems." Kalan could not help himself: despite the uncertain reputation of wyr hounds, he grinned. "I'd say the odds have just evened, wouldn't you?"

Kolthis's snarl would have done credit to the hounds, which growled again, displaying their teeth. Rhisart's gaze shifted to Kalan, then back to the hounds. "But wyrs, Kol ... They were Kharalth's gift to Blood, from when the Swarm first rose."

"The Defenders of Blood," Kalan said quietly. He had forgotten the story about Kharalth's gift, but it stirred now in his earliest memories, and he wondered if it had been his father who told it to him, or the mother whom he could barely remember.

"Fireside tales!" Kolthis retorted.

"Well, I won't kill them. Or the Storm Spear, if they take his part." Rhisart's voice was flat, and two of his comrades murmured agreement.

Kolthis swung around on the Bane Holder—before his smoothness dropped back into place and he shook his head. "Old Blood superstitions, Rhis. You should know better." He raised his hand conceding defeat. "You'll keep, Storm Spear, together with your tarnished following." His smile gleamed as he and his companions began to retreat, step by slow step. "Although you may regret lost opportunity when Sarein's hunters pull you down, since I doubt it's a swift death by the sword she has in mind."

The foremost hound rumbled a warning, and the assailants continued retreating until they disappeared around the curve of the tunnel with the wyr hounds following. "Let's go," Taly said, and Kalan nodded, although like her he kept his sword unsheathed. "I've never seen anything like that before, with the wyr hounds," she added, and he caught her sidelong glance. "They were loose without their handlers, too. That's not supposed to happen."

It happened the other night, Kalan thought. "I can't explain it," he said. For now, he preferred to keep speculation to himself. "But

I doubt Kolthis's parting threat was empty, so we'd better reach the Blood Gate ahead of Lady Sarein's hunters."

By unspoken consent they lengthened their stride. Soon afterward Kalan heard more booted feet jogging from the direction of the Blood Gate, and his sword hand tightened—but relaxed when Jad and his guards appeared, although all eight looked grim and strained. "The Night guards passed the gate without difficulty," Jad told them. "But when you didn't show—"

"We ran into Kolthis. He backed off," Taly said, clearly deciding details could wait, "but threatened us with Lady Sarein." She frowned. "Dab was right about not delaying."

We owe a lot to Dab, and to Bajan and Liy, Kalan thought, as they started forward again. "Did you see Liy?" he asked.

Jad nodded. "She's keeping watch at the gate." He studied Kalan. "If you put the sword away, we can act as if we're still escorting you."

"I wish we'd never drawn that duty," a guard behind Kalan muttered. Rhanar, he thought.

"My blame," Jad said heavily. Kalan could see the burden stamped into his face.

"No," Dain countered, "your honor. And ours." The others murmured agreement, although the look Rhanar threw Kalan suggested that he knew where blame lay.

"We've already had this out," Palla said. "Stand or fall, we'll do it together." But her shoulders were hunched, and Kalan knew it must feel like being hurled off a precipice: from all it meant to be an Honor Guard one day, to exile from House and keep the next.

Jad signaled the escort formation. "We're almost at the gate," he said, seconds before they rounded a last corner and found Liy waiting just inside the tunnel exit.

"I think all's clear," she told them. "No one's come since the Night company rode out." Worry clouded her assurance. "But you should still make haste."

"We should," Kalan agreed. He looked from Taly to Jad. "Ready?"

"Ready." They sounded sure, but Kalan imagined everyone in the company felt tense as they crossed the large square that lay between the keep proper and the Blood Gate. His pulse was fast and sweat prickled, expecting Kolthis to reappear or Lady Sarein's hunters to arrive. But no one did, and the guards on the gate were as uninterested as the wyr hounds on duty. The latter did not even raise their heads from their paws when the small company halted before the inner gate.

"The trickle's begun, I see." The officer of the watch began noting down their names. "We'll have the flood once the contest's fully done." Kalan thought his name might prove the stumbling block, but although he said Khar when asked, and the officer studied his face and insignia, the Storm Spear device did not seem to register. The Blood Gate, like the Gate of Winds in Night's chief stronghold, was a separate fortress with a distinct garrison, and the officer's reaction suggested that unless specific orders arrived, events in the keep proper, even an Honor Contest and duel, would remain of limited interest.

Liy whispered that she would go with them as far as the outer gate, but Kalan thought her excitement had begun fading into weariness as they passed beneath the inner portcullis and series of murder holes between the two gates. "Will you do one more thing for me?" he asked, removing one of his daggers as he walked. "Will you give this to Faro and tell him I said to bear it with honor, in my name and his own?"

"I will." Liy was very solemn as he handed her the sheathed blade, and she continued to clutch it to her chest when the outer gate opened. Once everyone had passed through and Kalan's eyes had adjusted to the twilight beyond the keep perimeter, he could see the Night guards waiting in the shadow of a rock outcrop, on the far side of the Red Keep's killing ground. To reach them, his own company had to descend the road that zigzagged up to the Blood Gate, then cross the open ground.

"So let's hike," Rhanar said, more sour than ever, and the small company started down the first, precipitous stretch of road. Kalan's shoulders crawled with awareness of the gate at their backs, bristling with archers and the giant, insect heads of siege engines within the protection of its storm ramparts.

They had just reached level ground when a commotion broke out behind them. "It's the sally port," Taly said, swinging around. Looking where she pointed, Kalan took in a sliver of light between overlapping sections of wall as the commotion resolved into hounds baying. He also saw the wyr hounds, thirteen swift, glowing-eyed projectiles hurtling down the near-vertical slope.

"Kharalth!" Jad said, as the baying fell silent. "Stay still, all of you."

Shouts sounded from the Blood Gate, but the light from the sally port had already shut off, its position lost again within the dusk. The hounds' eyes still glowed, on fire in the gloom as they raced closer. "Will we have to kill 'em?" Palla whispered, and Kalan heard Rhisart's reluctance in her voice.

"I don't think they're going to attack," he said, very quietly, because he knew precipitate movement or speech could change that. "They haven't been set to hunt us. I believe," he added slowly, "they may be accompanying us." Kalan felt the wonder of that as the thirteen dark shapes slowed, their luminous eyes fixed on him, before they flowed past and across the killing ground to fling themselves down, a watchful picket between the Night company and the Wall's darkness.

"Kharalth!" Jad said again, with feeling. But what Kalan was wondering, as the lead wyr rolled a brilliant eye toward their approach, was who had opened the sally port and released the thirteen from the Red Keep.

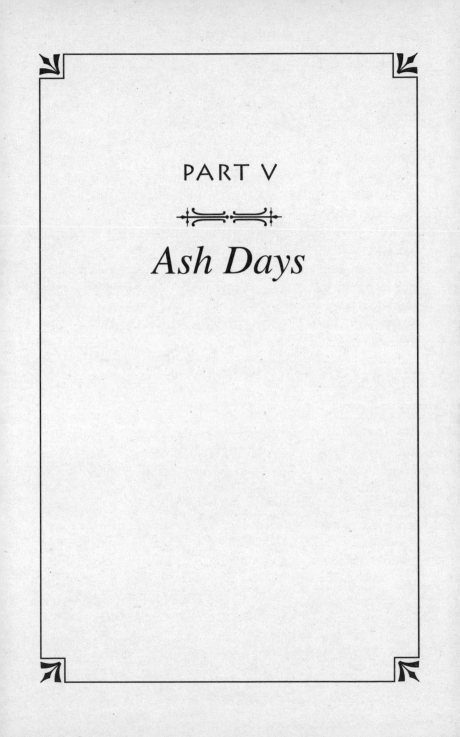

PART V

Ash Days

35

Dissonance

"**D**read Pass," Kalan's voice whispered, as though he were with Malian in her vision. A deep drift of smoke and fog pressed into her eyes and nose and throat, but the utter silence told her that she was alone. Eerie, she thought, and took a cautious step forward. Metal clanged softly, and when she settled onto her heels she found the fragments of a shield scattered among the stones. So this was where she had gotten to, again . . .

Malian guessed it must be later on in time from her previous vision, since the hot spots had died away. Only the smoke lingered, the last evidence of the confrontation that had riven the plain, as well as both antagonists and the hero's shield. Raven had said that Khelor ordered the bodies of both Yorindesarinen and the Chaos Worm buried, so even in the fog a few paces more should tell her whether Fire had yet arrived to claim the frost-fire sword.

Strange, Malian thought, rising, if I should witness their coming and see the young Raven with Khelor . . . Yet no stranger, she supposed, than her first vision of the Cave of Sleepers and the conversation with Amaliannarath's ghost. The dead Ascendant had called her namesake and asked who had named her—which Malian still didn't know. Raven had confirmed that her name *was* a diminutive of

Amaliannarath, but also that the Sworn and the Derai shared a wide pool of names in common. Once, Malian might have been disturbed that her name derived from one of the Sworn. But I'm growing hardened, she assured herself wryly.

Distracted by her thoughts of Amaliannarath, she almost stepped on Yorindesarinen's broken body. As in her Aeris vision, Nhenir was gone, but the Worm's bulk loomed nearby and the hero's hand still rested on her sword's hilt. A shiver ran through earth and air, and Malian felt the vision start to slip away. She gritted both her teeth and will until it steadied—only to wonder if she should have let it elude her after all, as the Worm's eyes began to open.

Flight is always an option, Malian told herself. Yet if the vision *was* important and she fled, it would only recur. So she held herself motionless, watching the membranes beneath the Worm's outer lids struggle to open. It *has* to be very close to death, she thought. Even so, when the last membrane finally lifted back, Malian knew that it could see her. The eyes were dull as the surrounding fog, but gradually a glow crept in, the saffron of coals in a dying fire.

"*. . . I shall not forget you.*" The whisper was a will-o'-the-wisp. "*I shall be waiting for your return.*"

Momentarily, all Malian could hear was her heart, beating out that she knew these words. Hylcarian, the remnant Golden Fire of Night, had spoken them to her as she fled the Keep of Winds. Yet if Hylcarian was trying to bridge the divide that existed between the Derai world and Haarth, including within the Gate of Dreams, surely he would speak through Yorindesarinen, not the Worm . . . *Surely*, Malian repeated, repelled—except revulsion, like all emotion, could muddy the seeing, so she distanced herself from it.

"*No, we did not die, but we came very close . . .* " She heard the echo of dying thunder, hollow around the whisper in her mind. "*Ghosts together . . . but I am weak . . .*"

Most of the phrases derived from Malian's exchanges with Hylcarian, but she did not recognize all of them. Could the Gate of Dreams gather up scraps of different conversations, she wondered, reassembling them to convey new meaning? The Huntmaster had warned Kalan that you never knew what powers might be watching and listening in the white mists. *Just as I,* Malian reflected, *am doing now.*

"Soon." The whisper repeated the Golden Fire's final word to her as she left the Keep of Winds. The membranes were sliding across the Worm's eyes again, the last glow dying—only to flare up again, a brighter amber veining the dull saffron. Even dying, the power of its gaze reminded Malian of when Nindorith had looked at her through both Shadow Band illusions and Nhenir's cloaking presence, in Caer Argent. *"Free me."* The beast's eyes clung to hers, its whisper permeating the fog. *"Free me, Child of Light!"*

Child of Light ... But the Worm's eyes had grown fixed, staring at nothing. The fog billowed, and the seer's vision bucked against Malian's hold like a horse. When it parted she saw an empty road beneath threatening sky. On it, a darkness with the suggestion of a man at its heart moved toward her.

I've seen you before as well, Malian thought, and let the last of her foreseeing dissipate.

Slowly, she stretched the trance's stillness away, recalling how the final vision had pursued her into southern Aralorn, but stopped after Stoneford. Malian had supposed that meant the figure in the darkness was Raven, following her south, but now that the vision had recurred it seemed unlikely. Emuun would have been tracking Jehane Mor's medallion around that same time, though, which made him the most likely reason for the vision to have returned.

Since the wayhouse, Malian and Raven had taken no chances around possible pursuit. They had switched between the two routes from Aeris to the River, again mixing their wary use of gates with horseback travel. As soon as they reached the Ijir's first navigable tributary, they had added in travel by water. Running water thwarted most Swarm magic, and Malian's cautious seeking had detected no pursuit. But since Emuun, like Raven, was immune to power, they had switched identities several times as well. The swords-for-hire had become caravan guards, then muleteers, and bargees once they reached the River.

To confuse the trail further, they had parted ways on finally reaching Ar. Patrol business had taken Raven into the white-walled city, while Malian bypassed it altogether. Too many there might recognize either the Band adept or the University scholar, and she had abandoned her bargee's disguise for the same reason. Now, in recognition that the Ash Days, which marked the seasonal shift from the autumn equinox to Autumn's Night—or Winter's Eve as some on the River called it—had overtaken her, she had become Ash, an itinerant mender of armor and weapons, and peddler of secondhand arms. This guise, she hoped, would see out the final leg of her journey to Hedeld.

Ash was gregarious, not particularly clean, and light fingered where opportunity allowed. The tinker's identity enabled Malian to wear a handful of weapons openly and to carry more, together with an array of tools, in packs strapped to either side of the lean, mean-spirited gray that had replaced Hani. Conscious of the frost-fire blade on her hip and its aeons-old bond to the House of Fire, Malian was careful to avoid the Patrol. She saw them often at a distance, or glimpsed the black sails of their galleys on the river, and—remembering her vision of Ar besieged—was glad they would remain in the River lands. War might still come here, but she suspected that even an aggressive enemy would think long and hard before biting off a mouthful of steel like the Patrol.

Malian wondered, too, whether that was why Raven, as the Patrol's Lord Captain, had responded with overt force to the Guild House massacre in Ij. The ancient treaty that charged the Patrol with defense of the Guild of Heralds was the apparent motivation, but there could have been other ways of fulfilling that obligation. Whereas the mobilization of the Patrol and the locking down of the River's largest city, together with road and river traffic as far west as Farelle, sent a clear message that the River would not be easy pickings for anyone contemplating invasion.

Including the Sworn *or* the Derai, Malian thought, releasing her final stretch and standing up. Mentally, she began checking last night's perimeter of psychic wards, while simultaneously going over Ash's array of weapons and her hideout arms. Her campsite was a ruined chapel to Seruth, situated amid heavily wooded terrain and so well concealed behind creepers and close-growing trees that she had nearly missed it the previous day, even with the map Raven had drawn her. The interior was more complete than it had appeared from the outside, with thick vines creating a secondary roof and much of the walls and floor remaining, despite thickly layered leaves underfoot. Bird droppings were splashed everywhere, and Malian could see evidence that larger animals had laired here in the past, but no signs of recent occupation.

"Hard to find but still providing reasonable shelter," she murmured, filling the gray's nosebag with oats Ash had pilfered, before grooms from the posting station had chased the tinker off. "A perfect hedge knight's—or vagabond's—hideout."

Her own breakfast was bread, cheese, and apples, and Malian considered the recent vision while she ate. She had seen the broken shield twice now, but still wanted to know what had become of its pieces. Yet even if Ornorith smiled and she found every splinter, reforging the shield seemed increasingly unlikely. I'd need to add in new metal, Malian thought, and Haarth ore might not bond with the adamantine steel. A remade shield would probably be considerably weaker than its predecessor as well. *"And that broke, despite supposedly having been made by a god."* She paused, then quoted softly: " *'Heaven's shield by the Chosen borne . . .'* "

" *'Terennin wrought me in time's dawn,'* " Nhenir concluded the ancient rhyme. *"But I was remade and did not break."*

"True," Malian murmured. She still frowned, because this morning's trance had been her first opportunity to seek after the shield since Aeris, and she was no closer to learning what had become of the shards. *"That suggests I have to try harder."* She grimaced. *"Or that what I saw is more important. Yet if it is . . . "*

She halted midway through the apple, puzzling again over why Hylcarian would speak through the Worm, in her vision, and not Yorindesarinen. On the other hand, the request to be freed fitted with the Golden Fire's reduced state, tied to the heart of the Old Keep, but also—less comfortably—with Raven's account of the Sundering. "But—" Malian said aloud, before completing her business with the apple. *"It called me Child of Light at the end. That's one of Yorindesarinen's names, not mine."*

"It could be the echo of a conversation that took place after the hero commanded me to leave her." Nhenir was cool-as-silver. *"Yet I would have said both Worm and hero were already well beyond that by then, even using mindspeech."*

"She was its greatest enemy." Malian shook her head. *"So why would it appeal to her, or to me, for that matter?"* The beast could, she supposed, have been in so much pain that it cried out for release, not realizing that its enemy was in similar straits. Yet that seemed an unlikely reason for it to figure in her foreseeing now. And it had not said "kill me," or even "release me," but "free me," which had a different ring. *"So most likely it* was *Hylcarian, seeking a means to reach me."*

The vision's implication could be that the shield's loss was irrevocable and she needed to focus on salvaging Hylcarian—and discovering whether any more of the entities that collectively formed the Golden Fire had survived the Night of Death. *"Right now, though,"* Malian said, shying the apple core through a gap in the wall, *"I need to clear my head."*

She donned Nhenir, currently disguised as the tinker's greasy leather cap, before knotting an equally grimy kerchief over the top and leading the gray from the ruin. Initially, she rode north to see if she could discern any sign of the Hedeld fort, but like the trading post it must lie farther toward the Wild Lands than she had realized. When she reached a high point on the road and saw nothing but trees interspersed with water courses and bog country, Malian knew that the River truly had given way to wilderness.

She studied the wild terrain for some time while the late autumn sun climbed to its zenith. When she had held still long enough, she began to hear the deep, wordless song of Haarth, which she had first encountered on Emer's Northern March. That first time, it had manifested as the call of a hidden path beside the river known as the Rindle. Later, Malian had heard it again through the singing green of Maraval forest, and the quiet of southern Aralorn with its chestnut woods and sleepy villages. The voice of this land, bordering wilderness, was more somber. The song of the wildfire and the flood, she thought. And because she was wearing Nhenir, she also heard another sound far beneath it: the faint, distant rumble of rocks, grinding deep in the earth.

Jaransor, the Hills of the Hawk, might lie well beyond the horizon, but Malian knew she would never forget the anger that smoldered beneath their tors. Hearing that savage grumble now, however muted by distance, she realized that the Rindle might not have been her first encounter with the song of Haarth, after all. Briefly, Malian felt as though the sun were an eye, gazing back at her from the noon sky. She also detected what might have been a flicker of power use to the southwest, but it vanished too swiftly to be sure.

Malian turned the gray south, both to increase her chance of detecting the anomaly again, but also to look for Raven on the road. Bypassing the ruin, she continued on to a woodcutters' village she had skirted the previous day. Studying it from concealment, she could see nothing out of place, although the smell of food reminded her that she had not eaten since early morning. Trading for a hot meal was an option, but she knew the villagers would regard Ash askance. Rightly, she thought, grinning, and headed back toward the chapel.

Despite the sun being well into its westward descent, Malian still drew rein when she spotted a large rock rising above the forest canopy. She had noticed it the day before but been intent on finding the ruin before nightfall. Now it struck her again that it would make an ideal vantage point for spying out this part of the forest, as well as being an interesting climb. She had to dismount to reach it, following a small, tumultuous watercourse that foamed around the rock's base, and concealed the gray in a nearby thicket.

The rock was steep, but the surface firm to climb, and the summit allowed Malian to study the terrain while remaining unseen herself. Threads of smoke, already distant, rose from the woodcutters' village, while birds were flocking back to the forest ahead of the coming night. When she lowered Nhenir's visor, Malian could detect sounds as soft as the pad of paws over damp earth, and the rustle of feathers among the treetops. She could hear a band of hunters, too, pitching camp in the deep woods beyond the creek, but otherwise the forest seemed unrelentingly peaceful.

"Bucolic," Nhenir supplied.

"That, too." Malian was about to raise the visor when she caught the dissonance. Concentrating, she made out the intermittent snap of broken stems accompanying a slow, heavy drag through nearby undergrowth. She could also hear the suppressed rasp that marked a wounded creature trying to keep silence, but finding every breath, let alone movement, a challenge. Soon, she had isolated the pattern: a lurch and drag forward, punctuated by a brief halt and labored breath.

The next stop was longer, and this time Malian heard a moan of pain, quickly cut off. Through Nhenir, she listened for any sound of pursuit, but could detect none. All the same, she was careful as she descended the rock and reentered the gray's thicket. The tinker's horse chanced a sly nip, but remained quiet as Malian studied the dense understory, using Nhenir to enhance her seeking after anything hidden between leaf and branch, light and shadow. The helm also sifted sounds: wind and water, falling leaves—and a very shallow, very faint, rise and fall of breath.

Sliding into the gloom beneath the trees, Malian stalked the flutter of breath through tangled undergrowth and gathering dusk. Even with Nhenir's visor lowered, she had to look hard to find her quarry, who had taken cover beneath a fallen tree. A curtain of brambles and vines protected the crawl space, and Malian had to snake through both to confirm that the prone figure was a woman and that she was still breathing.

Only just, Malian thought, dragging off a glove to be sure of the pulse. The woman was wearing the uniform of a Patrol river pilot, and between the deep gashes across her back and the quantity of blood staining her gambeson, it was a miracle she had survived this long. As gently as possible, Malian eased the wounded Patroler over, compressing her lips at the burn seared across chin and neck beneath a heat-twisted visor.

First things first, she told herself, and lay close beside the wounded woman, sharing her body's warmth while she considered options. The surest course would be to use a gate to reach the Band's headquarters in Ar, where there were skilled healers. If she took care, the unexpected arrival might not generate questions, although the wounded pilot undoubtedly would. But given how badly the woman was injured, Malian doubted she would survive exposure to the portal's power. Setting aside her habitual caution around gate use, opening one now also risked alerting the pilot's attackers. *"When the fact I can detect no pursuit suggests they believe their victim dead. Which she soon will be,"* Malian added, *"from cold and shock if not her wounds, if I don't get her to shelter."*

"You could just let her die." Nhenir was dispassionate.

"No. Derai don't abandon their own, and I've accepted Fire as mine. And the ruin's not far—but I'll have to get her onto the gray or carry her myself." Malian also had to extract the unconscious pilot from her hiding place, which she did by first extricating herself and then using the frost-fire sword to sheer through bramble and vine. Pulling the last of the tangle aside, she raised the pilot torso-to-torso with herself and prepared to lift the unconscious body across her shoulders. *"I just hope she survives this, let alone whatever healing I can dredge up once we reach the chapel."*

Nhenir did not respond, but the woman groaned, her eyelids fluttering. Her heartbeat was little more than a flutter, too, and Malian held her close, willing her own strength into the fragile pulse. The pilot's eyes had opened, but Malian was not sure how much she saw through the buckled visor—which could, she realized, have melted into the skin. Suppressing nausea, she continued supporting the woman's body and allowed the hand that wavered up to settle onto her own face.

"Mind's eye . . . " The pilot was wearing a glove, but Malian felt the brush of her mind as soon as the hand touched. She could also feel the woman's physical agony as the mindvoice whispered again. *"Take . . . "*

The flow of memories that accompanied the word was soft as an evening breeze, slipping through an open casement, and after a moment's initial startlement, Malian strengthened her mental defenses but allowed the transfer. *"Yris,"* she acknowledged, accepting the name that came with the memories. Closing her own hand over the pilot's, she held it in place to facilitate the exchange, but the connection between them was already faltering as the heart beating against hers grew fainter.

"You must close off the link," Nhenir cautioned. *"You must not be caught in her death."*

"Let me go . . . " Yris's murmur was simultaneous with the helm's warning, and Malian separated herself as gently as she could. The link was so weak now that it felt like brushing away a cobweb, and Yris's pulse, too, was almost gone. It fluttered again—once more, twice—before her body slumped. As soon as Malian lifted her palm clear, the pilot's hand fell away from her face.

"She's gone," Malian said, mostly to ease the moment, since Nhenir already knew.

"But she died well." Now the helm's coolness was all steel. *"With our help, she will take her enemy with her, down into the dark."*

36

The Language of Blood

The daylight had faded by the time Malian fetched the gray and got Yris's body across the saddle. She led the horse slowly through the gloom, but Raven still had not arrived when they reentered the ruin. An owl hooted from the forest as Malian laid Yris's body on a slab of rock rising out of the floor, which she guessed had been an altar. In the dim light, the pilot could have been one of the stone knights of Emer, carved upon a tomb, and the chapel seemed a fitting enough resting place. Tethering the gray to a sapling growing from a gap in the wall, Malian extracted a short-handled shovel from her baggage and cast around for a suitable grave site.

"So this is where the bitch got to." A vertical shimmer appeared in the blackness of the main door as a woodsman stepped through—but Malian recognized the voice, rough as gravel, from the Aeris fair. "Who'd have thought she'd open a gate on me, fleeing before I could steal her face?"

"I've been expecting you," Malian told him.

Emuun cocked his head as though listening for concealed meaning. "Have you now?" Malian tensed as he raised his left hand, but rather than a weapon, a greenish-white light flared against his palm, dispelling the shadows. The light came from a tiny cone lamp, similar to those that Night's initiates had carried on the Old Keep expedition. Emuun remained by the doorway, but the vertical shimmer kept moving, drifting further into the ruin. "You've changed your calling since Aeris, I see." Calculation colored the facestealer's tone. "Not, given your little display there, that I think you ever were a sword-for-hire."

He's trying to flush out answers, Malian thought, as the owl—or another of its kind—hooted again, closer to the chapel. She said nothing, simply waited while he studied her, and the line that appeared as part shimmer, part a flaw in the air, continued to float her way.

"In fact, you put me in mind of what our former Ijiri allies would call a Dancer of Kan." The face Emuun wore now was pockmarked and square-jawed, but the dark, hard eyes, like his voice, were unchanged from the night fair. "Except, that is, for the reek of power." He inhaled, a wolf absorbing scent. "With a Derai taint, too. Now why didn't I sniff *that* out in Aeris?"

Let him speculate, Malian thought, keeping her demeanor calm as he stepped forward. Her peripheral vision showed the flaw in the air still moving her way, and she imagined Emuun's current purpose was distraction. She was also aware that the flaw was using concealing magic. If she had not kept Nhenir's visor lowered, her seeking might detect its presence, but she would not be able to see it. As Yris, she thought, drawing on the memories the pilot had bequeathed her, had not become aware of it until too late.

Being immune, Emuun would know if she used power to investigate his familiar, so for the moment Malian focused on monitoring the information filtering to her through Nhenir. Beyond that, she was aware of the surrounding vastness of the forest and the sounds of night drawing in, with the song of Haarth's low note beneath it all. Pretending ignorance of his companion, she kept her eyes on the Darksworn as he studied her, his hard gaze intent.

"Nothing to say? Like what has become of your immune fellow traveler, for instance?" He paused. "Although you may prove more interesting. I resumed this hunt by doubling back on my original trail, enough to learn something of the agent Nindorith was pursuing when Ilkerineth's whelp died: a spy with an adept's power, using Haarth assassin's tricks, but with a taint of the Derai." His smile, too, was pure wolf. "I think perhaps I should gift you to the Prince of Lightning."

"If you can," Malian said softly.

An owl called again from almost overhead, and the second bird answered, a mournful echo from the wood. The drifting shimmer grew still as Emuun's wolf smile thinned. "Yes, whatever you are may be too dangerous to take chances with."

"Perceptive." Raven detached himself from the gap where the gray was tethered. He had resumed the hedge knight's amulets and shabby armor, and his visor was raised as he halted a few paces clear of Malian. "But as for the rest . . . Not this time, Emuun."

Emuun was staring, the last remnant of his wolf's smile wiped away. "It's not possible," he said slowly, as though struggling to accept the evidence of his senses. "You're dead. You all died with Amaliannarath, when she suicided in the void."

"Yet here I am." Raven was ironic. "You broke your own rule, Emuun. Didn't you always say that you only accepted a death once you'd seen the body?"

The Darksworn was motionless, silent—then Malian swallowed back revulsion as she realized that his form was shifting, the woodsman's stocky build transforming into a height and muscular grace that mirrored Raven's. The stolen face rippled, before transforming into a visage that could have been cast from one of the ancient hero masks that were said to be as old as the Derai. Or, Malian thought, chilled, those masks could have been molded from a face like this.

"I really should have guessed from Thanir's tale of an immune thwarting our work. But I'll confess I didn't." Emuun laughed, a bark of self-mockery. "You're right, too, I did break my own rule. Not a mistake I'll make again." His eyes narrowed. "But better if you *had* died, before sinking so low you'd put a dirty native adept, possibly even a Derai half-breed by her whiff, ahead of blood kinship and your Sworn heritage."

"All bonds, including my Sworn allegiance, were severed when Sun slew the Blood of Fire, my betrothed and all my kin among them." Raven's voice was the one he had used outside Aeris, speaking of Thanir. Hearing it, the hairs on Malian's arms and nape lifted, and she saw an answering muscle jump in Emuun's jaw. Energy glimmered along the vertical rift between light and air, and very slowly, it began moving again.

"So here you are, bent on interference—which always was one of your less attractive qualities, as I recall. But this—" Briefly, the hard stare flicked toward Malian. "It demeans you, First Kinsman."

If Sworn attitudes to outsiders were anything like the Derai's, he might well mean it. But mostly, Malian guessed, Emuun was trying to provoke Raven. She did not need Nhenir to read the subtle shift toward action in his stance, even as Raven regarded him with the hedge knight's most sardonic expression. "I see you've been consorting with natives yourself. When did the Great Djinn gift you one of their fire elementals?"

The rift swirled into life as Emuun's hand snapped closed, dousing the palm light, and Malian sprang sideways as a flung knife cleaved the space where she had been. She heard the ring of another blade, clearing its scabbard, and felt the flare of the elemental's magic, preparing to unleash the same fire that had seared Yris. Not this time, she thought—and spoke a phrase in the speech she had absorbed at midsummer, walking the path of earth and moon. The Jhainarian language of blood reverberated through the ruin, and the air around the elemental hardened, walling it in place.

Lifting her arm high, Malian let Yorindesarinen's armband blaze into silver-white life as Emuun cursed and hurled himself toward the trapped elemental. Being immune, he would pass her wall of power with impunity, and if he escaped into his freed familiar's warp of fire and air— No, Malian thought, and sprang to intercept, but before she could cast her Shadow Band throwing stars, Raven had brought Emuun down. Both warriors were gouging and grappling as they fell, much as the elemental was straining to throw off Malian's containment spell.

The energy within its rift was sluggish but slowly rebuilding momentum, and if it gained sufficient impetus might well breach her wall. But the language of blood was not just the speech the priestess-queens had wielded against Malian at midsummer. It was also the tongue that Zharaan and Kiyan had used to shut Salar's children out of Jhaine, and their predecessors had called on to still the Cataclysm. Now, Malian delved deep into its ancient structure and breathed out a profound exhalation of air and magic that coiled about the rift. The elemental within it fought back, twisting first one way then another as it struggled to transform into fire. A flame ignited, but wavered as Malian's incantation tightened, before disintegrating into sparks.

One by one the sparks snuffed out, but their initial snap had panicked the gray horse into a half rear, fighting his tether as the struggling warriors rolled toward him. The gray's forefeet struck the ground beside Emuun's head, and the Darksworn threw himself aside, tearing free of Raven's grip as the gray plunged again. The horse's shoulder caught Emuun as he started to rise, knocking him through the gap in the wall. The facestealer was staggering clear of it before Malian or Raven could reach him, although a second later they were both racing in pursuit.

Too much was at stake to let the Darksworn escape, regardless of whether he chose to come after them again himself or carried news of Raven, as well as Malian's blend of Haarth and the Derai, back to the Sworn. And Emuun *would* escape if they lost sight of him for a moment amid forest and night, his immunity eluding both Nhenir and Malian's seeking. So Malian willed herself on and let the armband blaze more brightly, illuminating their quarry as he dodged between its dazzle and the blackness of the undergrowth.

She snatched a glance toward Raven, who was keeping up despite running in mail, and realized that he was angling away from her on a trajectory designed to intersect Emuun's current direction. Malian's breath tore in her lungs as she urged her legs faster and cast her seeking wide, searching for terrain that might aid them. Instead she found a circle of warriors, at sufficient distance to escape her detection before now, but closing in—and she cursed herself for relying on the fact that Emuun had been alone, except for the elemental, in Yris's memories.

Ignoring the fire of muscle and breath, Malian closed the distance between herself and the Darksworn. Oddly, the only sound she could hear now was Haarth's somber melody, rising through the surge of her blood—which was also the surge of an owl's blood and sinew as it took flight. She saw Emuun through its predator's vision as it ghosted toward him, and recalled the tor hawk in Jaransor, flying into the Night Mare's eyes with extended claws and blinding wings. Opening her mind to both song and bird, she let the owl see her quarry both as she did and as it might perceive prey, fleeing across the forest floor.

The owl screeched and drove for Emuun's face in a flurry of pinions and claws. Startled, he threw up an arm to protect his eyes and lurched sideways. He regained his balance in an instant, but the distraction was enough for Malian to catch him. The Darksworn grunted as he spun around, coming at her with a fresh dagger in his right hand and a cestus wrapped around the left. She met him with the Derai-dan, in a flurry of strikes and blocks, kicks and evasions, that deflected the force of his blows. He was rock, but she was fire and tempered steel, and had been taught the Derai-dan by Asantir, who was a master . . .

Emuun grunted again, acknowledgment that she was holding her own. He would know, too, that Raven was close, so Malian was not surprised when he tried to break away, although when she sprang after him he retaliated with a battery of feet and fists. She darted and wove, then reeled as a blow from the cestus glanced off Nhenir. If it had been any lesser helmet, the glancing blow might have felled her. Even so, Malian lurched away from the strike—and Emuun was up and running, slipping through the night forest like an eel.

Malian's head rang, but she pushed to overhaul him again until every muscle screamed. Despite Nhenir, she could feel the beginnings of dizziness from the combination of the blow and the need for breath. Through the helm, she heard Raven a few seconds before he reappeared, cutting out of the trees to intercept Emuun—who saw him and veered off. Malian veered, too, suspended in what felt like a nightmare of pursuit and flight. She thought, for a few desperate moments, that Emuun might pull clear, until the owl—or another— swooped across his path again.

The Darksworn's swerve was minimal, but allowed Malian's burst of speed to bring her close enough for a flying tackle. They hit the ground together, exactly as he and Raven had in the chapel, and she felt his shoulders and back muscles bunch, preparing to throw her off—except Raven was already with her, driving a knee into Emuun's back and clamping his face in the dirt. Seizing opportunity, Malian slid a Band dart from her cuff and drove it into the Darksworn's neck.

He must be strong as a bull, she thought, because it was long seconds before his struggle against Raven's hold weakened and he finally succumbed to the drug. She bent to make sure he was unconscious before Raven released him, and as she straightened, Yris's memories reasserted themselves: Emuun ambushing the pilot with the elemental's blaze of fire, which blinded her, followed by Yris's desperate escape. The gate the pilot opened had been little more than a swamp hen's hop, skip, jump of flight, but it was enough to snatch herself from beneath Emuun's knife. "Yris." Malian murmured the name, part salute, part farewell, and let the armband fade to a dim glow. Her blood still raced, but both pulse and breath were steadier, and she saw that Raven had eased back onto his heels.

His expression was the measuring look she had first seen in the Long Pass. "He's not dead?"

Malian shook her head. "The dart was drugged, not poisoned." She hesitated, her gaze shifting from Raven to Emuun, facedown on the forest floor. Her shiver was partly reaction, partly re-noticing the night's chill. "He's your First Kinsman." Her eyes returned to Raven, recalling the words a siren worm had hissed through another vision six years before, when confronting Asantir. "Blood demands blood, isn't that the Sworn way, too? So I don't want his on my hands."

"If it comes to blood, Emuun's drenched with it. Yris's death is only the last of a multitude."

Malian nodded, uncertain how to interpret this as she peered into the darkness beneath the trees. "We're not alone out here. My seeking showed me other warriors, closing in on the ruin."

Raven had begun relieving Emuun of his weapons, an arsenal that would have put a Dancer of Kan to shame. "They're mine, warriors from my personal guard who were also to meet me here. A lieutenant, Sarathion, was with me, and Yris had gone ahead from Ar with a message for the muster. When we cut her trail and then Emuun's, we knew we had trouble. But I wanted to snare him, not send him to ground, so I ordered Sarathion to meet the escort and ensure they kept their distance."

Of course, Malian thought. She had grown used to the solitary hedge knight, but the Lord Captain of the Patrol and a prince of Fire—*the* Prince of Fire—was always going to have some sort of Honor Guard. Now that she was no longer engaged in a life or death pursuit through midnight woods, and had time to reflect, the explanation was obvious.

"I was not to know," Raven added, "that you would set yourself as bait, not just to trap a Darksworn facestealer, but one of the most dangerous there is."

Malian looked away from the forest and back to him. "You wanted to snare him, too," she pointed out. "The drug should hold him unconscious for several hours," she added, seeing he was using his sword belt to bind Emuun's arms.

Raven shook his head. "You saw how long it took to work on him, and Emuun could always resist Arcolin's potions as well. Amaliannarath believed the ability might be linked to his immunity to power, so we'll take no chances." He held out a hand. "I'll have yours, too, for his legs, until I can fetch a rope from my horse."

Silently, Malian unbuckled her belt and handed it to him, adding the leather ties Shadow Band adepts wound about their wrists. At the same time, she extended her seeking again. "Your guards are not far off now." Close enough to count, she added silently. Watching Raven work, she found herself putting other pieces in his puzzle together: from the night march to The Leas, to the way he had not needed the armring's light when he separated from her, cutting through the pitch-black woods to intercept Emuun.

"You can see in the dark." In retrospect it was obvious, but so unobtrusive she had never noticed.

"Not as well as Kalan, but like Girvase, well enough to be useful." She noted the initial lift of his brows, which suggested he had either thought she already knew or not considered it important enough to mention. And your hearing? she wondered, because despite being far enough away to remain undetected, he had still heard everything that passed between her and the in Butterworth. "A great many of us can," he continued, using the ties to reinforce the belt securing Emuun's arms. "It's one of the qualities, together with the helms, that began the River lore around the Patrol being demons."

"But Emuun can't," she said. Fortunately, she added silently, otherwise he would almost certainly have escaped.

Raven stood up. "No. But he has abilities enough. The only way to make sure of Emuun will be to kill him."

Was that an implied rebuke? Malian wondered as Raven left, carrying his scabbarded sword. She kept her own blade unsheathed, using Nhenir to monitor the newcomers' approach while she kept watch on Emuun. The similarity to Raven was less discernible in his unconscious features, she decided, possibly because of the cruelty stamped deep into his face.

She studied him a moment longer before turning away, but despite her familiarity with Nhenir's ways, she still started when a voice spoke, as clearly as if the speaker were beside her. "Apologies, sir, that we weren't in time to be useful."

"You kept back as ordered, Sarathion." Raven was matter-of-fact.

"Lady Malian found Yris before I did, but too late. Her body's in the ruined chapel, which we need to secure."

"The Heir of Night," a cool voice murmured, as though the words themselves tasted unpleasant.

"And Emuun, sir?" Sarathion asked.

"Captured. Lady Malian knocked him out with a Shadow Band narcotic, but I doubt he'll stay under long. We need to prepare for what that means."

"Keep Emuun prisoner?" A third warrior spoke, sounding grim. "We'll have our work cut out."

"Why did she take him alive?" It was the cool voice again. "Is extracting intelligence one of her Derai talents?"

"Stow it, Rhai," a woman said, and Malian heard the stir of armored bodies before Raven spoke again, his tone as even as the woman's had been blunt.

"She knows Emuun is my First Kinsman, Rhaikir. She didn't want his blood on her hands."

Put that way, it makes me sound squeamish, Malian thought, and grimaced.

"Once we've secured the ruin," Raven went on, "we'll hold him there while we bury Yris."

"We should bury him with her," the grim voice muttered.

"And not bother killing him first," another added.

"Not amusing, Ynvis." Sarathion was crisp, but Malian could imagine the answering shrugs.

The echo of the gesture was in the woman's voice when she replied. "This is Emuun we're talking about, Sarath."

"We are Fire," Raven said. Malian knew that flat tone from the banks of the Rindle. "So we won't be burying anyone alive. I'll not allow Emuun and Sun to drag us down to what they are."

That's the sort of thing Asantir used to say, Malian thought, to illustrate what she said my father wanted for Night and the Derai Alliance. Briefly, she saw her father's face as it had been in the vision that accompanied the return of the sword, and it occurred to her that if she continued on her current course, she might well bring Raven face-to-face with both the Earl of Night and his Commander.

"An interesting meeting," Nhenir observed, and Malian nodded.

The warriors' talk became sporadic once they reached the ruin, but she heard Raven dispatch Ynvis to retrieve his horse. The escort's horses had been left under guard, well clear of the chapel, while their riders advanced on foot. The woman, who was named Aithe, now departed with another guard to bring them to the ruin, too. And soon, Malian thought, Raven will return for Emuun and I'll have my first encounter with the House of Fire. The prospect made her frown even as she felt Nhenir's focus shift. A moment later, Emuun stirred.

That's not possible, Malian thought, echoing the Darksworn's own words from the ruin—except Emuun was rousing before her eyes, perhaps even more swiftly than Raven had anticipated. His body twitched, then stilled again, although his eyelids continued to move. Malian counted out a minute before his body shuddered a second time, then spasmed as he groaned, a hoarse, animal sound. Again his limbs quieted, although his eyelids continued to twitch. Finally, they jerked open.

"You." Several seconds elapsed before Emmun's vision fixed on her, but Malian saw recognition flare. "Blind." His pupils were dilated from the drug, but she could see them clearing as she watched. "Derai-dan . . . you . . . no half . . ." The slurred, hoarse voice stopped, then began again. "No half-breed," he got out at last. "You're . . . pure Derai."

37

✛═✛═✛

High Stakes

Speaking must have taken effort, because Emuun's eyes closed again and sweat sheened his face. Malian guessed he was fighting the drug's aftermath of lethargy and nausea, but doubted he would stay quiet for long. Resistant to drugs as well as magic, she thought, fascinated and appalled in equal part—and he perceives entirely too much. She eyed Raven's bonds with a far greater appreciation for his parting caution, and hoped they would prove robust. As if her thoughts had been a goad, Emuun's muscles bulged and blood suffused his face as he fought his bonds. Watching his neck swell, Malian wondered if he might burst a vein. Finally, his struggles ceased as abruptly as they had begun and he gasped for breath.

"You'll only injure yourself if you keep that up." She kept her voice broad with Ash's Terebanthi burr. "And I doubt you're immune to wound sores."

Emuun curled his lip at her. "Blind," he repeated, the word a little clearer this time. "Not just me . . . fooled. Nind'rith, too." She watched his brows and mouth both draw down, a second before his eyes opened again, their ancient darkness intent. "Ravir'n . . . always did know . . . how . . . to play . . . the long game . . . Why Amal'rath . . .

valued him ... even over Khelor." He stopped again, his breathing harsh. "If ... Ravir'n's playing ... then game's ... for high stakes."

Ravir'n must be Raven, Malian thought, careful to keep her gaze unrevealing. Through Nhenir, she was listening for Raven's return, but the Fire warriors appeared to be in the ruin still. Emuun's eyes had narrowed, and although sweat still beaded his lip, his expression was heavy with calculation. "Not just ... any Derai ... if *she* saw you ... Too strong." Systematically, he began testing Raven's restraints again, snarling when forced to admit defeat a second time—although almost immediately be began to laugh, a hoarse bark that ended in a cough. "Ravirien ... right. Should always see ... the body. To think of Aranraith ... not just believing ... Fire gone ... but holding back ... sixteen years ... Even working with Ilker'neth's witch to dispose ... of you ... clearing path for her whelp and ... counterprophecy."

What counterprophecy? Malian wondered. Slowly, Emuun's lips lifted into a cruel curve that bared his teeth. "Even Salar believed ... scion ... of the witch's blood would be the stake ... we finally drove ... through ... heart of thrice-cursed Derai ... Alliance. And all ... the time ... was you." He gasped out another coughing laugh. "Amalian'rath ... always deep minded ... must have *seen* ... "

Raven's not the only one who knows how to play, Malian reminded herself. All the same, she felt her expression stiffen and saw an answering glint in the Darksworn's gaze. His lip curled back again, and this time his speech was close to smooth. "I know Ravirien of old ... more than just First Kin, once we were as brothers ... in our war." His stare was an abyss, and despite his bonds Malian felt fear's cool touch, her muscles tightening as she sensed his facestealer's will reaching out to ensnare hers. "Having attached himself to you, he will seek to ... attach you in return. He always was astute."

And you, Malian thought, will say anything, distort everything, to drive a wedge between us. Knowing that doubt, like fear, provided an opening Emuun could exploit, she visualized a wall of glass about her power, its smooth surface repelling the tendril of his will—and could not resist letting a spark of the armring's fire singe its retreat. The Darksworn jerked back, cursing her, but the darkness of his eyes stayed cold as he began muttering a string of words that initially sounded like more vituperation. When the words came more swiftly, their cadence rising and falling, Malian realized that he was speaking a tongue similar to the language of blood. Only misshapen, she thought, hearing the allure-wrapped whisper that promised pulsing warmth and blood, pain and death. Beneath the surface glamour, she could see the invocation twisting into a maw that would soon gape wide. Only it was not a mouth but a portal, opening into a pit of magic.

Haarth magic, Malian thought, intrigued despite her danger, because Emuun was not opening the portal himself. Instead, his chant was invoking the opener's power. Her immediate reaction was that they should have gagged him. The second was to thrust the frost-fire sword through his throat—but she also wanted to learn more of this magic. Calling on the language of blood again, she wove an incantation to hold the River night closed.

Slowly, confronted by the rock of her will, Emuun's invocation faltered. Yet whoever was on the far side of the opening was holding the psychic equivalent of a foot in a chinked door. Grimly, Malian poured illusion shadows into the fracture. The contending power on the other side dispersed them almost at once, but in the split second of distraction, Malian forced the fissure shut.

Emuun choked as though she had stuffed a gag into his mouth— but just enough power must have leaked through, because his bonds began to smoke. His eyes blazed hate and triumph into hers as the leather disintegrated and he lurched to his feet. "Now," he spat, "let's see what you're really made of, without Ravirien at your back."

He ground out what sounded like another curse—and a cutlass flew off the arsenal Raven had set aside, and into his fist. His weapons must be bound to him—but Malian was already parrying, and the Darksworn pulled back, clearly remembering the frost-fire sword's effect in Aeris. He circled, muttering, and Malian felt the portal magic reawaken as she counterattacked.

The cutlass survived their whirlwind exchange, but Emuun was slick with sweat, his invocation coming in gasps as the drug's aftermath took its toll and Malian forced him back, step by step. Yet still he was dangerous: she could feel it through every clash of the blades and rasp of breath. And the unfamiliar power smoldered, searing her nostrils and eyes and throat as it struggled to reignite.

Musn't . . . let it . . . Summoning a reserve of breath, Malian shaped a single cantrip in the language of blood and drove it through her opponent's borrowed spell.

Emuun snarled and sprang forward, committing all his still-considerable strength to a strike that would sever head from shoulders if it cut home. Malian pivoted, the frost-fire sword rising to intercept— and a crossbow quarrel, shot out of the blackness of the forest, pierced Emuun through the eye. The Darksworn staggered, shock and pain transforming to blankness in his face. When he fell, it was the way a tree falls, straight and heavy to the ground.

The last trace of loaned magic vanished as Raven emerged from the trees and stared down at Emuun. Even with the armband's light, and Nhenir's power enhancing her own, Malian found it impossible to read his expression. When he spoke, his voice was quiet. "As you said, he was my First Kinsman. Better if his blood lies on my hands."

And *you* were right, Malian acknowledged silently: the only way to be sure of Emuun was to kill him. Moving slowly, she picked up her scabbard and resheathed the frost-fire sword. "He was invoking another power, using a tongue similar to Jhaine's language of blood, but infused with pain and death." The same way, Malian thought, the priestess-queens of Jhaine had desecrated the power that was their birthright. "It was magic of Haarth, not the Swa— orn, possibly another elemental trying to open a gate and rescue him."

"From the whiff of power I caught, I'd put money on one of the elemental's masters, or a cabal of them, since the Great Djinn rarely work alone." Raven's gaze narrowed on his kinsman's body. "Emuun must have shown them a way of extending their reach, because until now both the djinn and their lesser servants have been bound to the southern deserts." He paused. "His immunity came from his Fire mother, the facestealing from his Sun father, but he knew the runes as well as Arcolin or Thanir, and was adept at using them to glean others' magic for his own ends."

A magpie, Malian thought, but saw that Raven was watching her. "As you," he said, still quietly, "appear to have absorbed the Jhainarian language of blood from the Midsummer rite. In Ishnapur, the magi also call it the Language of Imuln. It's among the oldest magic in Haarth, as well as the strongest, but it comes at a price."

"Blood must be shed," she replied, as quiet as he. Drawing a dagger, she scored the tip across her palm, then stooped and pressed the bloodied line into the ground. Through the touch, she felt the song of Haarth again, a pulse within her hand. "I've already made one mistake tonight, using the Derai-dan. So you're right, best to avoid another."

He shook his head. "You used the language three times. Under the circumstances, it may be as well that Emuun died."

Malian frowned. "I thought that death was only required for the great workings. Like Kiyan, sacrificing himself so Zharaan could shut Salar's children out of Jhaine." Or the nine deaths, she thought, that had been required to prevent the Cataclysm destroying Haarth. Although really it had been eighteen, since the nine high priestesses had also died, their power drained performing the rite.

"The larger the working, the greater the offering." Raven spoke as though weighing his words. "In the Language of Imuln, blood and life are the same word. The way the story used to be told in Jhaine, that's why Kiyan knew his life would be necessary for Zharaan's rite to succeed. But what made the working so powerful, strong enough to keep the Sworn and their allies out to this day, was that Kiyan's sacrifice was primarily made, not out of fear or even necessity, but love."

A true offering, Malian thought, and supposed Yorindesarinen facing the Worm alone fell into the same category. She wrapped her jacket closer, her skin gooseflesh from the cold and the aftermath of the day's violence and death. Neither her Derai heritage nor Shadow Band training had yet exempted her from paying their toll. "I just didn't want to shout out Derai to any other Sworn who might be about."

Raven nodded. "Emuun will have suppressed any link to Nirn while he was on the run, but I imagine the sorcerer will feel his death. Sooner or later someone will investigate."

For the first time, Malian wondered how much of Emuun's conversation Raven might have overheard, returning ahead of the others, or whether he had only arrived in time for the brief, furious endgame. "Do you want to set another trap?" she asked.

"For now, I'd rather lose them." Raven glanced toward the sound of his guards approaching. "But facestealers must be burned, not buried or left to lie, so we'll place him in the chapel and set fire to both. That's Haarth practice, too, and since he was already a fugitive, with luck no one will look any further. Rhaikir's cadre can see to it and make sure our trail's wiped clear. And we'll find a better resting place for Yris."

"She deserves a place of honor." Among her own, Malian thought, assuming the Patrol had graveyards despite their longevity.

Before Raven could do more than nod, his warriors filtered out of the trees. Their eyes gleamed through lowered visors, although they were not wearing either Patrol helmets or the armor Malian recalled from the Cave of Sleepers. Their plain dark mail could have originated anywhere between Ij and Ishnapur, although the helms had a more southern aspect. I suppose they've had a millennium to build their armory, she thought, watching them study Emuun's body.

"Well, that makes life a lot simpler." She recognized Sarathion by his voice. "I did wonder how long we'd manage to hold him, especially on a march across wild country."

"He's carried a debt for our Kin and Blood a long time," said another warrior, one Malian had not heard speak before. "In the end, we'll hold all those who do to account."

Blood demands blood. Malian suppressed a shiver as she realized that Fire was resuming a conflict that had already been ancient before the Empire that Haarth called Old was founded. All the same, their mood was more somber than exultant, and she supposed the bonds of kinship must complicate the debt of blood.

We were as brothers in our war. Malian stifled another shiver as Emuun's words slithered across her mind. She was hungry as well as cold, and the day had been long. Stepping back, she tacitly ceded the site to what she guessed must be Rhaikir's cadre, preparing to wipe away any magical residue. Studying the shape of their power, she began to see what Raven had meant, outside Aeris, about turning aside unwelcome attention—and understand how the Patrol had been able to deflect doubt or questions until they and their helms of concealment were as much part of the River landscape as the Ijir itself.

An owl hooted again from the nearby trees, while farther off Malian heard the clip of many hooves on the forest road and guessed it was Aithe returning. As her attention shifted back to Emuun, her foreseeing flared, superimposing an image of Yorindesarinen's riven body over his corpse. The vision wavered, a candle flame against the void; when it steadied, the face of the dead hero was Malian's own.

Death down every path of seeing. This time, Malian could not repress her shudder as the image vanished and Raven and the cadre all looked her way. They must have detected the spark of power use, but no one spoke, and the warriors who had been about to lift Emuun onto a cloak tied between two spears resumed their work. They had barely disappeared into the trees when Aithe arrived to say that the horses were waiting on the road, at the point closest to the ruin.

No foreseeing is ever certain, Malian reminded herself, as Raven spoke quietly to Rhaikir. The cadre, she gathered, concentrating fiercely to combat the vision's chill, were to follow the main company to the muster ground once Emuun's body was burned and their work in the forest complete. She fell in beside Raven as the rest of the escort prepared to leave, but although she caught his brief, sidelong scrutiny, their walk to the road was a silent one.

When they reached the horses, Malian found that her gear,

together with the gray horse, had already been brought from the ruin. She could see Yris's cloak-wrapped body, too, trussed across the back of a horse as so many of the Normarch squires had been after the battle at The Leas. Sorrow for the pilot filled her, because although Yris had helped bring down her killer, Emuun's demise would not bring her back. Yet Malian knew that part of her melancholy arose from the fleeting glimpse of her own dead face. Self-pity, she told herself, and mounted up.

"Ready?" Raven asked, and Malian nodded, because however dark the road ahead, it was the only one open to her. She had made her choice six years ago, understanding the likelihood of her own death before she left the Wall. The owl's call, soft and sad from the trees, sounded like a farewell as she brought the gray alongside Raven's horse. Briefly, Malian wondered if it was the same bird that had helped her earlier. But the horses were already turning toward Hedeld and the Telimbras, their hooves muted by drifted leaves as they left the night, and the ruin, and Emuun's body to the pyre's leap of flame.

38

Dawn Wind

Fire's camp was not at the Hedeld fort, but in meadows close by the last, wild reaches of the Telimbras before it joined the Ijir. Familiar with night riding from her years with the Shadow Band, Malian had dozed in the saddle once they reached the main road north. Consequently, she was alert as she dismounted in a darkness that was still well shy of dawn, and knew there were not nearly enough tents for a muster of Fire's full force.

"This is just the vanguard," Raven said, when she asked. "The rest will wake when the preparations for the march are complete." There was no time for more questions, because the horses were being led away, the gray together with the rest. Malian saw her gear taken into a separate tent before entering the adjoining command pavilion with Raven, accompanied by Sarathion and Aithe. The interior was brightly lit, with maps and lists stacked on trestle tables, and more of Raven's officers waiting for them.

Malian estimated at least fifteen gathered about the long, central trestle, some in Patrol uniforms but most wearing the same plain armor as Raven's escort. For the first time, she saw Patrolers with their visors raised, but regardless of uniform, the expressions regarding her ranged from neutral to openly assessing. She detected something of the Cave of Sleepers, too, in the resolution that characterized their faces. Raven introduced everyone present, but she retained only a handful of names: Valadan, tall and stern faced, was second-in-command of Fire, while Kair was a cavalry commander, and Daile had come from the Hedeld fort ... Learning them all was going to take time. But a night's rest, Malian reflected wryly, should also help.

Unsurprisingly, the initial discussion centered on Emuun's death and the loss of Yris. When Malian recounted absorbing the pilot's dying gift of memory, she saw she had surprised those present. "I didn't think gifting was possible outside of Fire." Valadan frowned at Raven. "Do you think that's another consequence of the geas?"

"It turned out Amaliannarath and the sword made a second bargain." Raven was at his driest. "The blade's return was tied to Lady Malian accepting us, but before doing so, she asked if *we* were willing to accept *her*. When I said we were, an unforeseen effect may have been that she became part of Fire." Formally, he bowed apology to Malian. "I did not perceive that possibility until you told us what Yris did."

I didn't either, Malian thought, concealing her surprise. Valadan was still frowning, and she could see others visibly striving to absorb Raven's explanation. Finally, Sarathion spoke. "How would Yris know, though?"

Instinct, Malian thought. In Yris's last moments, intuition could have outweighed logic.

"She must have known that she could trust you," Daile said, his tone and look equally thoughtful.

"As for the Heir of Night taking us as her own," Sarathion continued slowly, "I thought we were going to have to earn a new place with our service, but also our deaths if need be?"

He did not speak her Derai title in Rhaikir's cool, dismissive manner, but Malian still understood that now was the moment she had to begin winning them in her own right. "It was a gift," she said quietly, "as much as a bargain, just as the return of the sword was, too, in the end." She waited, holding them with her stillness, the way

Asantir had once held the Old Keep rescue party to her, before their return to Night. "By its nature, a gift needn't be earned. As for service, you have delivered that many times over during your thousand years in the River." Her eyes met theirs, one by one. "Death may lie down every path of seeing," she said, and perhaps because of tiredness, she felt sorrow rise again, "but I do not want yours."

"Because life is your gift; I foresaw that long ago." The mindwhisper was a breath out of air and shadow, one Malian had heard twice before: first when she conversed with a ghost in a cave full of sleepers, and more recently in Stoneford, when Amaliannarath's shade had spoken to her again through the frost-fire sword. At the time, she had assumed it was part of the geas, but now she wondered—except there was no time for speculation as Valadan spoke again.

"If it was a gift, as you say, that would enhance Yris's ability to bequeath her memories to you. Does it also mean you will honor your pledge to accept us, regardless of whether we fight for you or not?"

"Effectively, Lady Malian already made that offer on our road here." Raven, too, spoke quietly. Several eyebrows rose, but Malian thought she detected an alteration in their regard—as if this particular group of Fire warriors was beginning to evaluate who she really was, rather than simply seeing a Derai and potential interloper. She inclined her head, acknowledging Raven, but answered Valadan.

"Yes. The alliance I have made is based on an exchange of gifts between equals: the Heir of the Derai and the Prince of Fire." She was conscious of a hush, not just outside in the night, or inside the tent, but within herself as understanding unfurled a deeper layer. "But it is as Chosen of Mhaelanar that I have taken Fire as my own, an acceptance that reaches beyond the old ties that bind the Derai and, I believe, the Sworn." Or severs them, she thought.

"Or severs them," Aithe murmured, and Malian wondered if they all felt the coolness that shivered through the lamplit tent.

"Perhaps," she agreed, and although she felt no stir of prophecy, her truth sense rang. "But it's past time for what was broken by the Sundering to be remade."

They were just words, and the deeds required to realize them likely to prove difficult if not impossible. Those gathered about her knew that, too. But this time, Malian was sure of the alteration as her gaze traveled around their watchful faces, a shift that said Raven's officers were prepared to give her the chance to make the words real.

Dawn was in the air when she left them, although the darkness outside remained unbroken and the air chill. Daile had brought more reports from the Patrol, but that was Raven's business unless it touched on her role as Chosen of Mhaelanar. *"My focus,"* Malian told both herself and Nhenir, *"needs to be on my return to the Wall, where the Sundering is only the final item on a long list of everything that needs to be remade, starting with the Alliance itself. And the Blood Oath must be overturned, reintegrating priest and warrior kind. At the same time, I will have to persuade the Nine Houses that a Darksworn army can fight alongside the Derai."* Her eyes lifted to where dawn would break above the forest's blackness. *"And then there's Hylcarian, and whatever others may remain from what we called the Golden Fire."* Seeking to restore their order was both duty and debt for the Chosen of Mhaelanar—if it could even be done.

"Like the shield," Nhenir murmured, and Malian checked a nod, aware of the sentries guarding the command tent. She was too keyed up to believe sleep would come quickly, so crossed to the nearest fire and added branches to build it up. She heard an exchange, too low to catch, among the sentries, before a warrior brought her a camp stool and a bowl of soup from the nearby mess tent. "Duar, Lady Malian," he said, when she asked his name, and she nodded, recognizing his grim voice from the forest.

She murmured her thanks, and he saluted before returning to his post. The camp was stirring, with warriors and horses moving through the darkness beyond the firelight, but no one intruded on her privacy. The soup was as warming as the fire, but weariness returned in its wake, blurring the individual flames into a wash of color. Like Yorindesarinen's fire, Malian thought, in the glade between worlds . . . She had foreseen so much in its heart, without realizing it at the time: Nherenor lying dead on the Caer Argent cobbles; Raven when he was young, at the point Amaliannarath snatched him clear of Sun's massacre; and Kalan, wearing warrior's garb and accompanying a Derai wedding caravan.

"*Kalan.*" Silently, she repeated his name, but knew it would do no good. The empathy bond between them, which otherwise might have allowed her to bridge the psychic gulf between the Wall and Haarth, was only one way. So although he might be able to reach through to her, she could not readily contact him.

Malian set down the empty bowl and watched the flames, absently tracing the pattern on her armring while her mind emptied of fear and doubt. Gradually her eyelids grew heavy and the flames receded, until she felt she was watching their dance from a vast distance, the colors constantly changing as the shapes disintegrated and reformed. Like figures, she thought dreamily, coming and going on a darkling plain where the aftermath of a great conflagration still smoldered . . .

A slight figure, in Derai armor but with a fearful, tear-stained countenance, crept close to a dead warrior, only to flee again as an army drew near, its banners like streaming flame. The army's leader bent and picked up a sword as the dance of flames leapt high. When they died away, a lone warrior stood amid the destruction. His black armor was honed to spur points at shoulder and elbow, but he ignored the dead hero and went to the Worm that lay nearby. The flames gusted as he stooped—and the warrior that straightened up again wore crimson and bronze. The banners that flew above the armed company behind him were crimson, too, flying beside garnet-and-gold pennants. They were the only color on all that vast plain, where the last brushfires had burned to ash and two mounds rose where Yorindesarinen and the Worm had lain.

The last warrior stood by the smaller mound for a long time, although he did not weep. Instead he turned and issued orders, and an eight-guard from among his following disinterred Yorindesarinen's body, transferring it to a coffin they had brought with them. Before the lid was closed, the commander took a ring from his finger and placed it on the dead hero's hand. *A friend gave it to me long ago . . .* He looks like Kalan, too, Malian thought, only older.

As if the thought had been a summons, the colors ran together and Kalan's face appeared in their midst. *"I am to fight a duel to the death,"* he said. A wood knot snapped out sparks. *". . . I have failed you . . . "*

The face dissipated as swiftly as it had taken form, and Malian was falling, falling—as though she could plumb the blaze and find Kalan, just as Tarathan had once found her in Yorindesarinen's fire. Only she was not within the Gate of Dreams and it was not Yorindesarinen's hand checking her pitch forward—

Malian jolted fully awake and sat back as Raven sank onto his heels beside her, his expression quizzical. "That wasn't quite what I envisaged when I said you had become part of Fire."

Surprised, Malian laughed, and saw heads turn in the periphery of her vision. Raven smiled, although that expression, too, was quizzical. "I believe we gave you a tent, if you want to sleep."

"You did. Initially, I wasn't sleepy." She paused as another of the escort brought Raven a stool as well. "I wanted to think," she added, when the guard had withdrawn.

"About last night? Or what was said in the tent?"

"Both." The recollection of Emuun's hoarse, gasping voice intruded, filled with a mockery directed at both the Sworn and her. Silently, Malian repeated his words without the gaps and hesitations: *Even Salar believed that a scion of the witch's blood would be the stake we finally drove through the heart of the thrice-cursed Derai Alliance. And all the time it was you.* Emuun had referred to a witch before that as well. The words had been mumbled, but with hindsight, Malian was sure that what he had said was *Ilkerineth's* witch. Before he fell, Nherenor had told her that he was Ilkerineth's son—while afterward, she had studied the Sworn youth's dead face and realized how closely he resembled her.

I guessed the truth then, Malian thought, but I wasn't prepared to admit it, even to myself. " 'A scion of the witch's blood,' " she repeated aloud, " 'and all the time it was you.' " Briefly, she outlined the gist of what Emuun had said, but kept the stake and his insinuations about Raven to herself. "If there's any truth in what he said, then Ilkerineth's witch has to be my mother: Nerion, daughter of Nerith," she added formally, "of the Sea Keep. My father told me she might have gone over to the Sworn, and it explains why Nherenor and I looked so alike. He was my half-brother."

We fought, she told herself, but it was the lurker poison that killed him. His death was not fratricide.

Raven's expression was as close to gentle as she had ever seen it. "Emuun knew that information can be most effective as a weapon when it comes in the guise of truth." He paused. "Ilkerineth lost his wife and children prior to the time of the Chaos Worm, when the maelstrom was quiescent and the Derai in the ascendant. So for him to have a son among the envoys in Emer, he had to have married again. The only question was who."

Especially since she bore him a child, Malian reflected, and began to comprehend the hope that might have led Amaliannarath to make her bargain with the sword. As for Nerion, in view of the circumstances surrounding her exile and suspected abuse in the Keep of Stone, Malian could see why she might have gone over to the Sworn. Yet Emuun's claim that Nerion had worked with Aranraith to bring about her own death was far more difficult to accept.

I've known it was a possibility since the attack on the Keep of Winds, Malian told herself now, but suspicion is one thing, confirmation entirely another . . . She thought she would have recognized the deceit if Emuun had lied outright, which made Raven's suggestion more likely, since truth slanted to achieve contrary ends was far harder for a truthsayer to detect. Nerion *might* have been trying to capture her six years ago, rather than to kill, but reexamination of those events—from the assault on the New Keep and Malian's escape into the Old, to the final flight into Jaransor—made her mother's intentions look doubtful at best.

Yet I liked Nherenor, Malian thought, and Kalan did, too. Her half-brother had been courageous and—remembering their encounter in the Caer Argent dawn—honorable as well. With hindsight, she realized it was probably significant that he had given his father's name, but not his mother's. "Although," she reasoned aloud, "Nerion of the Derai may have taken another name among the Sworn. Like you," she said to Raven. "You said in Stoneford that Aravenor was your true name, but Emuun called you Ravirien?"

He nodded—imperturbable, she thought, as the weight of a thousand years. "The past was dead, we felt that strongly when we first woke. Fire names would have given us away, in any case. So those of us who took service as the Patrol adopted Haarth names instead. A binding ceremony," he added, "in a sanctuary of Seruth."

Malian nodded, because on the River, Seruth was held to preside over new beginnings as well as journeys. "Aravenor was taken from my personal emblem, which is the hawk." Raven continued to study the flames. "The name means 'lord of the hawk' in the Old Empire's northern dialect, just as Jaransor was once J'ara Ensor, the hills of the hawk. A Hill chieftain first called me Raven, which was both chance and irony, since it's a shortening of Aravenor and resembled Ravirien." His grin, directed at the fire, was wry. "I still answer to it most days."

They were the hedge knight's words out of the Long Pass, which might have been why he used them, since Emuun had been right in calling him astute. Malian gazed into the blaze, thinking about her life's journey to this point, which of course had begun with Nerion, even if she could not remember her mother at all. What would she look like, Malian wondered, if I glimpsed her in the flames? But instead she saw Raven, riding the length and breadth of the Southern Realms along both high roads and back trails, serving as sword-for-hire and household warrior from Emer to Ishnapur through the course of a millennium. "Is there anywhere in the Southern Realms that you have not served?" she asked softly. "Even"—remembering the blood magic and the fire elemental—"Ishnapur and Jhaine?"

"I wanted to know this world: not just *where* we had come to, but *why* Amaliannarath might have foreseen that this was the place she needed to bring us." Beneath the hedge knight's imperturbability, Malian thought she detected the geas's legacy of mystery. "Over time, I went everywhere there were people, even Jhaine. I served among the Shah's auxiliaries, too, along Ishnapur's desert border. I learned a great deal about Haarth and its people, but I still don't fully understand the why."

And Amaliannarath, always deep minded, must have seen … Foreseen me, Malian thought: that's the implication. Emuun had said it to unsettle her, not knowing that in order to return the sword, Amaliannarath would have *had* to foresee both Haarth and the new Chosen of Mhaelanar. Yet Malian's truth sense told her that Raven was right, that was not all there was to the matter. As for Emuun, if she accepted his insinuations, she would also have to believe that the ghost Ascendant she had met in the Cave of Sleepers would have sacrificed herself and all of Fire's Blood, bar one, for what the Darksworn had described as a long game.

Returning Yorindesarinen's sword was also an unlikely move, even for those playing for high stakes. And no one, Malian thought, has tried to understand this world more than Raven, let alone serving it as he has. Despite, she added wryly, our Derai claim to be protecting Haarth with our Wall and our fractious—if not fratricidal—Alliance. She shivered, fratricide bringing her back to Nherenor, and thence to Nerion. Who hates my father, Malian thought somberly. She ran her hands over the tinker's patched knees, knowing that Nhairin and Kyr's accounts of her mother's exile, together with events six years ago, all pointed to that conclusion.

Eastward above forest and camp, the sky was growing lighter. Malian rubbed at her knees again, recalling the horror Nerion's possible defection had caused among the few Derai who suspected it. She knew that most in the Nine Houses would view her own alliance with Fire in the same light. On the other hand, the Blood Oath and Malian's exile meant the Derai Alliance was unlikely to follow her without a show of strength. Short of restoring the Golden Fire, an army at her back might well be the only argument that many Houses—starting with Blood and Adamant—would find persuasive.

Yet her fire vision suggested Kalan needed her on the Wall now, not long weeks or even months distant. *"I have failed you . . . "* Never, Malian thought, not in this realm or any other that lies beyond the Gate of Dreams. She spoke slowly. "I need to influence events on the Wall now, but the muster's going to take time, and a march across the Wild Lands on the eve of winter longer still. If I could use portals . . . " She paused, frowning. "But if other Sworn do investigate Emuun's death and detect portal use, it'll draw them like wasps to honey."

"And Thanir, in particular, may suspect Emuun of having pursued the Aeris sword-for-hire." Raven was measured, but Malian recognized the tone that said he was calculating odds. "Even without gates, you could take my personal guard as escort and travel fast, especially if you follow the Telimbras route north."

That might work, Malian thought, reckoning odds in her turn, especially since Raven's personal guard would be Fire's elite. With a small, mobile escort, she could also operate covertly until the main force arrived. "And assess the current disposition of the Nine Houses before declaring my hand," she said, thinking aloud, "as well as the level of Swarm threat. Although"—Malian hesitated before continuing—"with one of your cadres, perhaps some degree of portal use might be possible?" At least to get me as far as Jaransor, she added silently, since I still don't like the idea of using a portal to bridge the Wall-Haarth divide.

The fire collapsed and a log rolled out, but Raven seized it, tossing the branch back a second before it exploded in embers and sparks. "From what I saw on our journey here," he said, his eyes on the subsequent display, "you may be capable of sustaining a portal that would accommodate yourself and an escort. But it would take most, if not all, of Fire's cadres to have a hope of concealing it from the likes of Thanir, and we'll need them to screen the muster." He looked around at Malian as the branch gave a last, desultory snap. "We both know you'd travel fastest alone, but I'd prefer it if you didn't."

Because unlike the Shadow Band adept, Malian thought, an Heir of the Derai who makes alliances with princes should not place herself at risk. A bird called from the forest, a single note across the still-dark world; very soon now, it would be day. Raven ground out an errant spark beneath his boot. "We used to have squadrons dedicated to opening gates, and more to concealing them. Recruits with either ability didn't get to choose where they served. But those like you who could open a gate independently, let alone convey others, they were rare."

"Were they all of Fire's Blood?" Malian asked.

"The few with any substantial ability were. The minor talents died shoring up Amaliannarath at the last." He paused. "Even then we nearly didn't make it."

I'm sorry, Malian wanted to say, but knew the words were inadequate. A bird called again, a quicksilver bubble of sound, and this time another answered it. Her voice felt crow harsh by contrast. "I promise I won't slip away without your guards."

"I'll hold you to that," he replied, with the hedge knight's glint.

"I'm sure you will," she murmured, rising before exhaustion overtook her. She nodded, Crow's gesture from weeks on the road, before turning way. *"Although perhaps,"* she added to Nhenir, yawning as she entered her tent, *"I should have been more formal with his people watching."*

"Better," Nhenir observed, *"if Fire sees that the Heir of the Derai and their prince are easy with each other."*

"You're probably right." Malian discarded jacket and sword, lying down just as the full dawn chorus erupted. Perhaps because of the birds' tumult, her initial sleep was fitful, and fragments culled from recent events jerked her back into wakefulness several times. *"Dread Pass,"* Kalan whispered as mist poured into a narrow gap beneath high crags—only this time, shadowy figures climbed beneath its cover. A boot scraped, displacing a pebble, as warriors deployed about the gap.

"Dread Pass," another voice said. This time it was the High Steward Nhairin's voice out of childhood memory, inculcating geography. *"Morning guard it with their High Towers, or did ... "*

Nhairin, Malian thought, rousing again, whom I loved and trusted, but who turned out to be a traitor. The dawn wind stirred outside, cool as doubt, and she followed it with her farseeing: past the tramp of feet and ring of arms as the watch changed, out beyond the mingled scents of woodsmoke and breakfasts cooking, to reach the nearby Telimbras, pouring out of the north to join the Ijir. The River of No Return, she thought, her lids gritting together: it's as much a boundary between the Derai realm and Haarth as the Border Mark ...

Gradually, events, visions, and memory all faded into a drum of hooves that could have come from any of her many journeys. A deeper sleep followed, banishing the last of the hoofbeats, and no dream penetrated its layers. What did, finally, reach Malian was a single pure note that rose out of darkness like the first bird's call. The Song of Haarth, she thought, still mired in sleep. The note was achingly familiar, and Malian's seeking, stirring to pursue it, identified *north*. Yet she knew this was not the previous day's song of the Wild Lands, or part of Jaransor's grinding rumble—although when she roused sufficiently to hone her seeking, she discerned both wildness and an echo of Jaransor's power.

A line seared across Malian's inner sight and she smelled snow, mingled with the scent of birchwood fires as the fiery line became the hawk's flight, solitary above a winter plain. Her seeking quickened, and although her eyes remained closed she pushed her power hard. Now the curl of song was also a spring, bubbling up beneath another plain of wind and dust. Her seeking *became* the windhover, gliding this way and that on the currents of the air and all the time looking, searching—until Malian *saw* it, a Winter Country cairn in the midst of the Gray Lands, with the Song of Haarth rising beneath it. The spark of life force before the cairn would be the hound, Falath. She had seen him in her vision outside Tenneward Lodge, keeping his lonely vigil by Rowan Birchmoon's grave.

Her vision outside Tenneward Lodge ... Kalan had *said* it that night, she realized: that what they were seeing was an opening from Emer into the Gray Lands. But then events had overtaken them when the Darksworn came ... All the same, Malian thought, shocked fully awake, I should have remembered after Stoneford—especially as my visions since then have centered on Yorindesarinen's death and the fate of the shield. I'm also hearing and seeing Kalan still, although he *has* to be on the Wall by now.

"Which means," Malian told Nhenir, *"that I have been accessing the Derai side of the Gate of Dreams. But when I thought about it at all, I assumed it was an aftereffect of your Stoneford song."* Glimmerings and gaps, she added, when what I've needed—what I *need*—is a reliable bridge. Six years before, Nhenir had told her that she had the raw power to force a way through the psychic barrier, but warned that not only would brute force risk detection, a failed attempt might also widen the existing rift. *"But now ... "*

Malian sat up to find bright daylight outlining the tent flap, although the angle and length of the shadows suggested she had not slept long. "But now," she whispered, "I know a bridge exists." Because of you, she added silently to Rowan Birchmoon's memory. Somehow, in dying, you made your power into a conduit for the Song of Haarth—a wellspring emerging beneath the Gray Lands' cairn, but with its source deep in your own Winter Country. Deep in *Haarth*, Malian amended. That's why the visions of the cairn could reach me, first outside Tenneward Lodge and again in Stoneford. I saw it. I just didn't understand what it meant, although I should have.

In retrospect, it seemed obvious, a vision from the Wall side of the divide that was not just memory. Yet Malian also remembered how Tarathan, in bringing news of the Winter Woman's passing, had shared his belief that Rowan Birchmoon foresaw her own death. So why stay? Malian asked silently. Did you knowingly sacrifice yourself? Or was your love for my father, and the uncertainty of foreseeing, also part of the mix?

She knew from her own experience that motivation was rarely

simple, but this— "Even your death," she said aloud, "you made into a gift." She rested her forehead against drawn-up knees, trying to assimilate the magnitude of the offering, until Nhenir cut through her absorption.

"Riders are coming."

The drum of hoofbeats, Malian realized, straightening, was no longer confined to uneasy sleep. The riders were approaching fast, but she was fully armed and at the tent entrance before she distinguished Rhaikir's voice. "Fetch the prince!" he commanded, sounding both terse and exhausted.

The guards outside the tent sprang to attention as Malian stepped through. A return, she noted automatically, to the formality she had once taken for granted as Heir of Night. The newly arrived horses had been ridden hard, and their riders looked haggard, but Rhaikir and his second-in-command strode into the command tent without looking around. When Malian followed, the guards on duty there also stood to attention.

Raven and Valadan were already inside. Possibly, Malian thought, joining them, because they had never left. Rhaikir barely glanced her way before he resumed speaking. "We built the pyre and fired the chapel as ordered, but just before it really took hold—" He broke off, his gaze fixed on Raven. "The body vanished ahead of the flames reaching it. We felt no incursion of power, but one moment the body was there, the next gone. Just like that."

Another elemental? Malian wondered. Except from what she understood of the cadre's abilities, if they had not detected power use then it had to have been something far more covert. A rune triggered by his death, perhaps, since Raven had said Emuun was skilled in their use, or some form of desert magic that Fire had never encountered? Other possibilities intruded, including Kalan's tale of a siren worm's spirit, trying to return to the Swarm by way of the Gate of Dreams. To tell what it knew, Malian thought. When her eyes met Raven's, she knew they were both thinking the same thing: that before he died, Emuun had learned entirely too much.

"We'll have to delay the muster," Valadan said. "Best if there's nothing to find, should Sun start sniffing around. We can use one of the other forts to complete what we've begun here, then filter north by diverse routes."

"We can't delay the muster," Raven said, preempting Malian's protest. "Events are moving too fast for that."

"A thousand years—and now we're in a race?" Kair was grim.

Against time, Malian thought, but Raven was unmoved. "We all knew it could happen this way, when the moment came. You'll need to move fast as well," he told her. "And choose a captain for your escort. Someone you have confidence in."

Having attached himself to you, he will seek to attach you in return. Too late, Malian thought, her eyes narrowing on humor: at the price of Yorindesarinen's sword and an army, he's already managed that. Not that she had any complaints about her side of the bargain. And whatever darkness lay ahead, the only way to chart it was trust: of the sword and its bargain with Amaliannarath, and of Raven as she had come to know him, first in Emer and then in Aralorn, as well as on the road here. Most of all, she needed to trust her own judgment. "I have confidence in you," she told him, and smiled slightly at the stir among his officers. "But I understand that the Prince of Fire may need to march with his House."

"In Stoneford, I promised to ride in your shadow. Arguably, helping keep you alive is the most important charge on that pledge right now." Raven was matter-of-fact as he turned to Valadan. "I'd prefer to assess the situation on the Wall in person, in any case. We can establish a base while you manage the muster here, then get the army north. Liannar will continue to command on the River in my absence."

Valadan nodded, although Malian thought Rhaikir's gesture, abruptly cut off, might have been protest. Yet every instinct was telling her that she not only needed to move fast, but having Raven with her mattered, both now and in the immediate future. At the same time, the threat of Emuun's disappearance jostled with Kalan's situation, while her mind raced, recalling Lord Falk's visage, speaking out of an oak tree, and her flight from Nindorith in Caer Argent. Walking Imuln's path of earth and moon might have sealed her vanishing act, but before that Malian had eluded the Ascendant twice: first to surprise Nherenor above the Sondcendre ruin, and then diverting Nindorith's seeking into the Gate of Dreams.

Everyone was looking at her. Waiting for the Chosen of Mhaelanar to speak, Malian realized. Outside, the wind had strengthened. Through the tent opening, she could see one of the Patrol's black pennants, blowing toward the north. In her mind's eye, Malian visualized herself and Raven's small escort racing northward, too. Fear of delay surged, but she forced it down. "Show me the Telimbras route," she said, and made herself focus on the maps that lay on the table and debate over how soon a smaller, fast-moving company could reasonably expect to reach the Wall.

From there, the discussion shifted to logistics, approaching winter, and the need to protect lines of supply. Yet Malian's thoughts continued to race, traversing cairns again, encounters with Nindorith, and the siren worm slipping through white mists. She could not shake the sense, as weariness returned, of a vital detail or connection eluding her grasp—or the conviction that events were outstripping her, and time had already run out.

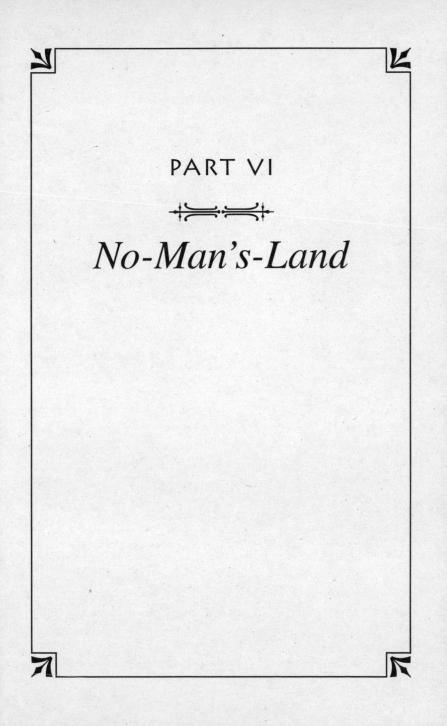

PART VI

No-Man's-Land

39

Traitor

"The country's crawling with 'spawn," Ter said, dismounting. "More than I've ever seen."

Garan and his unit were waiting in one of the dips in the plain deep enough to conceal their horses, until all the scouts sweeping the surrounding territory returned. With Ter and Innor now back, only Asha and Lawr remained outstanding. *They're experienced scouts,* Garan told himself, *who know to be cautious—especially since Ter's right, we're seeing too much darkspawn sign for this country.*

"Anyone would think—" Keron began, then stopped, shaking his head.

Best not to say it, Garan agreed silently, although he guessed they were all thinking it could be a sign the Wall was starting to fail. He rubbed at his rough growth of beard, aware that one of Sarus's favorite observations was that the fact Derai Houses had to ride regular boundary patrols at all meant the Wall must have been failing for a long time. This mission, though, was no boundary patrol, and they were closer to the Jaransor side of the Gray Lands now, rather than the Wall.

"It doesn't seem right," Keron muttered finally.

"It's not, Nine knows," Innor said, with feeling. "No one should have to stay away from keep and hearth this long. I suppose the ride to the River may've counted as adventure, but then we copped the Commander's nursemaid detail. And now we get this. What would you call hunting for a mazed ex-steward, Garan? More nursemaiding?"

"She's a traitor." Eanar spoke with a touch of defiance. He and Keron were the new recruits to Garan's unit of Night veterans, but Eanar came from Westwind Hold, where Nhairin had been confined. Garan suspected he construed Keep of Winds' honor guards being sent to retrieve the fugitive as a slight to his former comrades. "Mazed or not," Eanar persisted now, "she betrayed the Heir to her death in Jaransor."

There's more to that tale, Garan thought, aware of the quality of Nerys's silence where she was keeping watch. They had both been among those who helped Asantir engineer Malian's flight from Night six years before—while Ter and Innor had been with them on the earlier Old Keep expedition, and pledged themselves to Malian as Chosen of Mhaelanar afterward. Garan had sworn, too, together with Nerys and all the other expedition survivors except Asantir herself. The boy, Kalan, hadn't sworn either, he recalled now, aware of the whole raft of unspoken speculation between himself and Nerys on that topic, ever since the Red Keep.

Innor was nodding at Eanar's observation. "True enough, but Nhairin showed me kindness when I was new to both the keep and soldiering, so I prefer to remember her that way."

"If she wasn't mazed," Keron said tentatively, "she'd have been executed when they brought her back from Jaransor, wouldn't she?"

"She never disobeyed the Earl directly," Garan said quietly. "And if the Heir commanded her to assist the flight, a charge of treachery might not stick." That was Sister Korriya's opinion anyway, but if he were in Nhairin's shoes Garan would prefer not to face the test of Derai law.

Keron was nodding, although his expression, like Eanar's, suggested doubt. Ter, who was seeing to his horse, looked across at

Garan. "I don't think we're going to find her, though, do you? This country's immense, and even if she hasn't fallen foul of 'spawn . . ." His shrug covered all the other ills, from accident to starvation and exposure, that could befall someone alone, on foot, and ill-equipped, in the Gray Lands. "Winter'll be here soon, too."

"The Nine send we're in keep walls before then," Innor said fervently.

"I want to see the wedding," Keron put in. "Asha says it'll be a feast and carnival in one, being a marriage between two Houses. She says there won't have been a party like it since the Old Earl married."

Garan thought Asha might be right. He only retained a child's hazy recollection of Earl Tasarion's first wife, but he thought their wedding had been a quiet affair. Lord Tasarion had just become Heir, following the deaths of his older brother and sister, and for all Lady Nerion's Sea House connections, she was still of Night. But the Old Earl's wedding had happened well before any of those in the eight-guard were born. Grinning, he pointed this fact out. "So you can't rely on what Asha says, although I'm sure there'll be some sort of grand celebration."

"Seven days of feasting, was what I heard." Innor stared pointedly at the dried meat and hard bread she had taken from her saddlebag, then glanced at Garan slyly. "It's said to be an auspicious time for other weddings, too."

Ter winked, and even Nerys was grinning, although she kept her eyes on the plain. Garan cleared his throat. "We should all eat," he said, and made a business of rummaging in a saddlebag for his rations, unearthing a slender, leather scroll tube at the same time. Frowning, he considered Morning's simurgh seal before stuffing it back into the pack.

"Did the old Lady give you a present?" Innor asked, looking over his shoulder. "It's his smile," she informed the others. "That's why all the priestesses love him, old and young alike." She, Ter, and Nerys chuckled, while Eanar and Keron, both hold levies, exchanged uncertain looks. Even in the Keep of Winds, it was only recently—since the surprise Swarm attack, six years ago, and the subsequent inclusion of priest-kind initiates in the Old Keep watch—that anyone would contemplate making such a joke. Or I allow it, Garan reflected, in case I was thought tainted myself. As it was, he had fought almost as many rounds against fellow warriors, defending his willingness to serve with priest-kind in the early days of the new watch, as he ever had with darkspawn while on patrol. "What is it?" Innor persisted.

"An oddity." Garan shrugged to rob the evasion of offense before joining Nerys on the perimeter, where he chewed methodically on dried meat while his eyes traversed the terrain. But part of his mind remained on the scroll case, and the day Mother Sirit had given it to him, high on Morning's Tower of Watch. The rune scrolls it contained *were* an oddity, to Garan's mind, and his being given it odder still. And despite being with him at the time, Nerys had shrugged when he tried to make sense of matters afterward, as if to say the mystery would resolve at some stage, or it wouldn't. Typical Nerys, he thought now, with an inward grin—although if it doesn't resolve, I could end up carrying the cursed thing around forever.

Garan narrowed his eyes, intent on a distant wisp that could have been dust or a fragment of haze, while simultaneously recalling his fear that the scrolls could be some sort of death working. The old Lady of Morning had denied it, but her subsequent explanation had been cryptic, to say the least: *The scrolls are a gift for the one who wakes your oath. More than that I cannot say.*

"More than that I cannot say," Garan muttered, studying a wide sweep of plain. He knew Teron would accuse Sirit of being mysterious to cover either ignorance or ill intent—and Garan *had* been tempted to hurl the scroll case away on several occasions. But the recollection of Sirit's steadfast gaze, and the timbre of her voice, had always stopped him. When he reported the incident to Asantir in the Red Keep, she had been studying her chessboard and taken some time to answer. "What does your judgment advise?" she had asked finally. "Are you inclined to trust Sirit?"

I am, Garan thought now, as he had then. At the very least, he felt confident Sirit intended no harm to Night. He had been reassured, too, when the Sea envoy gifted a similar scroll to Khar, ahead of the Storm Spear's duel with Lord Parannis. *So I'm back where I started,* he reflected, *and must do as Nerys advises and let the matter play out.* "That wisp," he said. "What d'you think?"

Nerys shook her head, a gesture he knew meant she didn't know, rather than not being concerned. With so much 'spawn sign about, they could take nothing for granted, so Garan was relieved when Asha and Lawr finally rode in. "We may've found her tracks," Lawr said, "a fair way west of here. From what we saw, someone's been setting snares, but the prints suggest light boots. Hold-wear, not what you'd expect a hunter or scout to wear. And one leg's dragging," he added, a grin splitting his mask of dust.

Lame, Garan thought. *He's right, we've cut her trail at last.* "Eat and take a short rest," he told Lawr and Asha, "then we'll see how far the tracks take us. I want you two on point," he added, turning to Ter and Innor. "Let's make sure we stay the hunters, not become some Swarm minion's prey."

Even before they picked up Lawr's tracks, Garan had guessed where they were heading, although night and cold were both closing in by the time he sighted the rockpile that adjoined the Winter Woman's grave. "Would Nhairin know of the cairn?" Innor asked. She had ridden back to advise that the incidence of 'spawn sign was growing less frequent as they approached the cairn.

As if, Garan thought, *a larger predator has driven lesser minions off*—hardly a comforting reflection. "Any direction chosen by a mazed person is likely to be chance," he replied. Privately, in light of the past six years' experiences, he was not prepared to rule out uncanny influences.

"Assuming that's who we're tracking," Lawr said, his earlier triumph faded into weariness.

The lame leg makes it near certain, Garan thought, studying the rockpile's silhouette against the dusk. "Anyone wandering alone out here is clearly in trouble, so let's find whoever this is, regardless." The others nodded, although they all knew the wanderer could be a decoy, luring them into danger. "We don't want to disturb the hound, if he's still there, or spook anyone else, particularly our fugitive. So we'll ride in quietly, and when we're close enough Nerys and I'll scout the cairn on foot."

"Even if there's nothing to find," Innor murmured, "we'll have a decent campsite ... " Her voice faded, and Garan guessed the others, prompted by Innor's comment, would also be recalling how the hollow had housed a hunting camp when the Winter Woman was murdered. He was just thankful none of his eight had been part of that hunting party. The escort had been drawn from Lannorth's company—but the death of the Earl's consort was still every Night honor guard's shame, Garan reflected bleakly.

They halted in another dip, several hundred yards out from the rockpile, before he and Nerys took their bows and proceeded on foot, circling wide to find a vantage point that overlooked both cairn and rock stack. The hound, Falath, was a pale glimmer beside the tomb, with no sign of anyone else present. But the fugitive could easily lie concealed among the rocks, even if Falath would not allow entry into the cairn. We'll have to keep a close watch on both throughout the night, Garan decided, then search thoroughly by daylight.

Full dark was almost on them now, and the temperature dropping. Garan was about to send Nerys for the others when Falath sprang up and belled a warning—and was answered by a wolf's howl, wild and lonely from the plain. Assuming it really *was* a wolf. Instinctively, Garan fingered his bowstring, all too aware of his earlier suspicion that a greater predator might have driven lower-level darkspawn off. The second howl was prolonged, and Falath retreated into the cairn's mouth as the air around the tomb shimmered. Almost as though you could *see* the sound, Garan thought, like rings spreading out on water. Only in this case the center of the ripples was the cairn, not the wolf ...

Increasingly, the shimmer looked exactly like a halo about the moon, but when Garan glanced up, the sky was hidden behind cloud cover. Nerys stared at him, her expression a question, as the wolf howled again and the shimmer intensified—then splintered apart, opening into a long tunnel behind the tomb. Or perhaps it was opening *out* of the cairn: Garan was not quite sure. He could see whiteness, like Sirit's sea fog roiling around a spectral path, and riders in dark armor with chill flambeau lighting their way. The cold light glittered off jagged helms and rippled across the mail coifs veiling the lower part of the riders' faces. There's so many of them, Garan thought: this is a small army. He could see their line still stretching back along the tunnel, while the vanguard flowed out into the Gray Lands' night.

Automatically, his hand went to Eria's talisman, because the last time he had seen a similar opening, in the Old Keep of Winds, the Raptor of Darkness had manifested within it. Lady Malian opened a gate in the air, too, Garan reminded himself, to bring us all safely home. But Malian of Night had died in Jaransor six years ago—and this gateway was white and cold, not golden, as hers had been. Pushing down fear, Garan concentrated on what was happening. Horses filled the hollow now, their long manes tossing, and the phantom glow from flambeau and tunnel was reflected in their eyes. The same glow illuminated the foremost riders, drawn in close about a finely armored knight who remained intent on the tunnel opening.

Perhaps because of the talisman, Garan could sense the magic that connected the knight to the eldritch gate. The opener of ways, he thought, his mind racing even faster than his heart as he recalled Sirit's words: *Such oaths can always awaken, if one knows the way to unlock their bindings* . . . Something about the finely-armored figure drew Garan as well, tugging at him to rise and join the darkling army.

"Go!" he whispered to Nerys. "Get the others farther away. I'll follow when I've reckoned numbers and found out all I can of who and what they are." He fumbled at the talisman, because if he was taken, he did not want to provide any conduit back to Eria for the power unleashed in the hollow. As soon as he dragged the token over his head, the sense of magic faded. "Keep this safe for me." Nerys frowned as he thrust the disc into her hand. She had been with him that day on Morning's tower, but Garan still needed to be sure she understood. "We've found our opener of ways, so you, Ter, and Innor need to stay clear, because of the Old Keep oath."

For a moment he thought Nerys might argue, but instead she slithered backward into the night. Garan followed suit, working his way to a spot with better cover, which still provided a clear view of the hollow. By the time he was concealed in scrubby thorn, both the gateway and tunnel had disappeared, but the ghostly flambeau showed the knights establishing a perimeter and camp. Garan could not immediately locate Falath—but his attention was pulled away from the cairn as two knights dragged a struggling, shouting figure clear of the rockpile.

Garan tensed, recognizing Nhairin. She looked like she had been living rough for a considerable period, and as if it was only her captors' grasp that was keeping her upright. Because of her lame leg, Garan guessed, as Nhairin continued to resist. Her voice sounded hoarse from disuse, and initially he thought she was shouting her own name, because the distorted cries resembled "Nhairin." She was also shouting "no" at the same time, and what sounded like something about treachery. Eventually, though, Garan realized that the name Nhairin was yelling was "Nerion." The moment he did, the fragments of rumor and whispered surmise that had followed the Swarm's surprise attack on the Keep of Winds, six years ago, finally made sense.

An opener of ways: the epithet Sirit had used became a weight as Garan remembered that Malian of Night's power was believed to have come from her mother, Lady Nerion. And someone had *known* how to get into the Old Keep and bring down the New Keep's defensive wards . . . Garan gritted his teeth, remembering Night's tally of dead and injured from the Swarm attack and its aftermath. He wondered, too, if the reason Nhairin was keeping her face so resolutely averted was because one must never meet a demon's gaze—or the eyes of one who had fallen beneath a demon's sway. Although if so, that would suggest Nhairin was no longer mazed . . .

A slight sound made Garan whip around, only to relax as Asha and Lawr slid into the brush beside him. Next to Nerys, Lawr was their best archer, but more importantly, neither guard had been part of the Old Keep expedition or sworn the survivors' oath that Sirit had warned could be woken to life. Even so, he wished Nerys had understood that he meant for her to get the entire unit clear, regardless of whether they had sworn the oath or not.

"Nerys said you'd be needing this," Asha whispered, and handed him the scroll tube from his saddlebag.

Garan thought that if he had not already realized matters were serious, the fact Nerys had spoken would have convinced him. Emulating Khar ahead of the Red Keep duel, he stowed the tube inside his coat, but kept his eyes on the cairn. The lead knight had stepped clear of the others and was studying Nhairin, who still refused to look back. Garan was not surprised, when the knight lifted the veiling coif aside, to see a woman's face. Despite his hazy memories of Lady Nerion, he could not swear the visage carved from night's shadow and the flambeau's chill light was hers. But it *was* that of a huntress as she regarded Nhairin, who sagged against her captors' grasp and slowly sank to her knees, her head still bowed.

"My Nhairin." The huntress's voice carried to where the Night guards lay hidden. "I always hoped I would find you again." Stepping forward, she placed her hands on either side of Nhairin's face, turning the captive's gaze upward.

Asha hissed, her fingers shaping an ancient Derai ward against demon influence, as Nhairin choked out a harsh but inarticulate protest. "I could shoot her from here," Lawr whispered. "End it."

Except the Commander said we were to keep her alive, Garan thought. The chances were, too, that none of them would live long after Lawr's arrow flew. But Nhairin was locked rigid, her face a mask of shame and pain as she stared into the gaze bent on hers. Garan stared at the tableau of huntress and victim—and remembered the Tower of Watch, when Sirit had commissioned him to place her gift in the opener of ways' hands. And *he*, the Nine help him, had told her that he would. He guessed, too, that if the huntress-knight *was* Lady Nerion, then there was a fair chance she already knew the Night guards were watching. So he needed to seize the initiative.

"Nhairin is of Night," he said calmly, despite knowing the doom that had begun on the Tower of Watch was upon him. "And we were told to bring her back alive." Slipping clear of the scrub before the others could protest, he spoke softly over his shoulder. "Cover me if you can, but don't let yourselves be taken if this goes badly."

When this goes badly, he thought, extracting Sirit's scroll tube from his jacket. *I* must be the mazed one, not Nhairin. Even before he stood up, the huntress had turned his way. Her face was a mask of dark planes and sculpted hollows, and again Garan felt drawn to her. He resisted the sensation. "I have a gift for you," he called, feigning boldness: "From a Mother of Morning." And felt sure, as he started toward the cairn, that what came next would see his death.

40

Shadow Moon

Kalan climbed the same slope he had ascended in his Red Keep dreams, with every pebble rimed in frost and the moon a disc of pitted iron. The Wall was a ragged silhouette behind him, while the Gray Lands lay on the far side of the ridge. He could sense dawn, concealed just below the dark edge of the world, but the frost continued to tighten its grip until the last of the night rang with its stillness. Even so, the slope was steep and he was sweating beneath leather, wool, and mail before he reached the ridgeline with its spike of rocks and thorn scrub. The thorn was one of the few plants that grew in the barren terrain and its spines were fierce, so Kalan avoided the densest clumps. He wrapped his face, too, before lowering himself to the ground to avoid being skylined and snaking the last few yards to the crest.

The Gray Lands were as he remembered, deceptively flat until the plain broke against the dark brooding line of Jaransor to the west. Southward, it rose into the more gradual crests of the Barren Hills, while the paved road that ran the length of the Wall was a pale serpent beneath the pitted moon. At this point the terrain it traversed was a no-man's-land, where the territories of several Houses petered out into the plain. In his Red Keep dream, Kalan had seen a camp laid out below, with long bridal pennants hanging motionless above its defensive circle. In reality, the landscape beyond the ridge was empty except for a solitary wagon, foundered halfway down an embankment that supported one of the road's many bridges.

The ridge's height showed him the skeletal branching of the watercourse, extending out of the Wall's foothills and across the plain. Even Kalan's keen sight could not make out details from this distance, but he could see how the road angled as it entered the bridge. The wagon's position suggested it must have swung too wide, aiming for a better approach, and gone over the bank. At first Kalan thought it must have been abandoned, until he shifted to obtain a better view and caught a telltale spark of red below the bridge. He frowned, because the lone wagon suggested a small company, and in their situation he would not have risked a fire—but his main question was whether this was an independent company or one abandoned by the bridal caravan.

Kalan's frown deepened as he considered the latter possibility. He was well aware, from crossing the Gray Lands with Malian, six years before, that the dips and hollows masked by the plain's apparent flatness could hide an army. Especially, he thought, if that army used concealing magic. Given the perils of the terrain, he had dispensed with his wards once clear of Blood's territory, and now stretched his psychic awareness beyond the disabled wagon, but no hint of power brushed against it. Sound, too, would carry a long way in night and frost, but all he could hear was the occasional bark of a rat-fox. The luck of the unwary, perhaps, or the company might be stronger than a single wagon suggested. Either way, Kalan intended taking a closer look.

He slid away from the ridge before rising again and heading back to where Taly and Jad's eight-guard waited with the horses, concealed among rocks and the stunted scrub that characterized the Wall's boundary with the plain. They had all agreed—once Blood territory was behind them and the Night eight-guard had departed in search of their fugitive—to hide out in the foothills and shadow the Bride's caravan to Night. It was what Kalan had intended to do anyway, and he had guessed Taly would be of the same mind. But he had also known it was important to offer the former honor guards purpose as they struggled to adjust to their exile.

Caution had dictated they wait until the Bride's caravan passed well beyond Blood's official boundary before cutting its trail. As exiles, they might technically be safe once they passed Blood's border, but in reality remained at risk from patrols scouting beyond its bounds. So for the past few weeks they had hidden out among the tumbledown watchtowers and abandoned redoubts scattered through-out the marginal country between the Wall and the Gray Lands. Even in the Wall's settled season, the ruins' deep foundations still offered necessary protection from squalls or late storms. It was a safer option, Kalan had decided, than risking the shelters provided along the road, even if it meant having to travel further to intersect the caravan's progress. Both decisions had seemed correct at the time, because potential enemies were likely to wait until the slow-moving cavalcade was well out into no-man's-land before showing themselves. Now, though, with unease persistent as an itch between his shoulder blades, Kalan questioned his wisdom in delaying.

Rhanar and a pale-eyed hound rose from the shadows as he entered the rocks. Palla and another wyr would be keeping watch on the far side of the broken ground, but the remaining guards gathered close as Kalan rejoined them, while the wyr hounds watched, silver-eyed, from among the scrub. "Did you see the caravan?" Taly asked.

Kalan shook his head and saw her disappointment through the darkness. "There's a wrecked wagon, so that may mean the caval-cade's close. But I saw a campfire and people with the wagon, which suggests an independent company."

"With only one wagon?" Jad's tone said that didn't seem likely. "But for the caravan to abandon a wagon crew in this country . . ." Beside him, Dain's mouth pulled down.

"So what's our course now?" Taly asked. "I suppose we have to render assistance."

Kalan knew the question was for him, despite Jad's former command of the eight-guard. The entire company had tacitly accepted his leadership since quitting the Red Keep, partly because he had offered a course of action, but also because Jad was prepared to follow him. Even Rhanar, the most reserved toward him of all their company, accepted Kalan's orders. "We scout the surrounding area and the wagon's situation," he said. "It's possible they have an armed escort, in which case we'll keep clear. If not, I'll risk riding in, because even if they're not from the caravan they may know where it is."

No one argued, so Kalan sent Jad, together with Palla and her shield comrade, Machys, to scout deeper into the foothills. Dain and another guard, Aarion, went one way along the road, back toward Blood, and Jaras and Nhal started in the other. The wyr pack split up of its own accord, with a pair loping after each of the scouting parties while the remaining seven stayed with Kalan. "They like you, Storm Spear," Rhanar observed, his tone suggesting this was not necessarily a recommendation.

"How can you be sure it's not Taly they like?" Kalan countered, as they left the rocks.

The ensign, who was riding Tercel, grimaced at the bay's ears before returning her focus to the rough terrain. The frost was still intense, but the sky was lighter, and by the time they circled the base of the ridge a breeze had picked up. Taly frowned across the Gray Lands to the bridge. "We'll have to approach on foot to avoid being seen. Along the streambed maybe, although they'll be guarding that approach."

"We hope," Rhanar muttered.

"I'll go in," Kalan told them, dismounting. "You keep watching the plain." He did not need to tell them how deceptive it could be, but hoped the hounds' senses would help counter that. Only one pair padded after him, shifting in and out of the half-dark as he worked his way toward the watercourse. Once he dropped down into it, Kalan shielded himself using an Oakward weave, so anyone looking his way would see only a thread of stream between pale boulders, and the jagged tracery of scrub-choked banks. The shield should cover the wyr hounds, too, so long as they stayed close—although from what Kalan had seen, they shared Faro's aptitude for playing least-in-sight.

Despite the shielding magic, he still placed each footstep with care, aware how far the rattle of a stone would carry. He stopped a good spear's cast clear of the bridge, settling into a mix of scrub and boulders that provided a view of its underside. The bridge foundations still obscured most of the wagon company, but Kalan could pick out a sentry concealed by the parapet, and at least one more in the shadow of the buttress below, monitoring the stream approach. He could see picketed horses and mules as well, and a nearby scar of fresh dirt and mounded stone that looked like a grave. Someone must have died, he supposed, when the wagon went over the edge.

The pennant set into the mound stirred as the breeze gusted, and Kalan's eyes narrowed on the device. He could see it was not Blood crimson, but had to wait for a second gust to reveal the indigo field and mer-dragon badge of the Sea House. Both wyr hounds growled, an almost inaudible vibration from deep in their chests, and Kalan was tempted to echo the sound. Lord Nimor had a marine escort with him, which meant most scavengers and 'spawn would steer clear, but no wagon traveling with the Bride's caravan should be abandoned, its crew left to fend for themselves. If the worst happened and the Sea House's envoy—accredited to both Blood and Night in recognition of the significance of this wedding—was killed, then Lady Myrathis's honor would be stained irreparably in the eyes of the Nine Houses.

And since, exile or not, I'm still her champion, Kalan thought grimly, that makes Lord Nimor's safety my concern. Best to retreat now and ride in openly, he decided—but remained motionless as the sentry guarding the stream approach turned his way and he recognized Lord Nimor. The envoy was carrying a staff as tall as himself, one shod with steel for the road, and the angle of his head reminded Kalan of Laer when the weatherworker was listening to wind and wave. Reflexively, Kalan checked the direction of the breeze, but it was blowing toward his hiding place so would not carry scent or sound to the envoy. He was debating whether to reveal his presence and risk being shot out of hand by the sentry on the bridge, when someone called to Nimor from the far side of the buttress. As soon as the envoy moved that way, Kalan seized the opportunity to withdraw.

The long, early morning shadows were stretching out from the Wall when he rejoined Taly and Rhanar. Both frowned when he identified the stragglers as Sea; they all knew only the most exceptional circumstance, mostly likely grave danger to the Bride, could justify abandoning an envoy. "Even then . . . " Taly stared into the haze of distance. "No one outside the Red Keep would believe they were left against Lady Myr's wishes, but I know she would never have agreed to it."

With Kolthis as Honor Captain, Kalan thought, she might not have been informed, let alone offered a choice. He saw the same knowledge in Taly's face as she studied the wagon again. "If there was going to be a relief party," she added somberly, "it would've arrived by now."

"I think we can rule that out." That conclusion did nothing to reduce Kalan's unease, but at least the Sea Keepers could tell them if the cavalcade *was* in danger. "What about the plain?"

"Nothing," Rhanar said.

Taly nodded agreement. "The wyrs have stayed quiet, too."

Kalan regarded the hounds, uncertain how far they could be relied upon to detect darkspawn activity. Despite the day's apparent calm, he could not shake the tightness in his gut and studied the plain again, but could detect nothing out of place. "We'll ride in," he said finally, and remounted Madder.

Taly and Rhanar fell in to either side as he started for the bridge, with the wyr hounds loping alongside. Initially, they rode within the deep shadow cast by the Wall, but Kalan saw the moment when the bridge lookout spotted them. He halted Madder clear of arrow range and shouted out their identities, preempting a verbal challenge: "Khar of the Storm Spears, together with Taly and Rhanar, both of my company."

The Sea Keepers knew him and should recognize Taly's name from the duel, but the lookout kept an arrow trained on him anyway and was soon joined by two more archers. At the same time, Lord Nimor started out to meet him, flanked by his escort captain, Tyun, and a marine called Tehan, both carrying crossbows. Kalan dismounted again and removed his helmet when they drew close. "Khar of the Storm Spears," Lord Nimor said, and smiled, although he and the marines maintained a careful distance. "I wondered if we might encounter you again."

"I'm the Bride's champion," Kalan said, knowing that was explanation enough. The Honor Code was clear: an Earl might declare exile, but only the champion, or the one he or she defended, could sever the bond of honor between them. He tucked his helmet under one arm and gestured to the bridge with the other. "What happened here, Lord Nimor? I thought you would be traveling with the cavalcade."

"We were," the envoy replied, as Tehan snorted. "But the road edge collapsed beneath the wagon and our axle broke. Captain Kolthis then explained that the country was too dangerous for the caravan to wait on either repairs or salvage, or to spare any additional guards. I have my marine escort, the captain said, and the Sea House must look to its own."

Yet animosity from Blood toward Sea, Kalan thought, still would not justify marooning an accredited envoy in wild country. "What *is* the caravan's situation?" he asked.

"Kolthis is Honor Captain," Tehan muttered, as if that were sufficient answer.

Nimor shook his head. "Until yesterday he observed the formalities, although I have not been permitted to speak with Lady Myrathis. No one has. For her security, Kolthis says, although in fact there's been no threat to the cavalcade beyond the nature of this country."

"He's made it clear he considers her a poor excuse for a Daughter of Blood." Tehan nodded agreement as Taly cursed beneath her breath. "And most of the cavalcade follows his lead."

"What concerns me most," Tyun put in grimly, "is the axle. We assumed it failed because the wagon went over the edge, but once we looked closely we found it'd been tampered with. If not here, sooner or later the break would undoubtedly have occurred."

Kalan's unease sharpened into outright foreboding. "Is Bajan with the Honor Guard?" he inquired, as by tacit consent they all began walking toward the bridge. From what he could make out, the Sea Keepers were trying to repair the wagon, although they must have little hope of doing so without either a smithy or a replacement axle.

Nimor shook his head again. "He was one of those Kolthis vetoed as soon as he was made Honor Captain. Apparently that's the captain's prerogative, so Bajan returned to Bronze Hold with Lord Narn."

So now, with the Sea Keepers gone, Lady Myrathis would have no allies and few friends among the caravan. Nimor must have read Kalan's expression, because he nodded. "I agree. We need to rejoin the cavalcade as soon as possible. We would have pushed to do so yesterday, except the driver was badly injured when the wagon fell. He died despite my physician's efforts, but by then we had no hope of catching up before nightfall."

The Sea Keepers might never catch up, Kalan thought, if they insisted on trying to repair the wagon. He was on the point of saying so when he realized that the activity—and curses—around the foundered vehicle were not a repair attempt. Instead, the Sea Keepers were endeavoring to prevent the wagon tipping the rest of the way into the riverbed and smashing apart, while they removed its contents. These appeared to be necessities for the road, together with personal possessions, which were being ferried to the waiting mules. The quickest way to get the company on the road would be to help—and Taly and Rhanar must have reached the same conclusion because they were already dismounting.

Murn, Nimor's secretary, winked as they helped him with a particularly unwieldy sailbag. "It's the envoy's state robes," he said. Taly's expression suggested she was uncertain whether this was a joke or not, although Kalan thought the bag was too heavy for clothes. He left them to hoist it onto a mule while he returned for another load, but Tyun—working with two others to wedge the listing wagon more securely in place—waved him back. Halting, Kalan wiped his hands against his trousers and studied the sky. The sun had now risen above the Wall's dark mass, but the moon was still visible, a pale disc against the Wall's familiar leaden sky. He thought it seemed both frailer and less ominous than when he climbed the ridge in the dark.

And we're almost done here, Kalan told himself, with most of the day ahead, so we'll catch the caravan before nightfall. He turned as Taly and Murn rejoined him. "We're ready, sir," the secretary told Nimor, at the same time as the bridge lookout pointed toward the foothills.

"Riders incoming," he called, "with more wyr hounds."

It was only then, as the rest of the Sea company gathered, that Kalan realized he had not yet seen Faro. "Where," he asked Nimor, "is my page?"

The envoy sighed. "Not with us." He spread his hands. "He resented being given into our charge, and although he usually turned up for meals, otherwise he was off about his own business. I did warn him against leaving the caravan, but I didn't anticipate," he added ruefully, "that the caravan might leave us."

"I saw him last," Tehan put in, "observing some spine-legged creature on a thornbush. With everything else that happened, I didn't realize he wasn't with us until well after the last of the caravan disappeared." She pulled a face. "I've been trying to keep an eye on him ever since that so-called Honor Captain threatened to have him beaten."

"Beaten?" Kalan said, clamping down on his anger at the entire situation—although he supposed a threatened beating might justify Faro making himself scarce. "Because he was my page?"

"There's no love lost, that's certain." Tehan was cautious. "But Kolthis said Faro had been making a nuisance of himself, hanging around the Bride's pavilion and dogging her palanquin on the road."

"Was he?" Kalan asked, and frowned when Tehan nodded, because he had not thought Faro cared much for Lady Myrathis.

"He wouldn't tell us why," Nimor said, before Kalan could ask.

Taly looked perplexed. "I thought he couldn't speak."

"He can. He just doesn't very much." To others, Kalan thought, still frowning, because before they entered Blood territory and he had warned Faro against speaking at all, the boy would chatter incessantly whenever they were alone.

"He's a canny lad and good at lying low," Tehan said, sounding unhappy. "He'll know to keep clear of Kolthis until we return."

"Which we need to do as soon as possible." Nimor inclined his head in grave apology. "I'm sorry if we have failed in our charge, Khar, and so failed you."

Kalan nodded, accepting the apology, although his initial anger lingered. "How soon can we move out?"

"Murn says we're ready." Nimor waited for his secretary's nod before indicating the new arrivals. "Unless your friends need to rest and eat?"

But Jad, whose scouting party had joined up with Dain and Aarion, assured him they could report in and eat as they rode. "We saw fresh 'spawn-sign, plenty of it," he told Kalan as the Sea company mounted. "And riders' tracks, although they were older: long range scouts maybe, ahead of the caravan passing this way." Dain and Aarion had nothing further to add from scouting the road, beyond evidence of the caravan's passage. Once the Sea company and exiles rode on together, Kalan saw more such evidence, from wagon tracks and dropped belongings, to a trail of animal dung. Eventually they met Jaras and Nhal, riding back to the bridge, and their report reflected those from the other scouts.

The habitual Gray Lands' wind was blowing steadily now, but the grit from the plain was not thick enough to check their steady pace. It was during a break to spell the horses that Tyun, lying flat on a pile of rocks with a mariner's spyglass, picked out shapes in the distance. "They look like trees beside the road," he said, offering Kalan the spyglass. "But that's impossible out here."

Even with the glass, the haze prevented identification of the anomaly. But it was not, Kalan thought, his earlier foreboding returning, country where you wanted to detect anything out of place. The wyr hounds whined as if sharing his unease, and their agitation increased once the company moved on. They growled and bristled, staring across the plain until the riders caught their tension and eased blades in scabbards as they approached the tree-like shapes.

Definitely not trees, Kalan thought. He was almost sure they were standards, although the great banners looked misshapen. The way they hung motionless reminded him of his Red Keep dream, as though no wind blew where they stood. And there *was* something wrong about them, beyond the way the grotesque out-lines matched his memories of were-hunters and the Darksworn's bestial helms. The company around him murmured, infected by a similar apprehension, and Kalan wished the grit would clear—then checked Madder as the nearest standard moved. Behind him the entire company jolted to a halt, and the wyr hounds lifted their muzzles and howled.

The movement was crows, clustered on the standards and flap-ping up as the riders drew close. There were nine standards in all, but Kalan finally understood—from within the detachment that allowed him to assimilate exactly what the banners comprised—why they did not move with the wind. Rather than colors, stripped and mutilated bodies had been lashed to every cross-tree, with ears, lips and noses, breasts and genitals, cut away so only clotted wounds remained. This close, he could see the insects that crawled in the cavities, and the pecked-out eyes and guts where the crows had been at their business.

The deaths had not been swift or easy, there was no doubt in Kalan's mind about that. Despite the mutilation, he could still rec-ognize most of the dead faces from the Honor Contest. Rhisart hung on the standard closest to them, with one of his cronies, whose name Kalan did not know, a few paces further along. But it was the two bodies that hung at the far end of the grisly line that gave him pause.

Slowly, he walked Madder toward them and stared up at what was left of Malar and Tawrin.

"Do you know them?" Taly asked. She was the only one who had followed him, and Kalan was not sure whether she had done so voluntarily or been too shocked to prevent Tercel from following Madder. He could hear Rhanar cursing, a low continuous stream of vituperation, and someone else—Murn, he thought, without looking around—was murmuring the invocation for the dead.

"They're Sword warriors," he said. "We took ship together from Grayharbor." He wondered what had become of Orth and Kelyr, but turned as the rest of the company joined them. Everyone looked strained, while the wyr hounds continued to keen, although more softly now, as though recognizing the likely proximity of enemies.

"Rhisart and those with him were scouts," Nimor said. "Kolthis sent them out the day before yesterday. Rhisart questioned the order, I remember that, because one scouting party was already overdue and he was concerned the guard on the cavalcade would be too light."

"Rhisart questioned Kolthis?" Taly shook her head. "That doesn't sound right."

"He was right about the numbers," Tyun said, "but Kolthis ordered him to go anyway."

Kolthis, Kalan recalled, had been angered by Rhisart's refusal to attack the wyr hounds in the Red Keep—but he had not been the Bane Holder's captain then. For Rhisart to have publicly questioned an order now, something must have felt really wrong. Not, Kalan thought grimly, that it did him any good.

"Do we take them down?" Murn sounded uncertain.

"And say Hurulth's first rite, at least," Kion, the Sea physician, suggested.

"We leave them." Kalan heard his own harshness as he surveyed the grisly row again. "They are beyond caring, and our priority has to be the caravan."

"I agree," Nimor said, as grim as Kalan. "Undoubtedly, they're intended as a warning, so let others who pass by heed it."

Kalan turned Madder back onto the road, and first Taly and then the rest of the company followed, the wyr hounds flowing around them like a tide. They held the horses to a steady pace, but everyone was tense, intent on the surrounding terrain, and no one spoke.

41

┿━═━┿

Caravan

They found the caravan shortly after noon, far sooner than Kalan had expected because it was still encamped. Dain, who had been scouting ahead, rode back with the news, while Aarion awaited their arrival below a long rise in the road. "You'll see the camp over the crest," he told them. "It's too far to make out details, but something's not right."

If all had been right, Kalan thought, as Tyun dismounted with the spyglass, the caravan would have broken camp at dawn and they would have needed most of the day to catch it, despite its slow pace. From this distance, he did not need the glass to see there were no sentries on duty. Like my Red Keep dream, he thought—except the bridal banners were crimson streamers on the grit-laden wind, and carrion birds were circling the far side of the encampment.

"Whatever attracted them," Tyun said, his eye fixed to the spyglass, "there are people alive on this side of the camp. But they're concealed among the wagons."

"You and the envoy's party should stay here," Kalan said. He gestured toward Taly and Jad's eight. "We'll ride in."

Tyun nodded, but Nimor pursed his lips when they conveyed their plan. "How will you fare as exiles in a House of Blood camp, even if this is no-man's-land?"

It was the sort of question an envoy should think to ask, Kalan supposed. "Your wagon was sabotaged," he said, "so envoy or not, you can't approach first. And whatever's happening in the camp is primarily Blood's affair, and we're still Blood." Jad and his unit murmured their agreement. "So we'll ride in as what we are, Derai warriors on legitimate business."

"And find out what's going on," Taly added. She spoke crisply, but Kalan could hear her fear. Clearly Nimor did, too, because his expression lengthened—but he nodded agreement, and his company reformed into a small, bristling square while Kalan and the exiles rode on.

The camp was situated on a small hill that looked like the site of an old redoubt, with an earth dike ringing its base and a terraced upper slope. The cavalcade was large enough for its carts and wagons to circle the hillock twice. The outer circle reinforced the dike, with the main camp behind it, while the inner circle of carts was situated on the upper terrace, ringing the Bride's pavilion and a second tent. Another shallow stream curved around the side of the camp where the carrion eaters circled, although whatever had drawn their attention remained obscured.

No one challenged the exiles' approach, although Kalan detected surreptitious movement among the outer wagons. All his companions had settled shields onto their arms, except for Palla and Machys, who rode behind the rest with arrows ready. Kalan held Madder to a walk, studying the entrance into the camp, which ran through a gap in the old earthworks and between the wagons beyond. At the same time, he picked out several watchers crouched to either side of the gap. From what he could discern, the defenders were not guards, but retainers: the caravan's grooms and carters, farriers and cooks. Still no one challenged their approach, but Kalan held up his hand anyway, signaling a halt.

"I am Khar of the Storm Spears, the Bride of Blood's champion," he called, "together with Jad of the Red Keep and his unit, escorting the Sea envoy, Lord Nimor. Who's in charge here?"

At first no one answered, although Kalan saw more movement and caught a murmur he could not decipher. Finally, a man carrying a longbow rose to his feet, standing so he was still protected by the wagon. No arrow was fitted to the longbow, but Kalan was almost certain his companions would have arrows trained on the new arrivals. "I'm Sarr," the man called back, "a farrier with the camp. I wouldn't say I'm in charge, except of those on watch right now." He glanced down, and this time Kalan overheard his low-voiced query. "Are you sure it's the Storm Spear, Aiv?"

"It's his roan. I'd recognize that brute anywhere. And the others do look like Jad and his eight-guard."

"*Real* honor guards," another voice put in, just as low. "They have wyrs with them, too."

Sarr nodded, and spoke to Kalan again. "If you really are the Bride's champion, show us your face. Sir," he added.

The request was a fair one, despite providing a better target for archers within the camp. It also proved Sarr and his companions had no experience of facestealers. "Cover me," Kalan said to Palla and Machys, and removed his helmet.

The carrion birds had been attracted to the remains of the caravan's animal herd. "Slaughtered," Sarr said, showing Kalan and Jad the oxen, mules, and horses, all with their throats torn out or bellies gutted. "Those guarding them were slain, too. The attackers came out of nowhere in the predawn and ran the majority of the herd off. The rest they just killed, as though for the sheer pleasure of it." The farrier stopped, frowning. "When the alarm sounded, the rest of the camp came running, but no more guards. From what we've worked out, the remaining honor guards left sometime between the last change of watch and the attack."

"What, all of them?" Kalan heard his own incredulity, and Jad was shaking his head.

Sarr nodded. "All that were left, given the scouts already sent out. But these attackers—I've never even heard of such 'spawn, let alone seen 'em. But Aiv and Baris got a good look." The farrier turned to the two grooms, both of whom Kalan remembered from the Red Keep stables, when Aiv had called Madder a killer and Baris wanted the roan put down. The fourth sentry, a wagoner called Rigan, had remained on watch.

"They looked like a cross between beasts and men." Briefly, Aiv's expression worked. "Their speed was terrifying and none of our weapons, arrows or spears, could touch 'em."

Were-hunters, Kalan thought, remembering how the same thing had happened at The Leas until members of the Oakward countered their magic. Frowning, he studied the savaged bodies of the caravan's dead. "And these sentries really were the only guards left?"

"Other than the medical orderlies, and they're garrison auxiliaries, not Honor Guard." Kalan glimpsed bewilderment and fear beneath Sarr's surface calm. "Captain Kolthis had sent out so many scouting patrols there were barely enough guards left to secure the camp." Sarr paused. "He seemed to think that with so many of us ex-garrison, he could afford to do it, but most of us are too old for active service or were invalided out—"

He stopped as Aiv cut in, her voice tight. "Not just no guards, Storm Spear. No sign of 'em having left the camp, let alone which direction they might have gone, or why."

"The wind would disperse obvious tracks, especially in this country," Kalan pointed out. After a moment, Sarr and Aiv nodded, but Baris continued to stare at the line of dead.

"What about your wyr hounds?" Jad asked. "Have they vanished, too?"

"What wyr hounds?" Aiv demanded. "After a third of the Red Keep pack left with you, Captain Kolthis was adamant they couldn't be relied upon anymore, especially in open country. He said experienced warriors were far more dependable."

Convenient, Kalan thought, although he was not convinced Blood wyr hounds would have prevented the slaughter. "I take it no one's gone after the stock that was run off?"

Sarr and Aiv looked blank, but Baris turned on Kalan. "On foot? Pursuing what killed armed warriors on guard here?" The groom was shaking, his face twisted with loathing and fear.

Kalan kept his voice calm. "I didn't say I thought you should have gone. I asked if anyone had."

"Not that we know of." Sarr straightened, his expression turning bleak. "I know the caravan's crippled without 'em, but . . ."

"Baris is right," Kalan said, still calmly. "Pursuit would be folly." Suicide, he thought somberly, although with the camp immobilized and no guards to defend it, those who remained here were only marginally better off. And he had to assume the attack was just the opening gambit from an enemy who—adding the death standards to the crippled caravan—enjoyed toying with prey. Kalan read the same awareness in Jad's eyes, before swift footsteps made him turn.

"Khar!" Aarion, who had gone with Taly and Dain to find Lady Myrathis, spoke urgently: "Ensign Taly wants you at the Bride's pavilion now."

Sarr and Aiv's stricken exchange of glances told Kalan that checking the Bride's pavilion had never crossed their minds, which fitted with Tehan's suggestion that Myr was little more than a cipher to most of the camp. A vital cipher, he thought, his anger rising—before he reminded himself that in addition to the shock of the attack and the guards' disappearance, the retainers had also been catapulted into unaccustomed roles. He was still dumbfounded they had overlooked the Bride's safety, but berating them would not achieve what needed to be done now.

"You've done well," he said instead, "but we all need to do a lot more. Jad's an eight-leader, so I'm putting him in charge of securing the camp, but I'm relying on you, and those who've worked with you so far, to pull in everyone we'll need to make that happen. Fast," he added. Neither Sarr nor Aiv argued against his assumption of authority, and although Baris looked sullen, that could simply be a reaction to events. "Send Rhanar to bring Lord Nimor in," Kalan told Jad. "Brief him once he gets here and ask his permission for Tyun to help you organize a defense."

Kalan could not imagine the envoy refusing, but the distinction between Blood and Sea still needed to be respected. Leaving Jad to his work, he strode toward the heart of the camp with Aarion, two of the wyr hounds at their heels. "It's bad," Aarion said quietly. "A lot of dead, and we haven't found the Bride yet. But the rear of the pavilion, where Lady Myrathis and her governess had their compartments, has collapsed, so she could be under that."

Dead, abducted, missing ... Kalan lengthened his stride. The camp was eerily silent, with people either deployed into Sarr's watches or keeping to themselves. Everyone reacts differently, Kalan thought, watching one man go from wagon to wagon, methodically tightening straps and recoiling ropes. The only place they encountered something approaching normal activity was around a burned-out cook wagon, where several people were damping down the still-hot ashes. A woman turned as Kalan and Aarion passed and looked as though she intended speaking, but another grasped her arm, stopping her.

There were no retainers within the camp's inner circle, but Kalan detected the residue of power use as soon as he passed the cart barrier. Someone had used a great deal of it, probably during the night, and he identified the lingering occlusion from a shield-spell, willing away unwanted attention—which might explain why no one had thought to check on the Bride. He could detect other influences as well, all too faded to be sure of their purpose, although one hinted at allure. A melange, Kalan thought, and felt Yelusin's spark stir.

"You can see how the pavilion's collapsed." Aarion pointed. "When I left, Taly and Dain were planning to raise it. Jaras and Nhal checked Captain Kolthis's tent, but it's completely empty."

Nothing left behind, Kalan thought. Whoever Kolthis truly was, he was clearly done with being a warrior of Blood. Setting the implications of that aside, Kalan stepped through the pavilion's tied-back flaps. Despite being forewarned, he was still shaken by the carnage inside: pages, stewards, and attendants were strewn about the main compartment like broken dolls. The wyr pair trailing him keened on the same eerie, low-pitched note they had used beside the death standards. Walling off emotion, Kalan took time to study the dead faces but could not see any he knew. Including Faro, he thought, grimly aware that the boy was still missing.

He circled the remains of two guards, hacked apart at the entrance to the first of the inner compartments. The area beyond looked as though a whirlwind had been through it, with smashed camp furniture and belongings tossed about, but no more bodies. The rich furnishings and prevalence of Blood's hydra device suggested this had been the Bride's private apartment, which also pointed to Lady Myrathis having been abducted—although a successful abduction would not explain why time had been wasted tearing her quarters apart.

"Over here, sir," Aarion said, as the apartment's rear wall billowed and the subsided canvas began to rise. Kalan stooped through the entrance the honor guard held open and found the next section only partly upright. He sidestepped another dead warrior, sprawled beneath sagging canvas, and saw Taly beside a small pile of bodies, the uppermost wearing Blood uniform. Aarion, following him, paused to pull the body from beneath the canvas, revealing a crossbow bolt punched through gorget and throat. "From close range," the guard said, and Kalan nodded at the same time as Taly rolled the topmost corpse over. A knife had been driven into his eye, but it was harder to see what had slain the warrior beneath him until the ensign pointed to a tiny dart, again in the eye.

"Poison," she said, and hauled the second warrior aside, revealing a woman's blood-soaked body. The gore was probably not all hers, Kalan thought, although the congealing blood that covered her bruised face came from an ugly looking wound to her head. "It's Ilai," Taly told him. "She was one of Lady Liankhara's household before being assigned to the Bride's retinue." The ensign hesitated briefly: "As a wardrobe attendant."

Lady Liankhara, Kalan repeated silently, who is a Blood spy-master—while Ilai was clearly adept at more than looking after clothes. He supposed he must have seen her before, but it was impossible to tell through the blood and swelling, especially since Lady Myrathis's attendants had worn the same makeup masks as the Bride. When Kalan checked for a pulse, the flutter was slight but led him to look more intently for the equally faint rise and fall of breath. "She's alive," he said. "Aarion, get Lord Nimor's physician here."

Aarion left at as close to a run as the lopsided pavilion would allow, while Taly looked for something that wasn't shredded to keep Ilai warm. She finally came up with a tapestry that had only sustained one long rent, and when she spread it out Kalan recognized The Lovers. But Dain dragged his attention away, calling out from beyond another fold of drooping canvas. "Taly, I've found Mistress Ise. She's still alive, but only just."

"You go," Taly told Kalan. "I'll stay with Ilai until Kion arrives. But if Mistress Ise's alive . . . "

Then Lady Myrathis may be as well, Kalan finished silently. When he reached the next compartment, the old Rose woman was lying amid more wreckage, with her body curled around a sword that had been thrust up beneath her ribs. Her hands still clutched her gnarled walking stick, but what gave him pause was the aura of power, however frail, that surrounded her body. Frowning, Kalan stepped between a broken table and splintered chair to reach her side. The governess had woven a shield, he decided, studying the fading aura. She had concealed it very cleverly, too, using the larger working outside to disguise what she had done.

A Rose adept within Blood all these years, he thought—and no one any the wiser.

"Did you think, Storm Spear, that we would leave our own unprotected amid the barbarity of your House?" The mindwhisper was so soft that if Mistress Ise had spoken aloud Kalan would have had to bend close to hear.

"Did you manage to save Lady Myrathis?" he asked urgently. *"Is that what your shield spell was for?"*

"To conceal her escape, yes. She is with your page, who I hope may prove strong enough to save them both."

"Where—" Kalan began, but felt the headshake she was too weak to give.

"I don't know. There was no time. The enemy were already about their work, but we did what we could, Liankhara's agent and I . . . "

Liankhara's agent, Kalan thought: she must mean Ilai. *"Ilai still lives,"* he said, and felt her answering flicker of acknowledgment. He wanted to ask if she could not have used the shielding to save herself but already knew the answer. Only those with the very strongest gift could hide in plain sight. Otherwise, for a shield spell to work, there first had to be somewhere to hide.

"And I am too old to run. I have had my time and more but at least I could give those two their chance . . . " The mindwhisper wavered, then strengthened again. *"Liankhara's agent did well. She was a tiger . . . for ferocity."*

"A little Blood barbarity, eh?" Kalan caught the ghost of an answering chuckle, but the aura of power was dwindling fast now and Ise's life with it. He heard voices from the adjoining compartment, and a few seconds later Taly joined him. *"Taly is here,"* he told Ise, speaking aloud as well. The ensign knelt on the old woman's other side, her expression full of regret.

"She was always a good girl. Old Blood to the core . . . " The mindwhisper lapsed again, and this time it was Taly who checked for a pulse. *"To think,"* Ise murmured—mostly to herself this time, Kalan thought—*"I should live to see the line of Tavaral come into its own again . . . and the old Blood return. Myrathis . . . "* She convulsed, moaning aloud. "Myr . . . the web . . . take great care . . . "

"What does she mean?" Taly asked. "What web?"

Derai politics probably, Kalan thought, because the Rose had always been the Alliance's power brokers. He shook his head, indicating he did not know, as the last of Ise's aura winked out. "She's gone," he said. But at least he knew now that Lady Myrathis and Faro had fled rather than being taken prisoner. The need to find them drove him to his feet, only to almost trip on a silver tray lying beside the broken table.

"It's the tabletop," Taly said, as he propped it upright. The legs, carved into the shape of dragons, had been smashed to kindling, so Kalan pushed them aside with his foot as Dain pointed to the tent's outer wall.

"See how this has been cobbled together? Recently, by the look of the thread, and the tear in the fabric's clean. I'd say it was made by a knife."

"From in here, though, or outside?" Kalan slit the stitches and studied the camp beyond. A careful survey of the stony ground revealed no prints, and when he stepped through the gap the only out-of-place element was the burned cook-wagon. "I want this whole area cordoned off," he told Dain, reentering the tent. "The wind's probably obscured any tracks that weren't deliberately erased, but there may be a scent the hounds can follow." For the first time he felt glad of the spell that had kept others away until now. "Let's take no chances and get all the wyrs here."

Once Dain left, he went over the disordered interior again, startling when his boot brushed against Ise's walking stick and a jolt of power shocked through him. The spark of Yelusin's power flared in answer, and the wyr pair whined as Kalan studied the stick more closely. It looked like several thick vines twisted into a single staff and shod with steel, while the mother-of-pearl eyes set into the knotted head reminded him of those painted onto Sea House ships. They seemed to be looking back at him now, and the hair on his arms and nape lifted, especially when he saw the same eye etched into the locket about the old woman's neck. Yet when he touched the walking stick again, no further jolt came. Carefully, Kalan worked it free of Ise's hands and placed it beside the tray. "Will you make sure this and her other intact possessions, especially anything of value, are secured?" he asked Taly. "And whatever's left of Lady Myr's belongings as well?"

"I'll see to it." Carefully, the ensign unclasped the locket. "Mistress Ise always said this was to go to Lady Myr, since it contains a lock of Lady Mayaraní's hair. What about burial?" she asked, placing the locket on the tray.

Kalan drew his gauntlets back on. "It'll have to be a mass grave, both for the dead here and those guarding the herd." If we have time to dig it, he added silently, and left Taly covering Ise's body with her own cloak. Kion was intent on Ilai and did not glance up as he passed by, but Nimor was waiting by the pavilion entrance with two of his marines and turned at once, his expression a question. Kalan shook his head. "We haven't found the Bride yet." Or Faro either, he thought, while explaining what they knew. "But, we can't just focus on finding Lady Myrathis. With the caravan crippled and no guards, we must send for help at once."

If it's not already too late, he reflected, as Nimor nodded. "It's a Blood caravan," the envoy said, "so someone from Blood must go. But since the Keep of Stone is the nearest stronghold, it may help if I send someone, too." The Honor Code required that aid be rendered, but Nimor's tone, if not his words, suggested scant reliance on that. He would be as aware as Kalan of the rumors about recent House of Adamant aggression—and that the New Blood was not the only faction within the Nine Houses that wanted to pick and choose among the Code's tenets.

"Could we try for Night instead?" one of the marines asked.

Kalan shook his head. "It's too far, Reith. Both our messengers and a Night relief force would have to skirt Adamant and Stars' territory, and time is critical." He was also thinking of the death standards and his Emerian experience of were-hunts. "We have to send the best scouts we've got, but they'll need to be fighters, too."

Nimor nodded again. "I'll confirm with Tyun, but Namath's an experienced sea fighter and a keen hunter on land. He's cool headed, too."

Someone who'll remain calm in the face of potential Adamant antagonism, Kalan interpreted. That made Jad the obvious Blood choice, except he needed the eight-leader's experience here.

"Send me." Taly stepped clear of the inner tent, carrying a meager armload of unbroken possessions, including Ise's walking stick. "My home hold's small, so I've been riding boundary patrols since I was a page and am better than most at scouting." Her smile was a tight, half-moon curve that told Kalan she understood that volunteering could mean certain death. "When do we leave?"

"As soon as Murn can pen a formal request for aid," Nimor said briskly, "one that appoints both you and Namath as emissaries." He turned to Kalan. "Unless there's more you wish added?"

Kalan shook his head. "No, nothing. But make sure you're fully equipped," he told Taly. "And take Tercel. He's canny and enduring, and he'll fight for you."

"And I for him," she said, with the same tight smile. Her eyes held Kalan's. "Just make sure you find my Lady Mouse, wherever she's got to."

42

The Empty Plain

Two of the wyr hounds had accompanied Taly and Namath, but the eleven that remained disdained Myr's offered belongings. They rolled their ghostly eyes toward Kalan as if to say *they* did not need to be given a scent, and instead quartered the inner camp. Five sniffed around the pavilion before flattening their ears and growling at Kolthis's tent, a low rumble that began deep in their bellies and did not die away. The remaining six circled the cart barrier before ranging into the outer camp to investigate the burned wagon. When Kalan followed, the retainers there showed him how the fire had been set deliberately. Fuel had been gathered beneath the wagon, and the jar of lantern oil used to light it had been discarded nearby.

"It was started not long before the attack." The speaker was the same woman who had wanted to speak when Kalan and Aarion passed by earlier. "As a distraction, maybe, to draw our attention away from the perimeter and our herd."

"But it also roused us," a second woman said. She sounded reluctant—perhaps, Kalan thought, placing her, for the same reason she had stopped her companion from speaking before. Turning, he studied the pavilion again, because the fire would have diverted attention from anyone fleeing through the cut in its rear wall. By rousing the camp, the blaze could well have prevented more widespread killing, even if whoever set it had risked setting the entire camp alight—but the fire-starter might have decided that was the lesser danger. Or didn't consider the wider risk at all, Kalan reflected.

"Sir," the first woman said, then stopped. "The guards . . ."

The wyr hounds were tracking back toward the pavilion, their noses to the ground, but Kalan stopped himself from striding after them. "The Honor Guard's gone," he said, not softening the situation, "but my company and the Sea envoy's escort are seeing to the camp's defense. They'd welcome your assistance, once all's safe here."

"Yes, sir," she said. "Of course." The others nodded, too, and the low discussion that followed his departure suggested they meant it.

Regardless, I have to let Jad deal with that for now, Kalan thought, altering direction to rejoin Dain and Aarion as the wyr hounds started toward the dike. Once they reached it, they crossed onto the Gray Lands' side before stopping, their eyes intent on the plain. Kalan settled onto his heels beside them and studied the unrevealing terrain, trying to distinguish sounds beyond the camp's bustle and the incessant wind. He knew Faro could disguise his presence behind a wisp of haze or within the shadow of a rock, but the vital question was whether the boy was capable of concealing Lady Myrathis as well, the way Kalan had once hidden Malian in the Old Keep of Winds. Or they could be dead, Kalan thought: run down as they fled, or fallen victim to exposure and thirst. "We need to find out," he told the hounds, and stood up.

Eleven pairs of silver eyes turned his way at once, but with were-hunters about, Kalan had no intention of venturing the plain on foot. Instead he sent Aarion for their horses and thrust down impatience, surveying the landscape again. Yet the plain remained a blank, even the near-distance opaque with haze. The hounds were alert, although Kalan still retained doubts over their reliability. They've brought me this far, he thought—and turned at the first ring of hooves against stone to find Tehan and two of her fellow marines, Koris and Tymar, accompanying Aarion. "By Lord Nimor's order,"

Tehan said. "Besides, Aarion had his hands full managing your roan. He needed the help."

Aarion and Madder snorted in unison, and Dain chuckled before everyone sobered, preparing to mount. The roan tramped a circle, eager for action as Kalan settled in the saddle and the wyr pack advanced into the empty plain, their lean shadows streaming away in the lengthening afternoon. "We'll follow their lead," Kalan told the others, "but fan out behind them. Stay alert," he added, although he doubted they needed the reminder as the earthworks fell behind. Even armed and riding Madder, Kalan felt exposed, but shielding a moving group was always difficult; and more so when they were dispersed and he needed to conceal his working. Still, he did what he could to thicken the haze around both hounds and riders, creating the impression of a mirage, not substance, as they pushed farther into the plain.

"How far can they have gotten on foot, anyway?" Dain's mutter reached Kalan clearly from several horse lengths away. As if detecting the guard's doubt, the hound ahead of them growled as it leapt onto a low, flat-topped rock and peered over the edge—before growling again and turning glowing eyes on Kalan, at the same time as he felt its psychic summons.

The entire line of hounds halted as he dismounted and examined the print, part paw, part foot, pressed into sand on the rock's far side. A were-hunter, Kalan thought, and raised an arm to summon the other riders close. The print was smaller than those left by the herd's attackers, which suggested a forager, or a scout that had lain on the rock before leaping down. He surveyed the surrounding area again, alert for incongruity or potential hiding places, until he isolated a shadow that appeared deeper than the rest. Its shape suggested a shallow gully, the sort a stream might leave if it changed course. Kalan also began to sense a will at work, encouraging him to look away, to *not see* . . . Meeting the hound's spectral gaze, he slid the longbow from his shoulder.

Dain and the others followed as he led Madder forward, although they remained puzzled until the distance closed sufficiently for proximity to negate the shield spell, so everyone saw the narrow gash eroded out of the plain. Kalan sent Dain and Aarion to cover their progress from the gully rim, while Koris remained with the horses, and Tehan and Tymar accompanied him into the fissure on foot, quarrels already wound onto their crossbows. Cautiously, Kalan extended his own shield beneath the original working: sufficient, he hoped, to cover their advance, without alerting other hunters. The wyr hounds, too, were wary and stopped at the first bend, waiting for Kalan before scouting around the curve. The gully ahead was far deeper, and clogged by large boulders, but Kalan only felt the first insidious creep of tracking magic as they approached the second bend.

The wyr hounds remained silent, but all their hackles were up as Kalan eased forward to sight around the curve. Beyond it, the gully widened into an expanse of sand, rock, and thorn between eroded walls, before narrowing into a third bend. The densest cover was provided by a patch of thornbrush hugging the base of the gully wall. Gradually, Kalan pieced together a shape among the crisscross of spines and branches. It *was* some kind of were-hunter, he decided, but smaller than those he had encountered previously. He could chart the shape of its tracking magic now, bent on ferreting a way through the shield working that lingered in the wash. Frowning, Kalan tried to pinpoint the source of the shield, but the fissures caused by erosion appeared shallow, and the remaining brush was too sparse to hide anyone effectively. The boulders, too, were smaller and more scattered than in the preceding section.

Kalan was concentrating so intently that he almost missed the moment when the were-hunter moved. Initially, it was just one more shadow among many along the gully wall, but he got his first clear sighting when it slipped out of the thornbrush and behind a rock. The narrow, pointed face was manlike, but thick fur grew down onto it like a pelt and he could see the curve of incisors; the creature's arms and legs, too, ended in claws. Kalan felt the tracking magic strengthen as the hunter sapped its quarry's shield spell, and the sheltered gully felt stifling as the were-hunter crept forward. The narrow face alternated between snuffing first ground, then air, but its focus always returned to a stretch of wall more fissured than the rest, close by the third bend. Kalan studied the area of rock and shadow more closely and decided several of the fissures were deeper than they had first appeared. Eventually, a small ledge wavered into focus, halfway up the tallest crevice. The were-hunter must have seen it, too, because its bared incisors gleamed.

Kalan edged backward to fit an arrow to the longbow's string, before sliding back into position and waiting for a clear shot. The were-hunter was at the base of the cleft now, and Kalan could trace the course of its magic, questing upward. He also detected the first hint of a silhouette, crouched to the rear of the ledge, as the hunter studied the fissure—then leapt high, its extended talons raking the shelf. Steel flashed wildly as the shield spell shattered and a small form scrabbled backward. Simultaneously, Kalan loosed his arrow. The shaft pierced the were-hunter's neck at the base of the skull and its body convulsed, falling backward at the same time as a second arrow sprouted between its ribs.

Killed instantly, Kalan guessed—but the arrow through the ribs had not come from Dain or Aarion on the gully rim. Coolly, he readied another arrow, seconds before Orth and Kelyr appeared around the far bend. Both warriors were bloodstained, and Kelyr's left bicep was roughly bandaged, although his bow remained steady as the Sword warriors approached the fissure. Kelyr bent to examine the were-hunter's sprawled body, while Orth surveyed the crevice. He grunted, half turning away, then whipped back, reaching up one long arm and hooking Faro off the ledge with his longbow. The giant's other arm grabbed the boy out of his tumble and forced him to his knees. "I didn't think the Storm Spear would let you out of his sight, thief." Orth kicked Faro's dropped dagger aside. "But here you are, proof that Ornorith smiles after all."

Kelyr's gaze was quartering the gully. "Whoever's there," he called, his voice tight, "show yourself."

"Or I deal to the Haarth rat," Orth added. He shook Faro slowly, back and forward, and set a knife against his throat. The wyr hounds growled and bristled, starting forward as one, and Kelyr's arrow swung onto them. Moving slowly and deliberately, Kalan released his shield working and followed, keeping his arrow trained on Orth. Tehan and Tymar flanked him on either side while the wyr hounds continued to advance, their eyes silver flame.

"Call them off, Khar," Kelyr said. "Orth'll make the brat suffer if you don't."

The wyr hounds stopped, although their hackles still bristled. Faro was white, his face smudged with terror, desperation, and weariness. "We don't want to hurt him," Kelyr said, ignoring Orth's glower. "The country's crawling with 'spawn, more than we've ever seen, and we lost Tawrin and Malar during our last encounter with 'em." He paused, his eyes meeting Kalan's. "We want to come into the caravan."

"In that case," Kalan answered coolly, "I suggest you let Faro go."

"Do it, Orth," Kelyr said.

The giant's glower deepened, his head hunching into his shoulders. "We don't need them. Or this scum lover, thinking he can foist his Grayharbor gutter rat on the Derai."

The wyr hounds growled again, while Kelyr's face told Kalan what he thought of the Sword warriors' chances on their own. But it was Tehan who spoke. "What do you mean? A blind weatherworker could see the boy's Derai."

Kelyr's answering frown was uncertain, but Orth snorted. "So he's some fugitive priest's half-born brat—that's worse than a Haarth imposter."

"*Pure* Derai," Tehan clarified, shaking her head. "You don't think we'd let an imposter, or even a half-born, creep onto one of our ships, let alone carry him back to the Wall? That's not the sort of mistake we can afford to make."

For the first time, doubt flickered in Orth's expression. He did not appear to notice that Tehan had sidestepped the priest-kind angle—fortunately, Kalan thought. "Release the boy," he said, "and you can come into the caravan. You have my word." The Sword warriors might be brutes, but they were brutes who could fight, and the caravan needed every sword it could muster.

"Let him go, Orth," Kelyr said. He lowered his bow and the marines did the same, but Orth's head hunched lower.

"I say we keep hold of the boy as surety for the Storm Spear's good faith."

Even in Blood's camp? Kalan wanted to ask, but knew baiting Orth would not resolve matters. And although he still had an arrow trained on the Sword warrior, it would not beat the knife. Standoff, he thought, frustrated—at the same time as a rock flew out of the fissure and smacked into the giant's knife, knocking it from his hand.

"No shooting!" Kalan yelled, as Orth roared and Faro twisted free, pelting toward him. The wyr hounds surged forward, surrounding the boy in a protective circle. "Everyone hold!" Kalan commanded as the foremost hounds, their eyes still on fire, growled at the Sword warriors. Orth snarled in answer, his sword already out, but Kelyr had not fired—possibly because he had seen Dain and Aarion, arrows trained on them both from the gully rim.

"Orth," he warned, and Kalan saw the giant absorb the situation—before his glare focused on the fissure.

Oh no, Kalan thought, you don't. "Enough!" He spoke crisply, but lowered his own arrow at the same time. "You know as well as I do what we're facing and that we'll need every fighter, including both of you. So my offer to let you into the caravan stands, but this nonsense ends now. When we win clear," he said to Orth—if we do, he thought—"you and I can worry about settling scores."

Orth hesitated a moment longer before slamming his sword back into its scabbard. Scooping up his knife, he resheathed it more slowly. "Until this business is done," he said, and spat to one side.

"Until then," Kalan agreed. "Now, move away from the fissure." He watched Orth closely, but although the giant's glower was simultaneously calculating and reluctant, he retreated with Kelyr. "Don't take your eyes off them," Kalan told the marines, before moving forward. Seeing a gleam among the stones, he picked up Faro's knife—the same one he had charged Liy to pass on—and handed it back. "Well done," he said softly.

Faro's face was pinched small, his eyes huge with recent dread and unshed tears, but he drew himself straighter. "*She's* in there," he said gruffly, jerking his head toward the fissure. "Lady Myr. She's got a crossbow," he added.

"Ah." Of course, Kalan thought. A Daughter of Blood would have been taught to use weapons, but he had assumed, because of Lady Myr's diffidence, that the rock had been a lucky shot. Now he decided to err on the side of caution, and kept his approach to the fissure oblique. He could see no sign of Lady Myr from below, but pitched his voice to carry beyond the opening. "Lady Myrathis, it's Khar of the Storm Spears." He wished, momentarily, that Taly had not already left. "I've wyr hounds with me, and several of Lord Nimor's marines, so it's safe for you to come out. Or I can climb up to you," he added. "Just don't shoot me, all right?"

When no reply came, Kalan climbed level with the ledge and peered cautiously around the opening, to where Lady Myrathis was pressed into the rear of the shallow recess, her hands locked around the crossbow. "Lady Myr," he said quietly, "are you all right?"

"Yes," she whispered finally, and Kalan realized it might be as much reaction to her own daring as fear of Orth, or doubt of himself, that had made her freeze. "I couldn't believe it was really you. Or a rescue. I felt I wanted it to be true too much."

"It's true," he assured her. "Do you need help to leave?"

"No, I'll come out." He watched her shadow lower the crossbow then stand up. When she appeared in the entrance, he grinned at her.

"That was a fine shot with the rock, Lady Mouse."

She looked worn out, with her hair straggling down her back and dirt on her face and clothes, but now she flushed and looked away. "That's Dab's name for me, and Taly's," she said, then spoke again quickly, before Kalan could respond to the implied prohibition.

"They both always said I had a good eye." Her gaze returned to his. "I couldn't let the Sword warrior hurt Faro. But there were so many people close together and if I missed . . . The rock seemed better than the crossbow."

"Much better," Kalan agreed, as she took the hand he held out. The flush had drained away again, highlighting the shadows left by exhaustion and fear as Myr paused, her gaze searching his.

"Faro said that you would come, that you would save us, but I didn't believe it was possible." She slid a fleeting smile his way. "I'm glad you have, though."

"I think the pair of you did very well on your own." Kalan helped her descend and forbore to add that no one had been saved yet. Her eyes had already told him that she knew.

43

Bond of Honor

"I hate *him*," Faro said, his voice hoarse with the emotion, and Myr looked away from his contorted expression. Despite finding, during the course of their flight and the long hours spent in hiding, that the boy was not mute after all, she had noticed his continued reluctance to say Kolthis's name. Sometimes, too, he had seemed to struggle, as he was doing now, to get words out. His head jerked toward Myr. "I hated the way he watched her tent as well."

Myr kept her eyes lowered, partly as a defense against the circle of watching faces, but also because she knew her reddened eyes would betray that she had cried a great deal since returning to the camp. Not in front of anyone else—not even when Khar had told her that Ise and all her household except Ilai were dead—but afterward, when she was alone in what had once been Kolthis's tent. Under the circumstances, she had not wanted to return to the pavilion—and as for the smaller tent having been Kolthis's, a space comprising canvas and poles was not the person. Besides, Taly had already stowed Myr and Ise's few intact possessions there.

Taly, Myr thought drearily, who is somewhere out there in no-man's-land, trying to fetch help. She pushed down her fear that the ensign, too, might be dead by now and made herself concentrate on their council of war. They were gathered in the Sea envoy's large tent and Lord Nimor was attended by his secretary, Murn, and his escort captain, Tyun. Khar was accompanied by the former Honor Guard called Jad, who had been one of his seconds in the duel with Parannis. The eleven wyr hounds had crowded into the tent as well, and Faro was sitting with an arm draped about one of them.

Now he coughed. "Like a cat," he continued, his odd accent accentuated by weariness and remembered fear, "watching a mousehole. *His* face always changed, too, like someone else was looking out through a mask. And that other face—" Faro's arm tightened around the hound and he appeared to struggle with himself before getting the next words out. "It was cruel and cold. Very cold . . . " He shivered. "The other guards, the ones he kept close, always turned their heads when he turned his and looked exactly where he did. As though he was the only one that was real and the rest were like his shadow— only there were lots of them. It made my skin creep."

Myr shivered, too, because her skin had crawled on more than one occasion since departing Blood territory, although she had not known why. Now she imagined it might have been when Kolthis had been watching in the way Faro described, behavior that smacked of every fireside tale of possession Myr had either heard or read. Although a doubter, she supposed, would probably point out that Faro could be using those tales to embroider his own. Automatically, she glanced toward Lord Nimor, but his face gave nothing away.

Khar was studying his page. "I heard you'd been watching the pavilion closely."

Faro ducked his head. "I'm your page," he said gruffly, "and you're her champion. My mam always said nothing—no one—could change that, because it's a bond of honor . . . " Briefly, he looked uncertain, before his voice strengthened. "So that means I have to keep your pledge of faith, too, see?" Myr glanced up in time to see Tyun and Jad nod. Having experienced Faro's ability to find hiding places and keep out of sight during their flight, she doubted Kolthis had suspected how closely he was being observed. "I had to be a lot more careful, though, after he said he'd thrash me. Then yesterday, when I was tracking the insect, I saw *them*. Him and another beast-man like the one you shot, meeting out of sight of the caravan."

The boy shook himself like a dog. "So I laid low until it was dark before working my way into the inner camp and hiding out beneath one of the carts." He shivered again. "Nothing happened until the watch changed, but then the old guards didn't go off duty. Instead they joined with the newcomers and surrounded the pavilion. The way they watched it made me feel as though *he* was looking out of all their faces. That's when I knew I had to do something to draw them away." Faro's breath shuddered. "Or maybe I just had to distract *him*. I thought that, too."

"So you set the fire," Khar said.

Faro nodded. "I tried to be brave and clever," he whispered, "just like you would be."

Kharalthor and Hatha, Myr thought, would say something heartening but jocular in reply, while her other siblings would probably mock the expression of feeling. But Khar opened up his arms, and Faro relinquished his hold on the wyr hound and stumbled into them. "You were exceedingly brave," Khar told the head pressed against surcote and breastplate, "and exceptionally clever. I'm very proud of you."

Myr smoothed her pointed cuffs down over her hands, aware of the stab of an emotion she could not name, or did not wish to, but which might have been longing, or envy, or loss, or all three blended into one. When it dissipated, her fatigue and grief both felt more pronounced, but she managed a smile for Faro all the same. "And I am grateful. You were everything a champion's page should be, and more."

While I, she thought, recalling how they had crawled beneath wagons and clung to every shadow, was not brave at all. Once they struck out across the plain, she had been terrified by its openness. At any moment, she had expected the pursuing shout and thunder of hooves, or worse, the arrow or lance driving into flesh. Ise had insisted it was her duty to escape and ordered her to go—and Myr had obeyed, abandoning the person who had been her life's constant to save herself. Conduct unworthy, she told herself now, of a true Daughter of Blood.

Faro twisted to face her, although he still kept one arm tight around Khar. "I thought you weren't going to leave at all until the old lady made you." He scuffed one foot back, then forward again, darting a glance around the others' faces. "She said it was the Bride's *duty* to escape," he told them: "Because of the marriage treaty but also to thwart her enemies."

As though, Myr thought, he's defending me against my own unspoken accusation. Yet, if asked, she would have said that all his courage and cleverness had been for Khar's sake and because he hated Kolthis, not for her. Khar's eyes met hers above his page's head. "Mistress Ise was right," he said. Everyone else was quiet, although beyond the tent the camp was loud with activity. "The principal purpose of the caravan is to make sure the Bride reaches Night safely. But it's your duty, too, Lady Myrathis, as much if not more than anyone else's."

The others murmured agreement, but Myr frowned, mainly to prevent tears, before shaking her head. "I know I'm the figurehead, but I question whether this is just about me. The fact the caravan has been attacked at all, regardless of whether I live or die, will strike a powerful blow against Blood's prestige."

"Any such blow will be far less convincing if you live." Khar was dry. "Aside from that, I agree. If this had been solely about you, the enemy would have ignored the caravan and concentrated on hunting you."

Myr bowed her head, a Rose gesture that could indicate either acceptance or concession, although right now it mostly felt like exhaustion. "Given we agree that Lady Myrathis's survival is vital," Lord Nimor said, "there's one obvious course we haven't yet discussed."

"Riding hard for Night with Lady Myr and as many armed

fighters as we have mounts?" Khar was dispassionate. "I considered it, returning to the camp, but from what Kelyr said, this country's riddled with 'spawn and their scouting parties. And although he and Orth are experienced 'spawn fighters, they still lost two comrades in their last encounter." His change in tone told Myr there was more he wasn't saying. Something unpleasant, she thought, seeing the others' exchange of looks. "These particular Sword warriors are self-serving, too," he added, dry again. "If Kelyr and Orth had thought they could get clear, they wouldn't have joined the camp. Or stayed, once they learned that the only regular troops we have to defend it are Jad's eight and your marines."

Myr studied her linked palms and wondered if the reason Lord Nimor had raised flight as an option was because he was contemplating it himself. He was of Sea, after all, and owed Blood nothing, let alone fighting for a caravan that had deserted his company. She also understood that everyone currently in the tent would be prepared to abandon the camp in order to preserve her life. But what, Myr asked herself, do I want?

Tyun spoke across her train of thought. "I agree with Khar, sir. Given what we know, particularly about the level of infestation, defending the camp is our best course."

"So we'd best get on with defending it, since I believe we've learned all Lady Myrathis and Faro can tell us about what we're facing." Gently, Khar set Faro aside as he, Jad, and Tyun all prepared to leave.

Myr rose at the same time as Nimor and Murn also stood up. "There is one more matter." Despite a flutter of nervousness, she sounded calm, like a Daughter of Blood should. "With Captain Kolthis and all those in his chain of command gone, my understanding of the Code is that I must appoint a successor." Their collective look of surprise told her they *had* overlooked that. Yet the Code was clear. In a Blood camp and as the only member of the ruling kin present, she must appoint a new captain who would take charge of the remaining guard, or in this case, organize a new one.

Khar ran a hand over his hair, his expression rueful. "You're right, Lady Myrathis. And with an attack likely, and warriors of Orth and Kelyr's stamp in the camp, a chain of command's essential." Tyun and Jad exchanged glances, but nodded, and Nimor bowed, an envoy's flawless salute that acknowledged Myr's right.

As if, she thought wryly, I will do anything but confirm what is patently already the case. Nonetheless, if she did wish to be seen as a Daughter of Blood in truth, then she must play her part. At least she did not have to worry about finding suitable words, but could rely on the Code's formal phrases. Myr drew herself straighter. "Khar of the Storm Spears, I would be greatly honored if you would serve as my Honor Captain as well as my champion, and have those with you"—her gaze went to Jad—"form the core of a new Honor Guard."

The service she offered effectively rescinded her father's exile, so Myr was not surprised when Jad stood to attention—but she was dismayed when Khar remained silent. He had effectively taken command anyway, so his delay played to her misgivings: the possibility that an Honor Captain's service to Blood, as opposed to a champion's personal duty to her alone, might conflict with his oaths as a Storm Spear; or—more bitterly—that Khar, too, considered her unworthy. Doubt held Myr frozen, unable to look away so long as the silence stretched, but she was acutely aware of everyone watching, even the wyr hounds, jewel-eyed from every shadow.

"You honor me," Khar said finally, as the Code demanded, but before Myr could relax he spoke again. "Yet given what's happened with Kolthis, the camp needs to have confidence in its new captain. I entered your Honor Contest, but did not prove myself in the group contests. Arguably, too, Jad and Tyun, or potentially Lord Nimor, have more leadership experience."

Hatha, Myr knew, would pound her fist and say the decision had been made and that Blood warriors, even Storm Spears, did not refuse an Honor Captaincy. But she was not Hatha and the circumstances were irregular. She also thought the points Khar made were reasonable, so looked from Nimor to Jad. "What do you both say?"

Jad, as the other Blood warrior present, spoke first. "Supposedly, Kolthis did prove himself in those group contests. I doubt anyone in the camp will miss that irony. But we've been following Khar since we went into exile, and I'll continue to follow him, as will the rest of my eight."

Nimor looked thoughtful. "A champion in the arena is not the same as a commander in the field, that's very true. So it would be fair for you to inquire, Lady Myrathis, whether Khar has experienced such combat before, or withstood a situation of the sort we face now."

"Have you?" Myr asked Khar.

"I've done both," he replied, "but not commanded during a siege."

Nimor shook his head. "No one here can claim that experience, I believe."

"And from all I've seen during these past weeks," Jad observed, "you more than know your business. That's what counts." He spoke to Myr as much as Kalan, and she nodded.

"In that case, Khar of the Storm Spears, I still wish you to serve as Honor Captain. Do you accept?" Sensing his continued reluctance, Myr spoke with more assurance than she felt and was relieved when he bowed.

"I do, Lady Myrathis. You honor me," he said again, straightening. "Now, by your leave, I had best be about my work."

Myr bowed in reply, but although Khar waited for the formal gesture, she could see his focus was already elsewhere. The three warriors were discussing the measures currently being taken to fortify the camp before the tent flap fell behind them. Faro, together with all but two of the wyr hounds, slipped out in their wake. Tradition might say that the Red Keep wyr pack was bound to the ruling kin, but these hounds seemed far more attached to Khar and his page than to her— which doubtless proved the popular view that they were unreliable.

Or that tradition is wrong, Myr added silently, while the two remaining hounds stretched open their jaws, exactly as if they were laughing at her.

*

The service and duty to Blood inherent in the captaincy, Kalan told himself on quitting the tent, would only endure until Lady Myrathis entered the Keep of Winds and Night assumed responsibility for her safety. So despite his reluctance to accept the position, the likelihood of conflict with his loyalty to Malian was limited. In terms of the prominence the role would give him, the chances were that once they did reach Night—if they did—the furor over Kolthis and the Honor Guard's defection would ensure that a temporary Honor Captain, created in the field, received scant attention.

Kalan shook his head, reflecting on his childhood love for tales of forlorn charges and desperate defenses. Clearly, Ornorith of the Two Faces had been paying attention, since he was now charged with leading exactly such a defense, with nearly a thousand lives depending on his decisions. Still, at least many in the caravan had some garrison experience, which together with their overall numbers should give the camp a fighting chance.

When a wyr hound brushed against him, Kalan turned and saw Faro, dogging his shadow. "I'm your page," the boy said before Kalan could speak.

"Oh, that look!" Jad was grinning. "Hearing his accent, some may doubt Tehan's endorsement, but that look is pure Blood stubborn."

Sometime soon, Kalan thought, I'll have to discover what else Faro's mother taught him, beyond the rules that govern bonds of honor. And find out what he knows of his father. For now, though, it was one of many matters that would have to wait. "All right," he said, because Jad was right about the stubborn look, and so far none of his efforts to keep Faro out of harm's way had worked. "But you stay by me and follow orders. No arguments."

"May I live to see it," Tyun said, very dryly, and although Kalan could not disagree with the sentiment, he chose to ignore it.

44

⊹═══⊹

Listening to the Wind

Kalan spent what little remained of the day inspecting the camp. Jad and Tyun had already set watches and organized the Blood retainers into new companies, with the eight-guard broken up to lead each one. Tyun's marines were to be the reserve, shoring up weak points, since a force of any size would place the entire perimeter under pressure. Jad had also made sure the caravan's food and weapons were inventoried and every available container filled with water, before having the majority of both removed behind the inner defenses.

By the time Kalan reached the perimeter, sand and dirt to counter incendiaries had been stockpiled along the barricades. The wagon canopies had been taken down, both as proof against fire and to prevent enemies concealing themselves inside during an attack, and the area between the inner and outer defenses cleared of tents. The clearance would minimize the chance of fire taking hold and also provide a killing ground if the defenders were forced back to the inner camp. But we *have* to hold the dike, Kalan thought, otherwise the attackers will use its cover to fire on the inner camp with impunity. Once that happens, we'll be done for.

Frowning, he watched Sarr and his team deploy every available stave and metal bar into a sharpened palisade around the base of the earthworks. "I think you're right," he said aloud, "to assume enemy cavalry."

Tyun had left to oversee the first change of the new watches, but Jad nodded. Cavalry engagements might be rare in the Wall's mountainous terrain, but being on the plain changed the game—and removing the threat of opposing cavalry was another reason for the were-hunters to have targeted the camp's herd. "We'll keep our horses for Tyun's reserve and to use for sorties," Jad said. "The palisade will help counter enemy cavalry, and Aiv's teams are cutting thornbrush to barricade between the wagons and along the crest of the dike."

The thornbrush would help, but Kalan knew pikes would be essential to support the palisade. His gaze shifted from the outer defenses to the burned cook wagon, then back again. "Let's prepare what we need to fire the outer wagons if we are forced back."

More assumptions, he thought: that we'll manage a controlled retreat *and* have the conflagration too far underway for the wagons to be pushed against the inner defenses. They would also have to try and find a way to set the fires without sacrificing defenders, because anyone who remained behind would die—very possibly, if taken alive, like those who had ended on the death standards. Yet in view of the camp's size and the defensive preparations, Kalan remained optimistic that they could hold the outer perimeter. Warrior House discipline, he thought, should still counter the level of 'spawn incursion Kelyr had reported.

News of his Honor Captaincy had raced through the camp, so Kalan's inspection also enabled people to see and speak with him. He made a point of approaching any whisperers, huddled in their twos and threes, as well as those who appeared isolated or withdrawn. Nerves were on edge and tension high, but the undercurrent accompanying his progress was that if those elevated as a result of the Honor Contest had turned out to be traitors, then conversely, exile must prove the newcomers' worth. "Besides, they're here," one wagoner muttered, as Kalan and Jad moved on.

Yet treachery to Blood, Kalan reflected, all depended on where the defectors' original loyalty had been pledged. Or whether the honor guards had been ensorcelled or compelled in some way, as Faro's story suggested. Regardless, Kalan knew he could not rely on enemy infiltration being restricted to the Honor Guard. Even the Sword warriors could be facestealers masquerading as survivors, and Orth shooting the were-hunter a ploy to gain trust. Admittedly, once Myr and Faro were safe, the wyr hounds had lost interest in the Sword pair. Orth and Kelyr's obvious shock on learning of the death standards and their comrades' fate was also a point in their favor.

But I can't take anyone at face value, Kalan thought, not after what I learned of facestealers in Emer. He was also conscious that it was the Sword warriors' information about the level of Swarm incursion that had convinced him to dig in and defend the camp. Only time, he supposed, would bear out their veracity and his judgment. Meanwhile, he had emphasized to both the exiles and the Sea marines that the Sword pair were not to be trusted or allowed into the inner camp, ostensibly because of Orth's grudge against Lady Myrathis for having thrown the rock. Which given his disposition, Kalan reflected now, is reason enough.

The first campfires were being lit, and the wind dying as dusk thickened over the plain, although Kalan knew it would pick up again when full night fell. Sarr and those with him had completed their work on the palisade, and Jad was helping Aiv and her team work the last of the thornbrush into place. Six of the wyr hounds were patrolling the perimeter, but a glance back showed three still trailing him, together with a drooping Faro. "Asleep on your feet, I see."

Faro's head jerked up. "I'm awake!" He cast a longing glance toward the nearest campfire as cooking smells wafted cross the camp.

"We'll eat soon," Kalan told him, "once I've reported to Lady Myrathis." He had discussed the merits of a cold camp with Jad and Tyun, but their enemies already knew exactly where they were, and warmth and hot food would help morale. Turning, he saw Orth and

Kelyr sprawled by one of the nearby fires. They were watching him, although they did not move.

Faro followed his gaze. "Do we really need them?" he whispered.

Yes, Kalan thought. Briefly, he debated a conversation on the Code's stricture about succoring fellow Derai in the face of the Swarm, but decided against it. "Just make sure you stay away from them."

"I go where you go," Faro said, with the expression Jad had called pure Blood stubborn, then pointed. "Look! They're putting up your tent." Kalan had been concentrating on perimeter and plain, but now registered the garnet-and-gold panels rising above the inner camp. "I thought the ruling kin were going to burn it," Faro added, then clapped his hands over his mouth. "I'm sorry!"

"Don't be." All the same, Kalan was surprised the tent had not only survived the aftermath of the Honor Contest but turned up here. The mystery was resolved once they reached the inner camp and found Murn tidying away the sailbag he had claimed held Nimor's state robes.

"Which it does," the secretary informed them, grinning. "But Envoy Nimor only brought one set, so there was plenty of room for the tent as well. He said we couldn't let it be burned, and Captain-Lady Hatha vowed that if he beat her at cards, she'd see it found its way to us. The envoy's good at cards," he added, "but we didn't think the Captain-Lady was trying terribly hard to win. Since you're Honor Captain now, Lord Nimor and I thought you needed your own tent." Murn hesitated. "And that it might hearten the camp to see Storm Spear colors."

Faro was certainly beaming. "We should fly the oriflamme, too."

False colors, Kalan thought wryly.

"Are they?" The spark of Yelusin, quiet for so long, caught fire briefly.

"I might have lost it," Kalan said, then relented as Faro's face fell. "No, I have it still. After we've eaten you can help Murn raise it. Although I'm sure fires and hot food will do more to lift spirits," he told the secretary.

Murn shrugged. "According to Blood's fireside tales, it was often the Storm Spears that saw both their House and the Derai through similar defenses. Even we," he added, "remember them on our own memorial."

Kalan sensed the discussion was never going to go his way, so asked after Lady Myrathis instead. "No, don't wake her," he said, when Murn told him she was sleeping. He and Faro ate at the Sea company's fire, and Kalan only waited until the oriflamme was raised as promised before sending Faro to bed as well. "No discussion," he said, thinking the boy looked ready to keel over.

Faro visibly reconsidered argument. "Do I stay with the Sea Keepers?" he mumbled.

"The stealers," Kalan said, to tease him, then regretted it as Faro darted an abashed glance at Murn. The secretary looked startled, a mug paused halfway to his mouth. "No, you can use my tent, now it's up." Somehow, he didn't think he was going to be spending a lot of time there. "You're still my page," he added, to divert Faro's attention, and the boy beamed again.

Full darkness had fallen, and a shrill restless wind was rising when Kalan began another round of the outer defenses, keeping to the shadows thrown by wagons and dike. Two of the wyr hounds accompanied him, blending into the night so thoroughly even he had difficulty seeing them. He paused often, listening to the night sounds out of the Gray Lands, but could detect nothing amiss. The scattering of conversation from the nearby campfires was mixed. Whatever the camp's complement feared was to come, few were discussing it, and the only place Kalan lingered was near the Sword warriors' fire. Several of Sarr's palisade builders were there as well, and one kept peering toward where the oriflamme had risen in the last of the dusk. "I thought the Storm Spears were just fireside tales," he said finally.

Kelyr spoke from just beyond the fire's circle of light. "The story told in Swords is that their order was real enough, until the Earls of Blood exterminated them."

The palisade builders exchanged glances. "I don't know about that," a woman said finally, "but those things that massacred our herd were straight out of a fireside tale."

Orth's laugh grated out. "I always thought that fireside nonsense would bite you Bloodites on the arse one day."

Several of those around the fire muttered darkly, until one of their number chuckled. Kalan saw that it was Sarr, lying full length with his hands behind his head. "Looks like it's biting yours as well," the farrier said, grinning. Kalan heard Kelyr murmur a warning to Orth, who rose and stalked back to their bivouac, halfway between two fires. Kelyr waited a few minutes more before leaving, too, and Kalan ghosted after him, using a touch of concealing power to aid the darkness.

"The bastard was right," Kelyr told Orth. "We could all be caught like rats in a trap. But don't go killing him for saying so until we know this is over. Or Khar either."

Orth muttered a curse, and Kelyr began tossing a handful of knucklebones. "You know what's the biggest fireside tale in all this?" He snatched the knucklebones neatly out of the air. "It's the notion Blood's Bride could be half of the Rose, when the Rose never marries outside its own. Lovers maybe, but marriage . . . " Kelyr threw the knucklebones again. "If you ask me, someone's pulling a ruse on Night. Either that or they've already pulled one on Blood. Nine knows, the Bloodites seem gullible enough."

Orth spat. "Who cares? Like you keep saying, staying alive is what matters." Kelyr shrugged and continued playing with the knucklebones. If there was any comfort to be derived from their conversation, Kalan decided, moving on, it was that the pair made unlikely faces-tealers. As for Lady Myr's heritage, the straightforward explanation was that the rare or unusual was not the same as the impossible. Yet the more Kalan thought about alignments within the Nine Houses, the more he felt Kelyr was right. In terms of formal alliance, the Rose had stood aloof throughout Derai history, an apartness that had become isolation following the Great Betrayal. Traditionally, they were also the Derai's peacemakers and treaty brokers, as well as lovers of poetry and the arts, so Blood was hardly the obvious choice for a marriage outside their own ranks.

It would be interesting, Kalan thought, to know which House initiated the marriage and why the other then agreed to the alliance. Blood and Rose territories did not adjoin, and as far as he knew, Earl Sardon and Lady Mayaraní's marriage had not been a love match— which all added up to Lady Myrathis being as much an anomaly, lineage-wise, as her nature had made her growing up in Blood. Yet with Lady Mayaraní dying so soon after the marriage, any specula-tion caused by the alliance would have been forgotten, in the same way Myr had been overlooked.

Not everything that happens has meaning, Kalan told himself. Only this was a marriage between two Derai Houses, and such arrangements were always about advantage within the Alliance. First Blood and the Rose, he reflected, and now Night, as though someone is weaving new alignments: could that have been what Ise's dying caution meant? But rather than the old woman's fading whisper, he heard the drum of Grayharbor rain and Che'Ryl-g-Raham's murmur against his ear: *"I like puzzles."*

Briefly, Kalan held still, before shaking off both memory and speculation and joining Rhanar, who was captaining the current watch with a wagoner called Nai as his second. She was one of those with guard training who had been invalided out, in her case with a withered leg, a legacy of the plague years before Kalan was born. He suspected Rhanar had selected her as much for a similarly taciturn disposition as competence, since neither had much to say, beyond Rhanar's observation that the six wyr hounds were maintaining their perimeter patrol.

Nai pursed her lips. "They're different," she said. She bit off the second word as if she had already said too much, but Kalan guessed she was referring to the hounds' reputation for instability.

"Don't rely on them," he cautioned. "Even wyrs may not recognize these enemies."

"I'd prefer higher ramparts," Rhanar muttered.

Kalan nodded, because even with the dike's thornbrush crown the camp still felt horribly exposed compared to a keep or hold's walls. They were all silent, listening to the wind and watching the darkness, and Kalan wished he did not remember a similar sly, prying wind from his flight across the Gray Lands six years before. But he could not shake the recollection, or the certainty that a Swarm attack would use magic. Exactly as they did this morning, and in the Old Keep, as well as in Jaransor and Emer, he thought: they must laugh, seeing how we've hamstrung our ability to fight on equal terms.

He, though, was not hamstrung—and a shield spell constructed around the earthworks and palisade would protect the defenders from magical assault, including psychic attacks aimed at sapping the defenders' will to resist. It would also, Kalan thought, prevent the Swarm from scrying out the defense. Six years ago he had watched the herald, Jehane Mor, use a wall of air to fend off a Night Mare. Recalling her working now, he could see how it might provide a natural extension to a more regular shield spell. Kalan did not think such a working would last long against a major Swarm demon, but an infestation of lower-level 'spawn, even in unprecedented numbers, might be deterred by the unexpected magic use.

Anything that buys us time, he thought, and if larger scale magic's thrown at the camp as a result, it might alert the Houses that retain pretensions to power use. "I'm going out to take a look around," he told Rhanar and Nai. "See if I can detect anything more from beyond the perimeter." He knew Rhanar's frown was because the guard thought an Honor Captain should not put himself at risk, but where Jad would have spoken up, Rhanar remained silent. Kalan glanced around as the wyr hounds with him emerged from the darkness. "I won't be alone," he said, indicating their presence. "I won't go far either." He paused. "If I return without the hounds, don't let me into the camp before you have the other wyrs clear me. The same goes for anyone else wanting in, even if you believe you know them."

Rhanar's habitual dourness deepened, and Nai was frowning.

"That's fireside tale stuff," she said, then added slowly, "but you believe it."

Kalan nodded. "I do." This time Rhanar grimaced before shifting the barrier so Kalan and the wyr hounds could pass through. Despite shielding himself, Kalan still tensed as he moved beyond the protective earthworks. He continued a short distance into the plain, but aside from a rat-fox's bark, the night remained as empty as it had appeared from the camp. Any scouts, he decided, after listening and watching for some time, must be keeping their distance. Returning to a point clear of any sentry posts, he slipped between Sarr's stakes and placed his right hand against the rammed earth of the dike.

In Emer, the Oakward had taught him to listen to the magic that permeated Haarth. Yet even before Emer, as a novice in Night's Temple quarter, Kalan had been adept at assuming the likeness of stone and earth. Now he took a deep breath and stood motionless, building layers of shield and ward, first about himself and then around the camp. He infused the working with the fabric of the surrounding world: the dust and grit of the plain, the low shrill of the wind, and the incandescent glow of the hounds' eyes as they materialized out of the night.

The spark of Yelusin's power, which Kalan had carried since the *Che'Ryl-g-Raham*, flowered in answer, weaving through the new shield in the same way the remnant Fire had added her protection to his Red Keep wards. For a moment the wyr hounds' eyes were phosphorescence on a night sea, and Kalan smelled the ocean's tang. He let his awareness sink beneath it, deep into the fabric of the Gray Lands and adjoining foothills. Beyond both, the Wall's barrier rose, layer on layer, its roots of stone sunk deep into Haarth's alien ground. Yet the more Kalan extended his own shield spell, the more clearly he perceived places where the Wall's layered magic had grown thin.

Kalan sank deeper again, until he could detect Jaransor, lulled back into sleep on the far side of the plain but still grumbling with anger in its dreams. Winter, too, encroached on the periphery of his awareness, advancing inexorably on the world—and now his bones were rock and his flesh earth, the ebb and flow of his breath night itself. When he moved, Kalan felt as though he were grinding his way back to the surface of the plain. At midsummer, he had pulled power out of the earth to strengthen Audin when Orth seemed likely to kill his friend in the Caer Argent sword ring. Now he did the same thing on a vaster scale, placing both palms against the dike and pulling raw power out of the ground, channeling it first into the earthworks and palisade, then into his protective shield, before wrapping a rampart of air around both.

"*Stone,*" Kalan commanded, binding rock's essence into his working. And then: "*Earth,*" bolstering the foundations of the dike before drawing Haarth's power upward into an invisible shield wall. "*Air,*" he charged silently, and finally: "*Darkness.*" The concluding invocation transformed the shield into both fortification and psychic barricade, one that would simultaneously trick the eye and shield those within from magical assault. Slowly, because he, too, was encased in the working's essence of earth and stone, Kalan paced the circumference of the camp, locking the protective spell in place. The wyr hounds accompanied him, one always pressing close while the other maintained a wider orbit.

Kalan was over halfway around before he realized someone was reinforcing his working from within the camp. The power use was both deft and unobtrusive, but he dared not let his concentration waver in order to pursue its source. By the time his circumnavigation was complete, he had to lean against the earthworks while he tied the spell off, binding it into the physical structure of the dike. So long as the embankment endured, the shield should hold, even if he died.

I've done all I can, he thought, feeling exhaustion settle deep into sinew and bone. Now all I can do is wait and see.

45

✛═✛

Breakout

On the other side of the barricade the camp remained undisturbed, although Kalan heard Nai ask Rhanar whether he had been gone too long. "It's all right," he called softly, "I'm right here." Each word felt like a pebble, roughening his voice, and he trudged rather than walked back to the sentry post. Nai exhaled in relief when she saw the wyr hounds, and Rhanar worked the barricade apart to let Kalan and the hounds back through.

"Anything out there?" he asked.

"Not yet." The fires had burned low and most of those who weren't on watch were asleep, but Kalan saw that Orth was on his feet, glowering toward the inner camp. When Kalan followed his gaze, he saw a dark outline that he recognized as Nimor, leaning on his tall staff as he had only that morning, by the bridge.

"What put a thorn beneath his saddle?" Rhanar picked up the crossbow he had set aside to deal with the barricade, but he was watching Orth, not Nimor.

Kalan's night sight was keen enough to see the shadow of a second figure, also carrying a tall staff, standing behind Nimor. His body might feel more like slurry than rock, and his mind ache for sleep, but he guessed his day was not over yet. "Keep an eye on Orth," he told

Rhanar. His own focus remained on Nimor, although he caught the swing of Orth's head, tracking his progress toward the inner camp. Yet despite obvious suspicion, the giant stayed where he was—possibly because he had taken note of Rhanar's crossbow.

When Nimor stepped aside to let Kalan enter the inner camp, he saw the second staff-bearer was Murn. Once concealed from Orth's sight, he stopped and regarded them both. He had been suspicious before, but certainty still shocked him out of his exhaustion. "Khar of the Storm Spears," Nimor said, and indicated his tent. "May we talk?"

I think we should, Kalan thought, and nodded, following them toward the entrance. Yelme and Ler: reflexively, he recalled the names of the marines on guard as they allowed the wyr pair through with him. Once everyone was seated, the hounds settled at Kalan's feet. "I take it I must thank you for the help with the shield wall." He paused as the envoy and his secretary bowed. "You remind me of Laer, Lord Nimor, which makes me think you must both be weather-workers. Although he would never meet anyone's eyes, yet you do?"

Nimor nodded. "Weatherworking is our primary ability, but there are degrees of power, as I believe you know. Those who sail with our ships or safeguard the keep are the strongest of our order, but their power is frequently as chaotic as the forces they wrestle. That is why they never look at others directly, to avoid drawing them beneath their sway."

"You must be able to shield as well," Kalan said slowly. Not just to have helped me now, he thought, but to enter the Red Keep as you did.

"Most weatherworkers can, to some degree," Nimor replied, "although Murn's and my talent is insignificant besides yours."

"The rampart of air on top of the shieldwall is amazing." Momentarily, Murn's grin banished his impassivity. "I'd love to learn how you do that."

Despite his weariness, Kalan grinned back. "I'll show you, if we get out of this." Sobering, he shrugged. "Since you now know about me."

"I always knew," Nimor said quietly. "The ships told those they knew could be relied upon, and whom they thought needed to know." The envoy rose and bowed, a deeply formal gesture. "I am Sea's witness to the marriage between Blood and Night. The other part of my mission is to escort you." Because I'm carrying a spark of Yelusin, Kalan thought, as Nimor smiled. "Although having seen you construct your shield wall, I suspect it's more a case of your escorting us." His envoy's gravity returned as he resumed his seat. "Most weatherworkers have some farspeaking ability, too, and all Sea envoys have at least one farspeaker in their party. Murn is mine, and Namath, whom I sent with Ensign Taly, can manage a limited mindcall."

A marine can mindcall? Kalan thought, staring.

Murn coughed. "Most in Sea have power, however minimal. And we never swore the Blood Oath." The secretary sounded almost apologetic. "That fact's not a secret, it's just that no one ever asks, or hasn't for a very long time. Knowing how attitudes run, we don't volunteer the information either."

Especially, Kalan thought dryly, when it plays to your advantage. "You're a farspeaker?" he asked, before frowning at Nimor. "But you still let me send Taly and Namath out there?" The moment Kalan had spoken the words he stopped, inwardly cursing his tiredness. "Because you've already tried to farspeak, but failed," he said heavily. "Is that it?"

"Yes," Nimor confirmed quietly. "No-man's-land or not, Murn should be able to reach through to Adamant from here. He tried to do so while we waited outside the camp."

"But the camp's being blocked," Murn said. "The farspeaking fragmented into dissonance within a very short distance of the camp, no matter what I attempted, trying to push through the barrier."

Warded out—or in, Kalan thought grimly, which fits with the death standards and the were-hunters. "Would you have told me if I hadn't shielded the camp?" he asked, then shook his head. "Not that it alters our situation in any practical way."

"It doesn't," Nimor agreed, "but the fact you built your wall confirms that you, too, believe we're facing a large-scale Swarm incursion, one we'll need to work together to counter."

Meaning, Kalan thought, as their eyes held, that the only hope for the camp's survival may be to fight power with power. "Including sharing information," he said pointedly, then spoiled the effect by smothering a yawn.

Nimor inclined his head. "I agree. But there is one other matter, by your leave. Murn says you referred to us as stealers."

"Stealers?" Kalan glanced at Murn, caught between embarrassment and impatience. "I apologize if I gave offense."

"I wasn't offended," the secretary said quickly. "But I wondered if that is how the Storm Spears commonly speak of us?"

"Nine, no! It was a joke, that's all, because when I first met Faro that's how he referred to you." Kalan's impatience and weariness won out over diplomacy. "He didn't want me going anywhere near your ships. His mother, apparently, had warned him against you."

"Using that term?" Nimor was openly surprised.

"So he said. Does it matter?"

"It's just . . . unexpected," Murn told him, "since to the best of our knowledge the epithet died out hundreds of years ago. I know some families hold onto old customs, but even for Derai that's a long time when an expression's fallen out of use."

"I'm still trying to understand why it matters," Kalan said.

Murn grimaced. "Let's say it's a history we hoped we'd put behind us. After the Great Betrayal and the loss of the Golden Fire, we were desperate to protect our fleet. So much in the keeps and holds had depended on the Fire, and with it gone keeping the sea routes open was vital."

"For our survival," Kalan said, remembering his conversation with the *Che'Ryl-g-Raham*.

Murn nodded. "The ships were essential to supply the food, medicine, and other resources the Nine Houses so desperately required. To keep the ships sailing, Sea direly needed weatherworkers, farseers, shielders like yourself ..." He spread his hands, his expression unhappy.

"So you stole those with the powers you lacked." Despite his tiredness, Kalan could understand why the Sea House might want the history forgotten. "They call it pressing in the South, or slavery, depending on the circumstances. Practices," he added coolly, "that've been outlawed throughout the Southern Realms, with the possible exception of Lathayra."

Murn's unhappiness had grown more pronounced. "It's not a history we take pride in."

I imagine not, Kalan thought, before curiosity got the better of him. "What made you stop?" Deep in his mind, Yelusin's spark stirred.

"We believe it was part of what woke the ships to consciousness, a half century after the Betrayal. They roused as one and told us they could not endure such pollution on their decks. No vessel would leave port again until we swore, from the Sea Count to the most junior mariner, that the practice ended then and there."

"Many in Sea had opposed it bitterly in any case," Nimor said, "but were overruled by those who argued necessity. The other Houses," he added dryly, "also knew what we were doing, as the term 'stealers' indicates."

It was not, Kalan reflected, an activity that would pass unnoticed for long. The Oath would have been taking firm hold by that time, so he guessed it was mainly Stars and the priestly Houses that had borne the brunt of the stealing, which might explain Sea's subsequent political realignment closer to the warrior Houses. He could also see Nimor and Murn's point: for the term "stealers" and the fear that went with it to persist four hundred-odd years after the practice had ended *was* strange. "I agree Faro's use of the term is unusual," he said. "But under the circumstances, any mystery will have to wait."

"Our current circumstances," Nimor replied quietly, "are exactly why anomalies must be questioned."

They fear facestealers, Kalan realized, or some other Swarm

infiltrator—if a small one, in Faro's case. "The *Che'Ryl-g-Raham* allowed Faro to stow away," he pointed out. "That suggests any anomaly is unlikely to be a danger."

"It would not be the first time a ship, or the fleet collectively, has taken a greater risk for themselves, our House, and the Derai Alliance, than the rest of Sea feels comfortable with. Not least," Nimor observed, his dryness increasing, "because they love contests of wit and skill almost as much as they love mysteries."

"I like puzzles . . . " The memory of Che'Ryl-g-Raham's whisper almost made Kalan smile, except that might have insulted the envoy's gravity. "The Sea House was prepared to let me take responsibility for Faro before. Has that changed?"

"No." Nimor's look was level. "For now, we consider it sufficient to have drawn the matter to your attention."

For now, Kalan thought, and rose to his feet. "I thank you for the warning," he said formally, as Nimor and Murn stood, too, bowing in farewell. He passed Kion on the way out, and was aware of the physician's gaze, following him. I must look like I feel, Kalan supposed, as he crossed to the garnet-and-gold tent. One of the wyr hounds whined, pressing close, and he touched its head with one hand while opening the tent with the other. Night vision or not, he almost stepped on Faro, sleeping across the entrance. Guarding it, no doubt, since cots had been set up. The boy did not stir when Kalan stepped around him, although the wyr hound at his back opened a silver eye.

Whatever this business about stealers meant, it clearly didn't trouble the wyrs any more than it had the *Che'Ryl-g-Raham*. Although your character judgment, Kalan told Faro's hound silently, may be as flawed as your ability—or willingness—to identify Sea House power users. The beast gazed back at him, enigmatic, while Faro shifted, muttering something unintelligible. Derai flotsam, Kalan thought, cast adrift on Haarth's currents and now washed home again. Much the same, he realized, lying down, could be said of himself.

He dismissed the thought, but the day's events and details of the camp's defense crowded into its place. When he did sleep, Kelyr's voice pursued him: *"... the Rose never marries outside its own."* Opening his eyes, Kalan found himself standing on a dream plain, where the wind blew grit into his face and dispelled Kelyr's voice. When the grit dispersed, he was facing the cairn from his shared vision with Malian, during their brief sojourn at Tenneward Lodge. Malian had thought the cairn was Rowan Birchmoon's grave, but now the opening was darkness and the Huntmaster's crow gazed at Kalan from the lintel.

"There is always a price." The bird's soft rasp was half a caw. *"Who will pay it this time?"* The eye that met his was dark and searching. *"Who will pay?"* the crow asked again, taking flight and circling his head. *"Will you?"*

Aiv woke Kalan out of a dream in which the wind fretted along the edge of his shield-wall, scrying for entry. Behind it, he detected surreptitious movement in the darkness—and was on his feet before his eyes fully opened, feeling as though he had just crawled out from beneath a rockfall. The wyr hound with Faro was already standing, and the boy jerked upright as Kalan moved. "Are we attacked?" he demanded, staggering to pick up Kalan's helmet and shield.

"No," Kalan and Aiv answered together, the groom still outside the tent but holding the flap open. "Every horn in the camp would be blowing," Kalan added, and saw Aiv nod. She was Palla's watch second, which told him it must be shortly before dawn.

"We can't pinpoint anything," she said, as he armed himself. "But the wyrs won't settle, and those Sword warriors insist there's 'spawn about."

They're useful for something, then, Kalan thought, buckling on Asantir's swords. "I'll meet you at the inner barrier," he told Aiv, then knelt so his eyes met Faro's. "I want you to guard Lady Myrathis for me. Listen," he said, when the boy started to demur. "Now that I'm Honor Captain, I can't defend the camp and guard her at the same time. Not the way a champion should, so I need you to watch over her instead."

"Because I'm your page?" Faro's expression suggested he was reevaluating that honor.

"Yes," Kalan said, "and because you've saved her, and yourself, once already. If events go badly, I'm trusting you to do all you can to get her clear."

"But—" Faro objected, as Kalan relieved him of the helmet and shield.

"Everyone has their orders, Faro. I expect you to follow yours." Ignoring the boy's face of protest, he donned the helmet and slung the shield across his back before striding from the tent.

The two wyr hounds guarding Lady Myr's tent lifted their heads as he passed, and one of Nimor's sentries alerted someone inside the Sea pavilion. Otherwise the rest of the camp was asleep as Kalan and Aiv headed for the earthworks. Except Orth and Kelyr, Kalan amended, seeing them by Palla's command post. Both Sword warriors looked around, but for once Orth failed to glower before returning his attention to the plain. The two hounds with Kalan joined the six along the perimeter, their growling a low, constant reverberation. The night insects had fallen silent, and the wind had died away. Behind Kalan, Madder stamped and tossed his head, rousing the other mounts. Several whinnied, but no horse replied out of the Gray Lands.

It's too quiet, Kalan thought. "Rouse Jad and Tyun," he told Aiv. "Tell them to stand the camp to arms, but quietly: no alarm sounded and no lights. Let's keep whoever's out there guessing." He looked toward Kelyr and Orth, who had been put under Jad's command. "Time to join your company. I want everyone in their appointed place." Kalan turned back to the plain, but although he saw Kelyr's shrug from the corner of his eye, both Sword warriors obeyed the order.

"They could still be trouble," Palla muttered.

"Only if there's not enough fighting to keep them occupied," Kalan replied. Palla grinned, although without much mirth, and remained silent as the camp stirred to life and defenders mustered along the perimeter. The caravan did not contain enough bows for everyone in it, but each company could muster a double row of archers, with pikes and spears drawn up behind. The remainder of each unit carried a mix of swords, axes, and staffs. Those in support—who would resupply the fighters and drag clear the wounded, run messages, and fight fires—had at least a dagger for their defense. The latter teams comprised those too old or physically compromised to fight effectively, together with the camp's youngest: the scullions and horsegirls and errand runners, most of whom were little older than Faro.

Young or old, veteran or inexperienced, the tension in the camp stretched tight as Kalan dispatched runners to each of the newly formed companies, reiterating his orders to maintain silence, hold position, and only fire on his command. He still heard the stir of bodies and occasional mutter, but the unnatural silence continued as the night crept toward dawn—until a long line of were-hunters loped out of the Gray Lands' dark.

One moment the night was still, the next the plain was filled with advancing shadows and flaming eyes. The extent of the line told Kalan the attack must comprise multiple were-hunts: as many, if not more than had besieged the hill fort in northern Emer. He could also perceive the magical shimmer that would shatter spears and deflect arrows, exactly as those who experienced yesterday's attack had described. At the battle of The Leas, he and the other Oakwarders present had used a dispersal spell to counter the effect. Now, Kalan intended relying on his shield-wall to counteract the were-hunters protective magic once they reached it, enabling the defenders to fire into their ranks at point-blank range.

"Hold your fire!" he roared as an arrow flew, followed by a ragged volley that either fell short or disintegrated. "Wait for my order!" He could hear Nhal cursing the panicked archers, because the camp could not afford to waste arrows, and because Kalan was relying on the exiled honor guards to hold their companies in check. And on my shield-wall working, he reflected grimly, acknowledging the risk in allowing the attackers to get so close. The camp had not contained sufficient stakes for a closed palisade, so Sarr had spaced what they had for a cavalry attack—which meant the were-hunters could slip between them and onto the dike. Yet given the attackers' numbers, every arrow should hit home at such close range. And if Kalan's shield-wall worked, both rows of archers should be able to loose volleys before the were-hunters abandoned their magic for a purely physical assault. After that, it would all depend on the damage done by the volleys ...

Life is a risk, Kalan thought, and so—watching the were-hunters pick up speed—is death. "Hold until they reach the stakes!" His voice would carry to the attackers as well, but he doubted they could hear anything beyond the rush of their own momentum. "Then fire at will."

He could smell the fear rolling off the defenders, and someone nearby was praying to Mhaelanar, the Defender—although once the god's name had been uttered, the invocation seemed to be mainly *"please, please, please."* Which could mean anything, Kalan knew, from please don't let me fail, to please let me live. He noted, too, that it was Mhaelanar the prayer called on, rather than Kharalth with her fistful of skulls. A sideways glance showed him Darrar, one of Sarr's assistants. From what Kalan could see, the young farrier's face was as white as his grip on his bow. Beside him, Baris was equally pale, and while Aiv appeared composed, a muscle beside her mouth was spasming.

"Hold," Kalan commanded again. And all along the perimeter the defenders did, although the were-hunters were terrifying at close range. It was not just their numbers, but their size and speed, together with the bestial heads and savage maws. Their eyes flamed vermilion, carnelian, and orange, answering the wyr hounds' silver glow. Their expressions, to the extent Kalan could read them, suggested they expected to leap both stakes and dike, rolling over the defense like an incoming tide. Now their wavefront was just three strides away from Sarr's stakes, then two, then—

"Loose!" Kalan yelled. Several hundred bowstrings twanged,

releasing a deadly thicket of arrows, and the defenders shouted, as much from the release of tension as triumph when the volley found targets. Everywhere, were-hunters went down, some crumpling in midleap and falling back onto the stakes below, while others collapsed at the foot of the palisade. Some of the wounded pulled themselves clear, or else regained their feet and came on—with many going down again as the second rank of archers loosed their volley.

Despite the holes in their line, the were-hunter vanguard continued to press forward, while a second wave of attackers rolled in behind them. The camp's archers fell back as the pikemen advanced to defend the thornbrush rampart and the dike became a welter of leaping, snarling were-hunters, thrusting pikes, and screamed war cries. Kalan, who had withdrawn with the other archers, now drew the black blades and led the hand-to-hand fighters forward to cover the pikemen—although if the black blades sang, the sound was lost beneath the furor.

A were-hunter crashed through the thorns in front of him, and a wyr hound sprang to meet it as a second attacker sailed over the top. Kalan thrust the longsword into his assailant's chest, driving the short blade through the open maw of the beast that followed. Then Palla was there, her shield covering them both as the combat swayed back and forth, across and through the thornbrush barricade. The camp's line was holding, Kalan thought, as Palla cut down another were-hunter—and then as swiftly as battle had been joined the assault was over. The attackers broke off and retreated into the thinning dark, stopping only to pick up their wounded. The dead were left where they had fallen.

Dawn was imminent. Kalan could sense it as soon as his vision cleared and he recovered his breath. Despite having dead and wounded of their own to deal with, he forbade torches, which would aid archers outside the camp. A swift survey showed their losses were far less than he had feared and that none of the exiles had fallen, although scything claws had torn mail to rake Nhal's arm. The wounded were already being ferried to the Bride's pavilion, now the camp's infirmary, and Jad had squads checking underneath and within the wagonbeds for stragglers. One of the wyr hounds had a gash in its shoulder, while another's ear had been torn off, but otherwise they, too, had survived the encounter.

"Do we stand down?" Aiv asked.

"No." The attack might have failed, but Kalan doubted the assault was over. "We'll take what's left of the darkness to recover arrows and use the dead, theirs and ours, to reinforce the barricade." In the Emerian hill fort, wary of decomposition and disease, the Normarchers had dug a pit for the dead—but that fort had walls and a gate they could blockade. Later, on the way to Caer Argent, Ser Raven had discussed other assaults he had experienced, including one in Lathayra where a corral, with dead bodies used as sandbags, was the only perimeter.

Darrar, still white faced, looked shocked, while Baris swore beneath his breath before Palla ordered them both into a detail. The marines, whose reserve force had not been needed, provided cover for the defenders sent to retrieve arrows, while Jad's company ensured the fallen were-hunters were dead. Kalan was unsurprised to see Orth in the forefront, slicing ears from every corpse before Jad stopped him. "There's no time for that," the Blood guard said. Orth scowled, but accepted Jad's authority, and Kalan returned his attention to subtly shielding those outside his shield-wall. The camp's desperate activity, together with the defenders' relief at surviving the attack, helped mask the power use, and by the time everyone was back within the dike the world had grown gray.

The cooks began preparing a cold breakfast, which their assistants brought to each company in turn as the dawn wind riffled in off the Gray Lands. Someone among the enemy was using it to scry: Kalan could feel the seeker probing for weakness along his barrier. When the light brightened, he saw that yesterday's haze had thickened overnight, and he resisted the temptation to extend his psychic shield further out, just to see what brushed against its edge. The scrying, together with the wyr hounds' behavior, had already told him enough.

The hounds were intent on the plain, as though they could detect whatever the haze concealed, which perhaps they could. Yet even Kalan's keen sight showed him nothing, except on the stream side of the camp. There, the air wavered like heat haze in an Emerian summer, reminding him that a great deal of Swarm magic could not cross running water . . .

"Haze's clearing," Palla said, as the first pale sunlight broke through. Kalan nodded, concentrating on a shadowy outline that looked like banners stirring beyond the murk. A few seconds later the haze thinned further. "Nine preserve us!" Palla whispered, as a deep mutter of fear and dismay ran among the defenders.

They may have to, Kalan thought bleakly, remembering his dream of surreptitious movement in the night. The enemy must have used concealing magic, because what encircled the camp now was not a raiding party, or even a war band, but a legion, and there was no other way they could have gotten this close without being detected. Kalan scanned their ranks, registering massed pikes and archers, cavalry with the jagged helms he remembered from Jaransor, and a whole wing of were-hunters. But no major demons, as far as he could detect, and no sign of siege engines. He would take what comfort he could from that.

The camp had fallen silent, stunned perhaps, or despairing. Both were reasonable reactions, Kalan thought, given the size of the opposing force. He and Malian had known the Wall of Night was failing: the attack on the Keep of Winds six years before, the subsequent pursuit into Jaransor, and the Swarm's fomenting of unrest from Ij to Ishnapur had told them that. Yet incursion at this level made those events pale by comparison.

Because this, Kalan told himself grimly—a Darksworn legion in the Gray Lands, apparently undetected until now—means that somewhere the Wall has failed completely. This is breakout.

46

Line of Fire

Kalan's initial reaction was that Malian must be told, but he clamped down on his instinct to hurl a mindcall as far across distance as he could reach. Regardless of either the sensibilities of the camp, or the psychic divide between the Wall and Haarth, keeping the enemy guessing meant being circumspect with his use of power for as long as possible. "What's this?" Palla muttered, as the opposing ranks parted and a troop of mixed horse and foot, around one hundred strong, advanced into the place of honor and danger at the center of the enemy line. A collective hiss rose from the camp as the defenders recognized the armor of the caravan's Honor Guard—and deepened from groan to curse as the wind opened out the newcomers' pennant, revealing Kolthis's personal device.

"Treachery," Palla whispered, and Kalan heard the word repeated, the sound a wind through fallen leaves, as the exile turned her head aside and spat. "Kolthis," she said, as though the name itself were bile. "I always thought he was no plagues-rotted good."

"*Is* it the Honor Guard?" Darrar asked. "I mean, their visors are down so it could be anyone ..." His voice trailed off, but Kalan knew he and many others would be remembering the patrols that had never returned, even before the final disappearance of the remaining guards. We're looking at around half the original guard, he thought, and guessed those who could not be suborned would have paid the same price as Rhisart. Darrar was right, though. They could not be sure who was really behind those Blood visors, whether facestealers, turncoats, or—remembering his thoughts about possession—something altogether other.

"The traitors show their contempt for us and for Blood." Sarr spoke from his place in Jad's company, and although he was not shouting, his voice had the depth to carry along the earthworks. "Just as Kolthis did on the road here, because we're farriers and grooms, cooks and drivers, not keep garrison or Honor Guard. Now he thinks he'll sap our will with Blood armor and his traitor's banner, so we'll lie down and die before the fight is joined. But I say we show them the meaning of honor and what it means to be Blood. I say we make this a fight!"

"We fight!" those around him shouted. "For Blood!" First Palla's company on one side, then Rhanar's on the other joined in, until finally all the defenders were stamping their feet and clashing weapons against shields as they chanted: "Blood! Blood! Blood!"

Well done, Kalan thought, raising a hand to acknowledge Sarr as the Darksworn war horns sounded, followed by a long rumble of drums. He only hoped, as the enemy advance rolled forward, that the defenders' resolution would withstand the coming assault. The steady tramp of the foot soldiers shook the ground, kicking up veiling dust, but the were-hunters were advancing ahead of both. Their magic shimmered across the length of the attacking line, and Kalan knew he could not wait this time before letting his archers shoot. With the numbers they were facing, and lacking the element of surprise, the camp would be overwhelmed if he did.

"We'll have to shoot high and drop our arrows into the ranks behind the were-hunters," he told Palla. He glanced back to where Nimor and Murn stood with Tyun and the reserve, carrying their tall staffs and watching him as much as the enemy. Kalan hoped they could follow his lead, as they had with the shield-wall, when he initiated the Oakward's dispersal spell. Nimor inclined his head, an indication they were prepared to try. With luck, too, the enemy would not recognize the working, which might delay a counterspell. "We'll shoot as soon as they're in range."

Kalan dispatched runners with the order, and assessed the enemy advance again. The Darksworn cavalry had massed behind the foot soldiers, but he doubted they would charge until either enough of Sarr's stakes were down for riders to force a way through, or they could take advantage of the ground fighting to dispose of the palisade altogether. To hold the cavalry back and prevent that happening, the camp's archers would have to continue firing after battle along the dike was joined.

They had discussed all this, he and Jad and Tyun first, and then with the company commanders and their seconds, but not in the context of an attack of this magnitude. Now, the sheer weight of the force rolling toward them made all planning seem futile. The advance was right on longbow range now, the enemy archers preparing to fire. "'Ware, arrows!" Kalan shouted, a split second before the first volley arrived. The defenders yelled, ducking under cover or raising shields, and several voices cried out sharply. Kalan nodded to Palla, who lifted her horn and blew the exiles' own signal to loose arrows.

Bowstrings sang, and Kalan linked his psychic sense to the arrows' flight. The weatherworkers' power came in smoothly, supporting his as he wove the Oakward's dispersal spell, and the defenders' volley arched high over the were-hunters and down into the following ranks. Darksworn warriors fell, and in places their line grew ragged, but recovered swiftly. For a few furious minutes the flights of arrows crossed each other, but the Darksworn attack continued rolling forward. Kalan fired one last arrow as the were-hunters reached his shield barrier, but although their magic dissipated as it had before, their claws and jaws were also weapons. Behind them, the pike and crossbow companies came steadily on.

"Keep the archers firing," Kalan told Aiv, as their own pikemen engaged. Then he and Palla were running forward, and the morning blurred into hewing and hacking, blade against blade and muscle straining against muscle. When the weight of the heavily armored Darksworn infantry crashed into the defenders' line, the fighting along the earthworks wavered back, but the exiles rallied their companies and the defense steadied. At one point the enemy roared and pushed into a widening gap, before Tyun and the reserve reached them and the breach closed. All the same, Kalan thought—in a brief, clear moment when a pike spitted the assailant immediately in front of him—we'll be hard-pushed too hold. His archers were still firing, keeping the cavalry back, but the defenders' line was stretched and the opposing force kept pressing the attack.

Gritting his teeth, Kalan drove forward again, and this time he heard the black swords hum as he decapitated a were-hunter in midleap. The wyr hounds belled, leaping forward beside him, and Palla was shouting out a battle song that echoed the black blades' refrain. Others took it up, and the chant spread from company to company until the dike reverberated with its fierce rhythm. The defenders' line inched forward—and then, however impossibly, the attackers were falling back.

The retreat was a withdrawal in good order, not a rout. Yet why fall back at all? Kalan asked himself, as the Darksworn's covering fire eased and his own archers lowered their bows. The enemy had taken losses, but not nearly so many as the defenders. Another few minutes even, Kalan thought, and they might have had us. He shook his head, puzzlement still hovering as the roar of blood and breath began to ease, but he made himself focus on the damage taken by the camp. The wounded and dying were strewn the length of the perimeter, their cries replacing the clangor of battle. Further along the barricade, where the reserve had last seen action, a horse was screaming, but even as Kalan turned that way the sound abruptly cut off.

Someone must have put the animal down. Kalan, watching the orderlies and support teams labor to lift the wounded clear, knew the mercy stroke would be all that could be done for the worst injured. There were so many more dead this time, so many faces he could not name as he moved from company to company, even where the bodies had not been savaged by were-hunters. And too many of the fallen were the errand runners and scullions and horsegirls, their half-grown bodies smaller still in death. Among those Kalan knew, Tyun was down, wounded in the reserve action, while three of his marines, together with several more horses, were dead. Jaras was also dead, as were two of the wyr hounds: one pierced by a pike, the other torn apart by were-hunters.

"It was the strangest thing," Aarion told Kalan. Both wyr hounds had fallen in his quadrant of the dike, where the were-hunter attack had been particularly fierce. "When they fell, a light rose out of their bodies and went into the nearest living hound." He shook his head, wonder momentarily banishing grimness. "None of us have ever seen or heard of anything like it."

"And the traitors?" Dain asked, joining them. He indicated the bodies in Honor Guard armor that had fallen along the dike. "We should see if they're really our own."

Yet when Kalan checked, every face was known to him from the Honor Contest. So at least I know they're not face-stealers, he thought, straightening from his scrutiny of the last dead face.

"I thought we were dogmeat when they came against us here," Aarion said, "despite Sarr's fine speech. My ragged company against Honor Guards." He shook his head, unease coloring his tone. "But as soon as they reached the dike they fell to pieces, like puppets with their strings cut."

Once they passed my shield, Kalan thought, his lips pursed. "Let it—and them—lie for now," he replied. "Our chief business is preparing for the next assault." The exiles nodded, their expressions almost relieved as the discussion switched to attrition and resources.

"Arrows are my main concern," Dain said, dropping his voice. "We won't be able to retrieve 'em this time, not with their archers deployed. And although the caravan's well equipped for the usual dangers of the road, its reserves weren't meant for this level of attack."

Kolthis's defection guaranteed the enemy knew that, too, Kalan reflected. When he turned toward the inner camp, the oriflamme was a line of fire against the early morning sky, the Bride's former pavilion ghost white beneath its shadow. He stopped to speak with Jad, leaving him in command of the perimeter, and met Tehan as he crossed the inner barricade. She confirmed that the envoy and Murn had returned to Sea's tent, and that Tyun had several broken ribs. "So I'll be acting captain, with Reith taking over as second. Tyun also says that if we're to hold through another assault, we need you leading the mounted troop." Tehan's expression lightened briefly. "On your roan terror, he said."

Reflexively, Kalan scrubbed a hand across the crest of his helmet as he would his hair, but he had already reached the same conclusion, not least because it would give him a better overview of the action. "I take it Tyun's still conscious, then?"

Tehan nodded. "Lady Myrathis says he should do well enough, so long as infection doesn't set in."

"Lady Myr?" Kalan queried. But he was thinking that Manan, the Normarch healer, would say that in a makeshift camp, amidst this desolation of dirt and wind, it was all too easy for wounds to become infected.

"Apparently she knows some healing," Tehan replied. "She's been working with Kion and the orderlies since the first attack."

Of course, Kalan thought, remembering how she had cleaned and stitched Dab's wound. But he was still taken aback when he saw her assisting Kion in the pavilion, both her clothes and head covering spattered with blood. The Sea physician had an area screened off from the rest of the tent and was amputating a defender's arm below the shoulder. Lady Myr was pale but composed, her hands steady as she followed Kion's directions. Kalan, watching from the pavilion entrance, felt as though he were truly seeing her for the first time.

He did not intrude on their work, but recognized the unconscious amputee as Rigan, the driver who had been on watch when the exiles first rode in. He called us real honor guards, Kalan thought, but still we could not save him. Now, even if the caravan survived,

Rigan would have lost his current place in Blood together with his right arm, unless he could learn to drive with the left alone. Another place would be found for him, as was the Derai way, but it would be meaner and Rigan's place in Blood's halls lower, because that was also the custom in the warrior Houses.

Studying the rest of the pavilion, Kalan picked out Faro, fetching and carrying for the orderlies along the rows of wounded. The boy paused when he saw Kalan, but hurried on almost at once to a brazier where water was boiling. Kalan stepped outside briefly, to check that the perimeter was still quiet, before reentering the pavilion to speak with those who had sustained lesser injuries. He heard the murmur of "Storm Spear" and "the captain" run ahead of him along their rows, and those who could sat straighter, or maneuvered to watch his approach. Among them, Kalan recognized the woman who had been reluctant to speak, putting out yesterday's wagon fire. "We held them off, Captain," she whispered. "I didn't think we could, but we did."

"There's nothing wrong with my arms." The groom beside her had raised himself on one elbow. "I can fire a crossbow if I'm propped someplace useful, once this leg's been seen to."

It might come to that, Kalan knew, and sooner rather than later. "I can still run, too," a boy put in, from the groom's far side. He was an errand runner, and a were-hunter's talon had raked one side of his face. He held a bloodsoaked cloth clamped against it, and Kalan could see from the rest of his face that he had been crying. "I'll be up again soon, you'll see."

"Not before I've taken care of that wound," Lady Myr said, in her gentle way, from behind Kalan. She and Kion must have finished their work, and she had washed her hands and arms clean. Her eyes were shadowed, but she smiled fleetingly at Kalan as she knelt to inspect the boy's wound. Whatever she thought as she lifted the cloth, her expression remained steady.

"You're in good hands," Kalan said, stepping back.

"We'll be back with you, Captain, as soon as we're done here," the groom promised, and several of those around him echoed the pledge.

Kalan wondered if they realized their nurse was the Bride of Blood, since most would never have seen Lady Myr at close quarters, let alone wearing anything like her current bloodstained garb. He would have spoken to her but saw she was intent on the boy's wound, so he left to seek out Tyun.

"What's happening out there?" the marine captain asked, when Kalan finally located him.

"Nothing at present," Kalan said, smiling as Faro finally joined him. He had removed his gauntlets on entering the pavilion and now gave the boy's shoulder a brief, careful squeeze. Beneath his hand, the bones felt fragile as a bird's wing. "I'm sorry. For getting you into this," he added, when Faro looked puzzled. "I should have had Che'Ryl-g-Raham return you to Grayharbor."

Faro shook his head, his expression indicating that he would not have gone. Tyun smiled, despite his obvious pain. "He's Derai. He has a right to be with his own people."

Who exactly Faro's people were, among the Nine Houses, was still moot, Kalan reflected. "If Kion can spare you," he told the boy, "I need Madder's armor from my tent." Faro's eyes widened, but Kalan checked him before he could dash away. "Ask Kion first."

Tyun's look was wry. "Your lad's no fool, Khar. Like everyone else, he knows what we're facing."

"He's still a child," Kalan said.

Tyun nodded. "As you say. But we won't hold through another round like the last."

"I was surprised we held through that." Kalan kept his voice low. "We rallied at the end, but if they had pushed again—" His shrug finished the sentence. They both knew that although the enemy might have taken heavier casualties than perhaps anticipated, they would almost certainly have prevailed. The only rationale for withdrawal that Kalan could think of was that the opposing commander, while prepared to expend were-hunters and the former Blood Honor Guard, wanted to preserve the main Darksworn force. Especially, he thought now, if they can't rely on either reinforcements or resupply—which suggests they didn't get here by using portals. The Darksworn numbers, too, made portal use unlikely. Breach or not, the magnitude of power use and number of gates necessary to ferry a force that size would have triggered every residual ward and psychic defense left along the Wall.

From the Sea Keep to Swords, Kalan reflected grimly: I hope.

"They don't like taking losses." Tyun spoke slowly, partly because of his injuries, Kalan guessed, but also as though he were puzzling out an enigma. "I've seen it when we've fought their incursions at sea. Whenever victory means heavy losses, they'll pull back."

"We do the same to protect our ships," Nimor observed, arriving at his captain's side.

Preserving a scarce resource, Kalan thought, as he rose to acknowledge the envoy. He repeated the thought aloud. "But if so, why not let the were-hunters overrun the camp when they attacked the herd? Why allow those stranded here to prepare even a limited defense?"

The look Nimor and Tyun exchanged was as expressive as a shrug. "A divided command," Tyun said, "or decisions made for other than logical reasons, like an enemy that likes to toy with the prey. Or the kill being promised to one commander over another."

"We've seen how ready they are to expend the were-hunts," Nimor agreed. "It may be that a were-hunter victory is not palatable to those in command."

Emerian history, too, had its share of such accounts, where pride or personal differences between commanders had given aid to their enemies. Kalan only hoped that whatever was driving the Swarm's inconsistencies would continue to work in the camp's favor. "I'd better get back." He clasped Tyun's hand, before turning to Nimor. "You and Murn will be vital next time, I suspect."

The envoy nodded. "We'll be ready," he promised quietly.

Kalan looked around for Lady Myr as he left, but like Kion, she remained absorbed in her work. Faro was waiting outside with an armload of Madder's caparison, the armor stacked at his feet. "One of the horsegirls helped me with it," he said. His eyes met Kalan's. "Some of the orderlies were saying we're doomed, but I told 'em you'll find a way to save us."

Kalan wished he could share his confidence. Even if Taly and Namath had gotten through, and Adamant was already marching to the camp's aid, the defense would be hard-pressed to hold until a relief force arrived. Regardless of the enemy's attitude to sustaining losses, the numbers involved were too unequal, but he could not say that to Faro. "We all have to play our part," he said instead, "and not give up. Don't forget your primary orders," he added, picking up the armor.

Faro scowled. "She's got the whole camp. I don't see why she needs me as well."

Despite assault, injury, and death, Kalan still had to suppress a smile as he hefted the caparison over his shoulder. "Be worthy, my page," he said, and left—first to equip Madder, then rejoin Jad on the outer defenses. "Still quiet?" he asked.

"Ay but this lull reminds me of when a Wall storm's brewing." By tacit agreement, they stepped away from the wagons before Jad continued. "We've lost around ten percent of our total complement, more in some companies. I've reassigned defenders to even the squads up, but still . . . " He shrugged.

"Who've you appointed to replace Jaras?"

Jad's expression was half grin, half grimace: "Kelyr, with Orth as his second. Aside from the marines, they're the most experienced fighters available and they're used to working together. Rigan, Jaras's second, is badly wounded, too, so no one's being displaced—if we can even talk of that with companies that're less than a day old."

"Kelyr and Orth are the logical choice," Kalan agreed.

Jad glanced away, first to the perimeter, then the sky. "Mid-morning," he began—at the same time as the psychic wake from a portal opening broke against Kalan's shield-wall. War horns blew again from the Darksworn lines, and Kalan wondered, as he whistled for Madder, whether the camp would survive to see noon.

47

✛═══✛

Tempest

Maybe I was wrong about the portals, Kalan thought, swinging into Madder's saddle and turning toward the dike. Yet logic insisted the backwash of power had not been strong enough for a gate of any magnitude—and he refused to contemplate Malian's account of the demon, Nindorith, emerging through a similar portal in Caer Argent.

At first glance the Darksworn ranks appeared unchanged. But when Kalan stood up in his stirrups he detected a new banner, progressing from the legion's rear toward the front lines. The indigo standard bore the sun in gold, with a wash of red across its face, and Kalan recognized the device from Malian's description of that borne by Arcolin, the Swarm envoy to Emer. The Darksworns' forward ranks were opening now to allow a tall rider on an armored Emerian great horse to pass through. Not Tercel, Kalan reassured himself, identifying the coat beneath the caparison as gray, not bay. Despite the destrier's Emerian harness, the rider's black mail was Darksworn in style, and his indigo surcote also bore the red-washed sun. His visor, shaped into a raptor's beak, was closed.

An aura of power hung about the newcomer, and when Kalan looked more closely he could pick out calligraphy on both the helmet and mail. No, runes, he amended, studying the power that glittered in each swooping stroke. They linked one to the other, armoring the wearer in sorcery. According to Malian, Arcolin's face and hands had been painted with similar runes when he confronted her below Imuln's temple in Caer Argent—which tallied, Kalan supposed, with the presence of the red-washed sun device.

The horse stopped in the center of the Darksworn line while the rider surveyed the camp. The defenders stared back, as silent as if the newcomer had cast a mesmerizing spell. Through the medium of his shield-wall, Kalan could sense allure reaching out to enfold the camp, and wondered if a similar working had been used to glamour the Honor Guard from oaths and honor. He frowned when a swift check confirmed that his shielding was still intact, reluctantly impressed that even without magic, the rider had the presence to compel the camp's attention.

The glamour met the shield-wall and recoiled, but returned almost at once, prying along the psychic barrier for weakness. A growl of power rumbled across the plain and many defenders looked uneasily skyward, hearing the sound as thunder. Kalan, watching the rider's right arm rise, suspected the truth was as much to be feared as one of the dry electrical storms encountered in this country. He thought the rider was shouting words through the visor: the voice sounded hoarse, even strained, but that could be an effect of distance and the power being channeled. The runes on the rider's armor had grown dark, and the darkness within each character began to crawl. Like wasps in a nest, Kalan thought, intrigued and repulsed at the same time.

The glamour exploring his shield-wall vanished. Simultaneously, the Gray Lands' wind swung to the rider as though called and began driving toward the camp, swirling up stones and grit into a flying curtain. The defenders muttered among themselves, because although they might not hear the rider's chant as Kalan could, even the most resolute New Blooders would know this was no natural wind. As if mocking the defenders' uncertainty, dust devils whipped into life across the intervening ground—but a new breeze rose in answer, swift as dawn on the face of the sea, and blew away from the camp to meet the dust devils head on.

Kalan could have sworn the new breeze held the ocean's tang, and a quick glance back showed him Nimor and Murn by the inner barrier, with Reith and three more marines guarding them. He could sense the weatherworkers' focus on the sorcerer as the Sea wind strengthened, dispersing the dust devils and driving detritus back toward Darksworn lines. The runes on the sorcerer's armor writhed as the two winds buffeted each other, striving for mastery. Wildfire crackled toward the camp as the Sea breeze and Darksworn wind boomed together again, and many of the defenders cried out, clapping their hands over their ears.

By the time the boom faded and debris began to settle, both the contending winds had been extinguished and Murn's head was bowed, his weight resting on his staff. Nimor remained intent on the Darksworn sorcerer, who sat motionless, his arm still held high, while the ranks around him were equally unmoving. Waiting, Kalan thought, but for what? "What's happening?" a nearby defender asked, and Kalan heard the question repeated around the perimeter with varying degrees of doubt and fear.

"Stay calm and keep to your stations." He pitched his voice to project command and reassurance at the same time. "Keep your eyes on the enemy." Because, he added silently, as Jad and the other company leaders reiterated his orders, whatever's coming next has already started.

Madder stamped, tossing up his head as the pulsing from the sorcerer's runes intensified. From this distance, the armor itself appeared to be moving. The effect was disorientating, but Kalan forced himself to concentrate on the penumbra building above the runes. From what he could discern of its pattern, the sorcerer was creating a summoning spell. The Gray Lands' haze thickened and crept forward in answer, despite the wind that had sprung up again, spiraling fresh dust as the were-hunters advanced through the murk. Power was building around them, too, except this time it crackled rather than shimmered, as though infused with the sorcerer's wildfire.

Kalan had seen were-hunters use spells to increase their power before, when they sought to overwhelm the hill fort in Emer. Now their howls sounded in counterpoint to the rising wind, and the power surrounding them pulsed to the same rhythm as the runes. The grit thickened, whipping into whirlwinds that drove toward the camp like the earlier dust devils, only they were already larger and considerably more fierce.

The were-hunters were summoning a dust storm, Kalan realized—trying to break his shield-wall with a combined magical and physical assault. "Secure the perimeter," he shouted, and all around the earthworks he heard the exiles' voices, quelling panic and shouting to get the defenses tied down. "Take Madder and look to the horses," he told Tehan, dismounting and thrusting the roan's reins into her hand. "Have the envoy shelter them." If he can spare the power, Kalan thought. He could hear Nimor and Murn chanting aloud, a low steady counter to the tempest as the salt breeze sprang up again. The whirlwinds began to diminish and Kalan experienced a momentary hope—before the wind off the plain bellowed and a dark front of dust, stones, and grit came roaring in, overtaking the whirlwinds and battering the Sea breeze back.

"Hold fast!" Kalan shouted, as defenders screamed and a handful broke toward the inner camp. The camp's perimeter defenses were still their best protection against the storm's onslaught, whether real or magic, and the Darksworn host would be poised to attack as soon as the tempest had done its work. The runners wavered, some returning voluntarily before Tehan and the reserve turned the rest back. Kalan could hear Orth, threatening to kill anyone else that ran, his bull voice rising above the storm's shriek as the company leaders reiterated Kalan's exhortation to stand firm.

Murn had staggered before the counterattack, and Reith was supporting him. Simultaneously, Nimor's staff bucked against his grasp and he fought visibly to steady it. The best the weatherworkers were likely to achieve, Kalan gauged, would be to slow the storm's advance, rather than preventing the wall of murk from reaching them. The physical wind was already lashing the camp ahead of the tempest of power, tearing up everything that was not tied down, and the defenders were screaming, or cursing, or frozen, staring at the blackness bearing down on them.

"Remember you are Blood," Kalan shouted, at the full capacity of his lungs. He wished he could infuse them with fortitude in the same way he had strengthened his shield-wall with earth and stone. Instead of taking shelter himself, he remained upright, angled against the force of the wind with one hand locked onto the wagon behind him. He was in the clear space beyond fear now, where time stretched and he could take in the storm's entire front while simultaneously noting every swirl of dirt and wind-blasted stone flying their way. Kalan was aware, too, of those nearby watching him. He saw headshakes and heard imprecations, but gradually his calm spread outward, infecting those nearby with a similar composure that spread around the defenders' circle.

The storm wall towered overhead now, and the wyr hounds leapt onto the crest of the dike, their eyes on fire as they bayed defiance into the vortex. "Bravehearts!" Kalan shouted, and sprang up onto the wagon bed, one hand still locked onto its metal frame while using shielding to protect his eyes from flying grit. He laughed into the wind's fury, aware of every inch of his shield-wall, just as he was of his body's sinew and bone. An instant later both breath and laughter caught as the tempest of wind, magic, and debris smashed into the invisible barrier, clawing for a fissure to chisel open, or weakness to batter apart. Power and debris hurtled high above the impact before crashing back down and eddying around the perimeter of the camp— exactly as Kalan had seen the ocean pound in against the Sea Keep, only to founder about its deep foundations.

The wind, rudderless, roared back and forth across the plain. Most of the were-hunters had collapsed together with their conjuring, and the few who were still on their feet howled, a prolonged ululation to defeat and doubt. The Darksworn sorcerer had lowered his arm but remained unbowed, so Kalan guessed that his magic could not have been tied to that of the were-hunters, possibly because he would have to relinquish his protective penumbra for that. Or allow the were-hunters within it ... Both the runes and their associated swirl of power had faded now, but the sorcerer's raptor visor continued to regard the intact camp with the same savage expression.

Kalan felt the moment when the rider's attention fixed on him. One of the sorcerer's escort stepped close to the gray destrier, pointing from the oriflamme to the weatherworkers, but the rider's gaze did not waver. "He knows who his true opponent is," Tehan said, very quietly, as she and the reserve closed in behind Kalan. He nodded, holding the sorcerer's stare, then on impulse raised his arm in the salute used between adversaries on the Field of Blood. A ripple disturbed the opposing ranks, but no one responded, either in kind or to voice insult or defiance.

"'Ware arrows," Tehan murmured, and Kalan nodded again, jumping down from the wagon bed as the wyr hounds retreated from the dike's crest. The defenders were utterly silent, either staring at Kalan and the hounds or toward the weatherworkers. Murn was sitting on the ground with his head bowed, while Nimor leaned on his staff as though it was all that was holding him upright. Reith stood close beside the envoy, but his attention was on the Blood defenders. He had not stood the escort down, no doubt because he understood, as Kalan did also, that the camp's reaction to the tempest hung in the balance.

Clearly, the defenders must know that the storm sprang straight from what their House called fireside tales and it was only the old Derai power that had saved them. At another level, Kalan guessed that understanding was currently warring with five hundred years of Blood's fear and loathing for magic in any form. In all likelihood, too, the defenders would believe the Sea Keepers were solely responsible for the power that had protected them, reinforcing the Betrayal's deep divisions between the Houses.

Kalan frowned, weighing the frozen scene and its implications. He also registered Lady Myr's presence, standing with Faro in the entrance to the inner camp. They were both watching him and looked frightened. Not just because of the tempest they had survived, he suspected, but aware of the tension that could trigger at any moment, either to accusation or acclaim, relief or violence. Ignoring the strained atmosphere, he turned to Lady Myr and bowed—the same sword champion's bow, with the fingertips of his right hand laid against his heart, that he had made to her after his duel with Parannis. "Daughter of Blood," he said, tacitly reminding the defenders of why they were all here. And then, straightening: "We keep faith."

Lady Myr, as grave and graceful as though she still stood above the Red Keep's field of honor, did not let him down. Fanning her bloodstained skirt wide, she sank into a curtsey: first to Kalan, and then—as those around the perimeter turned to watch her—to Nimor and Murn, using the deep, deep courtesy the ruling kin reserved for those who had done the House of Blood great service.

Kolthis might have taken pains to emphasize her Rose heritage, but Lady Myrathis was still a Daughter of Blood and the Bride, and the gore on her clothing came from tending the camp's wounded. A single cheer sounded as she rose from her second curtsey: a hesitant, uncertain sound but a cheer nonetheless. Then everyone joined in, raggedly at first, before their relief and acclamation swelled into a roar. "Daughter of Blood," the defenders cried, as they had shouted for their House earlier in the day. And then, as Kalan bowed to Lady Myr again, "Storm Spear! Storm Spear! Storm Spear!"

"So now you know," Tehan said, to no one in particular and everybody nearby in general, "why we like to keep our weatherworkers close."

"But I'm only in the weatherworker reserve," Murn said plaintively, before swallowing the contents of the vial Kion placed in his hand. "If I was powerful enough for the sort of carry-on we just faced, I'd have been assigned to a ship, not secretarial duties."

Kalan, who had arrived to confer with Nimor, grinned as he was supposed to and clapped Murn on the shoulder, but he did not like the young weatherworker's pallor. Power was no more inexhaustible than physical strength, which was why the were-hunters had collapsed and Murn was still sitting on the ground. Behind him, he could hear a group of defenders still trying to puzzle out exactly what had happened. "Was that all weatherworking, then?" a voice he did not recognize asked.

"I thought Mhaelanar had placed his shield over us, just like the old tales say." That was Darrar, sounding solemn.

"Mhaelanar!" Orth snorted. "Priest-kind handiwork, more like!"

"Under the circumstances, perhaps we should just be glad it worked." Kelyr was very dry, and for once, rather than replying with challenge or derision, Orth remained silent.

"Ay, although it's not weatherworkers who'll see us through this, but the Storm Spear, mark my words."

The final speaker's pronouncement prompted a string of obscenities from Orth. Kalan thought Tehan must have caught the discussion, too, because she frowned toward the Sword warrior before observing, with apparent casualness, "The giant's no admirer of yours."

"Though I think he's starting to concede Khar has nerve," Jad said, joining them, "having seen him stare down that storm. Personally," he added to Kalan, "I thought you'd taken leave of your senses. As for saluting the enemy, that was just brazen."

"Impulse," Kalan replied lightly, and they all grinned, even if their humor was as much reaction as mirth. He was aware, too, that many of the defenders were still watching, either openly or pretending not to, as he and Nimor moved apart from the rest. Kalan kept his voice low. "Does Murn have the strength for another round?"

The envoy looked tired, too, but his reply was matter-of-fact. "We're both overmatched, no question of that. You, though—" He paused, but did not finish whatever he had started to say.

"Am still overmatched," Kalan replied, "because they have numbers. The were-hunters may have collapsed, but that doesn't necessarily mean they're dead. And the sorcerer appears relatively unscathed."

"Ay, he used their power to buffer his." Nimor's forefinger tapped against his staff. "I can't be sure, but I don't think he was the only adept to come through that portal."

So what are the others about? Kalan wondered, frowning toward enemy lines. If he were the opposing commander, he would be weighing the Darksworn's apparent reluctance to take losses against the time required to bring the shield-wall down, together with the likelihood that any prolonged expenditure of power would be detected, despite their psychic blockade of the camp. Yet I'll be cursed, he thought, if all I do is sit here and hope against hope, waiting for my enemy to act. "Could you manage a good strong following wind?" he asked Nimor. "The sort that will fan fire into a conflagration and push it fast toward the enemy?"

"They may just push it back at us," Nimor warned.

"Probably." Kalan's frown deepened, his eyes returning to the Darksworn force. "But fire's the next thing I'd try, in their place, and we've made all the preparations against it that we can. At least this way we may set them scrambling, and even if all that buys us is a little more time—" He let the sentence hang, but Nimor was nodding, and when Kalan turned and gave his orders, the defenders sprang to give them effect.

PART VII

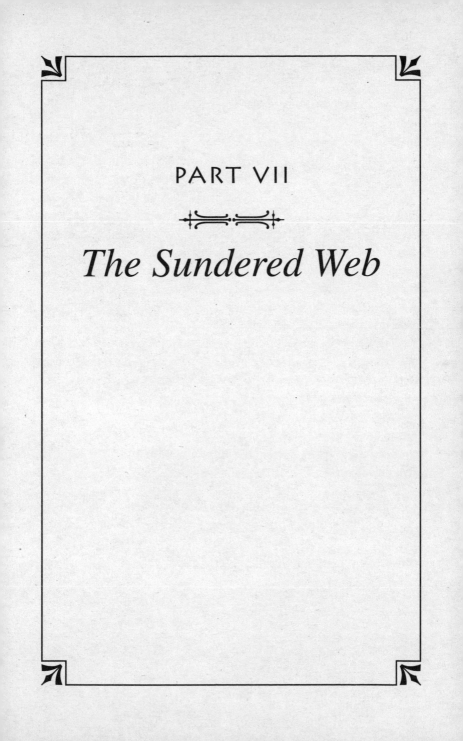

The Sundered Web

48

╪═══╪

Watchtower

"Still nothing," Rook said, and wanted to look away from the despair in the Blood ensign's face—what he could see of it, given the beating she had received. But looking away would only lead to another of Torlun's punishments designed to toughen him up, so Rook kept his eyes straight ahead. He knew Torlun would say the ensign's despair was because her attempt to deceive them had failed. Personally, Rook considered it far more likely she was afraid that all her comrades, and the Daughter of Blood she claimed to serve, were already dead.

"I'm still only in training," he said, for her sake as much as Torlun's. He *might* have caught the flare of a mindcall earlier, but the single flash was so faint it could equally well have signaled the beginning of his current headache. Rook was not prone to head-aches, but knew this one could stem from having overstrained his power—which might have compromised the farspeaking and could also explain his inability to reach the ensign's caravan. "I may be being walled out, too—" he began.

Torlun's gesture cut him off. "Beat her again," he said. Rook, still staring straight ahead, contemplated the shame of being assigned to his kinsman's service, even if Torlun was from the First Line of

Adamant's ruling kin, while he was only of the Third. Repugnance, however, did not alter the fact that he had been assigned to Torlun's company for the duration of this escort detail. He dared not look away either, as Corlin used his power to hold the Blood ensign immobile, even though her hands were already tied. Sird, another of Torlun's warrior-priests, channeled air and stone, using the ensign as a punching bag until she sagged to her knees.

The Sea marine was unconscious, sprawled where he had fallen when a stave connected with the base of his skull, cutting short his protest at the ensign's treatment. The marine's breathing was shallow, the wound still seeping blood, and Rook knew that he might not come around from such a blow. Compressing his lips, he refocused on the Blood ensign, who was sagging against Corlin's grip. One eye was already swollen closed and the rest of her face—and no doubt her body—was also a mess of swelling and blood. If she lived, she would be livid with bruising, but Rook did not think Torlun had any intention of letting her live.

"Blood must think we're all in the nursery still, to fall for what's obviously one of their own fireside tales." Torlun's eyes were narrowed on Sird's handiwork. "I'd have dreamed up a more plausible story than a 'spawn infestation large enough to attack a bridal caravan, let alone honor guards vanishing like ghosts."

Yet the marine supported the ensign's story, Rook thought. The pair bore a letter as well, one stamped with Lord Nimor's personal sigil, together with his diplomatic seal as Sea envoy. Rook found it difficult to believe Sea would publicly set their name to a trap of the kind Torlun perceived. But Orcis, standing in her Second's place on Torlun's right, was nodding agreement. "And Sea loan themselves to the ploy. Those curs always align with the strongest axis within the Alliance."

Rook considered trying to remind them of the instances in Derai history where farspeakers had been blocked out, to disastrous effect. Torlun's current expression, though, suggested that speaking would not only be futile, but could spark retribution as well.

"Pretending to have a Storm Spear initiating their request for aid does seem strange." Hur, the watchtower's commander, sounded worried. "Perhaps we should farspeak the Earl and council?"

Torlun's lip curled. "To be told what we already know: that if there *are* Storm Spears left on the Wall, they are not anywhere in Blood? I think not, Commander. Instead I will do what my Lord Grandfather expects and wring every piece of information out of this spy, before I expend a farspeaker's energy and intrude on his time." Torlun's hard stare bored into Rook, a warning that he had better perform when the moment to farspeak the Keep of Stone came.

"In that case, Sird should ease up or she'll die first." Rul was Torlun's half-brother and the Earl's personal emissary on this expedition. So far he had surveyed the proceedings without comment, but now picked up the discarded letter. "Knowing she's Ensign Talies of Clan Tavar and Brave Hold doesn't help us. Nor does constant repetition of her fireside tale, especially if we're to decide whether this Blood ruse threatens the safe arrival of our Stars' guests."

As always, Rook found it impossible to tell what Rul truly thought, but Torlun nodded, however reluctantly, and told Sird to stand back. "And bring her around," he added.

"Perhaps," Rul observed, "some scouts might also be in order, since the sentries have reported a creature—or possibly creatures—lurking outside arrow range. This Stars' visit is vital to our current interests, and although our guests' road may not lie through no-man's-land, we can't assume the Blood force will stay out there."

He did not need to add that the Earl of Adamant was hoping to negotiate a marriage treaty with Stars, as counterweight to the Blood–Night alliance. It was the obvious course, cementing the strongest of the priestly Houses to the only ally likely to give the warrior-kind pause. What no one seemed willing to discuss, according to Rook's kinswoman and closest friend, Onnorin, was the way it locked in the old enmities that had existed since the civil war, further widening divisions within the Alliance. Then again, Rook thought Onnorin might be the only person who saw that as an issue. She argued that the priestly Houses had let the situation play into Blood's hands by not offering an alternative marriage alliance to Night. But even she, Rook thought, would never dare say that to anyone except him.

The possibility of the Stars' embassy falling into Blood hands on the border of Adamant territory had obviously given Torlun pause. After a brief, frowning moment he nodded again, curtly this time, and told Orcis to send out scouts. Hur cleared his throat. "Once Blood realizes we're not going to fall for their ruse, they could strike against the watchtowers."

Torlun's stare was flat. "Let them try. They'll get a bloodying to equal their spy's if they do."

"Yes, sir." Rook wondered if anyone else had noticed Hur's hesitation. He guessed the commander wanted to make the same point he and Onnorin had often argued with their cadre comrades: that ultimately, small numbers of power users, which was all the watchtowers were able to accommodate, could be exhausted and then overwhelmed by a large enough conventional force. Hur would be conscious of that, stuck out here on the edge of Adamant territory, but Torlun was his superior in rank, as well as ruling kin, so Rook was not surprised the commander stayed silent.

Sird returned with water, which he hurled over the ensign's face and shoulders. When she stirred, groaning, he kicked her with his nailed sandal. "It occurs to me," Rul said, "that if there *were* truth to this stranded caravan tale, we should not let the gift slip through our fingers. Imagine the political advantage if the Daughter of Blood pledged to Night fell into Adamant's hands. It would be perfect fodder for your blood feud with Night's Commander as well, brother—unless your fervor for that has cooled?"

"Never!" Torlun snarled.

"It's a pity we have to wait on scouts." Rul was thoughtful. "Now if young Rook could only scry as well as farspeak . . ."

Well, I can't, Rook thought, at the same time as Torlun snorted. "He's not terribly useful for that either. But if we had farseers or scryers that could see beyond the end of their noses, we wouldn't waste time garrisoning these towers."

Rook decided that Torlun might be aggressive and physically strong, but he had obviously never spent much time looking at maps. Anyone who had—like Rook, Onnorin, and their cadre—would understand that the watchtowers were as much about asserting a physical claim to this border territory as gathering intelligence. Disbelief over Torlun's blindness helped Rook ignore the disparagement of his farspeaking ability. Despite being an initiate, he was among the strongest of Adamant's current farspeakers, which was why he had been selected for this mission. Although if Torlun was comparing contemporary farseers with those of legend, who could speak across worlds, then Rook supposed his assessment was accurate.

"We've no truthsayer either, unfortunately. But perhaps we could adapt our power and pry more information out of the spy, since beating clearly isn't working." Rul was still watching Rook, who longed to retort that his power didn't work that way—and he had no desire to try and make it do so. But unlike Torlun, Rul was clever, and there were unsavory rumors about what happened to those who crossed him. Rook knew, too, that most of those present would say he should be eager to serve his House in any way possible, and certainly owed nothing to an unknown Blood warrior foolhardy enough to enter an Adamant watchtower.

Trusting, Rook thought, in a Code that says the office of heralds and emissaries is sacrosanct and their persons must be protected. That reflection alone left a sour taste—and he could not help admiring the ensign's courage in refusing to forswear her mission, despite the punishment meted out. She reminded him of Onnorin, who had taken more than one beating, during their growing up together, that a lie would have prevented.

"The Stars company's been sighted, sir." Orcis rejoined them. "And the sentries glimpsed whatever's lurking in the rocks again, so I dispatched an eight-squad to escort our guests in."

Rul folded the letter. "Best if we stow the spies out of sight, since our Stars friends are reputed to be nice in their ways."

"Squeamish." Torlun was contemptuous. "Although I doubt they'd care. They've had no dealings with Night or Blood since the Betrayal War, and as for Sea . . . " He spat.

"Why risk their squeamishness? Also"—Rul's expression grew intent—"if there should prove to be something in the caravan tale, we don't want them reaping the benefit in our place."

Torlun shrugged, but jerked a thumb toward the storerooms built into the tower wall. "Sird, you and Corlin lock them in there." He watched the unconscious marine and the ensign, who was in little better shape, dragged away, before rounding on Hur. "Have the yard swept and fresh dirt laid over that blood. We'd better muster an honor escort as well, since we're to show this Stars lot respect."

The envoy turned out to be not only one of his House's ruling kin, but the Countess of Stars' second child. His silk and jewels, as well as the silver-chased armor of his company, thirty in number, made the dress uniforms of Adamant's warrior-priests look drab. "Popinjays," a sentry muttered, as Rook approached the watchtower's small hall. Rul had sent him to fetch a rare wine, brought from the Keep of Stone especially for their guests.

The sentry's watch partner rolled his eyes. "How much'd you bet against every one of them having a name longer than my arm?"

The first speaker shook her head. Rook, already slipping into a formal, processional step as he entered the hall, thought she was wise. The envoy might have introduced himself as Tirael, but Rook knew that any Son of Stars' full name would have at least five syllables. "Too long for everyday use," Tirael had said, smiling as he dismounted with a swirl of his blue-black cloak.

Torlun's expression, whenever he thought himself unobserved, made it clear he, too, considered the Stars' lord a popinjay. Rook had learned enough about his kinsman during their journey here to know Tirael's easy smile and the way he drawled his words would annoy

Torlun even more than the Son of Stars' finery. But rather than dwelling on that Rook needed to concentrate, because his headache had grown worse rather than better, and the elaborate panels of his dress tabard refused to stay swept behind his shoulders. Having them fall into the cups when he poured the wine would be bad enough, and spilling the wine even worse. Third Line of the ruling kin and initiate farspeaker or not, Torlun would punish him publicly for either solecism.

In the end, however, no mishap occurred and he poured the wine to the correct height in every cup. The cups were gold, with Adamant's sphinx emblem picked out in diamonds, which meant they were probably from the Earl's personal service. So *he* must have known the envoy was to be a Son of Stars, Rook thought: these cups would never have been brought to a border watchtower for anyone of lesser rank. He blinked when Tirael thanked him, but remembered to bow in acknowledgment of the courtesy. Torlun looked derisive but made no comment. Instead, Rul leaned forward, drawing the Son of Stars' attention. "I trust your journey was uneventful, Lord Tirael?"

"Entirely," Tirael replied. "But what of conditions here, since you had us escorted in?"

"This is a watchtower, on the border of no-man's-land." Torlun's shrug implied the escort had been routine.

Tirael turned his goblet, his jeweled rings winking in the lamplight that illuminated the tower's windowless interior. "We've been detecting signs of activity for several weeks now, first up near the high Wall, then moving down this way. Mostly it's been on your side of our border, in areas where neither of us has holds. Every time we've sent troops to investigate, we've found nothing concrete, but I wondered if you had noticed anything untoward?"

"I assure you, Son of Stars," Rul said, forestalling Torlun, "that Adamant has not been building up forces along your border, if that is what you mean."

"Not at all." Tirael's hand lifted in a gesture that was as graceful as it was apologetic. "I would have assumed a heavier than usual 'spawn incursion, except—"

"There are no passes in that part of the Wall," Torlun broke in impatiently. "There never have been."

Rul frowned at his half brother, an unspoken warning that whatever their guest chose to say, he should not be peremptorily interrupted. Tirael did not appear to have taken offense, although his escort captain's brows had lifted. "I am aware of that," the Son of Stars said, "hence our desire to know whether Adamant has also encountered unusual activity. One can never be too careful."

"No, indeed," Rul agreed. He lifted his cup in salute. "Your health, Lord Tirael. Ah," he added, drinking, "this is an outstanding vintage."

"From Lathayra, in the Southern Realms, I believe," Tirael replied. Rook noticed that he drank sparingly before proposing his own toast. "To your Earl and my Countess: honor on both our Houses. And Lady Yhle?" he inquired, when the toasts had been drunk. "Was she not able to accompany you, after all?"

Rook's face felt stiff with his effort to remain expressionless at the implication that Yhle, of all the Earl's many granddaughters among the First Line, was Adamant's nomination for the Stars' marriage. He guessed his blankness was probably just as telling—which was unfortunate, because the Son of Stars was looking his way.

"My First Kinswoman sits on our grandfather's council," Rul said smoothly. "Her obligations in that respect, as well as overseeing a fitting reception for your embassy, precluded her accompanying us. But she looks forward to welcoming you formally to the Keep of Stone."

Knowing Yhle's disdain for those not of Adamant, Rook thought that unlikely, but Tirael appeared to accept Rul's explanation. "And we to our arrival there," he replied.

"Ay." Torlun's chair scraped as he thrust it back. "So I'd best ensure arrangements for tomorrow's journey are in hand."

"I and my escort must do the same." Tirael, too, stood up. "Perhaps if someone could show us the resources placed at our disposal?"

"Everything in the watchtower is yours to command, both for your horses and yourselves," Rul assured him, rising as well. "Hur, if you or your Second could ensure Lord Tirael and our Stars guests obtain whatever they need?"

Torlun said nothing, but Rook recognized the set look that meant he was furious, and guessed he had intended returning to his business with the prisoners. Yet so long as the Stars knights were coming and going, Torlun would have to wait, and he did not like waiting. He barely nodded to Tirael before summoning Orcis with a jerk of his head and stalking from the hall

If the Son of Stars thought Torlun's behavior rude, he did not show it. Rul's expression had tightened, but he spread his hands. "My half brother is one of our rough diamonds, the more so for spending much of his life patrolling in dangerous conditions. I apologize for his abrupt manners, but assure you he means no offense."

"None is taken," Tirael murmured.

Eventually everyone filed out, leaving Rook to collect up the gold cups and remaining wine. Despite his headache, he could not shake the uncomfortable conviction that Tirael's account of unexplained activity along the Stars-Adamant border fitted with the prisoners' account of events in no-man's-land. Although that's not my responsibility to decide, he argued with himself: an initiate farspeaker has no right to interfere with council-level business.

Yet his unease sharpened when he took the cups into the scullery to wash and realized the prisoners had been left without water or food. In their condition, and without water, the marine in particular might not survive for Torlun to question further. So if I take them water and get caught, Rook thought, I can say it's to make sure Torlun gets the information he wants. He knew he would still be punished, but perhaps not so badly if his story was believed. Casually, he studied the ring of cellar and storeroom keys on their peg inside the scullery door, and then the kitchen beyond—but with so many additional mouths to feed, the watchtower's cooks were too busy to pay him any attention.

Slipping the keys into the wallet at his belt, Rook picked up a pair of waterbottles, connected by a strap, and filled them from the scullery pump. Afterward, he carried them openly across his shoulder while replacing the goblets in Rul's room, then returned to the yard by way of the kitchen stair, which Torlun and his elite company would not use.

Rook waited inside the doorway for some time, watching the yard. When it remained empty, he decided both hosts and guests must be fully occupied in stable or tower, and willed the situation to remain that way as he started across the cobbled expanse. Guards outside the storeroom would have sparked questions, so Torlun would be relying on the prisoners' condition, and the locked door, to keep them secure. In any case, even with twilight drawing in, there was nowhere for a fugitive to hide between the storeroom and the gate. Rook stiffened as the keyring clanked, coming out of his wallet, but the yard stayed clear and the storeroom key turned easily in the lock.

Once inside, he closed the door quickly and felt along the wall for the glim. When the light flared, he saw that both prisoners were conscious, and although their hands were still tied, the ensign had pushed herself into a sitting position. "I've brought you water." Rook studied the Blood warrior's battered face and one open eye, which measured him in return. Despite her beating, he sensed she would be dangerous if he untied her hands, so he trickled the water into her mouth until she indicated she had drunk enough. The marine required more help to sit up and drink, and Rook had to ease him back against the wall afterward. Almost of their own volition, his hands moved to check the injury at the base of the man's skull. Rook kept his touch as careful as possible, but remembering the force of the stave blow, he was not surprised when the marine winced away.

Trying to remember the lessons from his cadre's field-medic's class, Rook took the clean handkerchief from inside his dress tabard and wet it through. When he spread the cloth across the wound, he let a trickle of basic healing power seep through as well. The marine mumbled something unintelligible, while the ensign eyed the cloth and then Rook. "Why bother?" She spoke thickly. "Your leader will just have us beaten again." Until we die, that steady eye said, never leaving his; or we tell him whatever lies he wants to hear, since he will not accept the truth.

Rook knew she was right, but even if he could see a way to get them clear of the watchtower, the fugitives would not escape pursuit in their current condition. "I'm sorry," he said. "There's nothing I can do."

The ensign—Talies, he reminded himself—*was* like Onnorin, because her stare remained uncompromising. "Yet by doing nothing you not only condemn Namath and me, but potentially an entire Derai caravan, as well as the Sea envoy and a Daughter of Blood."

Rook wanted to protest that she was lying, and that besides, Blood was a warrior House and must fend for itself. But he found he could not meet her one eye and assert either of those things—or deny what she did not say: that he, like all Derai, owed a greater allegiance to the Alliance itself, beyond immediate loyalty to Earl and House. As if his discomfort had communicated itself to Namath, the marine struggled to raise himself up. His wavering focus was on the entrance, and Rook frowned, because the door he had thought closed was slowly edging outward. I can't have quite shut it, he thought—before both heart and breath jerked as the opening widened. He seized his dagger, only to stare, dumbfounded, as a wyr hound appeared in the gap.

Rook had seen wyr hounds before, but never one this large, and he had no idea how it could have gotten into the watchtower. Its answering stare was incandescent, and he only dragged his eyes away when footfalls sounded outside. Rook swallowed, aware just how thin his cover story would sound, now that discovery was upon him. Instinctively, he crouched lower as a man's shadow fell across the opening and the wyr hound turned—but although the yard beyond the storeroom was thick with dusk, Rook could not mistake the tall, elegant figure that blocked the doorway.

"Found," Tirael of Stars said, very softly, speaking over his shoulder to someone Rook could not see. His gaze rested on the wyr hound, then traveled past it to Talies and Namath. "The flicker of healing just now helped, but which of you, I wonder, mindcalled for aid?"

So there *had* been a mindcall, Rook thought, chagrined that he could have believed the brief flash was his headache starting. He was dismayed, too, that the healing he had considered too slight to be detectable had betrayed their whereabouts—to one whose House was the greatest enemy of the warrior-kind, he realized, frozen in place as Tirael pulled the door closed.

"A Blood warrior and a Sea marine." The Son of Stars' drawl was marked. "What could my hosts and prospective kin be thinking, to keep such intriguing company to themselves? Not that I don't appreciate the irony of a mindcall from either of you—however inadvertent on your part, Ensign, I'm sure—coming straight to Stars."

Rook was still frozen—but beside him, Talies made a convulsive effort to stand as Tirael, smiling and graceful still, drew the knife at his belt.

49

The Burned Man

The fire had raged between the camp and Darksworn lines for most of the afternoon, as contending winds pushed the flames first one way and then the other. Nimor and Murn endured far longer than Kalan had dared hope, and at one point the fire threatened the besiegers' position—only to race back toward the camp once the sorcerer returned to the front lines, his rune armor swirling. Darksworn archers followed in the fire's wake, shooting into the defenders through a veil of flame, and Nai was among those who fell. The weatherworkers smothered the fire in dust and grit before it reached the palisade, although Murn collapsed soon after and had to be carried to the infirmary. Yet despite the casualties, Kalan detected a general lift in spirits.

Because we managed to poke a stick into the Swarm hive, he thought, watching the sun sink through the lingering smoke—mainly because the enemy was taken by surprise. Knowing the caravan was pinned down and undermanned, the besiegers had not expected offensive action.

Darkness, however, always favored the Swarm. The were-hunters appeared to have withdrawn altogether following the tempest's failure, but what felt like a coterie of adepts launched a sustained attack against Kalan's shield-wall as soon as the sun vanished. The signature of the magic being used was as varied as the forms of assault, which shifted from continuous blasts of power to the psychic equivalent of sapping, and Kalan felt the strain almost at once. While none of the individual assailants appeared to wield power comparable to the rune-armored sorcerer, he knew their ability to work in unison, and in relays, presented a potent threat. He could feel the spark of Yelusin's power, shoring up his own, and the wyr hounds, too, stayed close, but within several hours he was having to repair fissures in the shield-wall and reinforce its foundations against the psychic sappers. If he had not grounded the shield-wall in the dike and the Gray Lands' earth, rather than relying on himself, Kalan suspected his situation would already be precarious.

The strain of first fanning the fire, then extinguishing it, had strained Nimor as well, but he returned to the defense when the Darksworn launched a succession of conventional forays. Each rush out of the darkness was accompanied by archers loosing incendiary arrows among the defenders, while a second wave of attackers focused on removing the defensive palisade. Time and again, Kalan led the reserve forward to protect the stakes. Without the palisade, the camp would lie open to cavalry attack, and although pikes and archers might hold the earthworks for a time, the defense was already stretched too thin. As the night advanced, he felt stretched as well. "At least we're spared the were-hunters," Nimor said, during one of the lulls. His searching look told Kalan he knew the barrage of power was taking its toll. "But they still have far too many minor adepts among their rank and file."

Agreed, Kalan thought grimly. "How's Murn bearing up?"

Nimor grimaced. "Still unconscious. And I could have used more time to recuperate after the fire. If only we had a Luck here, I could do more."

"Why a Luck?" Kalan asked, puzzled.

Nimor looked around, but only his marine escort stood within earshot. "The Lucks provide a conduit, so weatherworkers can draw on greater power at need, usually when outmatched by a great storm or the Swarm monsters that slip through where the ocean barrier is thin. The power can be drawn directly from the Luck, or from the ship itself." He paused, his weary expression settling into grim lines. "Possibly the worst abuse of the stealing era was that the Lucks were bound to the weatherworkers so their power could be drained completely at need. They were given no choice and a great many of them died." Nimor rested his forehead against his staff and spoke with his eyes closed. "The ships say it was this binding in particular—or rather its abuse, I suppose—that finally pulled them out of their limbo. That's when those we now call a Ship's Luck first acquired the name, although the association with the weatherworkers has since grown strong again."

Over four hundred years was a long enough time for that, Kalan supposed. He found focusing on something other than the siege, however briefly, was a respite in itself. "So they're still a conduit?"

"And a source of power," Nimor agreed, straightening, "only through choice, not compulsion. Lucks must serve freely and cannot be drained of their power and their lives, any more than a weatherworker or other adepts."

Except in circumstances like this where they drain themselves, Kalan reflected somberly, just as Murn had done. If the battery of power continued long enough, both he and Nimor would face the same situation. "I'll keep going as long as possible," the envoy told him quietly. Supporting you, his expression said: because without you and your wall, the camp will fall.

Kalan nodded. "Try and get some rest, if you can." If any of us can, he added silently, as Nimor left and he returned to monitoring the camp's defenses. The magical onslaught continued unabated, but it was some time before the next conventional assault rolled forward. This time the attackers maneuvered several long, rawhide-covered screens ahead of their advance, enabling their archers to dig in within easy range of the camp. Once close enough, the hides would provide shelter for foot assaults as well. "We'll need firepots," Jad said, joining him.

Without the were-hunters and their deflective magic present, enough arrows *might* get through, Kalan thought, calculating the odds. "But the rawhide still may not catch," he said, knowing the enemy would have their minor adepts deployed to make sure it didn't. "So we'll have to sortie once they're close enough." Yet as soon as the sortie party left the shield-wall they would be exposed to magical attack, which meant Kalan stretching himself further to try and protect them. "Tell Nimor he'll be needed."

Jad nodded, his expression grim. He looked grimmer still a short time later, when the camp's fire arrows smoldered into extinction on the rawhide screens. Shortly afterward, Palla led the sortie party out. The company comprised Sarr and a band of axe wielders, who would destroy the screens, together with fighters to protect them, while Kalan and the reserve provided mounted cover. At first, surprise and the sortie party's momentum worked to their advantage, although the initial clash was fierce. Kalan could detect no magical retaliation as Sarr and his axe team worked like those possessed, demolishing one screen and starting in on a second. "We're going to do it," Reith said, keeping pace beside him—an instant before a company of Darksworn cavalry charged out of the darkness.

Palla saw them and yelled for the sortie party to retreat. Kalan shouted, too, leading the reserve forward and simultaneously blocking the wave of terror sweeping ahead of the Darksworn. He saw Sarr look around, but rather than retreating in Palla's defensive formation, the farrier and several others renewed their effort to demolish the screen. "Leave it!" Kalan yelled, but doubted anyone heard as the Darksworn cavalry thundered down on them. The last thing he saw clearly before Madder crashed into the fray was Sarr fall, smashed to the ground by a war hammer.

The farrier's body disappeared as Madder maneuvered, striking out with hooves and teeth, and Kalan laid about him with the longer of the black blades. Reith was fighting alongside him for a time, then Ler took his place, covering the retreat until the Darksworn horn sounded again and more cavalry swept forward. Kalan yelled for the reserve to withdraw before they could be engulfed—at the same time as a glance back confirmed that the sortie party had reached the palisade, where Palla and a rearguard were holding the gap until the reserve passed through. Ler was still on his left as they retreated, while a surviving axe-wielder, bloodied but tenacious, clung onto Madder's right stirrup.

Covering arrow fire from the camp checked the Darksworn momentum, and the reserve were almost at the palisade when a barrage of power slammed into Kalan's shielding. The black blade vibrated like a struck bell as the Darksworn raced forward, and Kalan fought to steady himself and Madder. Palla shot an oncoming rider out of the saddle, advancing again with her rearguard to secure Kalan's right. The remaining wyr hounds closed around Ler, holding the retreat's left. "Well done," Kalan told Madder as the psychic attack eased—only to duck, using the black sword to extinguish an eldritch fireball streaking for his head. At the same time, he felt Nimor's power surge, destroying a second fireball before it reached Ler.

Palla was not so fortunate. She was still a step outside the palisade when another fireball exploded, blasting her backward as a fourth dissipated against the shield-wall. The fire engulfing her snuffed out as she was hurled through the protective barrier, but she was dead before Kalan could reach her and dismount. The exile's flesh was unmarked, but her mouth was stretched into a scream and her eyes were holes that stared at nothing. Grief tore at Kalan's throat and eyes—but there were so many dead, including Reith and Yelme from the reserve, as well as Sarr and most of his axe team. And still the assault of power hammered against his shield-wall.

Kalan knew Palla would understand, but still found it hard to turn away. When he did, Faro was beside him, holding Madder's reins. "Lady Myr told me to help," the boy said, the atrocious Grayharbor accent pronounced as his words tumbled over each other. "In case no one else could handle Madder."

Because you told her no one else could; I know your tricks, Kalan thought. But the boy *could* handle the big roan, so he would let him do it for now. "But when I need him again, Faro, you go back to Lady Myr."

Two of the wyr hounds trailed after Faro and Madder as all the horses were led away from the perimeter's increased risk of fire. The rest of the pack stayed with Kalan as he crossed to the nearest watch-post, where a brief survey showed enemy archers regrouping behind the two intact screens. Still enough to cause us grief, Kalan thought, but it'd be worse if Sarr and the others hadn't sacrificed themselves. "Nimor's still on his feet," Tehan said, as she and Jad arrived. She looked hollowed out from watching their dwindling numbers. "But he needs to rest before he'll be useful again."

Jad was equally strained. "I've redistributed Palla's armor and weapons," he told Kalan. "And put Orth in command of her company."

Kalan just nodded. There was nothing to be said and little else that could be done now, except try and hold on. He tended a gash in a wyr hound's shoulder himself once Jad and Tehan left, before resuming his watch on the plain. The harassing attacks continued, but in the hours that followed, only odd details pierced his weariness—like Orth looming out of the night to stare at him, before vanishing again. The incident occurred during one of the worst onslaughts of power against the shield-wall, when Kalan could barely move, let alone speak. Afterward, as his sense of time and events blurred, he decided he must have imagined the whole thing.

Later again, he thought a woman appeared in the shadows beside him. In silhouette, Kalan felt sure he knew her, but the face that looked his way was a blank mask, wrought from the plain's haze. The shock jolted him fully awake to find there was no woman present, just the wyr hounds pressed close with Faro burrowed into their midst. Kalan frowned, exasperated, until he realized that even while sleep-ing, the boy's power was buffering his. The Darksworn magic delving for the foundations of his shield working had died away, suggesting the opposing adepts had exhausted themselves at last or given in to bafflement . . . A ghost smile replaced Kalan's frown, because unless the enemy could comprehend the song of Haarth, they would never encompass his working.

A boot scuffed and he whipped around, but the newcomer was Jad. The woman with the blank face must have been a side effect of lack of sleep, Kalan decided—although, in fact, he felt a little more rested. "Dawn's coming." Jad sounded surprised they would see it. "Tehan says that Murn's conscious again, and it looks like Lady Myr's attendant will pull through."

"Good news." Especially, Kalan thought, if we can get Murn back on his feet. He shook Faro awake, and the boy glanced toward the Gray Lands as he scrambled up.

"I wanted . . . *want* to help," he said. Before Kalan could reply, the wyr hound closest to the dike growled, then all the hounds leapt up. A moment later, Orth bellowed an alarm.

"Get back to Lady Myr!" Kalan ordered Faro, running for Madder as Ler led the reserve forward. Once in the saddle, he could see the enemy marshaling, although no sign of imminent assault followed as night transformed into shadowed dawn. But something's afoot, Kalan thought, trying to assess the situation from the opposing commander's point-of-view. If the line of stakes was the equivalent of a sea wall, it had been eroded in several places. Yet for now the defense could cover the gaps. Only just, Kalan added. Still, a force reluctant to incur losses might not like the odds, especially while his shield-wall remained in place. And a full day had already passed, so every additional hour the defense held must tip the odds a little further toward survival, if only by increasing the chance the besiegers' presence would be detected.

So if I were the opposing commander, Kalan thought, I'd be looking for a new approach. As if affirming his conclusion, a group of riders gathered in the center of the opposing lines. The green pennant that signaled a parley flew above the blood-washed sun banner, and Kalan recognized the sorcerer beneath it, escorted by warriors wearing the jagged, bestial helms. "Do we honor the parley flag?" Jad asked, when Kalan and the reserve halted beside his company.

"So long as they're talking, they're not attacking," Kalan replied. "Do we have anything green to fly in answer?"

"The envoy has a parley pennant," Ler replied. "I can fetch it, if you're sure?"

Kalan was far from sure, but the delay alone made it worth listening to whatever the Darksworn had to say. "Yes," he told Ler. "Inform Lord Nimor what's afoot, and Lady Myrathis as well. But tell Tehan to keep them well back, since they're the most likely targets for treachery."

"Besides yourself," Jad observed, as the marine left. "This could be a ruse to lure you into the open."

"I've no intention of going out to meet them," Kalan assured him.

"You'd better have longbow archers to cover you anyway," Jad said, "and Rhanar and Machys are the best we have, besides yourself." He beckoned a runner, and the boy dashed away as Kalan checked that the sorcerer and his escort were still waiting. For a moment, doubt shook him—but as soon as Ler returned and the green pennant rose above the camp, the sorcerer's rune armor shimmered into life and the Darksworn contingent started forward. As far as Kalan could tell, studying their slow advance, Kolthis was either notable by his absence or not wearing Blood harness anymore. By the time the Darksworn passed into longbow range, Nimor had emerged from the inner camp with Myr and Faro, escorted by the wyr pair and Tehan's remaining marines. Shortly afterward, Rhanar and Machys arrived carrying their bows.

"Don't shoot, except on my order," Kalan told them. "Or Jad's, if I fall. And keep an eye on Orth, since I'm not sure he holds with parley flags and safe conducts." He may be right in this case, Kalan thought, remembering the death standards. Dismounting, he waited until the Darksworn reached the screens, then strode to the thorn-brush barricade. "Proceed no further," he called. "Stand and state your business with Blood."

The sorcerer advanced a horse-length ahead of his escort, before halting and raising his visor. Enemy or not, Kalan had to fight not to react, because the unmasked face was a mass of burn tissue, the skin stretched taut and shiny, its hue deepening to maroon in places. The scarring pulled down the rider's right eye, giving his face a lopsided effect that was compounded by his mouth, which looked as though the lips had melted into the surrounding flesh. In all that ruined face only the darkly blue eyes were still alive, their gaze burning as though the fire that had disfigured the man still lingered.

"I am Arcolin, of the Blood-Washed Sun." The Darksworn's voice was ruined as well: part hoarse rasp, part wheeze, as though the vocal cords had been seared. His gauntlet lifted, gesturing toward the oriflamme. "And you are Khar, the Storm Spear?"

Arcolin, Kalan thought, startled. Despite knowing both the name and the blood-washed sun device from Emer, the face before him did not fit Malian's description of the Darksworn envoy. "I am the captain who commands this camp," he replied.

"Captain or Storm Spear, it matters not." Still studying the oriflamme, Arcolin waved dismissal. "We have fought Derai captains and Storm Spears before and prevailed, as we shall prevail here. I think you know this."

"What I know," Kalan said, "is that no fight is lost until it's over. State your business with Blood or this parley is done."

The burned man's mouth parodied a smile. "Pressed true from the Storm Spear mold, I see, all bluntness and the business at hand. As for my mold—" His hand lifted, indicating his face. "I was not always as you see me now. Yet long hours of healing power were needed to restore even my current aspect." He likes talking, Kalan thought: Malian said it was his hallmark, that and poison, whether in the cup or on the blade. "It has been brought to my attention," the hoarse voice continued, "that you are harboring the one who did this to me."

Kalan had been wondering if the burns could be a legacy of the sorcerer's final encounter with Malian in Caer Argent, but now he frowned. Can he be referring to Sea House fire? he wondered, puzzled, before Arcolin spoke again. "In Grayharbor, Storm Spear. The deed was wrought by the boy you now claim as your page, when he called lighting and started the fires that burned me."

Faro. The ensuing silence thundered in Kalan's ears, while Arcolin regarded him with all the cruelty of a cat, for which the game is as vital as the kill. When Kalan replied, his lips felt stiff. "That's simply not possible." Except that Faro's shielding ability *was* comparable to his own and Jehane Mor's—and he was also recalling Nimor's observation that most weatherworkers could shield or far-speak to some degree.

"I see you harbor doubts, nonetheless," Arcolin observed softly. He raised his voice, speaking to the camp as well as Kalan. "You have taken the boy as your own, but who is to say he is not a Sea cuckoo, foisted upon Blood's nest? After all, you now know they have hood-winked Blood in other ways." The camp was silent, but Kalan could sense the defenders' absorption. "Or perhaps," Arcolin continued, "it's *his* power you are drawing on to protect your camp, for all that harboring one of his kind contravenes Blood's Oath. But what if I were to remove any further need for the boy's taint?"

"Does this mean you're finally coming to the point?" But Kalan had already guessed, with sick certainty, where this was heading.

Arcolin's smile twisted. "How remiss not to mention that I had an offer to make—not just to you and the Bride you serve, but to your camp." He paused, his gaze assessing the defenders, and again projected his voice to reach them. "Until now, my objective has been to put everyone in your caravan to the sword. But I will forgo that goal if you give me the boy. Your page, Storm Spear, in exchange for every other life in the camp: the Daughter of Blood, the Sea House envoy—everyone else walks free, in return for the boy."

Not just poison in the cup and on the blade, Kalan thought. Every word was a drip of venom. "And if we refuse?" he asked.

"I shall take the camp and the boy anyway. But I shall also aim to capture as many as possible alive and ensure their subsequent path to your Silent God is neither swift nor silent. When all are finally dead, I shall line the road from Blood to Night with their bodies."

Now Arcolin's smile, savage and satisfied, was for Kalan alone. "But it need not happen that way. So long as you give me your page, the assault ends for everyone else." He made a show of gathering his reins before speaking again. "I will wait an hour for your decision. But many lives in exchange for one, Storm Spear—acceptance should not take long." And as deliberately as they had paced forward, he and his escort rode away.

50

Chain of Command

The two wyr hounds with Faro were growling, but the boy seemed oblivious. He had stiffened as soon as the Swarm commander lifted his visor, and since then his eyes had never left Khar. Myr had been deeply shocked by the mutilated face, her clasp on Faro's shoulder an automatic reaction that she regretted at once. She had expected him to shrug it off, or obviously suffer the touch because they were in public, but instead he ignored it. It was only when Arcolin named Faro as the one who burned him—or caused him to be burned, Myr was unclear on that point—that she understood the boy was frozen with terror of the sorcerer, not horror at his ruined face. Whereas what frightened Myr was the weight of the camp's silence, and the rigidity of Khar's back as he watched the sorcerer withdraw.

He *can't* be considering the offer, she thought: surely he sees the deceit beneath the sorcerer's words? But even if Khar did perceive it, she was horribly afraid the other defenders did not. They were watching their numbers dwindle with every attack, and essential supplies—arrows, medicine, food, and water—were all running low. *Many lives in exchange for one.* Arcolin's words to Khar pulsed through Myr, and her fear deepened because she saw that the sorcerer's true bait was hope, when the defenders had thought there was none. And some among them—possibly many—might be willing to close their hearts and minds to its price.

They'll tell themselves Faro is priest-kind and an outsider, Myr thought. She shivered, recalling the rumors of infanticide committed against children with power in some Blood holds, which Ise had always tried to keep from her. Instinctively, she looked toward Nimor, but his expression was shuttered. Tehan and the marines with her looked grim, but their company's numbers were now so few, and their primary responsibility was to protect Sea's envoy . . . They may legitimately feel, Myr thought, that this is Blood's business to resolve.

As the only member of Blood's ruling kin present, that also made it her responsibility. If I'm to call myself a true Daughter of Blood, she added silently, as Khar turned to face the camp. Myr saw the way his expression hardened as he took in the drift of defenders toward his position. The archers who had been deployed to provide covering fire—Rhanar and Machys, she thought—slithered back from the dike's crest, but remained close by Khar. Myr could hear the company commanders exhorting the defenders to keep to their posts. The majority of those who had not already started toward Khar maintained position, although they were all more intent on the camp than on the plain. The Swords' giant, Orth, was standing a short distance away from Khar with what had been Palla's company. His body was angled between monitoring the plain and the camp, but his stare was openly malicious as he regarded Khar.

He disliked both the Storm Spear and Faro; Myr had seen that in the gully. Later, Khar had warned her against both Sword warriors and explained how Orth had besmirched his Earl's honor out of hatred for the priest-kind. So I have to assume, she thought, that he would gladly give Faro up. The boy, though, was still focused on Khar. Myr wondered if he, too, saw the grim, weary lines in the Storm Spear's face deepen as he confronted the array of expressions turned his way: the openly mutinous, those who looked sick and guilty at the same time—and those who would not look at him, or at Faro, at all.

Khar did not look toward Faro either, but Myr could not—would not—believe it was because he intended sacrificing his page. Technically, she could order him not to, but doubted she was capable of facing down both her Honor Captain and a hostile camp. The defenders might have cheered for her, and for Khar, too, only yesterday, but Myr knew how easily their mood could have swung the other way. Now the camp was so quiet she could hear the wind's low whine, bringing with it the jingle and stamp of the enemy cavalry. She shivered, her clasp tightening on Faro's shoulder, and a wyr hound pressed close, its great shoulder steady against her hip. Glancing down, she realized all the remaining wyrs had regrouped about her and Faro, their eyes a swordmetal sheen as they watched the outer camp.

Myr's attention had only shifted for a moment—but she jumped as Khar's voice snapped the camp's silence like the first whiplash of thunder heralding a Wall storm. "Return to your positions at once. The Swarm commander made no promises about ceasing hostilities during his hour. And I'd not rely on it if he had."

Almost every head swiveled toward the plain, and most of those who had left their places moved hurriedly back. Possibly, Myr thought, because for the first time since the siege began, Khar had named the Swarm. She wondered if she was the only one who felt chilled, hearing the word spoken, although she guessed everyone must know what they were facing, just preferred not to admit what fools Blood had been with their "fireside tales." The sullen looks cast Khar's way told Myr that many did not want to admit it now either, including most of those who had not given ground. Around a score, she estimated: enough to draw courage from each other's support.

One of the foremost folded his arms, his expression shifting from sullen to truculent. "If our duty's to see the Bride of Blood safe to Night, as we were told when leaving the Red Keep, then shouldn't we be discussing this Arcolin's offer?" His voice strengthened. "And since the boy's your page, Storm Spear, you should stand aside."

Myr was not sure whether it was the wyr hounds' presence that gave her courage, but suspected she was the most surprised person present when she spoke before Khar could answer. "I would never contemplate buying my safety at the expense of a child's life." Despite the stares that met her words, the shudder that ran through Myr was anger, not fear, and her voice rang clear. "Especially since the protection of children is one of the most deeply entrenched tenets of our Code. And Derai do not make bargains with the Swarm, least of all to give up our own. Even if we did, I believe this offer is no more than a ploy to sow dissension and undermine our resistance. One made with the knowledge," she added, "that we have fallen so far from what it means to be both Derai and Blood that we would contemplate taking this offer."

She had not won them over, she could see it. Too many expressions remained closed, too many eyes averted. "Fine words, Lady," the dissenter said. "But you're only half of Blood yourself, when all's said and done. Besides, maybe those who made the Code weren't thinking about situations like these."

As if his words had unleashed a flood, a flurry of other voices spoke on top of each other. "Baris is right. *She's* half Rose, not even a true Daughter of Blood. Why should we listen to her?"

"The Code can't intend that we have to put one boy, who may not even be Blood, ahead of all the lives in the camp."

"A fart for the Code, in the New Blood we make our own rules."

"The Storm Spear's no true Honor Captain either. He and his lot are outcasts. They've no right to decide for us." Myr could not see the speaker, because he was concealed behind others, but the wyr hounds growled as one. Several of the defenders closest to them stepped hurriedly back.

"Enough!" The blaze of Khar's anger banished any sign of weariness. "This is a Blood caravan on the Derai Wall, and each and every person in it is subject to the chain of command, which starts with the Daughter of Blood. And she has appointed me as her commander." His stare raked them all. "So I will not be standing aside from this decision or any other that needs to be made for the camp, just as I have not stood aside from fighting for it. And the Code," he added, his gaze boring into Baris, who took a step back, "was created for exactly these circumstances, not to be set aside whenever it causes inconvenience."

Several of the dissenters shifted uneasily, and no one spoke. In their place, Myr thought, I would not care to either. When Khar spoke again, his voice was quieter, the anger banked, if not cooled. "Do you really think it likely that a Swarm commander, having found a way to breach the Wall and bring a legion into the Gray Lands, will relinquish his primary objective for a personal vendetta? And that having assailed us with conventional assault and Swarm magic, both of which have failed to break our defense, he would not try guile? Say by offering a bargain he knows will sow what Lady Myrathis rightly called dissension in our ranks?" He paused, and now his quiet was hard-edged. "Even if you feel you can take that bargain and live with yourselves, ask who will defend you when the assault inevitably resumes. For I will not."

Orth laughed. Khar regarded him coolly, but Rhanar fingered the arrow still fitted to his bowstring. Machys, too, held an arrow steady, although it was not aimed at anyone. *Yet*, Myr thought, holding her breath. She knew Kharalthor and Hatha would agree that everyone in a field situation, whatever their role, was subject to the chain of command, which meant Khar would be within his rights to summarily execute anyone who incited mutiny. Except in a camp that needed every defender, that would also be doing Arcolin's work—which may have been why Khar's voice remained as level as his expression. "You find something in this amusing, Orth?"

"Ay, that Blood calls itself a warrior House." The giant's heavy gaze swept across Baris and those surrounding him, before he sneered at the answering grumble. "What I'd do, if I were that Swarm commander and you were fool enough to believe in my bargain, is take the boy and torture him in full view of the camp. Just to soften you lot up, ahead of attacking again when my fun with him was done." Orth paused, making a show of reflection. "Or maybe I'd wait until you'd broken camp and were marching off, thinking yourselves saved, before falling on you again. That way I'd minimize my losses and could savor watching you undo your own defense." The massive shoulders shrugged. "The only promise I'd keep is to make sure your deaths were slow afterward, and your remains used to decorate the road from Blood to Night."

Khar was maintaining an impassive facade, but Myr guessed he was as surprised as she was by the Sword warrior's support. Orth's words had certainly created dismay and doubt, especially among those surrounding Baris, and she saw both Rhanar and Machys relax. "Don't get me wrong," Orth continued, ostensibly addressing the dissenters, although Myr thought he was really speaking to Khar, "all I care about is survival. But that means this camp has to hold together. And the Bride may be only half of Blood like you say, but she's right about one thing." Without looking at Myr, he turned his head aside and spat. "Derai don't bargain with the Swarm."

Myr saw shame settle into the same faces that had remained unmoved by her words. Slowly, those about Baris began to disperse, and he, too, turned away before he could be left standing alone. Over, just like that, Myr thought, shivery with relief and reaction. When she glanced toward Faro, he was staring at his feet, so she could not even attempt to gauge his feelings—although she knew what her own would be in his place.

Khar waited until everyone was back with their companies, and he had conferred with Jad and the other commanders, before joining her and Nimor. "I can't linger with the camp on edge," he said, saluting first her, then the envoy. Myr could detect no anger in him now, just a matter-of-fact grimness as he glanced toward the plain. "And I doubt Arcolin's going to take refusal well."

Myr nodded, wanting to match his calm. But she still almost jerked her hand back in surprise when Khar took it, bowing over her fingers in the manner of the old stories. "Thank you," he said, straightening, and she nodded again, awkward with the old shyness. Should you have to thank a person, she wondered, for doing what was right? But it was not a topic that could be discussed with Faro present and Arcolin's hour passing. Myr hesitated, trying to think what she could say. "I, too, keep faith," she said finally.

"You do, indeed." Khar bowed again, before setting his hands on Faro's shoulders and kissing him on either cheek, a formal gesture Myr knew was aimed at the camp. "I promise you this, my Faro: Arcolin will never take you while I live." The boy made a strangled sound, and Khar shook his head. "But from now on you are not to leave Lady Myrathis and the inner camp for any reason, even to help me or Madder."

Rather than protesting, Faro nodded his bowed head. But Khar was already leaving, directing a salute between Myr and Nimor. Tehan accompanied him, with five of the wyr hounds loping at their heels, while the remaining four stayed with Myr and Faro. "We should go, too," Myr said, and Faro accompanied her silently, again without any sign of his usual reluctance He did not even look back as they reentered the inner camp with Nimor and his escort.

Myr hesitated between going straight to the infirmary or checking on Ilai first. She had organized the attendant's removal into her own tent once the pavilion began to fill up, thinking Ilai's recovery would benefit from the quieter space. Faro did not argue when she steered him in that direction now, and his head even came up once he stepped inside. Myr had used The Lovers to screen off a separate compartment for Ilai, and he walked right up to it, trailing his hand over hounds and crow and hind until Myr saw the attendant was asleep on the other side and beckoned him away.

Quietly, in order not to disturb Ilai, Myr damped a cloth so both she and Faro could wash their hands and faces before eating. She supposed it was foolish, in light of the camp's situation, but she found small routines comforting, like tidying her hair in front of the shield-mirror. Faro took her place immediately afterward, and Myr felt a glimmer of amusement, because he had also spent considerable time in front of its polished surface after helping her shift Ilai.

Setting out their small meal on Ise's table was reassuringly familiar, too, even if the tray was set on a crate instead of its dragon legs. But the moment Myr ran a hand over the battered surface, the memories associated with it tore at her and she had to exert all her willpower not to rest her head on the tray and weep. *I mustn't*, she thought, *or I won't be able to stop.* Yet still she crouched before it, her hands unmoving and her eyes gazing blankly at the tent canvas, until the sense of being watched intruded. Turning, Myr saw that Faro had stopped reordering his hair and was watching her through the mirror. "Thank you," he said abruptly, "for speaking for me out there."

Myr met his regard steadily. "Mostly, I said it wrong." *I was too esoteric*, she thought, *a Daughter of the Rose rather than of Blood.*

"At least you tried." Faro's reflection looked almost adult in its bleakness.

A sound from behind the tapestry made them turn, and when Myr lifted the heavy cloth aside, Ilai was awake. The angle of the cot allowed the attendant to see Faro, and her gaze—still bloodshot in her heavily bruised face—studied him before returning to Myr. "Tell me what's happened," she whispered. "The truth please, Lady Myrathis."

Myr nodded, despite finding it difficult to speak of Arcolin's offer with Faro there. Ilai's battered face hardened as she did so, her lips pressing into a thin line. "But how," the attendant said finally, addressing Faro, "could you possibly have burned him?"

"I didn't!" Faro sounded strained, as if getting words out was a struggle. "The lightning came down and struck him, and there was fire afterward. It wasn't anything to do with me."

"But you were there," Ilai said.

Faro's shoulders hunched. "It was the lightning," he protested, then started as a shadow fell across the tent floor. Myr's heart jumped, too, before she turned to see Nimor in the entrance.

The look the envoy bent on Faro was penetrating. "What circumstances, though, led you into such close contact with a lord of the Swarm?"

He must have overhead our conversation, Myr thought. She

wondered, too, why Nimor's question had not occurred to her before, when it was not only obvious but required an answer. "I'm not bad," Faro whispered. "*She* let me come on board. She wouldn't have done that if I was bad."

"She" must be the master of the ship that had brought him north, Myr supposed, but Nimor was shaking his head. "I did not say you were, but it would help if you answered my question."

Yet although Faro's face contorted with the effort to speak, no words emerged. Nimor's look of concern deepened, and Ilai shook her head, but Myr found she could not endure Faro's despairing struggle. "He's been through enough today," she told Nimor. Under different conditions, she would have smiled to hear Ise's tone of authority in her voice. When Faro did not seem to hear, she placed her hand on his arm. "It's all right," she told him softly, when his frightened eyes met hers. "We'll wait for Khar."

This time he nodded, relief banishing the contortion, and she handed him the leather strip he had dropped, so he could retie the mass of his braids together. His hands shook as he took it, and she thought that whatever Nimor suspected, Faro was an unlikely traitor. If he had wanted to betray her, he could already have done so twice over, both to Kolthis and the were-hunter in the gully. She could see Nimor marshaling further argument and steeled herself to counter them. But before the envoy could speak, a trumpet blast sounded across the plain, followed by a war cry roared from many throats.

The hour must be up, Myr thought, shaken because it seemed too soon. "They've attacked ahead of time," Nimor said tersely. His frown lingered on Faro, misgiving mingled with frustration before he shook his head. "You're right, Lady Myrathis, the puzzle will have to keep." He inclined his head, envoy to Daughter of Blood, and turned away.

When Faro darted out in his wake, Ilai beckoned Myr close. "The envoy thinks the boy may be a danger, and he could be right. Be careful of Faro, Lady Myrathis."

"I will," Myr promised, although she still thought that if Faro had intended to harm her, he could have done so long before now. Her head turned as a war horn answered the trumpet blast, followed by a long roll of drums. "Right now I had better see where he's got to." On leaving the tent, she saw Faro pressed between two carts on the inner barrier, with a wyr hound on either side. The remaining pair rose from beside the tent and followed her across to him. Faro shifted to make room, but did not look away from the plain as the enemy line, bristling beneath an array of battle colors, rolled toward the camp.

The enemy archers behind the screens were shooting steadily, forcing the defenders to hold cover. Just when Myr thought Khar must be waiting until the advance was at point-blank range, she heard him shout an order that was echoed around the perimeter. A line of arrows arched skyward before dropping down behind the screens, but although a large number struck home amid confusion and shouting, too many wavered off-line or disintegrated in midair. "They're using their magic," Faro said, in his oddly accented Derai. "It's always stronger the farther they are from our perimeter." His voice was gruff now, rather than strained, and she wondered if he really possessed power himself, as Arcolin had implied. "But still no beast-men." The boy sounded puzzled.

"They took huge losses yesterday," Myr reminded him. Like we have, she thought, only with no option of withdrawing to lick our wounds. The enemy horse archers were sweeping forward now, and beyond them she could see the remainder of the Swarm cavalry, drawn up in attack formation for the first time. She knew what Hatha would say that meant: the enemy must believe they could thin the defense sufficiently to bring a section of palisade down and allow their cavalry through . . . At which point, Myr thought, more coolly than she would have thought possible, the camp will be lost.

Now, though, the defenders were using fire arrows to shoot at the horse archers, but the coursers had obviously been trained to advance through fire, smoke, and noise—if they were not Swarm-bred demons themselves. Despite the incendiaries, the archers held formation, circling the dike and pouring a hail of arrows into the camp—before the attacking infantry roared again and picked up speed, crashing into the defenders along the earthworks. Metal clanged on metal, and more battle cries skirled before the confrontation steadied into formless shouting, with pikes thrusting back and forward across the barricade. The Swarm archers cut in on the edges of the pike melee, maneuvering to shoot the defenders, while skirmishers hacked at the palisade on either side of existing gaps.

Watching was unbearable, because there were too many weak points for the reserve to cover and several of the gaps were widening. But looking away was worse, and Myr's hands clenched tight, as if she might in some way secure the perimeter by willpower alone. She could pick out Khar on Madder, and the Sea marines with him, as well as Orth, because of his height, wielding what looked like a poleaxe among the pikes. Everyone else blurred into the ragged to-and-fro of fighting, in which Myr frequently found it impossible to distinguish either side as the dust swirled, let alone who had the advantage at any given moment.

Overall, though, she could not shake a sinking certainty that the defense was wavering, perhaps because Arcolin's offer had done its business, after all, and sapped the defenders' will to resist. The Swarm commander must have thought so, too, because a trumpet yelped from beneath his standard and the drums were beating again, quick and sharp. Slowly, the enemy cavalry began to move, closing the distance between their line and the beleaguered camp. "Kolthis," Faro said, pointing out the former Honor Captain's colors, which flew above a small knot of warriors in Blood armor.

Yes, Myr thought bitterly, *he* will want to be in on the kill.

Another trumpet call sounded, its clear note mocking her dread, and a second cavalry company followed the first. Myr closed her eyes, not wanting to see the defense fail and the Swarm's mounted force drive home the assault. But she opened them again at once, because keeping faith had to include not faltering while Khar and all those along the perimeter were fighting and dying for the camp's survival.

Beside her, both Faro and the wyr hounds stiffened, staring

beyond the stream boundary of the camp. "They're creeping up," he muttered. "I can see them, like shadows in the haze." Myr peered hard in the direction of his pointing hand but could not see anything. "There!" Faro said. "They're stealing in where the fighting's lightest."

If he's right, Myr thought, although she still could not see anything, then she should warn someone: Nimor, perhaps, or Murn, except he was still recuperating in Sea's tent. She hesitated—and as she did so the attackers roared. Myr swung around in time to see Dain and Aarion's companies crumble, and could only watch, appalled and helpless, as the gap around their position widened. A horn wound, exultant, from the opposing lines, and even though Khar and the reserve had already reached the collapse and were fighting desperately to stem it, the Swarm cavalry quickened their advance. Momentarily, Myr felt as though everything—the ongoing perimeter struggle and widening gap, the cavalry's gathering momentum, dust churning beneath the horses' hooves, and even her own heartbeat—hung in stasis, poised for the next swordstroke, or horse's stride, or catch of breath, that would seal the camp's fall.

"There!" Faro cried again. He tugged at her sleeve. "See, they're crossing the stream!"

Harried, Myr glanced toward the watercourse. This time she, too, saw the silhouette of riders through the haze that clung to it—a split-second before a company of riders surged out of the streambed and charged the Swarm flank.

The newcomers' armor was silver, with blue-black surcoats and a foam of plumes on their helms. Derai helmets, Myr saw, intent on the long silver pennant above their heads but unable to identify a device. Faro clambered onto a cart tongue, trying to see more, and Myr joined him as the oncoming company drove hard into the Swarm cavalry. The enemy line crumpled as some riders tried to turn and meet the unexpected attack, while the rest either scattered or were pushed back into their own ranks. The confusion spread as more Swarm troops wavered between pressing the assault and defending their flank.

As the attack faltered, the defenders rallied, but Myr could see how small the newcomers' force was. Only surprise had enabled so profound an effect, and now the Swarm flank was rallying about a mounted troop, led by a warrior whose helm was a grotesque parody of a bear. "No!" Faro's cry was half strangled. Myr cried out, too, as a smoky light poured out of the bear-helmed warrior and raced toward his opponents—only to shout again, in protest, denial, and amazement, as an answering, silver-violet blaze exploded from the newcomers' line.

The opposing magics writhed around each other like serpents as the two mounted companies thundered together and the shock of war cries and weapons rose. Light continued to surround all the combatants, but the contest between the leaders was plainly a trial of power as well as conventional strength and skill. Its ferocity made Myr's Honor Contest pale by comparison, and although the two appeared evenly matched, she thought the newcomer might be gaining ground. The melee about the two eddied, dust swirling around the trampling horses as weapons rose and fell—but Myr still saw the moment when the Derai leader's sword cut home and his opponent slewed sideways in a long, slow curve to the ground.

A cry of devastation rose above the battle din, and the Swarm troop scattered as the newcomers drove forward again. As if the cry had been a signal, the entire Swarm force began to retreat. Ignoring their disarray, Faro pointed again, and Myr saw a small party exit the watercourse and reach the perimeter with minimal interference. The group comprised a pair of the warriors in silver armor, with two wyr hounds shadowing a youth in priest's garb, a Sea marine who was swaying on his horse, and— "Taly!" Myr wanted to scream the ensign's name, but the sound emerged as a strangled whoop.

Faro had already turned back to the main conflict. Looking for Khar, Myr guessed. When she followed his example, she saw with relief that the Storm Spear and Madder appeared unharmed. But the aftermath of the assault would have rivaled any storm: the palisade was twisted or broken in numerous places, and a great many bodies clogged the gaps. The camp might have survived again, but it had only done so at considerable cost. Despite that, Khar was pulling the reserve together and sallying to meet the newcomers, who adjusted their approach to intersect his.

"It's some sort of bird," Faro said, distracting Myr, who saw he was staring at the newcomers' banner. He looked intrigued, and Myr finally understood why she had not seen any heraldic device earlier. The banner itself *was* the device: a phoenix wrought in silver and steel that rippled like a fish in the currents of the air.

"It's a phoenix," she told him, the wonder catching at her throat, "the banner of Stars!" The House of Yorindesarinen, she thought, and a great many other Derai heroes, too. Now Star knights had come to the aid of a Blood caravan, even though Stars was the House of Blood's greatest enemy among the Derai. Yet given what we're facing here, Myr reflected, we may need to redefine who we call enemy.

"*'Stars, the phoenix is their device,'*" Faro echoed, in the same half chant Myr had once used when reciting Ise's lessons back to her.

"The phoenix honors Terennin," she agreed, "whom Stars follow first amongst the Nine." The Star knights had joined with Khar and his company now, and after what appeared to be a brief discussion, the two captains took advantage of the Swarm retreat to destroy the remaining screens. Arrows flew their way, but this time it was the Swarm shafts that disintegrated in the air. A few ragged cheers sounded along the camp perimeter, but they were uncertain, at best, in the face of such clear evidence of power use. Succor from those we have been taught to despise, Myr thought, as Khar and his companions returned to the camp. She could see Taly's small party making their way around the perimeter to meet them, and longed to run and greet the ensign, hugging her close for the sheer fact that she was alive. But she knew what Taly herself would say: that a Daughter of Blood, let alone the Bride, needed to maintain the dignity of both her position and her House.

Just as Nimor, Myr realized, was remaining by the inner barrier rather than going to meet Khar and the Stars captain. Murn had joined his envoy, although he looked as if the effort of doing so had drained him. Silently, they all watched as Khar lifted his visor to speak to Taly, before turning back to the Stars leader. The two commanders grasped each other's forearms in the traditional greeting between warriors and equals—only this, Myr thought, as the two started her way, is Blood and *Stars*.

Not all the Stars company were accompanying their leader, presumably because that could be construed as a threat, with Stars officially a hostile House. From the numbers approaching, Myr guessed she would be meeting the captain and his officers, as well as Taly, the marine—who must be Namath, from Nimor's escort—and the youth in Stone priest's robes. "An Adamant initiate with a Stars company," Nimor observed. "I'll be interested to learn how that came about."

The youth seemed ill at ease, Myr thought, studying him, and Namath and Taly looked as though they had taken considerable damage in reaching Stars territory. She supposed they must have been forced that way by enemy patrols, despite Adamant being closer, although that did not explain the Adamant youth. Myr shook her head, puzzled, but there was no time to reflect further or do anything except descend from the cart and try to look like a Daughter of Blood and the Bride.

Faro jumped down, too, although he stood half concealed behind her as Khar and those with him dismounted and entered the inner camp on foot. A number of impressions stood out for Myr after that, beginning with Nimor and Murn coming to stand at her right hand—a courtesy, because she had no household of her own. She was aware, too, of Taly smiling at her out of a battered face, while the Adamant youth still looked uncomfortable, but curious as well. Khar was the depiction of exhaustion on his feet as he made the formal introductions, a roll call of Stars names and Stars faces. But from the moment the newcomers removed their helmets, they blurred into one face and one name.

"Tiraelisian, son and second child of the Countess of Stars," their leader said, speaking directly to her after Khar fell silent. He bowed low, but not before Myr took in pearl and silver, and a face as fair as the rare, clear dawns she had seen from the topmost tower of the Red Keep, breaking over the Wall ... No, she corrected, in an effort to keep hold on reality, his armor was silver and pearl, and he—Tiraelisian—had fair hair and gray eyes. The light of battle was still in his face, but he was smiling, too, as he straightened. "Honor on you, Lady Myrathis, and on your House."

And that, Myr felt certain, was the first time the formal salutation had been offered from Stars to Blood in the five hundred years since the Betrayal War. A murmur among the onlookers suggested she was not alone in her realization, but if Tiraelisian noticed, he did not show it. "I salute you, Lady, in my mother's name and on my own part." He paused before speaking again in his clear voice. "And greet you not only as Daughter of Blood and your House's Bride, but also as our kinswoman through your mother, Lady Mayaraní of the Rose."

Myr felt barely able to breathe, but was aware of the hush that had fallen and the way Nimor's brows had shot up. "Once I learned that you, kinswoman, were the Bride," Tiraelisian went on, "answering your Honor Captain's request for aid became a Matter of Kin and Blood."

"Kin and Blood," his officers said as one, and many others echoed the words.

"Light and safety on your path," Myr said, pulling herself together, although her thoughts continued to spin. Her bafflement centered on Ise and her father, because if they, or anyone else in Blood, had known that her mother—and therefore she herself—was kin to the Countess of Stars, no one had ever told her.

51

Out of Time

Kalan thought he had known what tiredness was when he constructed his shield-wall, but he had passed far beyond that
boundary now. His part in the recent battle had felt like instinct,
muscle memory, and a fair degree of Ornorith's luck—although the
heralds, he reminded himself, would say there was no such thing.
Listening to the account of Taly and Namath's mission to Adamant,
he was not sure he agreed. It seemed very like pure chance that
Tiraelisian—or Tirael, as he said they should call him—was on
his way to the Keep of Stone and so heard Namath's mindcall for
help, thrown out moments before the marine was knocked unconscious. Tirael had also detected the wyr hounds' presence outside
the Adamant watchtower and enough of their agitation to guess the
mindcall had come from there.

Just be glad he did, Kalan told himself. He was under no illusion
that only the boldness of Tirael's flank attack had saved the camp,
taking the Darksworn by surprise and playing to their reluctance to
take losses. Killing one of their captains appeared to have reinforced
that aversion, but more importantly, Arcolin would know the Derai
Alliance was now aware of his presence. In the sorcerer's place,
Kalan thought, pushing back against fatigue, I'd consider withdrawal:

either that or accept the losses involved and commit every resource to taking the camp. Arcolin's decision would depend on how important the camp was to whatever strategy the Darksworn were pursuing, as well as the feasibility of pulling back. If they were the intruders that Stars had detected, then any retreat along the same route would be a fighting one. Although now that the word's out, Kalan thought, they might as well fly their true colors and use gates—assuming they have that capability.

From what Tirael had indicated, the Darksworn were still screening their power use. Initially, all the Stars company had detected was a dissonance that intensified as they drew closer to the watchtower and no-man's-land. Rook, the young Adamant farspeaker, had experienced the backwash as a headache, but had not understood the cause until Vael, the Stars medic, explained. Vael had been kept busy, Kalan reflected, first pouring healing into Taly and Namath so they could survive the ride to the camp, and now helping Kion tend the wounded and dying in the infirmary.

Far too many wounded and dying, Kalan added grimly. Among the exiles, Dain and Nhal had fallen, and the reserve was reduced to ten. The enemy would have had us, he thought again, if the Star knights had not arrived. Yet uneasiness niggled, the sense that there might be a fact he had missed or detail he was overlooking. He ran over both their defenses and recent events, again in his mind, but could detect no previously unseen weakness. And Tirael's company, he reminded himself, also includes a farspeaker. The knight called Liad had contacted Stars when their company left the watchtower, which meant a relief force should already be on its way.

"You might say," Tirael said now, with a smile that belied his lazy manner, "that I'm counting on it."

Kalan nodded, reluctant to settle back in the camp chair in case he fell asleep. Holding their council within the Storm Spear's tent was a nuance both Myr and Nimor considered important in dealing with Stars, but which he could have done without. Even finding chairs had been a business, one that had fallen to Faro since Murn could still barely stand. The boy had returned in triumph with an assortment of seating, before Nimor drew Kalan aside to insist he be excluded from their discussions.

"A page wouldn't normally be included," Kalan had replied, but he knew Faro's unknown history with Arcolin made the precaution advisable. Frowning, he pulled his focus back to those gathered in the tent. He was seated at Lady Myr's right hand, with Taly on her left, but Jad was absent, because with Dain gone he could not be spared from the perimeter. Nimor had Murn and Tehan, while Tirael was accompanied by Elodin, his escort captain, and Liad. Namath was there because of his mission with Taly, and like her, looked much the worse for wear. The other person present was Rook, who so far had not spoken.

Whenever he thought himself unobserved, the young farspeaker looked both eager and absorbed, but his manner became guarded as soon as anyone looked his way. Kalan imagined that the wariness reflected the youth's position, which was undeniably difficult. Not only had events swept him into the midst of a Blood camp and Darksworn assault, but Adamant would almost certainly view his flight with Taly and Namath as treachery—which it was, when considered from the narrow perspective of one House alone, rather than a wider duty to the Derai Alliance. "What of Adamant?" Kalan asked him now. "Should we expect a force from the Keep of Stone?"

Rook straightened and spoke stiffly, as though making a report. "I tried to farspeak the keep before leaving Adamant territory, but the headache I had then made it difficult. Also, I'm still only an initiate, which may be why they didn't really listen." The wariness deepened into a bleakness that Kalan understood, because if the farspeaker's attempt to fulfill his duty and inform Adamant of events had failed, it made his situation even more precarious. Rook's gaze shifted to Tirael, the bleakness easing into admiration, then back to Kalan. "Lord Tirael and his knights were amazing, the way they crept out without anyone noticing. But I think Rul and Torlun will come after us, even though their force isn't large."

"Armed to the teeth and bristling with aggression," Elodin murmured.

Rather than taking offense, Rook nodded. "I was their only far-speaker, so they won't be able to send for aid that way, even when they find . . . " He swallowed, his expression closing in again. The Stars warriors all looked grim, too, but it was Taly who explained Rook's pause.

"There were more death standards on Adamant's border, Captain." Having taken note of Kalan's appointment, she was observing formalities. "The bodies were Adamant scouts who'd been sent out to investigate our story. But because it wasn't believed, they may not have taken their work seriously enough."

"I'm sorry," Kalan said to Rook, guessing he would have known the scouts.

The youth's expression worked briefly, before he bowed acknowledgment. When he straightened, he spoke as though working his thoughts through. "Rul and Torlun will probably send riders for aid when they find the bodies. And once they're reinforced, they'll definitely come here, because Rul said that if Ensign Talies's story was genuine—" He broke off.

"Then they would have to ensure," Tirael put in coolly, "that Lady Myrathis became Adamant's hostage against the closer alliance between Blood and Night. And added, no doubt, that they did not wish to share such bounty with Stars. You've given nothing away," he said, as Rook looked uneasy. "Even if I wasn't a truthsayer, I could read your Rul like trail sign."

Taly had taken that last remark well, Kalan thought, barely twitching at the mention of truthsaying. Although doubtless she was becoming hardened to the company of power users since the Stars company had rescued her. "He's not my Rul," Rook said defiantly. "I don't want to be like him, or Torlun. It's why I—" Flushing, he broke off again.

"Helped us," Taly supplied quietly, and he nodded, his expression set.

"You don't have to be like them," Kalan said. "Kinship, for all its importance, is an accident of birth. Who we associate with and how we act in this life is always choice, however much we may pretend otherwise, even to ourselves."

Rook nodded again, studying Kalan with open curiosity. Tirael looked quizzical, and Lady Myr was gravely attentive, as she had been throughout. Kalan was beginning to realize that was her innate nature as much as her Rose training. When she first met Tirael, he had thought she was dazzled by the Stars glamour, of which her new kinsman had more than his fair share, but now she was reserve to her fingertips.

Battleworn or not, Kalan had also felt certain, observing Myr then, that the kinship tie to Stars was as much a surprise to her as everyone else. Blood, the Rose, and Stars, he thought, shifting in his chair, ostensibly to get more comfortable but in reality to see Myr better. The web of alignments she embodied was proving to be spun more widely than anyone—with the probable exception of Ise—had realized. Now came the marriage into Night, which meant any child born as a result would be able to claim kinship ties into what were traditionally the three most powerful Derai Houses. Yet leaving Myr in ignorance of her heritage made her as much a Rose pawn as a Blood one. Put together with her Rose kin's apparent indifference to her existence, it suggested she might have been bred solely for that purpose.

Kalan shifted again, this time to conceal an instinctive revulsion. Deal with the Darksworn and the siege, he told himself sharply, and then with Adamant if you have to. Stars, too, if need be—for it had not escaped him that Myr and the camp would be as much in the power of a Stars rescue force as one from Adamant. "Right now, though," he said, coming back to the camp's defense, "I'll welcome any help that arrives, regardless of motivation. Or Ornorith may smile and the Swarm withdraw, but I'm assuming not."

They all nodded, and the subsequent discussion focused on the best disposition of the Stars newcomers. In the end Kalan decided to deploy them as the reserve, because it held the Stars company together as an effective fighting force. He was also uncertain how the Blood defenders—and Orth, he thought, with dour humor—would endure power users among their units. Utilizing the Star knights as his reserve also meant that he could substitute Tehan's marines for the fallen company leaders. "The reserve, though," he said, meeting Tirael's gaze squarely, "remains under my command."

"As does the camp." Tirael bowed, demonstrating that he had the traditional Stars grace as well as his House's glamour. Both drawl and smile were back in place as he regarded Kalan. "We are yours to command, my brother."

Nimor's brows rose, but he only spoke when discussions over the camp's food supplies—which were strained, but should hold if rations were cut again—concluded. "There is one more matter," he said, exactly as Myr had done two days before, and Kalan knew he meant Faro.

"You promised you wouldn't give me to *him*," Faro said, when everyone except Nimor, Myr, and Tirael had left, and Murn ushered him into the tent. Two wyr hounds stalked in after him, settling themselves with a *whuff* of breath that indicated they intended staying. Faro shook his head when Myr asked him if he wanted a chair. Instead he stood beside Kalan, not quite leaning on his chair-arm but close enough that Kalan could see he was rigid with tension.

"I won't," he replied. "But you need to explain how you crossed Arcolin's path, because now that he knows where you are and who you're with, he's going to keep coming after you." The despair in Faro's face suggested he already understood that, but try though he might, the boy could not answer Kalan's question.

Tirael, watching, grew more serious than Kalan had yet seen him. "He could be under some sort of compulsion," the Son of Stars said finally.

"I've never seen anything like it." Nimor was shaking his head. "We've been aware of Swarm activity in Grayharbor for some time, but when Faro stowed away on our ship no one detected anything amiss. I've had no reason for suspicion either, until now."

"He looks Blood-born," Tirael said to Nimor, "but if your ship accepted him . . . I don't suppose you're missing any weatherworkers?"

"Many lost," Nimor replied shortly, "but none unaccounted for."

Faro scowled from Tirael to Nimor. "My mam was an armorer, not one of your weatherworkers."

"Well, you can tell us that at least," Tirael observed. "What was her name?"

"Kara was what our Grayharbor neighbors called her, or Kara Armorer." Faro frowned, as though realizing that was unusual in Grayharbor, where people had family names, then shrugged. "But I just called her Mam." Obviously, his tone said, and Kalan's inward smile reflected Tirael's outward amusement.

The name Kara had a Blood ring: Kalan could see they all thought it might be one of the many variants of Kharalth. A Blood name did not lead readily to weatherworking, though—and if Faro had the ability, he was clearly unaware of it. Yet even the possibility raised the question of his father's identity. Kalan had already guessed that Faro did not know that either, even before the boy confirmed it, answering Tirael's next question. One of the Derai Lost remained an option, although from what Kalan now knew of Sea House ways, it was unlikely he would have originated there. In any case, Nimor had said there were no weatherworkers unaccounted for.

Another possibility was that Faro's father could have been—or was—a Darksworn. Arcolin himself had used weatherworking magic against the camp, while Nherenor and his knights had worn a lightning symbol in Caer Argent. The real question, Kalan thought, was whether a Blood Lost, which Faro's mother must have been, would have taken up with a Darksworn. She might not have known, of course—particularly if her lover was anything like Nherenor—and simply assumed Faro's father was a fellow Lost from another House.

It's all anomalies, Kalan decided, exasperated because he was too tired for this sort of puzzle. Yet *you* accept him, he added silently, meeting a wyr hound's lambent gaze—as the *Che'Ryl-g-Raham* did, too. Faro and Myr were both anomalies, he decided, remembering how he had used the same word in response to Kelyr's conjecture about her Rose lineage. It was Nimor, though, who had first applied the word to Faro. Straightening, Kalan repeated that thought aloud as he looked toward the envoy. "When you asked me about stealers," he added, since it was Faro's use of the term that had sparked their earlier discussion.

"Stealers?" Distaste clouded Tirael's expression. "I must admit, with calling lightning and the suggestion of compulsion— But all that was too long ago to explain Faro."

"Yes." Nimor was terse. "But when Khar used the term, which was what first gave me pause, he said he had it from Faro, who gleaned it from his mother."

Faro looked embarrassed, as he had when Kalan used the word in Murn's presence. "It's what she said: that you were stealers and I must never go anywhere near you or your ships."

"Yet she stayed in the main Haarth port for Sea House ships," Tirael pointed out, "whereas as an armorer, I imagine she could have gone anywhere."

"She was a *great* armorer," Faro said, quick and fierce. "She got sent all the most difficult repairs, even from the big cities of the River. Andron said she could've been rich, if she would only charge what her work was worth."

Which underlines Tirael's point, Kalan thought. He supposed Faro's mother may have thought wealth a greater risk than skill alone in terms of drawing attention, but none of this was leading anywhere. Nimor—all of us—will have to leave it, he decided.

But Myr, having listened intently throughout, was leaning forward. "'*Stars, the phoenix is their device,*'" she quoted softly. "That's what you said when we saw Lord Tirael's banner. Was it your mother who taught you the list of Houses and banners?" Faro nodded. "And when you learned them, what was the Earl of Blood's name?"

"Amrathin." The scuff of Faro's foot was loud. "I know it's Earl

Sardon now. Mam said you always have to update when people die, but the Houses and their devices endure."

Stunned, Kalan studied Faro as though he had never seen him before. Everyone else was watching, too, held in silent thrall as Myr nodded. "Mistress Ise said the same when she taught me. What about the Sea Count? And Stars?"

"*Tirunor for Sea, their insignia is the mer-dragon,*'" Faro adopted the half chant of rote. "*But they're stealers so you must never go near them. Telmirieneth leads Stars, the phoenix is their device; Night is Eanaran, the winged horse their emblem. The Rose is Nagoy . . .*'" His voice died as he stared around their faces. "What's wrong? Aren't I saying it right?"

"You're saying it perfectly," Myr assured him, still outwardly composed, although Kalan saw her hands shake before she concealed them in the folds of her skirt.

"Well, it explains the stealers," Tirael said, with an attempt at lightness.

"It's just not possible," Nimor protested. "There must be another explanation."

The wyr hounds, Kalan saw, were still tranquil, apparently indifferent to the consternation around them. "You were saying it perfectly," he agreed, putting an arm around Faro's shoulders. "But it isn't only Amrathin and Blood, you see. All the names are out of date. Over four hundred years out of date."

"Out of time," Tirael murmured. The gaze he bent on Faro was wondering, but the boy looked blank.

"Amrathin was the last Earl of the old line of Blood," Myr agreed. "And Kara is almost certainly a Blood name. So in a sense," she finished gently, "you've come home."

Kalan thought of the camp's reaction to Arcolin's proffered bargain and was not surprised when Faro shook his head. "Grayharbor was my home. I only ever lived there before now." He paused. "Maybe Mam did come from somewhere else, but Grayharbor's a port so lots of people there do. And she never talked about it." He

craned to look at Kalan. "Leti and Stefa's mam made them learn
stuff that was different from at the dame school, too, and they've
been Grayharbor people forever. My mam wasn't any older than
theirs either." Not four hundred years older, his eyes said; he looked
close to tears.

Kalan tightened his arm. "Whatever the mystery, it's clear you
don't know what it is. As for Arcolin, nothing's changed, including
your orders to remain in the inner camp."

Faro relaxed visibly. "Can I go, then?" he asked, and when Kalan
nodded he slipped away at once. The wyr hounds rose, too, and
padded after him.

"Should we keep a watch on him?" Nimor asked, once the tent
flap dropped.

Kalan listened to Faro's retreating footsteps before replying. "I
think the wyr hounds are already doing that."

Nimor's look said he knew Kalan was deliberately misinterpreting the question, but Myr spoke first. "Over four hundred years . . .
I would find that terrifying, but I don't think he really believes it."

"I agree with him," Nimor said, with undiplomatic bluntness.
"Even when we had the Golden Fire, there's absolutely no record of
Derai—or the Swarm, for that matter—being able to travel through
time."

Kalan regarded him. "There are records. One of my teachers
showed me an early account of our conflict with the Swarm, which
recorded a suspicion that some of their great powers might have the
ability to manipulate time. There's also Yorindesarinen's armring. *'I
move between worlds and time,'*" he quoted: "*'I seek out the hidden,
the lost I find.'*"

They were all silent—genuinely surprised, Kalan thought, even
Tirael, although he was the first to speak. "They teach you well
among the Storm Spears, it seems. But were any powers named? That
might throw light on the Swarm connection."

Kalan shook his head. "The writing was blurred by age and
waterstains."

"Even if your 'might' was certainty, Lord Tirael," Nimor said, sounding as weary of the business as Kalan felt, "why would a Swarm power, especially one from that far in our past, transport a Blood warrior from around four hundred years ago to the Grayharbor of today? It doesn't make sense. And Faro, as we all saw, knows nothing about it."

"Or doesn't know that he knows," Tirael murmured. "A compulsion could ensure that."

Kalan looked toward Myr, in case she wished to say more, but she shook her head. "I'd like to resolve the mystery," he said, rising. "Especially as Lady Myrathis has proven it's deep seated. But for now we'll just have to accept that there is one and remain cautious."

He could see Nimor was reluctant, despite his nod of agreement as they all stood. Tirael turned to Myr, his expression curious. "How did you know to ask about the Earls, kinswoman?"

"Partly it was the way Faro responded to seeing your banner. And Ise taught me about the 'stealing' "—her glance toward Nimor was apologetic—"but I don't know what made me put that together with the list of Houses and banners. I just did."

Possibly because of the simple act of standing up, Kalan's world was swaying, and he rested a hand on the chair to disguise it. By the time his surroundings steadied, Nimor was bowing Lady Myr toward the entrance, leaving him alone with Tirael. The Son of Stars surveyed him critically. "You need to rest."

Don't tempt me, Kalan thought. The assault on his shield-wall could resume at any moment, and he needed to repair the current damage before that happened. Tirael and his company might be power users, but without the protective barrier in place, he doubted they could defend the entire perimeter. And in view of his reflections around Myr, Adamant, and hostages, he was not sure how far he dared trust the Son of Stars.

Tirael was smiling faintly, as if discerning his reservations, which also made Kalan wonder about the limits to a strong truthsayer's ability. I should have asked Malian, he thought, because he felt certain the Son of Stars was very strong—although in this case he was probably just reading the face that Kalan was too weary to guard. "Why *did* you attack?" Kalan asked. "You could have waited until Stars' relief force arrived rather than hazarding your company. Most would say that was the prudent course."

Tirael shook his head, the smile lingering. "But am I prudent? My mother and sister would say not. Besides, the countryside's infested with darkspawn. So if discovered, our situation would have been equally precarious, while here we may make a real difference."

"You must know that your intervention already has." Kalan felt it was important to acknowledge that between them. "You turned the tide of the last attack."

"Perhaps," Tirael said, still light, "I am not brave enough to watch a camp massacred while I wait and watch. It takes, I fear, the kind of courage I lack."

Kalan nodded, recalling the way Lord Falk had spun his trap to draw out the facestealers and their allies in Emer. In doing so, the Castellan had hazarded even Ghiselaine of Ormond and the Emerian peace. Tirael's right, Kalan decided: that took a toughness I'm not sure I possess either.

"As for your getting rest," Tirael said into the pause, "perhaps you fear that I harbor similar ambitions to Adamant? But you won't be able to guard my young kinswoman from me, or them, if you die from exhaustion—or get yourself killed because of it. And I did pledge," he pointed out, "that we were yours to command. I think you know, too, that you have to trust someone, while our current circumstances make me trustworthy, at least until a Stars' force arrives. But," he drawled, before Kalan could respond, "if your reluctance is because you—single-handedly—have been holding the shield-wall protecting the camp, then hesitate no more. Elodin and her cadre may doubt their individual ability to build so impressive a construct, but are confident they can strengthen its weakened areas. They believe they can hold it, too, even against the sort of sustained assault we detected last night."

"You perceive a great deal," Kalan said slowly.

Tirael grinned. "There may be an imperceptive truthsayer in this world, but in general the two qualities are incompatible. And we still actually study power use in Stars, so I knew the shield-wall was no Sea House working. In fact," he added cheerfully, "as far as I can tell, it's unique, and I can assure you I admire it greatly. I'm also aware that it—and you—are the reason this camp and my kinswoman are still here." He paused. "And since she *is* blood kin, that places me in your debt."

Kalan stiffened. "I'm Lady Myrathis's champion and Honor Captain, which means there can be no question of debt. But if there were, it would concern her and me alone."

"Slapped down," Tirael said mournfully. "If I've transgressed against your Blood correctness, I apologize. What I was trying to convey, O Honorable Captain, was that you can and should get the sleep you need without fear for the camp. Beyond the fact that we're still outnumbered, of course."

Despite residual doubts, Kalan could not help liking the Son of Stars. He was reminded, too, of his Normarch friends, particularly Audin with his inborn assumption of leadership, and Girvase's willingness to test and challenge. "It's not just perception, though, is it?" he countered, adopting Girvase's approach. "Just how strong are you, I wonder, behind that manner you use to disguise it? And should I anticipate a relief force of similar caliber to your company?"

He had the satisfaction of seeing he had surprised Tirael, before the smile and the drawl returned. "It's not just shielding, though, is it?" the Son of Stars mocked, then grew more sober. "Even in Stars, I am regarded as a prodigy in these times, and my escort is also an elite. Only those who guard my mother, or my sister, the Heir, are comparable in strength. Nonetheless," he added softly, "I would not care to fight you, my brother."

That's the second time he's called me brother, Kalan thought. Still, Derai history contained many accounts in which brother, whether of blood or affection, betrayed brother—most famously, and disastrously, in Aikanor and Tasian's case. Best, Kalan decided, not to be swayed by the term. Yet Tirael was right. He did need rest, while the circumstances allowed for qualified trust, especially since the Darksworn, like the camp, appeared to be licking their wounds. "Or I you," he replied, still reserved, and supposed he was confirming every Stars axiom about humorless Blood warriors. Forcing a smile, he shrugged. "I've already given orders that everyone else is to rest in shifts, so as long as things stay quiet, I should heed my own advice." First, though, he would ensure that either Jad or Rhanar— now second in Dain's place—would remain on duty while he rested.

A huge yawn overtook him, and Tirael grinned before stepping into the entry. "We heard rumors that a Storm Spear had returned." The Son of Stars gestured around the garnet-and-gold interior. "But I didn't credit it until I saw the oriflamme. Four-hundred-odd years may not be so long for the Derai, but it's still a time." He paused, his expression arrested, then shrugged. "The same four-hundred-odd years since your Faro's list. But no doubt it's coincidence that it was the new line of Earls, after Amrathin, who really took against your order."

Except, Kalan thought as he followed Tirael outside, that Jehane Mor and Tarathan would almost certainly say that there was no such thing as coincidence, in the same way they did not believe in luck.

52

⊷⧫⊶

Path of Glory

Rook stared toward the Swarm lines and wondered whether he should have risked Torlun's retribution after all. His initial relief on realizing Tirael's arrival in the storeroom was a rescue, had swiftly given way to fear and nervous excitement as they crept from the watchtower, cloaked in Elodin and her cadre's shielding. Rook had felt elated, too, as the Stars company rode into the night bent on rescue, although doubt had crept in when he tried to farspeak the Keep of Stone and the duty farspeaker had reacted as if he was playing an initiate's prank. Nonetheless, the euphoria of stepping into what felt like one of the old heroic stories had soon reasserted itself as he watched the Stars warriors use their powers to negotiate the darkness and avoid enemy scouts.

Largely, Rook reflected now, because he had not felt in real danger until they encountered the death standards. The sour aftertaste of the vomit that had heaved out of his stomach then still lingered in his mouth, despite trying to wash it clean several times. By that stage, the Swarm aura had been clearly identifiable, but the Stars company had not turned back. And their charge had been magnificent. When Tirael made it clear that Rock would not be fighting, he had wavered between disappointment and secret relief—only to be caught up by exhilaration again when the Star knights charged. In that moment, it was only Taly's firm grasp on his arm that had stopped Rook from shouting a battle cry and charging after them.

Afterward, he had been buoyed by the excitement of entering the camp in company with Tirael and his knights. But during the recent council, Rook's sense of adventure had dissipated into weariness. The reality that he was alone in a camp that was potentially as hostile to him as the Swarm had sharpened, together with the realization that in farspeaking the Keep of Stone he had scuttled any suggestion that Tirael might have abducted him. In Adamant's eyes, Rook would be a confirmed traitor. The Earl and council might overlook Tirael's transgression because they wanted the Stars alliance, but they would not excuse his. Besides, Tirael had acted out of obligation to Kin and Blood, which overrode almost every other consideration. Adamant would not actually forgive the Son of Stars, of course, but retribution would be deferred until they had no more need of his House.

Until then, Rook thought bleakly, they will make me pay instead—and if my family don't disown me, Torlun and his faction will exact revenge on them as well. Even Onnorin, who was of the First Line of Adamant's ruling kin and the Earl's granddaughter, might suffer, since enough people knew she and Rook were close friends, as well as cadre comrades. Perhaps if I were braver, Rook thought, I would have stayed and faced Torlun. But he had known his First Kinsman's rage would probably have seen him crippled, if not killed, once Torlun discovered Rook had led Tirael to the prisoners. The Son of Stars had also thought that outcome likely, which was why he had insisted that Rook ride with his company and farspeak the Keep of Stone when they were clear of the watchtower. But now Tirael, like everyone else, had far more important matters to think about than the fate of a stray Adamant initiate.

Rook blinked, adjusting position as the Gray Lands' wind stung his eyes with grit. He was sitting with Taly and Namath on a row of casks outside the infirmary, waiting to see Vael. As well as curing Rook's headache, the Stars physician had poured healing power into both the former prisoners to get them to the camp, but he had been insistent that all three report for a more thorough check once circumstances allowed. Mostly, though, Rook was sticking with Taly and Namath because they tolerated his presence.

The Storm Spear's tent was visible from the casks, so Rook saw when the page called Faro emerged, followed closely by two wyr hounds. The next time the entry flap lifted, Lady Myrathis and the Sea envoy stepped out, and another pair of wyr hounds, which had been dozing in the shadow of the tent, rose and followed the Bride. The envoy was speaking to Lady Myrathis in a low grave voice, and both Taly and Namath watched with equal interest. When the envoy bowed and left her, the Bride lifted a hand and smiled their way. Having witnessed their reunion earlier in the day, Rook knew the smile was for Taly, but he pretended it might be for him.

Lady Myrathis was gentle and sweet natured, he thought, as she turned toward another tent: not at all what he had thought a Daughter of Blood would be. Rook could almost hear Onnorin's hoot, mocking him for sentimentality—but that made him think of the Keep of Stone and his family again. He blinked hard at the drear sky before making a show of rubbing his eyes, pretending it was because of the grit. When he looked around, Taly was watching him. The rope burns were still raw on her wrists, but because of Vael's work the swelling around her injured eye was subsiding and her good eye was clear. "Heart up," she said. "All's not lost yet."

"It's not the enemy," Rook said quickly, although in fact whenever he looked toward their massed ranks, a decidedly uncertain feeling churned in his stomach. "I was thinking about my family. And that I'll probably be exiled from Adamant."

Her clear eye grew thoughtful. "You should be all right, though. Lord Tirael seems honorable, and even if he has to consider the Adamant alliance, there's Lord Nimor as well." She nudged Namath. "Doesn't Sea always need farspeakers?"

Namath considered Rook. "We do," he said finally.

Rook had visited the Sea Keep once, when he was very young, and retained an impression of color and vitality, as well as the constant, powerful, mysterious presence of the ocean—which reminded him of a smaller mystery. "I thought Sea observed the Oath," he said to Namath, "but it was your mindcall that Lord Tirael heard." He could see from Taly's expression that she very much wanted to know the hows and whys as well, but would never ask.

The marine shrugged. "Sea observes what keeps us alive, and the ships sailing. Besides, most of us have some degree of power, which doesn't fit with the Oath." Namath's glance toward Taly held a hint of apology. "My flicker's just enough to know when an enemy's about and manage a mindcall for help."

"I did wonder how you always seemed to know where the 'spawn were before we walked into them," Taly said, "but put it down to years of experience."

"It's that, too," Namath agreed, before his gaze shifted to Rook, who was still trying to contain his shock. Adamant not only observed the Oath, but almost everyone in the Keep of Stone openly despised the warrior Houses and those without power. Even Derai with limited ability, like Namath, were very much looked down upon. "Given that jolt of healing you gave me in the shed," the marine went on, "I'd put coin on Peace taking you if no one else does."

Rook had not considered the healers of Meraun. "If I'm exiled for treachery," he said slowly, "they might not want me."

Taly's smile was crooked. "Captain Khar and I were banished for championing Lady Myr's cause in the Red Keep. If all else fails, you could always join us."

Rook eyed her doubtfully. "Even though you're all Blood warriors, while I'm priest-kind?"

Vael, who had arrived in time to hear this, glanced between them as he opened his physician's satchel. Taly nodded. "When you're outside both House and keep, the way we've been, many things don't seem as important as they once did." She hesitated. "My younger brother had the old power. Even when it was latent, I could never find him if he didn't want to be found, no matter how hard I tried."

Namath grunted. "Like young Faro."

"What happened?" Rook asked, remembering Adamant rumors about what Blood did to those who had the old power.

"It was like having a Wall storm in the house when his powers first manifested." Taly's tone turned dry. "But he wasn't murdered, if that's what you mean. Brave Hold's practice is expulsion to a temple of Kharalth, although I've heard many are sent on to other Houses."

"Or that's what you choose to believe happens." Vael was dispassionate as he examined Taly's recovering eye, his touch careful. "They could equally well be killed."

Taly was very still, and Rook did not think it was from the pain of her eye. "I think we would know," she said finally, her manner that of someone working matters through, rather than arguing. "Some things can't be completely hidden, like the way there are always whispers out of Oath and other hardline holds. But not Brave Hold and Clan Tavar."

A slight sound made Rook turn, and he saw that Captain Khar had come out of his tent with Tirael. He sat up straighter at once, but thought the captain looked odd, as though feeling a blow taken in the fighting. "We'll have to wait and see in terms of your vision," Vael was saying to Taly, "but overall you've been remarkably fortunate."

Because Sird likes to take his time, Rook thought, so he was only warming up when Lord Tirael's company was sighted. He could not say that, though, especially with Captain Khar looking directly at him. Torlun would say that Storm Spear or not, Khar was just another Blood warrior—but in the tent, the captain had spoken to Rook as if he was someone who mattered, not an initiate from an enemy House. Now, watching Khar fall into step with Tirael, Rook was seized by the desire to do something great and heroic, a deed that would save the camp and earn himself a place in the Storm Spear's company.

Vael was busy with Namath, and Taly—possibly because the healer had left a question mark over her vision—had withdrawn into herself. Rook concentrated on recalling the recent meeting and decided that it was not only a potential Adamant force that concerned

Khar: the Honor Captain had been reserved about a Stars rescue as well. I don't want Lady Myrathis to become anyone's hostage either, Rook decided. All the same, the beleaguered caravan did need someone to come to its aid. In fact, whenever he looked from the perimeter to the Swarm force beyond, Rook could not comprehend how the camp had survived this long.

During the meeting, Lord Nimor's secretary had explained how his farspeaking had been blocked by the enemy. But Murn was a weatherworker, so farspeaking would be his secondary power, whereas Rook was one of Adamant's strongest farspeakers, even if he was still an initiate. The besiegers' blockade might be weaker now, too, since they had expended so much power attacking the camp— and Rook had been trained to exploit weakness.

Frowning, he considered which House to farspeak. Blood had no 'speakers, and Sea and Swords were both too distant. The Rose probably is as well, Rook decided. That left Night, which was the caravan's destination anyway. Unlike Blood, Night still had a functioning Temple quarter, and Adamant's intelligence suggested they had been pushing the Oath's limitations in recent years. In fact, there had been Night initiates with the company that confronted Torlun earlier in the year, a fracas that resulted in the latter declaring blood feud against the Commander of Night. But if I'm already a traitor, Rook reasoned, I can't be any more of one for farspeaking Night, blood feud or not. He didn't know any Night adepts, though, or the disposition of their keep, so would have to find an alternate focus for his farspeaking.

"We should eat," Taly said, interrupting Rook's deliberations as Vael finished with Namath. "Then report for duty wherever we'll be useful."

"We could use extra hands here," Vael said. Rook felt guiltily sure the healer was looking at him, and resolved to return after the farspeaking. He avoided meeting Taly's and Namath's eyes, too, as they accompanied him to the only cookfire in the inner camp.

"My healing talent's only minor," he said, feeling the need to excuse himself. "So I've just been given basic training, enough to help get injured to an infirmary."

Namath studied him. "I wouldn't have called that jolt you gave me minor."

"Even if it is, you can still help those with more skill," Taly pointed out, making it clear where she thought his duty lay.

But helping in the infirmary wasn't the path of glory that Rook needed if he was to win a place with Khar—or Stars or Sea either. He chewed slowly, to make the meager meal last, and studied the inner camp for somewhere suitable to attempt his farspeaking. In the end he opted for the far side of the infirmary, which would screen him from both the other tent openings and the main crossing into the outer camp. The inner barrier would still be guarded, but with far less coming and going. In the meantime, Rook assured himself it was sound strategy to linger over his last hunk of bread until Taly and Namath finished theirs and left, even if an onlooker might have called it delay.

My younger brother had the old power ... Brave Hold and Clan Tavar: Kalan repeated Taly's words silently, watching the wind stir the tent's garnet-and-gold panels. And then, testing the word he could not say aloud: *sister.*

Kalan shook his head, because accepting comrades-in-arms at face value was the warrior life; more so when the warriors in question were exiles. So he had never delved beyond the names the others volunteered. Yet he, too, had been of Clan Tavar, out of Brave Hold, before the right to claim both was stripped away. The fact that it had never occurred to him Taly might be his sister, Talies, suggested that the rite of renunciation and expulsion might be more than a formality, after all. Their respective ages might also explain the lack of recognition, since Kalan had been seven when banished, and she no older than nine, at most.

You are no more son of mine. Six years ago, he had dreamed his father saying those words, and the rite made it equally true of his status as brother. The Blood Oath had not given any of them a choice, but Kalan had never forgotten his father's closed expression, or his siblings' hostility, as they performed the rite. Yet when he overheard Taly, she had sounded as though she remembered her lost brother with affection. *I was seven,* Kalan reminded himself again, *and she, being not much older, was probably equally bewildered by the turn of events.* He was sure of the present, though, and that he could not broach the subject until a day came when he could safely reveal his true identity.

" ' . . . *the line of Tavaral comes into its own again and the old Blood returns.*' " Yelusin's spark stirred, repeating Ise's words in his weary mind. Tavar, Tavaral: juxtaposed, the connection seemed obvious—except that Kalan's seven-year-old self had tried to bury the raw wound that he was no longer Clan Tavar. And whatever Ise might have meant, the most likely outcome if the camp survived was that Khar of the Storm Spears would vanish as mysteriously as he had appeared. While Taly and the other remaining exiles, Kalan felt sure, would find honorable service with Lady Myr in Night.

A wind gust shook the tent as his thoughts shifted to whether the Storm Spear's page should disappear with him. Myr's questions had revealed the depth of the mystery surrounding Faro, none of which pointed to easy assimilation into the Derai world. Especially, Kalan reflected grimly, with Arcolin hunting him. The business of the Darksworn's offer and the camp's response to it still turned his stomach—or would have if not for Myr, who had never wavered for a moment. Yet she could, as Daughter of Blood, have ordered him to accept Arcolin's bargain, placing him in the invidious position of either forswearing honor as her captain, or betraying Faro.

When it came to Lady Myr, Blood's loss was undoubtedly Night's gain. Kalan only hoped Earl Tasarion and those about him would see it. After this morning, in particular, he was far less sanguine about the marriage's success being none of his business. Increasingly, he felt that Myr's happiness was very much his concern, not just as an Honor

Captain or champion, but in the same way a younger sister's would be, or a close friend like Alianor in Emer.

You still can't interfere in an alliance between Houses, Kalan told himself. He did not think Myr would want him to either, any more than Taly would expect him to fight her battles. So he had best confine himself to looking after Faro, who *was* his responsibility, as much as the boy was anyone's. And get the sleep that will help me remain effective, he added. With no evidence of Swarm withdrawal, they were not saved yet, and the longer the lull continued, the more ominous he thought it—yet whenever he checked his psychic perimeter, he could detect nothing untoward.

Shortly afterward, Kalan fell asleep at last, although the dreams followed swiftly. The first, perhaps not surprisingly given his preoccupation with the camp's defense, picked up on the predawn's waking dream. Only this time, instead of a faceless woman examining the shield-wall from within the camp, a warrior in barbed, black armor approached from the plain. Were-hunters accompanied him, assuming their upright form rather than loping on all fours, and possibly because of their magic, no defender challenged their approach.

Were-hunters, Kalan thought, unease niggling again as the warrior sank onto his heels and rested one hand against the dike. Jeweled pins gleamed in his black hair, and the face that considered the shield-wall was all austere planes and sculpted angles. After a time, the warrior rose and departed with his were-hunt escort, their forms fraying into haze.

They approached through the Gate of Dreams, Kalan realized, that's why there was no challenge from the camp. He frowned, wondering where Elodin and the rest of Tirael's shielders were, or whether their talent did not include perception of the dream realm. Although because this was a dream, the warrior's approach could have happened earlier, or be yet to happen, or never happen at all—except Kalan could not shake the sense of danger pressing. He began to force himself back through the layers of exhaustion to wakefulness, but the dream countered, throwing him into his storm vision from the Red Keep.

Once again, the ocean was a dark, heaving mass and the sky riven by turbulence and fire. The same voices cried out in doubt and terror, culminating in the man who shouted above the tempest: *"She'll never hold unless— Do it, by the Nine. Live!"* The final words were new, but the vision rolled over Kalan like the mountainous waves and showed him the young woman from his Grayharbor dream, her face blotched with tears. The jeweled mesh no longer concealed her hair, revealing a weatherworker's cabled tresses.

"I'm sorry," she whispered, *"I'm sorry, I'm sorry."* Kalan still felt sure he knew her, but recognition eluded him. The Oakward taught patience in such cases, so he waited to see if the dream sequence would change its course, or continue as before—and found himself back in Myr's old rooms in the Red Keep. Fire shadows danced on the wall while the flames whispered secrets, and again Myr turned toward him.

"Who are you?" she asked. Her voice was steady, but Kalan could tell she was afraid. Yet when he stepped closer, all he could see was Faro's tearstained face, framed within the shield-mirror's tarnished oval.

"I'm sorry," the boy whispered. *"I'm sorry, I'm sorry."*

Kalan's sense of danger sharpened and he tried to shake free of the dream a second time, but again it would not let him. He could hear the Hunt of Mayanne now, baying out a paean to blood and death as it had in the Red Keep—only this time a new song, imperative and hornet-fierce, wove through the hounds' clamor. The Great Spear, Kalan thought, growing still, because he had never forgotten that dark voice, or the leaf-shaped blade with its collar of black, shining feathers. It had manifested through another dream, six years before, but the Huntmaster and his crow had maintained the time was not right; that the young Kalan was not strong enough to master the weapon.

Within his current dream, the hounds' baying grew wilder,

insistent as the spear's song and very near. *"We hunt! Awake!"* Wake up, Kalan told himself. He did not need to look to know the black-pearl ring would be glowing on his hand. *"Awake, Token-bearer. It is time!"*

It is time. Kalan could not see the spear, as he had in their first encounter, but the song that soared through his dream was as imperative as it had been six years ago. *"It is time, Kalan-hamar-khar ... "* This, he thought, was a different voice altogether, the words a moth-wing brush beneath the wild belling that sounded as close, now, as if the Hunt coursed through the inner camp. A moment later the pack were stalking into his tent, their eyes on fire—except these were not the Hunt of Mayanne's milk-white hounds, but dark sleek shapes.

"What," Kalan demanded of the wyr hounds that had followed him from the Red Keep, *"are you doing in my dream?"*

Eleven pairs of eyes regarded him. *"We are Maurid."* The mindvoice was stern and sonorous, the previous phantom whisper banished, and Kalan's heart leapt, as it had when the hounds first spoke to him directly in the tunnel beneath the Red Keep. Maurid, he thought, and felt Yelusin's spark quicken in unison with his pulse.

"No gate or door could hold us in the Red Keep. Did you think we could not pass the Gate of Dreams?" The incandescent eyes burned into his. *"Rise up, Scion of Tavaral, Kalan-hamar-khar. You must make haste: the sands are running."*

Breaking free of the dream's hold at last, Kalan woke to the camp's familiar sounds—but the ring on his hand glowed like the moon through cloud, and all eleven wyr hounds *were* in his tent, their eyes silver flame. *"Storm Spear, Token-bearer."* The voice of the Great Spear, too, had pursued him into the waking world: *"It is time."*

Myr, Kalan thought, because the sense of danger to her and Faro still pressed, but the spear's voice and the eyes of the hounds compelled him. And with the voice of the spear no longer contained by the Gate, the Hunt would be close behind. *"Storm Spear, Token-bearer—"*

"I'm hurrying!" he said. For the first time in six years, and without stopping to decide if it was something he could truly encompass himself, or whether the first and last time had been solely Malian's power, Kalan reentered the Gate of Dreams in his waking body. And the eleven wyr hounds flowed through after him.

53

Shadow Play

Once Rook was crouched in the lee of the infirmary, looking out at the expanse of the plain on one side and the vastness of the Wall on the other, the magnitude of his undertaking seemed far more daunting. I'm strong, he reminded himself, and skilled, too: all my teachers say so. In fact, he had already worked out that he could use Mhaelanar's sanctuary as a focus for his farspeaking, since Night followed Mhaelanar, the Defender, first among the Nine, and the sanctuary's altar, votive flame, and great shield of the god, were the same in every Derai temple. But once he focused on the dark mass of the Swarm force ringing the camp, Rook's recollection of his attempt—and failure—to farspeak the caravan from the watchtower reasserted itself.

Perhaps I should ask Captain Khar first, he thought uneasily. If he did that, though, the Honor Captain would probably ask Liad to do the farspeaking—and Rook's chance to prove himself would be lost. He reassured himself, too, that the fact the Swarms's battery of power hadn't resumed, must mean their adepts *were* exhausted, as Murn had been. So all Rook needed to do was find a place where the fabric of their working had frayed and his farspeaking could slip through, the way he'd practiced . . . He trickled a handful of dust and pebbles through his fingers and imagined Tirael calling *him* brother, as he had Khar—or Lady Myrathis gazing on him the way she had looked at Tirael when the Son of Stars first greeted her.

To *be* someone great, Rook thought, I have to *do* something great. Standing up, he squared his shoulders and stretched his psychic awareness to encompass first the camp, and then the Swarm blockade.

The camp *was* ringed about by power, he realized at once, awed. There was a shield-wall grounded beneath the old earthworks, which explained a great deal about why the defense had held this long. Beyond it Rook could discern the shape of the Swarm's psychic barrier, emulating the haze that thickened as it extended into distance. But the haze only appears to thicken, he thought, so the blockade could be the same . . . Cautiously, he extended his farspeaking, brushing along the invisible surface for a fissure wide enough to slip through. When the fabric of power proved impervious, he decided to explore whether the barrier dissipated with height, since several of his Adamant teachers believed that effect could explain why Swarm demons were able to ride the backs of Wall storms.

Part of Rook's awareness was still grounded in his body, with dust griming his sandals, a wall of canvas behind him, and interlocked carts ahead. The rest of his mind soared as high as the peaks of the Wall, where he could see the road stretching away from the beleaguered camp. The barrier did seem thinner, but Rook's farspeaking was also stretched, the first pain needling through body and mind. Suppressing doubt, he visualized following the road to the Keep of Winds, then gathered himself, stretching his farspeaking to its maximum extent, then pushing it further again. Momentarily, he thought connection flashed: flame rose on an altar, its spear of brightness reflected in a shield's face. Yes, Rook thought, *yes*. He began to formulate his message—but a cold wind funneled up from the plain and engulfed him, the image of the votive flame dispersed by a psychic gust. Dismayed, Rook tried to pull back, but found he could not.

"Well, well. What have we here?" The voice was both part of the wind and inside his head, but where the wind was brute force, the

voice was velvet and cruel as a cat's paw. *"A bug, scuttled out from behind its shield-wall. Shall I squash it, or play a little first?"*

"Even vermin may know something of value." The second voice hissed through the wind, piercing Rook like shards of ice. *"Let us make sure, before we amuse ourselves."*

"This bug is so pathetic that intelligence seems unlikely. But if it spares me a debt to Thanir . . ."

No, Rook thought, *no.* He tried to close his mind the way he had been taught, shutting out the ice that scythed through him, but each cut shredded his fragile resistance further. *Think of nothing,* his teachers always said, but all he could think of was the pain— and the memory of Taly's face as Sird pummeled her with power. Desperately, he seized on that image: Taly, resisting Torlun's inter-rogation in the watchtower bordering no-man's-land. Anything but the garnet-and-gold tent and the Storm Spear, except he was already thinking of them—

"Ah, the trumped-up captain from a forgotten order. But we already know about the Storm Spear." Impatience roughened the velvet voice. *"Can we use him to penetrate their shield-wall?"*

The cold voice was considering. *"It's more likely we'll lose our hold on him if we try, the same way my fire was extinguished crossing its protective barrier."*

"Ream the crawler, then, if he has nothing to offer. Just make sure he screams."

"Oh, he'll scream. But there may be something worth our while here yet . . . "

Rook was already screaming as the wind sliced through him, winnowing his memory of the Storm Spear's tent for details. The scream must have been only in his mind, though, because the frag-ment of awareness still grounded in his body knew the camp was going about its business, unperturbed. *Think of nothing*— Instead his mind snagged on the rhyme Khar had spoken, and he shrieked it out as the icy blades cut again. "I move between worlds, I move between worlds . . . " Desperately, Rook wished he could slip away from the pain and terror. "I move between worlds—" He screamed it out a third time, his mind and body raw.

"I move between worlds and time." The cool voice broke across him like a wave. Rook could have sworn he tasted the Sea Keep's salt on his lips as the wave held the flaying wind and the pain at bay. *"I seek out the hidden, the lost I find."* Now the wind was completely gone, and Rook hung suspended against a universe that was as much darkness as stars. He thought he could see it rotating, but that could just be the aftermath of the pain. Or perhaps he was the one being turned, a grain among constellations. Whatever power had snatched him from his torturers felt vast enough for that comparison. He felt, too, as though he had traveled as far from his body, and everything he knew, as he could get.

"I move between worlds and time," the cool voice repeated, and he found himself staring into eyes that were as dispassionate as the voice. Or perhaps he was looking through the eyes, into a mind . . . In any case, he felt transparent, as though the intelligence could read at a glance what the mind-flayer had tried to take by force. *"I seek out the hidden, the lost I find. And you, little mote, are undoubtedly lost."* Rook detected movement in the darkness surrounding the eyes, and gasped at what he saw—or perhaps the darkness was in the eyes, and the impossibly black pupils were chasms into which he was falling, falling . . . He spun again as he fell, the lost mote that the voice had called him. Only myself to blame, Rook thought, the words spinning with him: only myself to blame. But at least in the vastness there was no more pain.

"Clearly," Tirael's voice said, and it, too, was inside his mind, *"I should have kept a better eye on you."* Oddly, he still sounded lazy as he snatched Rook back from the darkness.

"The lost I find—and occasionally return, when I, too, am disposed to be kind . . . " The dispassionate voice faded, releasing Rook to the presence that he now perceived was more than just Tirael. Elodin was there, and the rest of the Stars escort, their combined power forming an anchor for Tirael and himself. A storm anchor,

Rook thought, another memory shaken out of his long ago Sea Keep visit. But slowly—slowly—the Star knights were reeling him in. He could hear their names weaving through the cable of power, as much a part of the strength anchoring him as their physical bodies would be. These were not the short names that made it easy for himself and others, but the full names that formed the essence of who and what they were: Elodinel, Liadinath, Vaelenor, Xerianor, Granianned . . . And both first, and last of all, Tiraelisian.

The Son of Stars' face was above him now, so Rook knew he must be lying on the ground in the inner camp. He tried to speak, despite his hold on consciousness slipping. "Storm," he managed to gasp out, although the word sounded strangled, and then " . . . eyes." But he needed to tell them what he had seen in or behind those eyes, in the darkness surrounding a cairn's mouth. Army, he thought, trying to lift himself up: army coming.

Tirael's hands were on his shoulders, holding him still. "Young idiot," he said, without any hint of levity. "What in the Nine's name did you think you were about? We may lose him yet," he added urgently. "Hurry, Vael."

Army, Rook thought again, and then—as the world diminished until all he could see was Tirael's gray eyes—you should marry Onnorin. She's strong, too, and honorable. The need to communicate was dwindling into dreaminess, haloed by dark, but Rook felt sorry he would never see Onnorin again. He hoped she would not be sad for long, or stop being one of the few people in the Keep of Stone who laughed . . .

He could still feel Tirael's grip on his mind and shoulders, but would have drifted further into the dreaminess if Vael's voice had not intruded, speaking with such precision it was almost a snap. "I've no idea why those Adamant fools thought farspeaking was his gift, because it's clearly healing—which may just save him now that the 'speaking's been ripped away." And although Rook tried to cling to the dreaminess, his head was tilted back and something bitter poured into his mouth.

Ripped away, Rook thought, but swallowed convulsively. The bitterness lingered, longer than anything except Tirael's gray stare, which continued to hold his as darkness closed in. He could hear the boom of the ocean, too, pounding into the foundations of the Sea Keep while he stood high above—so high that he was deafened when a thunderclap split the world apart.

Kalan ran, and the wyr hounds ran with him, deep within a Gate where the mists curved to form a tunnel and silhouettes gestured, a shadow theater along its walls. If the tunnel had a beginning and an end, Kalan could not detect it, but on this side of the Gate of Dreams his physical exhaustion had dropped away and keeping pace with the wyr hounds' speed was effortless. Despite their pace, Kalan held the strongest shield working he could manage, its edges blending into mist and the moon-glow cast by his ring. Perhaps because the shield filtered out other elements, the shadow theater grew clearer. Or, he thought, studying the images as best he could while running, they were the silhouettes of ancient dreams, a frieze cast against the greater Gate.

In one, a bloodstained, exhausted warrior and the equally bedraggled woman with him fought their way through harsh terrain, harried by the Swarm. It could have been the Wall, but Kalan felt that it was not: the peaks were not high enough. A few paces further on, the shadow pageant became leaping flames with a crow rising out of them. No, circling above them, Kalan thought, pausing to peer more closely and realizing the flames were from a pyre . . . But as soon as he paused, the images dispersed into mist.

"Do not stop!" the wyr hounds exhorted, racing on. As soon as Kalan sprang to catch up, the shadow play returned. Now, too, he could hear the Hunt's voice, baying of doom and war, and the dark thrum of the spear. No matter how fast Kalan ran, the belling drew closer, while the song lured him on. The next time he glanced at the silhouettes, the Hunt raced beside him, shadowy hounds with jaws agape. When, reluctantly, he looked again—this time without

checking his pace—there was only one hound and a warrior, as tall as Orth although of slimmer build, who stood with one hand in the great beast's mouth.

Kalan's heart jolted, remembering the Huntmaster's severed hand, but this warrior wore no mask. He did not see what became of the captive hand, for on the shadow wall a hind leapt away, and the entire milk-white pack slavered after her, their crimson eyes avid. He recalled Malian telling him how the hind in the Web of Mayanne had transformed into a unicorn that also fled ahead of the Hunt—but when he looked again both hind and hounds had vanished from the tunnel wall. Instead, the body of a warrior with one hand was being lowered into a grave. The shadow figures around him laid a spear upon his breast, and Kalan started, recognizing the narrow nave and undecorated surrounds from the Grayharbor sepulchre. When the shapes blurred into each other and grew clear again, the grave had been covered over by a steel panel that was twice the height of an infantryman's shield.

So now I know where the spear is, Kalan thought—but the Hunt was growing louder, the shadow pack racing along the wall again, just as the wyr hounds fled with him through the tunnel. *Make haste*: the words drummed through the rhythm of breath and blood, while his feet pounded out that the sands were running, running . . . Running *out*, Kalan told himself, yet dared not stop, even when the next long, curving bend revealed nothing new ahead.

Gradually another scene emerged on the walls of mist: a girl and a boy seated on a large block of stone amid snowy hills. The girl was braiding her hair while the boy surveyed his hands, one of which bore a black-pearl ring, so Kalan knew—although in fact he had known at once—that this was Malian and himself, in Jaransor. The night before this scene ocurred, both the Huntmaster and the Hunt of Mayanne had answered his need, thwarting the Night Mare that was hunting them. A little later that same morning, Malian would tell him about climbing a tower outside of time to find the moon-bright helm, and how the Huntmaster's crow had helped her reach the tower's crown.

Kalan saw the similarities with his current situation at once: the unending stair that Malian had climbed, and the corridor he ran through now without reaching a destination. *"I move between worlds and time."* He had quoted the phrase to Nimor, but the crow had suggested to Malian that it was a way of seeing time differently: not as a linear progression like the tunnel, but as a medium through which disparate places could exist in the same space at once. It was, Malian had said, trying to both explain and comprehend it herself, about accepting the oneness of all things. She had done that by seeing herself and the image that existed at the tower's pinnacle as one—which is not substantially different, Kalan thought, than stepping through the Gate of Dreams in my physical body and taking eleven wyr hounds with me. So if I can do the same thing using the sepulchre and will myself there . . .

He stopped running, and again the shadowy images faded. Steadying his breath, Kalan half closed his eyes and settled into a deeper awareness of himself and the hounds—both as unique identities and part of a collective one—within the Gate, before summoning up details of the Grayharbor tomb. First, he recalled the plain timeworn stone of the portico that was barely wider than the lane it stood in, and then the interior that was equally unadorned, down to the empty votive niches and layered dust throughout. He had tracked footprints through it, entering and leaving, and his breath had misted on the chill air as he examined the panel set into the floor . . .

Kalan's breath was misting again when he raised his eyes to the interior of the tomb. The door was closed, so there was no light except the muted glow from the pearl ring and the flame of the wyr hounds' eyes. The silence was profound, the voices of both Hunt and spear gone, and if Grayharbor lay beyond the mausoleum, no sound penetrated within. Kalan's skin prickled, but the Gate had shown the spear being buried here. "In the grave," he said. The words rang against the silence as he knelt and checked again for a means of opening the panel, but the join between steel and stone remained seamless. Frowning, he sat back—and the glimmer from his ring and the hounds' eyes snuffed out.

If it were not for his gift of seeing in the dark, Kalan would have been dead. One moment he was alone in the tomb, the next a shadowy warrior was upon him. Desperately, Kalan dove clear of the silent attack and got his shortsword out, blocking a vicious downstroke even as he rolled again, regaining his feet in the split-second respite. Another frantic block and feint enabled him to draw his second sword—and the black blades sang, absorbing the darkness that had filled the tomb. The glow from Kalan's ring returned, too, and he could see the wyr hounds, holding the milk-white pack at bay as the Hunt strove to materialize through the stone walls.

"Everything in your world will die if the Hunt breaks through Mayanne's weaving ... " The Huntmaster's voice was harsh in his memory. *". . . If the Hunt is roused, then the Huntmaster must master it."* And the ring was bound to the Hunt. Kalan understood, in retrospect, that the Hunt must have been waking for some time: at least since the Red Keep and very possibly since Emer. Yet so far he had seen no sign of the Huntmaster.

The shadow warrior attacked again, countering the power of the black swords with his own dark song. This time the contest felt more equal, but like the race through the tunnel, the combat also felt like a dream encounter, without either beginning or end despite the clash of steel and the striving of power against power. Kalan could also sense the wyr hounds' resistance beginning to fray, and responded out of instinct, directing both his urgency and will into the black blades. The shorter sword crooned, absorbing the wild magic that was seeping out of the Hunt and into the tomb. The wyr hounds growled in counterpoint, but the shadow warrior laughed, wild as the Hunt and dark as the spear's voice, and attacked with increased savagery.

"Of death my song and black my blade, for Kerem's hand by Alkiranth made." Kalan had quoted the rhyme to Asantir and the rest of the Old Keep rescue party, six years before, and now it reverberated through him as he drove forward, into the teeth of his

opponent's aggression. *"Kerem's arms were all black blades."* The
younger Kalan had said that, too, relating the legend that maintained
Kerem had been given the use of the god Tawr's weapons, including
his spear. *Kerem . . .* Almost imperceptibly, Kalan checked. His opponent crowed, apparently reading the hesitation as imminent victory.
Kalan disabused him of the notion as their blades clashed again and
both drew back, maneuvering within the tomb's narrow confines.

*" . . . anyone who grasps a Great Spear must be strong, lest the
weapon master the bearer."* The crow's voice whispered to Kalan
out of his first encounter with both Huntmaster and spear. And a
spear that had belonged to a god, and whose song meant death,
might well be indifferent to the prospect of the Hunt breaking free.
Within the Gate of Dreams, it could also be capable of transforma-
tion . . . Momentarily the shadow warrior hesitated, before his assault
redoubled in fury. Only this time, rather than countering through the
black swords, Kalan strengthened and extended his shield perimeter
instead.

" 'The Hunt wakes and must be mastered. Even a Great Spear
cannot argue with that.' " He grated out the Huntmaster's words.
" 'Such weapons choose their bearer.' As you chose me, six years ago,
and called me here now, saying that it was time. So either fulfill your
own choosing"—now Kalan drew deep, channeling all his remaining
reserves of power into the shield-working—"or find another spear-
bearer who is more to your taste. But I'm done with this game." And
he pushed his psychic shield forward, absorbing the shadow warrior
within its aegis.

The sword song soared, filling the sepulchre—and Kalan's adversary disappeared. The Hunt howled, the milk-white beasts flinging
themselves forward as the wyr hounds snarled in answer. A column
of light rose above the grave, and the Great Spear floated within it:
light and shadow played along the blue-black spearhead and across
the collar of dark shining feathers. *"Token-bearer."* The spear's
voice hummed, fierce with power, although if the weapon had indeed
shaped itself into the shadow warrior to test him, Kalan could detect

no remnant animosity. He dared not relinquish both swords with the Hunt still pressing, but he sheathed the shorter blade and shifted the longsword to his left hand. With his right, he reached into the column of light and grasped the spear that had almost certainly been Kerem's—and might once have been a god's.

Light, strength, and power flowed through Kalan until he felt as tall as the warrior in the shadow play. At the same time, the Hunt drew back, the great heads turning as though to listen—before one milk-white hound gave cry and leapt away, with the rest of the Hunt streaming after. Kalan knew an instant's relief, but already shadows were returning to the sepulchre walls, and the Huntmaster's crow took shape, gazing down on him from a spectral lintel. *"There is always a price,"* the bird reminded him. *"But who will pay? Will you?"*

Kalan's hold tightened on both spear and sword, but before he could reply, the beam of light vanished and an explosion tore through all three planes joined by his dreaming: the sepulchre, the Gate of Dreams, and the besieged camp.

54

The Lovers

Myr woke, uncertain whether it was minutes or hours since she had lain down, and found only her eyes would move. No wind disturbed the tent's interior, but the tapestry of The Lovers was billowing, and the same mist she remembered from the Red Keep had poured out of the mirror to surround her. The inkiness that limned the haze was deeper than any shadow, and darkness hovered at the apex of the tent and clung to its canvas panels.

Ilai. Myr tried to call the attendant's name, but her mouth proved incapable of opening. In any case, Ilai was injured and might also be immobilized. I have to help myself, Myr thought, although she could not think how. She was distracted, too, by the incessant whispering that filled the mist, recognizing its purport of insinuation and spite, even though the words were indistinct. It's a dark dream, she told herself: I just need to wake up. Except she knew that wasn't true. Whatever was happening in the tent was real.

In the Red Keep, the mist had retreated into the mirror when Khar appeared, but now long tendrils twitched toward the tapestry, only to scramble back, hissing, as The Lovers billowed out again. Whatever the mist was, it was afraid of The Lovers—but Myr's momentary hope died when she saw that the tapestry hounds' crimson eyes were locked on her, their savage jaws agape. The crow, too, watched her out of one sharp black eye, while the lovers remained oblivious, absorbed in each other.

"I'm sorry." Faro's whisper was so loud that Myr would have jumped if she could have moved at all. When her eyes slid sideways, she found him standing amid a wreathing of mist and shadow. Tears slid down his face and he was shaking; only the dagger in his hand was steady. Khar's gift dagger, Myr thought, as if that were somehow the most important aspect of the scene. But Faro was speaking again. "You may thank the Son of Stars for sealing your fate the moment he named you kin." The words were coming out of the page's mouth, yet Myr was certain he was not the one shaping them. "Ever since Yorindesarinen, we have made it our business to ensure that no more scions of Stars and Night are born into your Alliance."

The words were assured, but Faro's eyes were desperate, darting around the tent for a way out. Nimor was right to stress caution over the boy's past, Myr thought, and I was wrong. Although if she could only speak, reaching through to the Faro that still struggled, he might break free of whatever held him in its grip. But her voice remained frozen. All she could do was fix Faro with eyes that strove to remind him that she was Myr, who had fled Kolthis and the camp with him. Later they had crouched together in the gully, while a beast-man closed in on their hiding place . . .

"Can't!" The single word twisted out of Faro as if it wounded him, and the knife shook—but steadied again at once.

"I agree, it's a pity." Myr was unsure who the person speaking through the boy had addressed, but felt sure it was neither her nor Faro. When the boy jerked a step closer, the shadows around him ballooned like The Lovers and Myr glimpsed a warrior through their gloom, his armor honed to spur points at elbow and shoulder. "But even with the mirror present, the Storm Spear's presence counteracted much of my hold, as did the wyrs, always sticking to him like ticks."

Despite the knife, Myr's eyes were drawn to the shadows that crawled across the mirror's surface, while the mist continued to whisper malice. She shuddered inwardly, knowing both elements must have always been present, although she had never noticed anything unusual until the night Dab was wounded. But the tapestry gusted, pulling her attention back to Faro as he shuffled a step closer.

"They may call you Daughter of Blood," the entity speaking through the boy continued, "but that means even less now than it did when we gulled the Golden Fire, smelting a shard of your hero's shield into the mirror to disguise its essence, and so work our will on Aikanor. I doubt *you* have any more understanding of the forces shaping themselves around you than the Grayharbor brat, least of all why you must die." An adult's reflective note infused the child's strained voice. "Although the Derai's current state only makes your camp's resistance more intriguing. It should have been an easy mouthful, yet instead we've broken teeth on its defenses."

Whatever the Swarm had detected through the mirror and their hold on Faro, they still thought the boy was masquerading as Derai. So you're not infallible, Myr thought, watching Faro's mouth purse in another adult gesture. "More than time," the one controlling him said, "to be done with the entire business." The page's body snapped upright, and his next step was smooth. Only two more steps, or one if his stride was long enough, and both boy and blade would be within striking distance. Myr's heart hammered—but still she could not move.

Yet even in her fear, the part that was Ise's student, taught to observe and comprehend, thought how terrible this must be for Faro, his will trapped while his hand slew the person Khar had sworn to defend. She doubted the boy would live long afterward either, and sought his eyes again. *Remember*, she thought, focusing her will through her gaze: remember who *you* are—how you adore Khar, and love Madder and the wyr hounds. Remember your mother, who was the finest armorer in Grayharbor. Hold fast to all of them and what they mean to you.

As Myr concentrated, the shield's murmur began to acquire

meaning. A forest of skeleton leaves rustled, all assuring her that she was no Yorindesarinen to set the worlds alight with her power, just Myr the Mouse, the insignificant daughter of an abject line. All her endeavors, the dead leaves sighed, were doomed to futility ... But the Myr who had noted that the Swarm was not infallible whispered back, pointing out that mice could slip through the tiniest of spaces— perhaps even one as slender as a girl immobilized on a camp stretcher with only her eyes to save her. *"Heart up, Lady Mouse,"* Taly's voice encouraged her, out of memory. And again Myr threw all her heart and strength into reaching Faro, trapped behind his haunted eyes.

This time it was not just The Lovers: the entire tent shook as though a rogue wind had struck it. The tapestry hounds howled and Faro's eyes bulged, his body locked rigid as lightning forked through the apex of the tent and struck the tapestry. Myr smelled charred wool as more lightning crackled, but could only watch, both absorbed and terrified, as wildfire rippled across the ground. A strangled word that might have been "no," or "won't," crawled out of Faro's throat, and he dropped the dagger as if it burned him. The tent was blazing with energy, and Myr cried out, or tried to, as Ise's silver tray sailed through the air like a discus, knocking the shield-mirror to the floor. Wildfire danced across the tray's back as it covered the mirror, out-lining a riven phoenix in the silver—while Ise's walking stick sprang up, exactly as if an invisible hand had lifted it, and struck Faro down.

The mist vanished as the boy collapsed, leaving Myr free to move and speak. Her mouth felt as though cloth had been stuffed into it, and her limbs dragged as she sat up. When she looked around, she saw that the lightning had split the lovers in the tapestry asunder, but the crow still watched her from the warrior's half of the web. If a bird could be held to have an expression, Myr felt it looked sad. Faro was groaning, and she knew she should go to him, then see what had become of Ilai. She had just risen to her feet when sheet lightning flared outside—and the thunder that followed shook the world, tossing her down again.

*

The explosion that tore through the three planes had knocked Kalan off his feet. He could hear screams, shouting, and the clash of arms, but all at a distance. At first glance the sepulchre appeared untouched, but plaster dust fell from his body as he rose, and two of the wyr hounds lay unmoving. The other nine were whining and scrabbling up, their lost comrades' power glimmering about them, while the baying of the Hunt diminished at the same time as the roar of battle swelled.

Urgency drove Kalan, but he still paused when retrieving the spear. The hornet song had quieted, but the blade, which had been uncovered before, was now concealed by a leather hood. Exactly like the Huntmaster's spear, he thought—but the battle clangor intensified, forcing his attention back to the camp. He dared not linger, even to farewell the two dead wyrs, and made do with a parting salute.

The last time Kalan had exited the Gate in his physical body, it had been via a door that Malian created in the air. Now he visualized the interior of the Storm Spear's tent with himself inside it and the Great Spear in his hand, using the battle clamor as a grapple onto the daylight world. The wyr hounds belled their urgency, bridging the realms beside him, and Kalan's eyes opened to garnet-and-gold panels while his mind encompassed the hole that had been torn in his shield-wall. By the time he registered the barricade of Stars' power, spanning the breach, he was already on his feet. So far Tirael's company were holding—but although Kalan's barrier remained in place around the rest of the perimeter, the hole had undoubtedly weakened it. He could sense the magically induced onslaught of doubt and despair seeping through, and knew its trickle soon would become a flood. When it did, it would not matter whether the Star knights held the break or not. Everywhere else, the defense would fail.

Throwing open the tent flap, Kalan emerged into turmoil. The only still point was Murn, kneeling a few paces from the entrance with his forehead bowed against his staff. His head jerked up as Kalan emerged. "You're awake." The weatherworker hurried to rise and join Kalan as he strode toward the inner barrier. "No matter what I tried, I couldn't enter the tent."

If the inner camp was confusion, the outer was chaos. As soon as Kalan reached the carts, he saw that the psychic breach reflected a physical opening blasted through the earthworks. The blast had also revealed the tunnel used to reach the camp's perimeter undetected. Most of the enemy dead surrounding the opening were were-hunters, so now he knew where the remnant that survived Arcolin's tempest had gone. Together with their concealing magic, Kalan thought grimly, and cursed himself for missing the significance of their complete absence from the plain—while simultaneously noting that Tirael and his company were defending the breach physically, as well as spanning it with their power.

The rest of the defenders were holding on grimly as well, but everywhere Kalan looked the defense teetered on collapse. On the enemy side, a white-haired sorcerer with two adepts was stationed beneath the Darksworn's command standards, on an area of rising ground. Energy swirled around them as they battered the breach with power, pressing the Star knights hard. Otherwise, the assault was fiercest on the opposite side of the camp, where a section of palisade had come down and fighting swirled in and around the weakpoint—and a tide of magic, cold and deadly, was augmenting the Darksworn's physical attack. Nimor was there, shored up by his remaining escort, but Kalan doubted the envoy could hold for long.

Frowning, he identified Tercel in the midst of the chaos, and realized Taly was with Nimor, riding the bay charger and fighting with the battle fury of legend as she strove to reach Kolthis. The renegade Honor Captain was in the forefront of the second assault with the remnant Blood guards, and he, too, was cleaving a path toward Taly. "The ensign and Namath were with Lord Nimor and the others when the dike exploded." Murn's right hand clenched tight on his staff as he followed Kalan's gaze. "And as soon as Taly saw Kolthis, the battle fury seized her." If it was the true battle fury, Kalan knew that would account for why Taly appeared as indifferent to the aftermath of her watchtower injuries, as she was to the magical onslaught of doubt and despair. Both emotions, though, were stamped deep into Murn's face as he spoke again. "I should be with them, but Lord Nimor ordered me to rouse you, then prepare to defend the inner camp."

Nimor was right, Kalan thought. "Your presence on the dike would alter little now." He spoke with a calm he was far from feeling. "But I need you to get Tyun out here. Even from his stretcher he can marshal a defense. Tell him I want everyone in the infirmary who's capable of holding a weapon on the inner barrier, and every bow he can muster to cover a retreat." If the defenders retreated, they would all be dead soon afterward. In all likelihood, Murn knew that, too, but Kalan did not wait to find out. "Tell Kion and Vael I've ordered them out here with you. Their wounded will have to wait. Get the Adamant boy, too, and Faro. They'll both have to play their part." Throwing children into the breach, he thought: as if too many scullions and horsegirls and errand runners had not died already. "And look to Lady Myr," he added—although if she was with the healers, that made her as safe as anyone in the camp.

Kalan started to swing away, but Murn put out an urgent hand. "Lord Tirael shouted something as he left, about an army coming. From the way he yelled at me to tell you, I don't think he meant the Stars relief force."

If one Swarm legion had gotten through the Wall, then doubtless another could, too—while the Derai Alliance remained preoccupied with internal squabbles. But whatever might be coming, right now Nimor was weakening and more troops were advancing to support Kolthis's offensive, their battle drums rolling. Whistling to Madder, Kalan broke into a run, and the roan trumpeted in answer. Tearing his reins from the distracted horsegirl clutching them, the destrier plunged to meet Kalan, who vaulted into the saddle.

Tirael and his company were still holding as Madder turned, the breach about them choked with dead. A brief swirl among attackers and defenders revealed Jad and his company supporting them on the right, while Orth wielded his poleaxe to the left of the gap. On the opposite side of the camp, Taly and Kolthis were hacking at each other, locked knee to knee so the battle would not separate them. Beyond them, the blood-washed sun banner streamed above Arcolin as he led the fresh onslaught of troops on his Emerian destrier, surrounded by a knot of were-hunters.

A sledgehammer of sorcery, Kalan thought, poised to pulverize Nimor and the weakened shield-wall. Grimly, he urged Madder forward, the wyr hounds fanning to either side. *"If you are what I think,"* he told them, *"now is the time to unleash whatever power you possess!"*

"We are Maurid ... " The mindvoice vibrated, deep and somber, but was lost as Madder thundered toward the battle and the wyr hounds surged around him, baying—like the Hunt they had recently defied—to sunder worlds.

55

The Crow

The thunder had been deafening, but shouting and screams began to filter through to Myr as she pushed herself upright, and she could hear Faro groaning nearby. She wondered if the explosion had affected her vision, since the tent had grown dark again—then decided her mind must be playing tricks, because her brother Huern was there, silhouetted against a cave mouth that had materialized in the canvas wall. Both darkness and an intense cold were flowing through the opening, and Myr shivered as the silhouetted figure stepped fully into the tent. She had known he could not be Huern, but still stared, transfixed, as she recognized the warrior in barbed armor, glimpsed earlier through the shadows surrounding Faro. The austerity of his regard reminded Myr of Asantir, only without any of the Night Commander's warmth as he stepped toward her, kicking Ise's walking stick aside. Instinct commanded her to run, but even if she could have reached the entrance ahead of him, flight would mean abandoning Faro.

"Call for help if you wish, Daughter of Blood," the warrior said, with a courtesy Myr found more chilling than any Red Keep insult. "They will not hear you. Even if they did, they have more than enough to occupy them right now."

It helped, Myr found, to pretend to be unafraid even though she was: horribly so. "Who are you?" she asked, as Faro stopped groaning. "What are you doing here?" She sounded calm, she thought, as a Daughter of Blood should when facing danger.

"My name is Thanir, although I doubt it will mean anything to you." The warrior smiled at Faro as the boy's head wavered up. "I'm impressed, little rat. Most of all by your tenacity, although calling lightning should not be overlooked. You threw off my compulsion as well, which suggests I shall have to pay far more attention to what's being bred in Haarth. Yet you appear to have overlooked that you owe me a debt for your life, despite assuring me that I would not regret my generosity." The dark brows rose as the boy's head jerked in denial. "No? Ah, well . . ."

Thanir must have picked up Faro's knife, but Myr did not see it in his hand until he moved. As soon as she did, everything grew clear, like looking at a picture in which she observed herself stepping between Faro and the blade. Thanir's dispassionate expression did not change, and for a moment Myr thought nothing had happened— except the girl in the picture was sinking to her knees, folding forward over the hilt of the knife. In the picture there was blood, too, streaking Myr's hands and spreading across her clothes. She knew it was her own blood, not stains from helping in the infirmary, and the Faro in the picture was crying out and crawling to reach her. Myr thought the word he cried might have been *no* again, but his voice was too thickened by tears to be sure.

She swayed, her eyes fixing on the phoenix depicted on Ise's tray, as though it was not just Faro's arms, but the flame-etched image holding her up. Don't let him kill Faro as well, she thought—as if happier fireside stories might come true, too, and a bird engraved onto the back of a tray could save a life, just because it was the phoenix of Dawn-Eyed Terennin . . . The world beyond the bird of fire was all shadows, but Myr caught the gleam of another knife, this one with a lightning bolt engraved on the blade. When she fought to focus her vision and see who held it, she realized the severed tapestry had been lifted aside.

Ilai. Myr's whisper was only in her mind, because she was beyond speech. Yet what she was seeing still jarred, not just because of the unknown device on Ilai's knife, but because when the attendant stepped forward, she appeared to be uninjured. All the bruising had vanished from her face, and her eyes were clear as she held Thanir's dark gaze. "Not the child," she said.

The warrior bowed. "Lady of Ways," he replied. "I could assert that the boy is mine by virtue of the debt he owes me, to dispose of as I will."

"You could, but I would dispute your claim." Ilai's expression was as much a mask as any of the elaborate makeups she had painted over Myr's features, her cool eyes luminous in the dimness.

Thanir's face, too, might have been a mask. "You may find Arcolin more difficult to persuade." He continued to watch Ilai, his austerity grown thoughtful. "You're cleverer than he is, though, or even Nirn, to perceive that a shield-barrier, however powerful, cannot wall out what is already in. Although this one *is* impressive. I needed to rip a hole in its physical foundations before I could activate either the mirror or my hold on the boy." Apology tinged Thanir's thoughtfulness. "But much as I respect your cleverness, Lady, you are a long way from Ilkerineth's sheltering hand—and Aranraith will not be pleased to learn how you have opposed us here. Since he *has* ordered the boy killed, it would be ... inadvisable ... for you to cross him further."

"It would be equally inadvisable for you to threaten me, Thanir." Ilai's smile, like her voice, was thin as a blade's edge. "Do you really believe Ilkerineth would send me out alone? And the Bride was to have provided a cover for my entry into Night, so Sun's attack on her camp has equally undermined my and Lightning's plans. Nonetheless, I'm prepared to accept that with the maelstrom rising we cannot risk a new champion born from the bloodlines of Stars and Night." She paused. "The boy, however, is another matter. And his life is a small recompense when set against the debt the Sworn owe me."

Thanir's brows lifted. "You refer, I take it, to the way you opened through the Wall when fleeing your own kind? Yet since that was not done for our benefit, how can there be a debt?"

"My opening has facilitated much of what the Sworn have achieved over these past twenty years." Ilai was cool. "Besides, my sources tell me Aranraith ordered the boy killed in Grayharbor, which means you, Thanir, were the first to cross his will."

"Spies in our camp, eh?" The warrior's voice was fading, but he did not sound perturbed. Like his voice, the cave mouth was also receding, but Myr could still discern the tall figure in barbed armor, framed against it. "Well, I have warned you. Let that count in my favor when you next speak with Nindorith and the Prince of Lightning."

Faro, Myr thought hazily, had called lightning ... He was no prince, though. The shadows still clung, and the chill remained, but Thanir had gone. Myr's sense of distance from what was happening dissipated as well, replaced by pain. She found it difficult to see Ilai through the shadows, but heard her when she spoke. "I am truly sorry, Lady Mouse. I would have saved you if I could, and not only because you were my passport into Night." The cool voice paused. "But perhaps it's better this way. At least with Thanir, death is always clean, which it would not be with Arcolin or Nirn. And with both dike and shield-wall breached, the defense cannot last long."

She must have bent close, because now Myr could see her eyes, the color of twilit water and equally full of shadows. "I will return for the boy before that happens. But die knowing this, Lady Myrathis. They sought to use the mirror to suborn you, or whisper you into madness as they did Aikanor, but Salar's wiles could gain no hold over you. That in itself places you among the great heroes of the Derai."

Now I know I'm hallucinating, Myr thought. As if to confirm it, Ilai disappeared. Faro still seemed to be present because she could hear him crying, repeating the same words over and over: "I'm sorry, I'm sorry, I'm sorry." Somewhere beyond that, the hounds in the tapestry were baying after blood, although perhaps it was the wyr hounds she could hear, fighting for the camp.

So this is how it ends, she thought: alone except for a supposed Haarth urchin who turned out to be Derai. "It's not your fault," she tried to tell him, although she was not sure if her voice formed the words. "Not your fault, Faro." Nimor had been right, but so, too, had she and Khar—whatever the boy's part in this, he was debris caught in the flood, just as she was. Myr thought there was light where the shadow opening had been, though, so perhaps there would be a rescue for Faro, after all, if not for her. She was fairly sure there was not going to be anything for her, ever again.

I did my best, she told herself: to be a true Daughter of Blood and the Bride my House wanted, and to serve the Derai Alliance. But Taly was right. I should have practiced my weapons more, like she told me. Taly . . .

The hounds were louder now, and the light clearer. Myr could discern movement at its heart, although she could not make out details. She could hear that Faro was still crying, though, and tried to pat his hand by way of comfort, but was unable to feel whether she succeeded or not. I . . . should . . . have listened, she told herself again . . . to Taly . . .

The movement against the light was darkness, which felt right. Despite what she had imagined Ilai saying, Kharalth with her battle glory would not come for Myrathis the Mouse, who ran from arguments and hid in shadows. For a moment Myr felt sure it was the crow, fluttering out of the tapestry, but the face that stooped over hers was undoubtedly a woman's, even if the eyes were as sorrowful as the crow's had been, gazing down on her from the sundered web. "Who?" she tried to ask, and was glad the pain had grown remote again as the darkness pressed close.

"Emeriath," the stranger said, so perhaps Myr had managed the question after all. Emeriath, she knew, was from the heart of one of the old dark tales, a lady of Night who had been captured by the Swarm. Together with Kerem, who came to her rescue, Emeriath had trodden the Maze of Fire and escaped. A lady of Night, but there was a link to Stars as well . . .

Muzzily, Myr pondered whether Emeriath had been married to a Star lord: that might have been it. Even if she had not known she was dying, meeting a figure out of so old a story would have convinced her. Emeriath of the Sorrows was one of the lady's names, although Myr was not sure if Ise had called her that when she related the story, or whether the phrase had come from a book, or simply out of the light that shimmered around them. She looks sad anyway, Myr thought, as the lady spoke again.

"The spear has been claimed, but the Hunt is almost loose." The sorrow was in Emeriath's voice as well. "So now the hind must run, as she always does, or the fabric of existence will be torn apart."

"Captain Khar! The Storm Spear!" The defenders on the periphery of the assault were the first to absorb Madder's arrival, but the chant spread: "Storm Spear! Storm Spear!" The defense steadied as the refrain was taken up, but the pressure on them was clear. Kalan pushed his personal shielding to capacity as he reached Nimor, and the foremost attackers eddied back as their supporting power dissipated. Nimor's shoulders straightened, but neither he nor Kalan spoke because Arcolin was almost on them, his fresh troops pressing the assault.

Kolthis was dead, his bloodied body lying a few paces clear of his cast-down pennant, with the last of the forsworn Blood honor guards fallen around him. Some had no wounds, so Kalan supposed their lives must have been tied to Kolthis in some way. Taly was still fighting, although the sheen of her battle fury had dimmed as Arcolin's power built above the battle like a thunderhead. Disregarding Nimor, the Darksworn sorcerer extended his sword and pointed it straight at Kalan's heart.

Threat and promise, Kalan thought, as every glyph on Arcolin's armor flickered with its own unique sorcery, before blending into a nimbus that coiled about the sorcerer like a cat. It stalked Kalan with feline intensity, too, testing his shield for weakness while the runes whispered of lingering death, fomented in dark places and brewed out of blood and poison. The sorcerer's mindvoice twined through them, a rasp along the rim of Kalan's psychic shield.

"Thanir was right, after all. He said there was more to you than met the eye in the Red Keep. He warned, too, that it was wit, not luck, that ensured your survival, although Kolthis disagreed." The sorcerer's armored shoulders shrugged. *"But neither wit nor luck will save you or your camp now."* Kalan wondered how Arcolin knew he could hear him, but supposed the Darksworn must assume the ability came with his other powers. Or since he was a talker, he might not care either way.

More sorcery poured out of every rune and darkened the nimbus, which spiraled like the Gray Lands' dust devils as Arcolin advanced. Kalan spoke softly to reassure Madder and removed the leather casing from the Great Spear, releasing a glittering, hornet hum of power. Momentarily, the fighting on both sides faltered, before the were-hunters howled in answer and the nimbus drew in tight about Arcolin, pulsing to the same rhythm as the howls—then exploded toward Kalan and his shield. The Darksworn troops roared and charged behind the magic's blast, a flood tide of power and weapons, teeth and claws, intended to sweep the camp's last resistance away.

56

✛══✛

Spear Song

A net was dragging the darkness for Rook, hauling him back into the world of light. The net insisted that he was *needed* and refused to be gainsaid, even when he fought to sink back into the murk where there was no pain, and no shame of knowing he had brought calamity on them all by distracting Tirael and his company at a critical juncture in the camp's defense. The world had exploded, he remembered that as he was pulled inexorably back into consciousness—and now it was a confusion of yells and running feet, war horns and battle cries, the clash of steel and the screams of the dying.

Dying, Rook repeated, becoming aware that he was lying on a pallet close by the main entrance into the infirmary. And the attack on the camp included an onslaught of power, he could feel it even here. Shuddering, Rook curled into a ball against the aftermath of physical and psychic pain, and the return of memories in which the Swarm sorcerers tore at him, dissecting his farspeaking. *No*, he thought, curling tighter—but the net tugged at him: *dying.*

Instinct told Rook the summons did not refer to the camp's defenders, falling along the perimeter, but to a particular death that was calling out to him, or to his healing power. *Dying . . .* This time Rook followed the imperative tug, rolling from his pallet and crawling on hands and knees until he was clear of the infirmary. The pull strengthened once he staggered to his feet, drawing him toward the Bride's tent. He fumbled over the ties before realizing the flap was already unlaced—only to cry out, lurching to a halt, when he stepped inside. The interior smelled of blood and burning, and Lady Myrathis lay at the foot of a tapestry that had been torn, or burned, in two, with a knife thrust into her. Captain Khar's page crouched beside her, his face tracked with snot and tears and blood. Gore was smeared across his hands and clothes as well, but from what Rook could see, all the blood came from the Bride.

Dying. Yes, Rook thought, because he doubted anything could be done with such a wound, even by Vael or the Sea House physician. He knew he should not repeat his farspeaking mistake, but run and fetch both of them immediately. He also knew that if he did, they would arrive too late. It might well be too late already. And this, Rook told himself, is something I can do. To atone . . .

Dying. Something I can do. Atonement. The words were a refrain, but Rook was aware, as he knelt opposite the page, that without proper training or understanding limitations, what he intended doing could kill him and might not save the Daughter of Blood. But it was still something he could do, something that mattered. Sinking to his knees and placing his hands over hers, he tapped deep into whatever healing power he possessed and let it pour into Lady Myrathis.

Taly was shouting out Brave Hold's battle cry, but the Darksworn war cries drowned her voice as Madder and the wyr hounds leapt to meet Arcolin. Nimor's marines answered with a Sea House yell as the first rake of Arcolin's sorcery scored Kalan's shield—but the black spear absorbed the brunt of the assault and turned the remainder back toward the attackers. Wary of the spear's threat, the conventional forces parted, opening a path for the contest of power between Storm Spear and sorcerer. Arcolin snarled and sheathed his sword, pulling a spear of his own from the air. More runes were inscribed on both blade and shaft, the power twisting along them like flames. Kalan guessed that their touch, too, would burn—even as Arcolin spurred forward, striking at him simultaneously with both rune-spear and sorcery. This time, the magic clawed deeper into Kalan's shielding before he threw it off.

Madder sprang sideways, avoiding another spear thrust before wheeling to counterattack. Arcolin wove to one side, cloaked in the rune nimbus as the black spear thrummed and Madder spun about again, closing any potential gap before it opened up. Arcolin's sorcery snapped outward a second time, the runes crackling, and Kalan pushed his psychic shield forward to intercept. The collision of power resounded above the battle, and both sides faltered as the Great Spear's song swelled, cleaving a path through Arcolin's nimbus.

The sorcerer wrenched his horse away, spitting curses like lurker venom—because they *were* lurker venom, Kalan realized, expelling the psychic poison before it could dissolve his shield. Remembering Nherenor's fate, he reinforced his shielding as Arcolin assailed him again. A were-hunter abandoned its own magical protection in a bid to hamstring Madder, and the roan whirled, countering the threat with hooves and teeth. Kalan swung the spear like an Emerian ladyspike, and the sweep set Arcolin's horse back on its haunches as a wyr hound flung itself on the were-hunter.

The two rolled over in a snarl of claws and teeth, almost beneath Madder's hooves, before Kalan—wary of gutting strokes from below—kneed the destrier clear. His return sweep with the spear intercepted Arcolin's strike, and he felt the physical and psychic strain as the weapons locked: runes pulsing against spear song, sorcery against shield-magic. When a second were-hunter raced in, Kalan flattened himself against Madder's neck as the destrier pivoted to meet it, letting Arcolin's spear whistle overhead. Straightening, Kalan spitted the were-hunter as it sprang for him, but the spear caught when he tried to wrench it free. Clamping his knees against the roan's flanks, he abandoned his buckler and blocked Arcolin's counterstrike with Asantir's shortsword, before finally twisting the black spear free of the were-hunter's corpse.

Exultant, the spear thrummed its song of blood and death, while the sword sang in counterpoint, sparks of power flying as Kalan struck at the rune-spear again. He felt his weapons' power soar as the two songs merged and Arcolin retreated, hurling more poison-laced curses. When Kalan pressed his advantage, the sorcerer raised the rune-spear high and cracked out a command—and the remaining were-hunters sprang into Kalan's path.

He's withdrawing. The thought was fire in Kalan's mind as the black weapons keened in unison. The wyr hounds and the marines were still with him—although he thought both were fewer than they had been, as more Darksworn in their bestial helms pressed in on Nimor. The spear-and-sword song built again, gradually rolling back the were-hunters' magic, and Kalan became aware of Taly, reckless of Arcolin's power as she hewed down from Tercel's saddle, protecting his right. And like Taly with Kolthis, he was not prepared to let Arcolin escape. He had to finish the Darksworn or be finished, one or the other, both for the camp's sake and—at a far more personal level—for Faro's.

A fresh wave of were-hunter magic swept toward Kalan as the black blades keened again, echoing his resolve and sucking the opposing power into themselves, Kalan was certain he could feel the weapons' strength increase every time he struck home. Arcolin must have perceived the danger they presented because he was gathering his power, chanting runes that ignited in the air as he uttered them. His voice thundered, drowning out the battle roar, and the combat gradually grew dim.

The Darksworn sorcery, Kalan realized, was drawing him onto a Swarm plane where Arcolin's power would be enhanced and his own diminished. Grimly, he pulled the beleaguered earthworks and battle din back into focus as the Darksworn magic, shaped into a spear as black as his own, drove into his psychic shield. The resulting shock was so profound that both Kalan's mind and body reeled. He knew he was trying to urge Madder aside and duck again as Arcolin flung the rune-spear in the psychic attack's wake—but comprehended, with the slow-motion certainty of nightmare, that his evasion would not succeed.

A wyr hound leapt through the half-light between planes, intersecting the rune-spear's trajectory, and the cast meant for Kalan pierced its side. *"I am Maurid, we are ..."* The mindvoice was barely a whisper as the beast fell. The glow of its eyes was already fading as Kalan pulled himself fully back into the daylight world, in time to witness light rising from the hound's body. The black weapons wailed, striving to absorb the wyr power ahead of Arcolin's rune nimbus, which also surged forward. Another of the hounds was too quick for both, reaching its fallen comrade and absorbing the light as Kalan restrained his weapons and Madder sidled, keeping Arcolin in view.

Thwarted of the wyr hound's essence, the Darksworn retracted his nimbus again. Sorcery roiled about him like an electric storm, and the runes were a lurid blaze, their collective power spiraling into a vortex of energy and magic.

The spiral was some kind of pocket portal that he used to escape. I threw my dagger just as it closed ... Malian's description of her final encounter with Arcolin, beneath the great temple of Imuln in Caer Argent, resounded in Kalan's memory. Now this spiral, too, was spinning faster, its inside curve beginning to collapse in on itself with the Darksworn sorcerer at its heart—but Kalan was gripped by an older memory still, of Asantir casting her black spear through another portal in the Old Keep of Winds and slaying the demon at its heart.

A Great Spear was a very different proposition to a dagger. Yet sometimes, in order to gain all, one must risk all. Lord Falk had taught him that, among a great deal else. Channeling all the power he could draw into the spear, Kalan dropped his psychic shield and released the weapon in one great throw—through the closing portal, the protective nimbus, and the rune armor, to pierce Arcolin's heart.

Kalan just managed to restore his shield before the shockwave from the shattered portal reached him, but Madder still struggled to retain his footing as the reverberation shuddered out of the ground and into every bone. A voice was wailing and would not stop, but it was only as the aftershock cleared that Kalan realized it came from the Great Spear—which, rather than disintegrating with the portal like Asantir's weapon, had pinned Arcolin's body to the Gray Lands' earth.

Sheathing the shortsword first, Kalan worked the spear free. The wail faded altogether as he wiped the spearhead clean of blood, and the battle roar returned. The were-hunters were all dead, either bound to Arcolin's will, as the former Blood warriors had been to Kolthis, or too close to the sorcerous blast. Among Kalan's own, only Taly on Tercel, four marines, and six wyr hounds—all with heaving flanks and hanging heads, their fur thick with blood that was not their own—were still standing. Tehan was down with an ugly leg wound, her mouth clamped against the pain, and Nimor, collapsed onto a wagon tongue, was simply gray.

Kalan had hoped the Darksworn would be cast into disarray by Arcolin's death, but although the immediate attack had pulled back, the wider battle still raged. So either Arcolin was not the overall commander, or the Darksworn's second-in-command had stepped seamlessly into his place.

Despite aching in every bone and muscle, Kalan forced himself to assess the current situation. On the Darksworn side, a tall figure in black armor had joined the white-haired sorcerer, and shadows circled them both as the pressure on the breach intensified. The Star knights still held, but their bright armor was battle grimed and their numbers fewer, while the remainder of the defense, like the palisade, now presented as many gaps as ranks. Gathering Madder's reins, Kalan dispatched the few lingering runners to warn his commanders to be ready to fall back.

Although they'll already know, he thought, that it must come soon, or never ... "I'm needed in the main breach," he told Nimor and Taly. The envoy just nodded, while Taly raised a hand, her good eye intent on the Darksworn who had fled when Arcolin fell, but were now regrouping. She did not turn even when Kalan urged Madder to a run, the wyr hounds racing alongside.

Elodin and her cadre still had their power locked across the rupture in the shield-wall, but Kalan could sense their psychic strain, and also that Tirael and the rest of his knights were too hard-pressed to loan them much power. Swinging down beside the Son of Stars and slapping Madder away, he shouted to make himself heard. "Carve me a space forward of Elodin, my brother!"

"Forward?" Tirael shouted back. But even as Kalan nodded, the Son of Stars was yelling orders and battling into the enemy ranks with his knights about him. Kalan followed with the wyr hounds, and while the Star knights held the attackers back, he worked the butt of the Great Spear into the center of the breach. *"Now let's see what you're really made of,"* he told all three black blades—and thrust Asantir's swords into the ground on either side of the spear, creating a new barrier ahead of Elodin and her cadre's psychic shield.

The weapons crooned on a low note, each blade quivering as the energy storm pounding into the breach began to gyre around them. Whirlpools in the flood, Kalan thought, doing what he could to shield them from counterattack.

Rather than drawing back, the miasma of shadows around the opposing sorcerers thickened, and a pallid, green-tinged glow haloed the white-haired adept. "Here it comes," Tirael shouted, and Kalan could have sworn the Son of Stars was laughing as the black blades' song deepened. But one of his knights—Liad, Kalan thought—was shouting, too, and gesturing urgently toward the wider plain.

The wyr hounds pushed forward, wresting Kalan a momentary respite from the storm of power. Snatching at it, he saw a long, dark line emerging from the Gray Lands' haze. From the amount of dust kicked up, this had to be the vanguard of Murn's army, with the main force still concealed by the murk—and coming from entirely the wrong direction to be Derai.

Nothing to be done. The words spun in Kalan's mind like the flag wheels Southern Realms' traders used to ward their wagons against ill luck. Only in this case, Ornorith had turned her smiling face away at last, because the combination of the existing Darksworn force, together with the approaching tide, made the camp's survival impossible. Nothing at all to be done, Kalan thought—and shouted, a gut-wrenching yell of anger, frustration, and despair.

57

The Hind

The hounds in the tapestry were baying for blood and death, but there was light again, shimmering from the phoenix's silver into a clear, twilit green that haloed Emeriath's dark hair. The light slowed Myr's downward spiral, buoying her up so that she could take in details once more: like Emeriath's cloak of black plumage, and the solitary crow's feather that hung from her ear. Myr could discern the outline of someone else as well, who was the source of the green light. When she strained to see more clearly, she decided it might be Rook, the young Adamant farspeaker. She thought Faro was still present, too, even though he had fallen silent and she could no longer feel his hand beneath hers.

The hind must run. Myr repeated the words to herself, her eyes shifting beyond Emeriath to the hounds in the tapestry. They had always been lifelike, but now she could see the flow of muscle below the milk-white flesh and the way they jostled each other, making the tapestry billow as they fought to escape through the tear in its fabric. Myr could distinguish the bloodlust in the hounds' eyes, too, and the cruelty of their teeth. But she could no longer see the hind, lying at the lovers' feet.

The hind must run—but what, Myr wondered, if the hind is caught?

Perhaps she had spoken her thoughts aloud, or Emeriath could hear them in this realm between life and death. "Then the web of Mayanne will come undone," she told Myr gravely, "and the Hunt will be free to raven and slay across worlds and time. Yet we face the same danger now. When the Token-bearer claimed the Great Spear, the bonds that concealed it dissolved, as they were meant to do. But the spear, like the Token, is tied to the Hunt, so the violent explosion of power across the planes, and the sundering of the web that followed, has damaged Mayanne's weaving to a perilous extent."

Perhaps, Myr thought, her eyes shifting back to Emeriath, this Great Spear should have been left alone, then.

"If only that were possible," Emeriath said, her regret palpable. "But I have been in the tapestry for many aeons, and there is little I do not know of its workings. If the Wall of Night and all the realms tied to it are not to fall to what you call the Swarm, then the Token-bearer must take up the spear and the destiny that goes with it."

Myr knew there was an important question she needed to ask, now that the green light had stabilized her descent into darkness. Into death, she thought, with a detachment that Ise would have approved—but the question slipped from her grasp as her mind snagged on Emeriath's aeons. "How long," she asked instead, "since the spear was last claimed?"

"Since Kerem's day. Another should have taken it up, but the star-bright hero fell, and too much else fell with her." The tapestry shuddered, and the belling of the Hunt grew louder, filling Myr with dread. "You can hear them," Emeriath said. "The Token-bearer does as well, but that is to be expected." Her dark eyes were intent on Myr, although she spoke mostly to herself. "I wonder how much the Rose foresaw of this, when they sent the tapestry to the Red Keep with your mother?"

Amid so much she did not understand, Myr focused on the implication that Ise might have known the tapestry was more than it seemed. And her walking stick and the tray? she wondered, remembering how they had both come to life and thwarted Thanir's initial working.

"The Rose have always been charged with holding the Alliance together," Emeriath said softly, "so I guessed you were another step in their design to create a new champion. Now, though . . ." The sadness in her voice deepened. "I wonder if they foresaw that you and the Token-bearer would be brought together? This web is The Lovers, after all, and encompasses all the elements of the first weaving: the Champion, the Lady, and the hind that lies at their feet, the Sacrifice . . ."

She did not mention the crow, Myr noted, recalling how—despite her own doubts—Khar had been sure the bird belonged in the tapestry as well.

"And the child has so much power," Emeriath continued softly, at the same time as Myr felt Faro's hand beneath hers again. She guessed that like Rook—she was sure it *was* Rook—Faro was also partially in this half-realm, as well as being physically present in the tent. "It would be reasonable," Emeriath continued, "for any foreseeing to include him, too, and for the foreseer, or seers, to assume he was the sacrifice. Only he never heard the Hunt." She shook her dark head. "The wise know that foreseeing is never certain, and that like a river, the flow of events may switch course. But perhaps your duenna did not know what your hearing the milk-white hounds meant, or that it would bring the Rose's larger plans to nothing."

Myr might be dying, but she knew Emeriath meant that it was she, and not Faro, who was the sacrifice that was somehow connected to the hind. The woman with the cloak of crow's feathers was also implying that Ise might have undestood The Lovers' significance, and been prepared to sacrifice Faro, or even Myr herself. But Myr could not believe such a thing of Ise, whom she knew had loved her. She would never betray me, Myr protested silently. She could not believe that Ise would knowingly betray anyone else either.

Not even, doubt's small voice asked, *if she thought it was the only way to save the life contained in all the worlds?* Yet everything Ise herself had taught Myr cried out that no one could rightly force or manipulate another into the role of sacrifice, no matter how many others might benefit. The compulsion, she decided, not at all hazy now, would negate the sacrifice.

"The sacrifice must be willing," Emeriath agreed. "Even if that were not a universal principle, the original hind sacrificed herself and that flowed into the way the web was woven."

Am I willing, though? Myr wondered—but now the hounds were louder still, so there was no more time. She must find out what was required before the last of her life trickled away. "What would I have to do?" she whispered.

Emeriath bowed her head, the long crow's feather in her ear brushing across one shoulder. "Like the one you know as Ilai, I am also an opener of ways. I will make a path for your spirit to enter the tapestry and infuse the hind, which must then run, drawing the hounds deep into the web so its outer bindings may restore themselves."

Thanir *had* called Ilai something to do with ways. He had named her Lady, too, as though she were of comparable rank to the Derai's ruling kin. But Myr could no longer concern herself with that. "What if the hounds don't pursue the hind?"

"They always do," Emeriath replied. "That, too, is bound into Mayanne's weaving."

Myr tried to shut out the memory of the hounds' cruel teeth and savage eyes. She guessed that if the Hunt caught her, the hounds would rend her spirit as well as the hind's flesh, and then she would never come to Hurulth's Hall. Myr did not know if she was brave enough for any of that. Emeriath said nothing, simply waited, and perhaps because she wished to delay, the question that had escaped Myr earlier resurfaced. "Who is the Token-bearer?"

Surprise touched Emeriath's gravity. "I'm sorry, Myrathis, I thought you knew. He is the one you call Khar, the Storm Spear."

Myr felt an answering lurch through her whole being: *Khar*—who was her captain and her champion. And in all the sagas, the honor and obligation of the champion's bond was always two-way. "If the hind doesn't run, what will happen to him?"

"The same as to all who inhabit the worlds, only he will be among the first to die, because although he bears the Token, without the web the Hunt will not be able to be mastered."

I, too, keep faith. Myr thought of Khar as she had last seen him, dirty and sweaty and battleworn beside Tirael's dazzle. But Khar . . . "He is mine," she whispered. Myr knew her claim was grounded in honor, rather than the tie between lovers that her younger attendants had liked to sigh over—but that was still as true a bond as most could lay claim to in this world.

I'm dying anyway, she thought, but at least this way my death has meaning. And I will not allow Khar to die because I am unworthy of our bond. "Open your way," she told Emeriath, before she could waver.

Emeriath bowed. When she straightened, light glowed between her palms. She wove it from hand to hand, and with each repetition more of the light flowed off her hands and into the tapestry. As soon as Myr saw the path glimmering, she wanted to follow it, slipping away from the weight of her body. She thought she heard Rook cry out in protest or despair, or it might have been Faro, but the cry was already too distant for her to be sure. *I am saving them, too,* she told herself, *and Taly . . .*

Taly . . . With the final whisper of the ensign's name, the last of what had been Myr dissolved into the path of light. The tapestry shivered, the torn halves rippling in a wind that did not blow out of the Gray Lands, or off the Wall of Night, before it grew still again. And within the ages-old weave known as The Lovers, the hind sprang to her feet and fled.

58

Passage of Power

Every weapon along the perimeter rang in the aftermath of Kalan's shout, and both the attacking and defending ranks wavered as the wyr hounds howled in unison with the three black blades. Despite their shielding, Elodin and her comrades were shaking their heads as if to clear them, and the nearest Blood defenders were all staring at Kalan, their mouths agape. Kalan, as astonished as everyone else, saw that Tirael had raised his visor and was laughing—although he sobered as soon as his gaze returned to the plain. The stormfront of power still hovered, and the advancing force was now close enough to pick out the bristle of spears.

"Around three hundred heavy cavalry, by my estimate," Kalan said, when he dared trust his voice again. "But that's only the vanguard."

"Ay, there's more following," Tirael agreed, his eyes on the dust cloud.

Kalan nodded as despair, temporarily displaced by his shout, returned. The newcomers bore no pennants that he could see, and although the besiegers were deploying a skirmish line to meet them, they must know as well as he did that this was no Derai force. It seemed unlikely, too, that the Darksworn differences observed in

Emer would prevail to the extent of preserving Derai. No, Kalan thought, watching the power storm gather itself, they'll be united in wanting us dead. The assaulting ranks were rallying as well, now they realized no sorcerous offensive was going to follow his shout. Poised to give the order to fall back on the inner camp, Kalan shot another look toward the approaching force, assessing proximity and speed—and saw the skirmishers' line falter. An instant later their horns wound the alarm.

Trumpets yelped in answer from the Darksworn center, and the brew of power above it grumbled as both sorcerers turned toward the new threat. The skirmish line was falling back, and the full complement of Darksworn cavalry wheeling to face the newcomers' advance. The besiegers' trumpets brayed again, and their infantry began to retreat from the camp. Falling back on the rising ground, Kalan thought. In their place, uncertain of the newcomers' exact numbers, but seeing what the oncoming vanguard comprised, he would do the same—or withdraw altogether.

From what he had observed throughout the siege, the Darksworn instinct would be for withdrawal, but Kalan doubted they could do so now without a holding action, at least. The immediate danger to the camp was that a conventional engagement might trample right over the overstretched perimeter, in which case prudence suggested retreating behind the inner barrier. But if the gathered power storm was unleashed, then Kalan's remnant shield-wall was still the camp's surest defense—as it would be against any final blast of sorcerous spleen if the Darksworn withdrew.

So for now we'll hold position, Kalan decided, monitoring both the steadily closing forces and the boil of power. Beside him, Tirael and his knights were taking the respite; not speaking, just leaning on their weapons and observing developments. Gradually, their watchful silence spread, so the first trumpet call from the newcomers' ranks everyone heard. A moment later the unknown cavalry picked up speed, dust churning beneath hundreds of hooves. The same chill, livid fire that had burned Palla flared from the sorcerers' knoll toward the approaching force—only to rear up well short of their advancing line. Like water, Kalan thought, meeting an invisible wall.

"Strong shielding," Tirael said. Kalan nodded as the Darksworn cavalry raced to meet the newcomers, while rather than taking up defensive positions, their infantry continued to withdraw into the Gray Lands. Another wave of eldritch sorcery crackled across the open ground, only to dissipate a second time—and then there was no more time for large-scale power use as the converging lines pounded into each other.

Kalan narrowed his eyes, trying to assimilate what was happening amid the subsequent dust, and the hack and swirl of the melee. The Darksworn cavalry were using small-scale offensive sorceries that should have bolstered their attack, but the newcomers' shielding must have held at close quarters, because the magic gained no ground— and Kalan saw the moment when the Darksworn line faltered. Soon afterward, the initial clash became a string of skirmishes, before disintegrating into a running fight.

"Their sorcerers are abandoning the field," Tirael said, and Kalan realized he was right. The air above the rising ground was opening into a brume of shadow, shot through with tongues of fire. The way the shadows writhed, and the associated blast of freezing cold, reminded him of the Raptor's portal six years before—but already he was feeling the passage of power as the portal closed again, taking the sorcerers and their adepts with it. While the rest, Kalan thought, must fend for themselves.

Meanwhile, the running fight was increasingly spread out, although the Darksworn cavalry were still endeavoring to cover their infantry's retreat. The newcomers' battle line reformed and their main force continued in pursuit, while a smaller company veered toward the camp. "So now," Tirael said, as coolly as if they were spectators at a tourney engagement, "we'll see what this bodes for us."

By Kalan's estimation, the divergent company comprised around fifty horse. "No visible devices," the knight called Xer said, shading his eyes. "But is that a wolf with them?"

There *was* a wolf with the smaller company, Kalan saw, an old scarred veteran out of the Winter Country. I know you, he thought, his gaze narrowing on the beast. Elodin was nodding. "It's a wolf," she agreed. "And lack of insignia or not, they aren't marshaling power against us."

"Yet," Liad muttered. Like Elodin, Kalan detected no threat, but he, too, kept his shielding in place as he resheathed the black swords and retrieved the spear.

"Granian's our herald. She can issue challenge if you wish, my brother," Tirael murmured. But Kalan shook his head, because this was a Blood camp. Jad, who had been watching from his company's position to the right of the breach, crossed to join him as the newcomers stopped. The riders all wore plain armor that could have been crafted anywhere, although the veiling coifs were Ishnapuri in style.

Nherenor's Lightning knights had worn similar mail coifs in Caer Argent, but they had also displayed insignia—and Kalan was certain they would not have attacked the besiegers. He cleared his throat. "This is the camp of Lady Myrathis, the Bride of Blood. I am Khar of the Storm Spears, her Honor Captain." He was wryly aware how readily the Storm Spears' attribution came now. "In the name of the Nine, identify yourselves and state your business here. If you are friends, know yourselves welcome."

A finely armored rider advanced ahead of the rest, and Kalan guessed this must be a captain, if not the principal commander. "If deeds count as evidence, then I believe we may be accounted friends." The captain's voice rang clear despite the helmet, and Kalan had to fight to keep his demeanor impassive as she raised the visor, her gray eyes close to the wyr hounds' silver in its shadow. "We meet again, Khar of the Storm Spears, as I said we would." Kalan heard the defenders stir at that "again." "As to names and business, let all here know that I am Malian, Heir to the House of Night, returned to claim my place among the Nine Houses." She paused, her cool gaze shifting to meet Tirael's. Kalan guessed all present were acutely conscious, in that moment, of the bitter divide that had endured between

Stars and Night for five hundred years. "Kinsman," Malian said, and bowed from the saddle.

Tirael bowed in reply, graceful as always, although Kalan had no doubt he was thinking a great deal that his face did not reveal—including working out that any kinship bond had to derive from Malian's grandmother, Nerith of Sea, and her first, short-lived marriage to Serianrethen of Stars. "Returned with your army," Kalan observed, to bridge the pause, before adding privately, *"Are these the Lost?"*

"Not in the sense you mean," Malian said, answering both remarks. "Those who accompany me are new allies." The rider to her right inclined his head, so Kalan guessed this must be a leader among these allies. "As for our business here, we learned that a Darksworn legion had passed the Wall and besieged the Bride of Blood's camp." Her gesture indicated the battered perimeter, conveying regret. "I'm only sorry we couldn't reach you sooner."

Kalan was aware of the camp's silence, a weight at his back. "Our losses have been heavy," he said, not wanting to diminish that truth, "but we are all unreservedly glad of your arrival now." The nearby defenders murmured agreement, while Kalan tried to think what an Honor Captain who was truly of Blood would say next. "Lady Myrathis is the Bride of Blood and pledged in marriage to your father, the Earl of Night. As Night's Heir, I take it we may not only rely on your friendship and protection, but that of your allies?"

"You may." Malian was grave, her reply pitched to the camp. The defenders murmured again as Kalan drew the leather casing over the spear's blade, and Malian dismounted. The Code required that they now formally embrace, confirming good faith, but the remaining wyr hounds were ahead of Kalan as he stepped forward. A light that was more gilt than silver haloed each lean form as they paced to meet the Heir of Night.

"Chosen of Mhaelanar, Heir of the Derai. We are part of what was once Maurid, the Golden Fire of the House of Blood. We have waited long on your coming."

"We were Yelusin." The spark in Kalan's mind flowered into life. *"We, too, have waited for you and for this hour."*

Kalan wondered how many present could hear them, besides himself and Malian. Tirael and his company, probably, and Nimor if he were close enough. Yet he doubted that was all, despite Blood having turned away from the old ways.

Malian raised her right arm, Yorindesarinen's armring silver fire about her wrist. "*'I seek out the hidden, the lost I find.'*" She spoke quietly but her voice carried. "Maurid, Yelusin: you need wait no more. I am indeed the Chosen of Mhaelanar, returned at last to the Nine Houses."

Flying under her true colors with a vengeance, Kalan thought—but knew she was right to do so. Whatever either of them might have preferred before reaching the Wall, now the Swarm breakout required a bold and resolute answer. The sounds of distant conflict could still be heard, but the quiet in the camp was absolute. Many in it would recognize Maurid and Yelusin as the Golden Fires of Blood and Sea—and Malian had just claimed a title that was straight out of legend. *Chosen of Mhaelanar.* Small wonder, Kalan reflected dourly, that no one can speak. Even Tirael and his company were silent, perhaps recognizing Malian's armring, which was part of Yorindesarinen and Stars' legacy to the Derai, or simply appreciating that they were watching both history and lore twist into a new shape before their eyes.

And waiting, Kalan realized, for me to respond first. "Heir of Night and of the Derai, Chosen of Mhaelanar." He let Malian's titles resound through the hush. "I greet you in the name of Lady Myrathis, the Bride of Blood, and salute you on behalf of the Storm Spears. Welcome to the House of Blood's camp." Stepping forward, he offered the formal embrace and kiss on either cheek that the Code prescribed. *"How,"* he asked silently, *"did you know we were besieged?"*

"Wolf," she said softly, so only he would hear. "Rowan's death and his shaman's foreseeing drew him south. He's been scouting this country for months, waiting on my coming, and saw the darkspawn buildup."

Kalan's gaze went past her to the wolf, and he inclined his head as he stepped back. An uncertain cheer rose from the earthworks, indicative of bemusement and doubt, as much as thankfulness. Most of the defenders, Kalan suspected, would be grappling to assimilate the fact they were alive at all. *As I am,* he added, his eyes lifting briefly to the sun, settling west into ochre-streaked cloud. His tired mind burned with questions about Wolf and Malian's army, and how and when she had reached the Gray Lands, but getting answers would have to wait. Now he needed to ensure the dead were gathered up and the wounded tended, and the camp made as secure as possible before night fell.

First finish welcoming our rescuers to the camp, he reminded himself. Jad and Tirael came forward as Malian's companions dismounted, raising their visors and loosening helmets. Malian turned to introduce the warrior on her right, but he lifted his helmet clear first—and Kalan recognized Ser Raven, the hedge knight from Normarch and Caer Argent. *"How—"* he began silently, before pulling himself together. "Ser Raven," he said, still grappling to absorb the incongruity of the knight in this setting.

Ser Raven inclined his head. "Honor on you, Captain, and on your camp."

As in Emer, the knight gave little away, but Kalan was remembering how they had fought shoulder-to-shoulder at midsummer, to prevent a Darksworn coterie from assassinating Ghiselaine of Ormond. Stepping forward, he clasped the knight's hand and forearm. "Light and safety on your road, Ser Raven. I am surprised to see you here"—*very surprised,* he added silently—"but well met, nonetheless. So is this—" He let the sweep of his hand encompass both Malian's escort and the force pursuing the Darksworn.

"My personal guard," Raven replied, and Kalan caught a flicker in Malian's gray eyes, which vanished too quickly to decipher, "and the vanguard of a larger force."

New allies, indeed, Kalan thought, still trying to fit the knight into the puzzle of Malian's arrival. Explanations can wait, he reminded himself, as rapid footsteps made him turn. "Captain," Namath said urgently, "Murn asks that you come at once." The marine cleared his throat. "He said it concerns Lady Myrathis."

Myr. Kalan's eyes jerked toward the inner camp, then back to Malian. "Excuse me, Heir of Night." Even before she nodded, he had turned to Jad. "The perimeter's yours," he told him. "Lord Tirael, if you could see to our guests?" Striding clear, Kalan called Madder to him, but turned back to Namath from the saddle. "Fetch Taly as well." Mechanically, his eyes swept the disposition of the earthworks as he urged the destrier toward the inner barrier, where everyone from the infirmary who could manage a weapon was deployed along the line of carts. A true forlorn hope, Kalan thought, passing Madder's reins to the horsegirl who ran up. "Behave!" he ordered the roan, his focus on Myr's tent—although he nodded to a haggard-faced Tyun, whose stretcher had been raised onto a platform of barrels and sacks, presumably so he could better oversee the defense.

Murn, standing in the entrance to Myr's tent, looked even worse than the marine captain. "I'm sorry," the secretary said, "Vael has tried, but by the time I found her—" He broke off, his face working.

"Let me pass." Kalan's voice rasped so harshly he did not recognize it. Stepping inside, he was assailed by the acridity of burned wool—and the sight of Myr's bloodied body, with Faro and Rook collapsed beside her. *"No!"* Barely registering Vael's presence, he struggled to give his thoughts shape. *"She is dead. They are all dead."*

"Not all." Two of the wyr hounds remained at the entry, but the other four pressed close on either side of him. *"The child lives, and the other one . . ."*

But not Myr, Kalan wanted to shout at them, as he had yelled at the sight of the oncoming army: I have lost the life I swore to protect with my own. Fury seared through his initial shock, before he drove the turmoil back down. Opening his locked fists, he forced himself into a semblance of calm as the wyr hounds gave voice, mourning the passing of a Daughter of Blood.

"The child lives." Kalan blinked, thinking the hounds had spoken aloud, then realized it was Vael, raising his voice above their dirge. "And Rook may, Meraun willing." He paused, his eyes holding Kalan's. "I'm sorry," he said, as Murn had done. "There was nothing to be done for Lady Myrathis."

I'm sorry, I'm sorry, I'm sorry. This time the flag wheel in Kalan's head echoed the voice from his dream. Coming closer, he saw that Vael and the wyr hounds were right. Both Faro and Rook still lived, although the Adamant youth's breathing was shallow. When Vael went to the entrance, Kalan heard him giving instructions to Murn about stretchers and drugs—but all he could do was sink onto his heels by Myr's body and stare at the knife that had killed her.

The dagger, he thought numbly, that *I* gave to Faro. I was supposed to be her Honor Captain and champion, but instead I brought her murderer into the camp.

"No." The wyr hounds' whisper contradicted him at the same time as logic asserted itself, reminding him how easily Orth had overpowered Faro in the gully, and how he himself had disarmed the boy in the Red Keep stable. Any adult warrior entering the tent could have done the same, then used the knife for his or her own ends. And Myr's hand was clasped over Faro's, a gesture of comfort he doubted even she would offer her murderer.

You need to concentrate, Kalan told himself savagely, and learn whatever the tent's interior can tell you. He took in Ise's stick, hurled to the floor beside her silver tray, and the tapestry's sundered halves—but what brought him to his feet was the way the scene it depicted had changed.

In one half of the web, the lady had her hands pressed over her face. In the other, the warrior had turned away from her—and the crow, which had previously gazed down on them both, clung to his shoulder. Formerly, too, the hind had lain at the lovers' feet, while the hounds circled all. Now she fled from the warrior's side of the tapestry, with the milk-white pack in pursuit. The scene was so vivid that Kalan half expected the Hunt to spring to life, baying for the chase and the kill as it had within the Gate of Dreams. Instead he heard voices outside, responding to the wyr hounds' lament. And notwithstanding Myr's death, he was still Honor Captain and needed to confirm what had happened, and have her body laid out as befitted a Daughter of Blood. Rook and Faro, too, must either be treated here in the tent, or taken to the infirmary.

Kalan cast a last, lingering look toward the tapestry as Faro groaned, his limbs twitching. When the tent flap lifted, Malian stepped through, her eyes silver in the gloom. "She is dead." The way she spoke the words told Kalan she had heard his mental cry. "We have indeed come too late, for Lady Myrathis as for so many others. I am sorry."

Kalan did not need the bond between them to know her regret was genuine. But Malian had not known Myr, so primarily her grief would be for him, not the young woman who lay at their feet. She will mourn as decency requires, he thought, but as swiftly move on. He heard more voices outside, demanding explanations as the wyr hounds fell quiet and the opening lifted again. This time it was Taly who entered, only to stop as he had, white and stricken when she saw Myr. And for Taly, Kalan knew, there would be no easy moving on.

PART VIII

The Shield of Heaven

59

Chrysalis

Lady Myr's body had been taken to Khar's tent, where she would lie in whatever state the camp could manage. Everyone had stood with their heads bowed as her bier was borne out by Taly and the surviving Blood exiles—other than Jad, who remained on the perimeter. And Machys and Aarion had both wept. For some reason that was what Faro remembered most. That and Taly, who had shed no tears, her expression still as winter's frost, iron-hard across frozen ground.

Yet more than anyone else, perhaps even mistress Ise or Khar, Taly had truly loved Lady Myr.

Faro was ashamed, now, of the way he had despised Myr at first, simply because she had been visibly shaken by the fright he and Khar had given her, the first time they met on the Red Keep stairs. Afterward, too, she had embroiled Khar in a duel to the death, instead of defending what Faro had privately termed her own stupid honor. He had started to like her, though, when they fled the camp together. And in the end, Myr had stepped between him and Thanir's knife.

At least, Faro thought, Thanir wasn't able to make me kill her— although everyone will probably think I did, because he used my knife. The fact that the knife was the one Khar had given him, just made it all so much worse. Faro wondered what the Derai did to

murderers, whether they were hanged like in Grayharbor, and had to
fight not to cover his face with his hands and sob—not least because
his mam always said that crying because life went against you was
giving in to self-pity, which was unworthy conduct.

The healer, Vael, had checked Faro for injuries and cleaned away
the worst of the blood, before taking the still-unconscious Rook to
the infirmary. Afterward, Khar had sent almost everyone else away.
Now, besides Faro himself, only Khar, Nimor, and Tirael remained,
together with the two newcomers. Faro thought the lady looked like
a younger version of Ilai, while the tall warrior accompanying her
had eyes like Arcolin's, so darkly blue they were almost black. The
similarity made Faro want to shrink away and hide, despite having
overheard Nimor tell Murn that Khar had slain the sorcerer during
the battle. The envoy had said something about Yelusin as well, which
Faro had not properly understood, except to grasp that the ships'
closely guarded identity might have been revealed.

All the same, he still avoided the tall warrior's gaze, which was
keen enough to pick out secrets, exactly like the raven he was named
for. The lady was called Malian, and she seemed to know Khar well.
Faro could tell by the way she touched Khar's shoulder while moving
past him to study the tapestry. He also saw how Khar turned toward the
fleeting gesture, and to her. Once, Faro would have been jealous, as he
had been of Lady Myr at first, because he wanted Khar to belong only
to him. But not now, after Myr had died for him, when even remembering the old jealousy made Faro feel as if he had ill-wished her.

He wanted to ask what had happened to Thanir, but that would
have meant drawing attention to himself—and Faro already dreaded
their questions, which he would not be able to answer. His recollection of the time immediately before he fainted was vague, but some
of the impressions were so strange they seemed like fever dreams.
Particularly, Faro thought, the hounds in the tapestry appearing to
be alive, and the crow turning into a woman. He knew he hadn't
dreamed the lightning that burned the hanging, though. Not that it
changed anything. Myr was still dead.

I'm sorry, Faro cried silently, as he had when she was dying: I'm sorry, I'm sorry. They felt like the only words left in the world, and he wanted to cry them out to Khar, too, who so far had barely glanced his way. He knows it's my fault, Faro thought miserably. And because I'm his page, I've stained his honor as well as my own. The terror that Khar might disown him, because of that, was almost worse than the fear he might be hanged. Faro's only comfort was that the wyr hounds had stayed with him when he crept to one side of the tent, to be out of everyone's way. Yet he felt certain that when Khar left the camp, the hounds would accompany him, in the same way the original thirteen had bade Faro release them from the Red Keep so they could follow the Storm Spear into exile.

I always feel safer when they're with me, Faro thought. Then again, he had thought he would be safe from the demons that came to the Ship's Prow House if only he could reach the Derai Wall. His mam might have warned him against the Derai mariners and their stealing, but she had also told him how the Wall's great strongholds held back the darkness that crouched at the edge of the world. And at first Faro *had* felt safer, because when he was with Khar the nightmares that had stalked his sleep since the Ship's Prow House receded.

Once inside the Red Keep, he was always wary of the hard-faced Blood warriors and the stories whispered about the ruling kin—but he had only grown afraid again when Lord Huern's path crossed his, that day in the stable. From a distance, the Son of Blood might seem like anyone else, but up close . . . Faro had felt the chill that came off him, exactly like the demons in the Ship's Prow House, and when he looked sidelong, had felt sure he glimpsed jeweled pins, glimmering in braided hair. He had *wanted* to warn Khar, but whenever he tried—even when he wrestled to force words out, after Kolthis betrayed the camp and Khar rescued him and Lady Myr from the gully—his speech had remained locked.

Never speak of it, little rat. Let it be our secret, yours and mine. Faro guessed, now, that Thanir must have done something when he placed the two fingers over his lips that terrible night in Grayharbor.

Something that meant Faro *couldn't* speak of what happened, no matter how much he wanted to. So instead of being safe, he had brought the danger he feared with him, and Lady Myr had died because of it. And if he could not tell anyone what happened, then Thanir might find a way to use him again—and next time it might be Khar the dark warrior wanted dead. Despairing, Faro fought back another sob, even if what he dreaded most was that he had already lost Khar . . .

Despite his efforts, a sound between a hiccup and a sniff escaped, but it was Malian, not Khar, who looked his way. Her fingers still rested on the tapestry's burned edge, but her steady gaze held Faro transfixed—before she smiled faintly, then stooped to pick up Mistress Ise's staff, which was holding down the silver tray. "No!" Faro scrambled up, desperation wrenching the words out of him. "You mustn't!"

Malian checked. "Why not?" she asked. Now everyone was looking Faro's way, including Khar, although the Storm Spear's bleak expression did not change.

Faro could not answer, even indirectly, not even to share the conviction that when, ignorant of danger, he had looked into the shield-mirror that lay beneath the tray, Thanir and whoever else was on the other side must have looked back. Struggle though he might, no further explanation would emerge, only a combined plea and avowal as he turned to Khar. "I didn't kill her!"

"I know." Khar's face remained closed, though, and the hand he placed on Faro's shoulder was more weight than reassurance. "But you're going to have to find a way to tell us who did."

"He won't be able to." The warrior called Raven spoke for the first time. "Not until Thanir's compulsion has been removed. But that's only the surface layer. Beneath it, the boy's encased in warding, a prohibition so subtle it's almost invisible."

Speculation flared in Khar's face, before his expression closed in again. Tirael whistled softly, and Nimor was frowning. Only Malian and the wyr hounds appeared unaffected, although the hound closest to Faro whined a protest as his hand clenched on its fur.

"You did say there might be a compulsion." Nimor glanced toward Tirael.

"Yes." The Son of Stars was thoughtful. "But the structure of such workings, let alone unraveling them, has not been my study."

"I might be able to help," Malian said, in her cool way. Her regard was cool, too, as she studied Faro, who wanted to crawl away and hide again. But he knew none of those present, not even the wyr hounds, were going to let him out of their sight. So he hunched down into himself instead, while Malian turned to Khar. "How much do you know of his past?"

"Very little." Khar frowned. "Except that both the wyr hounds and a Sea ship have befriended him."

Nimor's mouth turned down at that, but he remained silent while Khar outlined the rest of their discussion from earlier that same day. When Lady Myr was still alive, Faro thought, miserably aware of all that had changed in so short a time. Malian looked intrigued by the suggestion that Faro's mam might have been over four hundred years old, but was more interested in Arcolin having been struck by lightning. "Because lightning was called here, too," she said, nodding at the tapestry, "which points to a Sea House influence."

"Or a Darksworn one," said Khar—reluctantly, Faro thought.

Tirael's brows lifted, while Nimor's drew together, but Malian pursed her lips. "Possibly." Faro could tell she did not think so, though, as she glanced at Raven. "What do you think?"

"It's unlikely." The warrior's eyes rested on Faro, who scowled back, resenting that someone could claim to see things in or around him that he didn't know about himself. "But if you know nothing," Raven continued, addressing him directly, "that suggests that for you, the warding has always been present."

"Something he was born with?" Tirael asked. "Is that even possible?"

"Well, you think he could be four hundred years old," Nimor said, beneath his breath. More than any of them, he looked drained, but the set of his mouth said he had no intention of leaving.

Malian inclined her head to the wyr hounds before sinking onto her heels before Faro. "I think we should remove the compulsion, at least." She met his gaze. "Do you agree?"

Faro had to check the vehemence of his nod, because he *did* agree—but he was also wary. "You look like Ilai. Only younger," he said, finding that was something he could say. "But your eyes are just like hers, even if yours don't change color."

The tent was hushed, despite the camp noises outside. Malian nodded. "Are they? What else can you tell me about her, Faro?"

Faro scowled again with the effort of remembering, and thinking what words he could use. "She saved me, and said she would come back for me before the camp fell." Since it hadn't fallen, after all, he supposed Ilai must have fled. "And she told Lady Myr she was sorry." Faro had been crying too hard to understand the reasons why, but he didn't want to admit that. "She was something to do with lightning as well. It was on her knife. And she said Lady Myr was a great hero." That had to do with the shield-mirror, but the compulsion locked his tongue when he even thought about trying to explain. Faro could see Khar behind Malian, but his face was so stern that it was a relief to focus on the cool eyes that looked like smoke. Rather than shifting between gray and green and blue, Faro reflected, the way Ilai's always had.

"I see. But I'm not her, Faro." Her gaze held his. "I am Malian of Night, and Khar and I have known each other since we were close to your age. You're what, ten, twelve?"

"Eleven," he mumbled.

"Eleven: a brave age. As I will need you to be brave now, and trust me, if I am to have this compulsion out of you. Then you will be free to tell us everything that's happened."

Free, Faro thought, and felt as though she had shown him dawn at the end of a long dark night. He was afraid, but he knew he could not turn away from the hope she offered. Not only to be rid of Thanir's hold on him, but to be able to tell Khar what had happened in the tent. "Please," he whispered.

"Be careful, Malian," Khar said, "especially with this deeper warding."

Faro had forgotten about that, but it was clear Malian had not. "Life is a risk," she said softly, as much to Faro as Khar, and he nodded, because his mam used to say similar things. Besides, accepting the risk was a way he could prove himself worthy of Myr's sacrifice. "But I will only look at whatever lies deeper," Malian promised, "unless I am very sure of my course. I don't think *they* would let me do otherwise," she added, nodding at the wyrs. She held out her hands. "When you're ready, place your hands in mine."

Do the hard thing quickly, that was what his mam always said. So Faro extended his hands straightaway. He felt Khar's shielding surround the tent as Malian's clasp tightened, conveying reassurance—but Faro still almost jerked free when he realized she was in his mind. He thought there was another presence joined to hers, as fine and elusive as moonlight, but he also felt the wyr hounds' solidity and understood they were with him still. *"Safe, you see?"* Malian's mindvoice murmured. *"I told you they would not let us go where we should not."*

Us, Faro thought. But he made himself relax and let his memories unfold: not just of recent events in the tent, but of the three strangers he had guided to the Ship's Prow House and the horror that ensued. Thanir's fingers rested against his mouth again, amid rain and fire and terror. *Never speak of it, little rat,* the obsidian voice whispered. *Let it be our secret, yours and mine.*

"Not anymore," Malian said aloud—and when she placed her own fingers on Faro's lips, he felt the invisible compulsion that had stitched them closed dissolve. "Clever," she added, and winked at Faro. "But not quite clever enough."

She was full of cleverness and secrets herself. Because she was in his mind, Faro could see that. Twisty, he thought. He felt rather than saw her smile, overhearing him, and caught the echo of a reply that was something about the moon's face being dark as well as bright. I'm like that, too, he thought dreamily, dark and light, whereas Khar is always bright, like the sun, and Lady Myr was clear water, with the light shining through . . .

Within the dreaminess, he realized that Malian was observing the reverse unfolding of his short life before the Ship's Prow House: his mam's death, and the years before that, living in the narrow rooms above the armorer's shop. She seemed very interested in his mam, as the wyr hounds were, too—but more so in a shadowy figure from his very earliest years that Faro had forgotten he remembered. The shadow sharpened as soon as Malian focused on the memory, and gradually became clearer still. Finally it was not a shadow at all, but a young woman gazing back at Faro through a frame of light. She was of the Sea House, he knew that at once because of her cabled hair and the rings in her ears, and he thought she would have been beautiful if she had not looked so sad. When he concentrated, he could hear what she was saying.

"*I was bound to the ship and to Ammaran, and despite his sacrifice, I cannot live now that both are gone. Every day I fade more. Only our child has held me this long, because he, too, is theirs. But you tell me our ships come here, so I must find a way to protect him—to hide him so no one will ever see, or know . . . And you, Kara, on your honor and your oath of fealty to Ammaran: you must protect him too.*"

"*My life for his, always. Fear not, Lady, I keep faith.*"

Mam's voice, although Faro could not see her, just the Sea woman's face bending over his. I keep faith, he thought. But those are Khar's words, the ones that belong to the Storm Spears.

"*Indeed.*" Malian's observation was as cool as silver, before she spoke out loud. "She must have spent the last of her strength weaving wards that turn away eyes and minds, not just from you, but from any thought of the Derai and the Wall of Night. The working's profound, but very elegant. Almost invisible, as Raven said. The Darksworn did not see it, that's certain, or I doubt Thanir would have let you go."

Faro shuddered, but felt deeply grateful to the unknown woman with her rings and cabled hair, at the same time as he wondered why his mam would say the Storm Spears' words. As though, he thought, puzzled, she was one.

"*Because* she was one. The weatherworker was your birth mother, Faro. Kara must have been your foster mother, but also a warrior, honor-sworn to Ammaran—who was your father."

"The last Heir to the old line of the Earls of Blood," Khar said. "He and his Honor Guard were lost sometime after the Betrayal War." Wonder stirred beneath his sternness. "A Blood father and a Sea mother: that explains a great deal."

Foster mother, not mother, Faro thought, bewildered. He caught a glimpse of *something* that surrounded him like a chrysalis, only spun from glass so it was invisible. But now a fracture ran through it, or perhaps it was the world as he had always known it that was splintering . . .

"I think you'll know about all of this," Malian said softly. "Kara will have told you, against the day when the wards—and their prohibition against knowing who you truly are—would lift."

But will I know what my mother was protecting me against? Faro wondered. And Ma— Kara, too? Or why the death of my father and a ship meant my mother couldn't live? Unless she had died of a broken heart, like they said in the stories . . . A vignette asserted itself, out of the Grayharbor years: Stefa and Leti's mam scoffing at just such a tale, sung in her inn one Summer's Eve—but his own mam saying no, in fact she had seen it. "And you so hard a case," the inn-wife had replied, shaking her head and smiling at the same time.

Kara *was* my mam, Faro thought. She was the one who had raised him, living in a narrow house in a backwater town, when she could have gone anywhere with her genius for making and mending armor. She had died there, too, far from home and House and kin. And perhaps, if Lady Myr had guessed right, over four hundred years out of her own time.

"The four-hundred-odd years *is* a mystery," Malian agreed. "But it's not the strangest I've ever encountered and still found to be true. As for the warding, it's a casing, not a working woven into your psyche or physical being, so not intended to be forever." Her cool eyes looked deep into his. "The key, I suspect, is for you to want to step clear."

The chrysalis was already fractured, but Faro hesitated, because if Malian was correct, it had protected him from Aranraith and those with him—while still allowing him, at great need, to call the lightning that was an inheritance from his mother. So I really did burn Arcolin, he thought, caught between remembered horror and satisfaction. Dark and light, he told himself, as the chrysalis split wider still. Only now Faro felt as though the fissures ran through him, too, despite what Malian had said.

"You are Derai," the wyr hounds answered. Their voices were in his mind, as they had been since the Red Keep whenever danger or need threatened. The *Che'Ryl-g-Raham*'s voice had been as well, when he sailed north. *"There were always reasons, beyond those the Alliance will admit to, why the Wall is named for Night. But the Derai world and all that goes with it is your birthright. The old Blood returns—and we have chosen the new to raise up with it, as was always our right."*

Faro knew they meant himself and Khar. He understood, too, through their wordless communication, why the wyr hound in the Red Keep stable had let Sarein to take its life. Allowing the attack had distracted attention from those the wyrs sought to protect, but the Daughter of Blood's knife stroke had also severed their last bond to the current ruling kin.

This time Faro heard the crack as a longer, deeper, fracture split his mother's working. *"The old Blood that is true will always come into its own again—and the new must be raised up when the old is found wanting."* His mam, who was also his father's Honor Lieutenant, had taught him that saying, along with so much else. Faro felt as though his eyes were full of the wyr hounds' light, a blaze that was in his mind as well, so that he knew Kara *had* been a Storm Spear—like his father, Ammaran, and all their company. Through the dazzle, he could feel Malian's hands holding him up as the last of the warding fell away and he spoke the words that were fire in his throat.

"I am Pha'Rho-l-Ynor. My mother was a weatherworker and navigator, also called Pha'Rho-l-Ynor after the ship of the same name. Through her and the name I bear, I brought a spark of Yelusin, once contained in the ship, *Pha'Rho-l-Ynor*, back to the Sea Keep fleet."

Malian had released his hands now, but Faro continued standing straight and tall. "My father was Ammaran, a Storm Spear and Heir of Blood." The fire was dying down, but he made himself meet Khar's eyes before his courage fled with it. "I have never lied to you. Everything I could say, I believed to be the truth. And I didn't kill Lady Myr. That was Thanir, although he tried to make me do it." Faro knew what had taken place was more complicated than that, because without Ilai's intervention, Thanir would have killed him as well. Right now, though, he was filled with the wyr hounds' words, that were also his mam's: *the old Blood comes into its own again.* "So Lady Myr was right, you see. I have come home."

And then, because it all felt like far too much, he did what he had once despised Myr for doing, and burst into tears.

60

Old Blood

"It's all right," Khar said. And it was, because he had put his arms around Faro. Beyond his tears, Faro could hear Malian telling the others what she had seen in his memories: the truth of Thanir's possession, and the mirror, and Myr's death. *I'm sorry*, he whispered again to her shade, *I'm sorry, I'm sorry . . .* But Ilai had said she was sorry, too, which Faro suspected only showed how little it meant, no matter how often the words thudded in time with his heart.

"Heir, eh?" Tirael spoke lightly, but Faro could tell he was serious. "That'll loose a wyr pack in the halls of Blood."

"Not just Blood," Nimor said tersely, "among the entire Nine Houses." He paused, his face haggard in the tent's dim light. "But *Pha'Rho-l-Ynor*, after more than four hundred years—"

"So you know of this ship?" Tirael asked.

"Oh, yes." Nimor rubbed his hands over his face. "We have a shrine in the Sea Keep, inscribed with the name of every vessel we lose. But the *Pha'Rho-l-Ynor . . .* " He paused. "The name of the ship's weatherworker was originally Taierin; she was also Count Tirunor's niece. Our history records that she stole the ship from its rightful navigator out of infatuation for Ammaran, who had more than his share of the old Derai glamour. He had come to Sea wanting a ship for some quest he was on, but the Count refused him. The ships were as valuable then as they are now, and the risks greater . . ." He paused again.

"And he was of Blood," Malian said quietly.

The envoy's eyes slid to hers before he nodded. "Probably. It was barely two generations since the Betrayal War, after all. Ammaran was also suspected of suffering from the Madness of Jaransor, having ventured there in pursuit of whatever quest drove him. In any event, he persuaded Taierin to commandeer the *Pha'Rho-l-Ynor*, usurping the role and name of the rightful navigator."

"It wasn't like that!" Faro said fiercely, from the shelter of Khar's arm. "My mam—Kara—said my father loved my mother above his own life!" He stopped, still trying to fit his new memories together with those he had always had. "She told me they married in secret, because Blood and Sea were close to enemies then, and sailed on *Pha'Rho-l-Ynor* because almost all the ship's crew supported my father's quest. When the navigator would not, they agreed my mother must replace him, which meant her taking the ship's name as well." Nimor shook his head but remained silent. "My father needed a ship," Faro went on, "because he had learned in Jaransor that what he sought lay in Haarth, but he didn't know how far south he would have to travel to find it. My mam said the crew agreed," he repeated. "She and my father's Honor Guard didn't take the ship by force."

"They couldn't have sailed it anyway," Khar said. "Or made a ship leave port against its will, I wouldn't have thought."

"But—" Nimor began, then paused, looking simultaneously uncertain and worn. "Tirunor must have thought differently," he said finally. "His Heir and a considerable fleet pursued the fugitives until they lost them in a great storm, one the *Pha'Rho-l-Ynor* never sailed out of."

"In that time," Khar said.

"So it would seem." Nimor sounded reluctant. "But the ship's name is on our memorial, so I think it must still have been lost."

"Mam said the storm was greater than anyone on the ship had

ever experienced." Faro mimicked his foster mother's somber intonation. "The seas were mountainous, as high as the Wall itself, and
Taierin believed there was some other power at work, beyond the
Great Ocean tempests. The winds shredded sails and rigging, many
were lost overboard, and the Luck died before the mainmast finally
snapped. That's when my father made my mother bind his power to
hers in the Luck's place, so her weatherworking would have greater
reserves and she could save the ship." Faro's voice shook, but Khar's
arm, which had lightened to a hand on his shoulder, helped him
remain steady. "He gave all his power and his life, but the ship was
still wrecked. As far as Mam knew, she and my true mother were
the only survivors."

Nimor looked shaken. "But—" he said, then stopped a second
time. The others watched him curiously until he spoke again. "As
far as we know, the remnant of what had once been Yelusin first
woke among the fleet that pursued the *Pha'Rho-l-Ynor*, when they
turned back because of the great storm. We always thought it was
because so many Lucks were lost as they fled before its fury." Nimor
sighed. "Perhaps the *Pha'Rho-l-Ynor* also woke at that time. But,"
he repeated, "if the essence of a lost ship had returned, especially
after so many centuries, it could not be kept hidden. The whole of
Sea would be alight with the news. Yet I heard nothing before I left."

"You weren't meant to!" Affronted, Faro nearly threw off Khar's
restraining hand. "Che'Ryl-g-Raham made me wait until the very last
night before we left with your company, and then go to the Ships'
Shrine just before dawn." He remembered how quiet it had been,
stealing away from Khar and the horses, then creeping along the dock
and into the dark shrine where the likeness of another ship's prow
had awaited his coming, its watchful eyes open. "I put my hand on
it, exactly like Che'Ryl-g-Raham said, and a light came out of me
and went into the shrine. *Pha'Rho-l-Ynor*'s name vanished off the
plinth at once, and I could hear all the other ships speaking to me
from around the harbor, welcoming me. But they said my road lay
with Khar, to the Red Keep and Blood." The old Blood returns, Faro

thought—and could see from the way Malian looked at him that she had observed that part of his memories, too.

"That makes sense, if your father was Heir," Tirael said, still sounding grave.

"Even over four hundred years ago." Faro could hear the same considering note in Khar's voice. "Kara must have realized something was badly amiss, though, even if she didn't know Haarth well, if at all, and was keeping away from Derai ships."

"It would explain why she never returned to Blood," Nimor agreed. "Because otherwise . . . However unacceptable the marriage may have been in those days, Faro was still Ammaran's legitimate son, and the last heir of the old line of Blood."

"Mam was always worried about the stealing," Faro told them confidently, because that was in his old memories. He frowned over the new ones. "But she said we couldn't go to Blood anyway, partly because of her being a Storm Spear, but also because of a new oath that she didn't like, both of which meant she wouldn't be able to protect me." Khar's hand tightened on his shoulder and the others exchanged looks that told Faro, quite clearly, that they thought Kara had been wise.

"So what now?" Nimor said slowly.

"I believe it's time we turned our attention to the shield-mirror," Malian said. Everyone else looked toward the silver tray, but Faro kept his eyes on a moth beating about the lantern, and concentrated fiercely on willing it away from the hot glass.

"I suppose we have to deal with it," Nimor said. He sounded as though he, like Faro, would much prefer not.

"From what I saw in Faro's memories," Malian replied, "it's far too malevolent to let lie, even overnight." Settling onto her heels, she lifted Mistress Ise's staff clear of the tray. "Interesting," she murmured, studying the twisted strands more closely, then looked up at Khar. "Between you and Nhenir, I think we can contain the shield's influence."

Khar nodded, and Faro felt the flare of his power, joining with the same moonlit presence that had been with Malian when she removed Thanir's compulsion. Tirael and Nimor both looked equally intent as Malian set the staff aside and examined the tray. "I'll lift it clear," she said, "but it had better be Raven who touches the mirror."

Faro craned around at once, realizing he had made the mistake of overlooking Malian's companion, who had been obscured from his gaze by Khar. Watching us all—and missing nothing, Faro thought, his own gaze sliding away as Raven stepped forward.

"Why Raven?" Tirael asked, looking from Malian to the tall warrior.

"Because I'm largely immune to power," Raven replied quietly.

The Son of Stars' brows rose, and Khar, too, looked around, his expression arrested, before turning back to the tray. "How do we deal with the shield-mirror permanently, though?" he said, as though thinking aloud. "I assume it can be melted down?"

"Not in any fire we could light in this camp." Malian's eyes met his again. "I propose using the frost-fire sword."

"You found it!" Khar exclaimed. Momentarily, delight broke through his grimness, so that he looked younger and less careworn than he had since the siege began.

"With Raven's help," Malian said, while Nimor and Tirael exchanged looks.

"Nhenir," the Son of Stars said, as though testing the name. "*And* the frost-fire sword. You really are the Chosen of Mhaelanar."

"I am," Malian replied, but with so much regret that Faro looked directly at her, even though that risked glimpsing the shield-mirror. "Unfortunately, if we destroy the mirror, which we must do, I fear the Shield of Stars, or Shield of Heaven will pass beyond my grasp. It was shattered in the battle with the Worm, but it seems one of the shards went into this mirror's making." She paused. "I've had several visions of the battlefield now, all focusing on the broken shield, and in one I saw Thanir. He took something from beneath the body of the Worm, almost certainly a shield fragment. From what I overheard in Faro's memories, the Swarm melded it into their shield-mirror, using the shard's disguising influence to infiltrate Night, where Aikanor fell beneath the mirror's sway."

Ilai had mentioned Aikanor, too, Faro thought, when she spoke to Lady Myr at the end—something about using the mirror to whisper him into Madness. Now Taierin's warding had been lifted, he knew this was one of the histories his mam had taught him: how Aikanor, the Heir of Night, had believed himself in love with Xeria, twin sister to his closest friend, Tasian of Stars. When she would not marry him, Aikanor had murdered Tasian and tried to seize Xeria by force, which plunged the Derai into civil war and ended with the Golden Fire being extinguished. By his mam's account, it was Xeria who had called down the Fire to thwart Aikanor and his adherents' attempt to assassinate their Derai enemies, at the peace feast intended to end the civil war.

But in relating these events, Mam had spoken of circumstances that were raw and recent and bitter, not the five-hundred-year-old history they were to everyone else in the tent. She had not known about the mirror, but Faro remembered Ilai saying that, unlike Aikanor, Lady Myr had not been susceptible to its influence. He wanted to remind everyone of that, but their faces and the wyr hounds' rigidity held him motionless. "Aikanor," Khar said, as though he had tasted something rotten.

Malian nodded. "What was intended, I suspect, to thwart another child born of Night and Stars by corrupting his feelings for Xeria, ended achieving so much more."

Tirael was white. "Tasian's murder, the whole wreckage of the Betrayal War, and the loss of the Golden Fire ..." Any trace of a drawl had vanished.

"The mirror may also explain why Xeria was *able* to wreak what she did." Malian was very quiet, almost stern. "We know she was extremely powerful, but even so, I've always wondered how she was able to override the Golden Fire's prohibition against striking at the Derai—especially since until then, the Fire had been resolutely neutral in the civil war." A silent growl vibrated through the wyr hounds. "We know she was no longer sane," Malian went on, "and sometimes that increases strength. But by that stage, even if part of the mirror was from Yorindesarinen's shield, the Swarm influence about Aikanor and those sworn to him must have been so strong it was growing discernible."

Khar scrubbed a hand over hair darkened by sweat and dust. "So when he initiated the Night of Death, Xeria persuaded the Fire they were striking against the Swarm. She probably believed it herself . . ."

"She must have," Malian said, more quietly still, "because she couldn't have hidden a lie from the Fire. And in one way, because of the mirror's hold over Aikanor, she was right."

The tent was so quiet that Faro could hear the warriors from Malian's escort, talking outside. He almost cried out as the moth finally came too close and singed its wings against the lantern glass. Crippled, it spiraled to the ground, where Malian saw its distress and killed it. Her movement broke up the tableau: Tirael rolled his shoulders as though sloughing off the old, dark history, while Khar bent to examine the line of solder running through the phoenix. "Was this more shards?"

Malian nodded. "Two of the larger pieces, I imagine." Her gaze went to Faro. "When you called your lightning, the power activated a residual virtue in the tray." Abashed, Faro fixed his eyes on the phoenix as everyone looked at him again. "Rithor," Malian said, reclaiming their attention, "was the only one of Yorindesarinen's squires who accompanied her against the Worm. The divisions within the Alliance must have been less entrenched in those days, because Rithor was of the Rose. Yorindesarinen sent him away before the final battle, but he can't have gone far because I *saw* him creep back afterward." She glanced at Raven. "I think Fire's arrival drove him off before he could retrieve more than the shield fragments. But," she finished softly, "if we looked far enough back along Mistress Ise's family tree, I suspect we'd find Rithor."

"So we know how the tray got here," Nimor said, almost explosively. "But how could the mirror get from the Old Keep of Winds on the Night of Death, to a place among Lady Myr's possessions?"

"How does the Sea Keep get an envoy and his secretary, both weatherworkers, past the Blood Gate?" Khar was grim again, lines drawn deep about his mouth. "It could have been brought to the Red Keep in the confusion that followed the Night of Death. All the normal bonds of Derai society had been frayed by the civil war, so I wouldn't rule out looting, even between supposed allies."

"Or the Swarm may have recovered it when they penetrated the Old Keep six years ago." Malian was calm. "If what we've learned through Faro is correct, a Swarm agent infiltrated Lady Myrathis's household, so planting the mirror is perfectly feasible. Still, we may never know exactly how it came about. But now," she said, steel tempering her calm, "we need to make an end."

She was careful, lifting the tray clear, but the shield-mirror beneath appeared dormant, and remained that way once Raven picked it up. Even Faro felt compelled to look more closely, despite his reluctance, and saw no movement in the shadowed depths. "The mirror may have to be activated from the other side," Raven said, propping it on a barrel set against the tent's main pole. "But whatever else went into its making, it stinks of Salar's handiwork."

Salar, Faro thought, his stomach churning as he remembered the Ship's Prow House, where the name had clearly referred to some greater demon that Nirn and the others feared. Ilai might have mentioned the name, too ... "Do it!" he said shrilly, but although Khar looked around, it was Malian who answered.

"Fear not, Pha'Rho-l-Ynor, I shall." Faro was reassured by her certainty, but almost immediately disappointed by the so-called frost-fire sword's plainness, once drawn. And rather than raising the sword high and shearing through the shield-mirror, the Heir of Night simply sighted along its length. As though she's getting the mirror in perspective, Faro thought, puzzled.

" 'Free me,' " Malian murmured—which sounded like she was repeating someone else's words. Clasping the hilt with both hands, she extended the blade until its tip touched the mirror, but even then she did not thrust the sword deep. Faro had just decided that being

Chosen of Mhaelanar couldn't be anything special—not like Khar defending the camp—when silver-white fire glittered along the blade and coruscated about its tip.

Electrified, he stared at the image of sword and flame reflected in the mirror's surface. Both remained frost-white, with lines spreading out from their reflection like fissures in ice, until the entire surface of the mirror was crackle glaze. "Free me," Malian repeated softly, before her voice rang out, commanding as a note struck on the great gong in Seruth's Grayharbor temple: "*Be* free!" The sword belled on the same note, the top of its range piercingly high, the bottom so profound Faro could feel the reverberation inside himself. From the strain in Khar's face, he thought that the sound must be testing his shielding, and wondered if he should help—the same way he and the wyr hounds had loaned Khar their strength last night, when the assault of power was at its height.

"Wait; watch." The wyr hounds' caution was also a command. The belling note was building rather than dying away, the invocation *'be free'* weaving through it like the entwined strands of Ise's staff. Both the actual and reflected swords blazed whiter until the mirror clanged, harsh with protest, and a sulfurous mist poured through the widening cracks in its surface. The sword belled again, insistent, and everyone except Malian—and Raven, Faro would remember afterward, wondering if that was what it meant to be immune—clapped their hands over their ears. Again the belling note swelled—and the mirror shattered into a cloud of steel fragments.

Faro expected the splinters to fall to the floor, but instead they revolved about the sword's white blade. Every revolution drew the filing cloud closer—like the moth and the lantern, he thought, riveted—until the first particle touched the sword's edge. *"Free ..."* The whisper was a breath out of the air as the entire cloud vanished. Nothing remained, not even specks of steel dust in the lantern's beam.

"Free," Malian said, remote as the moon. By the time she lowered the blade, its appearance was that of any other plain, workmanlike weapon. Tirael made a gesture, partly salute to Malian, partly valediction.

"It had to be done," Khar said somberly, as she sheathed the sword.

The others were silent, focused on the place where the mirror had been. Finally, Nimor shook his head as if to clear it. "There's still Lady Myrathis's vigil. We must keep that."

"You should rest first," Tirael told him. "We don't all have to keep the full vigil." But someone must: Faro knew that, too, from his mam's teaching. He supposed that would end being Taly, since Khar had already been delayed and must still make his captain's rounds of the camp. Nonetheless, as if glad of the excuse to leave, within a very few minutes everyone had moved outside. The Blood exiles, who were keeping the first honor watch for Lady Myr, were still deployed about the garnet-and-gold tent, so Faro guessed it could not be as late as he had thought.

Nimor stopped, intent on the solitary star that could be seen through the Gray Lands' cloud. "The pilot's star," he said softly, and even the wyr hounds turned their silver eyes skyward, following his gaze. No one spoke, but Faro knew they all understood that Nimor had not expected to see it again. "You know," the envoy continued, "there's still one thing I don't understand in all this."

"Only one," Tirael murmured.

Nimor ignored him, his eyes on the star. "I suppose Faro may know. But what quest was so pressing it sent an Heir of Blood into Jaransor, then led him to appropriate a Sea House ship?"

Faro shook his head, because if Mam knew, she had never said. In the brief silence that followed, Murn came out of the infirmary to join them. "Rook's awake and urgent to speak with you," he told Khar. "He won't settle until you come."

Khar nodded and started to turn away, but checked when Malian spoke. "What drove your stealing in those same times?" she said to Nimor. "Our Alliance had not only lost its bulwark against the Swarm, but the privation that followed the loss of the Golden Fire nearly destroyed us. As if that were not enough, the Blood Oath was taking hold, turning us more deeply against ourselves. We were like an animal in a trap, which sees gnawing off its own leg as the only way out." She paused. "What else *could* Ammaran have been doing, except seeking to restore the Golden Fire?"

One wyr hound moved sharply, but the rest stood motionless. "It seems obvious, once you frame it that way," Tirael said finally. "But even if Ammaran thought restoring the Fire possible, why voyage into the Southern Realms? What was he seeking there?"

"Power." Malian dropped the word into their midst like a pebble down a well. Faro could have sworn he heard the echo. "A source of power to draw on, since we had decimated our own." Her coolness was tempered again as she met their eyes one by one. "And now that we know the Wall has been breached at least once, while Yorindesarinen's shield is lost, we had better find a way to complete Ammaran's quest."

61

Storm Wrack

For the first time since the siege began, Kalan heard a rat-fox bark, farther out on the plain. The wind carried the coughing cry to him where he stood in the shadow of the breached earthworks, with part of his mind monitoring the muted sounds of both the camp and the wider night. The remainder of his attention was absorbed by the words Rook had spoken, risen onto one elbow in his urgency. At one level, the Adamant youth's account was a confusion of a crow woman come alive, who was also Emeriath out of legend, and how the hind in the tapestry must run. The rest was all too familiar: the Hunt striving to break free, precipitated by the finding and claiming of the spear.

My fault, Kalan thought, his jaw ground together. Not Faro's, for having crossed Thanir's path, or Tirael's for acknowledging Myr as kin: mine and this cursed ring's. He was tempted to drag it off and hurl it away, as his first instinct had been to cast The Lovers onto the nearest fire and watch it burn to ash—except he did not know what either action might mean for Myr's spirit, caught in the eternal cycle of hind and Hunt. Also, according to all Rook had witnessed with his power joined to Myr, and through her to Emeriath, the sacrifice must be willing. And Myr *had* been willing, not least for Kalan's sake.

"She said you were hers. Her champion and Honor Captain, I

suppose. That's when she agreed." Kalan heard Rook's words again, each one a reproach, although he knew that was not why the youth had told him of events in the tent. Yet so long as Myr was bound to the hind, her spirit would never come to the Hurulth's Hall. Rook, raised in Adamant, which served the Silent God first among the Nine, had not said that, but Kalan had spent seven years in Night's Temple quarter so he had not needed to be told.

I was supposed to champion and defend her, he thought, frowning at the ragged hole blasted through the dike, only to fail at the last. While she—the shy, the gentle, the one Blood considered unfit to be its Daughter—not only stepped between Faro and Thanir's knife, but into Mayanne's web to save us all. From what Malian had gleaned from Faro's memories, Myr had been naturally resistant to the mirror's influence as well. Otherwise, Kalan thought bitterly, she would doubtless have been permitted to live and take her place as Countess of Night. But then—less bitterly—she would not have been Myr . . .

Reason might assert that both the shield and The Lovers had been in place long before his arrival. Nonetheless, he had not paid either of them the attention they merited. *Because,* the voice of reason pointed out, *you had your mind on other imperatives, like a camp on the verge of annihilation.* Still, Kalan now knew how Lannorth must have felt, with Rowan Birchmoon dead on his watch. The situation was not the same since guards under his command had not slain Myr. Yet Faro's involvement, however unwitting, meant the parallel ran close enough.

The crow had warned him that the spear came at a price. I just assumed I would be the one to pay, Kalan thought. It *should* have been me. He could have wept, except the wind from the plain gusted, a grit-laden susurration to the futility of blame and might-have-beens. Dry-eyed, he stared into it, but felt as bleak as Taly had looked, keeping her vigil for the young woman she had called Lady Mouse. The ensign had insisted on honoring Myr with the rites of Hurulth, dismissing the New Blood's ritual of Kharalth—and Kalan could not bring himself to tell her both would be equally vain so long as Myr's spirit was bound into the Web of Mayanne.

On the far side of the camp someone was playing a flute. The sound was mournful, suiting his mood and the silence of those crouched around the fires. So many lost, Kalan thought: Palla and Dain, together with Jaras and Nhal from his exiled company; Reith and Yelme among so many other marines; and Sarr and Nai from the caravan. Baris, too, had fallen sometime before the end, and Orth was dead.

Kalan had seen the Sword warrior's body as he turned Madder to answer Murn's summons, cast up a few yards past the high-tide line of the final assault with a storm wrack of enemies about him. All Kalan's focus had been on Myr, so he had not fully assimilated the details absorbed at that time, including Orth's death, until much later. He might not mourn the Sword warrior as he did others, but could and would acknowledge that Orth had fought ferociously to the end—and cut down the support for Arcolin's offer to the camp as effectively as he had swung his poleaxe. Not from any change of heart toward Faro, but from his understanding of Arcolin's game and a hatred of the Swarm that outweighed other animosities.

The rat-fox barked again, and Kalan frowned, studying the shadow of Malian and Raven's warriors, keeping guard in the darkness beyond the camp. The main force of around six hundred horse, commanded by someone called Valadan, was still pursuing the besiegers. Almost inevitably, Kalan knew, their superior numbers would whittle the Darksworn cavalry away until the infantry were at their mercy. In the meantime, Malian's escort had been reinforced from the original vanguard, so now several hundred warriors guarded the camp.

All drawn from Raven's personal guard, apparently—yet try though he might, Kalan could not recall any Southern Realms' mercenary company of comparable size to the force that had rescued the camp. The warrior he had observed in the tent was subtly altered, too, from the hedge knight he had known in Emer. The old

Ser Raven had also kept in the background until need demanded, but this man was . . . Less rough-edged, Kalan decided finally, and more assured. If that's possible, he added wryly, remembering the hill fort and Caer Argent.

He felt confident Malian would explain more fully as soon as circumstances allowed. Meanwhile, the strengthened guard meant he need not fear either a surprise assault or harassment from the lower-level 'spawn infestation that had accompanied the legion. With Malian and her force present, he could even say that his job was done and walk away from the camp, losing himself and his grief in the vastness of the night . . .

The respite, Kalan decided after a few moments, lay in contemplating such a course, but without any serious intention of pursuing it. Especially since he was still the Honor Captain Myr had appointed, and would retain responsibility for the camp until alternate provision could be made. Still frowning, he turned back to the camp, and recognized Aiv, crouched by one of the fires with the remnant of Palla's company. Together with Rigan, who was still in the infirmary, she was the last of those who had helped Sarr secure the camp after Kolthis abandoned it.

Instead of passing unseen in the dark between the fires, Kalan turned aside and sank onto his heels beside her. Checking Aiv's move to rise, he held out his hands to the flames. "Where's Darrar?" he asked.

Aiv cleared her throat. "All the companies chose one of their number to keep the second honor watch for Lady Myrathis, and Darrar stands for us. The Sea company will keep the third watch, and Lord Tirael's knights will see the vigil out. The camp agreed while you were with the other captains." She hesitated. "We're all glad to see you unscathed, Captain Khar."

"And I you," Kalan replied as a series of murmurs endorsed Aiv's comment.

The groom glanced away, clearly uncomfortable in her role as spokesperson, but one of the others gestured her to continue. "I mean, we all know that none of us would be here if it weren't for you. Sir."

"Ay," an older man agreed. "Even this Heir of Night, the one they say is the new Chosen of Mhaelanar, only came to our rescue because of her friendship with you."

Nods greeted this, and Kalan saw the association with Malian had enhanced, not diminished, him in their eyes. No question, though, how quickly word got about. As if to confirm it, Aiv spoke again, very low. "Is it true what they say, that your page is a long-lost Heir of Blood?"

"He has ties to the old line of Blood," Kalan temporized. "That much is true." If that implied anything more was not the case, he would have to live with the stain on his honor—but Aiv's query had stirred fear to life, highlighting the danger of Faro's heritage. Tirael had implied it, with his remark about loosing a wyr pack in Blood's halls, while Nimor's response had anticipated the way current alignments within the Alliance would shift as Earls and their advisors scented advantage. Kalan had known the revelation of Pha'Rho-l-Ynor would cause a furor, but now realized that grief and other preoccupations had blinded him to what Tirael had seen at once: that the ruling kin's most likely response would be to seek Faro's death.

And I can't rule out Liankhara and others still having viable agents in the camp, he thought grimly. "The defense would not have held without each and every one of you," he told Aiv and her companions, deliberately returning to the previous subject. "Your stand here honors Blood."

Kalan noted the lift in their expressions as they murmured acknowledgment, and all those about the fire rose to their feet as he left. On reaching the inner camp, he saw the lamp inside Myr's tent had been relit—and since Malian and Raven's escort still waited, was unsurprised to find the two of them inside. Malian was seated on a folding stool, studying an ornate scroll with Ise's walking stick propped beside her, while Faro lay close by, fast asleep amid the wyr hounds.

"He wanted to keep the vigil," Malian said, following his gaze, "but fell asleep almost at once. I thought it best to bring him with us when we left."

"At least one of us is thinking clearly," Kalan said, relieved, then glanced from the walking stick to the scroll, his raised brows a question.

"It's the marriage contract," Malian told him.

Kalan's brows rose higher—until he reminded himself that as Heir of Night she had every right to look at it, now that Myr was gone. To cover his flash of disapproval, and subsequent surge of grief, he studied The Lovers again. "I hate the cursed thing," he said finally, turning back to Malian and Raven, "but I intend to keep it very safe." Settling into a camp chair, he told them all he knew or suspected of the tapestry's part in events.

"A complex weaving," Malian observed, then paused. "Honor and duty may count for a great deal, but I can see Lady Myrathis meant more to you."

Raven remained by the entrance, but Kalan could feel the shimmer of Nhenir's power as well, warding the tent and their conversation. "More than I realized. And it was my job to keep her alive." His voice roughened. "I failed in that."

Gentleness was not a quality he primarily associated with Malian, but Kalan heard it in her voice now. "I doubt she would see it that way."

He met her eyes. "But I do. And I'm still her champion, so I have to find a way to free her spirit, if I can. But you needn't fear," he added quietly, "that I'll fail you by turning away from immediate events to pursue a personal quest."

Malian shook her head. "From the beginning, we've been friends, not Heir and retainer. And friends come and go as they wish, choosing their own paths as need and wisdom dictate. So, the question of failing me does not arise."

Which is both freedom and a burden, Kalan thought wryly, since it leaves me with no one else to blame if my decisions go awry. His gaze returned to The Lovers and the young woman who stood alone, weeping—although he rather thought the symbolism might depict Faro's fate as much as Myr's. He met Malian's gaze again. "In terms of where I go from here, my dreams keep showing me Dread Pass, above the Towers of Morning."

She nodded. "I've detected that, through my visions. I also met Garan of Night and his eight-guard by Rowan Birchmoon's tomb. From what he told me, Morning and the pass are both dangerously vulnerable."

Garan had said the same thing to Asantir in the Red Keep, Kalan reflected. "In light of what's happened here, the pass must be secured."

"I agree." Malian was thoughtful, though. "But how sure are you of your dreams' truth? We know Nindorith manipulates both dreams and foreseeing, and the Darksworn might well try misdirection regarding their plans."

"So far, the other dreams around it have proven true." Kalan glanced toward Raven, watchful by the tent entrance, then back to Faro. "Including one that may be his great storm. *'Do it,'*" he quoted. "*'Live.'* I believe I dreamed Ammaran saying those words, presumably telling Taierin to use the Luck's binding. And there *was* another power loose in that storm." Kalan described the behemoth and the sky riven by more than lightning. "But how *Pha'Rho-l-Ynor*'s wreckage washed up four hundred years later, I still don't understand."

"I may, from what you describe." Raven spoke quietly from his place by the entrance. "Do you recall," he said to Malian, "my telling you how Amaliannarath brought us here, and that our few remaining adepts with any sort of talent for gates all died, shoring up her power at the last? And that even then we almost didn't make it?"

Amaliannarath, Kalan thought, cudgeling his tired brain to recall . . . But Malian was nodding. "She never intended bringing us back into time at all," Raven continued. "She had foreseen that we must sleep outside it and waken only when the circumstances were right. But she had expended too much of herself at the end and was already dying. She came out of the Gate of Dreams inadvertently, tearing a gap between it and Haarth, which is when our adepts died, joining their power to hers to rectify the error. That breach," he told Kalan, "is what you saw in your dream."

"'*I move between worlds and time,*'" Malian said softly. "Amaliannarath really did have that ability—but she came out of the gate *after* the time when she foresaw Fire waking. Before that could be corrected and the tear closed again, *Pha'Rho-l-Ynor* must have sailed through the anomaly and into our current time."

It does fit, Kalan thought. But Raven's reference to sleeping outside of time had prompted his recollection of Amaliannarath. "The Cavern of Sleepers and the warrior with the sword," he said. "Is *that* who you are?" Before Raven could reply, another realization made him swing back to Malian. "And the sword—was it the frost-fire blade all along?"

"It was," Malian agreed. "I found the Lost, too, but they were not inclined to return to the Wall." Her tone was wry, while her look said that she knew Kalan would appreciate their sentiment, which he did. He was fascinated by the rest of the story she proceeded to relate, supplemented by the occasional clarification or elaboration from Raven. At the end, he shook his head—although their tale of the frost-fire sword's path to reach Malian was no stranger than his own experience of a spear that had awaited him for what could have been aeons, in a tomb that had manifested on Haarth after having been raised in another place and time.

But still, Kalan thought, with another careful glance at Raven, who met his gaze levelly: Darksworn. *That* took considerable mental adjustment, and Kalan didn't know if he could have managed it without having known Raven in Emer first. "You had the sword all that time," he said, unable to keep the wonder from his voice. He frowned, though, reflecting on the rest of their story, because Malian could only have rendezvoused with the Patrol and Fire—Kalan shook his head again—around the time he was leaving the Red Keep. "There's no way," he said slowly, "you could have marched overland in that time."

Malian and Raven exchanged a glance. "No." Malian set the scroll aside. "By the time I reached the River, I knew events were moving more swiftly than we had hoped, and that I needed to reach the Wall sooner than the planned muster and march north would have allowed. But even once I understood that Rowan Birchmoon's grave provided a bridge between the Wall and the rest of Haarth, a portal would not have allowed the passage of sufficient numbers. Especially since," she added, with a flicker of the former hedge knight's own sardonic humor as she glanced at Raven, "you had extracted a promise that I would take your personal guard with me."

Two hundred horse, Kalan thought, appreciating Raven's old, imperturbable look. Or three hundred, if the entire vanguard comprised his personal guard . . . "But," Malian went on, "I reflected more deeply on the way the Wall-Haarth divide exists in both the daylight realm and the Gate of Dreams. I also recalled Yorindesarinen's path through the white mists, and what we know of how the siren worm infiltrated the Keep of Winds, six years ago. I thought further, too, on how I had used the Gate of Dreams to thwart Nindorith in Caer Argent. That it was *possible* to use the Gate in that way," she explained, meeting Kalan's gaze. "As well as the fact that you and I can pass the Gate in our physical bodies—while Fire has cadres dedicated to turning aside unwelcome attention. I also have Nhenir."

"So you opened up a way through the Gate of Dreams," Kalan said slowly, "and crossed over using the bridge provided by Rowan Birchmoon's power?"

Malian nodded. "The way was shaped from the fabric of the Gate, so I did not have to sustain it out of my own power in the same way I would a portal. That meant far greater numbers could pass through."

"Persuading the Gate to retain that shape," Raven observed, "still took its toll on you."

Persuading the Gate, thought Kalan. He cleared his throat. "I can see how that might be if it allowed the passage of your total force."

"That would have been a feat!" Malian shook her head. "No, only two hundred accompanied me through the Gate of Dreams. And you're right"—she glanced toward Raven—"even that pushed me to my limit. It was sufficient numbers, though, to fulfill my promise." Her gaze returned to Kalan. "The two hundred also ensured we'd have a fighting chance if our attempt at stealth failed, or we met a welcoming party on the Wall side." Briefly, the ghost of the excitement she must have felt on first working out the Gate of Dreams solution illuminated her face. "Rowan Birchmoon's bridge also meant Fire didn't have to wake on the Haarth side of the divide and *then* march north. We could wake them from this side."

She paused, growing sober again. "But Wolf was waiting for us near the cairn, and when he told us of the Darkswarm build up and how they were trailing the caravan, we sent out long-range scouts. Once their reports came in we knew we dared not delay, so only roused sufficient of Fire's strength to effect a rescue before we marched. And we had to march." Malian's expression, meeting Kalan's, conveyed both apology and regret. "The first crossing came close to exhausting me, and I could not have opened another way through the Gate so soon, let alone for a significantly larger force."

They came as soon as they could, Kalan told himself, despite the grief and bitterness that flared through his fatigue. He was all too aware that power could be exhausted as easily as physical strength, and what Malian had done . . . Shaking his head, he tried to encompass its magnitude. "But if only you could pass the Gate of Dreams in your physical body, how did the two hundred follow you?"

Malian's eyes narrowed—on recollection, he thought, seeing her absorption. "I've managed to take one or more with me at least twice before, most recently with Raven and his horses outside Aeris. So the process of opening up *this* way included persuading the Gate to allow the others through as well. It helped that Fire still has a handful of adepts with some dreaming ability," she admitted. "They were able to provide support."

Limited support, Kalan suspected, frowning. "If we're to believe Faro's memories, your ability to create such openings must come from your mother." Masquerading as Ilai, he thought soberly, remembering both the wounded attendant and the faceless woman from his predawn vision. He stiffened. "If she can do the same thing—"

Malian shook her head. "If she could have, I think she would by now. But her ability appears to be grounded in the physical realm—like the way she's supposed to have opened through the Wall, twenty-odd years ago."

The ability to pass the Gate of Dreams in one's physical body *is* extremely rare, Kalan reminded himself. And it was rarer still to be able to take others with you. He was still thinking about that when the clip of an approaching horse, followed by brisk footsteps entering the inner camp, made him turn. At the same time, Raven lifted the tent flap aside. "It's Aithe," the knight said, looking back at Malian. "She'll have brought dispatches from Valadan, but I'll deal with them by the escort's fire." His nod included Kalan, and then he was gone, the heavy canvas falling behind him.

For a moment they were both silent. Kalan listened to Raven's retreating footsteps, and then his voice, greeting the newly-arrived officer, while Malian appeared absorbed by the soldered phoenix. Her expression was so noncommittal that Kalan knew she was expecting all the questions about Raven, and her alliance with Fire, that he couldn't ask while the knight—or prince, he corrected himself—was present. Only I'm too tired for that, Kalan thought. Besides, he already knew the most important fact about Malian's new alliance, which was that it had saved the camp. And, he decided, realizing it was true, I trust her judgment.

He spread his hands, flexing fingers that were still stiff from grasping spear and sword. "Tell me about Wolf. You said he was drawn out of the Winter Country by Rowan Birchmoon's death?"

"And our return." Malian's gaze, lifting from the phoenix, grew reflective. "Partly because of the debt we owe Rowan and the Winter People for our rescue from Jaransor, and subsequent safe passage into the Southern Realms. But also, I suspect, because he wishes to be at the heart of what is coming, not just looking on from the periphery."

Kalan could understand that. He could also perceive the inherent danger of the wish. "Since he alerted you to the caravan's peril, I'm doubly in his debt." Wearily, he rubbed at the stubble on his chin. Garan's gesture, he realized, and wondered if the Night eight had found their fugitive. "Are Garan's eight still with you?"

Malian shook her head. "As soon as our scouts returned, I dispatched them to the Keep of Winds to rouse out Night."

"I'd better let Tirael know." Liad can farspeak the Stars force, Kalan thought, sure Tirael would agree that the last thing they needed right now was a Stars-Night confrontation. Rubbing his chin again, he studied Malian. "From what you said earlier, your plan is to concentrate on restoring the Golden Fire?"

"With the Swarm rising and all hope of the shield gone, I have to." Malian was matter-of-fact. "My only alternative is to summon the Council of the Derai and force the Nine Houses to accept me—and Fire. But that will take time I doubt we have."

And with the Alliance, it was always better to bargain from a position of strength. Assuming, Kalan told himself, that restoration of the Golden Fire is even possible. Silently, he reviewed the remnants they knew had survived. *"Hylcarian in Night, Yelusin with Sea, Maurid and Blood. I would put coin, though, on there being a remnant in Stars: a strong one, from what I've had seen of Tirael and his knights. And probably in the Rose,"* he added, his eyes on the walking stick at Malian's side. She nodded and picked it up, reexamining the twisted wood and mother-of-pearl eyes.

"Sea's ships have similar eyes painted onto their prows," Kalan told her. "In the Red Keep, it's the hydras. They're depicted everywhere, and you can always feel the eyes, watching you. I think that's where the bulk of Maurid's remnant resides, although he acts through the wyr hounds."

"The old Blood returns, and we have chosen the new to raise up with it." The mindwhisper was a ghost, its source uncertain. Had the mother-of-pearl eyes glowed briefly, Kalan wondered, or was it just a trick of the light? Automatically, he glanced toward the wyr hounds, but did not catch even the gleam of a ghostly eye.

"Five of the nine entities that once comprised the Golden Fire," Malian said. "But five isn't enough. We need all nine."

Kalan frowned, not wanting to contemplate the possibility that some, if not all, of the remaining four Fires might have been extinguished altogether. "If you could bring together the Blood of all Nine Houses, the combined power might be strong enough to wake any remnants that still lie dormant." He grimaced at her expression, which suggested that would be an achievement of similar magnitude to restoring the Golden Fire. "Even representatives from the Blood of each House might be sufficient," he continued doggedly. "Although if Xeria could call down all Nine at once during the Night of Death . . . "

"I should be able to restore them single-handedly?" Malian shook her head. "The leaders of all Nine Houses were already gathered that night, with the nine Fires drawn together as well, to foster the desired peace." Somberly, she traced the twisted strands of the walking stick. "I imagine, too, that by the time Xeria called down the conjoined Fire, many among the Nine Houses would have bound their power to hers in order to counter Aikanor's onslaught. So even once they realized what she intended, they may not have been able to break free. Effectively, though, she would not have acted alone."

I never considered that, Kalan thought. With an effort, he pulled himself back to his previous line of thought. "If representatives from the Blood of each House *were* enough, then we already have Tirael, Nimor, and Faro. And Rook, too, I believe, as well as you . . . " He shook his head, convinced his frown was in danger of becoming permanent. "But you'd still need some sort of focus for your working—something that unifies all nine entities that comprised the Golden Fire."

The walking stick revolved between Malian's hands, its mother-of-pearl eyes catching the light. "Like the table in the heart of the Old Keep of Winds," she suggested.

Exactly like the table, Kalan thought, excitement stirring with his memory of the twelve-sided room at the Old Keep's heart, with twelve doors opening into mist and fire, and the twelve-sided table at its center. One of those twelve panels had flared into golden life at Malian's touch, the winged horse of Night in flight across its surface . . .

The caravan would have provided excellent cover, he thought regretfully, for anyone as stealthy as Malian to access the Old Keep—only to realize immediately that she didn't need it. Six years ago they had both departed the heart of the Old Keep by physically crossing into the Gate of Dreams. In light of Malian's path back to the Wall, she should be able to reach the twelve-sided room again in the same way.

For a moment, regarding her, Kalan felt as though the mists of the Gate had already flowed between them. He told himself the urge to shiver was reaction and fatigue, but was still glad to be distracted by Faro, turning in his sleep. The boy soon quietened again, but Malian watched him for several moments more before turning back to Kalan. "The Golden Fire and our larger plans can wait, for tonight. But I'm not sure he can."

"No," Kalan agreed. "I'd keep him with me, but that won't ensure his safety. The Alliance would never allow my continued guardianship anyway, since he's kin to the Sea Count—and arguably, the Heir of Blood as well." Wary of Faro waking, Kalan switched to mindspeech. *"From what I saw of Blood's ruling kin, they'll only want him to ensure his death. But as he's a Son of Blood and Ammaran's heir, Earl Sardon will have the strongest claim to legal guardianship."* His eyes met Malian's. *"So perhaps the warding should have been left in place."*

Her answering look was steady. "He's called lightning twice now, which means he's a weatherworker like his mother and his training's already been delayed too long. The warding *had* to be undone."

Kalan's mouth thinned, reflecting on the unpalatable reality that untrained weatherworkers almost always went mad, unable to counteract the weather's sway over their power. He was surprised Faro's foster mother had not foreseen that risk. But perhaps because the boy looked all Blood, and if she saw no warning signs, Kara may have assumed his inheritance of power came solely from Ammaran. Still, at least the weatherworking should strengthen Sea's ability to claim custody—particularly since Blood's practice of banishing power users would negate Faro's right to the Heirship.

"But regardless of the Oath," Kalan told Malian silently, *"Blood's ruling kin will seek to ensure their tenure remains unassailable. So they'll still want Faro dead."* He paused. *"And once they realize that your claim to the Heirdom of Night and leadership of the Derai may overturn the Oath anyway . . . "* He let the implication hang.

Malian nodded, her expression deeply thoughtful. "Faro does need to be trained, and the sooner the better. It may not have to be on the Wall, though." Slowly, she rotated the walking stick. "The Lost declined rejoining the Derai, but I believe they would accept him. They are more than capable, too, of dealing with any Blood agents that reach them. Although with the Patrol, the Shadow Band, and the Oakward in between, I doubt there's much danger of that."

"No Sea ship would carry them south either. Yet the Alliance may say"—Kalan was wry—"that we have stolen him from his rightful guardians."

Malian's expression remained reflective. "Best, then, if we remove any grounds for such a charge." The stick circled slowly left, then back to the right. "With your permission, of course," she added.

I know that look, Kalan thought: she's up to something. "It's not my permission that matters," he said quietly, "but what's best for Faro, which has to include what he wants."

"I'll speak with him in the morning." Malian set the stick aside and retrieved the scroll. "But in the meantime, I believe he'll be safest in our camp."

Yes, Kalan thought, feeling the night's chill as he nodded. By tacit agreement they both stood up, but Malian put out a hand before he could turn to leave. "Besides Wolf, there's someone else with us that you know." She paused, a flicker of the very young Malian, from the Keep of Winds' days, in her gaze. "Kalan, I've found Nhairin."

62

The Gift

Faro, poised to sit up and declare that he wasn't leaving Khar, froze at the quality of the silence that followed Malian's words. A dangerous quiet, he thought, his skin prickling, and had to fight to keep his eyes closed. When Khar finally spoke, his voice was as hard as when he found Lady Myr dead. "Nhairin. Who betrayed us in Jaransor. Or does she blame it all on the Madness?"

Hearing that harsh note, Faro was thankful Malian had lifted Thanir's compulsion and allowed him to explain that he had not betrayed Lady Myr. Or not deliberately anyway, he thought, desolation returning with the memory of the Darksworn's hold over him. Outside, feet tramped past and voices spoke, momentarily distracting him as the guard changed. The honor watch for Lady Myr would be changing, too—but Faro knew that no matter how many came and went, Taly would not stir from her vigil.

I should be with her, he thought, before Malian reclaimed his attention, saying something about the Madness having played its part. "But she and Nerion share an empathy bond, Kalan, one very like ours."

Kalan, Faro repeated silently, hearing the name for the second time. "Their bond is also one way," Malian went on, "in Nerion's favor. And Nhairin has no power, or no other power, so could not close her out at need. When she first saw me at Rowan Birchmoon's cairn, she was terrified, believing Nerion had found her again." Malian paused before continuing, her tone as measured as the guards' tread. "From what I've learned since, Nerion was able to blur Nhairin's recollection of the times when she entered her mind and manipulated her will, but could not erase the occurrences completely. So to Nhairin, they seemed like dream memories."

"While her bond to Nerion provided a chink in Night's defences," Khar said, still harsh. "One the Darksworn prised open."

"Once they learned that Nerion's true father, my grandfather, was of Stars, not Night," Malian agreed, "and that for all their vigilance, a new Chosen of Mhaelanar *had* been born into the Derai."

Because of what Thanir had said about why Lady Myr must die, Faro understood that Malian's House of Stars heritage would mean the Swarm wanted to kill her, too. He lay very still, and when Malian spoke again, he thought she sounded sad.

"Nhairin loved Nerion, and loves her still, I believe, although there's too much bitterness now, piled on betrayal, to be sure. And she held my father at fault over Nerion's fate, and perhaps her own—but you heard that in Jaransor." Malian hesitated. "Yet because Nhairin always loved me as well, and was still Derai, she became a person at war within herself."

"If their bond's like ours, Nerion would always have known where she was, too. No wonder the Darksworn were able to follow us so unerringly." Khar's grimness sounded more tempered now. "I take it you've blocked their link?"

"I have. Otherwise Nerion could use Nhairin again in exactly the same way, now the Madness has lifted. That's why she was so terrified at the cairn." When Malian fell silent, Faro could hear the rise and fall of the wyr hounds' breath, their absorption matching his. "If that happened," Malian added, very softly, "I think it would destroy all that's left of my Nhairin."

"Probably." The tempered quality in Khar's voice strengthened. "But you know she may never have been your Nhairin. From what you've said she was always Nerion's—and could easily be so again, even with the old link closed off, if they ever meet in person."

"I do know that. Nhairin can never return to Night, regardless of whether my father would pardon her for what happened."

When Khar spoke again, Faro thought he sounded bleak. "Do you think Nerion ever cared about Nhairin at all, or only saw her as a tool?"

This time the silence was so prolonged that Faro risked peering through his lashes. "I don't know." Malian's expression was shuttered as she tapped the scroll she was holding against her opposite palm. "There's too much I don't know. Except," she added, with another brisk change of tone, "that you have a vigil that honor and the Code demand you keep, while we need to get Pha'Rho-l-Ynor to Fire's camp." The scroll tapped again as Faro hurriedly closed his eyes. "I may need this. I'll take the stick, too. And the tray, which is in a sense my own."

The wyr hounds rose as Malian spoke, but their voice spoke in Faro's mind, preventing him doing the same: *"Be still."* Startled, he opened his eyes to a glow of gilt-edged light haloing all six beasts. Light surrounded Khar as well—and Faro, transfixed, thought it looked like sunshine, glittering on the face of the sea. When the Storm Spear spoke, his voice was wrapped about with power. "The road to the Keep of Winds is no longer my path." Khar's eyes were intent on the wyrs, so Faro guessed he was speaking to them. "Nor is the restoration of the Golden Fire my task."

"No. But my thanks to you, Kalan-hamar-khar: Storm Spear." The Sea fleet's mindvoice resonated through Faro, as it had when he returned the essence of *Pha'Rho-l-Ynor* to the Ships' Shrine. From Malian's expression, he guessed she could hear it—hear *her*, Faro corrected himself—too. He almost forgot to breathe as the light about Khar rose into a single shimmering flame, then flowed toward Malian. The bracelet on her wrist blazed silver, and Faro thought he saw fire glimmer in her eyes, too, before the halo of sunlight disappeared.

Into her, Faro thought, wide-eyed—as it must have been in Khar all this time. But Malian's armring was still burning, and the light surrounding the wyrs was rising above their bodies, as it had whenever a hound died in the assault. Faro wanted to cry out in protest and beg the light not to abandon the wyr hounds and him, even though he guessed this was why the hounds had left the Red Keep. *"Be of good heart, Pha'Rho-l-Ynor."* The acknowledgment was a feather touch across his mind. *"You are right, this was always our purpose. Yet if all goes as we hope, it will not be farewell."*

What if it doesn't, though? Faro thought, feeling the slow slide of tears. But Maurid's light was already gone, streaming across the tent and into Malian of Night, and the six wyrs were silver-eyed hounds again, but nothing more.

In the end Faro was too drained to offer more than token argument when Khar insisted he go with Malian and Raven. He stumbled several times in the short walk to the escort's horses, and did not complain when he was put up in front of Raven and the warrior wrapped his cloak about them both, to thwart the cold and prying eyes. When they arrived in Fire's camp, Faro was given his own tent, and a warrior called Duar showed him how the flap lacing worked, so he could come and go as he pleased. But not leave, Faro thought, because when he checked he saw guards at the rear of the tent, as well as at the front. Everyone who spoke to him was kindly enough, but stern, and when they left him alone, Faro cried for the second time that night.

In the morning, he resolved, sniffing, he would find a way to persuade Khar to take him with him, after all. Or maybe it would be better to hide away, as he had on the *Che'Ryl-g-Raham*, until it was too late to send him back—although that would mean finding a way to escape from Fire's camp first. Somewhere in the middle of casting about for a means of eluding his guards, Faro fell asleep. When he woke, daylight was rippling across the tent canvas, and the surrounding camp was awake. He lay still, listening to its sounds, the same way he used to lie in his narrow bed above the armorer's shop and listen to Grayharbor waking.

When Mam was alive, Faro thought, tears pricking again. To comfort himself, he recalled the Ships' Shrine again, and the memory of all the vessels in the Sea Keep harbor welcoming him, as the *Che'Ryl-g-Raham* had welcomed him in Grayharbor. On the sea journey north, the ship had told him tales of the winds and tides that bore the ships up and down the long coast and out into deep waters, where they battled storms and monsters to keep the world safe. In the Sea Keep shrine, the ships had told him another story: how the vast power loose in the storm the *Pha'Rho-l-Ynor* sailed into, together with Ammaran's sacrifice of his life and power trying to save the ship and Taierin, was what had woken what remained of Yelusin—first in *Pha'Rho-l-Ynor*, and then in the rest of the Sea House fleet.

Raven had given that power a name, Faro thought—which he could not remember now—amid a great deal more that he did not fully understand. But he remembered the ships saying that Ammaran would have been trying to save him, as well as Taierin and the *Pha'Rho-l-Ynor*. Just like Lady Myr tried to save me, Faro reflected, feeling the ache of yesterday's events return. He knew what his mam would have said, though: that if he truly wanted to honor their memories and their sacrifice, then he needed to get up and shoulder his duty as they both had.

Only I have no duty, Faro thought. But he got up anyway, and confirmed that the guard about the tent remained in place. Because I'm important now, he told himself, and tried to decide how he felt about being a Son of Blood. On one hand, the House of Blood meant Khar and Lady Myr and Mam, and his father Ammaran. On the other, there were all his memories of the Red Keep, most particularly Parannis and Sarein—and Earl Sardon, whom he had heard the Sea Keepers say was prepared to see his own son slain on the Field of Blood. Faro couldn't quite understand what was so terrible about that, since the son was Parannis, but he was prepared to accept it was bad if the Sea Keepers thought so.

Now Khar and Malian believed Blood's ruling kin might try and have him killed, too. Faro had gleaned that from their voices and the pauses in their speech, as well as Malian's reference to Blood agents. As for Khar not being good enough to look after him, just because the Storm Spear wasn't one of the Derai's horrible nobility— "He's better than the lot of them!" Faro declared, then jumped as one of the guards outside bade someone good morning.

He recognized the voice that answered as Malian's and hastily checked his appearance, all his mam's newly remembered strictures about the courtesy to be shown Derai Earls and Heirs resurfacing. Malian was asking if she could enter before Faro had done more than straighten his tunic and tighten the tie about his braids, but since she added that she had brought breakfast, he said *yes* at once. When she stepped inside, the food smelled so good that he started eating as soon as she set the tray down. "There's more if you want it," she said, when he finished.

Faro shook his head, because after several days of siege rations, he was completely full. "Am I your prisoner?" he asked, deciding it was best to know.

"Not at all, Faro." Malian's regard was steady. "I have a matter to discuss with you, but if you wish to leave after that you will be free to do so. But both Khar and I would prefer you to stay here."

"You called him Kalan last night," Faro said.

"I did. It's the name I know him by. Yelusin and Maurid," she added casually, "call him Kalan-hamar-khar."

Like the long names of the ships, Faro thought, and—if he guessed right—Tirael and his Star knights, where each syllable spoke to the essence of their power. He wondered if he would ever grow into Pha'Rho-l-Ynor, because right now the name felt as alien to him as one of the great sea serpents in the *Che'Ryl-g-Raham*'s tales. Abruptly, he returned to what Malian had first said. "Because you both think I'll be safer here?"

"For now, although it's no more practical for you to remain with me than with Khar. And because you're a weatherworker, you must learn to manage your power."

"But not in the Sea Keep. Not even on the Wall." Faro's lip started to jut, before he remembered that would disgrace his mam's upbringing before one of the Derai great.

"So you did hear that. What you may not have caught is that because you're a minor, and of Blood's ruling line, Khar is concerned Earl Sardon may be able to claim legal guardianship."

No, Faro thought, panic rising. "But you can stop him. Can't you?" he asked uncertainly.

"I believe so. Under the law, marriage outweighs blood kinship's claim to legal custody. And although you're a minor, paper marriages for the purposes of guardianship were created for exactly that purpose. And we," Malian added, with the smile Faro was coming to think of as tricky, "have a legitimate contract between Blood and Night at our disposal. If you and I use it to marry, I will then be your legal guardian for the seven years until you come of age."

Faro knew his mouth was open, which his mam would have deplored, but could not help it. "You and me? But isn't the contract between Lady Myr and the Earl of Night?"

"The contracts are always between the Houses, specifying only that the marriage must take place between scions of the ruling kin. The details of names and signatures are filled in as part of the marriage ceremony. So the same contract will cover us, and using it will allow me to protect you." She paused. "And when the Swarm rises, as rise it will, our contract will also hold Blood to the Night alliance. Whether," she added, with an edge of steel, "they like it or not."

She *was* being tricky, Faro could see that. "But we would have to be married?"

"A paper marriage, yes."

"I still can't stay with you, though, because of the weatherworking?"

Malian nodded. "The marriage will give me an unassailable right to send you somewhere I consider safe, however. And as I discussed with Khar, there is another place your weatherworking could be trained." Quietly, she told him about the Derai Lost—although she said they called themselves the Ara-fyr—and how they lived a very long way from the Wall of Night. Almost, she said, as far as Ishnapur. "A very long way from Blood as well," she concluded, "and the Swarm."

"From Khar, too," Faro said.

"Yes." Malian was grave. "But Khar has traveled almost that far south before, and lived in those lands, so if we can make the Wall safe, he will come and see you there one day. When you are of age and can better look after yourself, you will also be free to return—if that is what you choose."

Almost as far as Ishnapur, Faro thought, remembering the mariner with her curved knives and curly-toed slippers. It would be a new adventure, too, of the good kind. And one day Khar would come, or he would return when he was grown up, like Malian said. "Will I have to go alone?" he asked finally.

"No," Malian said. "Because you are a minor, we can't live together as two grown-up people that marry would. But I am required to provide you with your own household: exactly the same as an Heir would have, including your own captain and guard, as well as a tutor and a steward. Khar has recommended Ensign Talies," she said, before he could speak, "and she has agreed, so long as you say yes. Nimor suggested Murn for your tutor, because although not a powerful weatherworker himself, he has been well taught and can oversee your training. And I," she added, "will send a strong company with you under Taly's captaincy. I know it won't be the same as with Khar, but you will not be alone, or friendless, or unprotected."

Taly, Faro thought, and Murn, both of whom he liked. "But it's only a paper marriage?" he asked again, to be sure.

"That is what it's called. It is a true marriage in law, but in addition to having separate households, we will not be permitted to make demands of each other's bodies, as grown-up people may do." She said that matter-of-factly, not sniggering or smirking as the Red Keep pages or Grayharbor street urchins would have done. "As I said, once the seven years are up you will be of age, with your power trained, so better able to protect yourself without need of our marriage." Fleetingly, she smiled. "I won't say free to choose your own path, because I think you've been doing that for some time."

"And after that," Faro said, focusing on what he thought was the important part, "we won't be married anymore?"

"Not unless we wish to be. There is," she explained, "what is called a renewal clause, but we both have to agree to it."

Faro knew she was tricky, and both dark and light as he could be, too, but he did not think she was trying to trick him. He also remembered how swiftly the fever had taken his mam, and how even those who were strong and sure, like Palla and Reith, or Orth with his brutal strength, could die in battle, just like that. "What if something happens to you?"

Again Malian nodded. "Your being with the Ara-fyr will be a secret, but I will also appoint Khar and Raven as your guardians in my place, should that prove necessary." She smiled. "And Raven, you may have noticed, comes with an army."

Faro could not help smiling back, because he *had* noticed that. "But I will see Khar again before I go?"

"He won't leave without saying good-bye," Malian promised, before growing serious again. "There is someone else I would like you to meet, who also needs a safe haven far from the Wall. Her name is Nhairin and she is an old friend of mine, one you will have heard us talk about last night. You may find her dour, but she will make an able steward for your household, and I would be grateful if you could take her under your protection."

Nhairin. Faro remembered Khar's anger on first hearing the name. He had softened later, though. And from what Malian had said, Nhairin had also suffered at the hands of the Swarm. "Mam was dour sometimes." He hesitated. "But I already know Taly and Murn . . . "

"I shall introduce you," Malian said, rising, "then you may talk together and decide. But if you can, Faro, be kind to my Nhairin. She has great need of it." In the morning light, her eyes were as much silver as smoke. "We'll keep the marriage ceremony brief, but Murn has confirmed the contracts are in order, so we can sign them whenever we want. The signing is the important part," she added, smiling again.

Faro knew she was saving him from his enemies and a life of fear, while making it seem like he could do her an equal favor by showing kindness to Nhairin. And last night, when they all watched the pilot star, she had taken his parents' quest as her own. Now he rose, too, shaken by the longing to give her something that really mattered in return.

"I heard what you and Khar said about the Golden Fire," he said quickly, before he lost his resolve. "How even with the twelve-sided table, you would still need the Blood of all the Nine Houses to focus the power. And if we're to marry I should make you a gift." When Malian remained silent, watching him, Faro hurried on. "I don't have anything of my own, but I do have an idea about the Blood—especially with so many Houses already represented here, like Khar said."

Malian's slim dark brows had risen, but Faro could see she was listening. "It's something Sea does with their mariners." His words tumbled over each other as he explained about Sea's death names and the scroll they had made for Khar, when he was fighting his duel to the death. "So his spirit wouldn't be lost, but tied to their mariners' shrine in the Sea Keep, the same way I carried a part of *Pha'Rho-l-Ynor* all that time."

Malian held up a hand. "You've got my attention, Faro, but you need to slow down. And breathe," she added, with a smile that was not at all tricky this time.

Obediently, Faro gulped in air. "We only used runes for Khar's scroll, but Murn said that very close kin and shield comrades often put a drop of blood beside their name, because blood is always strongest. But locks of hair are strong as well, so lots of mariners use them." He stopped, because Malian was extracting a narrow scroll tube from inside her jacket.

"Like this?" she asked, removing and unrolling a rectangle of linen so Faro could see its wreath made from locks of hair, together with silhouetted towers and the same calligraphy the Sea Keepers had used for Khar. Murn had said the symbols were runes, which he would teach Faro when there was time—but added that in scrolls like this, the characters always represented names.

"This is different from the Sea scroll," Faro said, indicating the wreath. "But you can see it's the same sort of thing." He looked up. "Where did it come from?"

"The House of Morning," Malian told him. "Apparently they also foresaw my coming. One of the Mothers sent it to me by Garan of Night's hand, together with a similar scroll from Peace. So now," she said, rerolling the linen, "the mystery is explained."

Silently, Faro went over the Houses with ruling kin present in the camp: Night, Stars, and Sea, Blood and Adamant—and now Morning had sent their own scroll *and* that of Peace. "Kelyr's of the Blood of Swords." This time he spoke slowly. "Orth was, too. I heard Kelyr say so when I was hiding from them in the *Che'Ryl-g-Raham*'s hold. Kelyr said their captain, Tirorn, would say he and Orth were shaming their inheritance of Sword's Blood. But Orth said all Tirorn's niceties had gotten him was dead." He left out the obscenities that Orth had spliced into his reply, which had been impressive even by the standards of Grayharbor's backstreets.

"Well, now, that is useful," Malian murmured. "But I can see there's more."

Faro hesitated. "Lady Myr was of the Rose as well as Blood," he said, stumbling over the words because he felt uncomfortable. "I don't think she would mind if we used her hair." In fact, he was sure Lady Myr would want them to take a lock of her hair if it would help.

"I may not need it, since I have the walking stick." Malian's eyes were close to silver again, and he could almost see the thoughts chasing each other behind her outward calm. "But if the Swarm wanted to kill both me and Lady Myr because of a grandparent's Stars blood, a lock of her hair may indeed serve for the Rose." To Faro's surprise, she bowed, the same grave salute the *Che'Ryl-g-Raham*'s Luck had made to Khar, pressing her palms together. "Thank you," she said. "If this is your bridegroom's gift, it is beyond compare."

And Faro was still blinking over that as the entry flap rose and fell, and she was gone.

63

Song of Farewell

The day was eerily quiet, the wind little more than a ripple as the camp set itself to rights and gathered its dead. The stillness infused the convalescents' tent, erected once someone had unearthed a manifest of the caravan's contents and a tent large enough to accommodate the overflow from the infirmary. Rook was glad the lack of wind meant one side could be rolled up, so he could see where the oriflamme had been struck above the garnet-and-gold tent. Blood's colors, together with a pennant of the ruling kin, hung in its place—to honor Lady Myrathis, he supposed. If he craned onto one elbow, he could see Elodin and Xer at the entrance, keeping the honor watch.

Once Rook regained consciousness, he had wanted to observe the Bride's vigil, too, but Kion would not allow it. The Sea physician had been reluctant to send for the Storm Spear as well, but Rook had insisted, urgent to tell Khar all he could recall of the dreamlike events surrounding the tapestry, the hind, and Lady Myrathis's death. Afterward, having seen Khar's face, Rook wondered if he should have kept the whole strange business to himself.

Telling him, he thought now, is probably just one more thing I've done wrong. Involuntarily, he flung an arm across his face, trying to deflect the memory of his disastrous attempt at farspeaking. All I achieved was to lose my ability altogether, he thought miserably. And I didn't save Lady Myrathis, either then or later. He gnawed his lip, not wanting to make excuses but still doubtful whehter any healer, however powerful or well trained, could overcome the fact that the Daughter of Blood had *chosen* to die.

Rook tightened his concealing arm, hoping that Rigan, the Blood wagoner on the adjoining pallet, would not see and make gruff, cheering remarks like "Heart up, lad." His fellow convalescent's alternate observations were that matters might not be as bad as first appeared, and tomorrow was always another day. *Obviously*, Rook thought—and grinned, just a little, thinking about what Onnorin would say if she could overhear. No doubt she would have several pithy observations to share on his current situation as well: the sole Adamant initiate in a tent full of convalescent Blood retainers, with a handful of Sea marines for leaven.

Mostly, the others ignored him, amusing themselves with games of chance or sharing the rumors that swirled in from the camp— including that the siege had been raised by the Chosen of Mhaelanar, returned to lead the Derai. Rigan, though, was inclined to be skeptical. "No point in getting carried away with fireside tales just because we've had a lucky reprieve. Next," he had added, grimacing, "we'll hear the Golden Fire's returned." In fact, Rook had overheard exactly that, but the account was so confused he tended to agree with Rigan. He had no chance to say so, though, because the wagoner had looked apologetic. "I expect you'd say differently in Adamant."

Not necessarily, Rook thought. He suspected Torlun and Rul would also scoff at the rumored return of the Chosen of Mhaelanar and the Golden Fire, as much if not more than any New Blooder. Still, he appreciated the belated courtesy, particularly since he knew Rigan was enduring considerable pain from the stump of his amputated arm. He was impressed, too, at the wagoner's unflagging optimism, even in the face of low-voiced conversations that suggested the Blood retainers' futures might be as uncertain as his own. "It doesn't matter how hard we fought," a woman called Aiv had said. With so much to be done in the camp, the convalescents had few visitors, but she had stopped by Rigan's pallet in the predawn dark. "No matter the circumstances of Lady Myrathis's death, the disgrace will cling when we return to the Red Keep."

"Ay," Rigan had agreed softly. "The ruling kin'll make us feel it, sure enough."

"You're Hold-born," Aiv had replied, "so at least you've somewhere else to go." Rook had heard similar conversations since then, and gathered that the future for retainers without Hold ties, or those who were seriously injured, like Rigan, was bleak. Under the circumstances, he was grateful they at least tolerated his presence. Kion had helped, letting fall that Rook was virtually an exile from Adamant, and had tried to save Lady Myrathis as well. Once that word spread, Rigan and those about him had edged from neutrality to cautiously including Rook in their conversation. But it was not until Namath visited Tehan that anyone got real news.

"The long-range scouts have just brought word," the marine said. "A Night brigade has been sighted, skirting Adamant territory and force-marching our way under their Commander's pennant."

Rook guessed the scouts must belong to the mysterious newcomers. His spirits lifted, because a strong Night force would ensure Torlun stayed well away, then fell again as Tehan said, "Lord Tirael will be leaving, then. He won't risk placing himself or his escort in Night's power."

But the rumors, Rook objected silently, say the Chosen of Mhaelanar is also the Heir of Night, yet Lord Tirael's still here. The force she led was not *of* Night, though. Could being Chosen of Mhaelanar *mean* being for all Derai, he wondered, not just for any one House—if that was even possible. Distracted, he missed the rest of what Namath said, but thought it was something about others leaving, too, which made sense. They would all go: Tirael and the Storm Spear, Envoy Nimor, and probably this Chosen of Mhaelanar as well.

Rook shifted, trying not to give in to fear, and to get more comfortable at the same time. When he glanced outside again he saw a horsegirl leading Taly's big bay past the tent. So something really is happening, he thought, frowning—and then his heart jumped, because once the bay had passed by he saw Lord Tirael approaching.

"Cursed Stars dandy!" the groom on Rigan's other side muttered.

"No one objected when he and his knights were holding the breach," Tehan said coolly.

"I don't object to him," Rigan replied cheerfully, "having heard how well he fights. But you've got to admit he's very gleamy."

Lord Tirael *was* gleamy, Rook conceded, now the blood and battle grime were gone from his silver-and-pearl armor. His fair hair, riffled by the wind from the plain, was almost as bright as the pale sunlight, even when he entered the tent. Hooking a stool close with his foot, he seated himself beside Rook. "How are you feeling?" he inquired, and Rook sensed Rigan grinning—inwardly, he hoped—at the Son of Stars' drawl.

"Much better," he replied, although the truth was, he still felt drained and shaky. He hesitated, wondering if he should try and apologize for the failed farspeaking, but Khar had checked his attempted apologies last night and he sensed Tirael would do the same now. "Namath said there's a Night force coming?" he said instead.

Tirael nodded acknowledgment to the marines. "Apparently so, which means the time has come for decisions, including what to do about you, young Rook."

Rook nodded, trying to appear adult and calm, although his pulse had quickened again. "I would bid you ride with me," Tirael said, "but that could create difficulties since I'm bound to honor the agreement between Adamant and Stars. If Adamant chooses to break it because of my part in these events, that will be different, of course."

They won't, Rook thought: they want the Stars alliance too much. But he suspected Tirael knew that. He would have liked to tell the Son of Stars that he must under no circumstances agree to marry Yhle, whose disposition resembled Torlun's—but despite Tirael's smile and easy manner, it felt like presumption, especially with the other convalescents listening. "Vael," Tirael continued, "tells me you have a considerable gift for healing." Namath had suggested the same, Rook recalled, catching the marine's nod from the corner of his eye. "He says you must go to Peace, where you will get the best teaching." Tirael paused. "Peace would probably take you anyway, but my father is of that House. If you wish, I can ask him to sponsor you."

I do wish, Rook thought. If another priestly House accepted him, that would help his family, and if he did well there, Adamant might even rescind his banishment—one day.

"I can see that's settled," Tirael said, smiling, and Rook nodded hastily. "But," the Son of Stars added, "I'm afraid there is a price."

Rook's breath caught, and he heard Rigan snort and someone else gasp. When he stole a glance at Tehan and Namath, they were both blank faced. Tirael tilted the stool back, relaxed and apparently oblivious to the surrounding disapproval, although the glimmer of a smile hinted otherwise. "Lady Malian needs a shaving of your hair," he said, "while I . . . I would like you to tell me more about Onnorin."

The marriage was for the best, Kalan told himself, returning to the camp after the brief ceremony that had formalized the union between the Heir of Night and Pha'Rho-l-Ynor, Ammaran's heir of House Blood. Nonetheless, he felt its unexpectedness, even if it was no more surprising than the alliance Malian had struck with Raven and Fire. Or Faro putting the Sea scroll that held Kalan's death name together with a way Malian could weave the Blood of the Nine Houses into her quest to restore the Golden Fire. She had told him she intended departing on that mission ahead of Night's arrival, and in view of the furor that was about to break loose among the Nine Houses, Kalan judged that he, too, should quietly withdraw.

But not without you, he told The Lovers silently, leaving the wyr hounds outside Myr's former tent while he folded the tapestry small enough to fit into his travel roll. When a pebble scuffed outside, he turned an instant before Tirael appeared, his plumed helmet under one arm. "So you're leaving, too," Kalan said, and the Son of Stars nodded.

"Needs must. Lady Myrathis was my kinswoman, but she was also pledged to Night, so honor and protocol both dictate that we defer." He shrugged. "Liad has farspoken the Stars' relief force, as you asked, and halted their advance. Night's Commander is reputed to be level-headed, but I see no point in testing either her or the individual warriors on either side. Our troops will be far better employed investigating whatever's been concealing this new way that's opened near our Wall border." Tirael spoke with his usual drawl, but his eyes belied his manner. "I'd be glad of you at my side when we do so. Come with me, my brother."

"I'm sorry," Kalan said, with genuine regret. "I have business that calls me elsewhere."

"The offer stands if you ever have need of a refuge, or simply for friendship's sake. Or it may be that I'll call for the Storm Spears' help to close this new way." Tirael smiled, before growing serious again. "For what it's worth, I think you have done the right thing by the boy. Nimor does, too, and we'll both hold what we know close."

Kalan nodded. "Thank you. And what becomes of Rook? Will he go to Peace?"

"He will. And Vael's support will allow him to ride with us now, at least as far as Stars' territory." Tirael glanced to where his knights were mustering, his mouth tightening as he regarded the riderless horses among their company, before he turned back. "Whatever transpires, I don't regret answering the call of Kin and Blood, but I don't want to provoke Adamant unnecessarily either. So Rook's traveling in our garb, and I'll send him straight on to Peace from our border. I am hoping," Tirael added, his smile returning, "he may recommend me to his kinswoman, Onnorin. Apparently she's one of the few people in the Keep of Stone who laughs." The smile deepened into self-mockery: "As well as being another of their Earl's many granddaughters and of the First Line of Adamant's Blood."

"So this alliance also includes a marriage?" Kalan said.

"So long as the current agreement holds—but I've drawn the line at living in the Keep of Stone. The Bride of Adamant will have to bear with the Citadel of Stars as well as with me." Tirael shrugged. "So I should be there when whatever business you're about is done."

"When it's done," Kalan agreed. He did not say that would only be when his business with the Wall and the Swarm was at an end, and after he had freed Myr's spirit from the tapestry, but he could tell Tirael sensed his reservation.

"You must not blame yourself for Lady Myr's death," the Son of Stars said, meeting Kalan's eyes with uncharacteristic gravity. "You did all that anyone could, then far more." Kalan shook his head, not arguing, but Tirael's expression clouded. "The Citadel of Stars will always be open to you," he said, and embraced Kalan formally. "Light and safety on your road, my brother."

"Honor to you and your House," Kalan replied, returning the embrace. He thought there could be no question of the honor in Tirael's case, and watched from the tent entrance until the Son of Stars mounted and the whole shining company, with a still-pale Rook in their midst, passed the inner barrier. As he, too, must go, having already charged Nimor with responsibility for the camp until Night reached it. Since Kalan doubted he would journey to the Keep of Winds any time soon, he had also left the black swords with the envoy, to be returned to Asantir on her arrival.

"He's right, you know." Taly was standing just clear of the tent entrance, so Kalan did not see her until he stepped beyond it to watch the Stars company depart the outer camp. Her battered face was healing, but she was still wearing her winter look; he guessed it would be a long time before that thawed. "About Lady Myr, I mean. You did do all that anyone could."

"I had thought you, of all people, would hold me to account."

Taly shook her head. "There's nothing you need account for. If you failed, then we all did. And you were the captain, you had to be on the perimeter. Whereas I could have stayed with Lady Myr during the final assault, but I didn't." Her straight, stern gaze met his. "I keep going over what happened, but no matter how many times I do, it never adds up to your failure."

"And if our places were reversed?" he asked. "Would you be telling yourself that you had done all you could?"

"Probably not." Her straight look continued to hold his. "But I would hope to have a friend, or many friends, who would continue to insist otherwise."

A friend, Kalan thought. He could say comrade-in-arms just as easily, but *sister* still felt like an unknown country. At one level, the questions were there: about their father and siblings, and what had befallen them. At another, he felt the weight of the years between them, almost fourteen now, and the heaviness of that first exile, sinking questions before they were asked. And always, the memory of his father's closed face and cold voice: *You are no more son of mine!*

"Look after Faro for me," he said, and she nodded.

"I will. He's a Son of Blood and should have one of his own House to guard him. It helps, too, having a new service." Taly did not add that it would never replace the old. She did not need to. Visibly changing the subject, she looked past him into the tent. "Lady Malian said you would take the web. The goods in the wagons are Faro's by right, now that he's signed the marriage contract, but most of them will be of no use to him so I've asked Nimor to see them returned to Blood. That'll create fewer arguments, too," she added. "But when Aiv hunted out the manifest, I saw Night's betrothal gift to Lady Myr listed: a suit of ceremonial Night armor. When I asked Faro, he agreed it should go to Lady Malian, by way of being returned to Night."

"She's Faro's guardian now *and* Heir of Night," Kalan said. "It's for her to say."

"You're still Honor Captain," Taly pointed out. "And it was a personal gift to Lady Myr. Until you quit the camp, it's for you to say." She paused. "On the way here, I saw Jad and the others with your horses. He said to tell you they were ready, whenever you wish to leave."

So they *are* coming, Kalan thought. "Yes, to the armor," he said. Stepping back inside the tent, he finished tying his travel roll around the tapestry. Lifting the roll onto his shoulder, he picked up the black spear. "Tell Faro I'll ride by Lady Malian's camp. And I'll be with Jad and the others soon."

Taly saluted before turning away, while the wyr hounds rose and padded beside Kalan to the garnet-and-gold tent. Two of the marines, Tymar and Koris, had replaced Tirael's Star knights on watch, but stepped aside to allow Kalan entry.

In a saga, the minstrel would doubtless say that Myr looked peaceful in death, or serene, but the truth, Kalan thought, was that like Palla, or Orth, or any of those lost in the siege, she simply looked dead. He had told Malian that Myr meant more to him than he realized—he had loved Jarna, in Emer, when he knew that he was not truly free to do so. Worse, he had let Jarna love him in return. So he had not permitted himself to love Myr, even when she grew dear to him, and deliberately steered his affection into a fraternal channel. Yet even if he had allowed stronger feelings, there could have been no good end to such a love, not for her and not for him either, given the places they both occupied in the Derai world.

If Myr were alive, Kalan would have bowed over her hands. Now he simply bowed before her bier, formally, as a champion bows, and an Honor Captain. He could have wept as well, but did not, because tears would do her no good, and there was no more time for weeping. "I will free your spirit," he said, to her dear, dead face. "I swear it, in my name and by all the Nine Gods. If I fail you Lady Myr, Lady Mouse, it will only be because I, too, am dead."

And the six remaining wyr hounds—that had once borne the essence of Maurid, the remnant Golden Fire of the House of Blood—howled their song of farewell.

When Kalan crossed into the outer camp, it was not just Jad and the remaining exiles, but Kelyr and a dozen caravan survivors, including Darrar and Aiv, who waited to leave with him. His brows rose at the sight of Kelyr, and the Sword warrior shrugged. "Fighting is what I know, but I doubt I'll be welcomed back into Swords. Kin and Blood was just an excuse," he said, before Kalan could ask. "Another of our number, Gol, had already sent written word of Tirorn's loss before we left Ij."

Kalan had met Gol in Emer but saw no need to say so. "You know what I am," he told Kelyr. His steady gaze went beyond the Sword warrior, first to Jad, then Rhanar, Machys, and Aarion, and finally to the caravan survivors. "I'm not only a Storm Spear, but an unbound power user as well, in defiance of the Blood Oath. A renegade," he said, to make the matter clear.

Kelyr shrugged again, cynical where Tirael would have been light. "You're confusing me with Orth. He was the one who hated power users, whereas most in Swords hold the Oath more lightly. Besides, I saw what you did here. Without you, the Sea pair, and the Star knights, this camp would've been lost. And now that I'm forsworn for a lock of hair," he added, "I may as well go all the way."

Several puzzled looks greeted his last words, but mostly it was nods. Jad and the exiles' expressions said they had made their choice long since and were ready to ride. "And you?" Kalan asked the caravan survivors. "You fought well, but fighting is not your business. It's what lies ahead, though, for anyone who rides with me."

"Yes, sir." Darrar cleared his throat. "With respect, if Lady Malian is the Chosen of Mhaelanar returned, then war's all that lies ahead for everyone." His boyishness, Kalan thought, had slipped away in the assault, erased by the shadow that lay on all their faces.

"You've been in the Red Keep, Captain," Aiv said, "so you know the ruling kin will make us suffer for the failure of their plans. And you needn't fear we'll hold you up. Envoy Nimor's given us Sea's spare horses, enough for all of us."

Any of them, Kalan knew, could be Blood agents—but the hounds were still wyrs and remained unperturbed. He looked at Jad, since the consequences of agreeing would fall heaviest on him. "What do you say?"

Jad grinned. "I think we can knock them into shape."

"You'd better be ready to go, then," he told the volunteers, with a glance at the horses mustered behind them, "because I'm leaving now."

"Yes, sir!" they chorused.

"Kelyr told us we'd have to be," Darrar added. Kelyr's expression was part irony, part self-derision, but he wiped both clear and saluted when Kalan looked his way.

"Then let's ride." Kalan tied on the travel roll, then swung into Madder's saddle before sliding the spear across his back. His small company formed up behind him, and Aarion unfurled the oriflamme. When Kalan turned Madder in a trampling circle, he saw that the rest of the camp was forming a ragged avenue along their route to the perimeter. Nimor raised a hand from the entrance into the inner camp, and although the rest of those gathered did not cheer, the words "Storm Spear, Storm Spear" were murmurous as the sea.

Madder tossed his mane and snorted, but stepped out smoothly. Jad followed immediately behind, together with Aarion and the banner. In only a few seconds they were past the lines of intent, watching faces and clear of the earthworks, crossing what had been killing ground to the Fire encampment.

The two hundred, too, were breaking camp, although Raven had promised Kalan a rear guard would remain on patrol, only falling back once the Night force arrived. A guard of honor was drawn up by the road, and he saw Malian waiting there, with Taly and Faro beside her. A moment later Faro broke away—or perhaps they had let him go—and pelted toward Madder, on a trajectory that seemed certain to end beneath the roan's hooves. Drawing rein, Kalan dismounted, and the boy ran full tilt into him.

"Promise," Faro whispered, his arms a stranglehold around Kalan's neck. "Promise me you'll come back. And that you'll come and find me. Promise me you'll live!"

"I promise to try," Kalan said, because it seemed easiest in the face of so much fierceness. He thought he might have to disengage Faro's arms, but even before Taly arrived, the boy had stepped back, his smile valiant despite a face wet with tears. Kalan remounted and saluted him, before signing for the oriflamme to dip: first to Faro, and again to Malian. And then he let Madder carry him away, from the Daughter of Blood that he had not saved, and the Son of Blood that he had, from the sister he could not acknowledge, and from the Heir of the Derai.

Epilogue

Wolf was waiting when Malian arrived back at Rowan Birchmoon's cairn just on the eve of Autumn's Night. The shaman had vanished about his own business while Malian was seeing Faro and his new household, accompanied by a sixty-strong Fire escort, safely on the first stage of their journey to southern Aralorn. Passing the Border Mark had been hard for Nhairin—but it's better for her this way, Malian told herself, as it is for Faro. Raven had rejoined Valadan, but the two hundred from his personal guard, including several of Rhaikir's cadres, were still with Malian. The adepts would establish an inner perimeter about the cairn, shielding what she was about to attempt.

Falath came to greet Malian as she dismounted in the gathering dusk, but drew back again as Wolf emerged from the nearby rocks. *"Remember your debt."* The wolf's eyes glowed topaz as the shaman's voice spoke in her mind. *"You promised Rowan to do all you could to save Haarth. Do not use her bridge to bring another Cataclysm."*

"I have not forgotten," Malian replied. *"I seek to honor both my debt and my promise to her in what I do now."* She could feel Maurid and Yelusin's power, concealed within hers—and the thread of answering magic from the walking stick in her left hand, imbued

with the name of its parent Fire—*Kamioriol*—that lay hidden in the one surviving rose vine in the Court of the Rose. The two soldered shards of Yorindesarinen's riven shield she carried on her back.

"Ammaran may have sought power in Haarth," she told Wolf, *"but I am the Chosen of Mhaelanar, and even without Yorindesarinen's shield I still have Nhenir and the frost-fire sword, as well as my armring. I'm carrying the essence of three remnant Fires as well."* Briefly, Malian's gaze shifted to Rhaikir, who still regarded her with reserve from among his adepts, before returning her attention to Wolf. She touched the breast of her jacket, where the seven rune scrolls from the Blood camp lay above her heart, together with the two from Morning and Peace: one for each of the Nine Houses of the Derai. *"I have these, too. But I still need Rowan's bridge into Haarth as my anchor. Because,"* she admitted, *"I don't know how deep into the Gate of Dreams this journey will take me.*

Wolf's regard was unblinking. *"That is also why I came. My shaman's power and blood kinship to Rowan will help moor you to her bridge."*

Blood is always strongest. Malian repeated Faro's words to herself. *But locks of hair are strong as well.* The only rune scroll that did not have both was the one for the Rose. But she had the walking stick, and a tress of Lady Mayaraní's hair—which Kalan and Taly had removed from a locket that belonged to Mistress Ise, both having been adamant that Lady Myr's body must lie undisturbed.

It will serve, Malian thought, and turned toward the cairn.

The day had been clear, so Nimor's pilot star and the waning moon both hung overhead, marking the opening in the roughly dressed stone as she rested a gentle hand on Falath's head. The darkness beyond the cairn's mouth was immense: a reminder, had Malian needed one, that she had no idea whether this would work, only whatever hope the remnant Fires saw—and the certainty that she had to try. Behind her, Rhaikir and the cadres were silent, Wolf a shadow in the dusk as she gave Falath a last pat and stepped into the mouth of the tomb.

Malian felt the stir of Wolf's magic, sealing the threshold behind her as Rhaikir and his adepts invoked their shielding circle. She had a brief, dizzying sense of the corvids' wings from her Stoneford fever, spiraling about her, before they dissipated into the murmur of Haarth's song, rising through the cairn's wellspring of power. Stepping forward, Malian placed her left hand on the pale boulder that served as a plinth. The armring flamed into silver life and the shadow of a gate rose before her, shaped out of mist and darkness. But before Malian could step forward, a phantom cavemouth appeared between it and her. *"We made a bargain, the sword and I."* Amaliannarath's mindvoice whispered out of the cavern's mouth and echoed from the frost-fire sword. *"As you did also, Namesake, in the Stoneford chapel."*

"To take Fire as my own," Malian said slowly. She hesitated, wondering if taking the ghost of one of the three sundered Ascendants on her quest to restore the Golden Fire could bring about Emuun's prediction that *she* would be the stake driven into the heart of the Derai Alliance. Yet having accepted the sword and pledged her word to Raven, Malian could see no alternative. She remembered, too, how Amaliannarath's ghost had spoken out of the blade in Stoneford. "So as long as I have the sword," she said aloud, "I will always carry you as well."

"A promise made to the dying," the ghost whispered. *"The sword carries a fragment of my essence as you now carry sparks of what were once Yelusin, Maurid, and Kamioriol. You will need us all, Child of Night."*

Did the sword foresee that, Malian wondered, as well as my need of Fire: is that why it made the bargain that binds me now? Nhenir was silent, and the fragments of Yelusin and Maurid were quiescent, too, which implied that this was her decision.

"It is." Now Nhenir did speak, silver in her mind. *"The Chosen of Mhaelanar must determine her own path."*

Only in this case, Malian thought, there is no other path. *"So be it,"* she said. The specter of the cave mouth vanished, leaving the gate of mist and shadow clear. Raising the armring high, Malian spoke the words inscribed inside its band: "'*I move through worlds and time . . .*'" And she did, stepping out of Rowan Birchmoon's cairn and into the Gate of Dreams, to stand before the psychic manifestation of the Gate of Winds that guarded the Derai realm—which had remained closed to her throughout six years of exile. Now, for the first time since she had ridden away from the Keep of Winds and her old life, Malian reached beyond the psychic barrier.

"'. . . *I seek out the hidden, the lost I find.*'" Silent as a ghost herself, inexorable as the passage of time, she descended through the vast, abandoned layers of the Old Keep and into the room that lay at its heart. "Hylcarian," she said, both aloud and with her mind's voice. "I have returned·as I said I would."

At first only silence answered, but gradually Malian felt the unfolding: as though a small space had opened to reveal a greater whole. Flame danced at the periphery of her vision. *"Child of Night."* The voice was fire's crackle through parched grass. *"Is my waiting done?"*

"It is. With your permission, I shall enter your secret heart, as I did once before when need drove me. But I do not come alone."

"So I perceive." The flicker of light became a sun rising in fire and gold. The voice was summer thunder, rumbling out of a clear sky. *"You are welcome into my heart, Child of Night. Yet although a child no longer, to enter you must still take the step of trust."*

Out beyond worlds, Malian knew, and time as well, like the tower she had climbed in Jaransor, and the cave Amaliannarath had made for her sleepers. Closing her eyes, Malian emptied her mind and heart, until all that remained was the murmur of Haarth's song and the darkness between worlds. Finally, her soul's eye opened into the heart of a blazing sun.

In the waking world, gazing into the face of the sun meant going blind—but the eye that was Malian's soul could not look away, and the brilliance was liquid fire along her veins. She was burning, *burning*, held in a crucible in which she, too, must be remade or die.

"Malian." The whisper was a tendril of silver spun across molten gold. She had heard it once before when she hung between life and death, only then it had been Darksworn sorcery that reached out to engulf her.

"Yorindesarinen." Malian was not sure whether she spoke in words or her entire being rang with the hero's name. The tendril became a kindling of white and indigo flame in a glade between worlds, and although Malian was still on fire, the surrounding conflagration was no longer molten. She watched Yorindesarinen's fire burn to gray ash, only to ignite again, brighter and stronger than before. A silver phoenix appeared in the flames, its tail an aurora and its eyes spring stars.

"I am Iriellirin. Your helm is wrought in my likeness and you bear my image on your back." The voice was both keen edged and bright as the bird soared out of the fire and settled on Malian's shoulder. *"You are dear to the greatest and most beloved of my daughters; my youngest son has given you a lock of his hair."* Silver claws dug deep but caused no pain, and the fire in her veins cooled.

"I am Yelusin." The spark within Malian danced free, expanding into an ocean of light. A mer-dragon swam out of it and curled about her, gazing down from the eyes painted on Sea House ships.

"I am Maurid." The hydra's essence also left Malian and grew, rearing multiple heads. *"My daughter is lost, but you protect my son. And you have left my new Blood free."*

"I am Kamioriol." Roses blossomed in the heart of the fire, exploding in fireworks, only to rebloom again. *"Myrathis was also mine and you bring Mayaraní with you. I mourn them both . . . "*

"I am Yyr." The gryphon of Swords circled.

"I am Iluthys . . . Thuunoth . . . Sirithilorn." The centaur of Peace gave way to the sphinx of Adamant, and then the sweep of the simurgh's wings.

"Namesake, I am Amaliannarath. The power released into Haarth through my dying reawakened my long-estranged sister, Yelusin. I crossed the void with Fire and brought you the hero's sword." The

golden conflagration stilled as the phantom voice spoke—before the crucible flared back into life. This time the protective entities were a firebreak, enclosing Malian as she stepped into its burning heart, the same way Tarathan had once entered Yorindesarinen's fire to find her. *Tarathan* ... His element was also fire, the magma that lay at the heart of the world, and momentarily, the Song of Haarth was all about her with its myriad voices. But the furnace roared again, and Malian spread her arms wide, expanding mind and heart and spirit to embrace it. When she opened her physical eyes at last, she was standing in a room with twelve walls and twelve doors, which blurred into a star-filled firmament.

The last time Malian had been here, the door frames had been golden flame and the space within them shimmering mist. Now each door was a sheet of fire and the arches above them constellations. The circular table still stood in the center of the room, its base an immense tree trunk, its surface divided into twelve equal parts by fiery lines. Six of the twelve parts remained as Malian had first seen them, cloudy and filled with indecipherable moving shapes. Five were now fields of gold containing a single, sharp-edged image: the phoenix of Stars and mer-dragon of Sea, the bloom of the Rose and the hydra of Blood, and the winged horse of Night. A sixth section glimmered white with a hint of rose-gold in its depths. Within it, the silhouette of a firedrake lay coiled amid silver and gold flame.

"Child of Night, Heir of the Derai, Chosen of Mhaelanar." Hylcarian's voice was light and warmth and heat. *"Welcome again, Malian, into my heart, which is also the heart of the Golden Fire."* The summer voice paused. *"Welcome, also, to our sister, long sundered."*

"Welcome," the others voices murmured, and then, speaking as one voice that resounded through Malian and the room, *"The maelstrom rises, Child of Night, and need presses. You must begin what you came here to do: restore us."*

Malian bowed, her palms placed together in the Blood of the Derai's ancient salute to the Golden Fire, which she had used to acknowledge Faro's gift of the rune scrolls. When she straightened, the table had altered shape so that she now saw it entirely as a tree, one so vast Malian was not sure even her soul's eye could encompass it. The trunk extended far below the tabletop and the roots delved deeper still, far back along the twists and turns of time. The canopy above her head held myriad stars and worlds, the slow spiral of galaxies, and the unfolding and closing in again of universes. "It's so huge," Malian whispered, mostly to herself, but of course they heard her.

"Once," Hylcarian told her, *"we were flame that moved in the darkness between its branches, before we acquired thought and will and form. When the ancestors of what you call the Derai and the Sworn were first born, we were drawn to the galaxy of their smaller sparks, shaping and reshaping ourselves until your forebears could see us clearly. Only then could they also hear us when we spoke, and learn to speak to us in return."*

"Until the maelstrom rose." All the entities present spoke as one, Amaliannarath's whisper weaving through the rest. *"Now, follow the sun's path about the table and lay each of your scrolls in their place."*

East to west, Malian thought, only where's north? But when she looked up, Nimor's pilot star hung over the winged horse, while one of the new constellations she had seen on her journey into southern Aralorn was rising above the phoenix opposite. *"Three times is best, one circuit for each of the Derai's three castes."* This was Nhenir's mindwhisper, but no voice of fire gainsaid the helm's advice. So Malian paced east to west around the table, laying down three of the nine scrolls with each pass: first Tirael's fair hair for Stars, with one of Nimor's cabled locks for Sea, and Lady Mayaraní's dark tress for the Rose. The second time around, she set down the scroll with a scraping from Rook's close-shaven head for Adamant, followed by the two that Garan had brought her from Peace and Morning. She kept her own for the third circuit, together with Faro's offering, and finally—and far from least, she supposed—Kelyr's scroll for Swords.

Nine of the table's twelve sections were gold now, the images of the simurgh and the centaur, the sphinx and the gryphon all burning bright. Malian halted by what she guessed was Fire's place, studying the firedrake and thinking that she should have made a scroll for Raven as well . . . Then again, he had said that Fire was making its alliance with her, rather than rejoining the Derai. Reluctantly, she looked beyond the firedrake to the two segments that remained clouded, any image no more than a turn of shadow within their murk. Salar and Nindorith: she was almost afraid to think their names, in case the Ascendants became aware of what she was doing.

"They will not know," Amaliannarath told her. *"The way here has been closed to both since the Sundering, as it was for me. I could not have come here now if you had not brought me and the others allowed me in. But I am dead, so can no longer be part of the crucible."*

"Yet even with you here," Malian said, "the table—like the Derai and the Sworn—is no longer whole. How much difference will that make, in seeking to restore the Fire?"

Malian sensed Hylcarian deliberate. *"We were born Twelve,"* he said finally, *"so even if the other two were present, Amaliannarath's loss might tip the scales against us."*

"I doubt Salar would be capable of reentering the crucible now." Amaliannarath was dispassionate. *"He has spent too long in the maelstrom."*

"But you are right to be concerned, Child of Night." Now the ten entities spoke as one. *"With three of the Twelve absent, we cannot assume that the alchemy of our beginning can be replicated. Restoration may fail, or what is reborn may be Other than what we were before."*

Yet even if the whole enterprise was doomed to failure from the outset, Malian knew she could not turn back. "If only the shield had remained whole and the arms of Yorindesarinen intact." She spoke her regret aloud. "They might have countered Amaliannarath's loss."

Hylcarian's thunder rumbled about tree and table. *"A buckler made of metal shattered. But* you, *Malian, are the shield of heaven, the aegis of Mhaelanar born into the world. Just as it was Yorindesarinen's will and courage that stopped the Worm, not the arms she bore."*

Again, the ten voices spoke as one. *"Do what* must *be done, Chosen of Mhaelanar. Take your god-forged sword and drive it into the table's heart."*

Not a stake, Malian thought, understanding at last, but a sword—for this place, with the table as its core, was undoubtedly the heart of the Derai Alliance. "Are you sure?" she asked at last. Her voice sounded small against the surrounding vastness, the intonation that of the child Malian, from when she had first come here.

"Child of Night, there is no other way." The summer thunder was muted now, Hylcarian's voice gentle. *"Iriellirin may wear the phoenix form, but we were all born from Terennin's fire, which must return to ash before it can reignite."*

"But you don't know for certain that it will."

"What in all the worlds and across time is ever certain? Yet even if everything we hope for comes to pass, we will not be reborn with the strength, built up over long aeons, that was ours before the Night of Death. That is part of the price we must pay to be made new."

The Night of Death ... Malian wanted to ask whether Raven's account of the Sundering was true and whether what she was about to do now could undo that, but the time for both questions and doubt was past. One way, or the other, she thought—and drew the frost-fire sword, the blade already glowing white as it cleared the sheath. The armring, too, was silver fire, and she knew that Nhenir, the moon-bright helm, would be as she had first seen it: black adamantine steel decorated with pearl and silver, with the phoenix wings swept up to either side and wrapped about the casque. Malian lowered the visor that was shaped into the dawn eyes of Terennin over her own, so no glamour or working born of power would cloud her vision, and closed both hands around the sword's hilt, raising it high.

"Now, Child of Night!" Ten voices reverberated as one between the fiery doors. Reaching deep within herself, Malian released the

power she had kept banked for so long, hiding from both the Derai and the Swarm. Wreathed in silver flame and anchored in the Song of Haarth, she drove the frost-fire sword down, deep into the table and through it, into the heart of the tree—and the twelve-sided room exploded in fire, hurling her into a void beyond thought, memory, and time.

Here ends the Wall of Night Book Three,
Daughter of Blood

+====+

To be continued in the Wall of Night Book Four,
The Chaos Gate

Glossary

Aarion: House of Blood Honor Guard in Jad's eight-unit

Aeln: Night honor guard in Asantir's escort

Aeris: city kingdom in the lands beyond the River

Aikanor: Heir of Night at the time of the Derai civil war and Great Betrayal

Aithe: lieutenant in the Prince of Fire's personal guard

Aiv: House of Blood groom

Alliance: alliance of the nine Houses of the Derai; also *Derai Alliance*

Amaliannarath: Darksworn Ascendant, most closely associated with the nation of Fire

Amarn: Darksworn adept, sworn to the sorcerer Nirn

Ammaran: Heir of Blood over four hundred years before, last of an older line

Amrathin: Earl of Blood over four hundred years before, last of an older line

Anchor, the: Grayharbor inn

Andron: smith to Grayharbor's town guard, also a fire-watch captain

Anvin: a Son of Blood, sixth child of the Earl of Blood; full brother to Kharalthor, Hatha, Liankhara, and Sardonya; half brother to Parannis and Sarein; also half brother to Myrathis

Ar: city of the River

Ara-fyr: border watch in southern Aralorn

Aralorn: realm of Haarth, located south of the River

Aralth: chamberlain to the Earl of Blood

Aranraith: a leader of the Darksworn, Prince of the House of Sun

Aravenor: Lord Captain of the Patrol

Arcolin: lieutenant to Aranraith; formerly Swarm envoy in Emer

Asantir: Commander of Night

Ascendant: Sworn term for three of their greatest powers, magical beings associated with each of their three nations respectively: Salar for Sun, Nindorith for Lightning, and Amaliannarath for Fire

Ash: River tinker

Asha: Night honor guard in Garan's eight-unit

Ash Days: the half way point between Autumn's Eve and Autumn's Night in Haarth's Southern Realms

Audin Sondargent: Emerian knight, nephew to the Duke of Emer

Autumn's Eve: the autumn equinox

Autumn's Night: the Southern Realms festival dedicated to Kan that marks the transition from autumn to winter; also known as Winter's Eve

Awl Lane: Grayharbor wynd, off Sailcloth Street

Bajan: House of Blood warrior from Bronze Hold

Banath: Honor Captain to the Earl of Blood

Bane Hold: satellite fortress of the House of Blood

Baris: House of Blood groom

Barren Hills: uninhabited hills to the north of Grayharbor and south of the Border Mark

Battlemaster: primary war leader of the House of Blood

Betrayal War: Derai civil war, five hundred years earlier; also *Great Betrayal*

black blades: weapons of power, commonly associated with the hero, Kerem

black spear: weapon of power; see also *Great Spear; black blades*

Blood: shortening of House of Blood*; may also refer to* Blood, the

Blood Gate: main entrance into the Red Keep and a fortress in its own right

Blood, the: includes the Earls of the Derai and any of their blood kin. Traditionally, the Blood have been closely linked to the power of the Golden Fire

Blood Oath, the: an oath that has bound the Derai since their civil war and institutionalizes the schism between the warrior and priestly castes; also *the Oath*

Border Mark: stone pillar that marks the boundary between the Gray Lands and the Barren Hills, and by implication, the Wall of Night and the rest of Haarth

Brave Hold: satellite fortress of the House of Blood

Bronze Hold: satellite fortress of the House of Blood

Brother Selmor: scholar priest in the Temple of Night

cadre: unit of Derai or Darksworn power users

Caer Argent: capital of Emer

Carick: graduate of the University in Ar, a city of the River lands, who journeyed to Emer as cartographer to its Duke

Cataclysm: period of extreme natural disaster, followed by war, that brought down Haarth's Old Empire; believed to have occurred as a result of the Derai's arrival on Haarth

Cave of Sleepers: cavern of sleeping warriors, deep within the Gate of Dreams

Cendreward: province of Emer

Chaos Worm: according to legend, the deadliest foe ever sent by the Swarm against the Derai; also *Worm; Worm of Chaos*

Che'Ryl-g-Raham: Sea House navigator for the ship of the same name

***Che'Ryl-g-Raham*, the:** Sea House ship

Child of Light: see *Yorindesarinen*

Child of Night: see *Malian*

Citadel of Stars: principal stronghold of the House of Stars

Chosen of Mhaelanar: prophesied hero who will lead the Derai for the final victory over the Swarm, to be born of the Houses of both Stars and Night; also *the one*

civil war: waged between the Derai Houses five hundred years ago; see also *Night of Death* and *Great Betrayal*

Cloud Hold: satellite fort of the Keep of Winds

Code, the: see *Honor Code*

Commander of Night: overall military Commander of the House of Night; see also *Asantir*

Corlin: warrior-priest from the House of Adamant

Court of the Rose: main stronghold of the House of the Rose

Crow: Southern Realms sword-for-hire, traveling with Raven

Crow, the: companion bird to the Huntmaster

Dab: Red Keep guard, assigned to Lady Myrathis; watch partner to Taly; also *Dabnor*

Daile: Patrol officer from the Hedeld fort

Dain: House of Blood honor guard, second in Jad's eight-unit

Dalay: senior Morning priest, deputy to Sirit

damosel: a young Emerian woman of knightly or noble birth

Dancer of Kan: follower of the god Kan, usually a member of the Ijiri Assassins' Guild or Ar's Shadow Band

darkspawn: term for low-level servants of the Swarm of Dark, also *'spawn*

Darksworn: vanguard of the Swarm of Dark

Darrar: House of Blood farrier

Daughter of Blood: title given to daughter of a ruler of Blood

Defenders of Blood: term for wyr hounds

Derai: warlike race, alien to Haarth, comprising an alliance of Nine Houses. They arrived on Haarth fifteen hundred years before, together with their traditional enemy, the Swarm of Dark. The Derai are fighting an aeons old war to prevent the Swarm obliterating the universe. They are divided into three societies or castes: warrior, priest, and a caste comprising both warrior and priestly talents but focused on specialist skills.

Derai-dan: Derai combat code, includes armed and unarmed techniques

Dread Pass: mountain pass in the Wall of Night

Duar: warrior in the Prince of Fire's personal guard

Eanar: Night honor guard in Garan's eight-unit

Eanaran: Earl of Night over four hundred years before

Earl: title for a hereditary ruler of a Derai House

eight-guard: Derai military unit; also eight-unit

elemental: magical entities associated with fire, air, water, or earth, servants to the Great Djinn; see also *fire elemental*

Elite Cairon: commander in Ar's Shadow Band

Elodin: Star knight, escort captain to Tirael; also Elodinel

Elv'Ar-i-Anor: Sea House ship

Emer: realm of Haarth, located south of the River

Emeriath: figure from Derai legend, associated with the hero Kerem

empathy bond: psychic link between two Derai that can be either one- or two-way, usually between blood kin, lovers, or very close friends

Emuun: agent of the Swarm, kinsman to Nirn

Eria: initiate Night priestess, serving in the Old Keep watch

facestealer: class of Swarm adept

Falath: Rowan Birchmoon's hound; keeps vigil by her grave

Farelle: city of the River

Faro: Grayharbor street urchin

fell lizard: class of Swarm minion

Fire: one of the three nations of the Sworn

fire elemental: specific magical entity derived from fire, a familiar to Emuun

First: captain of a Jhainarain Seven

First Kin: first degree of kinship within Derai society

First Line: refers to the Earl, his or her immediate family, and their First Kin among a House's ruling kindred

Forward Hold: satellite fortress of the House of Blood

Fray: lord of the House of Blood's Bane Hold

frost-fire sword: one of the three magical arms of the hero Yorindesarinen

Garan: eight-guard leader in the Earl of Night's Honor Guard

Gate of Dreams: supernatural realm between planes of existence; also the Gate

Gate of Winds: main entrance into the Keep of Winds and fortress in its own right

geas: magical binding the frost-fire sword placed on the House of Fire

Gervon: former facestealer in guise of priest of Serrut, and teacher at Normarch

Ghiselaine: Countess of Ormond, a region of Emer

Girvase: Emerian knight, trained at Normarch

Golden Fire: former allied power and bulwark of the Derai, that once burned throughout the Wall of Night's nine keeps

Granian: Star knight and herald; also Granianned

Grayharbor: port and northernmost town between the River and Wall of Night

Gray Lands: desolate plains that adjoin the Wall of Night

Gray Taan: weapons' trader in Terebanth

Great Betrayal: refers to both the Derai civil war and the peace feast that ended in slaughter, extinguishing the Golden Fire

Great Djinn: powers, native to Haarth, that inhabit the southern deserts

Great Gate: portal that Derai power wielders opened between worlds to allow the Alliance to come through to the world of Haarth

Great Spear: weapon of power; see also *black blades*

Guild House: place where heralds reside, found in every River city

Guild of Heralds: River-based society of messengers; see also *heralds*

Haarth: world in which this story is set

Haimyr the Golden: minstrel of Ij, friend and retainer to the Earl of Night

Halcyon: merchant ship, registered out of Port Farewell

Half-Blood: derogatory term for *Myrathis*

Hamar Sondsangre: of Aldermere, Kalan's Emerian identity

Hani: Aralorn Hill horse, belonging to Raven

Hatha: a Daughter of Blood, second child to the Earl of Blood; twin to Kharalthor and full sister to Huern, Liankhara, Sardonya, and Anvin; half sister to Parannis and Sarein; also half sister to Myrathis

Hedeld: trading post on the Telimbras, north of Ar, with a Patrol fort nearby

Heir: designated successor to the hereditary ruler of a Derai House

Heir of the Derai: alternate title for the Heir of Night, since Night leads the Nine Houses of the Derai; see also *Malian*

heralds: messengers sworn to the River-based Guild of Heralds

Heris: itinerant scribe, an identity adopted by Malian

High Hall: main hall of a Derai fortress

Hills of the Hawk: see *Jaransor*

hold: satellite forts of the main Derai keeps on the Wall

Honor Captain: commands a Derai Honor Guard

Honor Code: code governing honorable conduct in all aspects of Derai life, particularly combat and war; also *Derai Code;* the *Code*

Honor Contest: contest of arms to select a Derai *Honor Guard*

Honor Guard: elite guard units sworn to protect the lives of Derai leaders

House: Derai name encompassing each of the nine separate peoples who comprise the Derai Alliance; see also *Nine Houses*

House of Adamant: priestly House of the Derai Alliance

House of Blood: warrior House of the Derai Alliance

House of Morning: priestly House of the Derai Alliance

House of Night: warrior House of the Derai Alliance; the "first and oldest" House

House of Peace: priestly House of the Derai Alliance

House of Sea: House of the Derai Alliance, primarily mariners

House of Stars: House of the Derai Alliance, renowned as enchanters

House of Swords: warrior House of the Derai Alliance

House of the Rose: House of the Derai Alliance, primarily diplomats but also artists

Huern: a Son of Blood and third child to the Earl of Blood; full brother to Kharalthor, Hatha, Liankhara, Sardonya, and Anvin; half brother to Parannis and Sarein; also half brother to Myrathis

Huntmaster: master of the Hunt of Mayanne

Hunt of Mayanne: wild power that dwells beyond the Gate of Dreams; also "the Hunt"

Hur: House of Adamant watchtower commander

Hurulth: god of death, one of the Derai's Nine Gods, also *the Silent God*

Hurulth's Hall: a temple of Hurulth; also where Derai believe souls go after death

Hylcarian: formerly Golden Fire of the House of Night

Ij: the Golden, greatest city of the River

Ijir: main river of the lands known as the River

Ijiri: a person or thing native to Ij

Ilai: Liankhara of Blood's retainer, assigned to Myrathis

Ilkerineth: a leader of the Darksworn, Prince of Lightning

Iluthys: formerly Golden Fire of the House of Peace

immune: those immune to the effects of magic

Impassable Range: part of the Wall of Night, separates the Sea Keep from Morning

Imuln: Mother Goddess of the Southern Realms; also *Imulun* on the River

Innor: Night honor guard in Garan's eight-unit

Iriellirin: formerly Golden Fire of the House of Stars

Iriseult: last leader of the Second Line of Fire

Ise: duenna and former governess to Myrathis; also Mistress Ise

Ishnapur: fabled empire in the south of Haarth, borders the great deserts

Jad: eight-leader in the Earl of Blood's Honor Guard

Jaransor: hill range west of Gray Lands; also J'ara Ensor

Jaras: House of Blood honor guard in Jad's eight-unit

Jarna: Emerian knight, trained at Normarch

Jehane Mor: herald of the Guild, from the River's Terebanth Guild House

Jhainarian: people hailing from Jhaine

Jhaine: land in the Southern Realms of Haarth

Jharin: Darkswarm adept, sworn to the sorcerer Nirn

Kair: House of Fire cavalry commander

Kalan: friend of Malian, born to the House of Blood

Kamioriol: formerly the Golden Fire of the House of the Rose

Kan: one of the three gods of Haarth's Southern Realms; also Karn

Kara: Faro's mother, now deceased; also Kara Armorer

Keep of Bells: principal stronghold of the House of Peace

Keep of Stone: principal stronghold of the House of Adamant

Keep of Winds: principal stronghold of the House of Night

Kelmé: child prince from the early history of Ar

Kelyr: House of Swords warrior, companion to Orth

Kerem the Dark Handed: ancient hero of the Derai

Keron: Night honor guard in Garan's eight-unit

Khar: nom-de-guerre adopted by Kalan

Kharalth: Battle Goddess, one of the Nine Gods of the Derai.

Kharalthor: Battlemaster and Heir of Blood; twin to Hatha, and full
    brother to Huern, Liankhara, Sardonya, and Anvin; half brother
    to Parannis and Sarein; also half brother to Myrathis

Khelor: last leader of the First Line of Fire; also *Prince of Fire*

Kion: physician to the Sea envoy, Nimor

Kiyan: First to Queen Zharaan of Jhaine in the years after the
    Cataclysm

Kolthis: Red Keep guard, serves Huern

Koris: Sea House marine in Nimor's escort

Kylin: attendant to Myrathis

Kyr: Night honor guard, died in Jaransor six years before

Laer: weatherworker on the *Che'Ryl-g-Raham*

Lady Mouse: nickname for Myrathis of Blood; see also *Myr*

Lady of Grace: archaic Derai title

Lady of Ways: see *Nuithe*

language of blood: a magic of Jhaine, also known as the *Language
    of Imuln*

Lathayra: land in the Southern Realms of Haarth

Lawr: Night honor guard in Garan's eight-unit

Ler: Sea House marine, in Nimor's escort

Leti: innkeeper's daughter at Grayharbor's Anchor inn

Liad: Star knight and farspeaker; also Liadinath

Liankhara: a Daughter of Blood and spymaster; fourth child of the Earl of Blood; full sister to Kharalthor, Hatha, Huern, Sardonya, and Anvin; half sister to Parannis and Sarein; also half sister to Myrathis

Liannar: second-in-command of the Patrol

Lightning: one of the three nations of the Sworn

Lira: Night honor guard, died in Jaransor six years before

Little Pass: secondary pass into Emer, crosses to/from Aeris

Liy: page to Bajan of Bronze Hold

Long Pass: main pass between Emer and the River

Lord Captain: commander of the Patrol

Lord Falk: Castellan of Emer's Northern March

Lost, the: Derai with old powers who have fled the Wall of Night

Machys: House of Blood honor guard in Jad's eight-unit

Madder: Kalan's red roan warhorse, a gift from Jarna

Madness: condition associated with Jaransor, which affects Derai

maelstrom: Sworn name for the Swarm of Dark

Malar: House of Swords warrior, companion to Orth

Malian: only child of the Earl of the House of Night; also *Heir of Night*, the *Child of Night,* and *Chosen of Mhaelanar*

Malisande: friend to Ghiselaine of Ormond, killed by a shapechanger

march: a border territory of Emer

Marlinspike: Grayharbor inn

Matter of Kin and Blood: matter of great importance, usually life or House-threatening, that concerns the Blood of a Derai House; alternately Matter of Blood

Maurid: collective name the Red Keep wyr hounds give themselves

Mayanne: one of the Nine Gods of the Derai

Mayaraní: Lady Mayaraní of the Rose, deceased mother to Myrathis

Meraun: the Healer, one of the Nine Gods of the Derai

messenger horses: horses, usually black, belonging to the Derai messenger corps; famed for their endurance and speed

Meya: attendant to Ise

Mhaelanar: the Defender (or Defender of Heaven), one of the Nine Gods of the Derai, also called the Shield of the Derai

Midsummer: Emerian summer solstice festival

mindspeech: communicating directly from mind to mind, an old Derai power

moon-bright helm: see *Nhenir*

Morin: Night honor guard in Asantir's escort

Morning: see *House of Morning*

Murn: secretary to the Sea envoy

Myr: see *Myrathis*

Myrathis: a Daughter of Blood, ninth and youngest child of the Earl of Blood; also *Myr; Lady Mouse*

Myron: candlemaker's apprentice in Grayharbor

Nagoy: Count of the Rose over four hundred years before

Nai: House of Blood wagoner

Nalin: sergeant in the Earl of Blood's Honor Guard

Namath: Sea House marine

Narn: leads the House of Blood's Bronze Hold

nation: the three nations of the Darksworn: Fire, Lightning, and Sun

navigator: commander of a Sea House ship

Nerion: Malian's mother, the Earl of Night's former wife

Nerith: of the Sea Keep: Nerion's mother; Malian's grandmother

Nerys: Night honor guard in Garan's eight-unit

New Keep: the newer, inhabited stronghold of the Keep of Winds

Nhairin: former High Steward of the Keep of Winds

Nhal: House of Blood honor guard in Jad's eight-unit

Nhenir: magical helm of the hero Yorindesarinen; also *moon-bright helm*

Nherenor: Darksworn envoy, killed in Emer; son of Ilkerineth and Nuithe

Night: see *House of Night*

Night Mare: Swarm demon

Night of Death: peace feast at the end of the Derai civil war, which turned into another slaughter and culminated in the loss of the Golden Fire

Nimor: Sea House envoy to Myrathis's Honor Contest and wedding

Nindorith: Darksworn Ascendant, most closely associated with Lightning

Nine Gods: the nine gods of the Derai: Hurulth, Kharalth, Mayanne, Meraun, Mhaelanar, Ornorith, Tawr, Terennin, and Thiandriath

Nine Houses: nine Houses of the Derai Alliance

Nirn: Darksworn sorcerer, kinsman to Aranraith and Emuun

Normarch: stronghold of the Castellan of Emer's Northern March

northerner: Haarth term for a Derai

Northern March: border region of Emer

Nuithe: "dark heart" in the old Sworn tongue; Ilkerineth's wife and Nherenor's mother; also *Lady of Ways*

Oakward: secret society in Emer, said to resist evil

Oath Hold: fortress of the House of Blood; its leaders are maternal kin to Parannis and Sarein

Oath, the: see *Blood Oath*

Old Alth: senior wyr pack handler in the Red Keep

Old Earl: Earl Tasarion of Night's father; Malian's grandfather

Old Empire: empire said to have existed prior to the Derai arrival on Haarth, which stretched from Jaransor to Ishnapur

Old Keep: original Keep of Winds, now abandoned

One, the: prophesied hero who will come to unite the Derai and defeat the Swarm, predicted to be born of the Blood of the Houses of Night and Stars; see also *Chosen of Mhaelanar*

Onnorin: granddaughter of the Earl of Adamant; First Kinswoman to Rook

opener of ways: a class of adept

Orcis: warrior-priestess of the House of Adamant, Second to Torlun

Oriflame: standard of the Storm Spears

Ornorith: "of the Two Faces," the Derai Goddess of Luck; depicted as having two masked faces looking in opposite directions

Orriyn: Darksworn facestealer, died on Emer's Northern March; coterie-sister to Rhike and Gervon; see also *Selia*

Orth: warrior of the House of Swords

outsider: Derai term for anyone non-Derai

Palla: House of Blood honor guard in Jad's eight-unit

Paran: lord of Oath Hold, maternal grandfather of Parannis and Sarein

Paranna: of Oath Hold, Earl Sardon of Blood's second wife, mother to Parannis and Sarein

Parannis: a Son of Blood and seventh child to the Earl of Blood; twin to Sarein and half brother to Kharalthor, Hatha, Huern, Liankhara, Sardonya, and Anvin; also half brother to Myrathis

Patrol, the: corps that keeps the River's "peace of road and river"

Peta: Aralorn Hill horse, belonging to Raven

Pha'Rho-l-Ynor: Sea navigator lost four hundred years before; see also *Taierin*

Pha'Rho-l-Ynor, the: Sea House ship lost with all hands, over four hundred years before

Plain of Ash: mountain basin adjoining the Towers of Morning

Port Farewell: major trading port and capital of Aralorn

Power-born: Derai born with the old powers

Powers: supernatural and magical powers of the Derai, once used to combat the Swarm of Darkness. They include: the ability to command objects and forces, both natural and physical; understanding the speech of beasts and birds; acute eyesight and hearing, including seeing in the dark and hearing outside normal human range; chameleon ability to blend into surrounding materials and elements; dreaming; empathic spirit bond; farseeing and foreseeing; fire calling; illusion working; mindspeaking; mind- and spirit-walking; psychic shielding; prophecy; seeking; truthsaying; and weatherworking.

priestess-queens: rulers of Jhaine, nine in number

Prince of Fire: leader of the Sworn nation of Fire; see also *Khelor* and *Ravirien*

Prince of Lightning: leader of the Sworn nation of Lightning; see also *Ilkerineth*

Prince of the Sun: leader of the Sworn nation of the Sun; see also *Aranraith*

Raher: Emerian knight, trained at Normarch

Ralth: House of Blood warrior

Raptor of Darkness: major Swarm demon

Raven: Southern Realms hedge knight

Ravirien: prince of the Third Line of the Blood of Fire

Rayn: Grayharbor shipping clerk

Red Keep: principal stronghold of the House of Blood

Reith: Sea House marine, in Nimor's escort

Rhaikir: lieutenant in the Prince of Fire's personal guard

Rhanar: House of Blood honor guard in Jad's eight-unit

Rhi: House of Morning priestess

Rhike: Darksworn adept, died in Caer Argent

Rhisart: House of Blood warrior, from Bane Hold

Rigan: House of Blood wagoner

Rin: marine on the *Che'Ryl-g-Raham*

Rindle: river on Emer's Northern March

rites of Hurulth: vigil kept for Derai dead

Rithor: squire to Yorindesarinen at time of her battle with the Chaos Worm

River of No Return: see *Telimbras*

River, the: lands along the Ijir river, including the cities Ij, Terebanth, and Ar

Rook: initiate farspeaker from the House of Adamant

Rowan Birchmoon: Winter shaman, former consort to the Earl of Night; see also *Winter Woman*

Rul: personal emissary of the Earl of Adamant; half-brother to Torlun

ruling kin: ruling bloodline of a Derai House; see also *Blood, the*

Sailcloth Street: Grayharbor thoroughfare

Salar: Darksworn Ascendant, most closely associated with Sun

Salar's children: demons that ride Wall storms and slip through fissures in reality

Sarathion: lieutenant to the Lord Captain of the Patrol

Sardon: current Earl and hereditary ruler of the House of Blood

Sardonya: a Daughter of Blood and fifth child of the Earl of Blood; full sister to Kharalthor, Hatha, Huern, Liankhara, and Anvin; half sister to Parannis and Sarein; also half sister to Myrathis

Sarein: a Daughter of Blood and eighth child of the Earl of Blood; twin to Parannis and half sister to Kharalthor, Hatha, Huern, Liankhara, Sardonya, and Anvin; also half sister to Myrathis

Sarr: House of Blood farrier

Sarus: veteran sergeant of the Earl of Night's Honor Guard

Sea Count: hereditary ruler of the Sea House

Sea envoy: see *Nimor*

Sea House: House of the Derai Alliance, traditionally "the navigators"

Sea Keep: paramount stronghold of the Sea House

Sea Mew: coastal trader, registered out of Grayharbor

Second: second-in-command of a Derai military unit

Second Line: second line of a Derai House's Blood

seeing: the power to see and foretell future occurrences

seeker: one with power to seek out the hidden and find the lost

seeking: active use of a seeker's power

seer: one who has the power to see into the future

Selia: Normarch damosel, slain by the facestealer *Orriyn*

Serianrethen: a Son of Stars, first husband to Nerith of the Sea Keep

Ser Ombrose Sondargent: Duke of Emer's nephew and former champion, now turned rebel

Seruth: one of the three gods of the Southern Realms, the light-bringer, guardian of journeys and new beginnings; also Serrut in Emer

Seven, a: elite Jhainarian warriors bound together into a unit; escort of the priestess-queens of Jhaine; also used by Ishnapuri magi

Shadow Band: initiates of Kan, sworn to protect the rulers of Ar

shadow hunters: Thanir's cadres; see also *Darksworn*

Shah: ruler of Ishnapur

shielding: power to conceal objects and people physically and from magic

Shield of Heaven: one of the three magical arms of the hero Yorindesarinen; also Shield of Stars

Ship's Luck: weatherworker's companion on a Sea House ship

Ship's Prow House: Grayharbor residence

Ships' Shrine: sea keep memorial to lost ships

Silent God: Hurulth, the god of death, one of the Nine Gods of the Derai

Sird: warrior-priest from the House of Adamant

siren worm: minion of the Swarm

Sirit: elderly Morning priestess; also old Lady of Morning

Sirithilorn: formerly Golden Fire of the House of Morning

Sondcendre: noble house of the Emerian Cendreward

Son of Blood: title given to a son of an Earl of Blood

Song of Haarth: voice of the magic of Haarth

southern deserts: vast desert region lying to the south of Ishnapur

Southern Realms: lands of Haarth that lie between the River and Ishnapur; also called the Southern Lands

'spawn: see *darkspawn*

springtime love: Emerian tradition of courtly romance

Sri: House of Morning priestess

Stefa: innkeeper's daughter at Grayharbor's Anchor inn

Stoneford: village in southern Aralorn

Storm Spears: warrior society historically associated with the House of Blood

Summer's Eve: Emerian festival marking first new moon of summer

Sun: one of the three nations of the Sworn

Sundering: schism that separated the Darksworn from the Derai

Surinay: once of the House of Morning, now married to the Sea Count

Swarm Bestiary: an illustrated compendium of Swarm demons, minions, and darkspawn

Swarm of Dark: Derai's ancient enemy; vast entity comprising many fell creatures

Swarm, the: shortening for *Swarm of Dark*

Sworn: name the Darksworn give themselves

Taierin: weatherworker and niece to Count Tirunor, over four hundred years ago

taint: House of Blood term for priestly and old powers; also "tainted"

Taly: ensign in the Red Keep garrison, serves Myrathis; also Talies

Tarathan of Ar: herald of the Guild, from the River's Terebanth Guild House

Tasarion: current Earl and hereditary ruler of the House of Night

Tasian: former Heir of Stars whose murder precipitated the Derai civil war

Tavar: House of Blood clan, associated with Brave Hold

Tavaral: the Faithkeeper, a general in Yorindesarinen's time; he advanced to support the hero against the Chaos Worm, but came too late

Tawr: of the Spear, one of the Nine Gods of the Derai

Tawrin: House of Swords warrior, companion to Orth

Tehan: Sea House marine in Nimor's escort

Telimbras: river that runs the length of the Jaransor hills, bordering the Gray Lands, and eventually becomes a tributary of the Ijir; also *River of No Return*

Telmirieneth: Earl of Stars, over four hundred years before

Temorn: captain of marines on the *Che'Ryl-g-Raham*

Temple of Night: temple precinct in the Keep of Winds

Temple quarter: temple complex in a Derai keep, comprising the temples and adjunct buildings dedicated to all of the Nine Gods

Tenneward Lodge: country house of Lord Tenneward of Emer

Ter: Night honor guard in Garan's eight-unit

Tercel: bay warhorse, belonging to Kalan

Terebanth: city of the River

Terennin: Lord of the Dawn Eyes, one of the Nine Gods of the Derai, also known as both the Farseeing and Farseer

Teron: of Cloud Hold, sworn to the Earl of Night

Thanir: Darksworn warrior and mage, lieutenant to Aranraith

The Leas: site of a recent were-hunt led skirmish, on Emer's Northern March

Thiandriath: Lawgiver, one of the Nine Gods of the Derai

Third Line: third line of a Derai House's Blood

Thuunoth: former Golden Fire of the House of Adamant

Tirael: second son of the Countess of Stars; also Tiraelisian

Tirorn: House of Swords warrior and captain, nephew to the Sword Earl, also kinsman to Orth; lost in Ij

Tirunor: Sea Count, over four hundred years before

Token-bearer: one who bears *the Token*

Token, the: ring associated with the Hunt of Mayanne and its Huntmaster

Torlun: commands a House of Adamant company

Towers of Morning: principal stronghold of the House of Morning

Tymar: Sea House marine in Nimor's escort

Tyun: Sea House marine, captain of Nimor's guard

Vael: Star knight and healer; also Vaelenor

Valadan: marshal of the House of Fire, second-in-command of its armies

Valan: of Blood's Ward Hold, former suitor to Sardonya

Vela: attendant to Lady Myrathis

Wall of Night: vast mountain range garrisoned by the Derai Alliance that protects Haarth from the Swarm, said to have been created by the House of Night; also called the Shield-wall of Night, or Wall

wallspawn: Blood name for *darkspawn*

Ward Hold: satellite fortress of the House of Blood

weatherworker: Derai with the power to command natural elements

were-hunt: collective power of the Swarm, comprising were-hunters

Westwind Hold: satellite fort of the Keep of Winds

Wild Lands: vast wilderness lying between the Winter Country and the River

Winter Country: steppes in the north of Haarth

Winter People: nomads who dwell in the Winter Country

Winter Woman: see *Rowan Birchmoon*

Wolf: Winter Country shaman, Rowan Birchmoon's great-uncle

wolfpack: River and Emerian term for an outlaw band

wyr hounds: hounds unique to the Derai, able to detect psychic trails and powers

Xer: Star knight in Tirael's escort; also Xerianor

Xeria: House of Stars priestess during the civil war; she extinguished the Golden Fire

Yelme: Sea House marine in Nimor's escort

Yelusin: collective name Sea House ships give themselves

Yhle: granddaughter of the Earl of Adamant

Ynvis: warrior in the Prince of Fire's personal guard

Yorindesarinen: greatest hero of the Derai, Heir of Stars in her day: she slew the Worm of Chaos but died of the wounds received in that battle

Yris: Patrol river pilot

Yyr: formerly Golden Fire of the *House of Swords*

Zharaan: priestess-queen of Jhaine in the years following the Cataclysm

Zhineve-An: contemporary priestess-queen of Jhaine

Acknowledgments

The Chinese philosopher, Lao Tzu, famously said that *"A journey of a thousand miles begins with a single step."* Similarly, the journey of a book begins with the first word on a blank page—and in getting to that magical finale, "the end," a great many more words will have been written. A considerable number of people, too, will have been fellow travelers on the journey.

The first—but never the least—of these fellow travelers is my partner, Andrew, whose unflagging support, encouragement, and enthusiasm for the story helped keep me moving forward, even when the going was proverbially tough.

The journey of this book *was* a long one, and I sincerely thank my lead editor, Kate Nintzel (HarperVoyager USA), for her considerable patience and not inconsiderable grace throughout, as well as for her unwavering faith in, and commitment to, the ongoing Wall of Night story, and *Daughter of Blood* in particular. My UK editor, Jenni Hill, was new to the series when I began this book, and I am correspondingly grateful for her patience and continued support.

My agent Robin Rue of Writers House, and her colleagues Beth Miller and Angharad Kowal, have also played a vital part in enabling me to complete the book. I thank them most sincerely for all they have done and continue to do.

I am aware that there are many more people who work for my publishers and play an essential part in transforming what comes from me as "story" and "manuscript," into what readers experience as a "book." Most of these people are unknown to me personally, but I know they include dedicated professionals in the production team and art department, as well as marketing and publicity. I would like to take this opportunity to thank them all for their hard work, which is very much appreciated. And to particularly mention, with thanks, the few who are known to me, including my copyeditor, Peter Weissman; Joanna Kramer, Editorial Manager at Orbit; and the Hachette team here in New Zealand, including Melanee Winder, Susy Maddox, and Ruby Mitchell.

Many thanks go, as always, to those who were willing to read the manuscript-in-progress and provide insights, critique, and feedback, as well as to confirm specialist research and check specific facts. I would like to particularly thank Peter Fitzpatrick, Joanna Preston, Andrew Robins, Paul Waterhouse, Brynley Crosado, and Irene Williamson. I am also grateful to Dr. Robynanne Milford for answering early questions, and to Dr. Michael Rathbone for later reviewing the sections specifically dealing with injury and wounds, and their treatment.

In 2012, I was privileged to be an Ursula Bethell Writer-in-Residence at the University of Canterbury, which provided both financial and creative support during the early stages of *Daughter of Blood*. I would like to particularly thank Dr. Christina Stachurski, curator of the residency programme, as well as the University of Canterbury and its English Department, and *Toi Aotearoa*: Creative New Zealand, for making the residency opportunity possible.

I would also like to thank Samantha Webb for offering her fisher's hut as a writing retreat toward the end of the project. The quiet environment and uninterrupted time the hut provided was invaluable in finishing the book. I would also like to thank the permanent residents in the hut community for their welcome and support.

When *The Heir of Night* was published, I began a tradition of running a Tuckerization contest as part of the book launch. So when *The Gathering of the Lost* came out, part of the celebration included drawing a winner who would give her or his name to a character in *Daughter of Blood*. One of the provisions of the contest is that I reserve the right to *"adapt the winning name to best fit a fantasy character."* In this case, the winner was UK reader, Cheryl Graham—and although I am keenly aware of just how long Cheryl has had to wait to do so, I hope she will enjoy meeting her namesake, Che'Ryl-g-Raham. I note, needless to say, that the character created is entirely fictional.

Finally, I would like to thank all those readers who have not only read and enjoyed *The Heir of Night* and *The Gathering of The Lost*, but taken the time to write and tell me so—and then waited with patience (that word again!) and understanding for *Daughter of Blood* to complete its journey from the first word on the blank page, through to "the end." The same vote of thanks for patience, and I hope understanding, goes to all my readers.

extras

orbit

www.orbitbooks.net

about the author

Helen Lowe lives in Christchurch, New Zealand, and writes fantasy and science fiction novels, poetry and short fiction. She also hosts a monthly poetry feature on the New Zealand radio station Plains.

Her debut novel, *The Heir of Night*, won the Morningstar Award for best debut novel at the 2012 Gemmell Awards.

Find out more about Helen Lowe and other Orbit authors by registering for the free monthly newsletter at www.orbitbooks.net

if you enjoyed

DAUGHTER OF BLOOD

look out for

THIEF'S MAGIC

Millennium's Rule: Book One

by

Trudi Canavan

CHAPTER 1

The corpse's shrivelled, unbending fingers surrendered the bundle reluctantly. Wrestling the object out of the dead man's grip seemed disrespectful so Tyen worked slowly, gently lifting a hand when a blackened fingernail snagged on the covering. He'd touched the ancient dead so often they didn't sicken or frighten him now. Their desiccated flesh had long ago stopped being a source of transferable sickness, and he did not believe in ghosts.

When the mysterious bundle came free Tyen straightened and smiled in triumph. He wasn't as ruthless at collecting ancient artefacts as his fellow students and his teacher, but bringing home nothing from these research trips would see him fail to graduate as a sorcerer-archaeologist. He willed his tiny magic-fuelled flame closer.

The object's covering, like the tomb's occupant, was dry and stiff having, by his estimate, lain undisturbed for six hundred years. Thick leather darkened with age, it had no markings – no adornment, no precious stones or metals. As he tried to open it the wrapping snapped apart and something inside began to slide out. His pulse quickened as he caught the object . . .

. . . and his heart sank a little. No treasure lay in his hands. Just a book. Not even a jewel-encrusted, gold-embellished book.

Not that a book didn't have potential historical value, but compared to the glittering treasures Professor Kilraker's other two students had unearthed for the academy it was a disappointing find. After all the months of travel, research, digging and watching he had little to show for his own work. He had finally unearthed a tomb that hadn't already been ransacked by grave robbers and what did it contain? A plain stone coffin, an unadorned corpse and an old book.

Still, the old fossils at the Academy wouldn't regret sponsoring his journey if the book turned out to be significant. He examined it closely. Unlike the wrapping, the leather cover felt supple. The binding was in good condition. If he hadn't just broken apart the covering to get it out, he'd have guessed the book's age at no more than a hundred or so years. It had no title or text on the spine. Perhaps it had worn off. He opened it. No word marked the first page, so he turned it. The next was also blank and as he fanned through the rest of the pages he saw that they were as well.

He stared at it in disbelief. Why would anyone bury a blank book in a tomb, carefully wrapped and placed in the hands of the occupant? He looked at the corpse, but it offered no answer. Then something drew his eye back to the book, still open to one of the last pages. He looked closer.

A mark had appeared.

Next to it a dark patch formed, then dozens more. They spread and joined up.

Hello, they said. *My name is Vella.*

Tyen uttered a word his mother would have been shocked to hear if she had still been alive. Relief and wonder replaced disappointment. The book was magical. Though most sorcerous books used magic in minor and frivolous ways, they were so rare that the Academy would always take them for its collection. His trip hadn't been a waste.

So what did this book do? Why did text only appear when it was opened? Why did it have a name? More words formed on the page.

I've always had a name. I used to be a person. A living, breathing woman.

Tyen stared at the words. A chill ran down his spine, yet at the same time he felt a familiar thrill. Magic could sometimes be disturbing. It was often inexplicable. He liked that not everything about it was understood. It left room for new discoveries. Which was why he had chosen to study sorcery alongside history. In both fields there was an opportunity to make a name for himself.

He'd never heard of a person turning into a book before. *How is that possible?* he wondered.

I was made by a powerful sorcerer, replied the text. *He took my knowledge and flesh and transformed me.*

His skin tingled. The book had responded to the question he'd shaped in his mind. *Do you mean these pages are made of your flesh?* he asked.

Yes. My cover and pages are my skin. My binding is my hair, twisted together and sewn with needles fashioned from my bones and glue from tendons.

He shuddered. *And you're conscious?*

Yes.

You can hear my thoughts?

Yes, but only when you touch me. When not in contact with a living human, I am blind and deaf, trapped in the darkness with no sense of time passing. Not even sleeping. Not quite dead. The years of my life slipping past

– wasted.

Tyen stared down at the book. The words remained, nearly filling a page now, dark against the creamy vellum. Which was her skin . . .

It was grotesque and yet . . . all vellum was made of skin. While these pages were human skin, they felt no different to that made of animals. They were soft and pleasant to touch.

The book was not repulsive in the way an ancient, desiccated corpse was.

And it was so much more interesting. Conversing with it was akin to talking with the dead. If the book was as old as the tomb it knew about the time before it was laid there. Tyen smiled. He may not have found gold and jewels to help pay his way on this expedition, but the book could make up for that with historical information.

More text formed.

Contrary to appearances, I am not an "it".

Perhaps it was the effect of the light on the page, but the new words seemed a little larger and darker than the previous text. Tyen felt his face warm a little.

I'm sorry, Vella. It was bad mannered of me. I assure you, I meant no offence. It is not every day that a man addresses a talking book, and I am not entirely sure of the protocol.

She was a woman, he reminded himself. He ought to follow the etiquette he'd been raised to follow. Though talking to women could be fiendishly tricky, even when following all the rules about manners. It would be rude to begin their association by interrogating her about the past. Rules of conversation decreed he should ask after her wellbeing.

So . . . is it nice being a book?

When I am being held and read by someone nice, it is, she replied.

And when you are not, it is not? I can see that might be a disadvantage in your state, though one you must have anticipated before you became a book.

I would have, if I'd had foreknowledge of my fate.

So you did not choose to become a book. Why did your maker do that to you? Was it a punishment?

No, though perhaps it was natural justice for being too ambitious and vain. I sought his attention, and received more of it than I intended.

Why did you seek his attention?

He was famous. I wanted to impress him. I thought my friends would be envious.

And for that he turned you into a book. What manner of man could be so cruel?

He was the most powerful sorcerer of his time, Roporien the Clever.

Tyen caught his breath and a chill ran down his back.

Roporien! But he died over a thousand years ago!

Indeed.

Then you are . . .

At least as old as that. Though in my time it wasn't polite to comment on a woman's age.

He smiled. *It still isn't – and I don't think it ever will be. I apologise again.*

You are a polite young man. I will enjoy being owned by you.

You want me to own *you?* Tyen suddenly felt uncomfortable. He realised he now thought of the book as a person, and owning a person was slavery – an immoral and uncivilised practice that had been illegal for over a hundred years.

Better that than spend my existence in oblivion. Books don't last for ever, not even magical ones. Keep me. Make use of me. I can give you a wealth of knowledge. All I ask is that you hold me as often as possible so that I can spend my lifespan awake and aware.

I don't know . . . The man who created you did many terrible things – as you experienced yourself. I don't want to follow in his shadow. Then something occurred to him that made his skin creep. *Forgive me for being blunt about it, but his book, or any of his tools, could be designed for evil purposes. Are you one such tool?*

I was not designed so, but that does not mean I could not be used so. A tool is only as evil as the hand that uses it.

The familiarity of the saying was startling and unexpectedly reassuring. It was one that Professor Weldan liked. The old historian had always been suspicious of magical things.

How do I know you're not lying about not being evil?

I cannot lie.

Really? But what if you're lying about not being able to lie?

You'll have to work that one out for yourself.

Tyen frowned as he considered how he might devise a test for her, then realised something was buzzing right beside his ear. He shied away from the sensation, then breathed a sigh of relief as he saw it was Beetle, his little mechanical creation. More than a toy, yet not quite what he'd describe as a pet, it had proven to be a useful companion on the expedition.

The palm-sized insectoid swooped down to land on his shoulder, folded its iridescent blue wings, then whistled three times. Which was a warning that . . .

"Tyen!" . . . Miko, his friend and fellow archaeology student was approaching.

The voice echoed in the short passage leading from the outside world to the tomb. Tyen muttered a curse. He glanced down at the page. *Sorry, Vella. Have to go.* Footsteps neared the door of the tomb. With no time to slip her into his bag, he stuffed her down his shirt, where she settled against the waistband of his trousers. She was warm – which was a bit disturbing now that he knew she was a conscious thing created from human flesh – but he didn't have time to dwell on it. He turned to the door in time to see Miko stumble into view.

"Didn't think to bring a lamp?" he asked.

"No time," the other student gasped. "Kilraker sent me to get you. The others have gone back to the camp to pack up. We're leaving Mailand."

"Now?"

"Yes. *Now*," Miko replied.

Tyen looked back at the small tomb. Though Professor Kilraker liked to refer to these foreign trips as treasure hunts, his peers expected the students to bring back evidence that the journeys were also educational. Copying the faint decorations on the tomb walls would have given them something to mark. He thought wistfully of the new instant etchers that some of the richer professors and self-funded adventurers used to record their work. They were far beyond his meagre allowance. Even if they weren't, Kilraker wouldn't take them on expeditions because they were heavy and fragile.

Picking up his satchel, Tyen opened the flap. "Beetle. Inside." The insectoid scuttled down his arm into the bag. Tyen slung the strap over his head and shoulder and sent his flame into the passage.

"We have to hurry," Miko said, leading the way. "The locals heard about where you're digging. Must've been one of the boys Kilraker hired to deliver food who told them. A bunch are coming up the valley and they're sounding those battle horns they carry."

"They didn't want us digging here? Nobody told me that!"

"Kilraker said not to. He said you were bound to find something impressive, after all the research you did."

He reached the hole where Tyen had broken through into the passage and squeezed out. Tyen followed, letting the flame die as he climbed out into the bright afternoon sunlight. Dry heat enveloped him. Miko scrambled up the sides of the ditch. Following, Tyen looked back and surveyed his work. Nothing remained in the tomb that robbers would want, but he couldn't stand to leave it exposed to vermin and he felt guilty about unearthing a tomb the locals didn't wanted disturbed. Reaching out with his mind, he pulled magic to himself then moved the rocks and earth on either side back into the ditch.

"What are you *doing*?" Miko sounded exasperated.

"Filling it in."

"We don't have time!" Miko grabbed his arm and yanked him around so that they both looked down into the valley. He pointed. "See?"

The valley sides were near-vertical cliffs, and where the faces had crumbled over time piles of rubble had built up against the sides to form steep slopes. Tyen and Miko were standing atop of one of these.

At the bottom of the valley a long line of people was moving, faces tilted to search the scree above. One arm rose, pointing at Tyen and Miko. The rest stopped, then fists were raised.

A shiver went through Tyen, part fear, part guilt. Though the people inhabiting the remote valleys of Mailand were unrelated to the ancient race that had buried its dead in the tombs, they felt that such places of death should not be disturbed lest ghosts be awakened. They'd made this clear when Kilraker had arrived, and to previous archaeologists, but their protests had never been more than verbal and they'd indicated that some areas were less important than others. They must really be upset, if Kilraker had cut the expedition short.

Tyen opened his mouth to ask, when the ground beside him exploded. They both threw up their arms to shield their faces from the dust and stones.

"Can you protect us?" Miko asked.

"Yes. Give me a moment ..." Tyen gathered more magic. This time he stilled the air around them. Most of what a sorcerer did was either moving or stilling. Heating and cooling was another form of moving or stilling, only more intense and focused. As the dust settled beyond his shield he saw the locals had gathered together behind a brightly dressed woman who served as priestess and sorcerer to the locals. He took a step towards them.

"Are you mad?" Miko asked.

"What else can we do? We're trapped up here. We should just go talk to them. Explain that I didn't—"

The ground exploded again, this time much closer.

"They don't seem in the mood for talking."

"They won't hurt two sons of the Leratian Empire," Tyen reasoned. "Mailand gains a lot of profit from being one of the safer colonies."

Miko snorted. "Do you think the villagers care? They don't get any of the profit."

"Well . . . the Governors will punish them."

"They don't look too worried about that right now." Miko turned to stare up at the face of the cliff behind them. "I'm not waiting to see if they're bluffing." He set off along the edge of the slope where it met the cliff.

Tyen followed, keeping as close as possible to Miko so that he didn't have to stretch his shield far to cover them both. Stealing glances at the people below, he saw that they were hurrying up the slope, but the loose scree was slowing them down. The sorceress walked along the bottom, following them. He hoped this meant that, after using magic, she needed to move from the area she had depleted to access more. That would mean her reach wasn't as good as his.

She stopped and the air rippled before her, a pulse that rushed towards him. Realising that Miko had drawn ahead, Tyen drew more magic and spread the shield out to protect him.

The scree exploded a short distance below their feet. Tyen ignored the stones and dust bounding off his shield and hurried to catch up with Miko. His friend reached a crack in the cliff face. Setting his feet in the rough sides of the narrow opening and grasping the edges, he began to climb. Tyen tilted his head back. Though the crack continued a long way up the cliff face it didn't reach the top. Instead, at a point about three times his height, it widened to form a narrow cave.

"This looks like a bad idea," he muttered. Even if they didn't slip and break a limb, or worse, once in the cave they'd be trapped.

"It's our only option. They'll catch us if we head downhill," Miko said in a tight voice, without taking his attention from climbing. "Don't look up. Don't look down either. Just climb."

Though the crack was almost vertical, the edges were pitted and uneven, providing plenty of hand- and footholds. Swallowing hard, Tyen swung his satchel around to his back so he wouldn't crush Beetle between himself and the wall. He set his fingers and toes in the rough surface and hoisted himself upward.

At first it was easier than he'd expected, but soon his fingers, arms and legs were tiring and hurting from the strain. *I should have exercised more before coming here. I should have joined a sports club.* Then he shook his head. *No, there's no exercise I could have done that would have boosted* these *muscles except climbing cliff walls, and I've not heard of any clubs that consider* that *a recreational activity.*

The shield behind him shuddered at a sudden impact. He fed more magic to it, trying not to picture himself squashed like a bug on the cliff wall. Was Miko right about the locals? Would they dare to kill him? Or was the priestess simply gambling that he was a good enough sorcerer to ward off her attacks?

"Nearly there," Miko called.

Ignoring the fire in his fingers and calves, Tyen glanced up and saw Miko disappear into the cave. *Not far now*, he told himself. He forced his aching limbs to push and pull, carrying him upward towards the dark shadow of safety. Glancing up again and again, he saw he was a body's length away, then close enough that an outstretched arm would reach it. A vibration went through the stone beneath his hand and chips flew off the wall nearby. He found another foothold, pushed up, grabbed a handhold, pulled, felt the cool shadow of the cave on his face . . .

. . . then hands grabbed his armpits and hauled him up.

Miko didn't stop pulling until Tyen's legs were inside the cave. It was so narrow that Tyen's shoulders scraped along the walls. Looking downward, he saw that there was no floor to the fissure. The walls on either side simply drew closer together to form a crack that continued beneath him. Miko was bracing his boots on the walls on either side.

That "floor" was not level either. It sloped downward as the cave deepened, so Tyen's head was now lower than his legs. He felt the book slide up the inside of his shirt and tried to grab it, but Miko's arms got in the way. The book dropped down into the crack. He cursed and quickly created a flame. The book had come to rest far beyond his reach even if his arms had been skinny enough to fit into the gap.

Miko let go and gingerly turned around to examine the cave.

Ignoring him, Tyen pushed himself up into a crouch. He drew his bag around to the front and opened it. "Beetle," he hissed. The little machine stirred, then scurried out and up onto his arm. Tyen pointed at the crack. "Fetch book."

Beetle's wings buzzed an affirmative, then its body whirred as it scurried down Tyen's arm and into the crack. It had to spread its legs wide to fit in the narrow space where the book had lodged. Tyen breathed a sigh of relief as its tiny pincers seized the spine. As it emerged Tyen grabbed Vella and Beetle together and slipped them both inside his satchel.

"Hurry up! The professor's here!"

Tyen stood up. Miko looked upwards and pressed a finger to his lips. A faint, rhythmic sound echoed in the space.

"In the aircart?" Tyen shook his head. "I hope he knows the priestess is throwing rocks at us or it's going to be a very long journey home."

"I'm sure he's prepared for a fight." Miko turned away and continued along the crack. "I think we can climb up here. Come over and bring your light."

Standing up, Tyen made his way over. Past Miko the crack narrowed again, but rubble had filled the space, providing an uneven, steep, natural staircase. Above them was a slash of blue sky. Miko started to climb, but the rubble began to dislodge under his weight.

"So close," he said, looking up. "Can you lift me up there?"

"Maybe ... " Tyen concentrated on the magical atmosphere. Nobody had used magic in the cave for a long time. It was as smoothly dispersed and still as a pool of water on a windless day. And it was plentiful. He'd still not grown used to how much stronger and *available* magic was outside towns and cities. Unlike in the metropolis, where magic was constantly surging towards a more important use, here power pooled and lapped around him like a gentle fog. He'd only encountered Soot, the residue of magic that lingered everywhere in the city, in small, quickly dissipating smudges. "Looks possible," Tyen said. "Ready?"

Miko nodded.

Tyen drew a deep breath. He gathered magic and used it to still the air before Miko in a small, flat square.

"Step forward," he instructed.

Miko obeyed. Strengthening the square to hold the young man's weight, Tyen moved it slowly upwards. Throwing his arms out to keep his balance, Miko laughed nervously.

"Let me check there's nobody waiting up there before you lift me out," he called down to Tyen. After peering out of the opening, he grinned. "All clear."

As Miko stepped off the square a shout came from the cave entrance. Tyen twisted around to see one of the locals climbing inside. He drew magic to push the man out again, then hesitated. The drop outside could kill him. Instead he created another shield inside the entrance.

Looking around, he sensed the scarring of the magical atmosphere where it had been depleted, but more magic was already beginning to flow in to replace it. He took a little more to form another square then, hoping the locals would do nothing to spoil his concentration, stepped onto it and moved it upwards.

He'd never liked lifting himself, or anyone else, like this. If he lost focus or ran out of magic he'd never have time to recreate the square. Though it was possible to move a person rather than still the air below them, a lack of concentration or moving parts of them at different rates could cause injury or even death.

Reaching the top of the crack, Tyen emerged into sunlight. Past the edge of the cliff a large, lozenge-shaped hot-air-filled capsule hovered – the aircart. He stepped off the square onto the ground and hurried over to join Miko at the cliff edge.

The aircart was descending into the valley, the bulk of the capsule blocking the chassis hanging below it and its occupants from Tyen's view. Villagers were gathered at the base of the crack, some clinging to the cliff wall. The priestess was part way up the scree slope but her attention was now on the aircart.

"Professor!" he shouted, though he knew he was unlikely to be heard over the noise of the propellers. "Over here!"

The craft floated further from the cliff. Below, the priestess made a dramatic gesture, entirely for show since magic didn't require fancy physical movements. Tyen held his breath as a ripple of air rushed upward, then let it go as the force abruptly dispelled below the aircart with a dull thud that echoed through the valley.

The aircart began to rise. Soon Tyen could see below the capsule. The long, narrow chassis came into view, shaped rather like a canoe, with propeller arms extending to either side and a fan-like rudder at the rear. Professor Kilraker was in the driver's seat up front; his middle-aged servant, Drem, and the other student, Neel, stood clutching the rope railing and the struts that attached chassis to capsule. The trio would see him and Miko, if only they would turn around and look his way. He shouted and waved his arms, but they continued peering downward.

"Make a light or something," Miko said.

"They won't see it," Tyen said, but he took yet more magic and formed a new flame anyway, making it larger and brighter than the earlier ones in the hope it would be more visible in the bright sunlight. To his surprise, the professor looked over and saw them.

"Yes! Over here!" Miko shouted.

Kilraker turned the aircart to face the cliff edge, its propellers swivelling and buzzing. Bags and boxes had been strapped to either end of the chassis, suggesting there had not been time to pack their luggage in the hollow inside. At last the cart moved over the cliff top in a gust of familiar smells. Tyen breathed in the scent of resin-coated cloth, polished wood and pipe smoke and smiled. Miko grabbed the rope railing strung around the chassis, ducked under it and stepped on board.

"Sorry, boys," Kilraker said. "Expedition's over. No point sticking around when the locals get like this. Brace yourselves for some ear popping. We're going up."

As Tyen swung his satchel around to his back, ready to climb aboard, he thought of what lay inside. He didn't have any treasure to show off, but at least he had found something interesting. Ducking under the railing rope, he settled onto the narrow deck, legs dangling over the side. Miko sat down beside him. The aircart began to ascend rapidly, its nose slowly turning towards home.